I0650862

Crown of Vengeance

Crown of Vengeance

STEPHEN ZIMMER

SEVENTH STAR PRESS

Copyright © 2009 by Stephen Zimmer
All rights reserved. No portion of this book may be copied or transmitted
in any form, electronic or otherwise, without express written consent of
the publisher or author.

Cover art and illustrations: Matthew Perry
Cover art and illustrations in this book, © 2009 Matthew Perry &
Seventh Star Press, LLC.

Editor: Amanda DeBord

Published by Seventh Star Press, LLC.

ISBN Number   9780982565612

Library of Congress Control Number: 2009910166

Seventh Star Press
www.seventhstarpress.com
info@seventhstarpress.com

Publisher's Note:
Crown of Vengeance is a work of fiction. All names, characters, and places
are the product of the author's imagination, used in fictitious manner.
Any resemblances to actual persons, places, locales, events, etc.
is purely coincidental.

Printed in the United States of America

First Edition

DEDICATION

Book One in the Fires in Eden Series, and the series itself, is dedicated to my father, Dr. Stephen Zimmer, a brilliant scientist and incredible father, who continued to be generous and good to others despite having to endure true injustice over many very difficult years. I hope that he has walked in Eden, and what lies beyond it, where the many lives that he touched, the many people that he helped all throughout his life, and the dedicated, innovative research that he undertook to help those suffering with cancer, are the enduring treasures in a place where money and worldly status have no worth.

I also dedicate this series to everyone who suffers the kind of pain that comes with the loss of someone that you love dearly, something that time cannot heal in this world. It takes a lot of courage to get up and continue forward in the face of the unknown, and to take the risk of harboring hope in a world that increasingly embraces oblivion. May the destination of this story be similar to your own, so that everyone who has dared to love will find the fulfillment of true healing, in a place where life truly flourishes

ACKNOWLEDGEMENTS

Amanda Debord, my wondrous editor who has valiantly endured yet another step forward on my literary adventure. I hope that I have perhaps cut down the workload a little in advance, on this second project together. Thanks for being so wonderful to work with, and for not being inhibited in telling me what needs to be improved, where I've become too fascinated with historical details, and all the things that you've pointed out that have made the work better. I think the world of you, and will always work incredibly hard to make you proud that you chose to work with me!

Matthew Perry, illustrator and artist extraordinaire, and a loyal friend. I cannot say enough about how glad I am that you were willing to continue on this road, and that we were able to work together once again. I don't take anything for granted. This stage of the journey is far from easy, and your support during this time means more than you know. I will do my best to see all of this through, and I am very proud to have your considerable talents displayed on the cover of my book.

I can never express enough gratitude to my mother, Connie, who is definitely at fault for my great love of fantasy literature. As I often mention, it was she who read me The Hobbit and the Lord of the Rings trilogy aloud as a child, and got me hooked onto C.S. Lewis's Narnia series. Always supportive of my dreams, I could never have found better encouragement to persevere on a very arduous road. As I can never say enough, I love you, mom!

My unceasing respect and gratitude each and every one of the readers who joined me on the journey following the release of The Exodus Gate, the first step on the road, and to those who have joined with me since. An author is nothing without readers, and I could not move forward without you. I will always give you my utmost effort to bring you the best work that I possibly can, and I will always be looking for ways to improve in order to bring you exciting and thought-provoking stories, and satisfying series. My readers deserve that kind of respect and consideration at all times, something that I take very, very seriously.

"When I despair, I remember that all through history the way of truth and love has always won. There have been tyrants and murderers and for a time they seem invincible but in the end, they always fall - think of it, ALWAYS."
-Mahatma Gandhi

"The spread of evil is the symptom of a vacuum. Whenever evil wins, it is only by default: by the moral failure of those who evade the fact that there can be no compromise on basic principles."
-Ayn Rand

"There is no death, only a change between worlds."
-Seattle, Suquamish chief.

PROLOGUE

THE UNIFIER

A solitary figure stood gazing outward, at the edge of the crenellations ringing the circumference of the great tower soaring up from the top of the massive, mountain-citadel. Shrouded with a regal, proud air, The Unifier, the Lord of far more than Avanor, regarded the heart of His worldly dominion with an invigorating feeling of growing mastery.

Yet there was a deep concern weighing upon His mind, of a nature that rarely manifested to His pervasive senses.

The Unifier was a figure that embodied majesty and charisma, His captivating persona as legendary as the astounding feats that He had performed during His ascension to power. He was one of the most comely men to ever draw breath upon the face of Ave, and one would be very hard pressed to discover anyone who would dispute that observation.

He was fully six and a half feet tall, with a slightly olive tone to His smooth, unblemished skin. The immaculate state of His skin was noted by all who gained the privilege of close proximity to the Unifier. It was unmarred by scratch, bruise, or wrinkle, though His age was known to be great, and His travels extensive. It was regarded as yet another outward testimony to divine favor, as not even the immortal races fully escaped the ravages of time on their physical forms, whether Wizard, Elf, or the winged Elder in their skyward havens.

His large, even teeth were of the purest white, and His angular facial features seemed to be chiseled in, lending Him a strong mien with perfect proportion and balance. His face would have challenged the skills of the greatest of sculptors in endeavoring to replicate a close likeness, with its flawless symmetry and harmony.

The Unifier had short-cropped, coal-black hair that had a perceptible curl to its texture. His body was lithe and muscular, with wide shoulders tapering down to a narrow waist, with sculpted, long legs extending below.

The Unifier's luminous blue eyes were one of His most exceptional physical features. They always gave the impression of containing unimaginable depths within them, and it was known well that His eyes conveyed His moods with a mesmerizing power. The attribute was spoken of by those who had found favor with Him, and also by those who had found disfavor, and still survived to tell of their icy terror. The azure gaze held a mysterious, captivating quality, one that could make the most strong-minded and proud female swoon in euphoric vulnerability, or cause the most formidable of battle-hardened warriors to tremble in stark, quivering fright.

His exquisite physique was clad in a flowing tunic of pure white silk that descended all the way down to His ankles. It rippled in the high breezes, shimmering in the day's light.

The precious silk cloth used for the garment had been a gift from Theonia, acquired by the empire's merchants who had traded with the exotic lands to the far east. The ells of silk cloth had been the crowning element of a bounteous tribute from the Theonian Emperor, which had included a wealth of rare spices and other uncommon luxuries. Few ever undertook the long and perilous journeys along the Rising Sun Road to the eastern lands. Fewer still returned with such treasured items as that which had been enthusiastically presented to the Unifier, by the delegation sent to Avalos from the Emperor of Theonia. The quality of the immaculately woven silk was much rarer and finer than any now being produced within the Theonian Empire, who rigidly protected their indigenous silk trade. In the rays of the sun it looked as if it glowed from within, casting an angelic hue upon its exalted wearer.

The collar, hem, and sleeves of the tunic were brocaded with broad bands of magnificent, intersecting golden designs. The most expert hands in all of Avanor had labored relentlessly in fashioning the full-length tunic for the Unifier, sewing and cutting meticulously from the precious cloth. Through their painstaking skills they had rendered the Unifier a resplendent tribute of their own; a one-of-a-kind garment, for a man without peer.

The light tan shoes covering His feet were of the softest leather, coming from the rekka, a creature native to Kiruva. Even the most prolific of hunters and fur traders in that faraway, river-crossed land seldom encountered the small, cautious animal, rarer by far than ermine or sable. The hide of just one of the diminutive beasts alone was worth several quality war stallions, and two rekka had been used to fashion His footwear, part of a lavish gift from the last Grand Prince of Kiruva.

The Unifier's waist was tied about with a light belt woven of golden thread, which pulled His long tunic in, while also serving as a graceful adornment.

Truly, the Unifier was a vision of regality and grace, without equal.

The Unifier did not claim any one heritage, realm, or ethnicity, instead seeming to possess many lineages, hearkening from all the known lands of Ave. Though the subject was rarely raised directly in His presence, there was little to nothing known of His true origins. The only knowledge held by the scholars and monks was that He had risen up rather suddenly from the masses in Avanor, in a tumultuous age long ago.

His ascent had come at a dizzying in speed, a tale of epic proportion now sung by gleeman and bards across the lands. Coming during a bitter time of war and upheaval, the Unifier had swiftly become indispensable to Avanor. His reputation had spread like lightning, as He gave incomparably wise counsels to Avanor's lords, and was then involved in incredible, supernatural events that were witnessed by multitudes. How He had gained their ear in the first place was forgotten, but its affects were not.

He had been regarded by all as unwaveringly selfless, and as a dedicated peacemaker, helping the Duchy to avert many of the little internal wars between Avanoran barons that had caused so much suffering among the populace. In this area, He was far more effective than even the Western Church's Peace of the All-Father movement, which had been created to lessen the violence and ensuing suffering of the peasantry. The people of Avanor began to look to Him more than the Church, to resolve their dilemmas. Then, a very unexpected development had occurred, one that had surprised everyone.

The last titled Duke of Avanor, William The Bold, had lost his only heir to an unexpected illness, incurred during the onset of the young man's prime. It was a dark sickness that even the mystical powers of the Unifier had been unable to thwart.

Trusting nobody else, the old Duke had designated the powerful Duchy over to the Unifier upon his passing. The timing was most fortunate, as the populace saw it, as the declaration had preempted much further trouble when the Duke passed away rather abruptly, within just days of naming the Unifier to succeed him. The people lamented the Duke's fate, believing that tremendous grief had broken his will to live.

To the Unifier, the death of the young man and the Duke, and the timings of their demises, were not mysteries, but just a few of the secrets that He harbored. The Unifier had risen up with no established name or quality of lineage. Yet His charisma was without equal, and his powerful, commanding presence inspired people, both great and small, to follow Him.

He offered a compelling vision of a world governed by one order, a rule of law equal for everyone in it, in which all lands could prosper, and all wars would be brought to an end. The only conflict that He desired to prosecute was one that would achieve this unprecedented state in Ave, the War to End All Wars, seen as a very noble goal by the rulers of lands used to chaos and plight.

His incredible qualities, and the unparalleled vision that He embraced, were why there had been no subsequent challenge to His hold upon the Duchy of Avanor. At first, He had given no name, merely calling Himself the Servant of the People. By sole virtue of His magnetic persona, bringing even the most volatile of rival barons into cooperation for the betterment of Avanor, the Avanorans had soon begun referring to Him by the name that the world now knew Him by; the Unifier.

He had selected Avanor for two very specific reasons, one having to do with the solitary mountain looming over Avalos, and the other involving its storied people.

The land of Avanor had been fertile ground for the Unifier's ambition. The spreading of a new order and fighting a war to end all wars resonated strongly with the blood of Avanor's people, no strangers to martial adventures. From the days when Thrydrik the Wanderer and his Midragardan band had first been given rights to the land by King Louis I and intermarried with the Galleans, to the conquests in Norengal, Paleria, and Gael, to the raising of Kingdoms in the Sunlands during the Holy Wars, Avanor had made its presence known in blood and fire across the face of Ave.

History recorded many bold testimonies to the small, potent land, whose people had conquered kingdoms and triumphed against tremendous odds. They were an ideal kind of people to support the Unifier in the beginning of His rise. From the seat of Avanor, the Unifier had gone forward to build an initial alliance of Seven Kingdoms, which had spearheaded the influence and acquiescence that followed thereafter.

Few had objected to the rapid ascension, as none wished to be seen as in conflict with a being that most held to be personally blessed by the All-Father of the Western and Eastern Churches, or The One God, according to the followers of the Prophet. The fact that The Unifier did not show any signs of age was cited as a glorious sign that He was truly a rightly guided man. It was commonly held that no son of evil could transcend the very laws of life, gifted with such physical beauty and a silvered tongue. Even the Great Vicar of the West and the Grand Shepherd of the East refused to challenge these widespread beliefs, vigilant as they were against all forms of heresy.

To the more perceptive within the realm, it seemed as if time itself was moving faster. The Unifier would not have disagreed with their assessment, for things were indeed well in motion that led towards immense, unprecedented ends.

The harshest truth of it was that only the Unifier, and a handful of others, knew what the nature of those ends really were. Each and every day His influence was spreading farther, and that of His Enemy declined, continuing the legacy that had been born out of the blackest and most fiery pits, transcending time itself. From a fathomless fall, a glorious ascension was being forged by sheer force of will and power. The road of vengeance led steadfastly towards a resplendent crown, one that was now within grasp.

The Unifier silently gazed out over the mighty city of Avalos, and the luxuriant sheen of the ocean waters reaching out towards the west. The steady breezes coursing in off of the sea buffeted the pennons flying from the numerous towers of the titanic citadel, both on the terraces below, as well as from the singular, great standard flapping against the unsullied backdrop of the teal sky far overhead. The pennon snapped about vigorously in the high winds, exhibiting its blazing white star at the apex of the vast citadel.

The waters of the capacious harbor fed by the Saina River teemed with the sails of numerous ships, from very small vessels rowed by a single man, to great merchant round ships and oared galleys.

As it was nearly the summit of the day, the city below was abounding with activity, its traffic coursing steadily through its narrow streets. Large throngs were gathered within its great market squares, engaged in the day's business.

Graced with many great towers set at intervals between the robust gatehouses commanding the entrances to Avalos, the far ranging circuit walls on the city's outer edge hemmed in its most important elements. Beyond those walls, and past the clinging suburbs, the surrounding countryside could be seen for league upon league to the distant horizons.

The low, undulating terrain revealed the orderly, telltale signs of numerous cultivated fields and outlying villages. The rich green of the spring was emerging into its fullness, enlivening a beautiful panorama of sparkling blue waters, green and flowering trees, wavy grasses, and vivid meadows, arrayed amongst the signs of human construction and habitation.

Affording such a magnificent view, the apex of the citadel was not the only spectacular vantage point on the prominent mountain. The great citadel had been built according to the direction of an assemblage of the greatest architectural minds across the world of Ave. No less would have sufficed for the Unifier.

A small army of elite stonecutters, sculptors, and carpenters had found themselves completely engrossed for several years in building the principle edifices occupying the various terraces, aided by multitudes of porters and other manual laborers involved with the epic construction.

The great northeastern empire of Theonia, known for its lavish palaces, golden-domed churches, and spectacular craftsmanship in marble and stone, had sent its greatest builder and architect, Andronikos Comnenus. The Kingdom of Paleria, now a part of the Sacred Empire, had dispatched its best designers, who had guided the building of several wondrous castles that had been built deftly into the sides of mountains. Architects of Avanor and Norengal, renowned for having achieved many great successes in building powerful, nearly impregnable castles, had pushed themselves beyond any level that they had previously known in addressing the needs of fortification. Gallea, Ehrengard, Lambar, the Fahtamid Khalif, the Great Emir of Andamoor, and many others had contributed their most capable minds and bountiful resources.

Several individuals had been sent across tremendous distances, undertaking harrowing journeys just to bring their own insights and expertise to the awesome endeavor. A large proportion of these hailed from the exotic lands of the far east, the mysterious places where even the farthest-ranging adventurers rarely tread.

Also testifying powerfully to the unique nature of the citadel, and the exalted Lord that it was built for, the spectacular creation had not been completed without the involvement of a few contributors of an extremely unusual nature. An enigmatic group had suddenly manifested during the construction of the great palace and citadel, from origins known only to the Unifier. After their arrival they had gone into the depths of the mountain, only to emerge and depart swiftly upon the great palace-citadel's completion. The hidden individuals were uniformly very tall and lean, and impeccably silent and graceful in their movements. Dark face veils had shrouded their very faces, not entirely unlike the fashion common to many of the fanatical warriors of Andamoor.

Their presence known by their mere arrival, their separation from the laborers, artisans, and designers afterwards was rigidly maintained by a dedicated, ardent force culled from the elite of the Unifier's own garrisons. The very few persons who had come within any close proximity to these obscured figures had reported feeling a chilling fear, or an overwhelming sense of anxiety, take firm hold of them. Most, with nervous laughs, related that they had shrugged it off later as just a trick of a fanciful mind, or the result of too much fatigue incurred from overworking.

In just over ten years, with the efforts of so many thousands of laborers, innumerable oxen and horses, and countless thousands of pounds of gold and silver, the huge edifice sprouted and bloomed to ever greater heights on the mountainside. To the surrounding populace, the grandiose constructs seemed like a living, organic entity, vigorously rising up the side of the lone mountain that stood sentinel over Avalos.

Great quantities of rock and soil had first been removed from the mountain, as vast platforms were cut out and leveled, prepared for the buildings that were then erected upon their surfaces. Many laborers had kept pieces of the black rock as mementos, as it was of a unique kind, found only upon the mountain itself. Seven terraces were prepared in all, the largest at the base of the mountain, and six others rising in concentric fashion above the first.

As a whole, the citadel was an unparalleled, triumphant achievement, and a tribute of a magnitude never before seen in any realm of Ave. The end result was a fortress and palace complex unrivaled in its collective design, splendor, size, and strength.

The mountain citadel had been built for one singular purpose; to honor the eminent being that now stood silently on the high tower, gazing out over the capital city. No other place in Ave was more appropriate for the seat of His worldly power, the place from where the way was being prepared for the One whom He served.

The august figure did not move for quite some time, senses far beyond those of mortals telling Him that something momentous and profound was about to occur within the world. What it was, He could not yet tell, but He knew that it carried great danger, as much as it did tremendous potential.

He knew that His most challenging task would involve divining its nature, and turning it to His own purposes. He did not fear it in the slightest. Rather, He saw an opportunity beckoning; to hasten the day when the world itself would be cleansed, and then recreated, ushering in an age that could not arrive a moment too soon.

section 1

JANUS

"Daddy's gone."

The thunderous words hurled Janus Roland into a spinning descent, his chest tightening as his breath froze within him.

He had just gone to sleep, less than one hour before, after drifting off while reading a novel. The previous evening had been relaxing and uneventful, holding no warning that his entire world was about to be irrevocably shattered.

A surreal feeling enveloped him as he sat up from bed, as if he was in the midst of some feverish nightmare. Indeed, reality had been turned upside down, and from that moment on it was as if color had been drained out of everything.

The world was cast in a cold, sickly pallor from that moment of shock onward. If a hell existed, Janus would not have disputed that the immediate aftermath of that horrid night was a sharp taste of its environs.

In disbelief, snapped awake with heart pounding, he stumbled from his bedroom across the hallway from his parents' room. Kneeling by the side of the bed, as if in the midst of saying a prayer, was the still form of his father.

Janus knew the truth of it all from the moment that he set his eyes on the motionless form of his father, his hero and his best friend. Here was the man that Janus felt that he had so far let down by the lack of success in his own life, the one person that Janus so badly wanted to have reason to be proud of him.

From then on, Janus knew that he would never even have the chance to have his father see him realize any dreams.

Janus would never forget the cold, clammy feeling as he set his hand down upon his father's back, nor the discoloration that he noticed instantly in patches on his father's exposed skin.

This was not the man who had become his mentor, and who had been a loving and sacrificing father to his family. There was absolutely no presence of the beloved man within that bedroom. Janus' father was absent. The silent form by the bed was an empty husk.

Nevertheless, the folded hands up on the bed, in front of his father's face-down head, had been the very ones that had patted Janus on the back only the night before, as Janus talked of his enduring frustrations and obstacles in his life's path.

If there was one thing to be grateful of, it was the fact that Janus' father's face was set down into the mattress. Janus did not ever want to have the image of his father's death mask burned into his memory.

The rest of that night was a hellish blur, filled with dizzying images of blue and red lights circling in the court where Janus' parents lived. There were the neighbors groggily peering out of their windows and doors nearby, roused by the sudden commotion disturbing the formerly tranquil night.

The first to arrive had been a crew of firemen, who confirmed what Janus and his mother already knew. Others came, struggling with the removal of the body as Janus' father was a considerably large man. The sight of the men straining and struggling with the body through the front door was horribly distressful, looking as if they were removing nothing more than a bulky piece of furniture.

Janus had to remind himself in that moment that his father was not in that bag.

Janus did not even hear the words of the representatives from the funeral home later that night, as they kindly oversaw the details of the whole horrible process for the family.

A police officer had gently asked Janus and his mother several questions a little later, though every word spoken was left shrouded in mist.

The only thing that Janus could remember of the tall, young, light-haired officer was the manifest trace of compassion upon his face and within his tone. There was no mistaking that the officer abhorred having to ask the mandated legal questions required of the grieving wife and son.

In later days, Janus was grateful that his sister, living in another apartment, had been spared that whole surreal nightmare.

A part of Janus had died that night, as other parts of him had died before with each and every loss that he had suffered. Death had torn yet another precious life from Janus' world with pitiless abruptness, and this time it had taken one of the two most momentous individuals in his life. Death had shown once again its true face, the antithesis of life and goodness.

Janus already knew that the gaze from that malevolent visage spared nothing, manifesting its presence and ugliness under his own roof more than once before. Its malignant touch had withered away his first dog with a wasting disease, the first time that he had beheld its terrible countenance. It had been an ear-shattering thunderclap in the tranquil life of a ten-year-old boy. Death had then visited again, consuming his second dog with a horrid cancer. It had returned only a few years later, bringing another cancer upon his gray tabby cat, as if it were a diabolical encore.

That last visit of death, ending with an innocent, loving creature's still body wrapped in a blanket, shaved patches riddling the cat's emaciated form due to the multitude of desperate treatments to stave off the wicked assault, was still a raw wound when the most terrible visit of them all had come so suddenly upon Janus.

If there was one truth that had been ground into Janus through all of the previous experiences, it was that there was only life and the absence of life; the former being the purest of goods, and the latter the most corrupt of evils.

Janus loathed death, plainly, and simply. He regarded it with a burning hatred. It was the fact that death felt entirely out of place, like some terrible aberration, that always struck Janus in a quintessentially strange manner. Each life that death so callously destroyed was a life that was particular, unique, and irreplaceable in all of eternity.

There really was no comfort to be had. If there was anything on the other side of death, it was hidden from the view of those suffering its aftermath.

Janus struggled just to get through the days. The passage of time did not bring with it a return to functionality. Instead, a deep and abiding depression had crept in, rendering Janus listless and forlorn.

He could not see the point of it all, as every embrace of another life lead to a certain end filled with grief. The person that chose to love others in such a world was the greatest of fools. The more that one loved, the more pain that one eventually took upon oneself.

Janus soon found himself going through the motions of daily routines and work, while sinking into deep abysses when alone. He interacted with his friends, but knew that he was now a shell of his former self.

He found himself wondering at times just how much longer his friends' patience would last before they fully abandoned him to his morose new world.

Janus was encompassed with a dark mist. His spirit was crying out desperately inside for even a single chance to find his way out of the thick, cold murk; a chance to see the sun of life in an azure, timeless sky, and to feel its warm, vibrant rays against his face once again. Yet deep down in his heart, he knew that any such hope was merely wishful thinking.

Black oblivion was easier to accept.

MERSHAD

Mershad Shahab sat quietly and morosely in his assigned room at the university dormitory.

For Mershad the small space was a veritable sanctuary. Just outside the door to that room was a world growing darker and more unsettling by the day.

The television monitor in his room remained dark, and Mershad was increasingly reticent to turn it on. To him, it was just a window to the core of the very things that he so badly wanted to escape from.

The government of the United States had gone through the appearance of a deliberation, but in truth it was little more than a formality. Without much delay, the two chambers of Congress had authorized the president to use force in an ongoing dispute with a much smaller, weaker country far to the east.

That country, Iraq, just happened to be the birthplace of Mershad's parents, and was the current residence of nearly all of his blood relatives. Mershad, his two brothers, and his sister were the first in the entire family to be born in the USA.

Mershad's ancestral lands were indeed ruled by a heavy-handed dictator, but the strongman was of little threat to anyone beyond the country's borders. The country's military and economic power had eroded under withering sanctions in place for well more than a decade. The country could not even sustain electric power in its largest cities anymore, and its most basic infrastructure was crumbling.

Mershad could not believe the public campaign that had been unleashed to build up support for an attack. To him, the image created by the media versus the reality that he was well aware of was staggering.

It was heavily publicized that Iraq possessed weapons of great destructive potential, and would use them if not soon overthrown. Also put forth was the idea that the strongman ruler was in league with shadowy militants bent on holy war.

That postulation, to Mershad's amazement, ignored the seemingly obvious fact that those same militant organizations openly deemed the strongman to be one of their prime enemies. He was considered far too secular and worldly in their eyes, and was an opponent of their dreams of outright religious rule.

The media was filled with stories and images that painted a dark and foreboding picture of the dictator and the power that he wielded in Iraq. The tone of the stories had often taken on a hysterical and frenzied pitch. If one were to believe the reports, the strongman was a dire and immediate existential threat to the USA.

Underneath all of it, as Mershad well knew, were a couple of great prizes to be claimed. Iraq sat astride one of the world's largest sources of oil. Even more valuable in a political world, its location offered control of a strategic geography for wielding authority over the entire Middle East.

Through massive diplomacy, in many instances using outright bribery or coercion, a great coalition of nations was brought together. A huge military force was gradually amassed on the borders of Iraq, and it soon became apparent to all but the most naive that war was imminent.

The actual war had begun with a massive bombing conducted by hordes of aircraft and missiles. News networks, beamed across satellites, were awash with images of the tremendous, devastating assault. The highly surgical bombing attack was aided by new space-based weapon systems, technological wonders that filled the general public with an eerie sense of awe.

Shortly after the assault had begun, Mershad had heard an eruption of elated, spirited cheers from other students in the dormitory, as if they were spectators gathered at some sort of sporting event. Whenever he recalled those whoops of exuberance afterwards, he felt a chill seep into him.

Up and down the halls, students had gathered around the televisions, eating and drinking as if they were observing a sporting event, watching the images of destruction raining down upon Baghdad.

Mershad's extended family lived within that very same capital, and each vivid scene of the attack frightened and saddened him. Each massive explosion indicated within the reports, and shown in all their terrible might on the video coverage, could easily have been the last living moment of members of Mershad's very own family.

They were simple people, caught up in events far beyond their control. Their jobs as electricians, construction workers, working in restaurants, running small shops and the like were pursuits no different than those of the people of the USA.

Mershad had never personally been to his ancestral nation before, but he knew that the people of Iraq, such as his relatives, posed no grave threat to the world. Deep pain wracked Mershad's heart as he imagined the immense fear that must have been gripping his relatives and the millions of people who had been summarily condemned within that country.

Tallies of the destruction of infrastructure, casualty estimates, and sorties were little more than statistics for some sort of diabolical game. Interviewed military personnel seemed to barely be able to suppress the excitement that they felt towards the thunderous displays of martial prowess.

Mantras speaking of patriotism and troop support were repeated time and time again in the inundating media coverage. To the public, the whole episode was presented as another chapter in the stark conflict of good versus evil.

The only thing wrong with the scenario was that the defined enemy included Mershad's poor, struggling, extended family, and so very many others like them. Mershad wanted to scream out that good, real people were dying or having their lives irrevocably eviscerated.

The vivid new images pouring across the screens each day became increasingly chilling to Mershad's soul.

Resentment had quickly grown within Mershad towards the other students. It absolutely horrified him that most of the students did little to question or to even think about what was happening, and the underlying motivations. Only a few scattered bands of students bothered to voice any kind of opposition or protest. They were dismissed largely as malcontents, misguided or ignorant at best, unpatriotic to the edge of being treasonous at worst.

Then there was the way that his fellow citizens and students had begun to treat him. That was by far the most troubling for Mershad, a loyal USA citizen from the first second of his life onward.

The obvious stares, jostles, and insults had begun, and soon increased with frequency, a great many targeting his ethnicity. It was as if he were some covert sympathizer with the enemy, or a potential terrorist.

He had read the accounts of people physically assaulting others with his same ethnic background. He had to steel his mind to the relentless mental assault brought on by the harassment that he suffered. He also had to keep his awareness up, lest he find himself becoming a victim to an especially violent assault himself.

In a torturous silence, he feared and sorrowed for his family, and prayed that they might somehow escape the devastating onslaught. He also feared for the people of the country that he had pledged his allegiance to, many of whom had suddenly become so hostile to him.

As the days wore on, and the reports of destruction and civilian emergencies mounted ever higher, Mershad's heart grew unbearably heavier. He could do nothing to immunize or numb himself to the terrible realities.

Then matters became even worse. Some violent attacks had occurred around the world on interests related to the great economic powers of the United Nations. The attacks on innocent lives served to spiral the paranoia directed towards those of Mershad's ethnicity.

Mershad began walking with his eyes down, going to classes very early, and staying a few minutes afterwards to let the room empty out. He did not linger anywhere in public longer than he had to. He found himself spending most of his time either at the campus mosque, within the solemn refuge of his dorm room, or at the job that he held in the student cafeteria, washing dishes and doing some after hours custodial work.

He could not focus on his studies, his mind racing with a multitude of thoughts. His prayers had suffered in earnestness, as he had trouble reconciling how God could allow the traumatic, devastating attacks to fall so mercilessly upon the millions of innocents trapped within Iraq.

Sapped in mind, sapped in body, and sapped in spirit, Mershad had quickly lost the passionate and curious approach that he had always taken to life. His only relief was that his parents were safe, though their agonies were great as they had not been able to contact any of their relatives by phone or other means. Communications had been among the very first things taken out by the attacking coalition forces.

With the fate of the majority of his family shrouded in the ominous unknown, he and his parents had been given an arduous and sorrowful path to endure.

A few times, he had allowed himself to consider just quitting the university and moving back home. It seemed logical at times to weather the storm by just staying out of it. Each time, he had checked himself from giving in to the tempting urge. He knew that he had to continue forward and live his life, or the forces of ignorance would truly prevail.

In some ways, he found that his will to continue was in itself a shouted defiance at the organization and attitude of the world at large. While it gave him scant relief, it did harden his resolve just enough to keep the world from becoming overwhelming.

ERIN

The alarm clock continued to buzz annoyingly, while still failing to arouse Erin from the slumber that she had become so well accustomed to in recent years.

Over the years, Erin had developed a personal art form whenever it came to matters of comfort and ease. At the present moment, she had attained a virtual mastery of that art.

A few classes at the local community college and a part time job were now her only true responsibilities. Through the use of a shrewd form of diplomatic maneuvering, which required congeniality at times, and a display of hot temper at others, she had managed to achieve a state of existence where she received little resistance from family or friends for her choice of lifestyle.

Her routine held a few principal elements.

After the obligatory class or two, she headed to her restaurant job that lasted well into the evening. Following her shift, she patronized one of the local nightclubs or coffee shops.

Her network of haunts was largely nocturnal, such that she usually trudged back home just a few short hours before dawn.

Rolling over in bed, Erin reached across and smacked the alarm clock. She succeeded in silencing the irritating tone, her blow coming close to crippling the clock itself. Her mind caught somewhere in the nebulous area between the conscious and the subconscious, her thoughts slowly started to orient upon the new day.

The only class that had been scheduled for the day had already ended an hour ago. There was no test or papers due, and she had gotten home very late the previous evening, so she felt little guilt at having set the day's alarm well past the end of her scheduled class.

There was no work shift to worry about either, as it was her cherished day off from the drudgery of restaurant work.

She was aware that her friends Uli and Razor were going to have a little gathering later that evening at their apartment. Her closest friend, Lynn, had informed her of the fact the previous day.

There was still plenty of time left to go online and piddle around with a few friends within her electronic world, perhaps enjoy a new movie through the video on demand service, or watch some satellite television.

She knew that she possessed a luxurious buffer of time before she had to leave for Uli's apartment. With a satisfied purr, she rolled back over on the bed and let the subconscious win out for a little while longer.

LOGAN

Logan's ample black locks were tossed randomly about in the gusts of unseasonably chilly winds that swept down upon him as he continued walking down the street.

The night would fall soon enough, and for most persons that would be a signal for rest or for recreation.

For Logan, day, night, and hour were of little overall significance.

In fact, he had already felt a small pang of anxiety at having taken the long, late-afternoon walk through the old neighborhood by the university campus.

His early morning to late afternoon period had been entirely devoured by programming endeavors, as he worked feverishly on his latest digital magic. Piling up caffeinated beverages and hours alike, Logan finally found himself at the edge of exhaustion. His eyes were about to cross from constantly being chained to his monitors, poring over every element of code and pixel.

The three separate projects that he was currently laboring on were still not remotely close to the finish line. A consummate perfectionist, Logan had actually raised the ire of some clients by incurring a few short delays to bring projects in at a level that exceeded their original requests.

More often than not, though, he had endured a litany of revisions. Some clients requested things to be taken out that they themselves had demanded in the beginning. Others added things that they had at first declared that they absolutely did not want.

There were many moments where he just needed to walk away

from it all, and this late afternoon jaunt was one such time.

His stomach needing some sustenance, he had first gone to the little Chinese restaurant perched on the edge of the university campus. He had always admired the sheer drive of the restaurant's owner, who labored with a kindred orientation upon his craft of Chinese cuisine and restaurant management.

After downing a quart-sized plate of pork-fried rice and a ginger ale, Logan had decided to extend his break and go for a walk on the outskirts of the campus.

The campus itself, on which he had attended four semesters of classes before transferring to another college to finish his degree, was just across the road.

The street that bordered the western edge of the campus, near the block that held the Chinese restaurant, led straight downtown.

There was often an eclectic mix of individuals wandering about the collection of unique little shops adjacent to the campus area.

It was the sort of environment where nobody really stood out, where one could decide to sink into the background or shout out their presence proudly on a street corner. Logan was far more inclined towards the former, though he was sometimes amused when he witnessed the latter.

Glancing up the street, he could see a few garishly-dressed young individuals heading into a specialty bookstore. Just passing them, a scruffy man in a long overcoat was walking down his side of the street.

He was a tall man, with a mop of lengthy, tangled hair, and a long, unkempt beard, both whitened with advanced age. Logan surmised that he was one of the many homeless individuals that often lingered in the area.

While Logan did not have a lot of money on him, he opted to browse in a few of the music shops and art galleries.

Briskly, Logan walked up the street, passing a popular eatery that was open all hours and served as a hangout for many of the university students. Already, it held a substantial crowd inside.

Looking ahead, Logan saw that his path was about to directly cross with the homeless individual.

At a closer vantage, the man appeared to move a little easier than Logan would have guessed by the years that the man's appearance suggested. Logan attributed his overestimation of the man's age to his very weathered skin, making him look much older than he truly was.

His thick beard covered his mouth, and his uneven hair splayed over his shoulders, cascading down his back and chest. He looked to be almost six and a half feet tall, a full six inches taller than Logan.

The man had one particularly striking feature that caused Logan to nearly stop in his tracks. The man's eyes were like nothing that Logan had ever seen before.

They were a deep, rich blue that seemed to exude a tranquility and ease that Logan had never seen on the pained, troubled expressions on most of the homeless in the area.

"Can you help me get something to eat?" the man asked him in a calm, gentle voice.

The question caught Logan off guard, and he found himself staring into the man's striking eyes.

Recomposing himself, he replied, "No problem, let me check… see what I have … just a second."

Digging into his pockets, he found a few bills and a little change. Without counting it, knowing that it was not that much to begin with, he gave it all over to the older man.

The man accepted the money, folding his long fingers over it. He nodded slowly towards Logan, with an approving look.

"Thank you," the old man said in the gentle voice. "I have seen far fewer generous people these days. I do desire to repay you."

"It's no problem at all," Logan replied. "Call it a gift. No need for any repayment. We all need a break once in a while. I've had days I've been short too."

A slight grin came to the man's face, barely perceptible through his thick mass of facial hair.

"Thank you again, and have a nice day," the man replied, nodding again to Logan as he headed onward, right in the direction of the all-hours eatery.

Abruptly, as if he had forgotten to mention something important, the man paused and turned back towards Logan. He looked directly into Logan's eyes, with an unwavering gaze.

"Then my gift to you is this. Perceptions of the rightness of something can often be in error. Perceptions of the wrongfulness of something can also often be in error. It is always wisdom to look again closely. The true victory is in the correct judgment, and one can always change a judgement if one is still breathing. Things are often not as they appear. This is true on many levels, and in many ways. Bless you, for your kindness to a stranger, and remember this."

Turning back again, without waiting for a reply, the man resumed his path.

Logan watched the old man walk off. He did not have the first idea as to what to make of the old man's parting words.

Part of him wanted to brush the man off as merely another bizarre component of the colorful tapestry of a downtown and campus environment. Another part of him was not so hasty. The old man had spoken succinctly and intelligently, and Logan wondered what his story really was. Logan saw no real way to find out the truth, even as intriguing as the old man was. Letting off a little sigh, he finally shrugged and continued into the front door of the popular campus music store.

For the next thirty minutes or so, he browsed the music racks. If he had some money to spare, he knew that he could have easily spent it. As it was, he had to file away notes in his mind, at least until he had a little more discretionary income.

Without making any purchase, he walked out of the store and turned to head back. A few blocks away was his house, situated within an older neighborhood. It was well past the time that he needed to be returning to his work.

Looking ahead, he saw the homeless man that he had given money to. The old man was crossing the street about a block down from where he was.

Coming down towards the street from the opposite side was a person that Logan recognized, accompanied by two others that he did not. Logan paused to watch the inevitable crossing of paths, curious to witness the result.

The trio of neatly dressed, clean-shaven young men neared the old man as he stepped up onto the sidewalk. Logan recognized the young man in the middle as being from an immense church in town that Logan had done some work for on a few occasions.

Softball fields, classroom complexes, basketball gyms, auditoriums that could seat over five thousand individuals, and more occupied the monstrous church complex. Logan was well aware that many people moving to Lexington seeking to advance in the community joined the prominent, influential church.

Logan was sure that the three young men were probably doing a little better than himself in a financial sense, and surely were capable of helping the old man. He watched the developing encounter with a little interest.

The old man turned to them as they approached, and from his gestures Logan knew that the old man was soliciting some help from the three young men.

Logan watched with amusement as the three young men stiffened up a little as they neared the strange homeless man. Their body language was clear enough. They were well aware of the old man's overture and presence.

Two of the men soldiered onward, trying to act as if they did not even notice the old man. The third was shaking his head in the negative, at least giving the old man a response, though he barely broke stride to do so.

The homeless man did not exhibit any change in posture, as they passed, simply nodding to them and continuing on up the street. One of the two young men that had supposedly not taken account of the old man chanced a glance back at him, as the trio neared the side of the street that Logan was on.

Logan had not been surprised in the least by their rejection of the old man. Their response was exactly as he had predicted, though for the old man's sake he wished that he had not been accurate.

He almost broke into a laugh at the worried expression upon the face of the one looking back towards the old man, as if the fellow was deeply concerned that the old man might be following them to accost them.

Shaking his head, Logan chuckled to himself as he walked onward. He knew that the three had religion, but was not so sure that they had faith. Watching their encounter with the homeless man prompted him to muse for a few moments on the subject of religion, and how it was not necessarily the same thing as faith. It was an interest of his, at least on an intellectual level, even if he did not practice any particular form of it.

The concepts of free will, gods, devils, and destinies intrigued Logan well enough. He had absorbed quite enough about those topics over the years, at a parochial grade school and through regular independent reading that had given him a solid grasp of the world's various faiths.

There were some obvious conclusions that he had come to.

History marched onward as the dust of self-proclaimed prophets, predicting the world's end, had long since blown away in the winds of time. That same history also held a litany of figures who had shamed the faiths that they were public leaders of, while some of the most pious and reverent persons of history had been persecuted, defamed, and killed as heretics.

Logan had come to see religion as a creature that differed very little from the basic forces that ruled mankind. Adherence and affiliation to religion, in the proper context for a given culture, was used across the world to bring power, wealth, and influence in a manner that had little to do with the tenets of the various faiths themselves.

The inability of the public to recognize this reality had long angered Logan, and turned him away from any positive connotations when it came to matters of spirit. It had become difficult for him to separate the concepts of religion and faith.

The world was filled with many groups that were irrevocably convinced that they had full dominion on truth. At best, only one of them could be right. At worst, none of them were right. Looking at it from a detached perspective, it was a confounding situation.

Logan had plenty of reason to doubt that any of the ones that he was aware of had full dominion, based upon the fruits of their histories and efforts. He also had never personally experienced a miracle, had never seen a spirit, and nor had anyone else that he knew.

There was also the troubling notion that the things that his religiously oriented parents, and similar friends of theirs, prayed for fervently never seemed to come to pass, some becoming far worse in many cases. In contrast, the things desired by many non-religious individuals that Logan knew had come to fruition, often with ease and abundance.

Logan was certainly not the person to ask regarding his opinions on the power of prayer.

Over time, he had seen more than enough evidence to convince him that mankind was very astute at intricate fabrications and deceptions.

With all of his heart, just for once, he wanted to see and experience something absolutely undeniable with his own eyes. No third party accounts, not even eyewitness accounts, would be acceptable substitutes for his desired experience.

Then, and only then, he might find something to put his faith into. If that day ever happened, he knew that he could finally let loose of many inhibitions and misgivings, and pour his heart and soul into a faith, and gladly leave his dissatisfying agnosticism far behind.

Maybe someday it would happen.

Maybe it would not.

He was not going to hold his breath while waiting.

Looking down at his watch, he saw that he still had almost an hour to go before night arrived.   Time would soon become a blur again as he hurled himself into his projects and submitted the visionary to the mundane as best as he could.

As always, it was clients before creativity.

It was not a pleasant course of action, but it did bring in an income.

RYAN

Ryan and Antoine jogged across the main street, heading towards the heart of the city as the shifting hues of sunset crossed into the uniformity of night.

Artificial light and sprawling shadows settled across the reawakening streets.   The lull between the rush hour and the nightlife was over, and traffic was just starting to pick up again.

It would still be a few more hours before the city curfew took effect, nothing but a minor nuisance to the two street-honed teenagers.

Ryan had recently set his affections towards a young lady of his age named Pamela, who lived a couple of blocks over from his small, crowded home.   To his view, the relationship was proceeding nicely, though he hoped that she would shake off some other guys that she was seeing and commit fully to him.

Relationships with attractive females were not the only matters occupying his mind.

Ryan was becoming more than a little nervous about Antoine during the course of recent weeks.   Antoine had been acquiring some additional revenue through some drug trafficking on the streets.   At first, he had started dealing in order to keep himself supplied with his favorite pills.   The money and pills had brought him more attention from women in their peer group, and several that were older.   Antoine was increasingly becoming absorbed in the attention that he was receiving.   Ryan feared that Antoine was beginning to get overconfident and careless.

Ryan knew well enough that Antoine was not on the higher levels of the business that enjoyed both friendship and economic influence with elements of law enforcement.   Antoine was on the low level, a group whose members were readily expendable. From their number came the overwhelming bulk of the periodic drug busts and accompanying roundups that were portrayed so vividly in the media.

Ryan feared for his friend's growing recklessness, knowing that he was well within the target range of one of those kinds of roundups. Yet he could not dissuade him from his newfound lifestyle.

"So, what's up with you and Pamela?" Antoine remarked, as they turned off the main street and started down towards the north side of town.

"Not long, Antoine ... not much longer," Ryan retorted, a mischievous glint reflecting in his eyes. "She's getting close to being with me twenty-four-seven."

"I wouldn't let a girl even look like she was playin' around with me. But I don't blame you with her. She looks so fine," Antoine complimented, smiling broadly.

"She sure does," Ryan replied, exhibiting his boyish grin.

His friendly face and relatively lanky build had prevented him from ever developing an aura of intimidation.

Several unfortunate youths had, over the course of his life, found out intimately that his seemingly benign image did not represent the underlying substance. A scrappy youth with a penchant for mixed martial arts, he had a nearly fatalistic aptitude to take on any challengers.

The disposition had gotten him into a lot of trouble, when he had rendered his mother's live-in boyfriend unconscious after the man had started a drunken spree of violence upon her one night. Instead of being branded a hero, Ryan had been promptly placed into the juvenile detention center. His mother had been lukewarm to him, pulled between his intervention and the strange dependency that she had developed with her abusive boyfriend.

Ryan's pattern had not changed during his period of incarceration. There, he had gotten into several scrapes with some of the others being held there, and had even assaulted one of the security guards.

It had all started a downward spiral.

Soon he was disrupting his classes at school, which had gotten him placed in the city's special education facility. There, his continued unwillingness to back down from challenges had garnered him many more opportunities for trouble, and not all of them had been resounding victories.

Ryan had a social worker to report to, and had been forced to attend some different counseling programs. He strongly resented both conditions but over the past year had grudgingly been cooperating, largely because of his friend, a restaurant owner near downtown named Lee Chen. It was Lee that had helped him from falling headlong into an abyss.

Lee had taken an acute interest in Ryan, often commenting that he saw in him a stout heart and keen intelligence. Taking him under his wing, as a mentor of sorts, Lee had let Ryan help out at his restaurant.

The experience had been positive, settling Ryan down enough so that he cooperated with his legal requirements. He had to admit that it had gotten him out of the worst of the cyclical quagmire that had served as his day to day life.

Those who saw Ryan with Lee at the restaurant were treated to a different side of the youth. None would have guessed at his tendency for fighting and causing disturbances. Instead, they saw an energetic, if not fully articulate, young man who had an offbeat sense of humor.

Lee preferred to see Ryan stay in that world, and the two had started to argue more and more as Ryan had begun to spend an increasing amount of time with Antoine. Ironically, Ryan was trying harder to gain influence with Antoine before his friend got caught in the snares of law enforcement.

Yet Ryan did not dispute Lee's claim that the demeanor and outlook of the youth quickly reversed when he was on the street.

Lee's assessment was about to be put to the test again, as Ryan took note of some familiar faces after he and Antoine had traveled another two blocks off the main street. With easy strides, they continued to close the distance to where three other teenaged guys were loitering about a dim parking lot.

The tension rose quickly when Ryan and Antoine walked near the three youths, who gave them hard looks.

One of the guys yelled out sharply to Ryan, "Hey! What are you looking at? You got some problem?"

The trigger went off in Ryan's head, and he once again proved Lee's claims.

"Looking at? Absolutely nothing!" he retorted, a feral look coming into his eyes as he put a heavy emphasis upon the last words.

The other three responded with a series of expletives. Antoine stood with Ryan, as the shouting match drew the two sides steadily closer.

One of the three suddenly launched a high punch at Ryan. Blazingly fast, he avoided the punch and moved in, landing a crunching blow on the nearest youth's face, spinning and catching a second on the jaw with an elbow strike, and landing a solid kick to the third youth's right knee.

All three of them crumpled to the ground, pain and stunned amazement upon their faces.

"Yeah, I thought so," Ryan mocked them.

"You thought so?" came a fourth voice.

Out of the shadows came another youth, carrying a sleek, black object in his hand that was pointed right at Ryan.

"Are you so bad now?" the fourth youth roared, walking slowly and holding the pistol forward.

Ryan had been in such moments before, and it was no time for bluster and bravado. He and Antoine took off at a sprint without delay. It was several blocks more before they finally slowed down.

They had not been chased, the fourth youth having remained behind with his friends after likely feeling that he had won back some of his group's damaged pride. Ryan and Antoine continued onward at a comfortable pace, their breath slowly returning to normal.

When they were a considerable distance away, Antoine turned to Ryan with a grin. "You didn't even let me have a chance to get some hits in!"

Ryan chuckled. "Had to do it. Shut them up quick, didn't I?"

"Save some for me next time," Antoine said.

"Maybe," Ryan replied, grinning and exchanging a series of spirited hand slaps with his friend.

The two cavorted about the downtown area for the next few hours, joking and talking with several individuals as they encountered others that they knew.

It was an inexpensive and mildly entertaining way to pass the time, until the curfew hour approached.

The thought of the curfew often made them laugh. The only ones who followed it were the ones that never got into any trouble in the first place. The youth that had little to lose, and were adept at trouble, simply had a new thrill added to their adventures as they worked to avoid the officers of the law.

Ryan and Antoine knew that if they were caught, their parents would receive a citation and fine. The fine was the only aspect that would raise his mother's ire, and Antoine's mother and stepfather as well, as their interest in the two boys was negligible at best.

After a brief consultation, the two decided to go on up to Lee Chen's restaurant. Lee's Wok was a fairly lengthy trek from where they were, but they made the journey of several blocks to the south side of downtown without incident.

Only one police cruiser passed them on the way. The officer eyed them as he slowed down for a few seconds, making Ryan and Antoine tense as they prepared to run, but the officer abruptly sped up again and continued on down the street.

When they had finally reached the restaurant, Lee was diligently mopping up the floors as the place had closed around an hour prior to their arrival.

His short, straight black hair was under a white cap, and he was clad in his familiar apron, over a short-sleeved collared shirt and a pair of work slacks. His round face always seemed to be held in a positive countenance, though Ryan was well aware that the man dealt with constant stresses.

Lee was clean-shaven, except for the hints of a moustache below his nose, the latter being of a flatter profile. His dark eyes had a kindly look to them as he glanced up at their entrance, and he smiled amiably in greeting.

"Hi guys, I suppose I can't tell you two that we are already closed," he said, with his light Chinese accent.

"No you can't, Lee. You can't get rid of us. You know that…. So what's up?" Ryan asked. "How did we do tonight?"

"Not bad. Little above average. I may not be able to get rid of you, but I can't entertain you. I have to cut egg rolls tonight, both regular and vegetable, so I'll be here for awhile. What are you two up to?" Lee inquired of them.

"Not much, just hangin' around," Ryan replied, his voice lowering.

"Ryan got three at once tonight, you should have seen him!" Antoine said with a flare of excitement in his voice. He then quickly added, "They attacked him first, Lee. Ryan didn't start it."

Ryan frowned and gave Antoine a light elbow to the ribs. He did not regret the fight, but he was increasingly discovering that he did not like the feeling of Lee's disappointment.

As expected, the smile faded quickly from Lee's face. "Trouble again? Fighting does no good. It can only lead to bad things for you! You know that Ryan!"

"I do my best," Ryan mumbled in the aftermath of the scolding.

"I hope you are here to work tomorrow. We will need help, Ryan, and it will keep you from making bad decisions," Lee said curtly.

Ryan nodded. "I can be here, if you need help."

"I do. And remember, we close early on Sunday, and I'm hoping to watch some movies, just to give you two some advanced warning," Lee said, his tone lightening. "We can order some food in too."

Ryan knew that the invitation was largely for him, though Lee had politely extended it to his friend. Lee was not overly fond of Antoine, as Ryan was well aware.

"Are you going to go all out? Will it be Chinese?" Ryan quipped, seeing a chance to escape Lee's disapproving tones.

"No," Lee responded with a grin. "It must be something else. Pizza maybe."

"That'll do," Ryan said. "I'm in. And you?"

He glanced over at Antoine.

"I can't," Antoine replied. "I got some stuff I gotta take care of on Sunday."

As with every time that he was in Lee's presence, Antoine was careful to keep his street endeavors at a low profile. He need not have bothered, as Lee had long since figured out the truths about Antoine's activities.

Ryan had not denied the obvious many months ago when Lee had brought up the subject. His relationship with Lee had always been an open and honest one, and he was not about to let Antoine's foolhardy pursuits cause him to taint what was perhaps his only pure friendship.

"Well, I just remembered something. I will be there unless Pamela wants to do something," Ryan stated with a grin.

"Women, women," Lee said smiling, shaking his head. "They used to keep me busy, worried … and broke. Until I got smarter. Now I am much better off! Less headaches. More money in my pocket."

"Can't argue with that. You got me there," Ryan replied, laughing.

"It's the truth," Lee replied. He then shrugged his shoulders. "Well, you two are welcome to stay here, and have a soda, but keep the front door locked. I need to get to making egg rolls."

"You need to take a vacation, man," Antoine said.

"I would if I won a lottery. But I gotta pay the bills. Trying to take care of saving some money for my nephew," Lee replied. "And my mother is my priority."

"You probably haven't missed a day of work in a hundred years," Ryan joked.

"I look good for being over a hundred then!" Lee retorted, as he set the floor mop down.

Walking across the room, he bolted the front door and turned the light to the main dining room off.

"Now, on to the back," he remarked.

Ryan, with Antoine behind him, followed Lee as he walked through the gloom of the dining room and proceeded to the back kitchen.

Lee opened a refrigerator door and pulled out a couple bottles of soda, a popular, ginger ale-like soft drink made regionally. He used a bottle opener to remove the caps and handed them over to Ryan and Antoine.

For himself, he opened a can of cherry-citrus soda.

"You run on caffeine, man," Ryan chided, as Lee chugged down about half of the can in the first draught.

"Fuel for the fire, The Official Drink of Lee's Wok," Lee boasted, holding the can up and smirking, as if on a television commercial.

"Not bad, not bad," Antoine said, nodding his head. "If I was the company president, I'd hire ya to promote."

"Well, if you ever do, remember, I get ten percent," Ryan interjected. "I introduced you all."

"Good business mind, Mister Ryan," Lee remarked, setting the can down and going over to the refrigerator to get some ingredients out of storage.

"And if we get rich, you can take a vacation," Ryan said.

"Wouldn't that be nice, just to get away?" Lee responded, with wistful sigh. "Haven't been able to get away for years. Have to work so hard just to keep everything together."

"Maybe we will get away someday. But just don't forget to take me with you if you go somewhere exciting. I've never been out of this town, ever. I would like to see the world someday," Ryan said.

"By the time we can see the world, they'll probably be able to take us to other whole worlds," Lee jested.

The façade of humor did not mask the shimmer of a distant regret in his eyes, as he looked down at the egg roll ingredients in his hands.

Before too much emotion welled up, his stoic demeanor returned to take command of his features.

"But they say that the show must go on, right?" Lee asked, looking over at the other two.

Lee turned his attention towards working on the preparations for the next batch of egg rolls, the passing fancy of talking about personal dreams now pushed to the side by obligation.

"Need some help with that?" Ryan inquired.

Lee shrugged his shoulders. "Sure, if you don't have anything better to do."

"Well, if Pamela was around, I sure would," he wisecracked, walking over.

Antoine crossed his arms and leaned against the wall, drinking his beverage. "I'll hang around, but I'm outta this."

Lee chuckled. "I'm not sure I would eat an egg roll that you made."

Antoine just shook his head. "Okay, Lee, I'll cut you some slack. Let's just say I like to supervise."

"Remind me to talk to you when I hire a manager for the restaurant," Lee said with evident sarcasm, evoking some laughter from the other two.

For the next couple of hours, Ryan helped cut Lee's work load by almost a full third. As he put the freshly made egg rolls back for the next day, Lee thumbed through some bills in his pocket and gave a few over to Ryan.

Ryan never would have asked, knowing how many times Lee had fed him for free or given him a bonus on his work pay. He also knew not to refuse, as Lee tended to be offended by refusals of a gift or bonus.

Lee and Ryan worked together on the last few tasks involved with closing up the restaurant. When they left the building, Lee ended up giving them a ride in his car.

As he dropped Ryan off, Lee reminded him about the hours that he wanted him to work at the restaurant the next day, and then drove onward.

The rest of the evening was largely uneventful, involving little more than the intake of substances and the playing of some video games.

When dawn was finally coming around, and his eyelids had grown very heavy, he sprawled out on a couch to get a couple hours of sleep.

Fatigue ensured that he would not stay awake for much longer, but before he finally succumbed to sleep his thoughts lingered on the past evening and the feelings within him.

The night had left him with an empty void inside.

In his heart he found that he did not feel any pride at the fight that he had been in earlier in the night. The only warmth of the evening had come from being around Lee, one of the few lights in a very dark world.

He felt a pang of guilt about Lee finding out about the scuffle, and knew then that he wanted to make Lee proud of him. His own father had nothing to do with him, and Ryan rarely saw the man since his parents had split up. His mother had always been far more interested in her boyfriends than what was happening to him.

Only Lee expected something grander out of Ryan.

Lee was the only one that had expressed a better world being possible for Ryan.

The owner of that little restaurant had given him something to grasp onto, and for that he was growing ever more grateful. He felt extremely lucky just to realize what Lee's ongoing gift to him was.

Even though Lee would likely choose some bad movies to watch, Ryan found himself really looking forward to seeing his truest friend later that afternoon for work, and for some movies on Sunday.

The thought put a smile on his face that lingered as he drifted off to sleep.

LOGAN

Deep into the night, Logan wearily leaned back in his fabric-upholstered office chair, finally surrendering as he rested his hands upon the arm rests. He rubbed his strained eyes slowly.

As if his momentary detachment were some kind of cue, there came a gentle rap upon the wood of his front door.

Rising up with a groan, he stretched his stiffened limbs and made his way out of his home studio to the front of the house.

The identity of the figure standing on the front porch awaiting him was not a surprise, even at the very late hour. Shorter than Logan, stocky, with a face that was normally cherubic, Antonio Guerrero now displayed a quite dour expression.

Logan wordlessly opened the screen door, and Antonio nudged past him as he entered the apartment.

"I know, you are probably busy right now, but I need to vent," Antonio muttered in an obvious state of great frustration. "I am not going to take much more of this."

Behind Antonio, Logan battened down the hint of a rueful grin that had come to his own face, having been treated to comments and visits like this rather frequently as of late. It was not that he was callous, but rather that he was simply amazed that life always appeared to be so entirely predictable.

Late night, Logan could afford to give his friend a little more slack in terms of his time, and he had told him so. Antonio had certainly been making use of that invitation.

Logan did have some genuine sympathy for Antonio, who worked as a delivery person for a local pizza place, a horrific environment to Logan, who would have rather gone homeless than have subjected himself to such a place.

Antonio put in a lot of hours on the job, with frequent double shifts, and had incurred much wear and tear on his car that his pay could not keep up with. He got very little in the way of respect, from managers and customers alike, with a low hourly wage and sporadic tips that were more often than not miniscule.

It was not an environment overabundant in personal satisfactions, and as of late Antonio had begun to question the mere sanity of all of it. He had come to the conclusion that Logan had already made, and warned Antonio of, long before.

"No girlfriend, no real goals, and no money. That's what I realized today. I just exist to pay bills, and can barely do that, so that a select few can live in a paradise of wealth in some gated community," Antonio hissed with anger, clearly holding back a tide of frustration that had been long packed down deep inside of him. "And here I am, on another uneventful Friday night, making you listen to me tell you all my problems."

"We're friends, believe me, I wouldn't let just anyone vent in my living room. And it's not time to panic; you are just twenty-seven years old. Believe it or not, that is still young, Antonio," Logan encouraged, shutting the front door.

Logan gestured for Antonio to have a seat on a couch in the small living room at the front of the house. Antonio strode over and sank down heavily into the cushion.

He put his elbows on his knees, folding his hands in between, staring down at the rug underneath the low coffee table in front of him. He let his breath out slowly, as his shoulders sagged.

"You may be right, Logan," Antonio said in a tired voice, "but I'm starting to find myself thinking about all of this, and where I'm really going, more and more."

Logan understood his friend very well, and was glad that at least Antonio felt that he had an outlet with Logan. Antonio leaned toward being an introvert, and carried a tendency towards shyness around most others.

Logan knew that Antonio was allowing unhealthy pressures to build ever higher and higher, stoking a flaming resentment that was fanned into more of an inferno with each case of disrespectful treatment that he received.

Antonio did not ask for much, and certainly did not have enormous expectations out of life. Yet, when even a few tiny crumbs refused to fall off of life's tables, in an age when some feasted themselves to gluttony, even the most laid back of individuals could begin to simmer with a resentful ire.

Logan did not have many outlets for his own frustrations, but he had at least crafted some methods of containing his own outrage and disgust with the direction of the world.

Hurling himself into his work, the bulk of his energies were focused upon his small business. He had grasped the merciful art of blocking most negative thoughts out of his mind while he was immersed in tasks for clients, and clients were always capable of annoying him well enough.

"Want a soft drink? At this hour I need one myself. I'm getting a little groggy," Logan inquired.

He walked to his favorite high-backed chair, and lowered himself down on one knee. He had popped open the half-sized refrigerator just to the side of the chair, and pulled out two cans of soft drinks, before Antonio had even rendered an answer.

Almost like little fueling stations, Logan strategically kept stocked soft drinks at a few different points of the house. He did not deem it laziness, but rather efficiency. In an age where conserving energy was akin to adhering to religious dogma, he figured that he was just being logical and harmonizing with the times.

"Sure. Thanks," Antonio said, accepting the beverage. He opened it, took a long drink, and shook his head. His familiar and gentle smile, the epitome of good-natured miens, crept back onto his face. His voice was slightly apologetic, even if the weariness was still present. "Sorry about the outburst, Logan. Just everything is getting to me."

"Antonio, you know that if I could work magic, I would help you out right now," Logan smiled widely towards his friend, an expression that he only sparingly displayed. The smile then faded a little. "Only you, though. Most of the rest in this world can go to hell. If I can ever break through this trap of having to work for idiots, and live in a world governed by idiots, who were voted in by masses of even greater idiots, I will take care of things too. We will get the hell out of this town. We will take care of our own."

Antonio gestured over towards a fantastic poster framed on the wall to his left. It showed a vast castle with great towers set atop a lofty mountain, above which a great black dragon was flying. The roaring dragon was oriented towards one of the towers of the castle's outer wall, one massive set of talons reared back as if about to strike a blow.

"Be nice to go somewhere like there," Antonio said, staring into the large print.

Logan smiled again, with a wistful glint to his eyes as he gazed upon the image.

To Logan, the art spoke of a world of wonder, a world where the rules were fundamentally different, where anything might be possible, and where something new was around every corner. It spoke to him of majesty and dignity, a window into another world rich with excitement and an adventurous life.

"I've looked at that one quite a lot myself," Logan commented. "Yes, it would be great to go back to an age of castles, to a time and place when things like dragons really existed. But it just isn't possible, now is it?"

"No, I guess it isn't, but it doesn't hurt to dream," Antonio responded.

"No, it doesn't," Logan agreed. "I think I would go insane otherwise."

He paused for a moment in quiet reflection, and then looked over at his friend.

"I probably need another break myself, and I've been cooped up in here for too long today," Logan said, "Want to take a short walk?"

"Sounds good to me," Antonio agreed.

"Wait here, just a second," Logan instructed him.

It took a couple of minutes for Logan go check and make sure that everything that he had been working on when Antonio had knocked on his door was saved, protected, and in good order. Once satisfied, he returned back to the front living room.

"Ready?" Logan inquired, picking up a set of keys from where they were lying upon a small wooden stand, adjacent to a coat rack positioned behind the front door.

The two exited the house, with Logan tarrying again to lock the door and set his house's alarm system. It was nearly three in the morning when they started off down the quiet neighborhood street.

A tranquil atmosphere had settled over the neighborhood, as most of the occupants of the nearby houses had long since retired for the night. A few scattered lights were visible, shining forth from a few windows, but only the sound of a dog barking and some cars farther off broke the stillness.

A smooth breeze washed cool air upon the faces of the two young men, as they made their way along the sidewalk. The night sky held few clouds within it, and those that did ride the sky looked to be little more than stretched, thin wisps of vapor. The moon, nearly full, was bright and stood out strongly amid a host of visible stars.

The moonlight dappled the streets in pockets of light, even as it cast a wide variety of shadows from the towering oak, maple, and pine trees that populated the older neighborhood and lined its streets.

For about a block, until they had turned the corner to the right at an intersection, Logan and Antonio continued in relative silence. At the moment, the atmosphere was a welcome sliver of restful serenity.

Occasionally, there was the presence of a cat trotting in and out of the shadows by a house, or crouched attentively by the street. Here and there, a dog let loose a couple of small barks from within one of the fenced-in backyards that they passed.

Otherwise, there were very few distractions, save for the occasional car on its way home or cutting through the side roads.

Logan gazed up at the open sky, letting his eyes sweep across the huge ebon canopy, even as his lungs took in a long, slow breath of the fresh, cool air. To Logan, the night sky always hinted of the magical, as if something wondrous and mystical was playing just beyond the edge of his vision.

It always stoked the fires of his imagination, as for him it was like looking into a swathe of infinity whose immensity and scope was overwhelming to comprehend.

With Antonio dwelling silently in a brooding world of his own thoughts, Logan allowed his mind to wander. He had always envisioned the grander picture of life. It was much harder for him to focus on the smaller pictures that occupied the daily world. In his quiet, restrained world, his mind was still free to roam with willful abandon.

Even a glance at the deep night sky reinvigorated him. In a moment, he saw worlds of wonder, an endless diorama of possibilities and adventure.

When he read, he loved the authors that soared above the mundane, delving into the infinite possibilities of what could be. It was much the same with movies, video games, or any other type of medium that he might indulge in.

He had often been chastised by his parents for blurring the lines between reality and imagination in his mind. If anything, their berating of him had only made him more determined in his hopes that one day he could prove that there was far more to the world than the common experiences that seemed so all encompassing.

"Wouldn't it be great, if something totally unheard of, totally unbelievable, happened to us?" Logan commented suddenly, breaking the extended silence.

His eyes still panned across the sky.

"Like what?" Antonio asked.

"Something different. Something unexpected. Something unusual. Something completely exciting," Logan stated. "It wouldn't take me long to forget my routine existence."

"Wouldn't be much of a loss leaving our world behind," Antonio remarked, with a bitter smile. "Except for a few friends and family."

Logan smiled gently at his friend. "Other than a few people, it would be nice, wouldn't it?"

"I have never thought about anything that unusual actually happening, but I'm with you," Antonio said, grinning.

"We just get so used to the way that things are, and so used to knowing that if we drop a rock, it is going to fall down. We are so used to knowing that the sun will rise, and that fall will go to winter, winter to spring, spring to summer, and summer back to fall," Logan said. "What if all that was turned completely upside down? Just for once? What if you could think that the rock would rise up, or gravity was a non-factor, that you could even fly?"

"Never given a lot of thought to it, but I do see what you mean," Antonio said. "It would be something to be able to fly."

"Me too," Logan agreed firmly. "Just for once I wish the rules could be different. Just for once. Like this book I once read in school."

"The rules?" Antonio asked. "What book?"

"Just being able to walk through a simple closet, an ordinary thing of the world, and suddenly finding yourself in a whole new existence." Logan said, only partly responding to Antonio as he mused out loud about his innermost sentiments. His tone hardened, "A world where we wouldn't be beholden to the idiots, and could even become kings ourselves."

"I don't need to become a king, but a change for the better would be nice," Antonio replied.

Logan's thoughts began to drift once again as they continued on down the sidewalk. He held back the regrets about the world that he wished would exist.

Giving disappointments too much attention always left a bitter taste.

The truth was that Logan had often paused when opening a closet door after having read that book, a part of him believing that it was possible to find another world.

It was a part of him that his parents had once mocked, even if they had meant well, but it was a part of him that he was not about to part with.

DEREK

Derek Decker lay quietly in the welcome repose of his bedroom, a haven at the present moment.

Janus was downstairs, mercifully asleep on the couch. Derek knew that Janus had not wanted to go home that night, as his house had carried an unfathomable emptiness for him without the presence his father. He knew that there was really nothing that he could say to truly console his grieving friend, and that fact burned bitterly within him.

If there was one consummate truth about the physical world, it was that there was always more room for sorrows.

Even though Janus had been listless, as if he had been sapped of his very enthusiasm for life itself, Derek was resolved to keep Janus within some kind of sphere of activity. The abyss of grief, Derek felt, would only be magnified if Janus were left alone to the tortures of his traumatized mind and sorely wounded heart.

An idea had come to Derek's mind earlier that day.

A mutual friend of Derek and Janus, named Kent McNeeley, had a father who owned a house by a lakeside. The elongated, winding lake, far from secluded, was the scene of many buoyant social gatherings throughout the spring, summer, and into early autumn. One who was disposed to the outdoors could always indulge in the leisure of boating, fishing, or taking hikes in the wooded areas throughout the region. For Janus, a visit to the lake would be a full change of environment, and it would offer a degree of activity that would promise to keep his mind slightly occupied.

After wracking his brain, it was the best solution that Derek could find at the moment to try to help Janus find a spark of life again.

Derek would also have some more help at the lake. Kent McNeeley was a good acquaintance of Janus', and a very good friend of Derek's.

He knew that Kent's father lived in the city most of the year while running his real estate company. There was no doubt that it would take little convincing to get Kent to agree with Derek's plan.

The decision made, Derek made a mental note to himself to call Kent in the early morning, even if he knew that Kent would not be entirely happy about an early phone call.

Satisfied at settling upon a course of action, Derek finally let his mind relax.

Shutting his eyelids, he rolled over in his bed and finally gave his own body permission to sleep.

ERIN

Trudging in groggily at almost five in the morning, Erin made only a brief and necessary stop at the restroom, before lumbering on to her room and crashing almost fully clothed upon the bed.

The last two evenings had been nearly mirror images of each other, and she had been left with a sharp feeling of restless dissatisfaction at the conclusion of the night.

Erin was quickly tiring of the increasingly tedious setting of Uli's apartment, where she, Lynn, Razor, Uli, and some others had wasted away so many hours. The end to the nights arrived only when the natural, irresistible fatigue of the human body finally caught up with them.

On such nights, they rarely saw anything other than Uli's cramped living room, and Erin was sorely tired of that.

The rising tedium had served as a great motivation to Erin to speak her mind towards the end of the evening. Evidently, the boredom had been present in more than one of the others, as they had readily agreed that the group needed a change in scenery.

She did not make any move to set her alarm clock as her body settled into the mattress. Erin already knew that she would be calling in sick to her workplace, and not because she expected to be ill. She knew that she would be feeling healthy enough once she had gotten a few hours of sleep.

Once it was apparent that everyone needed a hiatus from the little apartment, a full consensus had then been reached for the following evening, one that Lynn, Razor, and Erin had readily agreed to. For once, Uli had shown some initiative in suggesting that they undergo a journey down to the great national forest, located just an hour away from their hometown.

Once there, they could hike towards an outcropping of rock that formed a natural bridge, and choose an optimal campsite in the vicinity for a night of relaxation and merriment. As it tended to be a popular camping area, Erin hoped that they would have some luck and that it would be devoid of very many others that evening.

A more cynical side of Erin mused that it would not be all that different from the past few nights, with the exception of a change of scenery. Virtually the only real difference would be that instead of carpets, walls, and sofas, they would have the bare earth, trees, and rocks as their surroundings for the same activities. Of course, to her greater view, there was little else to do, and it was as good of a plan as any other. At the very least, even if the company and general activity were the same, the ventilation would be much better.

section 11

MERSHAD

Mershad passed much of the day keeping to himself, content to be sequestered away within the solitude of his dormitory room. As it was the weekend, a good number of the other university students at the dormitory, mostly those who lived in the immediate region, had gone home for a couple of days. Even with the smattering of students that still remained, there was an unusual quietness permeating the residence building. For Mershad, the absence of most of the students was a great relief.

As usual, he had not needed the use of an alarm clock to rouse himself just before dawn broke. His internal body clock was very well attuned, after more than twenty-three years of practicing his faith. Following his morning prayers, the first of five designated periods of prayer each day, he allowed himself a little slack and dozed in his bed for a while longer.

After about an hour, the rest of the morning was spent leisurely; taking a long shower, making a small pot of coffee, and suffering through a little television.

As he had come to expect, the television was inundated with the latest updates about the ongoing war in the Middle East. The US-led coalition's forces had completed another flurry of thunderous air and missile attacks, and the newscasters were very upbeat about the recent reports from the battlefronts.

Only one of the aircraft from the coalition forces had been lost in the fray, and that lone plane's destruction was due to an engine failure, rather than enemy defenses. As Mershad and even the most casual of observers were well aware by now, the fighting was a one-sided affair that was degenerating quickly into a massacre. Unopposed in the skies, piloted and unmanned aircraft struck with unhindered impunity. Missiles launched from sea vessels offshore and military bases in the region raced towards their targets, guided meticulously by the latest systems, backed by the USA's unrivaled satellite network.

It was a deeply unsettling war to Mershad for other reasons as well. He could not see where older notions of honor and respect for one's opponent had a place in the modern ways of combat. It was not a war where adversaries clashed face to face, sword to sword, like the tales of the Crusades in the Middle Ages. Rather, it was one where one side's technological dominance enabled widespread slaying at a great distance. Operators of remotely controlled, unmanned aircraft could sit in full safety at consoles in air-conditioned rooms, located numerous miles from where their implements unleashed their deadly rain of fire and thunder.

Mershad could only handle a few minutes of the parade of images, and the accompanying stoic commentary by the ubiquitous retired generals that were surfacing regularly on the networks. He watched the screen with trepidation as a large building was turned into a pile of rubble in an instant, from aerial surveillance footage recording a missile strike's massive impact. With fear and sadness in his heart, he finally turned the television off.

In the early afternoon, he decided that the dorm room was too confining and that he needed a little fresh air. Chancing a foray out into the public, he procured lunch at one of the fast food outlets just across the street from his building.

Doing his best to avoid undue attention, he ordered the food to carry out, taking it back his room to eat in quiet. Once his hunger had been sated, he gathered up some books and his laptop computer.

Tucking them into a satchel and easing the shoulder strap over his right arm, he set off for a secluded spot that he preferred to visit when he needed space to think. The place was situated near the primary student center building, about a ten-minute walk from his dormitory. The center was located a little farther down on the west side of the campus's main boundaries, just off the downtown area of Lexington.

His favored area consisted of nothing more than a lowered expanse of open grass, which sat several yards underneath the street level as it was spread over a substantial sinkhole. A number of fully matured trees were arrayed about the area, forming a dynamic filter that cast direct light and shaded pools about in a number of different combinations and arrangements as each day proceeded.

It was set away from the main pedestrian thoroughfares of the campus, and the primary access points to the student center. As such, it tended to have a quiet and subdued atmosphere. Some students, like Mershad, had found the place to be a haven for a little time of reflection, or for some uninterrupted study.

The only frequent group of visitors to the area, and by far the most boisterous, were a bevy of gray squirrels that inhabited the area. The feisty creatures were fun to observe at times, as they endlessly scampered about the soft grass and scurried about the trunks of the trees. They lunged into their network of branches and traversed them with an impressive agility and dexterity that always amazed Mershad.

Mershad's ideal spot was a site tucked away almost directly under the street level, where he liked to sit with his back to the trunk of a maple tree.

Though he could still hear the cars going by overhead, the space afforded him a good nook where he could melt into the fabric of his personal oasis. With headphones on, he was lost in a world of his own.

Enough light cascaded down through the trees to enable him to study, and the hotter days were always disrupted by the cool, generous shade provided by the trees.

With the exception of a brief break for some dinner in the student center, Mershad consumed the rest of the day studying his notes and other course work materials. He took a couple of pauses for his appointed prayers, finding relief in the almost total vacancy of the area. During the time that he was there, only a handful of individuals strolled through the area, and none tarried upon the lawn.

The light of day finally waned, diffusing into night.

Though Mershad was tired of studying, he found that he did not yet want to leave the gentle confines. Putting his school materials away in the satchel, he stretched his legs out as he leaned back against the tree.

His eyes shutting, he took a deep breath of the evening air and settled into a serene repose.

"Mershad! Mershad!"

The voice startled him and caused him to flinch, even as he felt the light nudges of a hand upon his right shoulder. The sound of the voice, though passive and friendly in both tone and volume, snapped him wide-awake.

A few lights, whose fixtures were set within straight posts that were set in place at a few key intervals about the area, provided most of the available illumination. The rest came from moonlight, as the night was already a couple of hours old.

Looking up, he beheld the silhouette of Erika Laesig standing over him.

The sight of her brought an instant defensiveness to Mershad. Already introverted enough, his discomfort with women was compounded by some particular matters regarding the practice of his faith. Though she was a friend, he had never been quite settled in her presence.

She was perhaps the strongest female personality that he had ever encountered. He had met her about a year before, in one of his classes.

The first time that he had set his eyes upon her, he could not help but notice how stunning she was. About five-foot ten, she had a sleek, athletic build, and her movements were always imbued with balance and grace.

Though she had visible muscle tone evident whenever she wore short-sleeved shirts or shorts, her muscularity did not taint her femininity in any way. She was every bit a woman, one who exuded unequivocal strength in her appearance and demeanor.

Mershad had encountered many attractive women before, but Erika's attributes went far beyond matters of mere physical appearance. Each and every time that he had spoken at length with her, he recognized her considerable intelligence, as well as her real fervor for life.

She was studying to enter a career in social work, taking a path whose adherents truly had to have some passion about what they were doing. He certainly knew that those working actively in the field did not enter it for any hopes of attaining a great level of compensation. Erika was no exception, exhibiting the type of motivations that went well beyond the financial. She had very firm beliefs and attitudes about the rightness and necessity of what she had set out to do, and was very dedicated to acting upon them.

Though there was no warrant for it, he had never been able to elude the sense of intimidation that he felt whenever he was in her presence. That was his own problem to sort out, he knew, as she never did anything to intentionally make him feel awkward. If anything, she had always extended a welcoming attitude and warm kindness to him.

"Hi, Erika," he responded, his tone coming out a little meek compared to her own. He managed a grin as he came out of his foggy dreaminess. "So, you caught me napping."

Erika sat down on the ground before him, cross-legged. She was wearing a yellow, long-sleeved shirt and some dark jeans that followed her shapely contours very faithfully. Mershad felt a pang of guilt at having consciously focused upon her attractiveness right away.

She grinned at him. "I should have figured I would run into you out here. I usually don't go this way, but I just had an urge to cut through tonight, for whatever reason. I shouldn't have woken you up, but I haven't talked to you in a while, and I wanted to say hi. Hope you don't mind. What have you been up to today?"

Mershad certainly did not mind her decision to awaken him, though he felt awkward saying so. He gestured to his satchel. "Mainly, a lot of study. At least, until dark came. And good that you came, as I might have slept the entire night outside here otherwise."

"You are dedicated, and on the weekend too, when you should be relaxing a little," Erika quipped.

"No, not overly dedicated, it's more about anxiety with grades, I think," Mershad replied, suffering a laugh and still unable to shake the slight, underlying sense of unease. Small talk had never come easy to Mershad, not even with someone that he knew was a person with good intentions.

Erika laughed softly, with an understanding expression on her face. "I know the feeling, Mershad … believe me, I do … So, what's been going on with you lately? You've seemed pretty down in class this week."

"Not much, just trying to stay out of the way of trouble. You know, with the war and everything," Mershad said morosely. "You know what I'm talking about. The stuff I told you about a couple weeks ago".

Erika's brow furrowed, as her mouth grew taut. Her voice had an edge to it when she replied, "Just people with very small minds. I suppose that it doesn't help, even when you tell them that this is your country, and has always been your country … that you were born and raised here."

"I've told a few people that, including the fact that I've never even been out of this country. But there's a whole lot of people that just will not listen to anything," Mershad replied sadly, shaking his head. "They treat me like I am going to suddenly wrap myself up in bombs and blow myself up. I really wish I could escape everything for awhile. Probably would be much better to be anywhere but here."

"People are looking for ways to lash out. Everything around them is playing on their fears, every time they turn on the television or go online…. But it definitely doesn't excuse their behavior," Erika said.

She grew quiet, as if reflecting upon something bothersome, shaking her head slowly as she looked up through the trees for a moment. Erika brought her eyes back down after the extended pause and looked back to Mershad. "I have no way of knowing exactly what you are going through. I just know that you are caught up in the brunt of it all. And not by choice…."

Her voice trailed off into silence as they sat quietly together. After a few minutes had passed, Mershad finally broke the discomfiting stillness.

"Doesn't seem like its all going to end anytime soon. Like it's all becoming a never-ending war," Mershad murmured. He glanced over to

Erika. "And it's not like I wouldn't support going after murderers with a vengeance, especially ones doing it in the name of my religion. I'm not trying to impose anything on anyone, and I'd expect to be resisted if I was."

Erika suddenly elbowed Mershad playfully on his arm and grinned brightly. She then teased, "Like if I ever hear that you are working to make me wear head coverings, or try to take my beer away … don't be surprised if you have my work boot's indentation prominently displayed on your rear."

The two of them laughed together, and her words showed Mershad just how comfortable and honest she was with him. He did not take them as any offense, but rather as a strange kind of compliment.

"But I'm afraid fear has taken center stage. It paints with a broad stroke, and governs a lot of outlooks," Erika finished with unmistakable sympathy, after their laughter had died down.

Mershad glanced up at her, truly appreciative for the sincerity of her sentiments.

"I couldn't have said it much better myself, Erika. You do get it, but this is the way that things are, and I have to deal with it, whether I like it or not," Mershad responded.

He looked dejectedly back down at the ground, giving his visitor a distinct picture of despondence.

"Well, do you mind if I stay and hang out with you for a little while?" Erika inquired politely.

He was grateful for her uncanny perception, as he knew that she recognized Mershad's current need to have an outlet for the inner pressures that were churning so powerfully inside of him. Her empathic nature was one of the greatest gifts that he saw in her, which he knew would become very valuable to Erika in her chosen career.

Even so, he did not want to burden her.

"It is a Saturday night, Erika. I don't think I'm too much fun to be around lately," Mershad replied to her. "You need to go out and have some fun."

"You assume too much. I may not be too much fun either, you know. All I do lately is work out, work, go to school, and sleep," Erika commented, a brightening smile spreading across her face. "That does not exactly make for exciting times either, my friend."

Her beaming smile brought a lift to his spirits. She crawled up next to Mershad, and leaned back against the tree trunk to his immediate right.

"So, how come you never call me up to just go hang out or go hiking or something like that?" Erika said. "Sounds like you need to get away from the morons of the world from time to time, and I certainly would take the excuse. As for myself, I'm sick of hanging around guys that have a very limited range of things that they want to do, if you get my drift."

He did not doubt that she had attracted a lot of attention from the male student populace during her time at the school, and felt highly complimented that she had just tacitly expressed that she considered him as a different sort of man.

"I guess, as far as what I'm going through right now, that I don't want to drag anyone else through it," Mershad responded.

"Well, won't you at least give me a chance to take a stab at it?" Erika ventured. "I've got the time."

While he truly did not like to encumber others with his problems, he also knew that it was not healthy to leave the emotions stuffed inside of him. The latter proved to be the stronger impulse, as he glanced back over to her.

"Okay, but you have to let me know if it gets to be too boring, or if you get depressed just being around me," Mershad stated. He added more firmly. "Promise me that."

"I will, I promise," Erika remarked with a light grin, holding her hands up so that he could see that her fingers were not crossed.

"So do you know a way for me to escape somewhere, like in some movies and books?" he asked her, smiling. "Do you know of a time machine we can get a hold of? I always like the stories about going into other worlds."

"I wish I did know a way we could get one, because I'd use it myself. Believe it or not, I've been in a kind of a rut lately, and could use a decent adventure," she replied. "Every day is getting to be the same old, same old, if you know what I mean."

Mershad chuckled. "I know what you mean. Even without this war, I would have to say things are getting monotonous."

Her eyes then looked past him, drawing his attention with her gaze as she said, "Now that is a little unusual."

Mershad noticed some wisps of vapor that were drifting across the tops of the grass. Some other tendrils were pouring over the lip of the street level just behind them, and cascading down into the grassy area where the mists had begun to pool.

"That is odd ..." Mershad concurred. "I can't say I've watched it come in like that before."

"Guess we are in for a foggy night," she replied, shrugging and grinning amiably again. "Well, it's not a problem, is it? Mere fog isn't going to chase us out of here. So tell me a little more about yourself, I insist. We've talked so much in class, but I haven't had much time just to ask you about you."

"I guess you've asked for it, then," he replied, smiling. "Well, here begins your big Saturday night adventure. I guess I'll give you an overview at the beginning."

"I've always found it best to start on the first page," Erika retorted.

He started into the story of his parents, and his upbringing, as the fog began to accumulate among the trees and grow steadily thicker. It looked almost magical, illumined as it was by the silvery light of the full moon, and creating an effect of being in a different world; even if it was a very small one, with space for just two friends to talk.

The way things had been going, Mershad did not mind that at all.

LOGAN

Though it was an entirely new evening, a Saturday night that offered little chance of interruptions from nitpicking clients, Logan found himself more tense than he had been on the previous one.

His physical state was no better. His eyes were about to cross, following yet another marathon of monitor screens and tediously detailed adjustments.

Leaning back in his chair, he moaned at his stiffened lower back, and rubbed at his eyes. Glancing down at his watch, he saw that it was almost midnight.

"Any second now," Logan muttered prophetically.

A few moments later, he heard the distinctive sound of Antonio's car engine as his friend pulled up outside and parked in front of Logan's house.

The engine was shut off a moment later, followed by the sounds of the car door opening and closing. Logan listened to the thuds of the last few of Antonio's footsteps, as he neared the front door and knocked upon it.

"What's up, Antonio?" Logan greeted as he opened the door.

"No different than yesterday, personally, I mean," Antonio said grimly. He continued with his griping before Logan had a chance to respond. "Here I am on a Saturday night now, and guess what? It is still no different, treated like garbage, broke, the usual. Is anything ever going to happen to give us some hope of change. It is making me near crazy. But I did bring some food with me tonight."

He grinned as he held forth a small bag, loaded down with an assortment of burritos and soft tacos.

"Good thinking, Antonio, very good thinking …. You timed it well, I think that will hit the spot right about now," Logan commented, recognizing the familiar bag.

Reaching into the bag, he retrieved one of the soft tacos and unwrapped it. As he took a bite, he was quietly appreciative that Antonio had remembered that Logan liked the deluxe kind with sour cream.

"I think that it will too," Antonio responded, retrieving one of the burritos out for himself. "I forgot completely about lunch today. You know, pizza is about the last thing that I want to see or smell at the end of a workday. I didn't even realize I hadn't eaten today, until about ten minutes before I left work."

"Well, let's take care of this bag in its entirety. I'll get a few soft drinks out for my part of it, and we'll take a collective break from all of our headaches." Logan remarked between bites, finding out that he had incurred a substantial hunger since his late afternoon visit to Lee's Wok for yet another plate of pork-fried rice and a tall glass of ginger-ale.

After saving his files, and shutting down his main system, Logan returned to his living room where he and Antonio relaxed and finished off the rest of their meal.

Picking up a remote control, and sinking back into the lone couch, Antonio surfed through a good number of satellite channels. Images from reality shows, movies, and war coverage filled the screen, changing with each click. He finally settled on a music video show, but it served as little more than a backdrop for their conversation.

"So, no luck today? No dates?" Logan asked Antonio.

Antonio chuckled. "Who? Me? You know better than to ask, Logan. The way it seems, the minute I get a date, the world will probably end. That's about the extent of my luck right now."

"The possibilities in this town are pretty dry, you know that, Antonio," Logan said. "I wouldn't want to date ninety percent of the women around here anyway. It's one thing or another ... control ... money ... looks .... Whether you fit the proper image. Whether you attend the correct church. Whether you don't attend a church. And on and on. I could go on and on, but I won't. It's like you have to fulfill some kind of checklist with any of them. Just don't worry about it ... I know I've said it fourteen thousand times before. I say that we are just going to have to stick with things, and believe that something is going to break. And when we get the chance to turn the tables, we grab it. Something where we can set our own rules."

"I hope that it's sometime real soon," Antonio remarked before adding, after a pause, "I really don't need different rules overall, just a fair chance with the rules that there are."

"I'll take new rules if I can get them," Logan replied tersely. "The ones that are in place in this world don't offer much at all to most of us."

"Hard to please you," Antonio said, with a slight grin.

"Yeah, I guess I'm getting a little cynical, in my ripe old age of twenty-eight," Logan retorted, his momentary tension relaxing a little.

"Then I'm probably a little naive and gullible at the ripe young age of twenty-seven," Antonio countered, laughing.

"Maybe we both need to move more towards the center, they say balance is supposed to be best," Logan commented.

"Maybe so," Antonio agreed, leaning forward and popping open another can of soda. "So how's work coming along today? Workload getting any better?"

"Nope. More work than I seem to have hours for. The pay hasn't changed either. I just have to build up my credentials and reputation to get to where I can do a project that I choose to do for myself; One which will actually have a chance of getting out there into the public eye," Logan answered, somewhat more ruefully.

He stared off with a wistful expression, thinking of just how ephemeral that goal was beginning to appear. He knew that he was in a great rut, if not a kind of trap, in that he had attained a level that would keep him afloat but not get him far enough to accomplish what he wanted.

With financial obligations weighing upon him, he could not make risky changes at this point. Resentment about all of it was percolating within him.

"You have to suffer this stage to accomplish that, I've found, and that's still no guarantee," Logan stated dourly. "And you also have to block it all out of your mind, when most every dime that you get in compensation is immediately shuttled to the bank to cover bills. It's maddening, some days. It really is."

"I bet it is … I bet I make even better money than you right now, even with all the times that I get stiffed completely on tips," Antonio chided.

"You don't even want to know what my hourly rate comes out to," Logan answered, a bittersweet grin on his face as he shook his head. "It's not an enticing sum, I can guarantee you that much. I made the mistake of calculating it out once. Never going to do that again. Too depressing."

"But at least you get to get paid doing art, and you do like art, that's something," Antonio observed encouragingly. "I can't even really figure out what I like, but I can assure you that what I do like has absolutely nothing to do with driving pizzas around."

"Like I've always said, think of the things that you like as hobbies or pastimes, and then find a way to make a career out of it," Logan advised him.

"I might enjoy the food business more if I could make some real decisions on things that would make the business run better, and where I could make sure people don't get treated like I've been. Maybe something in management, but sure as the sun rises I'm not going to get many opportunities in my current situation," Antonio commented with a melancholic edge.

"I think that you can … You're smart enough, and you see what's wrong with things. Why not go back to school and work on finishing up a degree?" Logan suggested. "Maybe that could give you the boost."

"Too broke right now, and I'm in no position to get into further debt," Antonio said. "In a nutshell, that's the sum of it all."

Antonio then shook his head and laughed.

"And you know what, most of my co-workers who drive already have their degrees, and it hasn't done them any good," he stated. "Why would I think I would be any different?"

"Well … for whatever it's worth, if I ever make any money, I'll have to buy a restaurant, and get you to manage it. You'd better, because I have a short fuse when it comes to stupidity, and I'm sure you encounter a lot of that among your co-workers. So what do you say about that?" Logan offered, the corners of his lips turning up into a grin.

"Okay … I could deal with that," Antonio replied, nodding and grinning. "So you better double the number of clients that you take on, because I don't know how much longer my sanity will last."

Logan laughed. "That, my friend, is a very difficult proposition. If I take on even one more client, I'm afraid that my own sanity will crack."

"Dilemmas, dilemmas," Antonio sighed, as they sat in silence for a few moments.

"Well, after we finish up our sodas, what do you say to another neighborhood excursion?" Logan suggested. "Our walkabout cleared my head pretty good last night. And I want to take advantage of this weather, before it starts getting colder and rainier. They say a streak of bad weather is right around the corner."

"Sounds fine to me," Antonio agreed. He chuckled, "Who knows what we might get into?"

The two finished off their soft drinks while passively watching a few more music videos. When they were finally ready to go, Logan bagged up all of the garbage into the food bag. He carried it outside with him, and tossed it into a garbage can by his house as they set out for the night.

Once again, the night was fairly clear, mildly cool with perhaps only a slight increase in the amount of cloud cover. The night seemed to have its own glow about it, buoyed up by the illuminating power of the full moon.

"The first steps always feel so good, so free," Logan opined as they reached the sidewalk. He looked down towards the right. "What do you say? Let's take this direction tonight."

With no argument from Antonio, the pair headed up the street. Reaching his arms out wide, Logan stretched out and turned about in a full circle. All throughout the movement, he kept his eyes squarely focused on the star-filled sky above.

Gradually, he oriented his focus back onto the path that they were taking. A broad, weightless smile was on his face, as his cares seemed to melt away.

They were striding up towards the crest of a small hill. He turned towards Antonio. "Remember what I was talking about last night?"

Antonio nodded, and his eyes took on a hint of hope. "Yes, and I thought about that a little today. I agree with you … I wish that something really miraculous would happen. Could it really, do you think?"

Logan's eyes sparkled with the inner vision that he now held within him. The star-filled frontier of infinite space piqued his mind and imagination once again.

"What if? Just what if over the crest of that hill right ahead of us was an all new reality?" Logan asked his longtime friend, as a fire flared within him. "And your big adventure was really in the offing, something that would be more than anything than we have ever known before … Something that would enable us to show what we are really made of … Maybe a place where we could get in control of the rules, take charge of things, and set things to rights."

"I could do with just a different adventure, even if it isn't all that grand," Antonio joked. "But you are right. That would be something else, and if it could be grand, I wouldn't complain."

"Well, let's head for the top of the hill … who knows?" Logan said, picking up his pace a little.

Antonio had to spur himself forward to catch up with his suddenly inspired friend. The two walked quickly to the top of the hill.

They saw what they had seen so many times before, whenever they had walked up that sidewalk or driven their cars up the street.

A swathe of houses and the continuation of the road and its flanking sidewalks filled up their field of vision. Logan felt a little disappointment flash within him.

It was not that he expected to see anything else, but there was always that small, but potent, part of him that entertained the notion that the impossible was indeed possible. It was the brief glimmer of hope that maybe the very next horizon would reveal something altogether different and wonderful.

"Well, I guess we will have to climb the hill again on some other day, won't we?" Antonio remarked with a grin.

Logan shrugged in resignation. "I guess so. But at least we can console ourselves that we are just falling back to the status quo. I guess that there is something to be grateful about in that. Things could be worse."

"There is that," Antonio concurred.

"As strange as it sounds, I still feel disappointed," Logan said. His voice then brightened a little, as a more practical inspiration came to him.

"But you know what?"

"What's that?" Antonio asked.

"As random as this sounds, I have a sudden craving for a strawberry shake," Logan announced.

"We just started the walk," Antonio pointed out, "but if that's what you want to do."

"I'll splurge and pay for yours," Logan said. "Since I can't make up my mind tonight."

"Big spender," joked Antonio.

The two turned about, and made the brief trek back down the slope of the hill to Logan's house. Logan's black sports car was resting in its familiar place in the driveway.

He got his keys out of his pocket, unlocked the driver's side door, and pushed the button on it to open the lock on Antonio's passenger side.

Antonio settled into the bucket seat on his side, as Logan got in, set the key and turned the ignition, and gunned the engine to thundering life.

"I just love the sound of that," Logan remarked, sitting still for few moments as he listened to the steady, throaty rumble of his idling car.

Reaching down, he picked up his disc case and pulled out a release by a heavy rock act that was one of his favorites. Popping it in, he cranked up the stereo as the first drumbeats and guitar chords sounded, lowering his windows all the way down.

"Alright, let's go!" Logan said, backing the car out of the driveway.

Once oriented on the street, the car lurched into motion, as if it had a life of its own. In Logan's eyes, the car was a war horse. Behind the wheel, Logan often likened himself to a jousting knight, sitting proud and self-confident upon his very capable steed, a metal beast that could barely be reined in from exploding into a full-tilt, all-out charge.

They drove down to the end of the street and took a right, finally emerging out of the neighborhood as they turned onto one of the city's main roads. They proceeded through more several lights as they drove towards the south end of town, amid a sporadic amount of traffic out at the later hour.

Finally, they turned right at a junction by the largest city mall. The road ahead of them ran adjacent to a large public park that contained a long and winding creek. The other side primarily consisted of an extensive swathe of undeveloped, open fields.

The road itself was barely visible just a short distance away, enveloped within a dense fog.

"Time to click on the brights," Logan commented, as he flicked the lever that unleashed the car's high beams.

"That looks really thick," Antonio observed with a hint of curiosity, as they entered the fog's outer edges.

The words were an understatement, as the fog increased in density as they moved through it. The effect was highly unsettling to Logan. In just moments, the headlights of the car could only cut through a few feet, barely enough to keep the road beneath them in view.

DEREK

Though it was a Saturday, and no formal work was in the offing, Derek was up and out of bed well before dawn.

Following a brisk jog in the damp coolness of the early morning, he had proceeded through a series of calisthenics and a few of the martial arts routines that he had picked up during his four years of service in the military.

Regular workouts had chiseled his body into excellent condition, as well as giving him a way to clear his mind from any burdens besetting it.

Following the previous day, with his heart weighed down in the presence of Janus' great sorrows, it was much more difficult than usual to regain any clarity of thought.

Fortunately, he had succeeded in arranging for a substitute for his late afternoon shift, and the next day's as well, managing the produce section at the grocery superstore down the street. He had been compelled to barter off some favors for the late notice, which would result in his taking on some very inconvenient shifts over the next week, but he had agreed to the terms without any regret. The call of friendship had taken precedence.

Finished with the morning exercise and back in his house again, he had quickly discarded his sweat-saturated t-shirt into his laundry basket. Moving into the kitchen, he poured and imbibed a tall, cold glass of orange juice before picking up his satellite phone.

Clicking on Kent McNeeley's name, he rang the number repeatedly, clicking off the phone when it reached the voice mail, and redialing until his sluggish friend grudgingly answered.

Kent was not pleased at the hour of the phone call, especially given the fact that it was a Saturday morning. He proceeded to utter some extremely descriptive language from the other end that would have reddened most listeners' ears.

Knowing Kent well enough, Derek suffered the rant patiently as he stifled some amused laughter. Derek had inadvertently cost Kent his final hour of sleep before he had to go to work, which evidently was quite a major transgression in Kent's eyes.

Yet once the situation was explained, it did not take long at all for Kent to agree and his mood to change. He had even apologized for addressing Derek with such numerous expletives for having gotten him up so early.

Plans for Derek's jaunt were then set between the two of them, to be executed in the later afternoon.

Once off the phone, Derek treated himself to an extended, warm shower. The early morning workout and the massage of the pattering water from the shower left him feeling fully refreshed and ready for the day.

Janus was still asleep when Derek had finished with everything, as Derek had taken great care not to disturb his deeply grieving friend.

First turning the volume off on his speakers, he turned his personal computer system on. He indulged himself for a little while by catching up on several online sports articles, some current news, and the promotional sites for a few upcoming movies that he had been looking forward to.

He read over a few reports on the ongoing turmoil in the Middle East with some considerable interest, curious about some of the tactical approaches, the analysis of which appealed to his military background.

The motives behind the war, and the specific persons loudly championing it, though, had long filled his mouth with great distaste. To him, the conflict was about little more than power, made painfully obvious as the justifications offered to the public for the war had changed time and time again.

The nation under attack, with its decrepit, obsolete military, decayed under extensive previous sanctions, could not muster any threat to the USA, not in a hundred years. Even worse, a fragile lid kept on long simmering ethnic, religious, and tribal tensions within the area was about to be blown apart in the process of destroying the fully constrained regime that had been in power.

His heart went out to his brothers and sisters in the armed forces, many of whom who were undergoing their second, third, and even fourth tours of duty in the cauldron of Middle East conflicts. He would not hesitate to go overseas if his services were required, though he was grateful that he had not been recalled yet. Derek knew that his number would come up soon enough, though, as the military reserves and the National Guard regiments were now being used as frontline combat units.

His thoughts regarding the full situation were becoming very troubling, and for the first time he found that he had a nascent conflict building between his loyalty to the serving soldiers and the ideology of the war itself. While he would still serve if the call came, he knew that he could not condemn anyone who actively protested or opposed it. He had changed enough in the past year that he no longer held any animosity toward a fellow soldier that refused deployment.

In fact, some of the soldiers that had served multiple tours in the Middle East were now leaders in the opposition to the war. Derek did not see how anyone could question their integrity, for they certainly were no cowards and obviously cared for their country.

After perusing through some images of some of the latest hardware and technology being employed in the conflict, Derek heard Janus finally rustling behind him.

Turning around, he saw that Janus was slowly pulling himself up into a sitting position on the edge of the couch. Derek logged off his account, shut his system down, and rotated about to face his awakening friend.

"Get some rest, I hope?" Derek inquired.

Janus nodded, as he pulled aside the crumpled coverlet that he had borrowed for the night. Clothed in a t-shirt and sweats, Janus looked a little on the disheveled side.

"So, tell me what plans we have for today, because I don't have any myself," Janus said, only half in jest. Derek could hear the hollow, detached tone in Janus' voice.

Carefully, Derek explained the forthcoming excursion to Kent's father's lake house. Janus listlessly agreed to the trip, but the apathetic reaction did not dismay Derek in the least. He knew in his heart and mind that while a change of scenery would not be fully medicinal, it would be a much more palatable choice among the immediate options facing his beleaguered friend.

For the rest of the morning and early afternoon, the two friends casually watched Derek's flat screen digital television. Derek called and ordered some of Janus' favorite pizza to be delivered, but was left with several extra slices as his friend had still not regained much of his appetite. Though Janus politely responded to what little conversation Derek ventured, it was clear that Janus remained largely numb in spirit.

Time crawled by, but the hour for departure finally arrived.

"Looks like it is getting near time to go," Derek stated, peering down at his watch. "We still haven't packed up a change of clothes. You and I are about the same size. You can borrow a couple of my shirts and some jeans. That's all you'll need since we don't be gone too long."

Janus nodded, stretching his arms out, before slowly getting up out of the couch. He glanced back, "I guess I will get in a brief shower before we leave."

"Then I'll get the rest of it together, while you do that," Derek replied.

As Janus ambled towards the first floor bathroom, Derek trotted up the stairs to his bedroom to prepare for the coming trip.

Methodically, he packed up a few t-shirts, a couple pairs of jeans, and a few sweats to cover himself and Janus for the evening and next day. He added in another extra pair of underwear and socks for himself. He then pulled together some toothpaste, deodorant, shaving cream, razors, and other trip necessities into a small bag, and placed everything together neatly within a large suitcase.

Lugging it down to the living room, he waited and watched some more television as Janus finished up with his shower. Janus did not take long to dry off and get dressed, and less than thirty minutes later they were both in Derek's car and on the road.

Including a brief stop for fuel, the entire journey took up just a little more than an hour in order to reach the lake house.

The lake house was definitely not as secluded as Derek had initially envisioned it, back on the first time that he had visited the place a couple years prior. It was not in the middle of the wilderness on an otherwise uninhabited lakeshore, a mistaken preconception that Derek had quickly come to realize that first time. The house was one of several comprising a substantial community.

The houses were placed on sizeable plots of land lining the shore of an extensive, thin-bodied lake. There were a variety of stores conveniently situated just a couple of minutes away. A number of roads ran near to the place, two of which crossed the water via high bridges that were a good distance apart. The lake and its attendant community were nestled within a region that primarily consisted of forested ground and cleared farmlands.

The lake was not always the idyllic scene of tranquility that one would have suspected, and often being far from serene. There was always a steady traffic of watercraft skimming along the surface of the lake. Motorized boats, jet skis, and wave runners largely ran unimpeded, for there was rarely much interest from those owning property by the lake to see any appropriate resolutions enforced. Throughout the summer, it seemed as if there was a constant party occurring around the lake, whose focal point simply shifted among the various houses.

Despite the frequent presence of rambunctious activity, a person could still find ample relaxation and repose at the lake. It was a place for those who wanted to get a sense of seclusion, without ever truly leaving the conveniences of the modern world.

Kent's father, a fifty-six year old man named William McNeeley, was idly watching a soccer game on his satellite television when they arrived and entered the place. Derek was caught a little by surprise, as Kent had instructed Derek to just walk in the back door when they reached the lake house.

If a man could be the image of physical comfort, Derek found William McNeeley to be a likely candidate. Portly, and with a cherubic countenance to match, he greeted Derek and Janus warmly.

Mr. McNeeley was not far from taking an early retirement due to a rare arthritic condition. The condition had proven to be an arduous struggle for him during the summer, chaining him with frequent agony when the weather shifted to colder hues.

Derek had expected him to be away in the city, but the man seemed to have been anticipating them. Derek quickly surmised that Kent had explained the full situation to him. Mr. McNeeley also explained that Kent was running a little late from work, but would be arriving very shortly.

Derek knew that he did not have to convince Mr. McNeeley of Janus' need for a change of locales, just as he had not had to say anything to convince his son. From what Derek knew of him, Kent's father understood loss well enough. Just three years prior, he had lost his wife to cancer. She was his high-school sweetheart, and a woman that was inseparable from his own identity ever since they had married.

He had been by her side as she had wasted away and finally succumbed to the spreading, voracious cancer. It was not long after when he had purchased the lake house, selling his main house in the city and shifting over to an apartment for when he was in town for work.

After the initial greetings, Mr. McNeeley showed the two of them to guest bedrooms, located on the second level of the two-story structure.

He then informed them that he was going to travel back to town later that evening, to prepare early for the coming week, but that the three of them were welcome to stay for as long as they needed.

Derek recognized Mr. McNeeley's unstated meaning, a sincere, generous expression of compassion for Janus. It was reflected in the look within the man's tired eyes. It was humbling to witness, as Mr. McNeeley had not met Janus in person until that very day. Derek made a firm mental note to speak to Mr. McNeeley in private the next day, and thank him for the unconditional kindness.

William left shortly thereafter to go run some errands, leaving Derek and Janus to themselves with a full set of keys to the house. He had showed them where all of the fishing gear and other lake essentials were stored. He had also paused to show them that the refrigerator was fully stocked up with food, beer, and soft drinks, and stated that they were more than welcome to partake of whatever they wished.

About thirty minutes after William had departed, Kent arrived at last, still dressed in his work uniform. A younger, more athletic version of his father, he was about six feet in height. He had a slight paunch to his belly, but his squared shoulders and stout chest evidenced the presence of ample strength in him. With a round face and pug nose, he had an easy, charming smile. His dirty blonde hair was close cropped, and he had a trimmed goatee around his mouth.

With additional girth to his belly and a higher percentage of gray hairs, he could almost pass as a twin to his father. The sight of their physical similarities always amused Derek immensely, but from what he had learned about Kent's father, being like William McNeeley in any way could not be a bad thing.

Kent quickly took leave to shed his uniform and change. He rejoined the others back out in the living room, now in shorts and a t-shirt.

"We are forgetting one thing," he announced as he popped open a can of beer and sat down in a wide easy chair, setting two more unopened cans on the end table next to him. Without another word, he picked up a phone and proceeded to order three large pizzas, pausing only to get the others' input on toppings.

"We had some earlier, but we can roll with it again, I guess," Derek commented. "But I'm going to have to work out twice as hard tomorrow."

"I plan on working out hard, as far as curling twelve ounce weights is concerned," Kent said with a chuckle, grinning mischievously as he took a long draught of his beer for emphasis. He then said with a reassuring tone, "Don't worry, I've got it all covered. Nobody is going without here. Got paid today!"

Tilting his head back, he slugged the can down in prodigious gulps, crumpling the empty can when he was finished and setting it on the end table. He then emitted a resounding belch of sheer contentment, immediately opening up a second can.

Noticing Derek's bemused expression, he quipped, "Thirsty, you know."

Kent's loquacious, jovial mood provided a welcome levity that had been very absent in Derek's life recently. Not always the most articulate of individuals, Kent's good-hearted nature always tended to shine through brightly, and it was undeniably infectious.

Where Derek and Janus had to put some of their pizza back in the refrigerator, Kent ravenously finished his off completely. In the midst of downing the pizza, Kent was well into his third beer, accented by more sonorous belches. The latter were accompanied by dramatic facial expressions, as he tried to outdo each previous one in volume and resonance.

The speed of consumption continued to amaze Derek, and even Janus had a startled expression on his face.

"Hungry," Kent said, noticing both of their expressions. "And didn't I already mention thirsty?"

"Barbarian," Derek chided him, chuckling.

"If I am a barbarian, then we should go on a river raid! Lots of lake houses that are soft and ripe for plundering!" Kent retorted with fervor, smiling broadly. "Think you can handle the navigation? I'll take care of the raiding! Let me get my chain mail from the closet first!"

"Now there's a suggestion," Derek replied sarcastically, shaking his head as he chuckled. "But you might need me for tactics if the locals are prepared to resist."

"With you going with us, I'm not worried. If my sword and axe fail, you can back me up with your rifle on full auto," Kent said, laughing. He then added, with another copious swig of beer. "And you are driving."

A river jaunt did sound like a good idea at the moment to Derek, and they had more than one option available regarding their mode of travel.

Mr. McNeeley had purchased a shiny new speedboat about six months prior, which had some real kick in its engine. There were also two canoes resting upon on the shore, tethered to posts.

It did not have to be discussed openly as to which of the boats they would choose.

After Kent had finished off a couple more beers, when full night had fallen, the trio made their way down to a short quay at the water's edge. It ran alongside a small shed enclosure that sheltered the new speedboat within it.

Kent handed the speedboat's keys over to Derek, holding a couple more unopened beers in his other hand. The three of them settled into the vessel and made themselves comfortable.

Derek eased into the driver's seat and turned the key in the ignition. The engine growled to life, settling into a steady rumble. Slowly, he guided the boat out of the enclosure and out into the body of the lake.

In moments, they were cruising steadily along the water's surface, the wind beating against their faces. As they traveled, Derek again appreciated just how long the lake was. It seemed to go on forever, an endless panorama of houses, docks, and trees.

A number of lakeside residents were getting their nocturnal activities underway. They passed several houses exhibiting the beginnings of evening festivities. The thumping music and raucous chorus of voices coming from a couple of the ongoing parties indicated lake houses that would be very active well into the night.

Yet not every figure that came into sight was overly energetic or boisterous. At some points along the shore, Derek took notice of the nearly still forms of couples, young or older in age, enjoying the company of their significant other within the cool night's ambience down by the water's edge. Derek really liked such warm, peaceable sights, as he had seen quite enough of the other extremes in life.

As far as other watercraft, they only passed two other boats, both of which had their small engines off and were idly floating in the water. The silhouettes of fishermen were visible on both, still and silent as they waited for their bait to be taken.

Derek saw the fishermen turn their heads towards them as they passed. The night masked the likely glares on their faces. Derek knew that the fishermen were muttering low curses as he drove the boat by them, the water and their quarry momentarily disrupted.

Derek could only chuckle to himself and continue onward. The fishermen, after all, did not own exclusive rights to the lake. Engaged in an activity like fishing, they should be adept at patience anyway.

After some time, the trio finally drew close to the far end of the lake.

"Long … this is one long, long lake," Derek remarked as the end of the water came into sight at last.

"Yes. Yes it is," Kent said. "If you didn't know better, you'd probably think that this whole thing was a river. With the fairly narrow width of it, and all of the twists and turns that it takes along its path, it does kind of look like one."

"Just one of those rivers without a current," Derek retorted, chuckling.

"Well, whatever it is, let's head on back, and see what is happening at the other end," Kent said, as Derek turned the boat around. He then added, a little more spiritedly, as he finished another beer, "No promising sites to raid at this end, but there's another end to explore! Onward, sea raiders!"

"Sea raiders? So now this is an ocean?" Derek jested. Laughing, he shook his head, and set the boat forward on its course, simply glad that Kent was not driving.

JANUS

In the back of the speedboat, Janus just sat back and breathed slowly. He was content to simply let the cool breezes flow soothingly against the skin of his face as they resumed their trip back along the lake. The night sky was predominately clear, bestowing him with a beautiful view of the stars in the vast firmament above.

His mind, given the peace of the moment, and with such a tremendous vista of the heavens filling his eyes, wandered again towards thoughts of his father. He wondered whether somewhere, somehow, his father was even now watching over him. As was his new habit in such moments, Janus looked for any sign; in the stars, or on the gentle currents of air, or even on the few spare wisps of clouds that were drifting along in the sky.

The hardest part about death, he had surmised, apart from the abrupt and stark separation, was the state of the unknown, perhaps the worst element of it all by far. Janus knew that the separation would have been easier to bear with the comfort of knowing that his father still existed, and had reached a good destination.

Having been through the sorrows of deaths more than once before, he knew that the most sharply biting pains would eventually fade. Yet he also knew fully well that the hopes and worries would not, and nor would the sorrows.

Janus knew that life would go on, but with him there would be yet another scar on his spirit, and another weight on a heart grown far heavier over his brief years. Even worse, this newest scar was the largest that he had ever incurred.

Suddenly, as the darkness swarmed around him, he found that he needed the refuge of his mind.

He leaned his head back farther and closed his eyes, wondering what it would be like to have the surety of a healing end to life's journey. Imagination took root, sprouted, and flowered.

In his mind, he envisioned a shining road, leading to a gateway as resplendent as the sun itself. Beyond that gate would be realms where death had no name or claim, where all scars would be fully erased, and where the burdens would be lifted and tossed away in their entirety.

Janus imagined walking towards that radiant entrance, and what he might first see. In his mind's eye, he saw the outlines of many figures waiting for him before the gates, with one in the forefront of the gathering. In his inner vision, their details were obscured at first by the blinding light, but his heart knew who they were. He could feel the surging joy within him with each step that drew him closer to them, an electrifying thrill that infused the powerful emotions swirling within him.

As his eyes adjusted to the light, he beheld the face of his father, with an expression carefree and sparkling with life. Janus could feel the arms of his father wrapping around him in a welcoming embrace, even as he heard a chorus of human voices, as well as exuberant, excited barks, mixed with high pitched, chirruping sounds, all brimming with a boundless joy.

Such a glorious moment would only be the mere dawning of an eternal day, as he continued towards that gate with his heart rising and the jubilant throng of souls walking and padding along at his side. He knew that he could laugh, seeing familiar, beloved four-legged forms bounding along the edge of the pathway to the gate, imbued with the fullness of health and vitality.

His gaze would then focus in on the figure walking at his side, regarding that single face before he could even take in the endless, awesome beauty of the horizons spreading out to infinity beyond the great gates.

That moment would be the beginning of a reunion that would never be broken or tarnished by death or disease ever again; the beginning of a glorious and wonderful time that would never, ever end.

His heart ached thunderously with the burning desire for the realization of that luminous image, even as a few tears welled up in his eyes and began to trickle down his cheeks.

He wished that he could just know with reassurance that something like the vision in his mind could be real; that at the end of all things, his beloved family would all be there. For if a deity did love creation, and loved Janus, then his family was truly the expression, and face, of that love. With all of life's sorrows and struggles, it seemed like such a small comfort to ask for.

But, he was undeniably trapped in the physical world, bereft of knowing what was or was not out there beyond the senses. There was no gateway or conduit to other worlds, no matter how hard he wished that it could be otherwise.

Janus would simply have to pick himself up, bandage his soul's wounds that he knew would not heal in this lifetime, and trudge forward even if each ensuing step was harder to take. Only the passage of time itself would aid him.

"Man, that's pretty odd … came in quick, it looks like," Kent remarked, sharply breaking through the ambient noises of the boat's engine and the breezes wafting across them. "I know I haven't had that many beers."

"Real weird," Derek murmured. "There was nothing when we

came down the lake."

Janus could sense the absolute surprise reflected in the vocal tone of the others. He sighed and opened his eyes, to see what had so suddenly gripped their attentions. With the back of his right hand, we wiped the thin trails of wetness from his face.

The shoreline on both sides of the lake was still visible, but the headlights on the boat now formed solid beams. They could barely cut through the outskirts of a vapor that hovered over the water, rising up as a vast wall of fog about a hundred feet before them.

Janus shared the great puzzlement of the others. They had passed right through the area such a short time before. There had not been any fog or mist in the area whatsoever.

Janus took a deep breath, and his first impression was that something far beyond normal was occurring. He battened the thought back down, knowing fully well that it was just a rising fog caused by water and temperature shifts. It had just emerged much faster than he had thought that a fog could.

"What do you think caused it?" Janus asked them.

Kent shook his head. "I can't figure it out. Fog just doesn't form like this. Not this fast, at least. I don't know, maybe someone channeled a bunch of hot water into the lake or something, like their entire hot tub spilled over or something. Must be an amazing party going on nearby."

He laughed nervously, and Janus could see the anxiety in Kent's eyes.

"It would sure have to be a lot of hot water," Derek added, his eyes fixated upon the thick vapors looming ahead of them. "Pretty big hot tub."

"Maybe it is the mists of time, and we are going to end up on the shores of some ancient land," Kent remarked. "Then we can be like barbarian invaders and pillage and plunder. Let's stake our claims ... I get the wenches and beer, you guys can have the rest!"

"Creative, Kent, but probably not gonna happen," Derek said, a flicker of deep concern manifesting in his face.

Derek cut down the speed of the engine, until the boat was going at a slow crawl. The fog soon enveloped them entirely, shearing off any extended vision to any side of the boat.

"Lovely, just lovely," Kent remarked sourly. "We'll have to take it very slow, and very carefully."

"Maybe we should just stop," Derek suggested.

Janus concurred with Derek, as they were now unable to see more than a few feet ahead of them.

"We take it real slow, if we keep going. And we keep talking and listening, because if there are any other boats in this, they need to know we're here," Kent said, his lightheartedness dissipating rapidly, and his mood sobering up quickly.

Janus knew that the last thing that Kent wanted to do was to wreck Mr. McNeeley's boat. Each passing second invited that possibility.

"Keep talking. Keep it slow. Keep listening," Kent repeated again.

Janus did not argue with him, as his eyes strained to look through the shrouding fog.

ERIN

Erin, as was usual, slumbered lazily until it was almost three o'clock in the afternoon. There were no classes or work to be concerned with, though such things ultimately mattered little. Neither of those issues would have obstructed her intended pursuits for the coming evening.

It took about another half-hour to rouse herself sufficiently awake to take a shower, eat, and check up on her messages. By phone and computer, the messages were the typical kind, of a largely vacuous content.

It did not take her long to sift through them, responding to some and deleting most.

Time slogged onward, until Lynn finally arrived to pick her up for the planned excursion. Almost as an afterthought, Erin left a brief message behind for her parents that she was going to be out for the evening, camping with friends in the woods.

Slinging her large backpack over her shoulder, she locked the front door on the way out.

At a mini-mart near the main highway bypass, Lynn and Erin made their rendezvous with Razor, Uli, and the others that would be going on the camping trip. The group took a few moments to fuel the vehicles, and to procure an assortment of drinks and snacks, before finally setting off for their intended destination.

In total, the entourage consisted of a convoy of ten people situated in three different cars. The two-hour trip passed by quickly enough, the travel broken up by various antics as the cars took turns passing each other on the highway, the occupants giving each other obscene gestures.

It seemed like only moments before they were unloading the vehicles within an official national forest parking lot. Packs readied, and hiking boots laced, the ten started off together in a loose column onto the trail.

About two miles inward and upward, they broke off of the trail to find themselves a suitable spot for the evening. The park rangers required a minimum distance from the trails for overnight camping, but they elected to go well beyond that limited requirement, with Razor in the lead.

Eventually, they found themselves on the summit of a small hill, surrounded by thicker growths of brush. It was far away from any of the main trail paths, and required a little effort to reach.

It was not likely that the place would be disturbed by fellow hikers or park rangers. Razor, Lynn, and Uli quickly set to making a clearing for a small campfire, as the others staked out their camping spots.

A few tents were set up, three suited for single persons, and three larger capacity ones to accommodate the others, with two couples each claiming a tent.

It was not very long before the drinking and festivities began to get underway. The frivolity grew as the afternoon dipped into night, the sun tucking itself away below the hills.

As night drew onward, the group started to fragment as the flow of libations continued. A few of Erin's friends opted to go farther up the hill to get a grander view of the area, while one of the couples headed in the opposite direction to find some space for privacy.

Erin, Lynn, Uli, and Razor were the last four remaining around the campfire. Erin was simply glad that the quartet was not sitting in Uli's cluttered living room.

"Dissipation. Always happens on these trips," Lynn said, laughing in a carefree manner as she looked into the flames of the campfire.

"Dissipation, like this," Uli repeated, as he blew out a puff of smoke from the tightly rolled joint that he was taking deep inhalations from. The mind-numbing herb left a sweet smell hanging in the air, a scent that Erin had become quite accustomed to. Uli laughed hysterically.

"Surprised that you even know what that word means, Uli?" Erin teased, laughing, though her words had an intended jab within them.

"Don't care much 'bout words, but this will do," Razor said, carefully accepting the rolled herb from Uli.

He held it reverently, as he closed his eyes and inhaled upon the end of it. The others could see the flaring red of the other end as it burned down towards its stump. Razor held the smoke inside for several moments, before finally exhaling in a broad puff.

"So good to be here," Erin observed, without a trace of sarcasm. "Could do this every day, all day."

"Wouldn't you get bored?" Lynn asked. "I mean, I want to figure out something that makes me happy."

The others gave her strange looks in response, as usually occurred whenever Lynn invoked realities in the midst of a carefree party. Erin found such moments annoying, noticing that Lynn was bringing them out with greater frequency as of late.

"Don't get me wrong, I won't leave nights like this out of the equation," Lynn added, having recognized the sudden hesitation in the others.

Lynn laughed as the others relaxed. Erin refrained from expressing her personal irritation with Lynn, as there were other aggravations to express.

"Getting nagged to death, working for nothing, or wasting time at school ... those are the options life offers, if you want to get real about it," Erin said. She rested her chin in the cup of her right hand, propped up and braced by her arm, looking as if she were deeply contemplating the matter.

"World isn't changing anytime soon ... So, after some careful ... thought ... I'll settle for the herb. It's a lot easier on the stress levels," she then added, replacing the mock seriousness of her expression for a wide grin.

Accepting the remnant left from Razor, she took a deep inhalation of it, held it inside her lungs, and then slowly exhaled. She could feel her anxieties ebbing already.

"Got that right, 'bout that part, 'bout after some thought... I mean. That is ... cuz after the herb, there is no thought," Uli said, stammering through his words and barely making any sense. He guffawed in laughter, and the other three laughed heartily with him.

For the moment, none of the four had a care in the world. Erin was freed, and did not have to worry about school, work, or any other type of mundane activity. It was almost too good to be true.

The thoughts of that consuming liberation were embedded in the forefront of her mind as she excused herself from the group to attend to a call of nature. She fumbled about in her backpack for a flashlight. She clicked it on and a strong beam emerged. She was glad that she had just replaced all of the batteries.

Walking slowly to keep her balance, as she was feeling a little lightheaded, Erin made her way over to the far edge of the campsite. She carefully navigated the brush just beyond it until she deemed herself to be ensconced in full privacy.

Glancing around, she noticed some cool tendrils of vapor crossing over her. The silvery mist outlined the beam of her flashlight.

Looking about, her heart gave a flutter as she observed a significant amount of mist rolling swiftly in towards her. The light of the moon through the trees cast an eerie glow on the advancing fog, giving it a ghost-like aspect as it flowed through the depths of the dark foliage.

The strange phenomenon fully captured her attention, taking her mind instantly off of the task that she had left the campsite for. It was a few moments before she came out of her momentary stupor, and hurriedly finished her intended business.

Her nerves had started to rattle inside, for she had never seen a fog moving with such a fluid rapidity. Pulling her shorts and underpants back up, and taking a moment to compose herself, she hastened back to the campsite and implored Lynn to come back with her to see the eerie fog.

At first Lynn was reluctant to the overture by Erin, as she had gotten into a very relaxed, sleepy mood, seated close and comfortable by the warmth of the campfire. At Erin's very insistent urging, Lynn finally pushed herself up to where she could get her feet beneath her, and stood up.

She walked over to where Erin stood at the edge of the camp, with a look of mild irritation. Lynn's expression changed to one of curiosity as she noticed the utterly serious countenance upon her friend's face.

"What's going on?" Lynn asked her.

"You have to see it," Erin replied emphatically. "Just beyond here, not far at all."

Erin headed back into the woods, gesturing for Lynn to follow her. Her flashlight led the way, the beam soon being outlined again by the fog that it increasingly struggled to push through. She did not have to direct

Lynn's attention to the rising density of the fog, as Lynn noticed it clearly enough upon their arrival.

"Wow! I wonder where all that is coming from. Up on a hill too? Shouldn't fog lay low in valleys and such? Think that it will come in to cover the camp?" Lynn inquired with evident amazement at the aggressive behavior of the mist.

"Probably so," Erin replied, sharing the incredulity voiced by her friend. "Looks like it's coming in pretty quickly. Never seen fog behave like this."

"Yes, it is coming in quick, and no, I haven't seen anything like it. We should probably make sure that the others can find their way back to the camp, or there is a chance that they will get lost in this." Lynn remarked, looking down at the growing slivers of the vapor starting to envelop her own body.

Just a few feet beyond them, the density of the mist had formed into the beginnings of an impenetrable wall of fog. The full beam of the flashlight could not pierce the opaque mass at all.

Even more disturbing, the wall of fog seemed to creep closer with each passing second, swallowing the feeble attempts of the flashlight to cut through its relentless advance.

Within just moments, Erin could see that they would be fully surrounded.

LEE

Lee Chen attended diligently to his duties, enduring yet another exhausting day of managing the restaurant that bore his name.

He had arrived even earlier than usual that particular Saturday, to work on a valve problem in one of the restrooms after getting only four hours of sleep. Lee did not think much about how little sleep he had gotten, as it rarely reached even six hours on normal days.

The early morning maintenance was soon followed by a full afternoon and evening of almost constant activity; Clearing and cleaning tables, bringing out orders, cooking, passing out coupons, driving deliveries, taking orders, making schedule adjustments for employees, and all of the usual trials and travails of a restaurant owner-operator.

While never doing poorly, in terms of customer traffic, the restaurant's business had never seemed to grow enough to a point where he could hire the amount of help that was truly needed. Even with as much pressure as he constantly felt, he still could not ask the three employees in his hire to do any more than they were. They currently went above and beyond the call of duty on a regular basis. Lee was very grateful for their extra resilience, as quality workers were becoming something of a scarcity in his observation.

The pressures of what needed to be done, in contrast to the resources available to him, resulted in Lee's own efforts being stretched beyond the limits. Neither customer nor employee could often tell the full extent of the strain, for Lee held neither bitterness nor frustration within him.

His regular, friendly countenance, and stalwart perseverance on the most frenzied of days, was what had won him a core of regular customers and loyal employees. Though he did not take credit for it, it undoubtedly elevated the performance of his small, but earnest, staff.

When closing time finally did arrive, the most prominent desire in Lee's mind was simply rest. He looked very much forward to the following day, as the restaurant closed early on Sundays. He was eager to indulge in a few hours of blissful recreation, even if it was only to have Ryan over to drink sodas and watch movies.

Calling up a little extra resolve, he attended to the closing duties with Ryan and two members of his regular staff. They stacked the chairs on the tables and set about mopping up the floors. They cleaned the kitchen, including the woks, dishes, and the rest of his array of equipment.

At the very end, Ryan bagged up the trash and carried it out to the dumpsters, while Lee tallied up the register receipts and prepared a deposit bag.

Lee paid his two staff members a little extra bonus in cash, and thanked them for their sincere, solid efforts that day. Their job finished, they thanked Lee, wished him a good evening, and left for the night.

Circling around Ryan, Lee bolted the front door behind them and returned back towards the main counter. At last, the restaurant was silent and still, his work for the day finally at an identifiable end. The weight and tension dissipated from his shoulders at that moment, a feeling that he had come to savor at the culmination of a long day's work.

Ryan extended a can of cherry-flavored citrus soda to Lee, not having to ask as the soft drink was well known at the restaurant as being

Lee's favorite. Lee gave Ryan a tired smile as he accepted it.

Taking a deep breath, and following it with a long and gratifying draught of the beverage, Lee set it down and looked wearily towards Ryan.

"Good job tonight, Ryan. I appreciate your help a lot, I really do. It was a very hard day today, more than usual" Lee observed.

"No problem Lee. Did good biz today, from what I saw, didn't we?" Ryan replied, taking a sip out of his own can. He raised the can in a saluting gesture towards Lee, "To a good day, Lee!"

"Above average, I am happy to say," Lee replied. "Campus brought us a few more deliveries than I expected. You must have gotten some extra coupons out."

"I've passed out quite a few for the cause. But must have been giving them to all the wrong folks, because Bob wasn't too happy about the tips today," Ryan replied with a chuckle, referring to Lee's tried and true delivery driver.

The man had grumbled throughout the day about the frugal nature of the campus students. The language that he had used back in the kitchen had often been quite colorful. Lee and Ryan had laughed heartily at some of the creative and very descriptive anatomical suggestions that Bob had for the cheap students.

"Oh, he made us aware of that. But I made sure Bob got a little extra tonight," Lee said, a hint of worry on his face.

Bob was indispensable to his operation, knowing every optimal route and planning his deliveries to the height of efficiency. He did the work of two, maybe even three, mediocre drivers.

"I saw that. And Bob looked pretty happy about it. He'll stay around. Griping is natural to him, don't worry," Ryan said encouragingly. "And about those students. Just have them all work one day and night like this, and they will learn to tip really quickly. They should make it mandatory for cheap tippers."

"Very good point. I think that would work too. So, I noticed that you haven't bolted yet. Is Pamela busy tonight?" Lee asked him.

"Yeah, she sure is," Ryan replied at the mention of his girlfriend. "Says she is just going to stay home and get some rest tonight. You know what that means. But I'm not too worried. She plays a bit, but she knows who the real man is. Nothing else will compare. She'll learn!"

Lee chuckled as Ryan's youthful cockiness emerged. "I'm sure she'll realize who the real man is."

Ryan smiled. "Hey now, that better not be sarcasm. Don't you get in on disrespecting me."

Lee laughed heartily. "You worked well tonight, so I'll give you a break. Have you thought about what we should watch for the film festival at my house tomorrow evening, if you are up for some movies?"

"You need to get a game system, some day, Lee. And not a used one at the pawn shop. Get a cutting-edge console. But movies don't sound bad right now. I could do with just about anything at the moment, except some boring drama or silly chick flick," Ryan remarked.

"We'll figure something out, either on satellite or download," Lee replied, finishing off his soda. He crumpled the can in his hand and pitched it into a freshly lined trash bin that Ryan had prepared towards the end of the counter. "Well, there's the first start on tomorrow's trash load. I am about done here. Time to get some rest."

"And you are just going to leave me stranded facing a boring night. I'm not ready to go to sleep yet!" Ryan commented, as he started towards the door. His steps slowed as he approached the glass-faced door. "Looks like there is going to be a thick fog cover tonight!"

"Fog?" Lee replied in curiosity, coming out from behind the counter and walking down its length towards where Ryan stood gaping.

"Yeah, come over here. I could see it even as I walked towards the front door," Ryan said, turning back towards Lee while gesturing at the restaurant's entrance.

Lee walked past Ryan, his eyes fixated through the glass of the front door. He slowly unbolted the lock, and swung it open. Ryan followed close behind as they walked outside together.

As Ryan had observed, a rolling fog bank was gradually invading and conquering the city streets. The fog had already become an impenetrable mass just across the street from where the restaurant was located.

The tall street lamps near his restaurant cast a cramped glow, one that was visibly shrinking. The advancing vapors were steadily wafting in their direction, part of an enormous, rising tide.

"This is just plain strange. I don't understand it," Lee commented, staring at the unusual mists.

Enraptured, Lee continued to stand just outside of the unlocked restaurant with Ryan close by. The near proximity to the front door comforted him, as his eyes could not see more than twenty feet ahead of him.

The fog mass seemed to progress as if it had a mind of its own. It continued to engulf the area around them, as the density increased swiftly in the immediate vicinity of the restaurant.

"It is just fog, Lee, don't get too carried away," Ryan remarked.

He waved his hands about in the misty substance as it encircled them.

"It is, but I still haven't seen fog move like this," Lee commented. "Have you?"

Ryan shrugged and grinned. "Haven't given it too much thought."

The fog mass continued to shroud both them and the restaurant building itself, until they could not see ahead, behind, or to either side.

Though they were standing just a few feet in front of the restaurant, the familiar construction had been utterly consumed by the wafting sea. Looking down, Lee realized that he could not even see the ground.

The thickness of the fog was like nothing that Lee had ever experienced before.

Of that, he was most certain.

section iii

MERSHAD

Erika and Mershad sat silently as the mist continued to surround them with its cool embrace. The thick vapors had fully obstructed their vision of the trees that were less than ten feet away.

"This is some fog," Erika commented in a low voice.

"We'll have to take it slow, when we head out of here," Mershad said.

Erika looked over at him. "Probably won't vanish anytime soon, knowing my luck. Good thing we know the lay of the land."

"Yes, good for us that we do," Mershad responded, grinning at her though he felt a little nervous about blundering about in the dense haze.

"The cars must be slowed to a crawl as they come through up there," Erika stated, as she gestured upward towards where the roadway was. "Or they've stopped."

Mershad then noticed that a permeating silence had blanketed the area, with no sound of anyone or anything coming from the normally active street above them.

"I sure don't hear anything either," Mershad remarked. He slowly rose up to his feet, pulling his satchel over one shoulder. "Want to try and start navigating out of this?"

Erika nodded, getting up off the ground herself. "Otherwise we are going to be here all night. I think that this stuff is here to stay for awhile."

Mershad agreed with her, though he held no objections to spending more time talking with Erika. The lack of visibility simply made him nervous. At the very least the process of getting out of there would be easier to navigate with a friend.

"We'll have to go slowly," Mershad cautioned, taking the first step forward, grasping his satchel strap with his right hand. "Work our way to the sidewalk, and from there it should be easy enough."

"Sounds like a plan to me," Erika replied.

Erika walked closely by his side. They went painstakingly, step by step. There was just enough visibility that they became aware of trees before they smacked their faces into the hard trunks.

After they had moved about twenty arduous paces, Mershad noticed that their visibility was gradually increasing. He made no comment, continuing to press onward.

Looking down, he perceived that there were more leaves and twigs on the ground than he had observed before, even a fallen branch that he had not noticed on his way in. The university's maintenance staff usually kept the grounds around the student center very well groomed.

"We must have gotten changed around," Mershad said with some discomfort. "We should have hit the sidewalk by now. I know that we've been walking in the right direction."

"Well, this place is not that big, we'll run into it sooner or later," Erika added. "Besides, it looks like our visibility is increasing."

"Yes it is," Mershad replied, glad that she was noticing the improving visibility as well. It meant that it was not just his hopeful imagination.

He took a couple more steps, when he suddenly tripped and fell forward. With a startled outcry, he slung his hands forward in reflex, casting his satchel ahead as he braced for the expected impact.

"Are you okay?" Erika said in great concern, dropping to her knees next to him.

Groaning, Mershad shook his head as he brought himself up to his knees slowly. He had caught his fall at the last moment, and was not injured other than a few light scratches.

Brushing his chest off, he looked behind him. A large tree branch lay across his path.

"Wonderful," Mershad muttered, not wanting to know what had happened to his laptop. He looked sheepishly to Erika, highly embarrassed. "I didn't think there was anything on the ground. Didn't notice any fallen branches coming in here."

"It's okay. As long as you are okay," Erika said quickly, her eyes full of worry. "Let's find your satchel."

They both looked all around, but could see no sign of the satchel. Mershad was perplexed, as he knew that it could not have fallen very far from where he stood.

More than ever, the ground that Mershad could see beneath his feet looked markedly different than it had seemed before when he visited the area. There was a sprawling cover of debris, of fallen leaves, dirt, twigs, and grasses all about them, as if the surface of a wild forest. It was not the well-cropped, rich green lawn that he had walked through numerous times before. The feeling of unease grew faster within him.

Even stranger, the rate of improved visibility was accelerating, along with the emergence of a steady breeze that flowed all around them. It was as if the fog was reversing itself, departing as quickly as it had come.

Mershad and Erika remained wordless, fixed in place, their attentions captured by the bizarre phenomenon. Their range of sight increased by twenty, thirty, and then forty feet.

Trees began to appear out of the misty air, and the uneven contours of the ground, with the rough covering upon it, spread out in all directions around them. Mershad struggled to comprehend what was happening.

There was no sign of the sidewalk, the student center, or even a small patch of the rich, trimmed grass turf that they had been sitting on just minutes before. He barely moved a muscle as the fog steadily fell away, continuing to reveal the unexpected environment.

"What is going on here?" Mershad stammered, his eyes widened in trepidation as he looked around.

Erika shook her head in disbelief, staring ahead. Her voice was uncharacteristically full of anxiety. "I just don't know. I just don't know."

The fog proceeded to thin out on all sides. Strong rays of light began to cut through to them from above, a multitude of beams piercing the diminishing fog as they reached through the leaves and branches of the surrounding trees.

"What is this? What in the world is …" Erika began, her words trailing off as the air above them finally cleared up.

The strong light of a mid-day sun was revealed, cascading down from a nearly cloudless sky spread out far above the trees. It was a uniquely blue-greenish sky, like nothing that Mershad had ever seen before.

Mershad and Erika now found themselves in the midst of a great forest, with matured trees of several varieties rising up high all around them. The bright chirping of birds met their ears, coming from all around, amongst the lofty branches, but it was the surreal sky above that transfixed his initial attention.

ERIKA

Erika continued to stare upwards, entirely stunned.

There were no cloud masses to bar the view of the smooth, luxuriant sky, the light radiating from a solitary sun that seemed to be directly overhead.

The blue-greenish tint to the sky was remarkable.

It was turquoise, like the surface of the waters about the Caribbean islands that Erika had once taken a vacation to with friends, on a break from school.

Beautiful and vivid, it was nonetheless frightening. At the very least, though she did not consciously acknowledge it, the commanding presence of the sun was a stabilizing and comforting element to her jostled psyche.

"What do we do?" Mershad asked, his eyes still wide in a look of surprise and bewilderment.

"I have no idea," Erika said.

"This can't be a dream," Mershad remarked.

Some beads of sweat now stood out upon his forehead. He reached down and rubbed his arms, and even felt his own face, as if about to pinch it to test the reality of the moment.

He looked over towards Erika with a helpless expression. "This can't be a dream."

"I know that it isn't. I know when I am asleep, and when I am not," Erika said slowly. Her eyes were filled with fear, but she had already started to reach down into deep, internal reservoirs of personal strength to gain some elemental bearings. "This is real. Make no mistake about it. Whatever it is, we are both in it, it is real, and we had better acknowledge that first and foremost."

As she spoke the stark words, some more of that strength welled up in her. She took a few cautious steps forward.

Her shoes crunched on the debris-strewn forest floor. Mershad stared after her, until she turned and beckoned for him to follow her. Gingerly, he took a step, then a second, and slowly trailed after her.

She continued onward, feeling the hard ground beneath every step. Unexpectedly, she discovered that she was taking notice of the very air. It felt exceptionally fresh and clean within her lungs. She took many deep breaths of the sweet air into her, as her heart rate began to steady from the initial shock.

Though she was no naturalist, she knew that the trees around them were of types that she was familiar with. Likewise, the chirping and chattering coming from the branches above was akin to the sounds that she had heard before on wilderness hikes.

Other than the color of the sky itself, she could not help but think that they were not too far removed from the university. The state was filled with thickly forested areas, and as far as Erika knew, they were in any one of those regions. It was just a mystery as to how they had gotten there, perhaps something conjectured in some obscure journal of theoretical physics.

The continuing commotion in the branches attracted her attention. She looked upwards, searching for the squirrels that she expected were running about the trees, just as they did all around the university campus. She knew the sight of a few little squirrels would be something else to grasp onto, as her mind struggled with the unprecedented instability of reality itself.

Any hope that she had of taking another step towards calming her mind was swiftly evaporated.

The creatures making the ruckus in the trees looked like diminutive foxes. They had reddish fur, elongated snouts, and four narrow legs that ended in grasping appendages, like those of monkeys. Long bushy tails protruded out behind them.

Even more unusual, sprouting from their backs, were the presence of a pair of leathery wings that they kept tucked in as they skittered about the branches nimbly.

Erika gaped at the astonishing little creatures.

"What are those … animals?" Mershad asked, having taken note of the host of small creatures himself.

Erika was breathtaken, as one of the creatures glided gracefully through the air from the branch of one tree, over to the limb of another tree situated about thirty feet away. It moved with dexterity as it alighted smoothly upon the new branch, grasping it firmly, with exceptional balance. Folding its wings, its little eyes watched them intently, and though the creature looked cautious, it was clearly not overly afraid of the two humans.

"No idea," Erika replied. "I think we've just discovered a new animal. But wouldn't you know it? We don't have a camera with us."

Mershad shook his head. He looked far more worried than regretful about missing the opportunity to document a rare species. "This is getting crazy."

Though the environment held some features familiar to her, there was no denying now that there was something utterly alien about it as well. It was no longer just a matter of the anomalous sky.

She kept a wary eye on the little bat-foxes, not knowing whether or not they presented any kind of threat, but not about to underestimate them. Sometimes, the smallest of creatures could be the most deadly.

"Let's move on, this way," Erika suggested in a low voice.

Erika slowly turned to the right, beginning to carefully make her way from the area. She cast a sideways glance to make sure that Mershad was following her lead, but kept the greater part of her attention fixed upon the disposition of the little bat-fox creatures.

The creatures continued their high-pitched chatter among the branches, a few shifting their places amid the cluster of trees that they were situated within. To her immense relief, they made no moves to follow the two humans.

Erika had observed, with not a little worry, the fact that the creatures were not terribly startled by their presence. The creatures appeared to be no more wary than were the squirrels that heavily populated the university campus's grounds. Yet whether or not the little creatures were some sort of pack hunter in their own right, it soon became clear that humans were not likely their prime quarry. Erika and Mershad gradually lost sight of them, as the little beasts' hyper, high-pitched sounds faded farther behind.

Finally, she felt comfortable enough to turn around and face forward, picking up her pace a little in the process.

Erika looked over her shoulder several times to check on Mershad. "They are not coming after us, I'm pretty certain," she commented, as she recognized his lingering fear, her gaze sweeping around the area for a moment as an idea came to her.

She walked a few paces to the right, leaned over, and snapped off a branch that had been attached to a tree that had long since fallen to the floor of the forest. She stripped it of a few narrow offshoots, leaving behind a rather straight, sturdy piece of wood.

She extended it towards Mershad. "Here, take this. I'm pretty confident that those things in the trees could not take a solid hit from something like this."

Mershad reached out and took the offered branch, nodding to her. She watched his expression relax just a little as he gripped the stalwart branch, clearly feeling a little less vulnerable.

"And now for myself," she remarked, locating another suitable branch. Clasping it firmly, she held it out in front of her. "It will work fine. Just in case. But I don't think we will have much to fear from those little winged guys."

"My brain says we won't, but I just had no idea what they were," Mershad replied.

"Hence, precautions," Erika said, bringing the stick about in a powerful swing that swooshed through the air. As if taking her gesture as a cue, Mershad whipped his own branch-staff through the air.

"You've got the hang of it," Erika said approvingly, forcing a broad smile despite her ginger nerves. "Well, let's get going. We need to find someone or something more familiar in this area."

Erika started forward, resuming her long, easy strides. Mershad hustled up and walked along at her side, beginning to use his branch like a walking stick. She noticed that he glanced behind them less and less often, as they continued forth without incident through the forest for the next couple of hours.

To her relief, they encountered no more unusual creatures. More promising, they saw several birds that were of very familiar forms. Among those that she recognized were sparrows, finches, and even a couple of large, black crows. The familiar caws of the latter were welcome music to her ears.

Her tensions gradually lessened, and her spirit became more emboldened as they continued their long march beneath the trees. Mershad seemed content to walk in silence, but she suspected that under the surface his mind was racing with thoughts. She did not disturb him. Erika took the silent time to attend to her own thoughts. There was little else for her to do at the moment, except to avoid being lulled into complacency.

Erika could not begin to comprehend what had happened to her and Mershad. She had no idea as to what the fog was, or how they had gotten to the forest, much less why it had happened in the first place.

There had been no sensation of travel. The fog had merely appeared, and then departed, revealing a whole new environment around them.

Erika found that she was eminently grateful for the presence of another person with her during the harrowing experience, especially one that she already knew. She was not entirely sure if her mind could have handled such an event by herself. At the same time, she knew that while she derived some stability from having Mershad with her, she also had some new responsibilities.

With their whole world shaken, Erika knew that Mershad needed her as well, immersed as they were in an experience whose nature neither of them had an inkling of. She knew that she had to be as strong as she could for his sake, and resolved herself to that course even though she suspected that the fox-bats and the blue-green sky were not the last surprises that they would encounter.

LOGAN

"Thick. That's really, really thick," uttered Antonio.

Logan had no disagreements, seeing how the bright headlamps on the car, normally intensely illuminating, did little to cut through the dense mists all around them. His nerves were tingling as they crept through the fog. He feared that they were risking a collision any second with another car exhibiting less caution than they were.

"I've never been through fog like this. Nothing like this before. Never," Antonio said emphatically. "There's been fog on this road before, but I've never seen anything close."

They had already slowed down to barely a crawl, as their visibility lowered to just a few feet ahead. Logan felt increasingly vulnerable.

"Just our luck!" Logan finally snapped, frustrated and incredulous. "You know … we don't ask for much in this world. We just want to take a break to get a damn milk shake … and, lo and behold, the world's most dense fog bank ever has to manifest and roll in out of nowhere, right here, to make even getting a simple milk shake a major frigging endeavor!"

"Hard luck champion," observed Antonio, his right hand nervously clutching the passenger side door handle. "I think that we hold the titles in that division, counting all weight classes."

Again, Logan had no disputes.

The ride suddenly became extremely bumpy, as the smoothness of the paved road changed to the uneven surface of grass-covered ground. Logan's heart caught in his throat. Seeing a patch of grass in front of him, he feared that they had somehow gone off of the road.

Logan pulled the car up into a complete halt, not wanting to risk anything further. He cursed under his breath in frustration.

"What the hell is this? I know I didn't go off of the road. It was right there, even if I could only see a couple of feet. This ground just came out of nowhere, running right into the road."

"It's okay. It happens. People go off the road in bad visibility,"

Antonio said. "It's just good that you were going slow and we didn't wreck. No harm done."

Despite his friend's attempts at reassuring words, one glance told Logan that Antonio was a nervous wreck. Antonio's eyes had been riveted ahead, and Logan knew that Antonio had also seen that they had been squarely aligned on the road. Logan had not deviated from their course in the least.

"Well, I'll tell you what. I can't just pull the car around, and blindly head for the road. Who knows who else is trying to get through this? We wouldn't know until it's too late, in this kind of visibility," Logan vented, exasperated. "I think that we are stuck for a while, at least until this clears up somewhat."

Antonio nodded. "I understand. Well, let's get out of the car. Let's walk, and see how far it is to the road. We could easily hear another car coming, at least. And it might be safer that way, than being stationary targets in a parked car."

Having his car wrecked in the impenetrable fog was the last thing that Logan needed to have happen right then. He took a deep breath, beginning to get his bearings.

"Yeah, and that's about all that we can do right now," he declared, feeling more resolved. "I'm putting the hazards on, though, and keeping the lights on for a few minutes. Hopefully someone will make something out before they crash into it."

Taking the keys out of the ignition, he listened to the click as he pulled the hazard light switch. He then opened up his door and got out.

Antonio got out on his side, and the shutting of their doors was the only sound within the still, heavy air. Logan walked around the car to the rear, astounded at the sheer thickness of the fog. The flashing hazard lights were swallowed up just a few paces away.

With Antonio close behind him, he started forward, heading straight towards where he knew that the road had been. When they had gotten just a few feet away, they could not see any sign at all of the car behind them.

"Better not lose track of it," Logan growled. "We shouldn't stray out that far, but I know the road is right about where we are. We stopped almost immediately after I felt uneven ground."

"Should be real close," Antonio agreed.

"But I'm beginning to think that if another car comes through this,

I'd might want to be in a car when it hits, rather than be hit outside of a car," Logan remarked, drawing to a halt. "Don't forget, if they can't see the car with the lights on, then they certainly can't see us."

Antonio frowned as he thought about that troubling verity for a moment.

"I'll second that notion," he replied. He looked around then, his eyes narrowing in scrutiny as if taking note of something. "But maybe we won't have to wait for that long. It looks like things are starting to thin out already, or is it just my mind?"

Logan looked around himself, and quietly studied the mists pervading the air around them. After carefully watching it for a couple of minutes, it was clear that the fog was indeed thinning out, for their field of vision was observably expanding.

"Well, that's the first good news that we've had in quite a while," Logan replied sarcastically, turning around to head back towards the car.

After they had gotten about twenty feet, Logan, with Antonio following his cue, came to an abrupt halt.

"It should be here. We didn't get that far at all," Logan avowed. "Not far enough to lose track of the car."

"No we didn't," agreed Antonio firmly.

The amount of ground that they could see steadily continued to grow, as if the land itself were generating out of a gray void in all directions.

"Sure, it got stolen right after we moved. Like I am going to believe that. We should have seen it by now," Logan said, his ire and disbelief rising rapidly.

"We would have heard something if it did," Antonio reminded his friend, earnestly trying to soothe Logan's rising anger.

"I was just being sarcastic about the car being stolen. There isn't any way that could have happened, and I've still got the keys," Logan said sharply, holding the keys up in his hand for his friend to see. "But where is it then?"

"Right around here," Antonio said, looking equally mystified.

"Around where?" Logan stammered, holding his arms out wide.

"We didn't go that ... "

Rays of strong light cut through the fog from above them, and everything around them seemed to be lightening swiftly.

"What in the world is going on here?" muttered Logan.

He flinched in surprise as the misty cover above them parted and thinned out, letting through more of the piercing rays that soon became a flood of unmistakable daylight.

"Man … oh man … this is weird, way too weird," Antonio mumbled, as the advancing force of daylight routed the last remnants of the mists around them.

All evidence of the dense mass of fog was completely gone. So too was any sign of the road or the car.

Night had suddenly become day, the dark, black sky being fully replaced by a creamy, greenish-blue hue lit by a bright sun overhead. Stretched out before them were rolling grasslands that ended in a long line of woods just at the edge of their vision.

"This is weird, this is weird," Antonio said, repeating himself, as he gazed steadily into the unusual sky above. "Where are we?"

"Believe me, I'm wondering the same thing," Logan replied, his hardened demeanor shaken by the incredible changes that had taken place around them. Shading his eyes with his right hand, he turned slowly around in a full circle. There was nothing but the expanse of undulating grasslands and copses of trees in one direction. In the other was the line of woods that demarcated the beginning of an enormous, forested region.

Even more disturbing, there was no sign at all of the world that he knew; the encompassing diorama was fully devoid of any signs of human existence.

After a few more minutes passed, Logan slowly turned to look at Antonio. He found that his friend was looking expectantly towards him, a frightened, almost child-like expression spread on his face.

"So what do we do now?" Antonio asked, looking pleadingly at Logan, as if he would somehow have the answers.

"I have absolutely no clue," Logan responded regretfully, an edge to his voice.

Logan paused for a few more moments, gathering more composure, before continuing, "Maybe we should just wait and see what happens, and hope that someone turns up. Or we could just go wandering off in this place that we've never seen before."

The words were spoken flippantly, exuding a sarcasm that emphasized the seeming futility of it all.

"We'll probably get nowhere by just waiting for things to happen. It's never worked like that in all of my previous life, and I don't think my luck appears to be changing now, unless for the worse," Antonio said, his breath short as he struggled with his nervousness.

"Good point," Logan said curtly, placing his hands upon his hips.

With the tip of his right work boot, he idly dug around in the grass. He then shook his head and let out a deep, sustained exhalation, as if willing some of the coiling tension in him to ease out of his body. There was one thought that tilted the balance of the frustrating indecision now holding him in place.

"Maybe we shouldn't stand right out in the open, where anyone, or anything, can see us so easily," Logan said in an even, careful tone as he looked at Antonio. "Let's do something, at least so we don't lose our minds. Well, let's get a move on it, and maybe get ourselves just inside the borders of those woods, unless you have any objections."

"Sounds like the best option we've got," Antonio replied.

Following Logan's lead, they started off at a quick pace towards the extended tree line on the horizon. They constantly scanned around for the sight of anything that could give them any insights into the causes or full state of their current predicament. Their bolstered level of wariness heightened their senses, causing their attentions to snap in a flash towards a singular bird that flew across the sky.

"Well, it looks like we've got that little wish that you made last night," Antonio said, breaking the silence.

Logan rolled his eyes. "Sure did. I bet you are going to tell me to be careful what I wish for. Don't even say it. I can assure you that this isn't what I had in mind."

"I wasn't about to say it, but I'm frightened," Antonio admitted.

"And so am I," Logan replied, his face smiling ruefully at the open admission for just a moment. An edge of grim determination swelled in his voice as he continued, "But I'm not going to give in to this ridiculous event that's been foisted upon us. We are going to stick together to get through this crazy thing."

"We'll stick together," Antonio echoed, nodding quickly.

For the second time in recent moments, Antonio had the air of a scared child about him.

"Yes, together," Logan confirmed, before vowing angrily, shouting to the sky, "And I can assure you, that when I find out why this all happened, and who or what was responsible, we are going to set some things straight!"

Logan knew that they both harbored fears of the unknown, but where Antonio was willing to feel fragile and utterly helpless, the sheer fury of Logan's ire at their undeserved predicament reinforced his chosen course of action.

Fully resolved not to go down without a fight, and with a deep hunger to find out why they had been ripped away from their world, Logan clenched his jaws as he continued to ruminate upon their situation. He was committed to regaining the bearings in their lives once again. Their core foundations, those very elements that helped them rise to face the day from one morning to the next, had been severely violated. Yet as far as Logan was concerned, as a blaze of righteous anger was stoked within him, it would not be irrevocably violated.

JANUS

"This mist is absolutely insane. I can't see a damn thing!" Kent spat out angrily, cursing as he strained to look forward from the bow of the watercraft.

"We'll probably have to just cut the engine off," Derek replied calmly, though a look of concern shone in his eyes.

Janus fully concurred with Derek's choice, his own concern at possibly wrecking Kent's father's boat rapidly increasing. His confounded eyes told him in no uncertain terms that they would be wise to concede for the moment, rather than force themselves to take on any ill-advised risks in trying to blindly navigate through the mist.

The unusually dense fog choked off all visibility. Another boat could easily be just five feet away from them. Janus could only hope that they heard it, as he was certain that they would not see it until it was far too late.

After a moment, Janus voiced his full consent with Derek's proposition.

"Shouldn't we try and get somewhere?" Kent countered with a look of desperation. "We could be hit by anything."

Janus understood Kent's worries as well, as it was indeed quite unsettling floating about in the water, adrift within the midst of the impenetrable fog. Furthermore, any manner of objects might be close, from docks to shore ground. It was not just a matter of other boaters out on the lake.

"You are right. It's not just the other boats we have to worry about. I know what you are thinking, Kent. We could be beached any minute without warning," Janus said gently. "But if we cut the engine, we lessen any risks of damage to your father's boat, even if we were to run aground. And that way we will also be better able to hear something approaching us, so that we can try and warn them."

Kent stared at Janus, and then looked to Derek for a moment.

"Yeah, I guess that you guys are right. Damn! Why did this have to happen?" Kent stated in clear resignation. He nodded and gestured to Derek, indicating for him to go ahead and cut the engine off.

When the motor died down, all they could hear was the gentle sound of the water lapping up against the sides of the boat. A foreboding, eerie silence hung heavily in the air about them, the sheer lack of sounds escalating Janus' tensions. All throughout the sojourn, the wisps of music and laughter had carried through the air from the various houses. It was as if the fog closed off sound as much as it did sight.

For the next several minutes, they drifted idly in the water, listening intently for the sounds of any other boat or person. Kent kept the headlights on full beam, and they honked the horn periodically.

It did not take very long for their frustrations at the situation to mount steadily. Kent was the first to give voice to them.

"So, are we going to sit here all night? Are we?" It was evident that his patience was quickly wearing thin. "All I want to think about is drinking a few more beers, and then crashing for the night under warm covers, in a nice king-sized bed."

"Would be nice to round out the evening that way. If we could see for even ten feet ahead of us, I think we could go for it," Derek advised. "With the headlights on, and the horn and us calling out, we might be able to pull it off very slowly. But we can't even see five feet from the side of the boat. This fog is far too risky to try anything yet."

"It looks like we are going to have to wait," Janus added. "I don't like it either, but you might as well settle in, Kent."

Kent slumped back down into his chair, shaking his head in disbelief at the sour turn of fortune. "I guess that we are stuck."

Janus leaned back in his chair and closed his eyes. The moist air brushed against his face, and if they had been under any other circumstances he would not have found the feeling to be altogether unpleasant. In fact, its touch under other circumstances would have been rather soothing.

There was not much that he could do for the moment, and his strained emotions had already exhausted him considerably. The sustained idleness quickly added to his weariness, and he felt himself begin to slide towards unconsciousness. With an extended yawn, he slumped his chin down to rest. The tranquil refuge of a dreamless sleep tugged ever stronger at the edges of his lingering consciousness.

Consummately drowsy, he did not know whether he had momentarily fallen asleep, when Kent's sharp, raised voice roused him back to full wakefulness.

"It's thinning!" Kent exclaimed excitedly, from where he was still perched at the bow.

Janus leaned back up in his seat, and opened his eyes, feeling a heavy lethargy rooted throughout his body.

As Kent had indicated, the visibility beyond the sides of the boat had now increased to about fifteen feet. They were still surrounded by an outer boundary of dense fog, and could make no sign of the shore through it in any direction.

"Wanna go for it?" Kent queried impatiently.

"We can, but we've gotta be really careful, Kent, and do it my way, with horns, calls, and a very, very slow rate of speed," Derek said with manifest caution in his voice. "We do it systematically."

Janus had the sense that Derek much preferred to wait and see if the fog thinned out even further.

Kent nodded, "We'll do it your way, but let's get out of this."

Derek frowned slightly as he turned the key again, and the motor rumbled back to life. Slowly increasing the power, Derek set the boat forward once again. They were barely creeping along the water's surface. That much appeared to relax Kent considerably, who pulled back from his perch on the bow to come over to stand by Derek.

Kent, Janus, and Derek kept their eyes fixated upon the water just ahead of them. Janus could see that Derek's senses were on full alertness. His friend maintained a firm grip on the throttle, ready to cut the engine off at a moment's notice. Derek honked the horn frequently, to warn any others that might be in the immediate vicinity. They elicited no manner of response in return, and the only sounds to reach Janus' attentive ears were that of the boat itself.

The absence of any kind of response struck Janus as being very peculiar. He fully expected that their soundings would invoke at least a yell or call-out from a reveler or two, reacting to their horn signal from a party at one of the lake houses. Janus strained to hear even the slightest sound of music or talking, knowing that they were passing by houses on both sides of the narrow lake.

"Next problem," Derek then brought up suddenly. "How are we going to know where exactly we are supposed to go? We might be able to see ahead of us, and avoid crashing into somebody, but we can't make out any landmarks or houses. Unless, of course, you are really, really good at guessing, Kent."

"Once we pass under the main bridge, we know that we are close. And by then, the fog will probably have thinned enough so that we can get a glimpse of the shoreline," retorted Kent. "We just need to get in the vicinity. I need only a brief view of the dock areas, as I know most of the houses that are near to my dad's. I will only need to identify one to tell us exactly where we are."

"Well, then it won't be very long," Janus remarked with a little relief. He pointed off of the port side of the boat, "There's the shoreline, right over there."

"There we are. Easy enough," replied Kent enthusiastically. "All we have to do is follow along that shore, and we'll get there eventually. Take it in closer, as the water drops off deep right off the shore, all the way down the lake."

Derek steered the boat over a little closer to the shoreline. Janus observed that the visibility had increased by another few feet, even as Derek accelerated the watercraft.

Kent's face was filled with an expression of sheer relief. Yet as Janus looked at him, Kent's mien suddenly changed to one of shock as Janus felt the boat lurch to an abrupt halt.

Janus, Kent, and Derek all fell forward with the sudden stop. Kent's face was now a mask of confusion and fear.

"We are far enough off the shore. I know this lake well. It's got good depth right off the shoreline. What's this all about?" Kent said incredulously, anxiously looking over the side of the boat.

Janus joined him at his side.

Through the light from the front of the boat, he could see that they had effectively lodged the boat into an expanse of extremely shallow water.

For the next few moments, Derek tried to get the boat moving but it soon became very evident that it was fully immobilized in the muddy, shallow bottom.

"Great. That's all I need," Kent stammered.

Janus knew that Kent was thinking of his father, and how he would react to the news of having his boat run aground. Janus knew that any hopes that Kent still harbored of beers and rest had evaporated from his mind.

Kent looked towards the shore, several paces away. He announced with obvious unease, "Well, I'm going to find out where we are, at the least."

"Hey, be careful," Derek cautioned, stepping forward as Kent swung his legs over the side of the boat.

Kent's feet splashed into the cold water of the lake, but his weight was held up. He sloshed forward, examining the bow of the boat before looking back towards the others, his face illumined by the glow of the boat's headlights. "See, it's solid, and shallow. We can find out where we are, and maybe work on pushing the boat back out in a minute."

Kent stepped away then, trudging through the water as he made his way over to the shore. Striding up out of the water, he turned and gave the others a half-hearted smile that was accompanied by a thumbs-up gesture.

"It will just take a second, I'll find out where we are at," he called.

Turning his back to them, he walked up the shore and away from the water's edge, his form soon swallowed by the mist.

Derek and Janus sat patiently in the boat, the ponderous silence continuing its hold around them. They could hear nothing from the direction that Kent had gone.

The minutes continued to increase, one streaming into another without sight or sound of anything else. Janus finally placed his hands on the side of the boat, looking towards the shore.

He glanced back at Derek. "How long should we give him?"

"A few more minutes," Derek replied tersely, his features stoic and unreadable.

Janus knew that underneath it all, Derek was growing as concerned as he was. Kent had a jocular manner, but was not the reckless type of individual to indulge in trivial games during a situation such as this.

"Kent! Hey Kent!" Janus called out loudly, cupping his hands about his mouth. The shout broke through the still air with the equivalence of booming thunder.

There was no answer forthcoming.

"Kent! Hey! Where are you?" Derek yelled, even louder than Janus had.

The cumbersome silence around them remained, unrepentant and defiant.

Janus looked back towards Derek, his features grim. "I'm not liking this at all. Not one bit. I think I'd better go to the shoreline. What if he's tripped on something and hit his head, or something like that?"

"We shouldn't get completely split up," Derek advised. "We can leave the boat here. I don't think it is going anywhere for the moment."

Grabbing the side of the boat, Derek pivoted on the spot that his hands clutched as he jumped nimbly over the side of the vessel.

"Here, wait a second, let me test something," Derek said.

He brought his arm back over the side of the boat, just behind the wind-shield, braced himself, and tried to push it backward. After a moment, he changed his grip and tried the other direction.

Veins stood out on his forehead, and his muscles bulged with the considerable exertion. A muffled grunt escaped as he finally gave up the effort.

"Whatever we've managed to do, we've lodged it really good. I don't know how we've managed to get it stuck this firmly, but it is, and there's no sense disputing the reality of it. But as for our immediate worries, I don't think it is going anywhere, anytime soon. There's no current to speak of on this lake anyway," Derek remarked between rapid breaths. "Like I said, if we go after Kent, then I think we should stick together."

"Sounds like a solid plan to me," Janus readily agreed, not feeling eager to wander off into the engulfing mists by himself.

Janus swung his left leg over the side of the boat, holding onto its edge as he swung his other leg up and over. His feet plopped down with a splash as he came to stand in the ankle-deep water.

Derek and Janus walked towards the shoreline, calling out for Kent as they distanced themselves from the boat. They stopped for several moments to listen for a response, but the eerie quiet persisted. Janus found himself growing extremely worried. Something was simply not right about any of it.

"This isn't like Kent at all," Derek said curtly, glancing back to where the boat was lodged. "But I tell you what, I'm not going to be very happy at all if Kent is messing with us."

"That makes two of us, but I don't think that he would joke about something like this," Janus said. "He's a joker, but he's not a fool."

"For his sake, I sure hope so," Derek said, his snapping attitude revealing the great apprehension that was growing inside of him. He fixed his gaze forward. "Let's go!"

Their socks and shoes were soaked, weighing their steps down as they emerged from the lake and continued up the shore. The grass-covered land quickly inclined at the edge of the denser fog.

Derek used his hands to brace himself as he crept up the rising embankment through the fog. He proceeded very slowly, exercising extreme caution within the incredibly low visibility.

Janus emulated Derek's tactic and followed close behind. Their visibility had shrunk considerably again, which did little to allay Janus' worries.

After a brief, albeit steep, incline, the ground leveled out again and allowed for them both to stand up.

"Where do we go from here? We can't see anything," Derek commented, as Janus took a step forward to stand beside him.

The boat and the lakeside were no longer visible behind them. They were enveloped fully in the mist again, a world of gray with a patch of grass directly underfoot.

"Kent!" Janus called out one more time, the query proving naught in eliciting any clue as to Kent's whereabouts or condition. He turned towards Derek, "Let's go on."

He took a slow step forward, followed by another, as he proceeded cautiously through the fog. After he had taken several more steps, he noticed that his visibility was increasing again. The fog appeared to be thinning, and he wondered if the bulk of its density was concentrated closer to the water.

Ahead, there was a brighter luminescence that seemed to beckon to Janus. It increased in intensity with each and every step forward that he took.

With the rising visibility, he picked his pace up more confidently. He felt relieved that he could see for at least a few steps, just as the first shards of broad daylight burst suddenly through the last vestiges of the fog;

daylight that came from a stunning, greenish-blue sky.

Janus halted immediately, standing in a maelstrom of astonishment and wonder at the edge of the fog bank. He did not so much as move or speak, even as Derek drew up next to him a moment later.

Derek was equally speechless as he perceived the extraordinary sight. A remarkable and unexpected view was spread to the far horizons before them.

The land that was brilliantly revealed to their eyes flowed in a harmony of gently rising and falling contours, consisting of broad swathes of higher grasses that were broken up here and there by a few thick copses of trees. Off in the distance, towards the east, was a blurry, continuous line that signaled the beginnings of a vast forest that stretched beyond sight.

The strange hue of the sky compounded the shock of the unexpected scene unraveling before them. Janus finally turned about, the last wisps of fog vanishing at the edges of a modest river, gliding by along soft currents a few strides behind them.

The lake and the boat were nowhere to be seen.

"Janus! Derek!" cried out a very familiar voice to their right.

A couple of hundred yards off, running hurriedly towards them, was Kent. He closed the distance quickly, nearly tripping over his own feet in his fervent haste to get to where the other two were standing.

Janus' heart leaped as he saw Kent suddenly jump off to the side, as a loud, piercing screech erupted from the ground level.

A small lizard-like creature leapt up, startled from its hiding spot. Janus' eyes caught a brief flash of its greenish exterior as its scaly body caught the sunlight. Its powerful legs pumped desperately as it bounded away from Kent.

Janus watched the strange creature race into the distance, moving with incredible speed and agility. He had seen nothing like it in his life.

Janus looked back quickly to Kent. His expression was of outright fear, mingled with a wave of consummate relief at having found them. He stumbled forward again, quickly covering the last stretch of ground that still remained between them.

"You came out of nowhere, I thought I'd lost you guys forever," he stammered, wide-eyed and dangerously close to hyperventilation.

He looked to be on the cusp of hysteria. His eyes looked back in the direction where the lizard-creature had run, returning his attention a moment later towards Janus and Derek.

"You couldn't hear us calling for you?" Janus asked him.

Kent appeared perplexed, as his brow furrowed. "I didn't hear one word from you. I looked back, and I couldn't see you or the boat either. Then the fog had thinned enough so that I could see the river that's there now. You two were nowhere to be seen."

"Impossible. This is impossible," Derek said pointedly, pacing around in a circle and shaking his head. He opened and closed his eyes several times, as he stared around at the sights around them.

A soft breeze tossed some strands of hair into Janus' face, as he looked up into the teal sky in absolute incredulity. He had no inkling regarding an explanation for had just happened, his mind spinning as it tried to come up with a rationale.

"Where are we? What is this?" Kent asked Janus hurriedly, panic manifest in his tone and face.

Janus gave a pained smile, as he lowered his gaze towards Kent. He spoke gently to his friend, "Kent, can we all have just lost our minds? I don't think so, but I don't have any idea what this all is, or means."

"We are in the middle of nowhere. There's nothing out here, nothing at all! Wherever you look, nothing!" Kent declared.

He gave a wide, dramatic sweep of his hand as he spoke, the gesture taking in the full immensity of their unfamiliar environment. Janus' eyes followed Kent's gesture, and he could not deny that there was not one singular sign of any human presence or activity. It was a totality of open wilderness, beautiful and daunting at the same time.

"What is this place?" Kent prodded again, as if the others might actually know the answer. "Where are we?"

"I don't know, and Janus doesn't know!" Derek declared tersely.

Janus had never before seen Derek looking so exasperated, but like himself he knew that Derek was entirely devoid of answers. That cognizance alone was enough to add further to Janus' own increasing trepidation.

"I don't know either, Kent," Janus added quietly.

His nerves had already been frayed, and his emotions had long been spent, so there was little left within him to cope with the inherent shock of the moment.

There was no other way around it. Unless they were all suffering from a homogenous, mass hallucination, the impossible had become possible. His first inclination was that they had literally stepped right out of their own world, potentially into a world of a different time and place.

The scope of that notion was at once overwhelming, and mind-boggling. It also seemed totally absurd, and a part of Janus immediately dismissed the thought as a momentary shred of hysteria present within himself.

It was ridiculous to think that the stuff of dreams and fantastical tales had somehow manifested into a bold new existence, but there was a hard and undeniable reality to everything around them. Janus knew that whatever the case might be, they were at the mercy of something far beyond his comprehension.

"I'm going crazy … man, I am going crazy!" Kent said, his eyes gleaming with fear, moistening as tears of helplessness came into them.

He looked as if he were about to come apart at every seam.

Without a word, Derek walked with quick, purposeful strides over towards Kent. Derek reached out and grabbed him forcefully by the shoulders, bringing Kent around to face him directly as he waited for Kent to look back up.

"Come on Kent! Get a grip on yourself!" he said firmly. His gaze seemed composed of iron, as if compelling Kent to take some strength from it. Though he spoke to Kent with a commanding tone, Janus heard the strong sympathy and compassion underlying the words. "I don't blame you for feeling what you are feeling. But whatever all of this is, we are all in it together right now. And we have to work with what we've got."

Janus had nothing to add to Derek's statement, and he did not want to do anything to rattle Kent. He decided to demonstrate calmness while Kent's faculties swayed on the edge. Janus lowered himself down on the ground into a sitting position near to the other two.

He rested his arms across his knees, his right hand clasping the wrist of his left as he silently looked out over the quiet, grassy land. The breezes created gentle waves and undulations along its surface.

Derek slowly released his hold upon Kent, his voice coming low and much more gently, "Okay? Are you with us now? Come on, keep your cool now. We are going to need you."

Though a few tears had escaped and left tracks down his cheeks, and although he choked back a couple of muffled sobs, Kent at last nodded in agreement to Derek's words. Janus was watching out of the corner of his eyes, and he breathed a sigh of relief as he saw the reaction. Kent was still in a fragile state, but he was anchoring himself.

"Sit down, and get your breath," Derek advised Kent, gesturing towards the ground.

Kent took a seat near to Janus' side, and took several deep breaths as he struggled to regain his composure.

"No matter what, we'll have to deal with what we know, and what we have to work with," Derek iterated to Kent, sitting down to the other side of Janus.

Derek's words made good sense. No matter what, even if they were somehow sharing a strange dream together, they found themselves in an entirely unfamiliar location. Janus was not quite ready to accept what his heart was telling him, hoping instead that a rational explanation would emerge at any moment.

If Janus' first impressions, those resounding in his heart, were accurate, the lands around him were located nowhere within the state that he and his friends resided in.

The impenetrable fog that had covered their passage into this strange place was entirely dissipated, and Janus had no intimation as to how they could return back to the lake and the boat, much less his home.

In other circumstances, the extraordinary hue of the sky above them would have been a thing of majestic beauty to gaze upon, and the strange, lizard-like animal an object of great fascination and interest. As it was, Janus was far too unsettled to appreciate the unusual sights.

Even more daunting to their immediate prospects, they had no supplies of any kind, or even weapons.

Until something, or someone, familiar manifested, they had to act as if they had been set into the middle of a foreign wilderness, without any foreknowledge of its contents or environment. They had already seen a representative of the local fauna, and it was not illogical to believe that there might well be other unfamiliar species lurking about, perhaps some that were very dangerous.

At the moment, any signs of civilized society would be extremely welcome. An airplane in the sky, power lines, or even the sound of a car engine would be glorious music to Janus' ears.

The troubling prospects left him feeling very naked and highly vulnerable, as he sat in brooding silence with his friends on the grass, each of them trying to collect their thoughts together.

Janus did not try to interrupt Kent, and nor did Derek, even when they noticed that he had closed his eyes, and that his shoulders bobbed up and down with silent sobs.

The outpouring of emotion was no sign of weakness, nor any

indictment of Kent's strength or courage. Janus knew in his heart that Derek did not hold it to be such either.

Kent had been fully and brusquely immersed into an incomprehensible and overwhelming situation when he had been separated from the others. If anything, Janus was astounded that Kent had not entirely lost his mind. The mere fact that Kent was holding somewhat together, albeit shakily, instead testified to a considerable strength within him.

As Kent let his terrors and panic ebb through the sobs and tears, Janus contemplated Kent's ordeal.

Kent had entered this strange new place entirely alone when he had walked up the shore and away from the boat. He had endured a brief period where he had not known whether Derek or Janus would ever be reunited with him. For all Kent knew, he had been cast suddenly into an entirely strange place, and abandoned to face his fate alone.

If there was one small comfort remaining to Janus, it was that he and Derek had not been severed from the sense and bonds of familiarity and friendship that they shared with each other. In an inexplicable experience such as the one that they were now facing, such bonds were a tremendous boon, if not vital.

Janus knew that their bonds of friendship would now be about the only thing that they all could grasp onto. It was a very sobering realization, and it was abundantly clear to Janus that the welfare of the other two was indispensable to his own continued survival.

Reaching over, he patted Kent gently on the back.

LEE

"It's all around us now," Lee observed with fascination.

The fog had fully enveloped Lee, Ryan, and the entire restaurant. Looking behind him, Lee had been slightly unnerved to discover that he could not see the front facing of the restaurant anymore. There was not even a hint of it, walled off as it was by the opaque mists.

"It's so thick," Ryan commented. "Think that you can even drive in this stuff?"

Lee glanced over Ryan with an expression of disbelief. "Drive? Are you crazy?"

"Probably," retorted Ryan, laughing. "And if you are too afraid of a little fog, Lee … if it scares you too much, I would be glad to drive us out of here."

"Great idea. Turn my only car over to you," Lee replied with a tenor of sarcasm. "Have your license with you tonight? Oh, I forgot … you don't have one, do you?"

"Hasn't stopped me in the past," Ryan shot back, giving Lee a wink.

"No, and one of those trips got you a nice visit to court," Lee retorted. "We don't need any more of that."

"Hey, with fog this thick, the cops won't even be able to see us driving out of it," Ryan said. "Don't think they'll take too much notice of me."

"Not until we find ourselves crashing right into a cruiser, at least," Lee said, shaking his head. "That would be my luck if I ever threw you the keys."

"You have such little faith," Ryan said, chuckling.

"Not a matter of faith. I know you too well," Lee responded, grinning widely.

"That, you do, Lee," Ryan concurred, laughing.

"Well, what do you say? Instead of arguing about whether you or I drive, I think we should just wait this out for a little while back in the restaurant. If you are hungry, I can whip something up really quickly," Lee stated.

"It'd be lot better than standing out here," Ryan replied.

Lee and Ryan turned to go back to the restaurant. Lee was simply glad that he had only walked a few feet away from the building, continuing to be astounded at the sheer density of the fog. He stepped slowly, putting his hands ahead of him so that he did not walk face first into the façade of his restaurant.

Lee had traversed only about four short strides when he heard the ground crunch beneath his feet. Looking down, he saw the unmistakable appearance of a forest floor beneath his feet, solid earth covered by foliage debris and grass. He took one tentative stride directly backwards, but the soles of his shoes met more soil, leaves, and twigs, instead of pavement.

"What?" Ryan whispered at Lee's side. He had drawn to a halt and was also staring down at the ground.

Lee was confounded. He had walked those streets every day, and knew that there was nothing like what was now beneath his feet within any short distance of the restaurant.

The ground that he could see slowly started to grow, and all of it resembled the initial patch. Bringing his gaze back up, he saw that the fog was beginning to dissipate everywhere.

He took a deep breath, filled with tension as he waited for the fog to roll back and reveal the dark, starry firmament of a night sky. He knew that everything would be as it was once again.

There was a simple explanation. He and Ryan had somehow gotten misdirected in the fog, to where someone had dumped a pile of excavated dirt and debris. Lee must not have taken notice of it during the day, which was not a surprise as he always had twenty things on his mind at once.

To his amazement, everything around him was growing steadily brighter. Starting as a dim ambience, the light swelled considerably as the fog lessened in density.

Lee knew that the overall illumination was already well beyond the capability of street lamps, igniting his sense of alarm again. His mouth fell agape as the fog thinned further and began to part. He looked up, awestruck, into the depths of a bright, midday sky, visible through a matrix of intertwining branches that belonged to a host of trees surrounding them; a breathtaking, blue-green sky, of a hue that Lee had never before witnessed.

Lee began to turn around slowly, in complete circles, as it dawned on him that he was standing in the midst of a great forest. Rays of light filtered through the dense covering of leaves and branches overhead. The forest floor spread outward as far as he could see to the left and right, traveling up and around the slopes of large hills looming all about the bewildered two figures.

"You seein' what I'm seein'?" Ryan asked in a highly agitated voice. "Tell me you aren't seeing this."

"If you are seeing a big forest all around you, and a weird sky, then we are seeing the same thing," Lee responded in a low voice. His eyes darted in every direction, as he tried to find a modicum of sense in what he was experiencing.

The forty-three year old restaurant owner and the sixteen-year-old youth stood in stunned silence for several more minutes.

"So, what do we do now?" queried Ryan, finally breaching the impasse.

"That is the question of the hour," Lee stated. It took him another few moments to muster up the rest of his words. "Maybe we start walking. We should try to find out where we are, or if anything's around."

"I don't know. We don't know this place. We don't know what's around here. It might not be all that friendly. We don't know," Ryan said, his words tumbling out more quickly from his trembling mouth.

As stunned as Lee was, he still caught the tone and pace of Ryan's voice, and looked over towards the youth with understanding. Ryan's eyes exhibited the look of a frightened youth, certainly much more than the look of the hardened, street-smart young man that he saw himself as.

"I am open to suggestions, we can figure this out together," Lee said, keeping his voice calm so that he did not add any impetus to Ryan's rising panic. He did not want the young man to become unhinged, and he sensed an acute danger of that happening any moment.

Ryan paused a few moments before answering. Though Lee was anything but settled, Ryan finally seemed to draw some stability from the older man's composure.

"No, you are right. The top of the hill would be best. I can scale one of the trees there, and see if I can get a view of anything," Ryan said, as he started off towards the slope that Lee had been eyeing. "See if I can find a road or buildings … something like that."

Lee strode briskly next to Ryan, as the two mounted the long slope and finally reached the summit of the broad hill.

Near to the top, Ryan moved over to the base of a tall oak tree, which had strong lower branches extending out from the trunk just within reach of Ryan's fingers. He jumped up, grabbed the branch, and pulled himself up in a smooth motion. He methodically navigated up the heights of the tree, climbing from branch to branch with little difficulty.

Lee stood still on the ground below, a look of concern on his face as he watched the other's careful progress.

At long last, Ryan hugged the trunk of the tree as his feet rested upon one of the uppermost branches. His body weight caused a slight sway as he craned his neck to look out over the treetops.

Lee waited pensively as he watched Ryan scan the horizons. Lee remained tense as he saw that Ryan's expression remained unchanged.

Finally, Ryan looked back down towards Lee and shook his head in frustration. "Nothing. Nothing but a lot more of this," Ryan announced sourly.

With a resigned sigh, he held onto the tree and rested for several moments, looking outward as Lee patiently awaited his return below.

RYAN

Ryan's eyes drank in the uniform hue of the sky, bright and vibrant in the light of the sun directly over him. Though there was no sign of roads or buildings, it was a majestic vision.

"Amazing," Ryan murmured, shaking his head one more time, as he finally looked downward to begin his descent.

His nerves were teetering on the edge. Only minutes before, he had been standing in front of a restaurant just off the downtown area. He was now peering from the top of a tall tree, atop a hill in the midst of a forest that spread out in every direction as far as the eye could see.

Ryan had not gone more than a couple branches lower, gingerly bringing his weight to bear upon each one to make certain that they would hold his weight, when a dark shadow abruptly fell across him. His breath caught in his throat, as his eyes shot back towards the sky in alarm.

Gliding along the air currents was a very large, winged creature. It had a long, thin body that was covered with a light growth of purplish fur. Broad, membranous wings protruded from its back. A short, thick neck connected the body to an elongated head that resembled a cross between that of a serpent and a bird. Two narrow legs were tucked underneath its body, each ending in grasping talons whose ends looked wickedly sharp.

Ryan froze as the shadow from the animal crossed him and continued onward. It emitted a sustained, hollow cry that chilled his nerves.

The only comfort was that the flying monstrosity appeared to have not taken any notice of Ryan, as it showed no outward reaction to the young man's presence. As the creature glided into the distance, Ryan counted himself lucky and resumed his descent, quickly angling down from branch to branch with less caution and more urgency. He jumped down to the ground, bypassing one lower branch, and paced over to Lee.

Lee's face was one of sheer amazement, and his eyes remained fixed upward.

"I don't know what in the world that thing was, but it was big, and to be on the safe side, I am staying down here," Ryan announced.

"I think we'd better take things really carefully," Lee said, his eyes looking about warily as if the forest would suddenly come alive with an array of menacing, unknown threats. "I think we'd better not assume anything. I think that's the best thing to do right now."

"Let's get going, and be ready for the trees, if you see anything at all on the ground," Ryan responded. "I have no idea what that thing in the air was, and I wouldn't be sure that we won't run into even more creatures we don't know about ... ones down here that don't fly."

"I wouldn't be so sure about the trees either," Lee commented, eyes widening, "Look!"

He pointed towards the branches of a nearby tree.

Ryan followed Lee's gesture to find a small, furry canine-like creature staring quietly right at them. The tree that Ryan had climbed had been very close to the tree that this creature inhabited, and as his eyes met those of the creature he flinched reflexively in surprise.

A ray of sunlight glinted off of one of the sharp talons by which the small mammal clutched the tree branch. Tucked close into its sides were a pair of dark, leathery wings. Its beady eyes, set back behind the length of its extended snout, seemed to be furtively studying the two humans.

As if it now recognized that its presence had been discovered, it chittered excitedly and leaped abruptly from the tree, spreading its wings and gliding off into the depths of the forest.

"No, we can't be too sure," Ryan agreed, unnerved further and finding himself growing more fearful by the second.

"And we can't assume that smaller is any less of a threat," Lee added.

"Have any more encouraging things to say?" Ryan curtly riposted.

"Better figure the worst. At least things can only get better," Lee replied dourly.

Fully out of his element, Ryan was lost in a bizarre forest where the first two living creatures that he had set his eyes upon were entirely foreign to him. The specter of danger was palpably tangible to his senses, whether it lurked in the trees, the sky above, or upon the ground.

A freezing anxiety arose to grip him in the wake of his rapidly diminishing hopes. The feeling traveled through Ryan with a mildly paralyzing effect, and he felt as if the world itself was compressing him from all sides.

LEE

Lee saw the glistening forming across Ryan's eyes, feeling immediate empathy for the deep plight of the man-child. He knew that Ryan's fierce pride was straining to hold back any visible sign of weakness. Yet Lee also knew that something rigid and inflexible could be shattered in an instant when enough pressure had been applied.

Lee spoke to Ryan in as methodical and reassuring a voice as he could muster.

"We have some things to learn, probably a whole lot of things. We will simply learn whatever we have to know, to make it through all of this. There is no other choice, so let's set our minds on this one. I have your back covered, Ryan. I'm afraid, and there's no harm in saying so, but fear can't stop us from getting through this unless we let it."

"And these creatures? Do we stand a chance in a world like this, where we don't know the first thing about what's around us?" Ryan responded, his voice strained and shaking.

"Stop and think for a moment, Ryan. Remember, even in the world we are familiar with, the animals are stronger and faster," Lee replied. "Even an insect can carry several times its own bodyweight. But there is one thing that took us humans to the top of the heap, so that we didn't have to constantly huddle in fear, and hide from predators."

Purposefully, he slowly brought his right hand up, and tapped the side of his temple firmly to punctuate his words.

"It's this. Right in here. The mind. And we both still have that with us," Lee said.

"I don't see how I do. I can hardly think right now," Ryan retorted, staring downward.

"Okay, then maybe it is best that we find something that we can put our minds to. We need to know the lay of the land, we will need water eventually, and we'd better make ourselves some kind of weapon," Lee said, hoping that the simple logic of his words would find root in Ryan's troubled mind.

Ryan stood in rapt silence. His expression was dour, and Lee knew that Ryan's mood was vacillating between the opposing forces at work inside of him. Lee waited patiently on the young man. As if dragging a heavy weight, Ryan finally brought his eyes up to meet Lee's.

"It's worth a try," Ryan announced rigidly.

Once the youth had said the words, it was as if one part of him was unlocked and freed. He looked intently at the ground all around them, and without a word, walked over and picked up a fallen branch off of the forest floor. Placing one knee on the branch to pin it to the ground, he began ripping away the smaller offshoots growing out from it.

When he had stripped the branch bare, Ryan rose up and started walking back up towards the summit of the hill, continuing to examine the ground. Lee followed behind him quietly, continuing to watch.

Using the stripped branch, Ryan scraped around, revealing the rough edge of a jutting rock. Utilizing the edge of the rock, he patiently worked at one end of the branch until it was crudely sharpened.

He turned back to Lee, gripping the rough spear about midway down its shaft. Ryan looked into Lee's eyes, and something a little more firm and resolute was within his gaze now.

"Then we can start with this," Ryan proclaimed. "Start with the weapons, and then look to the rest."

Lee stifled a smile, proud. It was one less thing that he had to worry about in the midst of the unbelievable situation.

"Well done, a good job," Lee commented, with no hint of being patronizing, in sincere appreciation of the young man's fortitude.

Lee walked by Ryan, pausing momentarily to pat him gently upon the shoulder. Another elongated, stout branch, which probably had been broken off during a powerful storm, lay a few feet beyond them.

Lee picked up the branch and began to strip it.

ERIN

"Okay Lynn, what is this?" Erin asked, irritated and unnerved at the relentless fog swirling all around them.

The fog had encircled them fully, forbidding any forward vision and cooling the very air around them. She could feel the damp, chilly vapors brushing against her arms, face, and lower legs.

"Come on, Erin. It's time to get back around that fire," Lynn said resolutely, reaching out and taking her friend's hand.

"We can hardly see a thing, though," Erin replied, squeezing Lynn's hand firmly in her anxiety as they turned to make their way back to the campsite.

"Then we go slow, and we call out for directions. Just follow the voices of Uli and Razor in. We'll probably walk right into them. It won't be a problem at all," Lynn stated. She took a few cautious steps forward, gently tugging Erin into motion behind her. "Come on, let's start this way. Watch your step. Be careful."

Progress was painstakingly slow. The encumbering fog prevented Erin from catching even a glimpse of the campfire, though she was certain that it was just a short distance away.

"Hey! Razor! Uli!" Lynn called out loudly. "Where are you guys?" Her voice carried off through the fog, as silence settled back in around them.

They stood still for several moments, waiting for a reply from their friends to help with their bearings. None was forthcoming.

Again, Lynn yelled out to their compatriots, and once again there was no response.

"This is no time for jokes," murmured Erin in sharp displeasure, delicately stepping over the trunk of a fallen tree that was in their path. She did not recall stepping over a tree trunk when she had gone into the woods, and began to worry that they might have oriented themselves in the wrong direction.

"They had better not play around with us," Erin remarked acidly, her uneasiness fueling her vexation. "They know I will give them hell. Believe me, I will. Unholy hell."

"Tell me about it," Lynn concurred tersely. "But remember, they are just the type of dolts to try and pull something like that, especially if they figure out why we are calling out to them. They couldn't have packed up the camp and moved it away in a couple of minutes. We'll stumble into one of them sooner or later, no matter what."

"Hopefully sooner," Erin responded, shaken by the utter lack of visibility.

The two picked their way over yet another fallen tree. They continued onward cautiously, methodically making their way over a fairly open clearance of ground judging by the more sporadic contact with the trees looming out of the fog.

The ground seemed to be flatter, certainly more so than the downward sloping angle that the hillside had, but Erin attributed the perception to her momentary disorientation.

Both Lynn and Erin continued shouting out to their friends, repeatedly, with less than satisfactory results.

"This isn't it. The area where we were had a lot more trees," Lynn observed, a noticeable tension in her voice.

"Well, then let's turn back," Erin replied, matter-of-factly. It mystified her as to how they could possibly have gotten far away from the campsite.

"I wish it were that simple. Don't forget, there are cliffs not too far off from the camp. If we keep walking, we will have to go really slow. I don't want to step off the edge of a hundred and fifty foot drop, and I don't think that you do either."

Erin certainly had no argument to that.

The fog seemed to be thinning somewhat off to the right, as Erin could make out the outlines of trees a little farther away than before. Elsewhere, it was as dense as ever.

Lynn had evidently taken notice of the variance as well.

"Wait a second, Erin. Maybe we should go in this direction. It looks like the fog's not as thick that way," Lynn suggested. "At least it will be a little safer for us in this area, being able to see a little farther ahead."

"I'm with you on that," Erin agreed, relieved that they would have a few strides warning before coming to the edge of a lethal drop-off.

They took a few steps to the right. Erin reached out and felt the texture of one of the trees as they passed by it. She drew a little stability from the solidity of the trunk.

Gradually it became easier and easier to see farther into the trees ahead. The two women were finally able to concentrate more on the ground under them, than what was coming up immediately in front of them. Even so, Erin's sense of caution did not lessen.

As they continued forward, keeping a careful watch on the ground, Erin had no more doubts that their visibility was steadily increasing. Strangely, the illumination in the area was increasing as well.

"Full moon should be helping out, but this much?" Erin asked Lynn, taken aback by the rising ambience.

"I don't have an explanation for it," Lynn responded. "But you are right, it is getting much brighter around here."

They took a few more steps, when both Erin and Lynn came to a stop. Erin saw that the fog was visibly receding around them. Looking over at Lynn's bewildered expression, she knew that her friend was as struck with the bizarre phenomenon as she was.

With great apprehension, Erin stood with Lynn as they waited to see what the fog's dispersal would reveal. Hoping for a landmark, a sign of their campsite, or even a member of their group, she scanned the growing periphery with great scrutiny.

The amount of light continued to expand, until the last layers of fog started breaking up to reveal a blue-green sky spread far and wide above them. Forested hills rose up all around them, as they found themselves at the base of an incline that led towards a long ridgeline.

After the initial shock of the sight of daylight and unfamiliar terrain subsided, Erin looked to Lynn to see if her friend was as stunned as she was.

"Where are we? That's not normal. Something's wrong with my eyes," Erin said, looking at the teal hue of the sky, panic surging. "Something is wrong with me."

"Then something is wrong with me too," Lynn replied in a voice just above a whisper, her lips barely mouthing the words.

"Then what is it?" Erin asked Lynn after a few more uncomfortable moments had passed.

It was not what she had wanted to hear from Lynn. Erin had hoped that the problems rested with her alone, and that Lynn did not see what she was seeing. Whatever was affecting Erin's vision was also altering Lynn's.

"We've gotta find the others," Erin went on, before Lynn answered. "Something's gone wrong with us, Lynn."

"So that's how we walked all the way to the bottom of a hill, moved into another entirely different area, and found ourselves here? Is that right, Erin? And we've suddenly gone from night to broad daylight in less than half an hour? And how come everything but the sky is the right color, if something's wrong with our eyes?" Lynn queried.

Her barrage of words stung Erin. She wished with all her heart that they were experiencing some shared hallucination, but knew better.

Erin frowned as she looked over at Lynn. "Then how do you explain this?"

"You think I know?" Lynn countered sharply.

"We got lost in the fog, and lost sense of time," Erin said.

"For how many hours? And that explains the sky color?" Lynn shot back.

Erin glared at Lynn, unable to come up with a verbal response but not about to concede anything either. A heavy tension weighed the air between them down, as they continued to glower at each other.

They were given little time to resume their argument, as a loud, piercing screech shattered the still air. A broad, dark shadow swept across the ground, passing swiftly over their position and bringing their eyes hastily upwards.

"My god! What the hell is that?" Erin cried out, looking skyward, where she beheld the sight of a horrific-looking creature that was flying just above the tops of the trees. Its fierce, reptilian visage gazed down hungrily upon them, as it circled over their position.

The body of the fearsome creature was well over ten feet in length. Its extended jaws, opening with each ensuing outcry, revealed an arsenal of whetted teeth, arrayed into the unmistakable maw of a very formidable carnivore.

"Run! Just run!" Lynn yelled, giving Erin a hard shove to urge her onward.

Erin broke out of her momentary trance, lurching into a full run, needing little inspiration to hasten her strides. In an instant, both of the women were running as fast as they could across the forest ground. Lynn, with a slight lead, angled towards the rounded base of a nearby hill.

Behind them, the creature glided low just over the uppermost tree branches, relentlessly tracking the young women. The beast skimmed above the trees, its keen eyes searching carefully.

When it reached a larger break in the forest canopy, its wings tucked in suddenly, and it swooped downward with deadly grace and force as it leveled out beneath the trees.

The creature's wings folded close to its body whenever it passed by the trees in its path, spreading wide in the gaps between the trees, and snapping down in the open spaces, giving bursts to its pursuing flight. The beast closed fast upon the two desperate women running before it.

Legs straining to the limits, Erin and Lynn reached the bend at the base of the hill. Dodging trees, and adroitly leaping over another fallen tree trunk, the two women looked frantically about for escape.

"To the right!" Lynn shouted quickly, breaking sharply to her right, running towards a wide creek.

The creek had cut a deep embankment, as its waters coursed steadily along their meandering route. Erin realized Lynn's desperate notion at once.

Glancing back, Lynn checked to see that Erin was still close behind her. Erin was following right on her heels.

Erin looked over her own shoulder and stifled a scream as she saw that the huge predator was deftly flying just a few feet above the ground, gliding rapidly just a short distance behind.

It was closing on them far too fast.

"Down! And stay on this side of the bank!" Lynn yelled as they reached the lip of the bank.

In a flurry of motion that was a mixture of falling, twisting, and slipping, Lynn dropped and rotated to press herself against the near side of the bank. Erin tumbled in awkwardly behind her, almost falling out from the bank in the process. Swiftly, Lynn reached out and grabbed Erin's shirt, pulling her in tightly. Mud and water was spattered all over them.

A second later, the creature shrieked in rage. It hurtled by just overhead, streaking across the surface of the creek as its prey evaded its imminent grasp.

"It will probably turn around! Let's go!" Lynn said, anxiously watching the winged nightmare.

Once the beast came back from the other direction, their position would be abruptly turned from a means of refuge to one of vulnerability.

The cry of the monstrous creature suddenly changed pitches, as the sound of a great, sonorous roaring intermingled with it. The forest was filled with the deep-toned eruption, the furious cacophony shaking the air. Erin knew at once that the roar had not come from the flying entity.

The shrill shrieks of the flying monstrosity and the horrible roaring of the other denizen of the forest escalated, with both creatures now well beyond Erin's line of sight.

Erin was not about to wait to see what the cause of the tumult was, or what had become of the flying creature. Most certainly, she did not wish to see the source of the deafening roar.

Neither did Lynn evidently, who was already up and on the move, dragging Erin into step behind her and urging her to hurry. They dashed down along the edge of the creek, their frenzied steps throwing up splashes of water with each impact. Erin was pumping her legs as quickly as she could, several times almost stumbling and falling in her unrelenting haste.

Far behind them came anther loud, high-pitched cry from the winged creature. It carried a noticeably different tone. Unlike the cries that it had made before, this one sounded like a cry of tremendous agony.

It was followed a moment later by another thunderous roar. The piercing cry of the winged entity was then abruptly cut off, the roar ebbed, and the forest fell into silence once more.

The cessation of the chaotic dissonance did not lesson the frightful panic that Erin felt racing through her veins.

Erin and Lynn continued their urgent sprint, putting plenty of distance between themselves and the area where the creatures were. Only when her lungs were about to burst, and her leg muscles felt gelatinous from being pushed to their utmost limits, did they finally reduce their speed down to a jog and begin to reclaim their breath.

"What is going on …?" Erin asked between heavy gasps for air.

Inwardly, she cursed her life of sedate activity. Exhausted and winded, she knew that she was going to pay a very steep price for her prolonged lack of regular physical exercise.

Calling up all her willpower, she trudged onward, keeping by Lynn's side.

"I have … no idea," Lynn replied, between her own heaving gulps of breath.

Though in better physical shape than Erin, Lynn was still far from prepared for the ordeal that they found themselves in.

"Then, what do we do?" Erin asked, her voice despondent.

She looked to Lynn, as she took a few protracted breaths. Her heart continued to pound rapidly in her chest, strained by exertion and fear.

Lynn slowed down further, turning aside towards a spot where they could easily scramble up the bank. Before answering Erin, she dug into the incline, using her hands to help propel her upwards.

When she stood at the top, she turned around and looked down to where Erin had come to a stop at the base of the embankment.

"For now, we just keep going," Lynn said.

Leaning over and reaching out, she took Erin's hand and helped her up to the top of the bank. Standing at Lynn's side, Erin cast a distressed glance back down the creek. Fortunately, there was no sight or sound of any pursuit.

A wave of dizziness then came over Erin as she stood still, sweat beading and beginning to trickle down her warming face. The young woman then hunched over, her hands braced upon her knees. She felt a light wave of nausea. It was all that she could do to remain relaxed, and avoid the eruption of violent heaves.

"Breath slow," Lynn advised, placing a hand on her friend's back.

Erin closed her eyes and drew in a long inhalation, letting it out slowly. She repeated the process a couple more times.

"We keep going, but to where?" Erin asked between breaths, teetering on the edge of vomiting.

"I don't know," Lynn replied simply, after a long pause.

Erin glanced over at her friend, who had straightened up, placed hands on her hips, and was now looking around them.

The forest was quiescent, and the only sound in Erin's ears was that of leaves rustling in soft breezes. Whether it was paranoia, or just keen perception, Erin felt a prickly sensation along the nape of her neck. She sensed that they were being watched.

"Do you feel it?" Erin whispered curtly. "Like someone … or something … is watching us."

Lynn nodded quietly, her eyes wide as her gaze darted about.

"We'd better get something to hit back with," Lynn said at last, her eyes lowering as took a couple of steps away from the bank. She then warned, "We aren't going to be able to run much more."

Making her way over to a tree with low branches, she put both her arms out, wrapping her fingers around on a strong-looking branch. With a forceful, backward pull that engaged her body weight, Lynn snapped the branch off the tree.

Quickly, she set about stripping all of the extraneous shoots from the main branch.

"For you," Lynn announced to Erin, handing her the makeshift staff. "It won't be brittle, at least."

Lynn walked back over and repeated the process on a similarly stout-looking branch attached to a nearby tree.

"And for me," Lynn remarked as she bared the branch.

The branch felt solid enough in Erin's hands, and she knew that it could deliver a crunching impact. At the very least, Erin knew that they now possessed usable walking staves.

Erin set one end of the branch in the ground and straightened up, feeling another wave of dizziness and nausea pass over her. She leaned some of her weight upon the staff that she now held, closing her eyes and taking another couple of long, careful breaths.

Erin plodded over to where Lynn stood, her legs heavy and drained.

As their eyes met, Erin could see a reflection of the fear that she was still wrestling with.

"Just relax yourself Erin, as much as you can," urged Lynn, glancing downward.

Erin followed her friend's gaze, and noticed the whitened knuckles of her own right hand where she tightly gripped the wood staff.

Erin nodded slowly to Lynn, willing herself to relax her grip a little. "I'll try … but I don't know the first thing about what we're gonna do."

"And neither do I," Lynn replied. "We're both scared, just about out of our minds. We have to hope that this will all explain itself soon, and that we can somehow get out of here."

"Not very comforting," Erin said morosely. "And what if we can't?"

Lynn shook her head. "Don't think about that, Erin."

Erin looked downward, unable to meet her friend's eyes. She feared that Lynn would somehow be able to see inside her, as she slid further towards a state of sheer hopelessness.

They were completely lost, in the midst of an area that had already demonstrated that it held creatures of an inexplicable and terrifying nature within it. Erin did not have the first idea as to their whereabouts, and their lives had been threatened less than five minutes after becoming aware of their strange predicament.

"Come on, Erin, let's at least get moving," Lynn said. Branch in hand, her friend started off, following a path that ran atop the embankment, proceeding along the border of the creek.

Glancing down at the water, Erin saw that Lynn was heading upstream.

"Hey, wait up," Erin said, jogging hastily to catch up to her friend. "Why go this way? We don't know where we are, so we can't know where we are heading."

Lynn looked Erin in the eye as she continued her purposeful strides. "No … we don't know what is happening. But if the creature that put a stop to our pursuit is territorial, I want to keep moving away from it. As a matter of fact …"

Lynn's words trailed off as she turned aside, maneuvering back down the embankment and into the creek's bed.

"Let's keep our wits a little, and not leave any scent for anything to follow," Lynn stated.

Erin scrambled down the embankment, stepping into the water and feeling the cold chill as it soaked into her shoes. That was the least of her worries as she strolled alongside Lynn, continuing their arduous trek upstream.

After just a few moments, Lynn seemed engrossed in studying the rocks of the creek bed. Seeing a few that rose out of the water, she moved over towards one in particular, laying the end of her branch-staff upon the rock's edge.

She looked to Erin. "We can obscure our scents, and we can improve our weapons."

Lynn began to scrape the end of her crude staff against the rock edge, and Erin quickly realized what her friend was doing. Seeing another similar rock, she got started on the improvements to her own.

MERSHAD

Mershad and Erika continued walking at a comfortable pace, having already traveled for what certainly had to be several miles by then. Mershad had never walked so far in one single jaunt.

The scenery around them remained fairly constant. There was only a little fluctuation in elevation, as they wended their way around the bases of the encompassing hills. The plants, trees, and even animals remained largely familiar as well.

Yet twice more, they came upon more of the odd, tree-dwelling creatures that they had encountered shortly after their arrival within the strange locale. As before, there were no indications of threat from the unusual creatures, but the sightings reminded Mershad to not lapse in his focus.

"I believe that this forest could go on forever," Mershad remarked ruefully.

Though they had not pushed themselves overly hard, his legs were feeling entirely leaden. He was beginning to brace himself a little more with each step upon the stout branch that Erika had procured for him.

"I wish I was in your condition," he said through a tired grin.

"Need a break?" Erika asked him, looking at Mershad with care and concern. Her condition appeared to be holding strong. Her breath still came easy, and she was yet limber of step. She had since found herself another branch that she had deemed more suitable for her height, and was carrying it loosely at her side.

It came as no surprise to Mershad. He was well aware that she was accustomed to a regimen of regular exercise and activity. Mershad was not foolish enough to entertain any notions of sharing her endurance, honed and developed as it was through considerable exertion over a long period of time.

Mershad felt no loss of pride in being completely honest with her. He had no desire to quietly allow himself to sink into a completely exhausted state, especially not when they still lacked any clues as to their whereabouts. Neither could they afford to be lax regarding possible wilderness threats.

"Not just yet, but I promise that I will tell you, Erika, before I get into too much trouble. Who knows? Maybe we're just a little short of finding something that will let us know where we are," he replied.

"You'd better tell me," she replied firmly, still eyeing him carefully, before adding in a softer tone, "and I do hope that we find something soon, anything at all."

The two trekked onward for a couple more miles, sweat beading upon both of their foreheads. The late-afternoon weather was warm and mildly humid, broken up by the occasional breezes wafting through the trees. By the light of the sky above, Mershad judged that it was now just a few hours before evening arrived.

Mershad did not have any other options for estimating the time. Both his and Erika's watches were now useless, little more than decorative accessories, after the transfer through the fog. Both watches had come to a stop, and with the unexpected shift from night to day, he knew that trying to estimate a time would be largely futile.

Mershad was also feeling the initial pangs of thirst and hunger, a foreboding development that Mershad began to fear as it raised several new dangers to light. He had spoken about his concerns a little already to Erika, and found that her own worries were not much different.

Neither of them wanted to blindly sample just any sort of berry or nut, not even ones that they might deem to be edible, as they were not experts in woodland growths. Furthermore, they both had little experience with hunting, and did not have any ideas on making efficient netting or rigging poles for fishing.

Still, the inevitable had to be faced, whether they were prepared or not.

As he was worrying about the approaching difficulties, Mershad perked his head up as his ears took in the distinct sounds of running water. A few moments later, they came upon its source, a wide, deep creek whose current flowed at a mild pace.

"I hope that it's good water, because we are going to need it sooner or later. We've got nothing to boil it in, and I don't know how to start a fire," Mershad commented. "I ..."

"Shhh!" Erika warned abruptly, gesturing urgently for him to be completely quiet.

Her eyes widened as she stared ahead, her posture rigidly still. Mershad felt the hairs stand up on the back of his neck at her clear aura of alarm.

"Something is moving near," she whispered, indicating for him to lie down quietly upon the ground.

They both lowered themselves to the forest floor, and Mershad's heart began to pound rapidly in anxiety.

He listened intently, and it only took a moment for him to hear what had prompted Erika's sudden concern. It was the distant sounds of voices, moving through the brush and growing slowly louder. They were still faint, and he could not yet make out any of the words, but the voices were perhaps the most welcome sounds that Mershad had ever heard in his entire life.

The sky above them, though, was still of the unique, blue-green hue, and one glance at it served as a stark reminder to maintain caution. They could not afford to make any quick assumptions. If anything, the sudden upheaval in their personal worlds had instilled a strong sense of prudence in Mershad.

He glanced over at Erika. She nodded back at him, and gave him a slight smile, clearly looking pleased to hear other human voices.

Both of them strained their eyes to gain a better look at the approaching beings, and their ears to discern their specific words. After a few moments, the figures responsible for the voices came into view among the distant trees, accompanied by the crunches and snaps of their footsteps upon the debris on the ground. They were two men, walking at a slow pace.

One was a stocky male, with dark brown skin. He appeared to be in his mid-twenties. His short, coal black hair was shaved high on the sides of his head, and he sported a dark shadow of growth upon his face that would become a very dense beard if given time. He was dressed in dark khaki pants and a collared, short-sleeved shirt, with a single logo of some type over the left breast.

The other male, a light-skinned man, looked to be of approximately the same age. He was a little taller than the first, modest of build with a narrow waist, and had angular facial features with a strong jawline. He had dark eyebrows, and long, even locks of jet-black hair that descended to the top of his shoulders.

He was wearing gray jeans and a solid blue, long-sleeved shirt. His face was also covered with the stubble of a few days' growth.

One of the first things that Mershad noticed about them was that neither of the men looked to be very comfortable, as they were constantly looking around. They were talking in low voices, and it appeared as if they were keeping alert for an imminent danger. Their hands were empty, which surprised Mershad a little, given their obvious tension.

Mershad glanced over at Erika, and could see that they were both puzzled by the strange sight. The two men were clearly of a contemporary nature to their own, and their obvious discomfort strongly reflected the wary state of being that Mershad and Erika were in.

Yet despite the familiar signs, there was also the possibility that the men were yet another danger to be faced in this unpredictable and unknown place. The pair were headed right in their direction, and there was no real place to run to without being seen. A decision was being forced upon Erika and Mershad, which he knew that neither of them relished.

He gripped his branch-staff a little tighter, steeling his nerves as he looked back to Erika again. She quietly indicated her ears, then pointed towards the oncoming men, and proceeded to touch her mouth, as she silently mouthed some words.

Lip-reading as best as he possibly could, and using the gestures to augment the communication, he came to understand her intentions. She wanted them to remain quiet, and to try and listen to what the approaching males were saying before taking any action.

Nodding in agreement with her, he returned his attentions back to the two oncoming men to see what he could glean.

In the next few moments, he hoped that something could be learned from the men's conversation regarding their identity, or the circumstances that Mershad and Erika found themselves in. Enduring a few more tense moments would hopefully secure the knowledge that they needed to make a decision; to portray hostility, or to offer friendship.

LOGAN

"This is completely insane," Antonio said in a low, tense voice. "We'll have to figure out food shortly. There's the stream that we heard. I just hope that it's water fit for drinking. Last thing we need is to get sick."

"This is all insane, Antonio. Completely insane," Logan replied emphatically.

He looked over towards the stream that had just come into sight. It appeared to be ordinary water, but the way that things had been going, Logan feared that nothing could be taken for granted.

"I'm getting a little thirsty, and we do need water," Logan said. "Do you think there's anything to worry about? How could we even test it out anyway?"

Antonio shook his head with a nervous grin. "Drinking it straight? Not me. You can be the first."

Logan chuckled. "Thanks, but you better not be so flippant about this sort of thing. If I suddenly keel over and fall dead, you'll be in a world of hurt. Maybe we should save the taste testing as a very last resort."

Antonio stared towards the clear, gently flowing water. He slowed down and sighed, shaking his head.

"Sooner or later, if we are here for a while, we are going to have to take a risk and try it," Antonio said.

Logan stared down at the water as well, watching a few minnows darting about in its mild depths. He found that he was in a state of sheer disbelief, that something as simple as drinking water could unsettle him to such a tremendous degree.

His mind was getting the best of him in the wake of the dense fog and ensuing turmoil in his life. The realization annoyed him greatly, as he resolved himself to keep his reason intact.

"Well, at least we can keep close, until we absolutely need it. We can follow the course of the stream for a while," Logan suggested, looking back to Antonio. "And if we are going to be in these woods tonight, we need to begin coming up with some kind of plan."

"Where are we?" Antonio said, exasperated, in a raised voice that carried farther through the trees. "Can you tell me even that?"

Logan shot his friend an angry glare as he hissed, "Did you forget already what we agreed on when we entered the woods? Keep your voice down, Antonio. Even talking low like we have been might be too much of a risk."

It was almost as if Antonio was not listening to him. He saw a look of surprise and agitation spread abruptly across Antonio's face. He swiftly turned his head to share Antonio's angle of view.

His own heart skipped a beat.

Two human figures stood in plain sight about thirty feet away, almost directly in their path.

One was a young female of around twenty years of age. He was relieved to see that she was dressed simply in dark jeans and a yellow, long-sleeved t-shirt, the familiar attire giving him some hope. He was very thankful for the contemporary look, fathoming that she might possibly have some answers as to their whereabouts.

The other person was a shorter, thinner man with dark, olive-shaded skin. He was also clad in everyday clothing, wearing a collared shirt and jeans. The vestiges of extreme apprehension were stretched all over his face, though his mouth was turned up in the beginnings of a nervous smile.

Though both of them held sturdy branches in their hands, Logan felt no sense of threat coming from either. "Hi there … I didn't think we would find anyone out here," Logan said, breaking the momentary impasse. "Who are you?"

The icy tension that had risen upon their appearance quickly melted away in the wake of his words. He could see their postures relaxing just a little.

"My name is Erika, and this is my friend, Mershad," the woman replied, gesturing towards the male at her side. Her voice was steady and confident, and the look in her eye remained imbued with scrutiny.

There was a little awkwardness to the atmosphere. Logan got the distinct impression that, while both pairs were unsure of exactly how to proceed, they were both greatly relieved to have encountered the other. But, the guarded caution in the others strongly suggested that they were not entirely native to the local area. Their apparent discomfort was not a very encouraging aspect of their demeanors.

"I'm Logan, and this is Antonio," Logan responded. He ventured a little further with his words, deciding to take some light risks. "I suppose that you are not from around here, am I right?"

"No, and I would bet that you aren't either, correct?" Erika asked him.

She took a few deliberate steps forward. As if following her cue, the one named Mershad started forward, keeping close by her side.

"No, we aren't," Antonio answered, before blurting out, "and do you know anything about where we are right now?"

A discernable flicker of discouragement crossed through Erika's eyes at that moment, and Logan could see that she had been hoping to ask them the same thing.

"I'm not really sure," she responded, with a tinge of unease.

"And neither are we," Logan said, starting to see that the other two shared his and Antonio's predicament in some way. He then decided to say one more word. "Fog?"

He immediately saw the tidal wave of relief and recognition that hit their faces.

"So, have you two been in this place for very long?" Erika queried, somewhat hesitantly.

"Not really very long at all," Logan stated. "And we are totally out of place. If you know what I mean."

"The fog?" Mershad inquired cautiously.

Antonio nodded, as he replied, "Yes. One minute we were in fog, thicker than anything I've seen before, and the next minute we were here, just outside this forest. We didn't plan it."

"No, we certainly didn't. And yet here we are," Logan added, with a bitter edge to his tone.

"What were you all doing when the fog rolled in?" Antonio asked the newcomers.

"Just sitting and talking on our campus, at night, at the University of Lexington," Erika said. "The fog came in, and then night was day … and here we were."

"University of Lexington? Both of us are from Lexington," Logan replied, finding the increasing familiarity a welcome feast to his starved psyche. "Maybe there is something about that, unless you have any idea as to where this place is."

"No idea. Whatever has happened, we should stay together," Erika said. After a pause, she continued, "So, have you two discussed any plans for handling all of this?"

"Really … no," Antonio admitted. "We've just been walking for a little while. Haven't even tried to drink the water. What have you found out?"

"We've seen some rather unusual animals. And you already know about the strange color of the sky, but other than that, it seems enough like a normal forest," Erika remarked.

"There are some open grasslands, back in the direction from which we just came, and it isn't too far away," Logan said. "We decided that we definitely didn't want to stay out in the open, until we learned more about where we are. There are a lot more places to hide in a forest, and there are more possibilities for shelter. It didn't take us very long to decide to get out of the open and take our chances in here."

"The open grassland would be something different from what we've seen. We've just been walking through miles of forest and hills," Mershad added, gesturing behind and around him.

"As I assume we'll be staying together, what direction do you think we should try?" asked Logan.

"Maybe follow that. It might lead to a bigger body of water," Erika said, pointing over towards the nearby creek.

"Or it might go underground, with our luck," Mershad said dourly. "But it might be worth a try."

"I think it is worth a try, and we were about to follow its course for awhile. We also need to plan for food, shelter, and everything else. We don't even know if the water is safe to drink. I really hope one of you two is a woodland expert," Logan queried. "I hope your degrees were in forestry, and that at least one of you is an aspiring forest ranger."

"At the moment, I wish that were so, but I'm afraid that neither of us is. But there are more minds working together now. Maybe that can offset our lack of knowledge regarding all of this," Erika replied.

"Maybe it can," Logan said. He stepped forward and extended his hand, his somewhat stern countenance allowing a modest grin to emerge. "It is good to meet the two of you, and I'm glad that our paths crossed pretty quickly. It looks like we are going to be in this thing together."

Erika responded congenially, with a firm handshake, the others following suit.

"I'm not happy that you had to go through all of this, but we are very glad to find you as well," she said, the relief very evident in her expressive smile.

"Likewise," Logan replied, holding her deep gaze for a moment.

It took him a second to draw back from her warm, striking eyes. In the wake of his edgy nerves, he was starting to take more note of her considerable attractiveness.

With refreshed spirits and higher hopes, the foursome started along one side of the narrow brook, heading downstream. They compared their experiences and observations. From their collective best guess, the course of the creek meandered near to the outer border of the forest.

About an hour later, near to a cluster of oak trees, they stopped for a short respite. Taking their cue from Erika and Mershad, Logan and Antonio fashioned their own stout walking sticks out of branches during the break.

The quartet then resumed their travel at an easy pace, indulging in some light conversation as they began to relate more of their backgrounds and insights to each other.

The temperate flow of the creek next to them established a continual, relaxing backdrop, which further soothed Logan's wearied and harried mind. Yet despite the tranquil environs, they did not ignore caution. All continued to keep their eyes open for any signs of danger, and their voices remained subdued.

When the creek continued out beyond the edge of the forest, it was decided that they would keep within the cover of the trees. Turning to the left, they altered their path to shadow the forest's edge.

LEE

"Exactly what I was expecting on a Saturday night," Ryan said in frustration, taking a half-hearted stab at the ground with his crude spear. His voice was thick with sarcasm as he continued, "A nice, long nature hike, under a pretty aqua sky. Just what I was wanting."

The young man sat down heavily upon the trunk of a fallen tree, as Lee sat down close to him. Lee extended his legs out, to rest them and perhaps recoup some energy after several hours of what felt like aimless wandering. His stomach felt as if it were about to cramp, and a faint dizziness brought on by hunger and fatigue was just beginning to creep in.

"Not what you were expecting when you left the restaurant?" queried Lee ruefully.

"Didn't expect to go hiking, that's for sure," Ryan replied, with a bittersweet grin.

The youth slumped to the ground, leaning backwards against the prone trunk and letting out a fatigued groan. They sat together in silence for several minutes, as they both took in the serenity of their immediate surroundings. Breathing in the fresh air, they gradually allowed the aches and tingles in their muscles to settle down.

At long last, Ryan glanced up at Lee. "What's next?"

"There's the obvious. I know we're both getting hungry. And we should assume we're going to be here for awhile, so we'd better start thinking about things like that," Lee responded evenly.

"We barely know what is out there, and what we've already seen is not that encouraging," Ryan said.

"No, it's not," Lee said, thinking of the flying creature that had startled Ryan when he had climbed the high tree to espy their surroundings.

The broad forest, contoured by low hills and blanketed by teeming masses of trees, seemed to go on forever in all directions around them. As much as the forest seemed peaceable enough, that discovery was deeply troubling and weighed heavier with each passing hour upon Lee's mind.

"Should we stop and try to make some sort of camp then?" Ryan asked him.

"Probably wouldn't be a bad idea. And we will have to hunt soon, or take a chance on some berries, roots, or plants," Lee said. "I'm not familiar with a lot of things about this area, so we'll have to hope that we find some things that we are familiar with. Luckily, I know a little about mushrooms, herbs, and some things like that. We should ..."

"Hey! Lee!" Ryan exclaimed curtly, in a hushed voice, jolting his hand up abruptly in a gesture that demanded silence.

"What is it?" Lee asked in a whisper.

Ryan slowly got up to his feet, tilting his head slightly to the side, appearing to be listening to something.

Ryan finally whispered, "Something is coming ... this way."

Turning, he pointed emphatically over the tree trunk, in the direction to Lee's back. Lee quietly slid off of the tree trunk, and placed one knee on the ground as he rotated to face the woods alongside Ryan.

The fallen tree served as a capable barrier in front of them, easily large enough to hide behind. They remained as still as the thick length of dead wood lying right before them.

At first, Lee heard the unmistakable crunch of leaves and breaking twigs. Something larger, and not altogether stealthy, was indeed moving resolutely towards them through the woods. At a fair distance, Lee then caught sight of two human figures through breaks in the trees.

As they drew closer, Lee saw that the figures were two younger females. His hopes rose sharply with the recognition, instantly relieved to see the presence of other people within the strange woodlands.

Even so, he was not about to counsel recklessness, and wanted to make sure that Ryan retained some caution as well. He turned to Ryan before the other did something that might give away their hiding place.

"Let's go over there, a little more out of the way," Lee said, indicating the end of the fallen section of tree trunk, where it had broken off from its lower, rooted base. A narrow swath of arched wood and bark still attached the fallen section to the jagged lower portion that was still firmly anchored to the ground. "We can watch them coming with even less risk of being seen."

A small, triangular opening was formed near the ground, at the juncture between the fallen portion of the tree and the rooted lower trunk. To Lee, it appeared highly advantageous for engaging in concealed observation.

"Just keep down," Lee cautioned, as he took the lead.

Lee and Ryan crawled down towards the end of the tree, keeping to their bellies. Lee took painstaking care, and undertook a little extra exertion, so as not to cause much rustling as they moved across the leaves and brush lying beneath their knees and stomachs.

When he reached the small opening, he crouched to one side and left the other free for Ryan. He found that he had guessed correctly. The new vantage point did indeed offer an ideal place from which to watch and await the females without being too exposed.

Lee noticed right away that the dress of the women was contemporary, which came as further relief given the confounding nature of their experience so far. The recognition of that fueled Lee's hopes that everything was ultimately going to turn out to be some type of strange aberration, and that soon he and Ryan would be well on their way to forgetting about it all.

He got a good look at the full-faced young woman to the left, who had dark hair with streaks of deep red dyed into it. Her face and neck were glistening with sweat. As the women neared, he could see that her cheeks were flushed and that her eyes were reddened. Lee guessed this was the result of sustained crying, exhaustion, or a combination of both.

The young woman accompanying her was slightly taller, with long, straight dark hair. She appeared to be more composed than her companion, her expression taut and wary.

Their sluggish movements held the air of extreme fatigue, and both were using makeshift walking sticks crafted from stout tree branches. There was no question in Lee's mind now that they were both utterly tired, and had already been put through a great deal of exertion. Their wariness and fear were also manifestly evident as their eyes were constantly scanning the area around them.

While they did not talk, they trudged heavily forward. They continued to make more noise than Lee believed that they wished to, their steps crunching upon the forest floor. He also judged that they were not threatening to any degree, as far as he and Ryan were concerned.

Lee looked over to Ryan, and made a sharp motion for him to stay put, and to remain silent. Setting down his branch on the ground, and slowly straightening up, Lee walked calmly around the end of the broken tree stump to stand in clear, open view of the two women.

The two females flinched, and the one with the dyed-streaks of hair gasped, both quite startled at his sudden appearance. They reacted swiftly, rapidly collecting themselves and raising up their branches in firm grips, such that Lee could see that they had crudely sharpened the ends of their rough weapons. Lee resented causing them any further fright, but he wanted to make sure that they saw him first from a comfortable distance, both for their sakes as well as for Ryan and himself.

Lee slowly held both of his hands high, his palms openly exposed and empty. He opted for complete honesty, though he doubted that he would quickly gain any measure of trust from them.

"I am not a threat," Lee announced in an even tone of voice. "I wanted you to know I was here before you got any closer. I didn't mean to startle you, but it would have been more startling if I stood up right next to you."

As he spoke, he realized that he had taken it for granted that they all shared the same language. Fortunately, the women showed no confusion at his words.

The woman with the straight brown hair, a granite look embedded in her eye, asked firmly, "And who are you?"

Her eyes then flicked to each side, and she stole a quick glance backward. Lee could sense the immediate and sharp distrust that she had, as if his emergence was some part of a larger ruse or ambush.

As if to confirm his suspicion, she whispered to the other young woman, who kept a watch behind them as the first turned back to face Lee. Her countenance was grim, and Lee could see a little wild frenzy now playing about the edges of her gaze. He was certain that she had been through something quite terrible, and that it would not take all that much to cause her to snap violently.

Lee responded quickly, and as gently as he could. He decided to hold nothing back, hoping against hope that the other two found something in his words that struck a familiar chord within their own sphere of experience.

"My name is Lee Chen. I have no idea where I am. I got lost in a fog. And I found myself in this place. And you are the first people that I have seen," he stated calmly. "I am hoping you know where we are right now, but it looks like you don't either."

There was no mistaking the look of understanding that flashed across the other's face. She did not drop her guard for long, and her hardened façade returned as the flare of clear surprise at the mention of the word "fog" faded. Yet at the least, Lee had some of his instincts confirmed.

"I'm right, aren't I?" Lee pressed, deciding to go with the momentum and his gut feeling. "If I were to guess, I would guess that you were doing something quite normal, and then a fog came, and then you found yourselves in the middle of … who knows where we are. Maybe you even saw some strange things, or creatures? Different than anything you're used to."

The tensed, defensive look softened slightly in the eyes of the brown-haired young woman, if again only for a moment.

"And why should we believe you, that you aren't a threat to us?" she asked him tersely.

"I cannot prove to you why you should believe me. I have only my word. And I don't expect you to believe me. I almost don't believe myself, with what I've gone through," Lee replied.

He got the sense that there was something different and much darker about the experience that the other two had faced, as the edge of great fear remained at the fore in the young woman. Her companion had remained very disciplined and vigilant as she kept watch behind her friend, like one would be in the wake of going through something incredibly terrible.

Lee wished that he could fully reassure them with his words and demeanor, but knew that such a thing was well beyond his art. For a few moments, there was an unpleasant tension hanging in the air as the brown-haired woman carefully considered his words.

"You may be a danger to us, but I risked it," Lee then added.

The continuing level of mistrust, the obvious signs of weariness, and the protective postures of the two young women was evidence enough to Lee that he decided to take one further risk.

"Okay, I will be fully honest with you, in the hopes that you will trust me, and understand that we have been through something unexplainable ourselves.

"I have been defensive with you, as you are now being with us … Ryan, come on out," Lee said gently, turning slightly to face Ryan's obscured position.

Ryan hesitated for a moment, a hesitant look on his face.

"It's okay, Ryan," Lee encouraged. "Come out slowly, and stand up."

The woman with the dyed streaks turned and raised up her staff reflexively, her grip tightening upon it. The two women quickly backed up a few feet at the emergence of another man before them, casting glances to the back and sides, as if they feared that Lee was somehow triggering a trap. Seeing the gangly youth, they relaxed their rigid postures slightly, and Lee could see that they were beginning to perceive the truth in what he had been telling them.

"Explain more about how you got here, what you were doing, and where you are from," the girl with the straight brown hair demanded in a steeled tone, though her eyes gave away the sliver of hope that had now entered her. "Details are fine."

"I own Lee's Wok, down by the University of Lexington. Ryan is a friend of mine who works with me, and had joined me as I was closing the restaurant, earlier tonight … as it was night when all of this happened.

"We walked outside of the store when a large fog rolled in. It

138

was a fog like nothing I've ever seen before. It came in quickly, covering everything, and soon we were in the middle of it. The next thing that I knew, we were here in this hilly forest, in the middle of the day, with a sky completely different to any I've ever seen."

He shrugged his shoulders, and gave a sigh of resignation.

"What can I say? It wasn't our choice to be in the middle of this, and I don't know how we got here, and I really have no idea where here is, to begin with. Honest, that is all that I know," Lee stated.

The brown-haired girl nodded slowly in understanding. The hints of a smile slowly crept upon her face, reflecting familiarity as the various places were voiced. The other young woman then turned towards them fully, also exhibiting a relieved look. Both ceased casting furtive glances all about themselves.

"Then you are from Lexington too. And I know your restaurant. I've eaten there before, but not enough for you to know me," the brown-haired woman said. Her next words were as much for her own benefit, reasoning aloud as much as replying to Lee. "Wherever we are, I don't think it would be easy to make up a story that matched ours in so many ways."

Her companion with the dyed streaks, rigidly silent until then, finally entered into the conversation.

"You have great food at Lee's Wok. I've gotten deliveries from there more than once. I recognize you a little now. My name is Erin, and this is Lynn," the woman with the red-streaked hair introduced, stepping forward as a new series of tears began to roll down her face. "Right now, I am very, very happy to meet the man responsible for the food at Lee's Wok, more than you can ever know."

Lee smiled awkwardly, as Erin suddenly threw her arms around him, and proceeded to give him a tight hug.

"She tends to be emotional," Lynn remarked curtly, and Lee could see that Lynn was not at all pleased that Erin had completely let down her guard. "But we've been through more than a little so far."

"Very nice to meet the two of you," Lee said. "I'm Lee, and this is Ryan. I think that we are going to need each other's company, once we've compared the stories of our last few hours."

To Lee's surprise, Lynn seemed very enthusiastic to the idea. "We've already seen more than our share of things around here," she said, giving a slight shudder as she inwardly made some sort of terrible recollection.

"We've seen some really strange stuff too," Ryan said pensively, speaking up for the first time.

"Then you know that all this might be really, really dangerous, and that we need to be very careful," Lynn replied, looking about her, as if for emphasis. "I don't want to run into what we ran into just moments after coming here."

"I don't think that these would do much good at all against what we almost got caught by," Erin added, holding up her crude weapon. "It was horrible.

Ryan commented, "Then we are going to have to stay real alert, all of us together."

"First of all, we are all in the same boat. We don't have any idea of what or where this place is," Lynn said. "We were just out camping in the woods with our friends, down by the Gorge. The fog rolled in, just like you said, and Erin and I were suddenly alone in this place. Our friends and the camp were gone."

"I have no idea why," Erin said with evident frustration. "We didn't do anything to deserve this."

"What were you guys trying to do just now?" Lynn asked.

"Just trying to find out more about this place," Lee said. "And beginning to think about what we need to do for food and shelter."

Erin shook her head in agreement. "Like we've been doing, only we were forced to move pretty quick after getting here."

Lynn proceeded to relate the tale of their harrowing pursuit by the flying creature in detail, including the unexpected intervention by the unseen, roaring beast, and leading all the way up to the most recent moments where they encountered Lee and Ryan.

"Well, what do you think we should do? As in right now?" Ryan inquired when the women were finished with their account.

"I think the same things you two were about to do, just as a quartet now," Lynn said. "We don't have that many options. We need to figure out some kind of place to settle in when night comes, and we need to think about finding some kind of food."

"I don't even want to think about what comes out at night around here," remarked Erin somberly.

"Good thing there are four of us now. We can set watches with two at a time," Ryan observed.

"Each watch can be done with one of us, and one of the two of you," Lee quickly suggested, "if that would make you feel more at ease."

"Thank you," Lynn responded appreciatively.

"Well, then, let's try and find some food, and find some more things out about this place," Lee stated, before adding, "but hopefully no more creatures."

"We're in full agreement with you there," Lynn said.

After a few moments' discussion, they decided to start off in a direction that neither party had previously been going in. They made sure that it was one that definitely did not go anywhere near to the area where Erin and Lynn had encountered the fearsome woodland denizens.

Lee already had a good mental image of the flying beast that had pursued them, and he was not sure that he wanted one of the roaring creature that had inadvertently saved the two young women. It was abundantly clear that the young women did not want to risk an encounter with their unseen savior. Added to the flying creature that Ryan had seen from the treetops, at close range, it was indisputable that the forest sheltered some very dangerous residents.

In low voices that were near to whispers, Lynn and Erin spoke further with Ryan and Lee about their experiences. Lee was very glad for the new companionship, and felt a little better about their chances in a larger group of four. The two women seemed to have wits enough, though Lee's first impressions were that Lynn was the more focused of the two.

Having already traveled far that day, it was not all that long before the entire group possessed throbbing leg muscles that seemed ready to take on the consistency of jelly.

After recognizing that each of the others was in such a condition, they all finally decided to stop and search for a place to settle for the evening. They had not been lucky enough to blunder into something more familiar, like a building or a road, and it was becoming evident that they would be spending the night in the wilderness.

Lee thought back to the day's trek as the shadows began to lengthen. The distance that they had covered had been fairly substantial, likely far more than he ever would have thought himself capable of.

The rest of the day had gone mercifully without incident, free from the unorthodox creatures that they all had encountered after emerging from the fog into the strange forest. For Lee it was a tremendous relief, though he knew that the two women probably held much more gratitude for the absence of encounters with strange fauna.

The landscape had continued to remain much the same. It seemed like an endless series of slow rises and dips in the ground, surrounded by trees and brush that obscured any distant view. The continuous litany was broken only by the occasional encounter with a stream or creak. The air remained refreshingly clean to breathe, and the only sounds to reach Lee's ears were those of birds and their own footsteps.

The light of day continued to slowly decline, as the deepening pools of shadows expanded and started to fill the woods. Lee realized that the growing gloom in an unknown world would be much more menacing if they did not soon fabricate a makeshift shelter.

After the group had agreed upon a place that looked favorable, Lee instigated the formation of a basic shelter that took little time to erect. Using some long branches and a bevy of grasses, they worked together on fashioning a lean-to shelter at the base of a steeper hill. When finished, Lee saw that the small shelter had the added benefit of being relatively concealed.

Even with the shelter accomplished, Lee had some growing concerns as it came to light that the two women were relatively inexperienced in survival issues. He had hoped otherwise, given that they had been camping when the fog had enveloped them. As the women discovered the same general fact about Lee and Ryan, that they were not naturalists or versed in wilderness skills, a definite anxiety began to rise within the group.

Erin and Lynn's camping and hiking experiences had involved large numbers of people, equipped with plenty of modern conveniences such as sleeping bags and waterproof tents. The majority of their excursions were into the Gorge area in the Daniel Boone National Forest, with clearly marked trails and highly trained rangers in the vicinity.

Lee and Ryan's wilderness had always consisted of a jungle of concrete, metal, asphalt, and large numbers of people.

They were all finding themselves to be far out of their element, but Lee could see that necessity was quickly bringing them together for mutual support.

After some more conferring, it was decided that Lee's earlier idea of using one of the women and one of the men to serve in watch shifts would be implemented. The pair on watch, as well as those sleeping, would be situated within the little enclosure, so that none of them would be left too exposed out in the open.

With the evening's arrangements settled, they set out as a group in the waning daylight to search around the immediate area for any possible source of food. Lee did not expect instant success, but hoped that they could get some ideas for the coming day.

Lee urged the others to check into the beds of nearby creeks, suggesting that there might be the equivalent of frogs or crayfish lurking within the waters and grasses.

The others did not appear to find the idea altogether appetizing, and Erin looked entirely revolted by the suggestion. But Lee at least knew how to prepare both frogs and crayfish for consumption. He also realized that they would soon be eating tree bark if they did not find other solutions for sustenance.

The worries of the others turned out to be for naught, if just for the moment, as nothing was turned up from the couple of creeks that they probed.

Erin succeeded in discovering some mushrooms, which none of the group wanted to try. They had all heard stories about people eating the wrong kind of mushrooms, and none felt certain that what Erin had found was not one of the toxic varieties of the fungus. Lynn found some unrecognizable type of berries, which they also decided against trying for much the same reasons.

When the last vestiges of daylight finally ebbed, they all settled themselves into the enclosure with ravenous appetites harbored inside of them. Thirst overrode caution, and they drank abundantly from cold creek waters near their camping site, hoping that no contaminants were in the water. Bellies full of water helped to take a little of the edge off of them, but Lee knew that it would not be very long before solid food would become a major issue.

The night eased in upon the forest, and the sibilant sounds of insects chirping filled the woods all around them. There were only a couple of moments in which the woods went silent, which caused the group to tense at what was perhaps the passage of a larger creature nearby. Once, Lee's head shot up in alarm at what sounded like a far-off shriek. It took some time for his nerves to settle back down.

Good fortune prevailed overall, though, as there were no major disturbances throughout the rest of the evening, enabling those who were not on watch to allow themselves to surrender to sleep. The largely peaceable night also caused those who were on watch to struggle to stay awake, especially the first pair, as all four of them were entirely exhausted at the outset of the evening.

Lee had volunteered for the onerous duty of the first shift. He knew that it would be the toughest, and in that sense the most important, as it carried the greatest risk of leaving the group vulnerable by having those on watch inadvertently falling asleep.

Lee had been joined by Lynn for the unpleasant challenge, and to his delight soon found her to be very pleasant company. Yet in their great weariness they spoke rather sparingly, and when they did it was often only to help each other remain awake.

After the first shift had ended, and they had roused Ryan and Erin to take their places, Lee could barely keep his eyelids parted. The cloak of sleep came as a very welcome mercy, and not a moment too soon. Lee's consciousness tumbled into a dreamless sleep as he lay upon the hard, uneven ground.

The engulfing fatigue that plunged him into the dark depths of unconsciousness was not without its useful merits. He knew that otherwise he would likely have spent the entire night battling a rising tide of fears and anxieties, the greatest of which being that the sojourn that had begun that day in the peculiar forest would not be ending anytime soon.

JANUS

A few hours later, the mesmerizing sky began to dim as the sun descended towards the west. Janus was intrigued as to what kind of sunset would occur given the different hue of sky, but there were far more pressing matters at hand.

Though night was approaching, it was not yet fully dark. Janus, Derek, and Kent had been passing the time letting their bodies rest up a little.

There had been no major incidents during the past few hours. There were no signs of any sort of strange new life forms, like the creature in the grasses that Kent had startled upon their arrival. The only noises to be heard were that of the air sweeping through the high grasses, and the waters as they flowed through the channel of the river far behind them.

Growing tired with the inactivity, Janus stretched his limbs out and got to his feet slowly. Taking a deep breath, he walked well away from the others, until he was back at the river's edge. He looked all about for any sign of the boat.

To his continued dismay, there was no clue as to what had become of the vessel, and he felt a lump in his throat as a growing anxiety gripped him. He gazed back to where the unbroken line of trees heralded the beginnings of the vast forest. As the light dimmed, the shadowy boundary looked ever more mysterious and foreboding.

It was becoming evident that sooner or later they would have to begin thinking about getting something to eat. The forest would likely serve as their most opportune place to search, perhaps offering some nuts or berries. The river before him could well be teeming with fish, but they had no poles or nets available.

There was a small victory to be had nonetheless, in that there was plenty of accessible fresh water to go around. Cupping his hands, he knelt down and scooped up some handfuls of the water and drank it. He imbibed the cool liquid with relish, even as some of it dribbled down the sides of his mouth and neck.

He took in rapid breaths after the long draughts of water, still amazed at the clean feeling of the air as it passed into his lungs. He concentrated on gathering his wits, which was the most important asset that he still had available to him in this extraordinary place. He knew that they could not sit around and wait forever, but they had absolutely no idea as to how to get back to the lake.

With a barely audible sigh, he spun about and walked back down to where Kent and Derek were still resting.

"Anything new?" Derek inquired, idly looking up into the blue-green sky.

A couple of large, black ravens flew by overhead.

"Not always the best harbinger," Derek remarked with a rueful chuckle, watching the dark birds slowly fade into the distance.

"You mean the ravens?" Kent asked him.

"I'll explain it sometime later," Derek replied with a dismissive air.

Janus shook his head and frowned.

"What are you thinking about?" Derek asked him.

"Everything. Just what we do know," Janus responded dourly. "Boat's gone. There's a strange forest nearby. We have no idea what has happened or how it happened. The sky is entirely different to us, and we've already seen an animal that is very different from anything we've known.

My gut feeling is that none of it bodes very well."

"We'll have to head forth sometime and explore our surroundings. That much is obvious," Derek declared. "We'll look for some source of food too. Can't assume we'll be back home anytime soon."

"Not far at all from what was running through my mind," Janus said. "I wonder if there is anyone around this place, as far as people."

Janus let his breath ebb out in a long, controlled exhalation. He stood with his hands resting on his hips, looking down at the swaying grasses caught in the early evening breezes.

Under the circumstances, the most simple of things appeared daunting.

"There are others," a strong, deep voice intruded suddenly.

Janus whirled around, even as Derek jumped up immediately to his feet in a combative stance. Kent's eyes snapped wide open, and he twirled around with a mien of renewed panic, as he scrambled up to his feet and stood close to Derek.

All of their eyes were fixed upon the speaker, who had somehow managed to approach them without any of them having heard or seen anything.

The one who had addressed them was a tall man of very advanced years, clothed in full-length, blue garments. A wide-brimmed hat with a low, rounded crown topped his head.

Thick white eyebrows, a mass of long white hair, and an extensive white beard were among the most prominent features of the peculiar stranger. His long, sharp nose poked out over the abundant growth of facial hair, and a lone blue eye gazed intently at the three of them. His left eye was hidden from view, fully covered by a patch.

The elderly man looked to be very calm, even amiable in manner. "I mean no harm to any of you," he continued, before they had a chance to reply. "But there are others such as yourselves in these lands. In there!"

He extended his right arm, pointing to where the great forest began.

"There you will find others, who have gone through what you have gone through," he proceeded. "It is where you must start."

"Who are you?" were the first words out of Janus' mouth.

It was pretty evident that the man represented no great threat. Janus and his companions were physically capable enough, and he knew that Derek was an exceptional fighter if a greater danger arose.

"I am … a friend … names would mean little to you now, and perhaps be more trouble than it is worth," the old man replied. "Dire times indeed have struck this world, and there are very few that you can trust now. The violence across this world is great, and an unrivaled age begins. Everything is at stake. You must join the others who are here, who have come from your world."

The old man's remarks about two distinct worlds sent a deep feeling of unease rippling through Janus.

"Sounds absolutely wonderful. But perhaps you can tell us where the hell we are then," Derek retorted sharply, agitation and sarcasm lacing his words.

The old man did not respond to Derek's statement, nor did he seem to be offended by the curtness.

Instead, he calmly repeated his urging, "Go to the forest, and you shall find the others. I have matters of my own to attend to, but it is important that you know that others are nearby. Begin there."

With no further instruction or comment, the old man turned casually and started to walk off in a direction parallel to the forest. Janus noticed how easy and supple his movements were for an old man, and how his robes flowed gracefully with each long stride.

Janus glanced over at Derek, and discovered that the other's face was exhibiting the same utter confusion about the situation that he was feeling inside. Janus' eyes reverted back towards the old man as he continued heading away from them.

Janus and Derek simultaneously shook their heads in disbelief. Janus rolled his eyes and broke into a swift trot, hurrying to catch back up to the old man.

Without breaking stride or turning, the old man snapped his right hand up as Janus neared. Janus came to an abrupt halt, as the old man stopped and turned to look at him again.

This time, the sunlight caught his right eye directly, revealing it to be a bright, sparkling blue.

"I know that you are filled with questions. But it is best to keep the questions that you have to yourself for now, as any answers I give will only multiply your questions. I assure you, in time you shall know more. And as I have indicated, in time you shall find that you also know less, as each piece of knowledge beckons to several more," the old man told him.

The old man's voice then took on a very purposeful, careful tone.

"Here is some wisdom. You may find help from sources that you can see, and some help from sources that you cannot behold with the eyes that you see me with at this moment. See to your friends, and go find the others from your world. That is the best that you can do right now. I shall return to you soon enough."

Janus was entirely confounded by the enigmatic words of the older man. He failed to ask the old man about the issue of worlds, which had been at the tip of his tongue when he had hastened to catch the mysterious stranger. For no explicable reason, and perhaps only because he did not know what else to do, he heeded the man's words and pressed no further questions. He made no move to follow as the old man turned his back to Janus and resumed his walk.

A thousand questions were racing through his mind, but it was clear that the old man was not going to discuss anything further. With great reluctance, Janus turned and walked slowly back towards his two friends.

He knew that it was not a total loss. At the very least, they had encountered another person within this strange place, which was becoming more bizarre by the moment.

"I have no idea," were the first words that he heard from Derek as he drew near to the other two.

Derek was shaking his head and looking down at the ground. When he looked back up, he had an expression of sheer bewilderment.

"I don't even know where to begin," Derek spat out. "Or even which way is up, or which way is down right now."

His friend's tremendous mystification matched his own. "I don't either, Derek," Janus replied. "The world is upside down." He looked back in the direction that the old man had gone, only to find that the stranger was no longer in view. His brow furrowed for a moment, as he did not think that the old man had been walking quickly enough to travel entirely out of sight. The path that he had taken out in the open should have kept him in their sight for quite awhile.

"Who do you think that was?" Kent said, staring into the distance. Neither of the others answered him immediately.

"An old, bearded man in blue robes and a wide hat. That's what we know. Here and gone already," Janus finally replied, with an edge of tension to his words.

"So what did you find out? What did you ask him? Did you ask him where are we?" Kent asked.

"No closer to that answer," Janus said with frustration. "You heard him, and know as much as I do. He warned us not to trust anyone, that things are violent here, and that there are others from our world in the forest."

"And that we need to find them," Derek added.

"That explains a helluva lot," Kent quipped in irritation. "And what's the bit about 'our world'? So, we are in another world, aren't we? That's for sure, I suppose, just looking up at that sky and seeing that lizard thing earlier. Well, then, maybe we shouldn't stay out in the open for too much longer. Where do you all propose going?"

"What about the forest?" Janus inquired.

"What about it? How can we just trust that guy?" Derek asked. "Who knows what's in there?"

"He's the first sign of sentient life that we've seen in this place, and we've gotta move on sometime," Janus rationalized. "The forest probably has our best hopes of finding something to eat. And if there was a threat involved with the old man, then don't you think that it would have come upon us when we were idly sitting here, and were completely unaware of his approach to within a few feet of us? If an old man snuck up on us so easily, then anyone could have ... or might yet, if we sit around here forever. That's the way I see it."

Derek immediately harmonized with Janus' logic. "I've never been that oblivious before, having someone sneak up on me like that. You're right, Janus, regarding your comments about the threat. But still, what reason do we have to trust him? Even he warned us not to trust anyone."

"Maybe because we don't know anything. And what if what he said turns out to be true? About this really being a different world? And about some others from our own world also being here, in the forest? If this unintended arrival in this world could happen to us, then it could have happened to others, right? Maybe there is a real reason why we are here," Janus responded, though he found the sentiments incredible to fathom even as he spoke of them.

"Maybe there are others, and maybe there aren't," Kent interjected. "I, for one, sure as hell do not want to place my life into the hands of an old stranger ... especially if this is another world.

"I don't care if he's the best older sneak in the universe, and could have crept up on us, and cut our throats in broad daylight, right in the middle of a barren desert plain, with us wide awake and sitting back to back looking out in every direction. You're giving him way too much credit for trustworthiness, too soon … way too much."

"Then I wouldn't expect you to follow the suggestion," Janus retorted in a more resolved tone, drawing upon a sudden dose of inspiration and willpower that rose within him. "I'll test it out myself, and Derek can stay with you here. Right now we don't have many, if any, options, and at some point we need to begin to understand this place."

"And what if it is some kind of trap?" Kent asked with a trace of fear splayed upon his face.

"If it is, then those enemies would move on us sooner or later anyway. The old man got up to us without us catching a glimpse of him, like I said. We all know that. And like I said, it wouldn't be too hard for others to do the same, I'm afraid, unless we get our heads on straight and figure some things out," Janus stated.

"So what are you going to test out? You don't seriously mean in there, do you?" Kent asked incredulously, gesturing towards the darkening boundary of the forest.

"I'm going to go on a little trek, just a very short one, and I will be back before nightfall," Janus said. "I just want to get a better idea of what's going on, and maybe even see if I can find something we can consider eating. Is that okay with you both?"

Derek nodded, and Janus was appreciative that he had heeded Janus' unspoken wish. Janus knew that Derek understood that it would be foolhardy to even suggest leaving Kent alone, especially after the horrific trauma that he had been through in the moments when he had been trapped alone in this foreign place.

From the stoic look on Derek's face, Janus knew that he had made solid, nearly irrefutable points to his friend.

Janus' own appetite was just starting to nag at him, but he knew that food would not be the only need of theirs in the coming days. They would have to begin making some headway in several areas, and take some chances, if they were going to survive for very long in this strange new environment. To remain ensconced in indecision was accepting almost certain ruin.

Unless they suddenly woke up and found out that this was all some sort of unbelievable, shared dream, or were suddenly whisked back to their familiar grounds, they would have to begin facing the stark reality of their situation.

"I'll return before nightfall, remember that," Janus said, mustering as much confidence as he could into his voice as he started off.

Janus then turned his full attention on the scene ahead, increasing his stride until he was almost jogging. The riverside and his friends fell farther behind him, as the distant line of trees steadily rose up to greet him.

If this was indeed another world, he hoped that the progress of time, and the passage of day into night, went at a similar rate to that which he was used to.

He felt a mounting trepidation as he drew closer to the line of trees. His imagination started to unfurl as he wondered what manner of life might be within the shadows of the forest. The first animal that they had encountered seemed to indicate that there would indeed be some surprises, though the trees themselves looked to be normal enough.

His imagination starting to run amok, he silently admonished himself to regain his grip upon his fraying nerves. His steps crunched beneath him as his shoes met a higher concentration of twigs and fallen leaves. Before he knew it, the forest suddenly loomed right before him. With a deep breath as he girded his resolve, he stepped forward into the trees and was enveloped within just a few strides.

The trees of the forest were fairly well spaced apart, proud, older sentinels that had long since carved out their space and spread their branches wide above to secure it. The ground itself was carpeted by low growths of grasses, moss, and wildflowers, and pockets of more significant brush grew wherever adequate light was available through the foliage canopy.

Walking out of the clear, unobstructed daylight and abruptly entering into the dimmer forest environs jogged Janus' senses. He decided to pause for a moment to let his eyes adjust to the shadowy depths around him.

He could perceive the thumping beat of his own heart, feeling much smaller as he tried to gaze through the assemblage of towering trees ahead of him. His mind started to play tricks with him again, cruelly reminding him that he was too far from his friends to get help if something truly unexpected and threatening did occur.

There was a discernible stillness to the air, an unsettling disquiet that made his pulse race a bit faster. Glancing around, Janus searched for something that could be used as a weapon. He conceded that anything he found might not be very effective against whatever might ultimately lurk within the depths of such a forest, but he knew that it would suffice to provide him some confidence.

Studying the trees, he saw that some of them had sturdy-looking lower branches that were not too big to be snapped off and utilized as a rough staff, or club-like weapon.

Without further delay, he walked over to the nearest tree and fixed his attention upon a suitable branch. As he set his hands upon the tree branch, readying to put his muscle and weight into bending it to break it off, his ears heard a strong male voice call out. "Excuse me!"

Janus whirled about, nearly falling over in his haste and panic. He faced the four strange people now a few short paces before him, three males and a female. Unlike the old man, they all wore familiar styles of clothes, and to all appearances looked like people of his own community.

Janus' jaws clenched. His mind immediately set itself to analyzing possible options for defense, and for considering potential escape routes. He cautiously backed up a few steps in the direction of the forest's edge. His muscles bunched in readiness to run at the slightest provocation.

"Let me guess … you were doing your own thing, in a world that made a lot more sense than this one. Then a fog came … and next you found yourself in this world, wondering what the hell happened … just like us," a tall man with dark hair addressed him, the one that had first spoken.

Though he had a very stern countenance, and his words were firm, Janus did not sense any imminent threat from the speaker.

Janus must have looked quite puzzled, as one of the other males, a stockier Hispanic fellow, ventured, "I'm sure you have no idea of what this world is, and probably neither does anyone that might be with you. Am I right? You know what I am talking about? I bet you do know."

It then crossed Janus' mind that perhaps these were the individuals that the old man had so recently spoken of.

"Have you seen an old man near here, in blue, robe-like clothing, and with a long, white beard?" Janus queried cautiously.

To his disappointment, all of the others answered in the negative, a couple of them looking perplexed at his question.

"Then tell me something of your story," Janus told them, darting his gaze behind him as he took another couple of slow steps backward.

The serious-looking male who had first addressed him proceeded to explain the details of their situation. He described taking a car ride with his friend, who was evidently the second speaker, and encountering a similar, impenetrable fog, then undergoing an inexplicable arrival into the new environment. He spoke of later meeting the woman and the other man while wandering within the woods.

The woman in the group then interjected at that point to relate the origins of their own escapade, which had evidently begun at the University of Lexington's campus. The dark-haired man finished the story with a brief description of the things that they had since discovered about the forest, with a few comments added in by the woman.

In many ways, the stories carried great similarities to Janus and his friends' recent experiences. He was incredibly relieved to see that they all appeared to come from the same town that he and his friends did.

He knew exactly where the grassy, tree-dotted haven that the woman had spoken of was, situated along one side of the student center at the University of Lexington. He knew the road by the mall that the dark-haired man and his friend had taken, when they had become immersed in the strange mist.

There was little doubt that they all shared some common origins. If they were to be believed, then the others were in the very same predicament as Janus, Derek, and Kent. The two pairs had come together randomly in the middle of the forest, just as Janus was meeting them now.

It did not take Janus long at all to recognize that a group of seven would have a much better chance of success within this foreign territory than one group of three, and another of four. The temptation of increased numbers put a tremendous pressure on Janus to accept their story at its face value.

He carefully regarded them as various thoughts and emotions pulled inside of him.

At last, he stated, "Here's my own situation."

The other four listened attentively as he spoke of his own ordeal. He detailed the boat trip, coming to the shore in the fog, and the recent visit of the old man.

When he had finished, the woman among the quartet, a tall beauty with flowing black hair and expressive dark eyes, said, "Maybe that old man you talked about did know something. Maybe he was speaking about us specifically.

"But I know one thing for certain, I think that we had all better stick together, for our own sakes at the least. I think that it is pretty clear by now that this isn't a place that any of us are familiar with. Maybe not even our world, the more I see of it. None of us can argue that by now. And if we are to go much further, then we'd better get introductions taken care of."

Janus paused for an extended moment, held back by some last vestiges of extreme caution. He looked into each of their eyes, one by one.

"Agreed," Janus finally answered, trusting to his impulses. He offered them a smile. "My name is Janus Roland."

Janus shook each of their hands, as each of them gave him their names in turn.

The attractive woman's name was Erika Laesig, and the dark-haired man with the austere countenance was called Logan Danner. The stoutly built male was Antonio Guerrero. The shorter, lean male with a darker complexion, who looked to be of Middle Eastern descent, was named Mershad Shahab.

"I need to go back to my friends, as they need to know of this right away. They won't exactly be expecting this, so you might as well come along with me," Janus indicated, as they finished their introductions with each other.

The quartet of new acquaintances followed behind, keeping a little distance between themselves and Janus. Seeing their own caution was a reassurance to Janus as he settled into a brisk stride, leading them back out of the forest and into the open.

Janus called out, waving to get Derek and Kent's attention as soon as they emerged from the cover of the woods.

Derek and Kent saw them right away, standing quietly and awaiting their approach. Both looked very attentive, sizing up the four individuals coming in Janus' wake. After watching them approach for a few moments, Derek started forward, breaking into a jog as he moved away from Kent to intercept the others.

"Janus!" he called, his eyes fixed upon the other four. "What's up?"

Janus replied, as he slowed down to meet Derek's approach. "The old man appears to have been right. These people with me are all from Lexington, and have been through the same kind of thing as us, with the fog and everything else. They're in the same mess as we are."

Derek's eyes looked over the foursome that was now drawing close, resting his evaluating gaze upon each one of them. The careful, appraising look in his eye gave away the fact that he was even less inclined towards trust than Janus had been.

Janus could tell that his friend was fully on his guard, watching very alertly for any sudden moves or other troubling indications.

Janus turned to look at the others, as they drew to within a few paces of him and came to a stop themselves.

"This is my friend Derek Decker, and over there is Kent McNeeley," Janus told them.

He then proceeded to introduce the four to Derek, who still kept his own distance from them. Kent had strolled over in the interim, and was now standing by Derek's side.

Janus found that he was even more convinced about the other four at that moment. In his mind, he knew that if they bore any ill will towards Janus and his friends, it was definitely not to their advantage to allow the three men to come together in a group.

"Probably best if you tell your story in your own words to them," Janus said to the quartet.

"I understand," Erika replied with a nod, glancing towards Derek and Kent.

The stories were then shared again, which helped to break the tension a little with Derek. He asked them a few pointed questions regarding some elements of what they had seen in the forest, clearly looking to gather useful insights about their new environment.

Following the retelling of the stories, they all came to agreement that they would remain together from that point onward. With the light around them continuing to ebb towards their first night in this region, it was abundantly clear that some kind of plans had to be made.

The group of seven slowly made their way back to the edge of the forest. Dividing tasks up, they set about to building a shelter for the night, as well as looking around for any source of food that they could find.

The shelter that they erected was crude, but would likely suffice even if some rain fell during the night. It was arranged as a rough, semi-circular lean-to around the massive diameter of an ancient oak tree. Gathered brush and foliage were arranged to form layers atop a lattice of thin branches harvested from the nearby trees.

Only a few sour tasting berries were turned up in the search for food, unripe versions of a wild berry that Derek was familiar with. To help offset the worsening hunger pangs, all of the group members had to settle for drinking copious amounts of cool water from a stream that was located near to the site of the shelter.

The most obvious concerns were gradually voiced by more than one member of the newly formed group. Very soon, unless they uncovered a few naturally growing, edible sources, they would have to turn to other options for food. It would likely mean trying to hunt some of the local fauna, or perhaps figure out a workable method for fishing in the streams.

Of their group, only Derek and Kent had hunted before, but even that was not a full assurance of success. Their hunting had been done with guns, and the group currently had no firearms with them, or even bows.

Just as the shelter was finished, the night finally settled in around them with a sharp drop in temperature. As cooler winds coursed throughout the trees around them, bringing a steady rustling to the teeming leaves, Janus' eyes were attracted to every break in the branch canopy overhead.

The glittering spectacle that was unfolding in the skies above them was an experience that he would not soon forget. It was yet another piece of evidence that they were indeed in a strange new world, but it was nonetheless incredible to behold.

There were a great many more stars visible in the deep sky above than there ever were in the skies of Janus' own world. They were also arranged into unfamiliar patterns, a bevy of new and strange constellations.

Similar to his world, a circular orb rose resolutely up into the sky as the night marched forward. Nearly a full circle, its light provided a fair amount of illumination as it reached down to break up the deep shadows beneath the trees.

Unlike in his world, however, a second orb soon came into view, smaller than the first, but most certainly another moon.

Janus sat awestruck at the development, not believing his own eyes. He heard the gasp of one of the others as they took note of the undeniable presence of a second, gleaming moon.

"I think that confirms it," Janus heard Erika saying to one of the others.

Several members of the group talked for a long time about the presence of the second moon and what it heralded. Janus had nothing to add to their discussion, and sat quietly as he continued to stare above in amazement and awe.

The blue-green sky had been no anomaly, and the strange creatures that had been witnessed were not merely undiscovered species. They were truly within a foreign world, a concept that Janus found to be utterly staggering.

Even Derek had grown very quiet and pensive, and Janus knew that fear's chilly touch had not spared his stalwart and undeniably tough friend.

A thousand more questions were rising up within him, and it was all that he could do to suppress his spreading anxieties.

Each of the others dealt with the reality in their own way. Kent and Antonio gave voice to their laments, while Erika and Logan tried to instill some courage in the others, though Janus could still sense the nervousness behind their words. Mershad's reaction was much like Janus and Derek, as he dwelled upon the revelation in a contemplative silence.

The chirping of insects droned on steadily in the background, as Janus watched the two moons slowly crossing the sky overhead with a feeling of wonder and trepidation. He tucked his knees up to his chest, clasping his hands together.

The old man had been right. The answer that they were in a new world stoked the fires of new inquiries, and Janus saw the wisdom in keeping things to their most basic element.

Dawn would bring with it a host of new worries and pressing matters, and Janus could only hope that the old man would return to them. If this was a world that was entering a violent age, and most could not be trusted, then Janus was not eager to have too many random encounters before they knew the lay of the land.

In due time, the full weight of the day finally caught up to each of the seven. They were all emotionally drained, and the four that Janus had met in the woods had already hiked a considerable distance, and were physically very weary. The seven were unified in their exhaustion, and despite the troubling certainty that this was indeed a foreign world, their bodies' demands for rest finally became irresistible.

Before their focus faded completely, they quickly organized watch shifts for the night, with Derek and Erika taking the first one together. Janus had been ready to endure the challenge, but drew the second shift. He was quietly relieved that he was spared the early task and could get a little immediate rest.

He crawled into the shelter of branches and brush. He kept to one of the two open ends of the semicircular lean-to, so that he did not disturb Mershad and Kent when he was roused for his designated watch.

As he cushioned his head upon his tucked arm, he found that the hard ground was unforgiving, and that the air was thicker in the confined space. Yet neither discomfort proved to be an impediment to sleep as his weariness became irrepressible.

Listening with fading awareness to the litany of trees and insects, Janus finally drifted off into the arms of a deep and abiding sleep.

section iv

LOGAN

When daylight finally arrived, it was accompanied by a faint tremor that reverberated steadily through the ground.

A sound like the distant rumbling of thunder, heralding a faraway storm, traveled through the early morning air. After a little time had passed, it became quite evident that both the noise and the potency of the tremors were increasing.

Logan, whose own restlessness had prompted him to take the final watch of the night with Derek, affording Erika a little more rest, had readily noticed the first subtle disturbances. The night had passed without incident, though the relative tranquility had not lulled the senses of either of them into complacency during their appointed watch.

Their presence in an utterly foreign world had helped to keep Logan's own senses keen to the slightest sound or aberration. Furthermore, as Logan had come to appreciate, Derek already possessed an exceptionally alert, very disciplined disposition.

There was little incentive to any other orientation anyway, as, to Logan's perspective, there was not much comfort to be had at hand. When he had decided to ask Erika to take over for the final watch shift, his back had felt like it had been transformed into dry wood after struggling in vain to sleep for a few scant hours upon the hard, unforgiving ground. Even after much stretching, there still were some serious kinks in his back that he had not yet been able to work out.

Logan and Derek's looks of apprehension had increased, as the rumbles grew ever louder and the vibrations became stronger. Logan's own unease stemmed from the feeling that the seeming thunder did not have the usual quality of a natural storm. He dreaded to think about what kind of unwelcome surprise might be greeting them, to start off this new day in an utterly strange land.

Mershad rose up from the ground nearby, where he had recently adjusted his orientation towards the light of the rising sun. He had just concluded some prayers, his pre-dawn prostration instantly revealing to Logan that Mershad was of the Islamic faith.

Mershad's widened eyes and nervous demeanor reflected how he was feeling about the vibrations and rumbles. He looked to Logan and Derek, and all three nodded solemnly to each other as an unspoken consensus was reached.

Without sparing a further moment, the three roused all of the others from their slumber. The tremors persisted all the while, continuing in an unrelenting, ascending pulsation.

"What is it?" Kent asked Logan, groaning as he was shaken firmly upon the shoulder.

Logan backed out of Kent's way, urging, "Get up! Something's happening!"

Kent looked to be in a very disheveled state as he emerged out from under the makeshift shelter, a nervous frown upon his face as he squinted into the bright morning light. His eyes darted about warily as he became more cognizant of the disturbing sensations. The audible rumbles and shaking in the ground brought an increasingly apprehensive look to Kent's face.

"I have no idea what it is," Logan replied to Kent's unvoiced query.

"That's not like any storm or earthquake that I have ever been around before," Kent remarked to Logan and Derek, as the latter approached them.

"No, it isn't," Derek replied curtly.

"It doesn't recede or ebb," Erika added firmly, as she came over to stand by them, her eyes already quite awake and alert.

Her brow furrowed as she concentrated, methodically looking to all directions. She finally squared her body almost directly towards the west, where the trio of Janus, Kent, and Derek had originally entered the borders of the forest.

"I'm pretty sure that it is coming from out there, straight in that direction," she declared, pointing off through the trees. "And surprises aren't always good. Maybe we should look into it for ourselves ... before something looks into us."

Antonio and Janus had emerged into the morning light by then, crawling out from deeper within the crude shelter of branches and foliage. They were swiftly brought up to date by the others, as a frown darkened Janus' countenance, and anxiety gripped Antonio's.

One by one, the others all looked about, concentrating upon the strength of the sounds and vibrations. Logan and the others gradually arrived at their own best conclusions, and announced them in turn, collectively finding that Erika was entirely correct in her assessment.

The increasing rumbles hailed to them through the forest from the immediate west.

"Come on then!" Derek pressed the others adamantly. "Erika's right. We need to find out. I don't like surprises to begin with, and I like to at least know what I'm facing, especially if some potential trouble is afoot."

Logan nodded in agreement, before declaring, "I'll come with you, Derek."

Mershad and Erika then volunteered in turn, right before Antonio spoke up.

"Shouldn't a couple of us stay back at the camp?" Antonio inquired, looking nervous. "And I'm not the fastest runner, if you guys need to get back here in a hurry."

"And neither am I," Kent then added, with a veneer of clear diffidence.

Logan glanced over at Derek, who was looking more impatient by the second. Logan understood where Kent's trepidation came from. From talking to Derek, he knew that Kent had already been through quite an ordeal when he had become stranded alone for a brief time in the new world.

"Maybe a few of us should stay here, to keep an eye on our camp," Logan suggested. He then eyed Janus and Kent. "Maybe you two should say here with Antonio. Leave at least three together."

"Fine with me," Kent responded, looking a little relieved at not being compelled to court potential danger right away.

Janus looked a little reluctant to stay behind, a slight frown returning to his face, but finally nodded after a long pause.

"Then we're decided," Derek said bluntly. He clapped his hands together sharply, the noise cracking the air loudly in the tense atmosphere. "Come on, let's get going! Let's get near to the treeline, and we'll see what comes next."

Breaking into a run, Derek took the lead and bolted off for the edge of the forest to the west. Needing no further inspiration, Logan, Erika, and Mershad followed immediately after him, running hard a few steps behind.

Derek outran all three of the others, covering the distance to the forest's edge rather quickly. He slowed down only when the trees had started to noticeably thin. Finally coming to a complete stop, he then crept forward silently and carefully from a crouched position towards the outermost edge of the trees.

Erika was the next to arrive in the vicinity, followed by Logan, and then Mershad. They each slowed as they neared Derek, stalking up towards him and silently taking a cue from his manifest caution. They each emulated his form as best as they could, Logan and Erika having more success in the endeavor than Mershad, whose efforts at stealthier movement appeared a little awkward.

Derek glanced back occasionally to note their progress, saying nothing, and evidently satisfied at the wary approach that the others were taking. Even so, there was something in Derek's gaze that caught Logan's attention, though the man's face continued to remain impassive as they crept up to his position.

The reason for the strange look within Derek's eyes became abundantly clear just a few moments later.

Through a break in the trees, Logan beheld the grassy plain beyond. His eyes widened in reflex at the incredible sight that abruptly swamped his eyes. His breath was also snatched away by the unexpected, overwhelming vision erupting boldly before the four shocked observers.

The massive scene spread out upon the plains was simply staggering in scope, difficult to absorb as it bombarded the senses, and almost impossible to believe. Where the open grassland swept out towards the far horizons, there was a gargantuan, moving presence.

Without question, it was the source of the sonorous rumbles, as well as the substantial tremors that continued to course through the ground.

Sprawling out right before their eyes was the passage of a vast army on the march, many thousands in number. Even more astounding, it appeared to be an army from an age that Logan would have thought to be long lost within the mists of time.

It was as if the pages of medieval history had vibrantly come to life within this astounding new world. At his side, Mershad gasped in undeniable awe, as a wave of lightheadedness flowed through Logan. He struggled to make some sense out of what he was seeing, his mind and heart racing. Not a single word was shared among the four observers.

Logan and the others gradually recovered from their momentary trance brought on by the enormous spectacle. Derek was the first to come back to full focus, lowering himself slowly to the ground and beckoning for the others to do likewise.

Once they were all prostrate, they crawled forward on their bellies with Derek until they were close behind the trunks of the trees nearest to the edge of the grassy, windswept expanse. Logan's form grew rigidly still after he halted, a combination of wonder and fear fixing him firmly in place.

Even if he had the eyes of a hawk, Logan would still have been overwhelmed at the variety of sights, not to mention the sheer size of the column of warriors that meandered far beyond the limits of his vision to the south. He was already resigned to settling in for an extended duration. With the column's size and rate of march, Logan estimated that it would take a very long time for the entire army to pass by their position. The immensity of the scene wholly enveloped his attention, and he did not so much as cast a glance towards his companions.

Stretching far off to the left, well past the edge of his range of vision, was a continuous stream of warriors. Some mounted, and many others on foot, all were arrayed in an organized, column formation. The fresh daylight glinted in abundance, reflecting off steel all the way down the incredible length of the column.

The bristling expanse of spears in view resembled a new, deadlier version of the rolling grasslands that the army was passing through. Unlike the abundant, swaying grasses all around the column, the tract of upright blades of iron grass was not swayed in the least by the billowing winds.

Leading the extensive column was a vanguard of mounted warriors, iron helms shining brightly underneath a host of fluttering banners and pennons.

The forms of their horses exuded strength, the equines all displaying a sleek, well-cared for appearance as they traveled forward at an easy gait. Many of the horses were garbed in white caparisons, which appeared to have a quilted or padded design to them.

The riders in the vanguard were all clad in what looked to be black woolen habits, fitted with hoods that were currently pulled back. Upon the left breasts of the riders' habits, on their red banners and pennons, and rendered upon the black facings of the long triangular or almond-shaped shields, slung over their backs via guige straps, was the image of a white, upright spear.

Carrying long lances, the warriors all had swords sheathed in the scabbards at their waists.

Logan watched the vanguard contingent trot by with rapt interest. It was still difficult for him to fully accept that he was really witnessing such a remarkable sight, even as the ground steadily vibrated beneath his body.

The black-garbed mounted force was followed soon after by a great number of marching foot soldiers. The masses of infantry provided a living screen of protection for the extensive baggage train in their midst.

Four-wheeled wagons and two-wheeled carts rumbled forward slowly, some pulled by horses and others by teams of plodding oxen. Wagon drivers used shouts and long switches to spur the brawny creatures forward. Packhorses laden down with all manner of hide pouches, water skins, and other materials trundled along among the wheeled elements of the baggage train.

Many of the marching figures in the looser throng surrounding the carts and wagons carried spears, while others held crossbows or bows. Several were bearing a very unique type of long-hafted axe, guisarmes with lengthy, curved blades.

Two distinct lines of marching figures strode in disciplined order along the forest-side of the baggage train. The men of the inner line were all bearing crossbows, the belt hooks used for loading them jangling downward from their waists.

Just outside of them in an even line was a file of spearmen with tall, rectangular shields. Mail-coated, with iron half-helms, they formed a living screen for the crossbowmen to their left.

The orderly lines of spearmen and crossbowmen warily eyed the forest's edge, compelling Logan to not move a muscle lest the cascade of eyes sweeping along the edge of the trees take notice of him.

Out from the flank closest to the outskirts of the forest were intermittent formations of mounted warriors. Logan could not help but think that many of the riders in these periodic bands were knights.

The particular riders catching Logan's eyes exhibited an unrivaled splendor that was set well apart from all others in the column, whether on foot, or with them on horse. Logan found his eyes roving from one impressive form to another, each one a grand sight in and of themselves.

Several individuals displayed matching colors between their sleeveless, knee-length surcoats, triangular shield facings, and the draping bards adorning their war stallions. Luxuriant blues, vibrant reds, bright yellows, deep greens, and other lush hues formed the bases of their rich trappings.

Some of these warriors had additional designs displayed on their outer surcoats, shields, and bards. Stylized lions clawed viciously at unseen adversaries, while great birds of prey spread their beaks apart, loosing piercing battle cries. Dragons opened their mighty jaws wide, as if about to loose torrents of scorching flame. Wolves bared their knife-like fangs menacingly, caught in mid-bound as they raced across some invisible terrain.

On other shields, surcoats, and caparisons, the displays were simpler. Straight bars, chevrons, and other geometric elements were set in various arrangements against the solid hues of their backgrounds.

The stately riders, like those of less prominent appearance accompanying them, had their heads turned towards the forest. The expressions of many knights were hidden behind the iron visors of cylindrical half-helms, or encompassed within full great helms, flat-topped and barrel-round.

After watching the procession of warriors for quite some time, Logan's eyes were drawn towards an exceptionally sizeable banner pulled forth by a large team of burly oxen. The great banner undulated in the robust breezes from the top of a high mast, exhibiting a prominent sigil upon its surface.

It was of a golden fleur-de-lis. Set against a deep blue background, the proud image of the fleur-de-lis was striking to behold.

The stout wagon trundled onward, carrying the banner along with it to the north, and the river of warriors continued to flow by for what seemed to be an interminable length of time to Logan. Without needing to count, he knew with surety that several thousand men had already passed by their position. He longed to stretch his tightening limbs, doing his utmost to block out of his mind any physical discomforts that arose in the extended duration.

Lying on his belly in a prone position was fortuitous in that he was not in a more contorted pose that might have quickly become unbearable to maintain. He was even able to prop his head up on the back of his arms, though he did so very slowly and cautiously.

He had no other choice available other than to wait with his equally silent companions, continuing their prolonged vigil at the edge of the forest. Even modest movements were very likely to be seen by the more diligent elements of the marching force. It was nerve-wracking enough worrying about discovery, even being as rigidly still as he was.

Just as Logan grew acclimated to the sight of the marching formation and his nerves had settled a little more, another unexpected, and breathtaking, element manifested. The hairs immediately stood out on the nape of his neck as the first of many utterly strange, fearsome-looking creatures started appearing shortly beyond the mid-way juncture of the huge force's passage.

Even farther out towards the forest from the core of the dense marching column, pacing lithely along the ground, were what looked to be a type of massive, dark-furred cat. The great beasts were noticeably larger than an adult male lion, which was the closest animal that Logan could relate the burly felines to. There were several of the stunning beasts in the first wave to come into view, stepping with feline grace and brimming with powerful muscularity.

The powerful cats' broad heads turned from side to side, their ears twitching separately and reactively, in sharp alertness to every sound. An extensive, wicked-looking set of frontal canines was visible, fully exposed and descending to sharp points just below their great jaws. The veritable daggers gave the creatures an appearance acutely reminiscent of the prehistoric sabretooths whose images Logan had often pored over with fascination as a child.

Proud of posture, the impressive creatures were restrained by long, thick leather cords, attached to iron-studded collars fitted around their ample necks. The leashes were held at the opposite ends in the firm grips of handlers of a very unusual appearance, who jogged effortlessly behind the steady gait of the cats.

The handlers were as fascinating as the great sabretoothed cats, and Logan stared at them in wonder and disbelief. They were of the same race as the small contingent of warriors that came up close behind the first group of great cats. There were around a hundred of the peculiar, bi-pedal creatures in all, including both the handlers and the armed company.

Their appearance was like that of a large rodent that could walk upright, like a human. Their height was many inches shorter than that of average human adults, the taller ones among them being only about five feet tall. A coat of coarse, dark fur fully covered bodies that were lean and sinewy, with long, narrow limbs.

The extraordinary creatures walked with a discernable spring to their every step, evidencing a natural supremacy of agility in relation to their nearby human companions.

The rodent-like creatures, or rat-men, were clad in what looked to be close-fitting, dark tunics that ended just below their midsections,

tied above their hips with narrow hide belts. Their clothing was otherwise scanty, as they wore no type of footwear or other significant pieces of attire. A few hints of smaller adornments, largely in the form of snug-fitting neck rings, could be seen amongst them.

Most of the rat-men carried thin javelins, which they rested in small clusters upon their shoulders as they trotted forward. Others had short quivers affixed to their belts, with strung bows scaled to their more diminutive size that were carried over their shoulders. Simple leather sheaths affixed to their belts held what looked to be lengthy daggers, or perhaps short swords.

Their high-pitched, chittering voices carried faintly across the air to Logan and the others, as the larger company of rat-men passed by their hiding spot, following in the wake of their cat-handling brethren.

While the huge cats and the rat-beings were shocking enough in appearance, it was the presence of a third variety of inhuman creature whose emergence brought Logan's breath to a momentary standstill. He almost had to remind himself to allow air into his lungs, as awed as he was by the newest sight in the column.

Logan could barely believe his own senses, as a group of monstrosities lumbered up into plain sight from the far end of the column. Though few in number, the gigantic brutes would easily have sufficed to serve as a rear guard all by themselves.

Like the rat-men, they were also marching a little farther out to the side of the humans. The enormous creatures trod by the men rapidly, taking huge strides up the flank of the main column. Horses whinnied and snorted in agitation, and many of the men cast fearful glances in the direction of the daunting entities.

The collective presence of the striding juggernauts was awesome to behold, and Logan could not imagine anything that could offer a challenge to such mighty beings. Towering over the tallest of the men, including those mounted upon great steeds, the behemoth creatures moved on powerfully muscled, thick legs that looked to be as stout as tree trunks.

Easily over nine hundred pounds on average, the massive creatures had a dark, greenish outer hide. They were clad in little more than crudely fashioned, short-sleeved hide tunics that extended down to the tops of their bulky knees. The earthen-hued tunics were slit at the sides up to the waist, having a protective quality in that the hide they were fashioned from was thick, and of a toughened constitution.

CROWN OF VENGEANCE

Resting upon bullish necks, their great heads featured elongated snouts, which exhibited thick, short tusks that sprouted prominently up from their lower jaws. Deep-set eyes peered out from underneath pronounced brow ridges. A dense, bristly mane of hair started high on their heads and ran down the back of their necks, giving the creatures a natural crest.

Brawny, bulging arms gripped oversized, single-bladed war axes, or great iron maces with flanged heads, not one of which could have been wielded by the strongest of humans within the entire column. The thick hafts of the mighty weapons rested upon the beasts' broad shoulders as they carried them along.

Logan began to notice that all of the creatures had what looked like great scars running along their upper right arms. He would have attributed the blemishes to the beasts' coarse appearances, if it were not for the fact that many of the creatures had scars bearing an uncannily close resemblance to those of others within their group. To him, there was little chance that the groups of scars sharing very similar shapes were mere coincidences.

The largest among the massive beasts strode at the forefront of the awe-inspiring group. It wore a longer-sleeved hide tunic of a decidedly better craftsmanship, further differentiating the beast from its other hulking brethren.

The exceptional creature glanced back occasionally at the others, glowering, growling angrily, or erupting with a few harsh, unintelligible words.

By their reactions and postures, it was very clear to Logan that the other brutish creatures readily deferred to the greater one's authority. There was absolutely no sign of challenge or resistance to their obvious leader.

Logan had previously noticed that there had been a considerable amount of conversation occurring among the human infantry with the baggage train. Aside from the ordered, more attentive lines of spearmen and crossbowmen to their right, many of the marching men had relaxed expressions and casual postures as they interacted with each other. It was now apparent that most of the humans were greatly discomfited by the close proximity of the huge, bestial warriors.

The humans grew pensively silent, a hush falling over them as they nervously watched the contingent of gigantic creatures, around a dozen in number, tromp heavily by them. Even the throngs of mounted warriors, including the proud-looking ones of a knightly character, seemed to shy away from the beasts by angling their mounts closer to the main column, or spurring themselves farther ahead.

Only when the giant brutes had gone well past them did the humans in the main column begin to resume their interactions again; and even that seemed to be done with great hesitancy.

Packhorses, a great number of lightly clad riders, more throngs of infantry, and a couple more of the mounted contingents with knightly elements followed the baggage train, before the far end of the column came into sight at last.

Logan set his eyes upon the final contingent, feeling a wave of relief pass over him at the recognition of the column's end. He was aching to move his limbs and taut muscles, though he was firmly resolved to remain still until the last of the force had traveled well past his group.

Trotting in formation, and bringing up the rear, the mounted warriors echoed the vanguard in that they had a very cohesive appearance, with a paucity of variation in their attire and equipment.

Most of the riders were garbed in white surcoats, and the rest in black ones, all of which bore the image of a red, upright spear affixed just over the left breast. They carried lances and swords, similar to those in the leading formation. Their limbs were fully covered in mail, with many having added protection on the thighs and knees.

Also like those in the forefront of the column, the warriors of the rearguard displayed a distinctive design upon their numerous pennons, banners, and facings of their wide, triangular shields. Roughly the upper quarter of the banners, pennons, and shields was solid black, with the rest of the ensigns being white.

A slight variant on this arrangement was in evidence, in which the colors were reversed in their position, and equal in proportion to each other. These latter versions contained an additional element, a black spear that was placed atop the white background of the upper half.

The black and white arrangement on the shields, pennons, and banners was combined with the red on white scheme on the rider's white surcoats in the trappers covering their elegant mounts. The red spear image graced the neck and hindquarters on a white portion of the trapper that encompassed the horses' heads, necks, and the upper half of their bodies. The lower half of the equine garb was solid black.

The faces that Logan could see among the men of the final group were uniformly bearded, and of steely countenance, as they rode tall in their saddles, scanning the forest's edge continuously with their eyes.

The rearguard contingent was not overly numerous, soon proceeding by Logan and the others as they left the plains open once again and followed the rest of the great force heading due north. It was still quite some time before there was any hint of movement or discussion among the four observers.

Logan stared off towards the end of the column as it headed away, gradually growing smaller in the distance. The ground still reverberated underneath, but he could tell that vibrations were beginning to ebb in strength.

He was still incredulous at what he had just witnessed over the past few hours. It was as if something of an astonishing nature had been summoned right from the depths of a long-forgotten history, to live and breathe in the world once again. Yet the history that Logan was familiar with did not contain everything that had been present within that huge, marching army.

"I think that we should head back … right now," Logan suggested at long last, speaking in little more than a whisper as the rearguard of the column shrank to the cusp of vanishing from sight, far off to the right.

Logan glanced at his companions, and quickly saw that he had voiced the inner sentiments of the other three with him. He received nods from them in response, with no arguments.

Peering from the ground level, where he was positioned behind the thick, arching roots of one of the trees, Derek held up a hand for the others to wait. He looked away and remained fixated upon the end of the column until it was no longer in sight. All the while, Logan noticed that Derek's jaws were clenched in rigid tension, reflecting an intense level of concentration.

The sight of Derek's great pensiveness helped to mitigate Logan's impatience to fully stretch out his muscles and return back to the campsite. He did not doubt that Derek had a good purpose for his continued delay, trusting to the other's judgment as he was from a military background.

Derek's head then slowly swiveled in the direction where the army had come from, staring off resolutely towards the south for several minutes. To Logan, the passing of those few minutes seemed like hours, but he did not disturb Derek's scrutiny.

"Keep it very slow, and keep it low," Derek finally told the others in a subdued, yet adamant tone, his words unmistakably akin to an order.

"Back up on the ground, and maintain your low profile. Use your whole body, from your knees to your arms. No matter what, no quick movements. We're taking no chances."

Logan did not blame Derek for the extreme caution, his mind still swimming with images of the massive column and its extraordinary non-human elements. Though the column was now well into the distance, the sounds of its passage and the vibrations had not faded entirely. The lingering sensations were good reminders to not let down his guard.

Derek kept up his wary vigil while the others began to move backwards. Crawling upon his belly, Logan wiggled methodically farther and farther back away from outer edges of the forest.

"No quick movements," Derek repeated again as the others carefully progressed. "And don't rise up until I tell you to."

Derek finally began to move back from the last of the trees, after the others had covered a modest distance. He moved a little more quickly, elbows and knees working in efficient concert, and soon caught up to Logan.

"Keep it low, and keep going," Derek reiterated as he slowed down to keep pace with the other three.

Logan glanced over at Derek, and saw that he was staring hard at each of them to convey the gravity of his meaning. He gave a curt nod of acknowledgement to Derek in response.

Mershad and Erika were also faithfully doing as Derek wished, working slowly and meticulously towards the relative concealment of the deeper forest shadows. The wooded depths offered the promise of shielding the quartet from the eyes of anything out on the plains, and Logan could not avail himself of that reassuring shroud of tree and brush a moment too soon.

Logan's heart continued to beat fast as they crept backwards, his renewing fears causing him to half-imagine that shrill cries of discovery would erupt at any given moment. He blanched thinking about one of the green-hided brutes storming down upon him, swinging one of those great iron maces down upon his vulnerable flesh and bones. One thunderous blow from such a huge weapon, wielded with the kind of force that the lumbering hulks were undoubtedly capable of, would reduce him to pulp in an instant.

The group did not cease in their crawling until they were well out of sight of the grassy plains. Logan's elbows were scraped up from the extended, rough contact with the debris-strewn ground. Some small insects had also managed to climb up onto him, which he brushed off vigorously as he felt the tingle of their steps upon his bare arms.

Derek finally signaled to the others that they could safely rise from the ground level. Quietly, they all got up to their feet, took a moment to stretch, and readied to continue back towards their makeshift camp.

It felt good just to stand again, though Logan had to contend with a slight wave of disorientation after having endured such an extended period of rigid concentration in a prone position.

While regaining his equilibrium, Logan was momentarily startled by the sudden flutter of a couple of large ravens. His heart leapt in his chest as the two birds lifted off of a tree branch that he and his companions were crossing under. Seeing the dark birds flying off swiftly into the forest, Logan closed his eyes and breathed out a long sigh of relief. His rattled nerves began to settle back as prepared to resume his forward step, simply glad to see the feathered denizens rather than massive forms bristling with muscles, claws, and sabre-long teeth.

"We can risk a faster pace," Derek then told them, also having twirled about in quick reflex at the abrupt commotion caused by the two sizeable ravens. Logan could see hints of relief reflected in the stoic man's face.

After taking a couple of moments to regroup and regain their composure, the four picked up their pace behind Derek until they were back in a full run. Logan's shoes pounded on the forest floor, as he focused his eyes upon Derek's back at their lead. Ericka was just a few strides behind Derek, with Mershad a short distance in back of Logan. The four covered the remaining ground swiftly.

When they reached their camp, they skittered to a halt. Mershad almost tripped over his feet in the process and slammed into Logan's back. Logan caught and steadied the young man, who was breathing heavily, before turning quickly to the sight that had stunned all of them.

Janus', Antonio's, and Kent's heads snapped about towards the other four with looks of surprise, clearly startled as the four bounded into the camp area. They were gathered around a tall, white-haired old man, clad in a wide-brimmed hat and long, flowing blue robes. The loose-fitting clothing on the old man did not hide the considerable broadness of the stranger's shoulders, made more apparent by his very erect posture and confident disposition. Interestingly, the old man had remained entirely calm when the others had burst into the camp, showing no reaction whatsoever to their sudden emergence.

Logan's first reaction was to look all around the area rapidly, though he quickly discovered that the old man was the only individual outside of his own group within sight. The unexpected encounter disrupted Logan's lingering tensions for only a moment, as the air and ground still carried hints of the army passing towards the north.

Adding to the abrupt mystery, Logan noticed that Derek had a look of recognition upon his face as he looked towards the old man. Showing no signs of alarm at the presence of the stranger, Derek strode over towards Janus and came to stand by his friend's side. Erika and Mershad stood quietly at Logan's side, watching the others with caution.

Logan watched the unfolding scene with growing interest and puzzlement, as the words of the old man cut through the air.

"Forces in thrall to the Unifier pass near to you, though others would say that those are Gallean forces. In truth, they are all of the Unifier, in this darkening age," the old man stated, his words carrying a distinct tinge of distaste. "You must not tarry in this place much longer, lest you fall into their hands. Go to the east. Others of a different mind will be found there. Ones who can be of help."

The old man then turned to face the newcomers who yet kept their distance, stepping slowly towards Erika, Mershad, and Logan. He moved with an easy, effortless step, showing no sign of infirmity or frailty despite his seemingly ancient years.

Logan found himself staring right into the old man's lone blue eye, for the other was fully covered by a patch. Logan could not read the expression of the stranger, as the old man's mouth was nestled within an abundance of white that descended to his upper chest.

The transfixing gaze appeared to be generating a jeweled sparkle within its cerulean depths, a timeless evocation that belied the apparent age of the stranger's physical appearance. It was a look brimming with vitality, alertness, and wisdom, and the stranger's seemingly advanced years were as nothing in context of the ageless look reflected in that single, mesmerizing eye.

Logan tried to concentrate upon the old man, but found that it was increasingly difficult to gather his thoughts, as if his mental focus was slipping, and swiftly becoming hazy. For no explicable reason, the new development did not frighten Logan in the least. If anything, he felt an absence of danger in the immediate presence of the old man, and even his badly shaken nerves were bolstered by the inexplicable placidity that washed over him.

"And you three, with your friend over there, have all seen the strength of the Unifier's forces for yourselves. Your own eyes do not lie. You saw what you saw, a river of power that is nothing compared to the vast seas of power beyond it," the old man stated firmly, his voice deep and resonant.

"The Unifier?" Derek responded from next to Janus, "Who is the Unifier? And where is that army going?"

"Some would say those forces herald the genesis of a new order, brought forth out of the lands of Avanor, a land far to the west from where you now stand. The truly wise would see something from a much older order, one more ancient than the world itself," the blue-robed man explained somberly. "The Unifier. ... A leader cloaked in fair countenance, attractive and charming to all who behold Him, but wielding a terrible, dominating force that comes from the very depths of the Abyssal Realms themselves."

The old man paused, and his countenance darkened, as if contemplating a particularly troubling thought. When he continued again, his voice was lower, and his tone deeply solemn.

"And the true wisdom is this; the Unifier is just a steward. He is a steward of another far more powerful Entity ... though very few in this world, in lands under His influence, would be willing to say so openly. And still others are foolish enough to embrace Him knowingly, even aware that He is a steward, and conscious of the One that He is a steward for. Such are the ones who are most steeped in madness within this troubled world."

"And the army we just saw?" Derek prodded insistently. "Where are they headed to?"

"The lands that you are in, right now," the old man replied without hesitation.

"Then we should get the hell out of here, it would seem to me," Derek stated tersely. He glanced to the three that had remained behind in the camp, Janus, Kent, and Antonio, his next words directed squarely at them. "We just saw an entire army march by at the edge of the woods. You probably wouldn't believe me, but it was like something right out of a medieval time. Spears, armor, horses, swords ... even knights ... all that, and more. Things you probably won't believe at first. It was an enormous army, thousands and thousands strong, and it was the source of all the noise and shaking that we all experienced."

"Things I wouldn't believe?" Janus asked him. "What do you mean?"

Derek hesitated, and when he answered Janus, his voice took on a tension that Logan had not heard within it before.

"There were ... creatures...." Derek said, his brow furrowing, as if it was difficult for him to make the declaration. "Of kinds that I have no idea what they were. I still can't believe what I just saw, but I saw it, and so did Erika, Mershad, and Logan. We can't deny it. And I do know that we don't want to run into any of these creatures. Not in the least."

The old man held his hand up, drawing everyone's immediate attention.

"Before you worry yourself too much, that army will not come in here just yet," he stated. "They are still assembling, gathering, and preparing for what will come. The Unifier's hunger turns to the last lands that will not bend their knees to Him in submission, but know that those forces that you saw will not move on these woodlands just yet. You still have some time, and you will need what I have come here to give you."

The old man had a large pouch affixed to the belt at his waist, from which he withdrew a number of small amulets hanging from thin, hide necklaces. Logan noticed that a radiant golden ring, inlaid with a spectacular blue gemstone, rested upon one of the old man's long fingers.

The elongated, thin leather strips of hide procured from the leather pouch were each threaded through a metallic amulet. The amulet looked to be crafted of iron, inlaid with a small blue gemstone that was of the same kind as that on the old man's ring.

The stone on the old man's finger was large and round, while each of the stones in the amulets was cut into a very unique shape. The stones were nearly in the form of the letter "F," with a distinctive difference. The two horizontal lines extending to the right of the vertical line were parallel, but slanted downward in a diagonal fashion.

The metal that the blue stones were set into framed them exquisitely, closely following the outer contours of the shaped stones. The complete pendants, including both stone and setting, were not overly large. Each could fit comfortably into the palm of a person's hand.

"Take these, and wear them, at all times. They will help to get you through this time and place," the old man announced, extending the first one towards Mershad.

Mershad accepted it a little gingerly, holding it out in front of him as he peered intently at the strange amulet. The old man moved onward, bestowing one necklace upon each member of the remaining group, until seven of the amulets had been distributed in all.

When he was finished passing out the necklaces, he advised them, "Walk this land with caution, and always be wary, for these are the most perilous of times for the world of Ave."

The name of the new world sounded so graceful and elegant to Logan's ears, pronounced 'ah-vay' by the elderly man. He wondered whether it carried the same meaning as a Latin word from his own world.

The words of caution from the old man were not necessary. Logan was not about to let his guard down, though he regarded it as unbelievably bad fortune if he and the others had truly stepped into another world that was wreathed in its most perilous age.

"Who are … you? And why … would you bother to help us?" Erika interjected, with a little strain in her voice, as if the question took a very conscious effort to utter. Logan could read confusion and mild exasperation on her face, as if she was struggling with herself.

She had asked what was probably the most obvious of questions, the one that should have been on the tips of all seven of their tongues. Yet not one of them had asked it, and Erika had only done so with evident difficulty.

Even as she voiced the question, Logan took notice that his nerves were indeed dulled. He knew that he should be feeling much more guarded and scrupulous in the face of an enigmatic stranger, especially one passing out distinctively shaped amulets fitted with blue gemstones. Yet it was as if he could not gain a tight enough grip upon his own thoughts to be concerned with what was transpiring. The mere sight of the old man seemed to be instantly soothing and reassuring, and there was no feeling of alarm anywhere within Logan.

The old man smiled gently at Erika, with the kindly warmth of a caring grandfather.

"It is good to be overly cautious in this age," he responded in an amiable tone. "I am a friend, one who has been waiting for those such as you for a very, very long time. I only wish to be of help to you, the truth of which you all will know in a time to come.

"As I said to Janus yesterday, it is best that you limit your questions now, as any answers will only open up far more questions than you are ready to grapple with. Such is the true nature of knowledge, and what the seven of you are now being faced with could overwhelm you, if you are not careful. Heed my advice; take this journey a small step at a time."

The others exchanged mystified glances with each other at the strange answer. Logan looked towards Janus, and then back to Derek, as full realization struck him. He understood then that this old man was the unusual figure that they had mentioned encountering soon after their arrival out of the mists.

Kent, who Logan also knew had seen the old man before, then asked the stranger, "I don't understand any of this. And it sounds like you aren't going to help us clear things up quickly … but don't you at least have a name we can call you?"

The old man smiled again, and for a moment there was an amused glitter within his eye.

"Not all things at once, my young friend," the stranger replied evenly. "I am simply a Wanderer through this wide world. One that has long sought wisdom, and has paid a great price for gaining it."

The old man looked slowly around to each of the seven gathered around him. The others all remained silent and mindful, and even Kent did not offer objection to the unsatisfying answer to his question. The stranger seemed to be able to hold onto their undivided attention with merely a glance.

He uttered no other words, as his scrutiny finally ended with Logan. The encompassing gaze notably remained with Logan for a few seconds longer than it had with the others. Logan could not fathom why that was so, though the extended attention seemed very peculiar to him.

"You will be given guidance soon enough," he told all of them, as he swept his gaze across all of their faces.

As if some kind of hold had been lifted, Logan felt the clarity of his thoughts begin to sharpen. With a sparkle in his eye, the old man turned away from them and started off into the woods with his long robes flowing about him.

His parting words carried back to them.

"Wear my gifts about your necks. They will bring you understanding. You will need them, if you wish to gain answers faster."

Snapping fully out of the trance-like state, Logan regained mastery over the rest of his senses. He watched with amazement until the old man was out of sight, bewildered by the whole encounter.

"Hey, I wonder how much this would go for. Have to get a jewelry shop to price this one out when we get back," Kent quipped.

His jesting words broke the awkward silence weighing heavy in the air, as Kent casually looped his pendant around his neck. Grinning wide, Kent added, "So, do I look like a good model for this? Gotta be worth a little money ... I'm sure of it."

"But it won't be worth much if we get caught around here," Logan stated.

A darker expression rose upon his face as he looked off in the direction where the old man had headed in. His mind filled again with vivid images of the enormous army, most especially the massive saber-toothed cats, the rat-men, and the burly monstrosities with their huge, wicked-looking axes.

"Are we all losing our minds? Why trust him?" Logan questioned the others. "Why trust anyone? What do we really know? But I think we do need to get a move on things here."

Derek's expression was very austere, as he looked over to Janus and Kent. "That was definitely the old man we saw yesterday ... did he say anything else to you when we were gone?"

Janus nodded. "No doubt, it was the same man. He had appeared to us right before the four of you returned. I have no idea why he has such an interest in us, but he appears to be trying to help. He doesn't seem to be dangerous, and if he was, wouldn't he have done something yesterday, or just now?"

Derek shrugged, "Don't ask me. Nothing makes sense anymore."

"We should get going," Logan interjected. "Medieval army or strange old man, I'm not about to trust anything or anyone. Derek's right. Nothing makes sense."

"I sure can't make much sense out of what that man said. I wish I had asked him some more questions. It was like my mind grew sluggish, and I couldn't think of much to say," Erika said, accurately describing the sensation that Logan had felt throughout the encounter. "It was all I could do to just to ask him who he was. Like I had to force the words out of my mouth."

She fingered her necklace for a moment, gazing down at the deep blue gemstone. Her glance prompted Logan to turn his attention to his

own.

It appeared to be safe enough, a simple pendant of metal and gemstone. With a shrug, Logan finally slipped it on around his own neck. Looking back up, Logan was about to make another comment, when he saw the forest come alive all around them.

Seemingly out of nowhere, to their sides, to the front, and to the back of them, a large number of lithely moving figures emerged right from the trees and shadows themselves. All of them were armed, bearing various types of weapons, and their attentions were resolutely fixed upon Logan and his companions.

In appearance and attire, they were nothing like the ones that Logan had recently witnessed, comprising the huge column marching out on the plains. If anything, they immediately reminded him of the native peoples of his own country.

The weapons were poised for use, bringing a clenching feeling to Logan's gut as the air swarmed with tension.

A good number of the warriors surrounding them held curving, wooden clubs of war. The gracefully cut, slender arching shafts ended in dense, rounded balls of solid wood. Some of the shafts were carved to resemble serpents or other animals, whose open jaws cradled the orbs of wood at their ends. On others, the facing of the spherical ends had been carved into the visage of a human face.

A few of the warriors had feather-fletched arrows notched on bows, which were partially drawn back and trained directly upon their targets; Logan and his six companions. Logan took uneasy account of more than one sharp iron arrowhead pointed coldly and impassively at his own body. The feeling was deeply unsettling, like nothing that he had ever experienced before.

Still other warriors bore axes with hafts of modest length, weapons clearly designed to be wielded with one arm. The hafts were fitted at their ends with small, single-edged blades of iron that had a slender horizontal profile. The axe blades gleamed dangerously as they reflected the sunlight breaking through the leaves of the trees above them.

Short bone-handled knives were suspended down the center of many of the figures' chests, encased within sheaths graced with intricate quill-work and fringes of metal-banded tassels lining the openings.

The warriors themselves were very simply garbed. Though some wore longer hide tunics on their upper bodies, most were bare of chest.

The latter were clad with some type of buckskin waist-skirt, not unlike a kilt, or a hide or woolen breechcloth that ran through their legs, looping up and over a waist belt. All wore hide leggings to the mid-thigh, and had moccasins covering their feet.

Their faces and exposed skin were covered in painted strips of red and black. Slightly obscured by the striping were a plethora of tattooed designs, some of recognizable animal or nature designs, and others geometric patterns.

The warriors did exhibit a considerable amount of ornamentation, as bands of quill-decorated hide, feathers, or small shell beads, wrapped around their upper arms or at the knees, were quite prevalent amongst them. Earrings and nose rings were in regular evidence, some of the former being substantial, looping designs made of shell. A few had their ears adorned with puffy, globular adornments of swan down.

There was a complete lack of facial hair on the men, and even their heads were largely shorn of hair. Most wore styles with thick tufts sprouting atop their heads, the centered tufts decorated with feathers or other smaller items.

Their facial features, on the average, were very angular in nature, with high-set cheekbones and prominent noses, lending many of them an almost hawk-like profile. Their dark eyes were piercing and humorless. Almost all had leaner, sinewy bodies, infused with a well-defined muscularity.

Logan and the others instinctively grouped together in a circle, facing outward with their backs to each other. He could not see any other clear options, as they were completely surrounded by the stern-looking warriors. It was certainly not in their interest to profess to fight.

"Stay where you are!" one of the nearest of the warriors commanded them in a hard, resolute tone.

Despite the black and red paint, and several tattoos, the warrior had a very handsome visage. He possessed a balanced symmetry to his wide, expressive eyes, full lips, and slightly broader nose, which complimented an ovular face. He was among the taller of the surrounding warriors, with a sculpted body that brought out his well-defined chest and bulging shoulder muscles.

He was every inch the image of strength and vitality, and definitely did not look like the kind of man that one would want to cross. Logan looked slowly to the others with him, seeing looks of utter confusion on the faces of some, and comprehension on the faces of others.

"Who are you? Why are you in these lands?" the figure then inquired, with manifest caution underlying his insistent manner.

"My name is Erika," Erika then responded, "and we really don't know where we are, why we are here, or even what is happening."

Logan glanced towards his companions again.

The perplexity had seemed to increase on the faces of those who had looked the most confused when the warrior had initially spoken. They were eyeing Erika sharply, and Logan could see the questioning look in their gazes.

It was then that he took note that the ones wearing the pendants, like himself and Erika, looked to be the most comfortable. A distinct thought came to him, but he was not yet ready to try and test it. A throng of fierce-looking warriors of unknown intent, bristling with weapons, prompted him to severe caution. He did not want to make one comment or gesture that would be misconstrued to an unfavorable result. Nobody had to tell them that their lives were hanging in the balance.

"I'm Kent," Kent replied nervously, after Erika had spoken, his eyes wide with anxiety. He suddenly stammered out, "We don't know where we are, and if we trespassed, we did not mean it. She's right, we don't know what's happening here."

The others remained quiet, staying rigidly in place. The ones without the pendants on continued to look dumbfounded, and appeared to be growing increasingly worried.

Only Derek did not look to be overly ruffled by the unexpected developments unfolding all around them, his eyes constantly roving among the warriors. From what Logan had come to know of Derek, he surmised that his disciplined companion was carefully assessing the warriors' intentions. He wished that he could ask Derek what his initial impressions of them were.

Logan pondered some of the thoughts tugging more strongly upon his mind. He had found it very intriguing that the old stranger in the blue garments, clearly a native to this strange world, had spoken the language of Logan's group without any difficulty. It was even more curious that these woodland warriors spoke Logan's own tongue so fluently.

Logan was not about to believe that everyone within an entirely new world spoke his language. Something very strange was occurring.

He glanced down at the blue stone pendant, as comprehension

advanced in his mind. Though he knew he was taking a risk, he felt that he had to alert his companions that had not yet donned the amulets. The exchange with the surrounding warriors was tenuous at best, and Logan wanted everyone to be able to answer if questioned.

"It's something with the pendants," he whispered to Janus, Derek, and Antonio. "Trust me."

The others looked towards him with puzzlement. Even Derek's brow furrowed at Logan's words.

The warrior addressing them abruptly looked to Logan with a sharp gaze, before glancing back quickly to Erika. Logan froze in place, hoping that his whisper had not provoked the warrior.

The warrior then looked past all of them, towards a couple of warriors that had just emerged from the woods. The two were now standing directly opposite him, on the other side of the trapped group.

"They do not wield the dark magic," one of the pair of emerging warriors proclaimed, holding out what appeared to be a large quartz crystal for all to see in his right hand. He stared intently at its glittering surface, before looking back up again. He nodded and continued in a confident tone. "I am sure of it. The woman is not a witch, and the men are not shamans. They do not use the dark magic."

The first warrior that had addressed them, the one that clearly appeared to be the band's leader, looked back to Logan's group. His steely look echoed the unyielding tension in the air as he silently regarded them.

"Who are you? What are you doing in these woods?" he demanded. "Each of you, speak your answer."

"I am Erika, and I do not know how I came to be here," Erika answered, the first of the seven to venture a response.

"My name is Kent … McNeeley. And it is no different with me," Kent stated nervously. "I have no idea where we are right now, or how we got here. I swear. That's the truth."

Logan and Mershad answered similarly, but when it came to the last three in their group, there was an uncomfortable pause. Janus, Antonio, and Derek looked both confused and incredulous.

A look of frustration quickly grew upon the leader's face during the uneasy delay. He turned his attention back towards Erika, even as Logan whispered to the remaining three.

"Just tell them your name, and why we are here," he urged.

The leader of the warriors whipped about, and riveted immediately upon Logan.

"They heard me as easily as you did. Why do they not answer me?" the warrior challenged Logan. "Tell your companions to answer. Your lives may depend on it. We will take no chances here."

As if for emphasis, he raised up the axe gripped in his hand, his chiseled arm muscles flexing at the movement. Logan had little doubt as he watched the fluid movement that the warrior was well-seasoned with the deadly weapon.

Logan imagined the axe hurling forward in a flash, its blade embedding deep in the warrior's intended target. He certainly did not want that gleaming axe-head to be lodged in his own flesh and bone.

"I don't know, but I have an idea why they cannot answer you," Logan replied quickly, trying to keep his timbre as respectful as he could. "They cannot understand you, as we can."

He hoped against hope that the hard-looking warrior deemed his tone to be polite enough. He looked to the three without the pendants, his mind still very conscious of the sharp edge of the axe gripped in the warrior's right hand.

There was no harm in answering the question that had been asked, and they were not in any position to bargain.

"Tell him your names. Answer him," Logan insisted, looking to the other three. "Do you not understand him?"

Derek shook his head first, followed by Antonio and Janus.

"Not a word," Derek confessed tersely. "I do not know how you are speaking with them. They don't speak our language."

"What did he say?" the leader of the warriors questioned Logan curtly, heightened agitation flowing within his words.

Logan looked back to the warrior, becoming more certain of his analysis. Derek had spoken loud enough to be easily heard by the leader, but it was quite apparent that the leader had not understood him.

"He doesn't understand you, and he doesn't understand why we can understand you," Logan offered to the leader carefully, whose impassive expression did not change with the answer.

Derek then asked Logan in a low voice, "How do you understand him?"

"Put the pendants on," Logan instructed him. He turned back towards the leader. "I think we can speak with you, because of these...."

He slowly brought up his right hand and fingered the blue stone resting upon his chest, lifting it up to display the object to the leader. The hardened warrior seemed to be further perplexed, and his eyes narrowed as he stared intently at the amulet. It was the most significant reaction yet that Logan had seen from the leader, and his interest in the pendant was very evident.

"I do not understand this. I understand you, the woman, and the other two. I see that all understand you when you speak. But you speak in our language. And these three do not understand us, and I do not understand their speech," the figure said, his words outlining the confusing scenario.

The leader's eyes flicked between the four wearing the pendants and the other three who were not. He seemed to be searching and studying them at the same time, his brow furrowing more in the intensity of his gaze.

"It must be some kind of magic, but they are not witches, shaman, or sorcerers. My vision is the same as that of Eagle Spirit. There is no dark magic here," the second warrior that had emerged from behind Logan with a quartz crystal emphasized.

The lead warrior looked solemnly towards the crystal-bearing warrior, before quietly continuing in his scrutiny of Logan's group. He regarded them for a few more minutes, which seemed like hours to Logan.

As if he came to the same understanding that Logan had reached, the leader stated at last, "Have them place the necklaces on. We will see if you speak truly."

Logan passed on the directive from the warrior, with his own addendum. "Put your pendants on, but do it slowly."

The others cooperated, and carefully donned their amulets, looking back to Logan, the warrior-leader, and all the others when they had done so.

"I will ask you again, who are you? Do you serve the Unifier?" the leader asked the trio.

Though a part of him had fully expected the reaction, Logan was still amazed as he saw the wonder dawning upon the faces of the others, as they suddenly comprehended the warrior's words. In that moment, Logan knew that the strange old man in the blue robes had rendered each of them a most valuable gift. Yet whether the stranger had given it to them for reasons of good or for ill, Logan could still not tell for sure.

Presently, the gift was unquestionably an extraordinary blessing. The fact that the presence of the pendants also seemed acceptable, or at least tolerable, to the armed warriors surrounding them was certainly not a detriment either. Eyeing the arrows trained upon them, as well as the axes and the formidable-looking war clubs, Logan did not want to fathom what might have befallen his group had it been otherwise.

The implications of it all were unfolding quickly upon him. However inexplicable, a genuine type of magic was at work. The realization staggered Logan's mind.

"No, we don't serve any Unifier, and I don't even know who this Unifier is," Derek replied slowly, the echoes of his astonishment lingering in his face. "We are lost, far from our own world. I don't even know where we are right now."

An energetic murmur rippled through the gathering of warriors as they heard Derek speak. Logan could see their amazement, knowing that they understood his words after he had put on the pendant.

Janus and Antonio then voiced their agreement with Derek. As if it was an afterthought, all three then proceeded to give their names to the leader.

"Where did you get those?" the leader questioned the group, gesturing towards the amulets that had so evidently enabled their ability to converse.

"A stranger to us. An old man, with a long white beard and dressed in blue robes. He wore a patch over one eye, and would not give us his name," Erika replied. "He only said that he was a wanderer through this world. He is the only person we have met since we have been here."

Logan's apprehension grew as Erika spoke, hoping that the strange old man was not by some ill twist of fate a great enemy of these warriors. The only thing that now existed in Logan's world was the expression of the leader's face, as he tensely awaited the man's reaction to Erika's statement.

To Logan's great relief, the warrior's posture relaxed, even to the point that there was the hint of a smile on his otherwise indifferent face.

"So, the Wanderer favors you. That is a good sign indeed," the leader commented, his lightened tone reflecting the visible ebb of tautness from his face.

"What about the army we saw back there?" Logan ventured cautiously, casting a glance back towards the west. "Who were they?"

Several looks were exchanged among the surrounding warriors.

The leader tensed again at the mention of the army, and for a moment Logan feared that he had just blundered into making an unnecessary provocation.

Fortunately, the leader's face settled back once again, after a moment's pause.

"I might ask you the same question," the leader replied somberly. "The Unifier brings many from other lands. Some from very far away. I see clearly that you are not of our land. What are we to think? Yet the Wanderer favors you greatly. He could not be fooled by the arts of the Unifier. And if you worked the dark magic, the crystals would not be deceived. I do not yet understand any of this...."

The last words seemed like an exasperated confession, as the leader fell into an extended silence. Logan could see the frustration plainly enough upon the warrior's face, and knew that he and the others were not yet out of danger.

Derek then declared, "We have nothing to do with that army back there. Not one thing. Honest. We have no idea about what that army is, what it is about, or where it is going. We truly know nothing. We simply heard its passage when we awoke this morning, and went to see what it was."

"See if any have the markings," the leader urged, addressing some of the warriors to his right.

The indicated warriors stepped forward without hesitation, directly approaching the seven. Logan and his companions offered them no resistance, as the warriors grasped their wrists with firm grips, looking very closely and carefully at their bare arms. Logan wondered what they could possibly be searching for, as he continued to cooperate fully with the unexplained inspection.

"Nothing," one of the other warriors reported at last. "None of them bear the markings."

At the warrior's response, the leader let a small smile emerge. The grip on the shaft of his axe noticeably relaxed, as he lowered it down slowly to rest at his side.

"That is another good sign. It seems more likely that you are speaking the truth. For those pledged in full loyalty to the Unifier bear the markings, and it is certain that you are at least not one of them," the leader said, his tone considerably warmer. "I did not think that the Wanderer could be deceived, especially by a dedicated servant of the Unifier. Such a taint cannot escape the Wanderer's gaze."

The leader hesitated, and his voice took on a more somber tone, as the slight smile faded into a stony mien. His eyes flitted between all of them, not meeting their eyes, but looking lower on their bodies.

"But there is still so much about you that is unknown. Your strange garments are different than anything I have ever seen. Not in any of my travels have I seen such garments.

"I once journeyed to large trade gatherings in the great city of Carcasse, within Gallea. Garments from far places in this world were traded there, yet nothing like those that you now wear."

The leader's voice then took on the air of a rendered judgement, as his gaze rose back up to meet theirs.

"As there is much that we do not understand about you, all of you must return with us to our village. You have not yet been found to be enemies, and as such, you will be treated as guests, with honor. You will receive food and shelter in our village, but you may not travel free until the Council says that you can do so."

His eyes narrowed to a penetrating glare, the lines on his face becoming as rigid as stone. "But if you are liars about your purpose and allegiances, you will not walk alive from these woods."

Logan had no doubts at all that the leader and his surrounding warriors could fulfill that grim pronouncement quite capably, and swiftly.

The leader looked off towards the west, as if he was taking momentary notice of the distant, marching army. The rumbles were not entirely gone, though the very faint sensations had dwindled to the brink of becoming completely imperceptible.

"You shall walk with us, as we must go from here now," the leader stated firmly, turning back to them.

He gestured for Logan and the others to approach him, as the full group of warriors gathered closer together, in apparent readiness to move onward.

"I am called Ayenwatha," he introduced himself. "And know that you are considered guests of the Onan tribe, one of the tribes of the Five Realms of the Sacred Fire."

At a signal from Ayenwatha, the combined group then moved out, proceeding deeper into the forest towards the east. Logan was simply glad that they were heading away from the direction where the marching army had been, relieved to be putting some distance between his group and the massive force.

The ground underfoot finally carried no more traces of the army, and the tranquil sounds of the living forest filled the air once again. The wind flowed through the leaves of the trees overhead, creating brief openings that sprinkled rays of sunlight onto the lower growths, which were inundated with snowy white flowers. Had circumstances been otherwise, Logan would have rapidly found himself taken in by the timeless serenity reigning all around him.

Ayenwatha remained close to where Logan walked alongside Janus, just ahead of their other five companions. Logan chanced a look back towards the others. None looked to be the worse for wear. He exchanged a glance with Antonio, who gave him a rueful grin.

Logan discovered that each of the seven members of his group had a tribal warrior striding close behind them, as they traveled in a loose column through the woods. The implications were clear enough. The seven might well be considered guests, but their escorts were taking no chances.

He was not about to do anything to provoke the black and red painted warriors. He had already espied some grisly mementos being carried by a few of them. Bloodied swathes of skin, with locks of hair still attached, hung from the hide belts of those that bore them along.

Logan had a fairly good idea of what it meant to be considered as an enemy of the tribal warriors.

JANUS

The leader of the band of warriors gradually eased into open conversation with Janus and the others as they continued forth through the sprawling forest. Janus listened with great interest to Ayenwatha's words, hoping to learn a little bit more about the lands within the new world around him.

Their new host, Ayenwatha, was a war leader within his Onan tribe, referred to among his people as a war sachem. The Onan, in turn, were part of a broader alliance of five great tribes.

That alliance, called the Five Realms, had come together for common protection and fellowship long ago, under the guidance of a very wise individual, named Deganawida, who was deeply revered by all the tribes.

Ayenwatha also informed them that he was of the Firaken clan, reflecting no small amount of pride in his expression and voice. Though Janus did not have the first idea as to what a Firaken was, or what it meant to be in such a clan, he could sense that clan affiliation was a very important element of the tribal society.

Janus was also able to glean more about the enigmatic figure known as the Unifier. Ayenwatha's tone was little different than that of the old wanderer when he was speaking of the highly mysterious Unifier.

There was no mistaking the bitter hatred that Ayenwatha felt towards the Unifier, an animosity that clearly reflected the feelings of all the tribal warriors. To Ayenwatha's knowledge, the Five Realms were one of the few civilizations remaining in the whole known world that still remained openly opposed to the Unifier.

Ayenwatha related that a state of war had recently arisen between the Five Realms and the followers of the Unifier, who would accept nothing less than the utter submission of his people. The Five Realms had long before rejected the Unifier's overtures to seek the tribes' loyalty to Him, which Ayenwatha described as a tacit demand to submit fully to the Unifier's authority.

A stark, more overtly worded demand recently delivered to the tribes had been refused outright by their Grand Council. It was a fateful rejection, which the tribal sachems had known would likely conjure up a violent, raging storm upon their own people.

As luck would have it, Janus and his companions had come into the tribal lands just as those storm clouds were building to the verge of bursting. That fully explained the extreme caution displayed by the warriors when they had emerged to confront Janus' group.

Ayenwatha informed Janus and the others that his Onan war party had been shadowing the army that they had witnessed from the edge of the forest.

The large force's appearance along their borders, Ayenwatha believed, was the sign that an invasion was imminent. Ayenwatha surmised that the force was making its way towards a position central to the westernmost borders of the tribal lands, a place that also afforded access to ample amounts of fresh water in the forms of a sizeable lake and attendant streams.

According to Ayenwatha, it was an ideal locale for a massive number of warriors and animals, putting the enemy force in an advantageous position where they were well-poised to cleave through the heart of the tribal lands.

Janus learned that the bordering kingdom where this force had mustered and come from was called Gallea. According to Ayenwatha, it was just one of many strong kingdoms that had implicitly submitted their authority to the Unifier.

Janus could tell that Ayenwatha greatly lamented the impending conflict. The war sachem remarked that Gallea had not always shown such outward hostility to his people. Ayenwatha spoke with a very conspicuous sense of wonder about a great Gallean city called Carcasse, which he had once been to in earlier, and more peaceful, times. He described with unmistakable admiration how the city was surrounded with high stone walls, and many prominent towers, filled with traders and guests from all over the Gallean realm and far beyond.

The tribes had until fairly recently enjoyed a steady trade with the Galleans, as there was evidently a large demand in the Gallean markets for beaver furs. In return, the tribes had regularly obtained many iron implements, such as cooking pots, axe, arrow, and spear heads, and knife blades.

Ayenwatha spoke with outright fascination of other massive, stone-walled fortresses that he had seen on his journeys into the Gallean lands. These were not cities, he explained, but rather where the Gallean sachems, as he called the Gallean leaders, resided with their families.

Ayenwatha held a high and very respectful regard for his tribe's powerful neighbor. It was obviously a point of considerable distress that Gallea had fully enjoined with the Unifier, enough such that it was gathering its military might to threaten and beset Ayenwatha's woodland people.

Derek had then interjected into the discussion, querying Ayenwatha regarding the non-humans that he, Logan, Erika, and Mershad had seen marching with the great enemy force.

The presence of non-human races had been an incredible revelation, one that greatly intrigued Janus, as he had remained behind in the camp when the others had gone forth to investigate the source of the tremors. He too wanted to learn a little more about the strange beasts that Derek, Logan, Mershad, and Erika had seen and described.

From the snippets of their descriptions and other comments, Janus had been able to cobble together a rough mental image of the unusual denizens of this new, mystifying world. As Ayenwatha elaborated in response to Derek's inquiry, that picture became much more clear.

The non-humans that Derek and the three others had seen amongst the marching forces were not from Gallea, but had been summoned from other, faraway lands. Like the Galleans, they were each just another part of the enormous coalition being gathered under the Unifier's dominion.

The rat-like beings were called Atagar, from a distant land called Yanith. They were reputed to be nimble, formidable fighters, highly-suited to a forest environment as they occupied one themselves back in their native lands. With their natural abilities, it had come as little surprise to Ayenwatha that they had been brought in for an attack upon the woodland tribes.

The cat-like creatures with the extensive canines that accompanied the Atagar also came from Yanith. Not unlike war dogs used by humans, these creatures, called Licanthers, were raised and trained by the Atagar to serve as guardians, companions, and living weapons of war.

Hearing about the fearsome Licanthers, Janus was not sure that he ever wanted to see one within any short distance of himself. It was disconcerting enough just to know that such fantastical entities truly existed, and were not simply beasts of myth or legend.

The massive, brutish creatures witnessed by Janus' companions were called Gigans. Ayenwatha explained that they were native to the north-central regions along the borders of a very large realm called Kiruva, a place that Ayenwatha claimed he knew little about. As a whole, the Gigans were still fairly unfamiliar to the tribal people, but Janus could tell that Ayenwatha was not eager to discover all of the attributes of the hulking race.

It was hard for Janus to envision these weapon-wielding behemoths, but he could tell that Derek had been entirely awed by them. That was enough to daunt Janus, as Derek was not one to be easily impressed.

Janus also learned that the Five Realms were not likely to be the only ones that were imminently coming under the shadow of assault from the Unifier. From some trading exchanges with other people still friendly to the Five Realms, Ayenwatha had learned that the far-reaching power of the Unifier was already moving to conquer another large kingdom that had steadfastly refused Him.

It was a realm located across the waters of the ocean to the south of the Five Realms, called the Kingdom of Saxany.

The Unifier, from His citadel in Avanor, had also begun turning

His eyes towards a land known as Midragard. Janus could sense the marked distress that Ayenwatha felt at this prospect in particular, quickly recognizing that Ayenwatha felt an affinity for the Midragardans.

The people of Midragard were apparently masters of the oceans, great seafarers whose main homelands were located much farther to the south. They had numerous settlements stretching far beyond the main lands of Midragard, even including some on islands located just offshore of the Five Realms to the east.

The seafaring people, according to Ayenwatha, were legendary warriors and traders, whose travels in war and trade had taken them to many foreign lands.

Once ferocious raiders of the tribal lands, the Midragardans were now in a longstanding state of friendship with the five tribes. The enmity that formerly existed between Ayenwatha's people and the Midragardans had ebbed over time, finally disappearing as open trade replaced violence.

The relationship had grown strong, bringing the Five Realms more than just material items of trade. The Midragardans brought Ayenwatha word of rumors and happenings from many distant lands. It had been Midragardans that had brought Ayenwatha the tidings of war involving Saxany.

While Janus could sense that such reports were troubling enough to Ayenwatha, he understood that the sachem's own concerns were very immediate in nature. Ayenwatha's war party had been tracking and shadowing the marching army beyond the border for the better part of the last two days. Prior to encountering Janus' group, the war band had been very close to returning back to the Onan village called the Place of Far Seeing, where the eternal Sacred Fire of the Five Realms was kept. This village, as Janus learned, also happened to be Ayenwatha's own home village.

Ayenwatha's war party been sent out by the village to learn everything that they could of the enemy forces, in order to gain as much information as possible for the consideration of future councils.

There had been some fighting over the course of the two days, though none of the enemy that had been encountered by Ayenwatha's band had escaped the forest. Janus had seen the evidence of those melees in the form of the gruesome scalps being carried by a few of the warriors.

It had been late in that very morning that the war party had become aware of the seven humans' presence within the woods. They had come upon their campsite not long thereafter.

Derek perked up and drew closer when Ayenwatha spoke of how the war party had fanned out and quickly surrounded the campsite, moving into place right after the Wanderer, as Ayenwatha referred to the old man, had departed. Oddly, they had not encountered the Wanderer as they had closed in and encircled the seven foreigners, though there were only a handful of moments between the old man's departure and their emergence. Once they had taken their positions, Ayenwatha's warriors had been content to stay concealed for a few more moments, as they observed the unusually attired, strange interlopers.

Janus was sure that the revelation of the warriors' successful encroachment and surveillance was of great interest to his friend, who prided himself on his own senses and acute alertness.

"A whole war party … encircled us, and crept up, without anything seeming remotely amiss," Derek murmured to Janus, the appreciation for the skills of the tribal warriors very evident in his voice.

Janus realized how lucky they were to all be wearing their own clothes. As Ayenwatha explained it, their unfamiliar attire was the sole factor that had stayed the hand of the war band from killing them outright. Their highly unusual clothing had prevented the tribal warriors from instantly mistaking the seven to be some sort of scouting offshoot from the nearby enemy forces.

After the brief observation, Ayenwatha had come to the fortunate decision that there was a real possibility that Janus and his companions were not aligned with the forces of the Unifier. It was at that juncture that Ayenwatha and the warriors had made their presence known.

The thought of how precariously close Janus and the others from his world had come to dying that day was quite sobering to contemplate.

Janus and his companions were not the only ones hungry for new information. It did not take long for Ayenwatha to begin probing for answers to his own questions, regarding the seven and their recent experiences.

Janus related in detail his own interactions with the Wanderer. It was clear that the tribal people regarded the Wanderer with great esteem, holding a deep respect for his wisdom in particular.

While frustrating to Janus, Ayenwatha offered nothing specific about the old man's nature, even though Janus could clearly sense that there was much more that Ayenwatha could have said about the Wanderer.

Janus felt a tantalizing urge to try and press Ayenwatha on the matter, but then thought better of it.

Janus did learn that the Wanderer was known to possess great powers, gifts that Ayenwatha said came from the One Spirit, which the Wanderer used to help humankind and all of creation. Ayenwatha was insistent to assure Janus and the others that the Wanderer was no shaman or witch, and that his powers had nothing at all to do with dark magic.

Janus had already noticed that Ayenwatha's war band had shown a pressing interest in determining whether Janus and his companions were shamans or witches. The determination of their status in that regard had appeared to be of the utmost importance to the tribal contingent. The seven had been carefully evaluated by the quartz-holding warriors, and had been deemed blameless of such pursuits.

That judgement, in Janus' estimation, had also been immensely fortunate for his group, with dire consequences had it gone otherwise. With the very adamant declaration of the Wanderer's full innocence in relation to dark magic, the truth was made very clear to Janus. The tribal culture that Ayenwatha was from regarded witches, shamans, and dark sorcerers as baleful adversaries, in a very hostile sense. The practicing of dark magic was most certainly among the most serious of transgressions in the eyes of the tribal people, an odious and unforgivable affront to their culture and beliefs.

A few of the other warriors in the immediate vicinity of Janus and the others had then begun to relate their own tales concerning the Wanderer.

Every story and encounter regarding the Wanderer boded no ill or danger for those that had experienced his presence. Rather, all of the described experiences of the tribal people with the Wanderer were of a very positive nature. Janus was left with few doubts that his own encounter with the esoteric, woodland wanderer had been a stroke of excellent fortune. Without the pendants the Wanderer had given them, he did not wish to think of what might have happened after the tribal warriors had come forth from the shadows.

With the tone of a jest, Ayenwatha had then remarked that the Wanderer had often appeared to his eyes and sensibilities to be a wayward elder from Midragard. According to Ayenwatha, the Wanderer's fair countenance, luxuriant blue eye, staunch fortitude, and seemingly relentless passion for adventuring strongly reflected the kind of blood found flowing in Midragardan veins.

The only significant difference in Ayenwatha's eyes was that the Wanderer had always been encountered solely by the tribal people within their own woodlands, well within the territories of the Five Realms. The tribal people had never met the Wanderer out upon the Great Waters, or around the Midragardans that they interacted with. In fact, the Midragardans that Ayenwatha knew had claimed to have had no encounters with the Wanderer. As the sachem stated with emphasis, had the Wanderer been of a Midragardan origin, it was inconceivable that the Wanderer would have had no interactions with Midragardans living and traveling in the vicinity of the tribal lands. It was also unbelievable that he had never been seen out on the seas that the Midragardans so loved.

Janus steadily came to realize that it was the great reverence that the tribes held for the Wanderer that had also helped the cause of the seven lost foreigners. The warriors undoubtedly had been encouraged to even greater restraint when it had been revealed that the seven exiles had not only interacted favorably with the venerable, blue-robed elder, but had also been bestowed by the Wanderer with powerful gifts.

Janus gave a brief shudder as he considered again just how perilously close they had all been dancing to the edge of a razor sharp blade. One slight inclination by Ayenwatha in another direction could well have resulted in arrows hissing from the forest to impale Janus and all the others, before they even knew what was happening.

Ayenwatha was rife with curiosity about the seven exiles, and Janus was not surprised when the warrior-leader began to venture the inevitable cascade of questions regarding the foreigners and their circumstances.

Logan and Erika took most of the turns explaining the course of the events that had brought them to the very moment where Ayenwatha and his warriors had revealed themselves. Janus did not mind the others speaking for the group, as it gave him some more time to observe the reactions and responses of their host.

Ayenwatha listened to the accounts with manifest interest, and undisguised fascination. Janus could tell that it was very difficult for Ayenwatha to even conceive of the concept of someone coming from another entire world.

Ayenwatha rarely interrupted, openly encouraging all of them to go into great detail. Many of the surrounding warriors walking with them edged closer to catch pieces of what was certainly to them a wild and incredible tale.

As Janus watched Ayenwatha closely, he eventually came to understand that Ayenwatha was no individual to be underestimated, or taken lightly. The sachem possessed a subtle intelligence, and was clever in using it, as Janus slowly realized what the sachem was truly up to in the prolonged dialogue with his comrades.

Ayenwatha's questions kept the others talking, often backtracking over areas that they had covered before. Janus came to understand that there was a cogent reason for the seeming redundancy.

It dawned upon Janus that the sachem's desire for considerable detail was not the result of simply wanting to feed casual interests. As he listened to the foreigners, Ayenwatha was actively sifting through the many elements of their story. He was looking for any inconsistencies or conflicts in their accounts, as well as working to gain deeper insights, seeking to discover anything that would tell him more about the real truth involving the seven's unexpected presence in the lands of his people.

Janus hoped that the greater amount of information given by his companions was reinforcing to Ayenwatha. Everything being said by them regarding their ordeal was the truth, and not some intentionally deceptive concoction.

From Ayenwatha's continuing relaxed posture and amiable countenance, Janus suspected that their stories were measuring up well with the war sachem's assessments. Janus felt confident, as the sachem's correlation of the group's various accounts would have revealed no incongruities, for there were none to be had.

Like the crystals, Ayenwatha's pursuit of extensive detail was merely another bout of testing, woven shrewdly into an atmosphere of casual conversation.

"I believe that great magic was used upon you. It was wielded against you, or for you," Ayenwatha remarked at long last, after the stories of the group's travails had been thoroughly rendered. "But which kind of magic, I cannot yet tell. Perhaps it was the miraculous work of the One Spirit, the Creator and Sky Lord. Maybe it was the Mother of the World, whom the Sky Lord sent to us ... or the Light Brother. Maybe it was the work of the Dark Brother, or malevolent spirits from deep in the underworld. Who can now say? Even so, in time, I am sure that it will become clear which kind of magic brought you into our lands. There is much to consider, and ..."

Ayenwatha's words were interrupted as the sound of flapping wings filtered down from the skies above the thickly foliated tree branches. Abruptly becoming silent, the war sachem froze in place, right as all of the other warriors snapped to a halt.

Janus instantly took their cue and stood still, holding his breath as he watched Ayenwatha for an indication of what to do. The sound of the wings grew louder, as if something was approaching. From what he could tell, whatever was coming was not far above the trees.

"Down, all of you, and press against the trees," Ayenwatha commanded them sharply, in a voice laced with urgency.

The other warriors had already faded into the forest's foliage, dissolving into undergrowth and shadows. For them, the act of vanishing into their surroundings was probably a mere reflex. For Janus and most of the others with him, everything was unfamiliar, including the nature of this new world's dangers. Only Derek could have been expected to possess some kinship with the instinctive responses of a trained warrior.

Following Ayenwatha's directive, Janus crouched low and pressed himself tightly against the trunk of a great maple tree. Looking around, he saw that the others of his group had taken similar positions at the bases of nearby trees.

Like himself, most of the others looked anxious and uncertain, and only Derek looked to be confident and more at ease with the task. Ayenwatha moved around quickly, nimble and light of step, as he took appraisal of the seven and their postures. His purpose became apparent as he made Antonio adjust his body position, aligning him closer to the base of the tree that he had sought cover under. The flapping sounds drew ever nearer, prompting Janus to start looking skyward.

"The sky scouts of the Unifier's forces are above us. Stay still. Stay to the trees and do not move at all. Do not speak, until I tell you it is safe," Ayenwatha cautioned them as he moved to a tree close by, drawing Janus' attention back to the war sachem.

Ayenwatha then nodded towards the skies, compelling Janus to look upward again. Through the few breaks of light in the interlaced mass of branches and leaves overhead, Janus observed a number of winged forms passing through the air a short distance above the tree canopy.

A rapidly occurring assortment of brief glimpses transpired, as the winged group flew over the war band and the exiles. Shadows flitted all over the ground with their passage. Janus remained motionless, staring intently above, though he could not make out much detail out about the flying creatures. He did see enough to determine that whatever the winged creatures might be, they were large, and they were bearing riders.

A sizeable group continued over their positions, and by Janus' best estimations it was at least twenty riders strong. After several more tense moments, the flapping of the wings faded and the skies became fully silent once again.

Cautiously, Ayenwatha crept out from his own hiding place, looking upward and listening carefully. After waiting for many long moments, he finally raised his hands to his lips and gave a signal that sounded like the call of a bird. The trilling call brought all of the warriors forth from the shadows, and they reassembled in the area around Ayenwatha and the seven.

"You may be at ease now," Ayenwatha said to the exiles, indicating for them to come forward from their places. Derek and the others converged, rising up and striding from the trees towards Ayenwatha, one by one.

Ayenwatha waited until all seven of the foreigners had drawn near to him before continuing. His voice was thick with anger. "Those wings herald the doom of our lands, and the power that commands them is the bane of all our people … and, in truth, the bane of all people."

"What … were those?" Logan asked Ayenwatha in a low voice, standing at Janus' side with a furrowed brow.

Janus looked back to the sachem, the same question perched on the tip of his own tongue. Shifting over a couple of paces to stand next to Logan, Antonio kept his widened eyes fixated towards the skies.

Janus glanced over at Kent, who was at his other shoulder.

The right side of Kent's face looked like tree bark, from where he had mashed his face into the trunk that he had taken cover by. One half of his face smooth, the other the inverse pattern of the bark, the resulting effect was undeniably comical. Janus had to stifle the chuckle that threatened to burst forth, given the very serious circumstances.

"The Unifier calls upon the power of many lands, and the forces gathering against us have far greater numbers than do we. It is no different with their sky warriors. We have winged steeds, but we must keep our steeds upon the ground, lest we become overwhelmed by their numbers in the sky," Ayenwatha replied in a grave tone. "The enemy has brought a very fierce race with them from afar, warriors whose great steeds are stronger and faster than are ours.

"It is said that the dog-faced warriors that ride upon those steeds come from the great, mountainous lands to the west of the Gigan lands, those huge creatures that some among you saw marching with the human forces this day. The dog-faced ones are powerful and courageous warriors, known as Trogens."

Janus could hear the sincere respect that Ayenwatha held towards these particular enemies, though Janus had not the first inkling of what Trogens were.

There was so much to assimilate since that morning. Learning of the existence of a strange race of dog-faced warriors riding upon winged beasts was now added to everything else. Janus already had to contend with thoughts of the passing of a massive army on the brink of war, Ayenwatha and his people, Gigans, Atagar, Licanthers, the Wanderer, all manner of foreign realms, the apparent reality of magic, and the talk of the foreboding Unifier.

Janus had no answers for any of it, and it was almost enough to send his head spinning. From a quick look at each of the others of his party, it did not look like any of them had a full grasp of things either.

Starkly confronted by the growing maelstrom of an unknown, very dangerous world, Janus knew that, like himself, his companions were only just beginning the quest of coming to terms with their new reality. It was a challenge that none of them had chosen, but one that all would have to face outright.

"We must not delay here," Ayenwatha said after a few more uncomfortable moments, "We must continue onward to the village."

There were no arguments forthcoming from anyone, warrior or exile alike, as Ayenwatha resumed the march, leading the war band at a brisk pace through the woods.

LOGAN

The Onan village to which Logan and the others were escorted was a fountainhead of tranquil imagery, from its own majestic, hilltop perch, to the sights within the scenic, forested terrain leading up to the prominent rise.

The village was nestled within a territory that was rich in beech and birch trees, as well as the white flowers amply decorating the ground that Logan had seen everywhere within the forest domain. The village itself surmounted a great hill, but the signs of human habitation came into view well before the party reached the base of its long slope.

The war party had announced its presence early on the approach to the hill, with a series of spirited cries and whoops that had carried far through the trees and hills. Logan had quickly perceived the rising enthusiasm running through the warriors, noticing at the same time that the group's pace had picked up significantly. With the upswing in mood and the brazen outcries, he had known that it was not going to be much farther to their destination.

The next indication of their close proximity to the village came shortly thereafter. A couple of warriors that had been sent running ahead a short while earlier returned back to the war band. They had not come back alone, as they were accompanied by a small number of tribal women.

The faces of the women beamed radiantly when they came into sight and saw the rest of the war party. They quickly took notice of Logan and his six companions, eyes widening as they studied the strange appearances and clothing of the foreigners. An even more amazed look arose upon their faces when it was explained to them that the seven were not captives taken in battle.

The women's purpose in meeting the war party was then revealed, though the women did not cease in casting furtive glances towards Logan and the others.

The rather grisly scalps that had been carried along by the warriors were then affixed to small rings that were set atop long, red-painted poles brought by the women. Once the scalps were attached, they took up the poles again as the group resumed its march through the woods. The women carried the poles upright and held high, like a standard, as they walked at the forefront of the war band.

The next tribal people that the party encountered were a number of men who had been engaged in hard labor. That was made quite apparent from the glisten of sweat covering their bared skin, their weary countenances, and the heavier breathing pervasive among them. Sunlight reflected off of many axe heads, the short wooden hafts held firmly within the hands of several of the men.

Many were bare of chest, wearing little more than a kind of hide breechcloth, of the type that went between their legs and was tucked over a hide belt in front and back. They wore no body paint, though a copious array of tattoos, reflecting the diversity of design seen upon the warriors, were worked into the skin of their lean bodies.

Though they had come to a complete halt in their labors at the approach of the war party, their undertaking was clear to Logan. They had been embroiled in the task of felling several trees within an area that was evidently being cleared for some future use.

The men, like the women carrying the poles, were elated at the sight of the returning war band. They hastened over and exchanged informal, fervent greetings with the warriors, several individuals in both groups clearly displaying affinity towards each other.

The men eyed Logan and his companions very closely, as Ayenwatha and the other warriors spoke briefly with them. The march was resumed again very shortly, as the men from the nascent clearing brought their hand axes along with them, falling in with the growing procession.

The enlarged group had not gone much farther when they ran into yet more members of the tribe that had been toiling with the land. In broad swathes of ground that had been fully cleared of trees, now teeming with small dirt mounds, a number of women had been laboring amid some newly sprouted crops.

Scattered throughout the mounds and growths, the women were fully oriented upon the war party's presence by the time that it drew into their sight. Joyous smiles spread quickly, and within moments the throng of women was converging upon the marching group.

The war party came to yet another halt at that juncture. As the women gathered all around, Logan took the opportunity to study the females of the tribe a little more carefully.

The majority of the women was clad in one of two general styles of attire. One group wore wrap-around garments, not unlike long skirts, which were accompanied with cape-like tops on their upper bodies. Others were clad in full-length tunics. Both styles were fashioned of buckskin, most being left in a natural color, with a few dyed to darker hues.

The outer surfacing of the hide attire showed ample variation in the quill and beadwork patterns worked skillfully into them. Flowers, birds, and intertwining swirls gracefully ascended the women in beautiful displays of natural elements.

Richly decorated moccasins adorned the feet of the women, filled abundantly with even more dyed quill-work and beaded embellishments. On many of the pairs the ornamentation was augmented further around the high ankles of the moccasins, with fringes created from deer-hair tassels, each of them bound by little metallic cones.

The women had been using hoes crafted of wood and bone in their labors among the developing crop. Looking again at the planting area, Logan then noticed that the burgeoning yield was not uniform in nature. Rather, it contained multiple elements that had been planted purposefully together.

One of those crop elements was rising from the tops of the small dirt mounds, the growths roughly a span high. Another distinct element was sprouting on the surface of the mounds as well, maturing close to the taller, vertical growths. A third distinctive crop was fanning out from the base of the mounds, filling in the flatter ground in between the low rises.

"What are you growing here?" Logan had managed to ask Ayenwatha, as he stared out over the field. "Has it been planted for long?"

"When the leaf of the oak is the size of a squirrel's foot, the Three Siblings are brought forth," Ayenwatha replied, as if quoting some tribal maxim.

"The Three Siblings?" Logan asked curiously, wanting to learn something more of the intriguing people that were taking Logan and his companions in.

Ayenwatha related to Logan that the Three Siblings were the primary crops of the tribal people. As Ayenwatha explained it, maize stalks would rise up from the mounds of soil, and beans would then grow upward along the rising stalks, using them as support. The third of the Siblings, squash, would grow profusely all over the lower ground, thickly covering the spaces in between the small mounds with their broad leaves.

Logan nodded, as he looked around at the women now fully gathered all around them.

The women, who mostly ranged from young adulthood to middle age, displayed a great exuberance at the arrival of the war band. Like the others that the war band had come across, they looked upon Logan and the others with both curiosity and a little trepidation exhibited in their faces.

A few children, likely having mothers amongst the field laborers, soon made their presence known among the throng greeting the war party. The little ones worked their way eagerly to the forefront of the gathered women, taking quick note of the interesting newcomers among the war party.

The youngest among them were entirely unclothed, much to Logan's surprise and slight awkwardness. The presence of clothing, and the amount of it, increased with their age, with the oldest of the children being garbed in very similar manners to the adults.

The children chattered and giggled excitedly, talking amongst themselves as well as calling out to the warriors. They all remained close to the adult women, clearly keeping a little cautious distance from the strangers.

A few of the warriors laughed merrily and teased the children, who appeared to be utterly fascinated with the seven guests, making no effort to hide their feelings. Many little mouths fell agape, eyes widening with incredulity and amazement at the sight of the peculiar clothes and foreign appearances of Logan's group.

The mothers, trying to maintain a certain level of composure, endeavored to deflect the flurry of hushed and blurted questions cast at them by the inquisitive, unsubtle youth.

The women from the crop field subsequently joined their number to the swelling entourage, as the group continued onward following the short delay. The children, though staying intensely interested in the exiles, maintained a healthy distance from the foreigners as they trotted out to the sides of the war party.

The expanding party proceeded on past the field, finally moving towards the base of the village's great hill, which came into sight through the trees, the prominent elevation looming high above everything around it.

The village was quite an impressive sight seen from below, drawing Logan's eyes immediately upward as he strode out from the trees and walked forward under the open sky. The summit of the large hill had been entirely cleared of trees and brush, as had the slopes. An encompassing wooden palisade of vertical stakes had been erected all along the contours of the hilltop's outer edges.

Just beyond a thin strip of ground at the base of the palisade were some earthworks, which consisted of a broad ditch and outer embankment that had been cut into the hillside itself. The ditch and embankment looked as if it would be a very potent obstacle to any threat seeking to reach the palisade itself.

The long walk up the slope to the village was accompanied by an increasing amount of jubilance and fanfare from the tribal people. The returning warriors shouted and cried out boisterously as they approached the timber crown surmounting the hilltop. The women carrying the poles with the scalps, still at the forefront of the entire procession, called out in loud, resonant voices, before breaking into vibrant, chant-like singing. They waved the poles back and forward, proudly heralding the return of the war party.

Several other tribal warriors filed out of the narrow entrance in the palisade wall to greet the party as they ascended the lengthy slope. The emerging warriors were not covered in the red and black paint, such as that gracing all the members of the war party. Like all the groups that the war party had recently come across, they also looked happy and very relieved to see the approaching contingent.

Also similar to all of the others, they took an immediate, profound interest in the seven foreigners.

The chorus of animated cries and vibrant songs filled the air underneath the bright silken skies, as the war band funneled through a gap in the earthen embankment and continued forth through the village entrance, with the rest of the crowd in their wake. Within the palisade's narrow entryway was a considerable expanse of open ground, which was occupied by numerous wooden structures.

Most of the edifices were of a generally similar, elongated appearance, which varied only in their absolute lengths. They ranged from a few dozen feet up to some greater ones that were well over a couple hundred feet long. Sprinkled in amongst them were a few smaller, circular wooden huts, as well as some tall vertical posts, which displayed an array of surface carvings.

Another similarly narrow opening within the outer palisade was evident at the far end of the large enclosure, placed just opposite to the one that Logan and his companions had just passed through.

A number of high wooden platforms, accessible by steep sets of narrow, ladder-like steps, each provided with thin timber railing, had been erected at several locations along the inside of the palisade. From their positioning and height, it was very obvious to Logan that these platforms were intended for defensive purposes.

As Logan gazed out over the grounds of the enclosure and the structures within it, he noted that the largest of the elongated buildings was placed at what looked to be the very center of the village. A garden plot brimming with what looked to be young tobacco plants sat just adjacent to it. Smaller such garden plots accompanied some of the other lengthy edifices.

The particular construction of the dominant form of building was made very evident a few moments later, as Logan set his eyes upon a mid-sized structure of the type that was currently undergoing an extension in its length. Materials such as stacks of bark sheaths, various poles derived from saplings and thicker tree sections, and coils of hempen rope were clustered near to the skeletal framing of the extension.

The longhouses were covered in a type of elm bark paneling or sheathing, affixed over a framework of tied elm poles. Sapling poles bent into arches formed ceiling rafters.

From the look of the unfinished structure, it could be seen that the longhouses were divided into chamber-like increments within their interiors. There was a sheltered entrance at each end of the longhouses, where bark panels were hung over their entryways with images worked upon their facings.

Logan did not have long to regard the construct, or much of anything else. Villagers quickly surrounded the group, pressing in close, with more streaming in every moment towards the increasing mass by the entrance. They emerged from within and around the many structures, hurrying in from farther areas of the village's interior, ceasing whatever tasks they had been engaged in.

A few women off to Logan's right got up from where they had been arraying gathered berries on the surfaces of bark trays. Another woman set down a long wooden pestle by a mortar that looked like a hollowed-out tree trunk, releasing her grip on the narrow midsection, spanning between the two thick ends with rounded heads.

A little baby was resting securely in a wooden cradle-board, suspended from a peg fixed into a high, stout timber post near to her. She paused only long enough to gather up the decorated cradle-board and her baby, a plump little urchin swaddled in dark cloth wrapping that was ornamented with light-colored beadwork.

Logan caught the sight of a number of horses gathered off to the left. They were not saddled, but it was clear that they were being prepared for a journey. All were bearing loads that consisted of hide pouches or stacks of furred skins. Several men were striding away from them, moving to join the rest of the villagers.

More young children were now emerging from where they had been playing deeper amongst the longhouses and huts, accompanied by a bevy of dogs. Bounding alongside them, the canines wagged their tails vigorously in the growing commotion.

The children's jubilant cries and excited shrieks were mixed with the playful barking of the dogs, putting a cheerful tint upon the living, dynamic picture evolving before Logan's eyes.

Logan almost chuckled aloud as he beheld the extremely humorous sight of one particularly chubby little fellow, who was trotting as best as he possibly could to keep up with the other children. The little one's shaky balance showed that it had not been all that long since he had ceased crawling as his primary method of movement.

Logan winced as one of the accompanying dogs nearly tripped the little fellow up, causing him to totter for a second. Logan breathed a sigh of relief as the child stabilized, managing somehow to remain upright.

The broad mixture of old men and women, children, young adults, and several more warriors all appeared eager to get a closer look at the eccentric appearances of the strangers brought back by the war party. They herded around the seven, those farther in back craning their necks and jostling to get better positions, their eyes drinking in the sight of Logan and his companions.

Among the last of the villagers to arrive to the throng around Logan's group were some of the most intriguing individuals of all.

A few older women, of particularly stately bearings, methodically came up join the gathering. Several younger members of the tribe escorted these women with obvious reverence. The crowd parted wide to allow the elderly women access to the forefront of the assemblage, many conceding their prime locations in deference to the women.

One of the elderly women caught Logan's attention in particular, as she came to stand almost directly before him. She was wearing a full-length, black-dyed buckskin dress, richly ornamented with dyed quill-work. A distinctive image was visible on the front of her tunic-dress, surrounded by a bevy of swirls and floral representations. It featured a large, semicircular shape, which arched over a pair of parallel lines, whose width spanned to the ends of the semicircle.

The old woman gazed upon Logan with an impassive expression resting upon her heavily creased face. The look in her dark eyes was alert and penetrating, and he wished that he could read her thoughts.

Another distinctive individual caught Logan's attention in a similar way, an older man whose approach was also accompanied by gestures of respect and deference among the other villagers. Like the elderly woman, he came to stand close to Logan.

He was wearing a headdress fashioned from the thick-furred skin of a brown bear. The bear's upper jaws crowned the old man's head, lending his stern, eagle-like visage even more strength as he stared fixedly towards the foreigners.

Logan held the man's eyes for only a moment, before his attention was taken in again by the swirl of faces all around. The tribal people were still cheering and lauding the warriors, but it was becoming abundantly clear that burning questions were on the tips of all their tongues. Murmurs ran abundantly through the crowd, coming from lips set underneath eyes that were intently scrutinizing Logan's group.

Before the tension at the unanswered inquiries became too uncomfortably palpable, Ayenwatha stepped forward from the war band and swept his gaze over all of them. A hush fell upon the crowd at his movement, as a host of expectant eyes turned to regard him.

"My brothers and sisters of the Onan, of the village of the Place of Far Seeing, the war party has returned … and with very good tidings. We have not lost even one of our brothers, while gaining a victory over the enemies that would seek to do us harm," Ayenwatha announced, his tone resonant, and unmistakably proud as it carried over all the gathering.

As if to emphasize the triumphant result of the excursion, the women bearing the scalps waved the poles back and forward again in a salutatory fashion. The gesture elicited a chorus of whoops, cries, and cheers that pierced the air.

Logan could both see and feel the ecstatic surge of delight at the news of the full survival of the war party. The exuberance was especially reflected within the faces of many women that had begun to step forward to greet individual warriors in the band. All of these women wore their hair with a single, long braid down their backs.

Logan did not have to ask anyone regarding the identity of the women stepping forward. Their faces emanated the lightness of sheer relief, along with the radiance of unrestrained joy and affection towards their returned husbands.

The scalp-poles were then given over to some of these women. The particular woman that received the pole displaying multiple scalps had a sparkling expression as she accepted it from the female bearer. She gazed back proudly at the warrior that she had just been embracing, raising the pole high and letting out an energetic, victorious whoop, flashing a dazzling smile at him. The other women receiving scalp-poles had similarly beaming expressions and reactions as they turned to regard their husbands, who, Logan fathomed, were undoubtedly the ones responsible for the war trophies. Following the handing over of the scalp-poles, it took a few more moments for the renewed adulation to settle down again.

The crowd then became subdued once more, as Ayenwatha resumed his address, turning to look upon the seven foreigners as he spoke. To Logan, it felt as if the air immediately thickened with the multitude of inquisitive stares that fell in mass upon him and his fellow exiles. The pervasive stillness held the acute, weighty sensation of the enveloping throng collectively holding their breaths.

"As you can see with your own eyes, we have seven with us who are not of the tribes … and who are not of these lands. They were not taken as prisoners by our war party, and do not appear to be of the enemy. Their stay among us is still to be decided," Ayenwatha stated firmly. "But know that they carried no sign of the dark magic. The crystals speak truly, and it is certain that they do not practice the dark ways.

"For now, they are to be my guests. They are to be treated as guests of the Onan, while their fate among our people will be decided by our village council."

Logan could read a wide range of responses within the faces and eyes oriented towards the seven strangers. Mistrust, apprehension, hostility, and even some smatterings of welcome were displayed in the variety of expressions in view around him.

The diverse reactions left him in a more uncertain state, after having just gained a little more confidence while traveling along with the war party. Though Ayenwatha had treated Logan and the others politely enough, it was now very clear that the seven were still facing a very unpredictable situation.

"Prepare now for the welcome, with meat and the sweetness of the maple," Ayenwatha then announced, his words bringing a little of the former levity back to the atmosphere. Though many of the tribal people continued to stare at Logan and the other newcomers, Ayenwatha's words were greeted with considerable enthusiasm.

Logan looked to the sachem for some indication as to what was to come next. Ayenwatha's eyes roved across the faces of the crowd, and looked well beyond the gathering, as if searching for someone in particular.

Ayenwatha then turned and conferred in private with some of the warriors that had initially come out of the village to greet them. All that Logan was able to gather were some passing references to a person named Deganawida. From what he could glean from snippets of their conversation, the desired individual was not currently within the village.

Ayenwatha looked visibly displeased at the news of the person's absence, and Logan found himself wondering who the sought individual might be.

The sachem then turned his attention back to the seven exiles. He gestured for them to follow, as he stepped forward and guided Logan and the others onward, heading deeper into the village. The crowd dutifully parted aside to allow all of them a channel to pass through, and Logan could feel the heavy stares that lingered to his sides and back as they proceeded through the congested assemblage.

Ayenwatha, a few escorting warriors, and the seven foreigners passed deep into the midst of the elongated structures. They finally drew near to the cluster of greater longhouses that Logan had espied earlier, in the village's center.

The sachem led them straight towards the end of one of the extensive longhouses. Ayenwatha did not break stride as he pushed aside a hide flap spanning the sheltered opening and proceeded inside. As he passed just beneath the bark panel suspended over the entryway, Logan carefully eyed the symbol depicted upon it.

The symbol was that of a very unusual, six-legged beast, sharp of fang with decidedly cat-like features. He hoped that such an unusual creature was just a mythical depiction, a construct of tribal imagination, and not any actual representation of what lay out in the surrounding forest; the forest which Logan and the others had just been walking through.

Passing under the sheltered porch-entrance, the group filed through the hide-draped opening into a sort of vestibule. It held within it a number of barrels fashioned out of bark sheaths, as well as a quantity of corn-husk baskets and pottery containers. The object of greatest abundance stored within the space was firewood, the sections of which had been collected and piled into many sizeable stacks.

The group did not linger within the storage area as they headed straight through another opening a few paces immediately ahead, similar to the entryway behind them. Once through it, they found themselves within the first interior chamber of an inhabited longhouse.

Ayenwatha drew to a halt within the chamber, as if to indulge the visitors' curiosities. Logan was grateful for the pause, as he gazed around at a fully finished living chamber. It was a segment of the same type that he had just seen in the process of being crafted outside, the extension to the mid-sized longhouse near the village entrance.

To each side of Logan's group were raised, bark-covered platforms, set at about a sitting level for an average adult. Upon the platforms were long corn-husk mats and several animal skins, both of which Logan figured were used for sleeping at night.

Over their heads, running along each side of the chamber, and also constructed of thick sheets of bark, were shelves being used for the storage of foodstuffs, tools, weapons, hides, and other various items. Some of the implements in view were very interesting in appearance, catching Logan's attention momentarily. One of these items looked like a racquet of some type, perhaps giving a hint as to the kind of sport engaged in by the tribes. Nearby was a pair of matching objects that featured latticed, broad bodies, looking distinctly like a set of snow shoes.

Logan could see the edges of shallow pits that had been dug out directly beneath the lower sleeping platforms. The pits also appeared to be for storage, as he could see the dark shapes of objects contained within them, though their specific forms were shrouded in deep shadow.

A few feet of open space extended along the side walls from each end of the lower platforms, the small areas holding more bark barrels, as well as a few stacks of firewood. A bark-panel wall, pierced by a narrow opening, divided the living chamber from the next compartment in the longhouse sequence.

While the upper and lower platforms arranged on each half of the chamber, as well as the storage spaces, inherently mirrored their opposite sides, not everything within the section was duplicated. Set into the middle of the compartment was a singular fire pit, which was presumably shared in common by the occupants of the two analogous living spaces.

Farther above Logan, hanging from the elm-pole rafters of the ceiling, were what appeared to several braided bunches of corn, as well as long strips of some type of dried meat or fish. There was also a small hole in the ceiling that was positioned directly over the fire pit, presumably for the escape of smoke.

Despite the smoke hole, Logan could quickly see that ventilation in the chamber was very limited, and that any fire burning in the hearth pit would quickly render the room congested and hazy. Even without an active fire burning the air was thicker to the lungs, and heavily laced with strong, musky scents. Logan surmised that it would not take very much to make the interior conditions unbearable to his own senses.

"There are two families to each chamber, one living on each side," Ayenwatha explained, as Logan and the others continued to gaze around. "For now, you will be staying in this longhouse, which is of my own Firaken Clan, for I am responsible for your presence in the village. Now, come forward with me, and I will take you to your quarters."

Ayenwatha led them onward, across the chamber, passing through the next opening and continuing through the midst of several more similar dwelling spaces until they finally came to one that had very few signs of habitation. If anything, it appeared to be wholly abandoned.

The chamber's upper shelves, rafters, hearth pit, and open spaces were largely barren, save for a few mats, hides, a couple stacks of firewood, and a few other elements.

Ayenwatha drew to a stop in the chamber, and turned to face the group as they gathered around him. "This chamber is where you may rest amongst yourselves for now. It is not being occupied at the moment. A terrible sickness claimed many from the village a few seasons ago, and not all chambers in the great longhouses have been reoccupied. I must go now, to tell the others of everything that has happened, and of you. I will return for you when I am finished."

Ayenwatha then walked through the middle of the group and made his way out of the chamber, heading back the way they had come, leaving the seven exiles all by themselves for the first time since they had been surrounded. A few moments after Ayenwatha had left, the group began to quietly spread out within their assigned living quarters.

Logan walked away from the others, heading towards the lower platform that was set to the right side of the opening through which they had entered the chamber. Antonio followed after him a few moments later, and the two friends sat down side by side upon the platform's edge. Feeling the rough, uneven surface beneath him, Logan knew that it would take some time getting used to the furnishings.

Logan glanced over to his right, towards Antonio. In that moment, Logan realized that the two of them, so used to confiding closely in each other over recent years, had not spoken much at all together since they had joined up with Erika and Mershad in the forest.

"So much change, so fast," Logan muttered, low enough that his words were delivered in relative privacy.

Antonio replied in an equally subdued voice, "Everything is moving fast. Makes me feel kind of helpless. I don't think we have real freedom anymore. None at all. Any way you look at it. And I mean … any way."

He pointedly glanced over at the opening that Ayenwatha had just departed through. Logan followed his friend's gaze and saw that there were a few of Ayenwatha's warriors lingering quietly within the adjacent chamber. Seeing their presence, Logan had little doubt that if he, or any of his companions, were to walk through the next opening into the other abutting chamber, they would likely encounter another warrior or two.

For the time being, it was abundantly clear that the seven were not going to be allowed to exit the longhouse of their own accord. Their hosts were treating them with a cordial respect, perhaps even generously given the circumstances, but it was still one that had its precautions and firm parameters.

"We will work with whatever we've got," Logan finally replied, staring at the forms of the warriors for a moment longer before returning his gaze back to Antonio. "Really, it's just like every day back in our own world. We didn't control those circumstances either. We did whatever we had to do … in response to whatever we had before us."

Logan paused, and then gave Antonio a rueful grin. "Though I admit the things facing us back home were a whole lot more familiar to us."

"But where is this all headed to?" Antonio asked with a forlorn expression. Logan could see the fear glistening in his friend's eyes. "If it wasn't for the fact that we're going through it hour by hour together, it would be hard for me to believe any of this is even real. But I know it is no dream …."

Logan shook his head, "I don't know. The best thing that's happened is that we haven't panicked too much. I know that we're all scared. I would be a fool and a liar to say otherwise. But we can't lose control now, and we can't start panicking. Things would get much worse, very quickly. We have to keep our wits about ourselves, even if it all looks like murk and storms ahead."

Antonio nodded with a pensive expression at Logan's advice. Logan knew that his friend would likely heed the sentiments that he had voiced, even if Antonio was none too happy about their current state of affairs; prisoners in a foreign land that had a blackening cloud of war spreading over it.

Logan looked over at the rest of the group. Two were milling about the opening to the chamber on his left, while a couple more were occupying the surface of the platform opposite to him.

Kent, clearly restless, was working to climb up to the overhead platform on the other side of the chamber. Logan watched him idly, somewhat curious as to what Kent was up to.

"So what do you think of the others? Do you think that everyone else can hold themselves together for long?" Antonio asked Logan.

Logan, continuing to watch Kent's upward progress, nodded affirmatively. "I think so. I think they all can. Especially Derek. He's probably our best fighter, if things come down to something that needed that, and he's got a military background. We talked about it during our turn together on the night's watch. And I really think Erika and Janus are very capable individuals too. She's a strong one, with a lot of willpower. Janus is one of those quiet, tenacious types. He's not one that would easily let us down.

"As for Kent, it is a little questionable, but he seems to be managing okay for the moment. And Mershad … I don't know enough about him yet, but my gut tells me he's good. But I honestly think all of them will be fine. I really do."

"Well, let's make the best of it then, like you say. Everyone in this room is kind of like our family now, in a way," Antonio observed. His grin, likely meant to be encouraging, was laced with nervousness. "I …."

"No weapons! Put that down! And come down here, right now!"

Antonio flinched as their conversation was curtly interrupted, a stern, authoritative voice coming from the opening that they had entered the chamber through.

Kent had succeeded in climbing up to the overhead platform, and had been marveling at one of the ball-ended, carved timber war clubs that he had found lying up there. His expression in the wake of the admonishment was not far from that of a naughty child caught red-handed.

Kent set the club down slowly, and carefully climbed back down to the ground level. His face was flush as he turned around to face the others.

"Sorry, sorry, I just was curious about what was up there, that's all," Kent said gently to the strong-looking warrior that was now standing in the entryway, glowering at him. Kent held his hands up, palms open, in a placating gesture.

The plainly irritated warrior moved quickly past Kent, climbing up swiftly to the upper platform and retrieving the weapon. He took a few moments to search about the platform before coming back down. Crossing the chamber, he climbed and checked the other higher platform.

The warrior appeared to be more annoyed with the fact that the weapon was up there, than he was angered with Kent's transgression. Once back on the ground again, the warrior turned to face all of the chamber's occupants, fixing each of them with a sharp, piercing glance. His dark eyes held a hardened, inflexible look within them.

"No weapons!" he said firmly.

"Kent, sit still! Can't you at least do that for a few minutes?" Derek vented, with obvious exasperation. Derek looked over to the warrior, and spoke politely. "I apologize for our friend. He did not mean to provoke, he's just very curious about everything here. All of this is new to us."

Janus rolled his eyes from where he stood next to Derek. He turned to Erika and Mershad, chuckling. "Kids. Can't always watch them."

The others returned a nervous, low laughter from where they were sitting on the lower platform. The warrior in the doorway relaxed his posture somewhat as Kent shuffled away from the platform, to come over and stand by Derek and Janus. Another warrior had come up to stand next to the first one by then, and neither showed any impending signs of leaving, or ceasing in their supervision of the seven foreigners.

Turning his head, Logan saw that a third warrior had taken up a vigil in the chamber's other opening. Like the other two, he gazed with a humorless expression upon Logan's group. The sight of the warrior instantly confirmed Logan's earlier suspicions regarding the possibility of guarding occupants within the other adjacent chamber.

Though they were not making any special effort to intimidate, the presence of the three warriors had the instant effect of dampening all conversation within the room. Sitting down upon various edges of the lower platforms on each side of the chamber, Logan and the others quietly bided their time.

Looking sullen and castigated, Kent moved deeper on the platform towards the chamber wall. He lay on his back across one of the animal skins and stared up at underside of the upper platform, brooding in the tense stillness of the chamber.

The warrior that had initially spoken then handed the confiscated war club over to his companion, and calmly walked over to the platform, looking down at Kent.

"Use the mat, place it underneath you against the wood," he instructed Kent in a slightly softer tone of voice, gesturing towards one of the corn-husk mats lying close by. "It will be more comfortable for you."

Finally understanding the warrior's intent, Kent nodded and sat up. He pulled the nearby mat over, pulled the animal skin onto it, and shifted his body to lie atop all of it. The warrior seemed satisfied, turning and walking quietly back to the chamber's entryway.

Despite the considerate gesture by the warrior, the time nonetheless continued to pass by with a heavy, pensive silence pervading the chamber. Logan stared down at the empty fire pit a few feet in front of him, letting his mind slowly drift off.

It may have been hours or just minutes later, but Logan's sluggish attention was fully roused as the warriors in the doorway straightened up suddenly, and the sound of low voices came to his ears. The two warriors to Logan's left proceeded to step aside, clearing the opening, amid a general sound of shuffling and shifting in the adjacent chamber.

The warrior in the opposite chamber opening had an attentive look upon his face, his gaze no longer fixed upon the occupants of the chamber, but rather on the other entryway. Logan followed the warrior's eyes back across the room, to see what had compelled his attention.

A tall, older man with gray-streaked long hair then walked through the opening to Logan's left, followed a step behind by Ayenwatha.

The older man had a hardened look woven into his amply creased face. Though clearly a man very advanced of years, his authoritative presence was accompanied by an aura of strength.

Wide-set, straight lines of a lighter hue streaked down his face. Showing prominently against the darker skin of his weathered face, the set of markings spanned from under the older man's right eye down to just below his sharp chin. They looked like old scars, from the raking claws of some great, predatory beast.

He wore a banded type of headdress, the wide part circling about his head generously decorated with colorful bead and quill-work. Out of the center of the headdress emerged a plumage of long feathers, mixed with what looked to be clusters of horsehair. Two prominent feathers rose straight upward from the apex of the head covering.

The arms of his knee-length, buckskin tunic and leggings exhibited ornamented garters. They were wrapped snugly about his upper arms and at his knees, with the ending lengths dangling down from where they were tied off. An elaborate, multicolored strap traveled across his chest from the right shoulder down to his waist, where it secured a similarly decorated pouch.

His feet were clad in bead-decorated, moosehair-tasseled moccasins, and his ears exhibited long, circular earrings that were crafted of alternating dark and light hued shell beads.

"Deganawida, Great Sachem of the Onan Tribe, first on the seat of the Grand Council, Headman of the village of the Place of Far Seeing," Ayenwatha announced.

Logan regarded the regal-looking old man carefully, recalling the name from the inquiries made by Ayenwatha when they had first entered into the village. Logan felt certain that the man now standing before them was the person that had been spoken of.

The seven occupants of the chamber arose at his entrance, giving nods and awkward bows towards Deganawida. Logan was one of the latter, not really knowing what the proper gesture of respect was for the Onan tribe's particular culture. He endeavored not to make lingering eye contact with the old sachem, figuring that might well be taken as an affront.

There was a hint of amusement gracing the older man's face when Logan glanced up, as if the sachem had perceived their cultural confusion.

"Deganawida has come here to speak with you himself … about your coming, and about your purpose here," Ayenwatha informed the seven in a low voice. He then took a step backward into the opening to the chamber, turning and leaving Deganawida by himself with the seven.

The old sachem looked towards the seven, regarding each one of them intently for a few moments, before moving his gaze onward to the next. To Logan, the sachem's methodical and scrutinizing manner evoked thoughts of the blue-robed Wanderer back in the woods.

When the sachem's gaze encompassed him, Logan inadvertently caught the older man's direct stare. The quality of it caused him to hesitate, despite his inclination to avoid meeting the old man's eyes.

The alert, penetrating look within the sachem's sparkling, dark eyes elicited even more comparisons to the Wanderer. It was as if Deganawida was looking through Logan's skin, to something far more inward.

Logan had the inexplicable sensation that the tribal elder's eyes could willfully look even deeper than his very thoughts. The feeling was quite unsettling, in that Logan was left in an unprecedented state of nakedness, one that went far beyond a mere lack of physical clothing.

"I have heard that you are not from our lands, or any that we know of. I have heard it said that some great magic is responsible for your presence here in the tribal lands. I have also heard that you spoke with a special man, the Wanderer, who is well known to us in our lands. I would like to hear you speak more about all of these things," Deganawida told them. His voice matched his august appearance. It was low, resonant, and, although gentle in tone, carried an unmistakable air of authority just underneath its surface.

Logan looked to each of the others, and saw various degrees of caution and hesitancy in his companions. After a long pause, he finally took the initiative and started to relate their story to the prominent sachem.

On the way to the village, Logan and Erika had done most of the talking on behalf of the group. This time, Janus and Derek interchanged more often with Logan and Erika, as the four fleshed out the account of their strange experience with considerable detail. Kent, Mershad, and Antonio looked apprehensive and very uncomfortable, more than content to keep quiet and let their companions do the telling.

The tribal elder showed no reactions or emotion during the telling of their story. His attention was studious and ardently focused, as if he were pondering every single word that the visitors uttered. Even after the tale had been finished, he stayed silent, and appeared to be in deep contemplation for several minutes before he finally spoke aloud again.

"You speak of an incredible journey. One that is difficult to imagine. The gift of the Wanderer helps your speech, but I can tell by your appearances that you are not from any land that I have ever heard spoken of within this world. I do not sense any lies in your words. I do see your confusion, and I feel your fear. These are not the things I would see in a gathering whose purpose was bent upon deception and evil.

"Yet all things within this world have both good and evil within them, to a greater or lesser amount. It lies within each of us to decide which to empower, and it is possible that you may yet have darker things hidden that I cannot yet sense.

"Even so, I believe your words, and, as Ayenwatha has done, I can do no less than offer you a refuge and welcome within our village. I do not know if you will remain safe, even here in the midst of our people. As you have learned, the forces of the Unifier draw very near, and the skies are increasingly filled with the dark storms of war. That is something beyond your power, or ours, to determine. What will come, will come.

"For today, you may eat well and rest. I will leave you to yourselves now, but I would like for you to join me for a feast, and a celebration of life, this very evening."

Deganawida then displayed a hint of a smile, one that emanated a kindly, compassionate warmth. The effect was enhanced within his dark eyes, the surfaces of which seemed to glitter from an inner light.

While there was little doubt that Deganawida had a very intense interest in the newcomers, Logan was relieved to see the signs of an affable disposition in the tribal sachem.

Deganawida turned and withdrew from the chamber. There was a momentary delay, as Logan strained futilely to make out the substance of a low conversation that then ensued in the adjacent chamber. Finally surrendering in his efforts, Logan stared impatiently towards the opening until Ayenwatha finally entered to rejoin them.

"Deganawida sees good within you," Ayenwatha greeted them with a smile. The warrior appeared to be very pleased with whatever initial evaluation the great sachem had just rendered, further allaying Logan's anxieties. "It is our way to respect each individual as a creation of the One Spirit, but we also cannot endanger the village.

"I will speak further with Deganawida, and it may be that you will be allowed to walk outside the village … but warriors of the village must always go with you. I hope that you understand this necessity. These are not usual times … for you, or for us. For now, rest, and soon you shall eat and drink to your fill."

Without further comment, or waiting for any sort of reply, Ayenwatha turned and walked out of the chamber, leaving the seven alone to themselves once more.

Logan glanced over at his companions. He could sense that all of their moods had been given a lift upwards, likely encouraged by the favorable reaction of Deganawida, and the lightened mood that had just been exhibited by Ayenwatha.

All of them looked to be very fatigued, a fact that quickly emerged in the conversations that then took place amongst themselves. It was unanimously, and swiftly, decided that they should all make use of the time available, and take full advantage of the chance for a little rest.

Logan had no arguments, as there was little else to do to occupy the time. It would be a little easier to relax in their current environment. There was no need for a watch anymore, as they were under considerable guard within the center of the village, and within the longhouse itself.

For the first time since they had come into the new world, Logan realized that there was little risk in letting his own guard down for awhile. Even so, he knew that it would still be a very hard thing to do, with every part of his being still set on edge.

Spreading themselves throughout the two similarly arrayed halves of the chamber, the seven took their places upon the raised platforms. Using the animal skins and cornhusk mats, they wearily adjusted their positions, lay down, and gave themselves over to rest.

Logan soon found that the harder surface of the platform was rather uncomfortable, even with mats and skins providing a buffer between his body and the bark platform. It was nonetheless a great improvement over the altogether unforgiving bare earth, on which he had restlessly spent the previous night.

Yet the platform was not the only source of discomfort for Logan. His own stomach had begun to incur the first pangs of a steadily growing hunger. Logan's only comfort was that he knew that when they were roused awake, the feast that had been declared by Deganawida would be imminent.

As sorely tired as he was, the hard platform and empty stomach proved to be of little impediment. The discomforts faded along with his consciousness on his drift into a deep and welcome slumber.

LEE

"Ooooohhhh," exclaimed Lee, stretching as he took in a deep breath of the new morning's crisp air.

Reaching down, he cupped some of the cool creek water within his hands and generously splashed it all over his face. He blinked his eyes rapidly, shuddering as the cold water trickled down his face, neck, and chest. The vibrant feel of the chilly water was instantly invigorating, melting away the lethargy that had still clung to him long after he had opened his eyes to the new day.

Clasping his hands above his head and arching his back, he again stretched, endeavoring to rid himself of the lingering rigidity in his body that had formed as a result of sleeping for hours upon the hard, unforgiving ground. A few cracks and pops sounded as he worked his back and limbs.

"Body stiffen up, old man?" Ryan asked, chuckling as he came up to stand at Lee's right side. In his right hand, he held both his and Lee's sharpened stakes. "Accommodations not good enough around here? Didn't you request extra pillows?"

Lee shot Ryan a bemused glance, a last few drops of water dribbling off of his face and hair. "Very, very funny, and good morning to yourself. But if you could talk to the cook, I'm starved. Or, maybe you can fix something up? Whip something together. You know I've taught you a few things."

"Supplies are low, and the wok is currently under repair," Ryan retorted with a half-hearted grin.

Lee could see right through the teenager's façade of humor. The young man was feeling very grim about their meal prospects. The topic was the greatest worry weighing down upon Lee's mind, ever since morning had arrived and confirmed that the previous day was no dream.

"Then we need to take care of it," Lee replied firmly.

"What the hell can we do about it?" Ryan queried in a voice laden with frustration. He handed Lee's stake over, adding in a lower, tense tone, "And here, we probably shouldn't walk around without these real close at hand."

"What can we do about it? Take some risks. Let's go see what we can find," Lee responded, sounding more confident than he felt, feeling the stout, bark-covered haft of the crude weapon. He glanced down at the stake in his hand, and then over at the one in Ryan's. "We have something to work with, at the least."

"What about the ladies?" Ryan asked.

"I've already talked to Lynn. She was the first to get up today, evidently. Took over early from Erin's last watch. I told Lynn to stay and watch the camp, and that we'd go and see about food. If we don't succeed, we can switch teams whenever Erin gets up. They can give it a try," Lee said, stepping to the brim of the creek's bank.

He looked across to where the water trundled along the brim of the far bank, gauging the distance.

"I'd bet it'll be awhile before that girl gets up," Ryan remarked sarcastically.

"I'd bet too. Which is why we should go now, while we are ready and rested," Lee responded.

With a leap, he hurtled the span of the creek. His feet squished into the soft footing on the opposite side, splattering a little mud and water all around.

"Coming?" Lee inquired of Ryan, turning back towards the youth.

Ryan tensed, took a step, and propelled himself across, his youthful spring and longer legs taking him a little farther than Lee. Lee winced as Ryan descended, fully resigned to being amply covered with splotches of mud. Fortunately, Ryan landed upon a more solid swathe of ground, and did not spatter Lee with the impact of his landing.

"The question really is, are you ready?" Ryan asked Lee, sparks of excitement reflected in his eyes. "Hmmmm, old man?"

Lee was glad to see the flair of youthful adventure within Ryan's face, as his own mind was more oriented upon the very troublesome concerns regarding their unfamiliarity with the immediate environment and its denizens. He wished that he could embrace it all more like an adventure, and was not about to do anything to dampen Ryan's current spiritedness.

"Yes, yes, the old man is ready," Lee replied with sharp sarcasm.

Ryan took a step away from the bank. He pointed the sharp end of his stake towards the depths of the woods beyond, while looking back at Lee.

"Then shall we?" he asked, with raised eyebrows and a grin.

"Just remember, use gestures from here on out," Lee said, holding his finger to his mouth as he stepped by Ryan. "We make enough noise moving. Let's try and not add to it."

Ryan nodded as they set forth together. The two of them stepped softly, both careful in their efforts to remain as silent as possible.

Lee did not want to wander very far from the camp, as the last thing that needed to happen was for them to become lost. He took great care to make several mental notes of their surroundings. He pinpointed their pathway as best as he could, cataloging distinctive landmarks in the forms of certain trees, as well as some uniquely shaped rocks. Committing them to memory, he knew that the natural signs would be their lifeline on the way back.

He had no idea of what he and Ryan might come across on the excursion in the forest, being that he was no experienced outdoorsman. Theirs was to be a foray of sheer opportunism, delving into the unknown.

On the gathering side of things, their miniature quest remained a dismal failure, as they failed to locate any nuts or berries of a recognizably safe nature in the general vicinity of the camp. Anything they found turned out to have a very questionable appearance, and Lee was not about to chance a possible threat to their health. If any of them were to get sick, the prospects of treating the illness were very remote at best.

They had an altogether different experience in regards to hunting. About an hour and a half into their sojourn, Lee heard a couple of high-pitched screeches coming from deeper within the trees and brush, somewhere directly ahead of them. He signaled immediately to Ryan, to duck down and take cover behind some nearby trees.

Situated close together, Lee and Ryan waited in crouched positions, poised in a state of keen alertness.

Several minutes later, a group of four apparently flightless birds, each at least three feet tall and heavier of body, came into sight. Spread apart at staggered depths, they stalked slowly forward as their eyes swept through the area.

The heavy-bodied birds had large, and sharp-ended, curved beaks at the ends of their sizeable heads, which provided conspicuous evidence that the creatures were predators to be respected. Their stout bodies rested upon pairs of long, powerful legs, equipped with sets of horrific-looking talons. They had a very limber, muted step, and their purposeful movements gave off the appearance that they were ready to explode into rapid motion at any moment. The creatures also possessed two very undersized wings, readily confirming their flightless nature.

It was quite clear to Lee that their darker plumage was very advantageous to moving stealthily amid a world of shadows, brush, and earthy colors. They blended extremely well with the background, and it was plainly fortuitous that the area that Lee and Ryan had been trekking through contained only sparse, patchy areas of undergrowth.

To Lee, the creatures looked like they had emerged right out of a far distant past. He was simply glad that they were the size that they were, and not like some of the monstrosities of a very similar type that had walked the prehistoric ages of his own world.

While Lee realized the dangerous nature of the predatory birds, he also recognized a prime opportunity at hand. Though the large birds were themselves hunters, they were now about to become the hunted.

Lee gestured for Ryan to remain idle, while he kept his eyes riveted upon the approaching quartet of birds. The birds continued to methodically step through the area, fanning out broader as they looked about for smaller game.

Holding his position behind the tree, Lee waited patiently while he slowly brought his stake up in both hands to a level plane. When his arms came to rest, the sharp end was pointed towards the nearest of the birds. He kept a strong, firm grip upon the stake, the muscles of his arms, back, and shoulders tensing in readiness.

About a minute later, one of the other birds stepped over very close to where Lee was hiding. Lee carefully shifted the point of the stake to align with the advancing creature. It had just started to pass by the trunk of the tree, and in another stride or two would be in a position where it would not fail to discover Lee.

Lee was not about to let that transpire. Having kept rigidly still, he remained poised, a serpent coiled to strike. The very instant that the bird poked its head by the tree that Lee was behind, it found itself abruptly impaled with a powerful thrust of the makeshift spear. His robust strike was well-executed, bringing his body's weight and momentum fully behind it, and driven all the more forcefully by Lee's growing hunger.

The blow landed squarely in the bird's body, the sheer force knocking it backward and slamming it down into the ground. Spiked and grievously wounded, it made a loud squawk of dismay, which instantly roused the others of its group.

Lee yelled loudly at the birds, hoping to startle and scatter them. Instead of taking to flight, the others three birds recovered quickly, spreading out as they started towards Lee. Lee's heart sank precipitously, seeing their aggressive intention.

Secondly, and even more worrisome, Ryan was nowhere to be found.

"I need some help here, Ryan!" Lee shouted in panic.

His voice echoed off into the woods, without any reply other than the sounds of the predators encroaching upon him.

Lee yanked the crude pike out of the bird lying before him, raised his leg, and stomped down as hard as he could upon the creature's neck area, feeling his heel crack bone. The bird underneath him thrashed once more, before falling entirely still.

The other three continued to close in upon him. Lee raised his spear up, and readied in desperation to fight them.

Ryan entered the fray at that moment, yelling at the top of his lungs as he rushed out and skewered one of the incoming birds, taking it completely by surprise. The blow did not land as flush as Lee's had, but it knocked the bird off its talons and to the ground.

In burst of adrenalized vigor, Ryan hurled himself forth and threw his weight fully upon the end of the stake. His efforts drove the wood through further, and effectively pinned the writhing bird to the ground.

The two remaining birds were momentarily distracted and confused by the sudden attack of the shouting newcomer, enabling Lee a prime opportunity to strike cleanly and formidably. He focused and delivered another solid strike with his crude spear.

Yet another thrashing bird hit the ground, expiring a moment later after Lee had moved in and landed a couple of vicious kicks to its head, the last one crushing its skull.

The lone remaining bird, seeing the violent fates of its comrades, and no longer finding any strength in numbers, whirled about with a resounding cry, and bounded briskly off into the depths of the forest. Its body melted into the shadows and brush, vanishing in just a few strides.

"A lot harder than I thought," Lee remarked between heavy breaths, looking towards the depths of the forest that had engulfed the surviving bird's fleeing form. "Didn't think they would attack us. I hate surprises."

"Yeah, it was alot harder," Ryan agreed, then adding with a grin, "But at least we got something."

"And you took long enough," Lee retorted accusingly, with a grin that was only half in jest. His heart was still racing from the uncertain moment when the three birds had stalked him.

"Timing is everything," Ryan responded without hesitation. "Worked too, didn't it?"

"Okay, I'll give you that," Lee conceded, though not entirely assuaged. "But you still took your sweet time."

The three slain birds were now fully motionless, hard-won prizes for Lee and Ryan's efforts. Lee pulled his spear out of the dead creature that it was currently lodged in. He took a few moments to walk around and make certain that the other two fallen birds were indeed dead before trying to handle them. Lee knew that just one slash delivered from one of the powerful talons, or a lone, hard strike from the creatures' sharp beaks, could quite possibly cripple or kill him.

Each of the creatures weighed somewhere between sixty to seventy pounds. "We'll have to settle for two on one trip, it looks like," Ryan said, straining to heave one of the carcasses up and over his right shoulder.

Lee shrugged. "We've got more than enough here, and we don't have any place to store the excess."

"I hate wasting it, since we killed it," Ryan stated, looking over at the third bird. "Maybe we should come back for it."

"I think the meat will be made good use of, long before we can get back," Lee said, looking up into the surrounding trees. His eyes remained fixed on the branches above them. "They aren't going to be upset if we leave the bird. And I don't think they'll wait very long when we are out of sight. In fact, you and I are probably now heroes to them."

"What?" Ryan queried, before following Lee's glance on up into the boughs of the trees. He flinched in surprise at the sight.

A number of small, rodent-like creatures were cautiously emerging into sight on many of the upper branches.

They were chittering in high-pitched, squeaky voices, and their long snouts vigorously sniffed at the air in apparent excitement, likely emboldened by the sight of the three dead birds. Were it not for their prehensile tails, anchoring their dark-furred bodies to the tree limbs, Lee would not have doubted that their raised level of fervor would have caused more than a few of them to tumble out of the trees in the expanding commotion.

Lee understood immediately what the lay of the land was.

In more usual settings within this new world, it was creatures such as those above that were eaten by the carnivorous birds now lying below. Caught foraging on the forest floor, before they could reach the refuge of the trees, the creatures that Lee now saw all around him would be very easy prey for the large, predatory birds.

In what was probably a most glorious moment among their furry little race, their great nemesis's body would now be serving as a feast for their own kind.

Lee surmised that with the killing of three out of the four birds, he and Ryan had effectively decimated the rodent-like creatures' main threat within the area. If the small tree-dwelling creatures had been able to speak a succinct language, Lee would not have been surprised if they acclaimed the two humans as saviors.

Ryan grinned as he stared at the odd little creatures. "Yeah, we probably are heroes to the little guys. And you know what? I don't mind that. Nature's not really a very friendly thing, you know?"

"In reality it can be pretty brutal, and the tables aren't often turned, so they should celebrate it while they can," Lee remarked. He slung a bird carcass over his own right shoulder, with a grunt accompanying the exertion. "But we gotta survive. And so do they. So that's that. Now what do you say to getting some breakfast going?"

"And making up for a few other meals … but you clean it," Ryan replied as they started on their way back. "And I'm not watching. I prefer to get meat already cut and readied."

"I thought you young people were afraid of nothing," Lee chided, laughing. "Well, you can be happy that we landed birds. I've prepared chicken and duck more times than you can count. This will be on a bit of a bigger scale, but I'm sure the approach is not too different. But you are not off the hook. While I'm on this, you work on a fire."

"Don't know how," Ryan said.

"I'd bet one of the women might still have a lighter in her pocket," Lee said with a wink. "Didn't you notice Erin's coughing?"

"Good point," Ryan replied.

In time, they reached the campsite and set about their tasks. As Lee had suggested, Erin was a habitual smoker and did indeed have a lighter in one of her pockets.

In another moment of fortune, it was discovered that Lynn had one as well. She half-reluctantly confessed that her uses for it went further beyond tobacco. She also had a small pocket-knife in her possession, which Lee enthusiastically borrowed to help with his immediate tasks.

Ryan helped Lee get the carcasses carried over to the creek. Ryan soon disappeared as Lee started attending to the job of preparing the newly acquired food. The process was not as hygienic as Lee would have liked, as well as being much more awkward, but with some effort he finally accomplished his task.

When he finally came back, lugging several cut sections of meat in his hands, Ryan and Lynn had a small part of the ground cleared, and demarcated with a ring of stones. A fire was burning steadily inside a hollowed out area located within the stone circle.

Fashioning some rough spits, Lee soon had the meat cooking. The flames licked at the fresh meat, as the juices hissed and crackled in the heat.

In minutes, the scents wafting off of their cooking breakfast inundated the air. Lee's mouth watered in anticipation, buoyed by his gaping hunger, but he noticed that Erin was looking very sullen and hanging far back from the fire. Erin quickly saw that Lee was staring at her, and apparently recognized his puzzlement with her demeanor.

"I'm not eating that," she remarked edgily, her nose turned upward. In a tone that sounded like a judgement being delivered on all the others, she stated curtly, "I'm a vegetarian."

Lee chuckled openly, unable to hold back his amusement given their stark circumstances and options.

Ryan evidently could not hold back his incredulity either. "Oh, your kind really amaze me. See these? They are called canine teeth … C-A-N-I-N-E! They are used for eating meat," Ryan said in a patronizing tone, as he pointed at the sharp teeth in his own mouth.

"And what about it?" she snapped back hotly at him.

"Herbivores are not equipped with them. Omnivores and carnivores are," Ryan replied in the same condescending tone. "Oh, and did you know that your jaw moves back and forth, and also moves up and down? That's what a natural omnivore's jaws do."

"So what?" Erin replied irritably, her face now a hard scowl.

"Oh, and guess what else? Large brains in humans came about because of meat consumption," Ryan continued, clearly deriving some amusement from her vexation by that point. "I won't get into what that implies for the future of vegetarians, other than your brains will probably shrink over the generations, but you had better consider yourself real lucky that we can eat meat. Otherwise you would have had to continue starving."

Lynn half-heartedly moved to defend her friend at that moment, interrupting Ryan abruptly, "Take it easy on her now. She's been that way for years. Not my thing either, but it's what she wants to be. And we really do need to find some other food sources around here, eventually."

"And I will find something else," Erin added obstinately. "We'll find something soon enough."

Lee shrugged, but was not about to change his plans. "Have it your way then, but I'm going to eat now, and I'm eating what we manage to find. There's no menus out here. Just reality."

"Makes two of us," Ryan commented with a glare at Erin.

"I can't deny it either," Lynn said, with a sideways grin to the two men, out of Erin's line of sight, which showed that she understood their mystification at her friend's obstinacy.

They were able to satiate their hunger easily, for there was an overabundance of food for one meal with what Ryan and Lee had procured. Even with the crude manner that Lee had been forced to use to prepare it, the meat was surprisingly good. It had a tender, juicy quality that was not unlike well-prepared turkey, a quite pleasant surprise in the midst of the wilderness.

Erin watched the others eating from a few feet away, with a series of disgusted, sullen looks parading upon her face. Her juvenile display was almost to the point of being obnoxious, as far as Lee was concerned.

If she had intended to ruin Lee's enjoyment of the meal, it was to no avail. With each and every bite, Lee felt stronger, and more revived, while he knew that she was left lightheaded with an expanding hunger, by her own stubborn choice.

Finally, Erin got up with a curt exhale and stomped off into the forest. Lee was incredulous at the highly immature response of the young woman, especially from one whose life had hung by a precarious thread just mere moments after her entrance into this dangerous new world.

"No time for philosophical debates," Lee said. "We have to live. A starving lion wouldn't have any problem making short work of her."

"Exactly," Ryan said. "Neither would a shark."

"Which brings me to another point," Lee said quickly. A scowl crossed his face as he stared off towards where Erin had disappeared. "After what I've seen, there's no place for childish tantrums and stomping off into these woods alone."

He looked over to Ryan.

"True enough, I'll keep an eye on her, and try to talk her back here," Ryan said, getting up, picking up his stake, and setting out after Erin.

"Do it quickly," Lee called after him.

Ryan paused to pick up Erin's own makeshift weapon, which she had left behind in her ire.

"She gets impulsive," explained Lynn with an apologetic air, watching Ryan heading onward after her friend.

"Impulsive can mean getting killed here very quickly, I'm afraid. We don't know much about our whereabouts," Lee said. "I just learned a very good lesson, almost a very hard one."

He proceeded to tell Lynn more detail about their earlier encounter with the predatory birds, emphasizing the unpleasant surprises that had manifested. Lynn's eyes widened as the full tale was told, as Lee quickly discovered that she had only heard the basic elements from Ryan upon their return.

Erin appeared back at the campsite several minutes later. She was bearing a couple of branches loaded with berries, a petulant look fixed upon her face.

Ryan emerged into sight behind her a few seconds later, shrugging his shoulders at Lee with a look of exasperation. He was still carrying her makeshift weapon.

Erin looked towards Lee, and her face beamed with a look of triumph. Sitting down, she picked, chewed, and swallowed a mouthful of the berries. She then held out the branches towards Lee.

"See, this is called persistence," she declared acidly.

She took off a few more berries and ate them.

"She wouldn't listen to me," Ryan said. "I don't know about those. You and I both were worried about whether or not those were safe to eat."

Lee grew concerned as he watched her, as she had already proceeded well past the point of caution. The berries that she was eating he had indeed seen on his recent foray, and he had deemed it best to avoid them entirely.

His caution was affirmed a short time later, when Erin's haughty smile swiftly faded, her face growing very pale. Dropping the remaining berries, she clutched at her stomach and started to heave.

Lee, Ryan, and Lynn jumped up immediately and ran over to the stricken young woman, reaching Erin as she violently regurgitated her recent findings back onto the ground. After a few more heaves, when nothing more was coming out of her mouth, her breathing slowly settled back down.

The others gently helped Erin lay on the ground, easing her down carefully. Once Erin was prone, Lynn darted off towards the creek. She returned shortly with a piece of cloth that had been torn off of her own shirt, dampened with water. Kneeling by her friend, she wiped Erin's brow and patted the cloth lightly about her face.

The next couple of hours were filled with tension. Lee silently stood by the others with Erin, a great apprehension taking hold of him regarding the nature of the berries that she had consumed. He felt both anger and concern as he peered down upon the young woman, knowing that her suffering was wholly unnecessary. Her breathing was short and rapid, and her face reflected considerable pain as she cradled her stomach in a fetal position. The most bothersome aspect of it all was that Lee had no idea as to the outcome of her folly.

Only time would reveal the full answer.

As the moments passed, Erin went through another couple bouts of dry heaving, her stomach already having been thoroughly emptied. Her pallor continued to be troubling. Yet just when Lee had begun to dread the worst, her physical signs appeared to stabilize, and then slowly began to improve. Her breathing became more regular, and her face slowly showed less strain.

"Don't ever do that again," Lee remarked firmly, when it finally became abundantly clear that she was not mortally poisoned.

Erin's reaction to his words demonstrated that her constitution was returning in full. She did not give him the courtesy of a verbal reply, simply shooting Lee a hardened, annoyed look, as if to say that she absolutely refused to concede anything to him.

"Pride isn't going to get you very far under our circumstances!" Lee fumed with exasperation, throwing up his hands and tromping back towards the center of the camp.

Ryan shook his head and trotted after Lee.

Behind them, Lynn helped Erin back to a sitting position, and cautiously pulled her back up to her feet. She slowly guided Erin across the campsite, assisting her back under the shade of the shelter that they had fashioned.

"She'll rest better out of the open. So what now?" Lynn asked the other two, after she had emerged from the shelter and returned to join them. As if to answer their unspoken queries, she stated, "What she did was completely idiotic. I'm not supporting her stupid choice, but she's my friend."

"And we'll stand by her too, Lynn, as we're in this mess together," Lee replied without equivocation. "Even though I won't hesitate to point out when she's being a total fool."

"I'm with Lee, on both counts," Ryan added.

Lynn nodded to both of the males, "I appreciate all of that. She filters me out often enough, so it's good that you two are blunt with her. Maybe something will eventually get through her thick head."

"So what do you suggest we do now?" Lee asked, changing the subject back to the decisions imminently facing them. "Your guess is as good as mine."

"Try and find somebody, or something," Lynn answered. "It's all we really can do, when we have no idea where in this world we are."

"If there even is somebody out there," Ryan commented ruefully.

"We've got to at least look," Lynn replied.

"Then let's start doing it right now," Ryan said impatiently. After an extended pause, his next words took on a tinge of anger and desperation. "Let's get on it!"

Lee knew that the sharp edge just exhibited in the young man was stoked by the torrent of worries swirling within him. He could not blame Ryan for his great trepidation. Lee shared it too, and was simply a little better able to stifle his own worries, packing them deeper down inside.

"After a minute or two," Lynn stated firmly, steadily meeting Ryan's heated gaze. "Whether her fault or not, let Erin get a little of her strength back."

Ryan sat down with a huff, rolling his eyes. "Then I'm sitting."

Lee replied gently, "We will wait, Lynn, but we need to learn everything we can about this world. And we need to learn very fast, if we are going to have a chance to make it very far. Now we know of those aggressive birds. Now we know about those berries. Two steps on that journey."

As if to accentuate his point, Lee walked over and picked up Lynn's stake where she had set it down. Returning, he handed it over to her.

"And you keep this near you, at all times," Lee said adamantly.

Lynn set the end of the stake into the ground, gripped in both of her hands as she lowered her eyes to the ground before her. Lee said nothing more as he turned and stepped over to Ryan's side. He lowered himself down, patting the youth reassuringly upon the shoulder as he took a place by him. Lynn sat down with them a few moments later.

Few words passed between the trio, as time marched relentlessly onward.

After about another hour had passed, Erin came out from the

shelter and broke the impasse, indicating that she felt that she could handle some slow hiking. The group gathered its belongings together and left the campsite behind. Setting off at an easy pace, they halted sporadically, mainly to allow Erin to rest for a few moments.

While clearly not feeling fully well, Erin proved to be capable of handling the rather leisurely rate of travel without major incident, or sign of undue strain. A few times Lee considered urging her to press herself a little harder, but he bit back his impulses, simply grateful that she was cooperating without an acerbic display of attitude.

The landscape that they traveled through remained largely unchanged, as the litany of trees, hilly terrain, wide forest creeks, and narrow streams continued.

Majestic oaks allowed considerable sunlight to reach the forest floor, resulting in the flourishing of ferns, violets, and other types of plants low to the ground. Tall beeches, with their smooth gray surfaces, heralded the presence of minimal undergrowth beneath their ample, thick-shading canopies. Beautiful hazel trees with their dangling, cylindrical flower clusters, hardwood ash trees, and great pines were just some of the other types of woodland sentinels populating the area that they walked through.

The signs of animal life were minimal, confined primarily to a few more sightings of the strange, tree dwelling mammals that seemed to be prevalent to the region that they were traversing.

There were also a number of rather ordinary birds, of kinds much more familiar to Lee's eyes. The diminutive sparrows emitting their sustained chirping, the blackbirds with their eyes ringed in yellow, and a few warblers, grey-backed with reddish undersides, were all witnessed by Lee as they hiked through the woodlands.

The birds were largely resting among the branches of the trees, sending their various calls out through the peaceful forest air. Lee passed the time by watching a few of them alighting upon, or taking off from, the living roosts. He watched them dart and glide amongst the trees, with some lifting out of sight on a climb skyward.

The afternoon slowly dissolved as the shadows lengthened, announcing the approach of the early stages of evening. By that time, it seemed to Lee as if his body was being sapped of energy with every passing moment. He had begun to envy Ryan and the two girls, who possessed natural, extra reservoirs of youthful stamina.

Yet despite the youth of the other three, all things were not equal in relation to their various conditions. Ryan and Lynn were holding up to the trek very well, while Erin now appeared to be toiling just to keep moving forward.

Just as Lee was about to call for an extended halt, for both his sake and Erin's, they finally came upon a break in the trees and brush. They had just skirted around the base of yet another one of the ubiquitous, forested hills that dominated the region that they were passing through. The denser foliage gave way fairly abruptly, as an entirely new, magnificent vision was unveiled before them.

A series of very low, grassy hills undulated in what was essentially a broad, rolling plain, broken up only by pockets of brush strewn randomly about. The low waves in the sea of windswept grasses spread out to the farthest edges of their vision.

"Progress, I hope," Ryan remarked, as the four of them looked out over the markedly different terrain.

"And maybe danger," Lynn quickly returned, not looking very confident at the significant change in geography.

Lee could not blame Lynn's apparent misgivings, as the new territory offered its own set of daunting concerns. It was considerably more open and exposed, especially if they were to try to walk out into it.

They would easily be visible for miles around, especially to any eyes watching from a higher vantage point. It was not lost on Lee that all four in the group had already witnessed formidable flying entities traversing the skies of this strange world.

Yet there was no imminent threat in view, or even a remote sign of danger. A very large, heavy-bodied bird with a substantial wingspan, chestnut-breasted with a white underside, flew calmly over the grassy surface, showing no apparent urgency in its easygoing flight.

Erin slumped down to the ground at the edge of the trees, breathing heavily as the others hesitated. Her body had been taxed to a much greater extent than the others had been. She looked to be genuinely grateful for the stop, rather than for any notable change in geography.

Lee stood silently, peering off towards the distant horizon, looking carefully to both sky and ground. He slowly dropped to one knee, and placed his hand upon the ground.

He had intended to simply brace himself, resting a little as he stared out over the open expanse. Yet something tugged at his instincts almost instantly, as his palm connected with the land.

He felt that there was something faint under his hand, like a barely perceptible tremor, though it was not strong enough for surety. A frown crossed his face, his expression swiftly growing pensive. There was not enough in the feeling coming from beneath his palm to convince him, but the foreboding sense prevented him from dismissing it outright.

"Let's go!" Ryan said from behind Lee, taking a couple of steps forward.

Lee shook his head curtly, snapping his hand up to get Ryan to halt when the youth had reached his side. The young man was just a couple of steps away from leaving the cover of the trees.

Lee said emphatically, "There's something here. Let's pull back behind the trees for now … at least while we rest."

Ryan groaned in frustration, as the others walked back a few strides, deeper into the cover of the trees. They waited in silence, hungry and tired, for nearly an hour.

Even if Lee could not say exactly what it was, he was increasingly certain that something was amiss. All of his instincts screamed out to him to heed his caution and stay away from the open ground.

Lee continued to feel the vibrations in the earth beneath, soon perceiving that they were growing stronger. It was clear from their moods that Lynn and Ryan were becoming quite restless, although Erin was still weary enough to value the extended respite. Lee had just begun to ponder whether his mind was playing tricks on him in his fatigued state, when their eyes were all suddenly drawn towards one of the low, grass-blanketed hills off to the right.

A light thumping sound, in a conspicuously galloping rhythm, filled their ears and grew steadily louder. Lee gestured urgently for all of them to get down and press their bodies to the ground.

There was no argument from any of the others as they hurriedly lay down flat upon the hard earth. Lee's heart leaped and pounded, and he doubted that any of the others had a slow heartbeat in the sharply heightened anxiety of the moment. The rumbling beats swelled, the vibrations under Lee becoming ever more prominent. His eyes remained locked on the plains before them.

About a minute later, a number of mounted riders burst into full view.

Lee drank in the startling sight, spellbound at what he saw. Stunned,

Lee stared at the throng of figures, taking in their strange appearances.

The riders were sitting in wood-framed saddles, astride horses of a strong, muscular build. Most of the riders were armed with long lances, the spear-blades featuring iron lugs at their bases that jutted straight out to the sides.

Near to the lead of the group was a rider bearing a special lance, to which a wedge-shaped pennon was affixed. The pennon was of alternating blue and gold stripes, with a fringe of red tassels lining the curving outer edge. It flapped vigorously as it cut through the air above the galloping riders.

All of the riders wore long cloaks, pinned at the right shoulder. Round shields of various colors were slung over their backs, suspended from leather straps. Iron bosses glinted in the daylight where they protruded from the middle of the large shields.

The riders' heads were protected in a variety of half-helms. Some were of a rounded type, with chain mail aventails affixed to extend the wearer added neck protection. Others were of a more crested profile, protruding slightly in the rear. A few were crafted of segmented iron plates, with descending nasal guards in front.

The riders' upper bodies were clad in coats of mail, and a few wore chain mail chausses, providing additional protection on their thighs down to the tops of their knees.

A bearded rider just ahead of the pennon-bearer suddenly raised his sword high, drawing Lee's attention. Sunlight gleamed off the golden inlay on the hazelnut-shaped pommel and short, straight quillons. Long locks of dark hair whipped around from where they flowed out from the base of his half-helm, as the sword-wielder cried out loudly to the others, eliciting a spirited shout in response.

This warrior had additional protective elements, distinguishing him from the rest of the riders. Unique among the group, he possessed a pair of splinted iron greaves that protected his lower legs, echoing similar vambraces encasing his lower arms.

The horses were being spurred forward with a desperate urgency, driven at a full gallop as they pounded swiftly across the open ground.

Lee ripped his gaze away from the remarkable sight, and glanced quickly over to the others with him. Wide looks of amazement were exchanged among his companions, before they turned their full attention back towards the oncoming cluster of riders.

Loud cries, and a flurry of sounds resembling growls and barks, then filled the air, as the throng of horses was swiftly brought to a halt. The riders bore looks of utter surprise, as they looked up into the sky, right in the area over where Lee and the others were hiding.

Lee's heart thundered more furiously at the new chorus of sounds, which were directly over his position.

The riders scattered in all directions, as a number of dark shadows sped across the ground towards them. Lee saw the deep, racing shadows from the first moment that they broke out along the surface of the grasses. He looked up into the sky, just as a horde of stunning forms burst into full view.

Lee had never seen anything like the flying entities now soaring low over the grassy plains, conveyed forth by sweeping sets of dark, membranous wings. They were entirely unique to his experience, giant, four-legged creatures. Even more incredible, they were bearing armed riders.

The winged creatures themselves had a slightly sloped frame, rising from their lower hips to the frontal portion of their bodies. They had large heads, with short muzzles that harbored broad, powerful jaws. Large, triangular ears rose up on each side of their heads, positioned near to the crown.

Covering the backs and sides of the flying creatures was a shaggy mass of long, coarse, dark brown fur. Around their wide necks and chests, from the backs of their upright ears to the tops of their shoulders, they displayed a distinctive, light yellow mane.

Four legs, lean and sinewy, were tucked underneath their bodies, the limbs ending in broad paws that were each equipped with a set of sharp claws. The short fur covering their legs held a distinct coloration pattern, with alternating light and dark rings running from their wide paws on up to their undersides.

As Lee caught his first clear glimpses of the profiles of the riders upon on the winged steeds, time screeched to a standstill. They were undeniably inhuman.

Lee's mind scrambled to recover from his initial shock, as the fliers guided their winged steeds directly towards the scattering horsemen with exceptional skill, and a deadly grace. Nearly fifty of them had now swept into Lee's view, racing towards the dispersing horsemen far beneath them. At first, they drove the horsemen farther away from the forest's edge, forcing a few that had been charging directly towards the trees to veer away just a short distance from reaching the woods.

Several of the fliers curved about, as if seeking to corral the dispersing horse riders closer together. In the process, they presented Lee with a full, frontal view of their forms.

Lee's mouth dropped agape.

The considerable size of the winged steeds was wholly necessary to bear the imposing riders aloft, while still retaining agility, maneuverability, and speed. The warriors had thick, powerful chests and torsos, complimented by broad backs and shoulders, and long, brawny limbs.

Their strong upper bodies were clothed in knee-length, earthen colored tunics, which were worn underneath protective hide jerkins. Leggings, or perhaps woolen trousers, completed their primary attire. Their hide shoes or boots were set firmly into bronze stirrups of a simple, stout design.

The fronts of many of the outer jerkins were richly decorated, exhibiting a variety of designs that contrasted with the darker color of the hide. Many of the fliers were also wearing amulets around their broad, muscular necks.

Thick, very long locks of dark hair flowed out copiously from underneath boiled leather caps, or simple iron half-helms, buffeted about vigorously within the winds.

Their faces were fully exposed to Lee in the broad daylight, displaying the most striking features of all. Their non-human visages contained a protruding muzzle, one that had a thick-set appearance short in length, and broad in width. Opening their jaws wide to emit their deep, sonorous war cries, they showed off the extensive canines contained within their considerable maws.

Many of the beast-men were carrying extensive lances, fitted with broad, elongated spear blades unmistakably suited for slashing as much as thrusting. Others bore a formidable-looking, sword-like weapon, which had a quite lengthy, heavy blade. It had no cross guard above the short hilt, or pommel beneath. The weapon's broad, protracted blade had a gently curving, saber-like profile to it, singled-edged, and ending in a wickedly sharp point.

A few of the fliers bore a particularly fearsome-looking, long-hafted weapon. A two-handed weapon, its single-edged blade was both longer and heavier than that of the sword-like weapon, while being of a generally similar profile. It was not a spear, but rather a cutting weapon, able to be utilized like a great axe.

Several fliers pursuing the horsemen held short javelins in overhand grips, while a handful of others were clustering in a hovering pattern, bearing great longbows fashioned of a single stave of wood. Arrows fletched with large, black feathers were being set to the bowstrings as the archers searched out targets below.

Many of the airborne warriors bore rectangular shields, crafted of wooden planking faced with plain hide coverings. The shields were suspended by thick leather straps across their shoulders and backs, keeping their hands freed up. The warriors' left hands held onto the reins of their sky steeds tightly, while they brandished their weapons in their right.

As Lee looked out upon the developing melee, the first of the sky riders swooped downward at a high speed that was a challenge to follow with the eye.

The iron-helmed flier at the lead of the attackers roared a furious battle cry, bringing its steed swiftly lower with a few others diving in its wake. Wielding one of the sword-like weapons, the lead warrior kept its arm forward of its steed's wings, holding the blade angled back. The sky rider adroitly guided its steed to come up on the shield side of a horse rider that was racing just ahead.

The winged steed stretched its wings out and glided through the short remaining distance, closing quickly as it allowed its rider to bring the blade back farther for a powerful attack. The sky warrior did not strike at the horse rider, but rather slashed viciously at his mount, blood spraying in the aftermath.

Crumbling to the ground with a hideous scream and a mortal wound to its neck, the horse threw its rider off. The man flew forward, and cried out in pain as he slammed hard into the unyielding ground just a few strides ahead of his horse.

The rider had not even regained his feet when a second flier swooped in, bearing one of the long-hafted weapons with the extensive, heavy blades. With a frenzied battle cry, the sky rider whipped the great weapon through the air with both of its heavily muscled arms. The blade cleaved right through the man's head, the headless body wavering for a moment before slumping to the ground. The flier shook the bloodied weapon vigorously, uttering another loud war cry as the winged steed carried them onward.

The horse riders were continuing to spray outward, into all directions, perhaps hoping to confuse the attackers that so greatly outnumbered them up above. If so, it soon became apparent that their efforts were in vain, as the fliers swarming the area were gradually singling out horse riders, honing in on them with lethal intent.

The fliers who had long bows were now loosing arrows from their hovering mounts, the missiles streaking towards their intended targets. The ones with javelins were jettisoning their own missiles, by robust throws from steeds kept to a slow, steady glide.

Outnumbered and confined to the ground, it soon became quite clear that the horse riders were at a great disadvantage.

Using their long lances, and in some cases resorting to javelins themselves, the horse riders did whatever they could to repel and frustrate the attacks, at least whenever their assailants came close enough.

Lee saw one horseman come to the aid of another whose assailant was closing in fast. Racing his horse up alongside the gliding enemy warrior, the human sent a javelin hurtling to lodge in the body of the attacker, just as its long blade was about to arc down towards the other human rider.

The victory was short lived, as the javelin-thrower did not see the thrust of the spear from another non-human warrior coming from behind him, impaling his own body scant moments after he had interceded for his comrade.

A bloody, furious struggle evolved, though the horse riders were steadily whittled down in the relentless, overwhelming assault by the aerial attackers.

Lee could not help but be impressed at the incredible skill of the non-human warriors. Even their winged steeds were living weapons, working in close harmony with their riders.

In a couple of instances, Lee saw the sky steeds utilize their powerful claws effectively, lowering their legs and viciously raking humans right off the backs of their galloping horses.

The sky riders continued to work in close concert with each other. Several endeavored to herd the beleaguered horse riders back in, while others rushed in immediately to finish off the dazed and injured riders that had been knocked from their mounts.

On occasion, such as when a horseman whirled to present lance and shield to the flying attacker, there was a firm attempt to continue the attack. Yet more often than not in such instances, the assailants from above merely banked their steeds away from their approach before the horseman could have any chance to inflict damage.

Lee did witness one horseman who was able to get in a lethal thrust against one of the attackers. The horseman's spear rushed up from a strong, overhand grip to meet the forward momentum of the incoming sky rider, the force of both movements converging to spike the attacker. The horseman immediately had to let go of his deeply lodged weapon, as the beast-man's body was blasted right from its low saddle.

The triumph was temporary, as another sky-borne warrior dove in to avenge its fallen comrade. Before the horseman could unsheathe his own sword and bring it up to fend off the assault, he was beheaded by the heavy blade of the attacker's sword-like weapon.

Cries of agony were filling the air, coming from horses, humans, and a few of the inhuman assailants and their unusual, flying steeds. The end of the battle was approaching from what Lee could tell, and the result looked inevitable.

Several of the skyward warriors began to land their steeds upon the ground. The massive riders leaped off of their mounts with astonishing dexterity, especially given their considerable size. Readying their weapons and shields, they charged with a raging fury at the surviving human warriors that had been unhorsed. Their sharp, long teeth were bared in a feral mask of maddened frenzy as they brandished their weapons.

The dismounted human warriors responded with a fiery resolve of their own, several drawing swords out to meet the onslaught from their fearsome attackers. They showed no outward signs of fear, and now that the fighting field had been more leveled, proceeded to acquit themselves better.

They shouted out their own raucous battle cries, the words seeming to charge them with impetus and tenacity.

The sounds of clashing steel were added to the chorus of the fray, along with the thuds and cracks of heavy blows upon the thick wooden planking of both round and rectangular shields.

The awesome strength of the inhuman attackers was made very apparent, as round shields held by the defenders were broken asunder. Chunks of wood exploded out in showers of shards and splinters, fracturing under the heavy blades of the beast-men's sword-like weapons, and the even more unique, long-hafted ones.

There was no give on either side. The attackers roared with a deep, wrathful vigor, and the men shouted angrily back in response, each side matching the other's mettle.

Lee's heart grew heavy as he watched the combat, knowing that the fates of the human defenders were almost certainly sealed. Gradually, a small remnant of the surviving horsemen was herded together by a encroaching circle of the bestial warriors. With no route of escape left, the humans were forced into a last stand against their relentless oppressors.

Weapons clashed fiercely, flesh and muscle was pierced and slashed, and bones were crushed. Casualties were incurred upon both sides during the last, frenzied moments of the fighting.

The last of the men to fall was the apparent leader of the horsemen, the one wearing the vambraces and greaves that Lee had witnessed riding close to the standard-bearer at the onset of the fight.

Lee was a little surprised that the beast-men took any risks with the lone remaining human, trapped as he was without hope of escape. The archers among the sky warriors could have taken him down with little difficulty, but those that still held their bows had lowered them, and held no arrows in their free hands.

The valiant human fighter undoubtedly understood his dire situation, but if he felt any fear, it did not show. His blade flashed in the sun as he wielded it adroitly, bringing down one of the beast-men after deftly avoiding the cleaving blow of a long-hafted weapon.

He did not hesitate as his mortally-stricken opponent stumbled and pitched over to lie still, already lunging towards another tall enemy warrior. Delivering a gash to the thigh of the enemy fighter, the man held his ground as his bleeding attacker gave way and backed up a step.

The man then straightened up and got into a balanced stance, as one particular sky rider shouldered past its comrades to confront the fierce human warrior. A terrible scowl was on the face of the new challenger, and the other sky warriors, including the one that had just been wounded, stepped back a couple of paces to give the two combatants a wider berth.

It was the sky rider that had led the attackers out over the plains, the first one of them to descend. Lee deemed that the warrior was the human's counterpart among the airborne force.

The sky rider was a very mighty specimen amongst the inhuman warriors. Seen close to its comrades, it was quite evident that the warrior far surpassed the exceptional stature and mass inherent in its kind.

The human fighter staggered as the clang of the first blow echoed loudly across the grassland, having barely blocked the first strike of his towering opponent. With a loud cry, the human used his shield to barrel directly forward, driving his much larger opponent back a step as their shields collided.

Shuffling back quickly to create some space, the human fighter set himself again, taking up a balanced position and coldly eyeing the beast-man. With a roar, the sky rider stomped forward and raised its sword-like weapon up to strike again.

The human warrior acquitted himself well in the ensuing fight, but was finally hewn down after a rabid exchange of blows with the brawny, iron-helmed warrior.

Wielding the huge, sword-like weapon with amazing speed, the sky warrior finally found an opening in the human's defenses after a few previous attempts had been capably blocked by the horseman's own blade and shield. The sky warrior's blade raced into a slim gap of space as the human's sword was caught on the other's large shield.

Lee felt a pang of sadness as the brave human warrior dropped to his knees in the wake of the devastating slash, before toppling over to the ground, dead at the feet of his slayer.

Curiously, after the human leader had been felled, and the field of battle had fallen eerily silent, the savage posture of the inhuman warriors dissipated rapidly. The fighting over, it was as if the blood-lust that they had exhibited suddenly released its grip upon them.

The huge sky warrior knelt down upon one knee at the side of the horsemen's slain leader. With a massive hand, the sky rider picked up the fallen warrior's sword, from where it had fallen from his grasp, and carefully returned it to the dead man's grip. The sky warrior, who had only recently been a tempest of martial ardor, looked uncannily gentle in its movements.

There was a respectful aspect to the purposeful gesture, and Lee could not help but think that the hulking warrior was honoring the skill and fortitude of its fallen opponent.

No more than seven or eight of the attacking war band had been killed in the fighting, with a few more wounded, in comparison with every last one of the horse riders being slain.

A few horses had died as well, though a great majority had made it through the battle without serious injury. Several of the rider-less horses were wandering aimlessly nearby, or cantering farther off in continued fright, with nobody left to guide them.

The victorious attackers proceeded to systematically check the corpses littering the area, and to Lee's eyes they appeared to be making sure that the humans were indeed dead. No human survivors were discovered, but there were a few critically injured horses in the vicinity that still had breath in them. Without hesitation, and without any sign of pleasure, the inhuman warriors quickly put the beasts out of their misery with focused, singular blows.

The bestial faces of the warriors, and their absolute ferocity in battle, were quite unsettling, in a primeval way. Yet Lee observed that these warriors were not simply animalistic barbarians. Their complex nature was acutely reflected in the way in which they went around the fallen humans, and attended to the mortally wounded steeds.

A couple of sideways glances revealed that Lee's companions were similarly spellbound by the sights and frozen in place, with nary a breath to disturb the air and invite discovery.

As Lee continued to observe them, the creatures spoke to each other from time to time in a guttural language. Though rough in manner, it was very clear that the warriors were highly disciplined and well-organized. Watching their exchanges, Lee was left with no doubts that the huge one that had felled the human leader did indeed hold the primary authority over the entire group.

The extraordinary winged steeds that the beast-men rode lingered in patience for their masters, a few emitting low whines or barks. A couple of the ones situated closer together nipped and snarled at each other.

When the riders were completely finished with their inspection of the battlefield, the huge leader shouted to all of them. At the leader's call, there was a little spark of hesitance, which flared suddenly into reticence among the others. The leader seemed to be expecting the reaction, speaking sharply as the others cast glances about at the fallen humans and those of their own race.

At first, Lee had been sure that the taciturn response had something to do with the fallen non-human warriors, but the more that he watched their deliberate glances include the human warriors, he was not quite so sure.

The leader shook its great head emphatically from side to side, in an unmistakable negation to the unvoiced objection that the others were clearly referencing.

The leader then spoke again, its tone changing and lowering in volume, as its next words came out slower. Lee was positive that the leader was addressing the unspoken desire within the others in a more sympathetic fashion.

The leader glanced around at the corpses, shook its head again, and finished its address with a few words that took on a more authoritive timbre. The other warriors seemed to be largely assuaged from whatever issue had initially troubled them. A few of them hurriedly went over to their fallen brethren, carefully removing amulets and other small objects from the bodies of the dead beast-men.

Before standing back up, the living warriors bowed their heads, some laying their massive hands upon the shoulders of the prone bodies. Lee could see their lips moving as they uttered last words at the sides of their comrades.

The few sky steeds that had carried the fallen among the beast-men were then wrangled and brought together with the others. Lee took note that these had not strayed far from the vicinity of the rest of the steeds. All of the warriors eventually proceeded to stride back to their winged steeds and mount them.

The huge leader was the last one into the saddle. A few moments later, after a loud cry from the prominent warrior, the riders spurred their exotic steeds into motion. The creatures spread their wings, lurched into a short, bounding run, and leaped towards the sky. With powerful, snapping flaps, the mounts carried their riders up into the air. The steeds with empty saddles followed the cue of their brethren, as if trained, pursuing the others off of the ground and up towards the sky.

Lee watched the steeds beat their wings vigorously as they climbed towards the heavens, gaining height steadily on a sharp incline. In a loose formation, the great steeds finally leveled out, as they carried the throng of menacing sky riders across the rolling plains, heading into the distance towards the west and the setting sun.

Lee and the others remained motionless long after the riders were just mere specks on the far horizon. Nobody so much as moved or spoke, until those specks had completely disappeared from view.

"Don't ask me," Lee commented at last, his eyes slowly lowering to gaze upon the garish collection of corpses strewn all about the grounds ahead of them.

His heart sank.

A predatory, bird-like creature, like that faced by Erin and Lynn upon their entrance into the new world, was one type of danger. Bands of well-armed fighters, fully equipped with iron weapons and riding upon incredible winged steeds, was another level of threat entirely.

"Maybe we could use some weapons, from out there," Ryan then suggested, pointing out towards the dead warriors. "These stakes aren't going to do us much good, especially if we run into either of those who were in the fight."

Lee was impressed by Ryan's proposition, especially the fact that he had not assumed that the humans would automatically be receptive to their group. It reminded Lee to maintain a better wariness himself, and to presume nothing about the things of this new world, no matter how familiar they might look at first.

"I think that's an excellent idea. We should take advantage of it while we know that the area is clear right now," Lee concurred.

"I'm not going out there," Erin stated flatly. "No way. If those things come back, there is no way we are going to get away. If a couple dozen armed fighters on horses can't survive, then how the hell will four of us?"

Without saying a word, Lynn got up with a somber expression and started forward. Just a few strides carried her out of the shelter of the forest, and out under the open sky.

She paused for a moment, and turned back to the others. Her eyes fixed solidly upon Erin.

"We can't just wait for the trouble to find us. This might be a chance that we won't have again, or anytime soon," she stated. "We have to try and be prepared somehow, and I would rather do it with what those dead men were carrying, than with the sticks we have now."

Lee got up and trotted out after her. Ryan finally got to his feet and jogged to catch up with them, after some initial hesitation.

"Let's get it done quickly," Lee remarked to them.

Erin remained behind, clearly not willing to budge from her hiding place.

Lee reached the first of the dead human fighters, one of those who had taken part in the final stand. His heart raced, and he momentarily shivered as he looked down upon the dead man's inert face.

The man's glassy, lifeless gaze stared back up at him. A gaping wound had been opened in his chest, where a large spear blade had been lodged and then ripped back out. Blood soaked the ground around the body, though the flow of it had ceased.

Lee glanced towards Lynn, who was standing by another fallen human warrior. A few tears had come to her eyes, as she stared in an almost mesmerized fashion into the stark visage of death beneath her.

Taking a deep breath, and struggling to regain his composure, Lee forced his eyes back to the slain human underneath him. The man looked to be in his early twenties, his weathered face unable to mask the youthful luster that still lingered underneath the hardened edges.

The light of life was entirely absent, but the man's face had settled into a peaceful expression that conflicted profoundly with the brutal violence of his demise.

Lee had to pause again, as this experience was something that he was not well prepared for. The males in their twenties that he had previously known were normally busy with school or work, their concerns related to careers, relationships, or entertainment.

Lee certainly did not come from an environment where bodies were left torn and broken under an impassive sky, sprawled right before his very eyes.

He was not so naïve to think that his own world was immune from such horrid things. Terrible sights occurred frequently, indeed every day, in the far corners of that world. It was simply that he did not encounter such awful visions so closely, and intimately, in the world he had left behind. He was certainly not steeled for what he was now seeing all around him.

Lee glanced again towards Lynn.

She had averted her eyes from the warrior's face, turning her head to the side as she picked up a sword that was lying near to the fallen man. She gripped the hilt and raised the weapon upward, the flesh of her hand pressed against the short, straight cross-guard.

The blade was long and straight, double-edged with a broad fuller running down its center. The hilt had a tightly-wound leather grip, and a multi-lobbed pommel.

As she lifted the sword, Lee saw that it was a little heavy for her to lift in one hand. She then gripped it in both hands, taking a hesitant, awkward swing through the air with the blade. With two hands, Lynn demonstrated that she held enough strength to swing the weapon with some purpose.

Lee then picked up a sword from the man at his feet, very comparable to the one that Lynn had taken, except for its hazelnut-shaped pommel. He kept the sword with him as he walked onward, feeling the considerable weight of it tugging at his arm. He proceeded a little farther out, striding over to another fallen warrior, whose horse's body lay nearby. Eyeing the dead horse, he moved over to it, to see what might be found attached to the saddle and harnessing.

He searched through the man's equipment, discovering a strung longbow and a quiver that was almost full of arrows.

"We could use that, for sure," Ryan stated, from where he was strolling close to Lee.

Lee glanced up to him. "See if you can find some food on the slain horses. And remember to keep up a lookout. Any sign of anything whatsoever, and we bolt immediately for the woods. Got it?"

Ryan nodded, looking back up the sky and sweeping his gaze slowly across the horizons.

Lee did the same, and to his great relief the skies were empty of everything save for some drifting clouds and a descending, reddish sun. He shortly resumed his search, pausing occasionally to take appraisal of the horizons.

Among the corpses of the horses and men, Lee, Ryan, and Lynn found some leather pouches that held a small quantity of dried, salty meat, hard bread, and a little fresh water that was contained in leather skins.

Lee also took an interest in the large, single-edged daggers that many of the men had carried, claiming one of them for himself.

In addition, he gathered up all the small silvery coins that he came across among the possessions of the slain men. While most of the coins were fully intact, a portion of them had been cut into halves. A quick look at the half-coins told Lee that they were of the very same minting as the rest of the coins, though he wondered as to why they were not complete.

Knowing that the small silver coins held more hints about the world that Lee was now in, he examined several of the fully intact ones very closely. He turned them over in his hand, and held them up to bathe in the still-ample sunlight. Lee ran his ringers slowly over their edges, as if he could somehow absorb what the little silvery pieces had to tell him.

The coins were all of the same size, roughly a little smaller than the size of Lee's thumbprint. They did not have a smooth surfacing, even in the areas without an image or letter displayed.

The obverse facing of the coins showed the side profiles of male figures, with lettering running around the circumference of the entire coin. The reverse side held more similar lettering around the edges, with a spear-shaped symbol occupying most of the inner surface.

Most of the coins, including all of the coins in the best condition, held the image of one particular man, who possessed a strong chin, nose, and full beard. Lee wondered who the man depicted on the coin was, assuming him to be a ruler or leader of the realm that the horse riders were a part of.

He also wondered what the prominently displayed spear shape symbolized, figuring that it was more iconic in nature than merely a simple representation of a common weapon.

The images, and Lee's inability to read the lettering, created a little more frustration in him. Lee could not decipher anything specific from them. Having taken more time than he intended to with the coins, he placed them all back into his pocket. The questions that he had would have to be pondered at a later time.

When they finally finished gathering up foodstuffs, weapons, and other items, Lee and Ryan had each procured a bow, quiver with arrows, and a sword. Ryan had also taken up a hand axe, whose edge had been honed incredibly sharp.

Both had ended up leaving the long lances born by the horsemen where they lay about the ground.

Lee had taken a moment to consider the spears, with their sizeable iron blades and flaring wings of iron near the sockets. Though feeling reticent about the choice, he had opted not to take one.

They were most certainly solid weapons, and they could be used to keep an opponent at a distance. Yet there was no question that they would be entirely too cumbersome for Lee or any of the others to carry along, and he did not have any training in how to properly use them.

Lee and Ryan also claimed a couple of the very few remaining undamaged round shields, with their raised iron bosses set within the center. Lee looked at the narrow protrusions extending from the apex of the dome-like bosses, instantly realizing the potential of the shields as weapons themselves.

Ryan's shield was solid red, with a yellow line around the rim, while Lee's had broad, swirling segments of alternating red and blue upon its facing.

The shield was heavy, with a grip in the center placed just behind the iron boss. Lee was grateful for the thick, buckled leather strap on it, which he used to suspend and carry the shield over his back.

Some of the better items uncovered were small iron objects that were kept with pieces of flint. That alone promised to solve one looming problem that Lee saw coming, of what to do when they no longer had access to the fire-making implements from their former world. The two women's lighters would not last forever.

Almost as an afterthought, he and Ryan added a couple of small, single-edged knives to their expanding collection of items. Lee surmised that the knives would come in very handy as tools, and would certainly be much more efficient in the shaping of wood than using the edges of rocks.

All the while, the dead bodies that they searched among continued to bother Lee's conscience. The apprehension and misgivings that he felt mounted with each individual that he came across.

Even so, he could not help but continue to marvel at the nature of the fallen warriors' equipment and appearances, as if they had stepped right out of the mists of time. His fascination was tempered by the stark reality of what had recently happened, as he found himself increasingly saddened by their terrible fates.

For the most part, Lee tried to keep the haunting feelings at bay, while going about his chosen task. He paused several times during the search, taking a moment to closely regard more than one of the individual men. He wondered what kind of men each of them were, and what kind of society they were a part of.

He wondered whether they were good men at heart, or whether he and his companions would have had something to fear from them. His thoughts lingered and dwelled with each new face that he came upon, and he felt a deep pang of regret as he knew that they would not be able to bury the men, or even burn their corpses.

Every one of the dead men had a mother, something that Lee pondered deeply as he thought of his own elderly mother. He thought of how traumatic something like this would be if it had happened to him, abandoned to rot out on some empty, windswept plain.

Lee bit back a swell of great frustration as he thought of the men's family, friends, and others who would long wonder what had befallen the warriors that had been a regular part of their lives.

Lee wished dearly that he could do something for the men, but survival demanded cruel indifference. He accepted that he and his companions would be unable to attend to the men in any significant manner. It was unavoidable that their bodies would be left behind as simple fodder for carrion, and the drawn-out decay of the elements and time.

The utter helplessness of the situation pained Lee immensely, especially as he thought of everything in a much more personal sense, but there was really no choice. Each time the waves of sad regrets came over him, he clenched his jaws and went back to searching the bodies with a single-minded resolve.

The humans were not the only ones to cause him distress, as the bodies of the larger race of attackers proved to be another matter entirely.

Lee finally worked up enough nerve to examine a couple of the dead beast-men. He shuddered as he peered down at their inhuman visages. Up close, he saw that they had the broad, powerful jaws of a large canine, with huge, sharp teeth to match. Their pupils, staring lifelessly towards the sky above, were also similar to those of a dog or wolf.

Carefully, Lee removed one of the leather half-helms from one of the daunting creatures. He flinched in surprise as he saw that they had pointed ears, which were placed a little higher up on their heads, and oriented more forward, than were those on a human.

The removal of the half-helm also revealed the wide, high foreheads that the creatures had, with a hairline raised much higher than that of an average human. Their dense, thick locks of hair framed their faces and heads, looking much like a dark mane.

Yet as bestial as their intimidating forms were, so were they unmistakably human-like. Two arms culminating in massive, five-fingered hands, two legs, and several other aspects were akin to a human's features.

Up close, Lee felt more than a little fear as he looked upon their bulging, corded muscularity. These were undoubtedly extremely strong creatures, an observation confirmed when Lee tried to heave up one of the intriguing long-hafted weapons with the equally lengthy blades.

Lee could lift the weapon up, but only slowly, and with great effort. He certainly could not wield it for its intended purpose.

It was no surprise that the weapons of these creatures were quite useless to Lee, or to anyone else within his party. Lee watched as Ryan came to a similar conclusion, as the young man had to use two hands just to heave up one of the beast-men's sword-like weapons.

It took Lee only one attempt to realize that using one of their great bows would be impossible. He could not pull back the string more than a little, despite putting a tremendous effort into the endeavor. Ryan tried himself, and, though he strained immensely, could do little better than Lee.

All the while, Lynn had kept largely to herself. She had retained the initial sword that she had found. In addition, she had acquired a couple of the larger daggers with the broad, single-edged blades. Both daggers rested in well-crafted sheaths of leather and wood, reinforced with multiple bronze rings set near to their mouths, with bronze chapes capping the bottom.

One of the final things that Lee examined closely before departing the open ground was the pennon borne at the forefront of the contingent of horsemen. The haft that it was attached to had been severed through during the fighting, cleaved just below the curving pennon by one of the heavy blades of the attacking warriors.

Lee held the pennon gently in his hands, looking down at the tasseled fringe and the alternating blue and gold stripes of the ensign itself. As with the coins, he knew that the pennon held in its very hues and patterns some more information about the lands of the horse riders.

Setting down the pennon respectfully, Lee turned to look for the others and finish up their task.

Once all were laden down with their newfound items, and had satisfactorily concluded their exploration of the area, they returned together towards the safer harbor of the woods. Night was now falling over the forested hills and the rolling, grassy plains, twilight having settled in full upon the land as the sun sank beneath the western horizon. Lee looked about in the violet hues, and grimly realized that he and his companions probably would not be able to tell if any sky born threats were approaching.

While gaining the cover of the forest was imperative, Lee was simply glad to leave the grisly scene behind him. At the end of it all, he felt drained, and somewhat guilty. He loathed the great necessity of requisitioning the items off of the corpses of the valorous men, while leaving their bodies entirely exposed to the outer elements and hungry scavengers.

His mind told him otherwise, that there was no good choice, but that ultimately proved to be of little comfort in his very wearied state of emotional turmoil. Lee could only hope that in time he could fully reconcile with the dire needs of his group's immediate situation, and that the troubling images bombarding him during the search would not often assault his dreams at night.

When they returned to the woods, and were under the thickly

foliated boughs once again, Lee and the others found that Erin was still crouching right where they had left her. She was glaring at them, with a deep frown etched upon her face.

"Thanks for the help," Ryan remarked sarcastically, as he drew near to her.

Lynn was evidently in no mood for Erin's disposition either, as she glowered at her friend. Without saying a word, she slowly withdrew one of the large daggers that she had found out of its sheath, and shoved its hilt towards her stubborn friend.

"You might want this," Lynn said curtly. "This should do a lot better than sticks if we run into more creatures, and can't outrun them."

Erin gingerly fingered the offered weapon. Surprisingly, she made a grimace as she took it in her hand and looked at it. She made no gesture of gratitude to Lynn for having thought of her in procuring the weapon, a response that instantly annoyed Lee.

"What, are you against this too?" Ryan inquired aggressively.

Erin shot him a hard look. Her tone was flippant. "So I don't fool around with weapons much, or really care for them either."

"Well, you'd better start right now, because I sure as hell don't think that the things that we've seen can be easily reasoned with," Ryan snapped. He gestured behind him, up towards the darkened skies. "Not the thing that flew after you, not the things that were just flying out there, and I doubt those beast men that were riding them. And who knows about the ones on the horses? Humans can be dangerous too.

"It's pretty clear that this isn't our world, and it definitely is like being in a whole different age. You'd better start caring real quick, Erin, about the rest of this group. If you choose not to eat, and continue to be stupid about that, that's your problem. But you'd sure as hell better help us defend ourselves, because that's my problem too … and if you don't like it, you can take a walk right now."

Erin looked entirely incredulous at the open berating by Ryan. More distressing, Lee could see the defensive hardening of resolve in her eyes.

Whether or not there would be any appeal to logic was no longer of a concern to Lee. The moment was degenerating quickly, into something that none of the group needed.

"Ryan, Erin, everyone!" Lee interjected firmly. "We've all gotta stay clear-headed, no matter how upset we get at anything."

"We do," Lynn then concurred in a low voice, nodding to Lee. She turned her head and looked with a stony expression towards Erin. "We can't let emotions get in control. Lee's right. We've gotta use our heads."

Lee was immensely relieved. He knew that while he had some influence with Ryan, Lynn had the greater insight by far into her recalcitrant friend. There was little doubt that Lynn's words were directed right at Erin, as much as they were also a reinforcement to Lee's response.

Ryan took a long, slow breath, though not before shooting another angry, darting glance at Erin. He finally stated in a tense, low voice, "I guess so."

"And things are a little better. We do have some more proper food now," Lee said, holding up one of the leather pouches that he had taken from the saddle of one of the slain horses. "That's some good news, at least."

Erin stared at the large pouch, and then looked back to Lee. After a tense delay, she finally nodded, which was about as good as Lee believed that he could hope for.

Lee, Ryan, and Lynn then proceeded to occupy their time with dividing up the rest of the items. They continued until everyone had some type of pouch to carry things in, along with food rations and weapons.

Not all of the food rations were designated for storage.

The salty, tough dried meat could well have been the most succulent of roasts to Lee's starved palate.

All four of them wolfed down some chunks of the hard bread, not complaining for a moment regarding its texture, and thorough plainness. Lee improvised, using some of the water from the skins that he had found to soften up his own piece. It was a tactic emulated rather quickly by the others.

Even Erin's spirits lifted somewhat as they consumed some of the food together. The peaceful sounds of an undisturbed forest returned to reign all around them. The evening air cascaded down with an increasing coolness, seeming to accompany the gradual relaxation of Lee's own emotions.

The gentle ambience, caressing winds passing through the leaves, chirping insects delivering their timeless forest song, and the soft blanket of evening serenity were healing salves to Lee's body, mind, and spirit. They were most welcome conditions, especially after the furious, desperate sounds and sights of battle, and the investigation of the bloodied field in the fighting's aftermath.

"Never thought I would be that enamored about the noises of insects," Lynn remarked, echoing Lee's own thoughts as she chewed on her last morsel of bread. Reaching down, she tenderly massaged the area around her knees, slowly kneading her skin and muscles with her fingers.

Lee, seated a few feet to her right, leaned back against a tree trunk and stretched his legs outward. He closed his eyes, letting out a sigh as he lowered his hands to rest in his lap.

"It feels good just to relax for few a moments, without a hungry stomach," Lee replied after a few moments. "I just wish we could call it a day right now."

"But we can't ... I bet you were about to say that, weren't you?" Ryan queried dourly.

"At least we can take a break for little while, can't we?" Erin interjected with a plaintive tone. "Days and nights seem so long in this place anyway."

"It would be nice, wouldn't it?" Lee responded. He then shook his head regretfully, and his voice took on an equally melancholy timbre, "But there is a little more to the situation right now. There's something I just realized."

Lee could not believe that until that very moment he had completely overlooked the thought that was now foremost in his mind.

"So what more can there be right now?" Erin spat out, her ire rising once again. "I want to rest!"

"Rest for a few more minutes," Lee replied rather gently, in response to her vitriolic tone. He greatly desired rest himself, and his sympathy outweighed his ongoing irritation with her attitude. "But I was just thinking that we don't really want to stay at the site of recent battle. You never know what kind of attention it might bring. Wild ... or intelligent."

His logic and tone evidently caused Erin to choke back any further responses, as she held her tongue and stared off in sullen silence.

"Lee, you're right. I didn't think of that," Lynn said, as a look of grave concern emerged swiftly within her eyes. She cast a nervous glance off in the direction of the grassy plains.

"And no argument here," Ryan muttered.

"I still think we can risk taking a few moments, to settle ourselves and recoup our strength a little bit," Lee said. "We just need to be out of here when daybreak comes."

Taking the sustaining night sounds as a comforting sign, and letting his eyes close again, Lee implored the tightened muscles in his body to relax. He concentrated upon his sorely taxed, stiffened muscles one group at a time.

As the tightness in his physical body gradually eased, he thought about an interesting comment that Erin had made regarding the days and nights seeming long. The days within the new world did indeed seem to be lengthier, but whether that was because time was truly different, or instead a perception shaped by their unfamiliar circumstances, Lee could not yet tell for sure.

Whatever the case was, he did wish that they could afford to take a longer rest than was possible. Yet Lee knew that they needed to be vigilant, and vacate the premises well before dawn. Added to that was the need to locate another favorable area to settle down in.

Lee was not looking forward to setting up another makeshift shelter, beginning to dread the idea that it would soon become a regular practice. He let out another extended sigh, and reminded himself that very little in his life would be the same from that moment onward. At the very least, they now had some decent weapons and supplies in their possession.

He had almost fallen entirely asleep after his body had relaxed, but he was somehow able to hold onto the edge of his focus. After roughly an hour had passed, Lee judged that they had delayed long enough.

He got up and roused the rest of the drowsy group. Exhibiting varying degrees of reluctance at having to cease their rest, the others joined Lee in gathering up their newly procured items as they prepared to press onward.

The dual moons provided just enough light to see by, though Lee was not altogether pleased by the necessity of traveling through the forest at night. Keeping the grassy plains on their right, and the shadowy depths of the woodlands on their left, they marched in weary silence for several hours before finally halting. The moons had trekked across a fair span of the night sky overhead when they drew to a stop, and Lee was satisfied that they had put a considerable distance between themselves and the scene of the fighting.

Though very tired, none of others complained at having to erect another rough shelter, as the prospect of sleeping fully bared to the elements was very uninviting. The effort was made a little easier with the sharp iron implements now at their disposal.

Also easing the stress of the moment was the availability of a bit of dried meat, bread, and a few drinks of water. The rations of drink and food staved off the biting feelings of hunger that had arisen during the long hike, if not erasing them completely.

With the tree-covered expanse of hills to one side, and the broad, grassy plains to the other, Lee and his companions at last settled down for a truly extended rest.

This time, with a little luck, it would not be interrupted until the break of day.

DRAGOL

Flying at the head of a small patrol, Dragol gestured downward to where the fallen corpses of the Saxan horsemen, Trogen warriors, and a few horses were just beginning their lengthy process of decomposition. Some carrion eaters were already busy indulging themselves in a grisly, gluttonous feast, the sight instantly raising Dragol's ire.

A couple of Trogen warriors in the modest war band broke away from the main body of the formation, in order to survey the surrounding area from their high elevation. As always, it was necessary to make certain that no imminent enemy presence was lurking about. Dragol watched the pair carefully as they coursed low over the edge of the dense forest. Encouragingly, there were no wisps of campfires lingering in the air over the forest, but the enemy was cautious, and nothing could be taken for granted.

After a few passes up and down the woodland boundary, the warriors settled into a circular pattern high over the area of the previous day's fighting. Dawn had already broken for quite some time, and there was ample visibility within the new morning's light.

The sky riders finally signaled back to Dragol that they had seen nothing amiss. Knowing well the keen eyes of the particular Trogens that he had assigned to such scouting tasks, Dragol was more than satisfied with their evaluation.

With a firm jerk upon the leather reins of his winged Harrak steed Rodor, Dragol guided the great beast swiftly in descent.

As the shadows of Dragol and his sky riders crossed over the carnage-strewn battle site, the winged carrion eaters took to immediate flight, and the four-legged ones scattered off rapidly in the direction of the nearby forest.

Alighting smoothly upon the ground, Dragol quickly unbuckled the straps securing him to the low saddle. They were a necessary precaution during longer distance traveling, though most Trogens, like Dragol, often left the straps hanging free during battle, so as to enable better movement in combat.

Bringing his right leg back around, he swung down off of his steed in a continuous, and oft-repeated, movement. Dragol then took a step forward, and gave Rodor a firm pat on the side of the creature's amply muscled neck.

"Gather up swords, mail shirts, and any other valuables," Dragol shouted out to the others, as they landed nearby. Dismounting hurriedly, the other Trogens moved rapidly to obey his orders, and strip the dead bodies.

Dragol did not like returning to the site of the previous day's fighting. He had endured a very restless night, once again despising the fact that they were under strict commands not to bring any undue attention to themselves.

With night falling, and with the war band far away from their base camp, Dragol had to strictly adhere to his orders as darkness approached. He would have been tempted otherwise, had the circumstances been different.

His war band had been aghast when he had commanded them to depart without attending to the fallen warriors. Even the greatly hated Elven warriors, who fell in battle, were given the honors accorded to those deemed to have a genuine warrior's heart. Dragol had been forced from extending any such honors, to either the capable Saxan horseman or to his own brave Trogens.

He was not supposed to tarry and allow any proper respects to be given now, though his conscience was again tearing at him from within.

A few Harraks, the steadfast, flying war steeds of the Trogens, had been brought along by the war band without riders. Instead of carrying warriors, they had large hempen sacks or small wooden chests strapped to their backs, in addition to coiled lengths of hide cordage. Their purpose was specific. The patrol had returned to the site to bear back any quality weapons and equipment that might be found.

Leaving the unattended implements behind for the night had been a risk, though it was one that had been unavoidable with night falling, and such a far distance to return. As they had flown away, Dragol had known that they would have to return briefly. Well-crafted swords, iron helms, and chain mail shirts were of great value to the enemy, and it was Dragol's task to deprive the enemy of their further use.

Dragol strolled slowly among the bodies of the fallen warriors, his mind a tumult of thoughts and misgivings. He clenched his powerful jaws tightly at each troubling sight of one of the fallen Trogens, resenting his orders more and more with each passing moment. His mood blackened, as the bitterness flowed through him, bolstered by the each sight of a brave Trogen warrior who would not be honored properly.

The Trogen leader was not made to brood for very long. Dragol's dark simmering was abruptly interrupted, as an unsettling discovery was brought to his attention.

"Others were here. Since the fighting. They were not Saxans. They could not even be Midragardans," a stout Trogen with very broad shoulders reported quickly to Dragol, after hastening up to the massive Trogen chieftain. "They took very little with them, and left all the mail shirts and helms behind. No true warrior in these lands would leave such items unclaimed. Their tracks go back to the woods, and are very different in shape from those made by the humans of these lands."

"And have you have examined the tracks?" Dragol asked the other Trogen, instantly curious about the very strange tidings.

The development was mystifying, for no Saxan party would have missed the chance to reclaim so many mail shirts, swords, helms, and other weapons. The armor and the weapons of the horse riders represented months upon months of hard, skilled labor by many blacksmiths. Such a quantity could not be replaced by the time that the full war broke out.

"Yes. They lead straight towards the woods. Three sets of footprints. A taller human, and two others, more average in height. They took a couple of shields, some swords, and some of the foodstuffs. Maybe a few more small items. Nothing from our fallen warriors. It also seems that they were not using any horses, or any other manner of steed," the Trogen warrior answered.

"Where did they go in the woods?" Dragol asked, his eyes narrowing. The fact that they had not taken anything from the Trogen dead was even more perplexing, as even one Trogen weapon, like a longblade, would be solid, irrefutable proof to carry to anyone in order to testify to the presence of Dragol's kind in Saxan lands.

"They rested, and then traveled onward, keeping to the edge of the forest at first," the other Trogen replied. "But I came back to report to you, and did not follow those tracks very far."

Dragol grew silent, as he considered the other's discoveries carefully, mulling everything over. The other Trogen waited patiently for his response.

"Then we will have to search them out, for nobody must know of the Avanoran army approaching this territory," Dragol finally responded in a firm tone.

He glared in the direction of the woods, knowing that the day was suddenly becoming quite problematic. Dragol was not privy to all the particulars of the events that were unfolding, but he clearly understood the core elements.

The invasion of Saxany was now imminent, which left little room for error on his part. Vast forces massed deep in Ehrengard to the west were even now crossing the eastern edges of that land, as they moved resolutely towards the borders of Saxany. Soon the juggernaut would cross that short stretch of borderland, and seek to hammer right through the center of the Saxan Kingdom. The numbers comprising the looming invasion were staggering, unlike any that had ever been assembled within the current age, or likely any other age.

A smaller Avanoran force, which was a modestly sized army in itself, would soon be breaking off from the teeming masses to head directly through the region where Dragol was now standing. The Avanorans' unimpeded passage, and the crucial matter of determining their most advantageous route of travel, were squarely upon the shoulders of Dragol and the other Trogens.

Dragol understood that this second, offshoot force was integral to the overall invasion campaign. Its task was to penetrate the Saxan lands in such a way that the forces assembling for the defense of the Saxan Kingdom, against the main thrust of the invasion, could be outflanked, and then cut off from their own main route of escape.

The Trogen leader saw the simple brilliance in the plans envisioned by the powers in Avanor. The great hammer that was the primary invasion force would smash the defenders against the anvil formed by the smaller force.

Given what he thought of humankind, Dragol sometimes found himself wondering as to why the Saxans were so resolved to fight. He did not doubt that they were well aware of the immensity of the force that was being sent against them.

Most other human-ruled lands had capitulated to, or placated, Avanor without a battle having ever taken place. Why the Saxans were among the very few exceptions remained a question, though it made Dragol respect them more than those lands that had acquiesced and surrendered their ultimate sovereignty so easily.

It was in such moments of rumination that he acutely remembered his own troubled homelands, and the age-old, relentless struggles of the Trogens against the Elven menace.

The Trogens' long-established nemesis held numerous advantages in the great conflict between the two races, but no matter how powerful the Elves were, no worthy Trogen would ever capitulate in the fight. The Trogens had suffered terribly for ages, but as a whole they still remained unconquered. Every last Trogen would resist until the Trogen population held captive within Elven lands was freed, and the shadow of the Elves' persecution was fully removed from Trogen lands.

Seen in the light of his own kind's struggle, Dragol could certainly relate to the spirited, defiant response of the Saxans. Their great resolve against insurmountable odds made him respect them all the more, which was precisely why his burden in the present moment was made that much more difficult. In the pure core of his heart, he wanted to extend honor to the Saxan dead as well as his own.

"Get the Harraks heading back to the camp, with the best weaponry and mail that can be taken from here. Take an escort of five warriors, and press with all haste to the encampment. The rest of us will set off to search after these unknown scavengers," Dragol stated to the other Trogen.

"It shall be done," the Trogen answered, lowering his golden eyes and giving a slight bow of the head.

Dragol then personally selected the five warrior escorts that would return with the confiscated swords, helms, and mail shirts. All were exceptional fighters, which would help offset the lack of numbers in the returning party. The Saxans had not yet appeared upon their own breed of sky steeds, to challenge the Trogens in the skies over their lands, but Dragol was not about to become reckless in carrying out his charges.

The orders were promptly carried out. The pack-bearing Harraks were soon loaded up to capacity with the remaining weapons, both Trogen and Saxan, and any other prominent items that could be salvaged and denied to the enemy.

Accompanied by the six Trogen warriors, the small group of Harraks was spurred forward and off of the ground. The contingent flew off at a slow pace, laden with the confiscated items.

Dragol watched their departure for a few moments, and then brought his eyes back to his immediate surroundings. He gnashed his teeth in bitter regret as his eyes came across the body of a particular young Trogen warrior that had fallen the previous day. He knew the warrior well, who had been one of his personal favorites.

The dead warrior's amulet, set with large claws from the great forest wolverines for which his clan was named, had already been retrieved. Small personal items, especially those things that related to a warrior's clan affiliation, had been immediately taken so that the warriors could be honored and remembered at a later time. Items such as the amulet would be passed on with great reverence, to be held with pride by others in the clan that the slain warrior had belonged to.

Dragol simply wished that he could set fire to the bodies of the brave Trogen warriors, as well as to those of the equally courageous enemy fighters. None of them deserved to have their remains be food for carrion. All of the slain fighters deserved a welcome place in Elysium.

Yet he knew that he could not allow their bodies to be consumed by flame. The smoke from the open fires would signal to the enemy for leagues around. It would mark the vital territory for a wary enemy, one that could adjust and more capably prepare for the approaching incursion.

In war, even the slightest change in timing or advantage could become critical to the outcome.

Dragol tore his eyes away, and with a loud cry he summoned the other Trogens back to their steeds. He mounted his stalwart, dutiful Harrak, which had remained in place for him where he had left it. He took up the creature's reins after buckling the straps that secured him to the low saddle.

Dragol, with fifteen other riders gathered about him, gave another resonant shout. At the signal, the steeds surged forward in a staggered line, sprang upward, and ascended into the air on the strength of their powerful wings. The Trogens headed off in the direction of the forest, almost immediately reaching its border following the take-off from the ground.

Dragol skimmed with the others a short distance above the surface of the trees, his eyes watching closely for any signs of movement. He signaled to the others to be as quiet as possible. The group glided in relative silence over the woodlands as they headed southward, the wind whistling by their heads as they cut through the air. Rodor bumped and rocked lightly as they shadowed the border of the forest, and Dragol settled into his saddle, acclimating to the familiar sensations of air travel. With little turbulence, there was not much to distract him from the search.

Dragol hoped to sight, and then close in upon, their quarry soon. He did not like having to deviate from the main tasks facing the Trogen warriors.

The amount of territory that could be covered from the sky was substantial, and would easily encompass any distance achieved by a party on foot. Whoever had visited the battle site had a full day's lead, though, and the Trogens only knew of the initial direction that they had taken.

Some luck would be needed, but Dragol was not overly worried. Unlike the dilemma that the Trogens had faced at the end of the previous day's fighting, which had forced them to depart for the evening, there was plenty of daylight remaining this time.

Whether sooner or later in the day, Dragol was confident that the unidentified visitors to the battle site would eventually be discovered.

LOGAN

The pleasant aromas of succulent meats permeated the air, as the seven exiles feasted upon the ample bounty provided for them by Deganawida and the village. The prodigious feast was attended by a substantial number of the villagers within the large, open longhouse that it was held in.

The meal itself was quite varied, with the predominant element being a kind of corn meal porridge that was prepared with oils and deer meat. A good-sized quantity of turkey was provided, the meat being the result of a recently successful hunt.

There was also a very tasty, unleavened bread that was served. The distinctive bread was derived from corn flour and contained an abundance of dried berries within it, the latter adding an appreciable amount of flavor.

Wild greens of a few varieties were included in the evening's fare, as well as what looked to be several distinct types of edible forest roots. Also gathered in from the munificence of the surrounding forests were an assortment of nuts and berries.

A much smaller quantity of pigeon meat was presented, with evident pride reflected on the faces of the women tending to the seven guests of the village.

Logan sensed instantly that the fowl was considered to be a valued delicacy by the tribal people. As such, he feigned extra gratitude to the women, even though he found the deer and turkey meats much more suited to his own palate.

He largely ate out of a small wooden bowl, using his hands or a wooden spoon, the latter designed with a short, upright handle, surmounted with the carved figure of a bear.

The tribal women administering the feast smiled warmly, and appeared to be of a genuinely amiable disposition. The women encouraged the guests to eat heartily, as they tended to them from large kettles of brass and bulbous cooking pots of clay that were located within the broad chamber.

It did not take long before it became quite hazy in the crowded chamber. The air grew thicker as low ventilation impeded the efficient escape of smoke from the great central hearth fire.

Logan would not have initially guessed just how good the food tasted. The components of the meal were not especially fancy, in and of themselves. While not elaborate, each bite brought with it a wealth of pleasure, certainly when compared to the uncertain fare that he and the others had been recently facing, out on their own within the new world.

Logan was content to simply eat and observe their hosts, absorbing everything that he could about his new patrons. Their customs and practices were different from anything that he was used to, and he knew that specific meaning was woven deeply into their gestures and items.

Such meaning and ceremony had been made very apparent when Erika had accepted a special gift on behalf of the group, from Deganawida himself.

The medallion had been given to the otherworlders during a small ceremony that had taken place just before the feast. Crafted of a host of small bead-like shells, the flat, circular object was predominantly purple, with the exception of a white circle formed within the medallion's center.

The shell medallion, according to Ayenwatha, had been given to the seven as a sign of fully open and truthful relations between themselves and the Onan tribe. The medallion was an emblem of the tribe's sincere intentions toward the seven. The importance of the solemn gesture was not lost on Logan, and, from what he could tell, the others of his group also understood it clearly enough.

He could already sense that the spirits of the entire group had improved greatly since their arrival in the village. The short rest, the plenteous meal, and the symbolic extension of good intentions by the tribal people, in the form of the purple and white shell medallion, had indeed been a boon to their beleaguered hearts.

The prevailing mood of the villagers had also helped to reinforce the better feelings. They were jubilant, and not just because of the presence of the seven special guests.

The successful return of the war party was also being celebrated and commemorated at the feast. That exposed Logan and the other six to even more depths of tribal custom and cultural values.

After the presentation of the medallion, Logan and the others had been treated to several tribal songs, which were delivered in a rhythmic, chant-like fashion. Rattles of folded hickory bark, gourd rattles set upon short handles, and water drums, with hide drumming surfaces stretched upon cylindrical wooden bodies, accompanied the chorus of human voices.

The tones from the water drums were quite varied, which Logan had known was due to the amounts of liquid contained within them. The chants, and the rhythmic sounds of drums and rattles, gradually lulled him into a partially entranced state, as he immersed himself in the mesmerizing tribal music.

Only occasionally did he come out of his semi-trance, in order to ask a question, or instead listen to some brief explanation offered to him by Ayenwatha in regard to one of the chanted songs.

Logan had been fascinated when it was explained to him that there was a unique and personal nature to one of the performances then being delivered by a solitary male warrior. According to Ayenwatha, the man who was singing it before them was the only person who ever performed that particular song.

From what Ayenwatha had gone on to explain, the man had received the song directly from his father before him, and would one day pass it on to his own son.

Logan had been very curious about that particular song. His interest stemmed from the fact that he had recognized the man chanting the song, right when it had begun. The man was one of the warriors that had been among Ayenwatha's war band, who had helped to escort Logan and the others back to the village.

The warrior had evidently performed some valorous acts in driving off some Gallean scouts that had been venturing deeper into the forest. He had killed three of the interlopers before they could reach the open ground beyond the forest's edge. It had been his wife that had been given the pole with the multiple scalps.

The warrior, following his personal song, had then sung his full account of the martial deeds, laced within a story of the entire encounter.

To Logan, the overtly boastful song took on the open flavor of self-aggrandizement. Yet all the tribal listeners seemed to be quite enthralled with the warrior, and very pleased with the song nonetheless. It was as if the crowd's willing embrace of the man's lauding of his own deeds was a kind of recognition in itself.

Finally, the sequence of songs came to an end. The air within the open longhouse soon filled with laughter and conversation as the main portion of the meal ensued. Stomach rumbling, Logan had been very glad when the first portions of the feast were served.

"This is one of the best meals I've ever had!" Antonio exclaimed, his cheeks puffed up with an overly full mouth of the tender turkey meat.

As if to accent his words, juices trickled down each side of his stuffed mouth.

Ayenwatha grinned proudly at the compliment. "I am glad that our humble offerings please you, Antonio."

"Very much so," Antonio managed to articulate, despite having taken another plentiful bite of the turkey.

"We truly thank you," Erika then said, looking to both Ayenwatha and Deganawida. "This is more than we could ever have hoped to expect when we were wandering around lost in the woods. It is a tremendous feast, and we are very grateful for it."

From his expression, Deganawida seemed to be particularly amused by her comments.

CROWN OF VENGEANCE

"Thank you, Erika," Deganawida responded. "With the threats of war, we have not been feasting often, and our hunters have been forced to be much more careful. We have not been able to undertake large deer hunts, though it was fortunate that some deer and turkey were recently taken. I had feared that we would not be able to extend to you a proper feast, given the troubles that you have been through."

"This is far more of a feast than I'm ever used to," Derek remarked, scooping up another heaping spoonful of the hominy.

"I hope we are not causing any burdens for you, if food is scarcer in these times," Janus added in a conciliatory tone. "Please do not feel any pressure to do anything special for us. We are just happy to be your guests, and to have a safe refuge, and to have anything to eat. That's enough for us."

Ayenwatha smiled. "We are very pleased to grant you what we are able. It is just that if these were not times of probable war, it would be a much greater feast. The darkness coming from the Unifier dampens much in these lands."

Erika then asked the two tribal leaders, "You speak of this Unifier again.... If I may ask, who is He? And where did He come from?"

Deganawida looked away for a moment, as a sad look crept into his eyes. He gently cleared his throat, and gazed upon Erika and the others for an extended pause, before answering her query.

"What we see today, the world facing all of us now, could only rightly be spoken of in a very long tale. This darkness that we confront now is something that I know has been many ages in coming, for such momentous things do not happen with a single pass of the moons.

"I have long watched this Unifier, and pondered every tiding involving Him. I have learned much in the years that have passed, and have questioned many learned people.

"The Unifier's rise was accompanied by displays of great strength, demonstrating signs of power and offering an abundance of trade and glory to those that followed Him. Destruction came to those that did not, or who resisted ... individual people at first, and now entire realms.

"Avanor, the land of the Unifier, was a territory caught up in the ebb and flow of kings and lords. The Unifier liberated the people of Avanor from the great burdens of being caught between the desires of Gallea and Norengal, and the lords who were, in truth, beholden to both.

"The fighting between lords at the time of the Unifier's rise was terrible, all throughout the lands. Even the Peace of the All-Father declared by the Western Church did little to ease the sufferings of the common people.

"In such a dark hour, the rulers of the lands, who could not keep control of their own realms, were pulled towards giving full powers over to Him.

"All of this, I am now certain, was intended by Him from the beginning.

"In time, the Unifier grew a mighty circle around Him. Many powerful sorcerers steeped in the mystic arts committed to Him, or were brought up within His mighty citadel. It is said that many Wizards, indeed some of the greatest among them, heeded His seductive call.

"In time, there arose many more wars and times of great trouble, beset with famine and disease. The Unifier's rise did not end strife. Yet none would dare question Him, for all rulers' efforts had turned towards achieving the unity that He had offered; to all who would bow their will to His.

"This promise ... this offer of a world placed under full order and control, was unprecedented. It was a promise to elevate the rulers of the world's kingdoms to be at the side of a great throne astride the entire world. It offered a height of power previously unknown, and one that would be unassailable when brought into being. This promise proved irresistible to those lusting after power and wealth.

"A gathering of realms was begun, even if it was only in a secret understanding that the common people were very unaware of.

"The Unifier's greater vision was made clear to the rulers attracted to His seductions and promises. They were told that when the Unifier's new world came to pass, the means of trade would be governed under one standard. In addition, all people would one day be identified under a common standard as well, even with marks upon their bodies such as those now said to be on the skin of rulers and others who have fully committed to Him. These were powerful enticements to those already steeped in a love of dominion.

"Peace. Prosperity. Order. The end of all chaos and wars. These things were at the behest of the rulers of all realms, if they only would join with the Unifier. Who could argue with such ends?

"It is no secret that if the Unifier achieves His vision, His rule will one day supersede that of all realms. The world's rulers merely think that they will continue in their own power, and have a seat at the Unifier's table.

"It is my fear that it will not be long before the Unifier is openly declared to be the supreme authority of the world, over all manner of rulers and kingdoms. Delirious in promises of power and wealth, the world's rulers will acclaim Him as such.

"For those so used to the things of control and power, they willfully deceive themselves, victims of the same overtures and maneuvers that they have often used in securing power in their own realms.

"So very few stand opposed to Him now. Only three realms that I know of, with any strength to resist, remain steadfastly opposed; the realms of Saxany, Midragard, and the tribes of the Five Realms, of which our tribe is one.

"Perhaps there are more, somewhere within the far reaches of Ave, but it is certain that these three lands bravely refuse to bend their knee to Him. For our choice, as one of these three lands, we face terrible lies and accusations, as the storms of war gather upon the horizon. We are deemed a wicked and vile people for opposing the completion of the Unifier's vision, for merely wishing to retain our own sovereignty, and self-determination for our own people.

"I am under no illusions. It is certain that we are about to face a time of great tribulation."

As Deganawida finished his somber oration, there was a heavy silence hanging over all of those who were listening nearby. The telling had quickly sobered the jovial nature that had taken root and flowered during the feast.

"It is not all that strange, to my ears," Logan commented quietly to Janus, who sat at his right side. "I've often thought that's where our own world seems headed. A domination of all, by an elite few. Just not as far along as this world is, apparently."

"I saw that all too clearly as well," Janus murmured in reply. "And maybe it is farther along in our world than we think. The powerful have always had an insatiable desire for control, evidently no matter what world they happen to reside in."

"You can't appease those types, that's for sure," Logan agreed, drifting off into contemplative silence once more. He found himself wondering as to why the populaces influenced by the Unifier could become so vigorously stirred to war.

There seemed to be so little that the tribal people could offer those who lusted after wealth and power. He had seen the considerable trappings of the marching army that had been assembled in the west. They hailed from a very material culture, one that was most certainly abundant in metals, fabrics, well-bred horses, and many other signs that hinted to a society rife with luxuries.

The tribes, on the other hand, did not seem to possess any great material wealth. Other than a few decorative, crescent-shaped silver gorgets, Logan had seen little sign of precious metals amongst the villagers, most of whose possessions derived from corn husk, timber, or hide. Logan could not see the allure inherent in launching a war against such a people, and figured that the motivations had to come from another kind of source.

There had to be a reason, even if it was from a distorted and manipulated perspective. Logan could also not overlook the distinct possibility that there may well have been something done to provoke the lands to the west.

He had only heard one side of the story, after all.

Logan looked over to Deganawida, who was gazing upon the seven with a thoughtful countenance. A slight grin, tinged with sadness, slowly came to the old sachem's face.

The uncomfortable silence around Logan deepened, as all seemed to be waiting for Deganawida to break the impasse.

"Do not trouble yourselves, honored guests of the Onan. Now is a time to leave the worries of the world behind us, at least for a little while," Deganawida said at last. His voice was soothing, as he smiled reassuringly at the others. "Perhaps it would be better to let me tell you a happier tale, one about the origin of the five tribes, and how the Five Realms came together."

One by one, Logan and the other exiles nodded to Deganawida. For his part, Logan was ready to hear about something a little less foreboding.

The old sachem needed little further encouragement. Without delay, he began to relate the account of the origins of the Five Realms.

The tribes, as it turned out, had not always been so cohesive with each other. The tale of it all was quite fascinating, and featured a powerful Wizard from whom Deganawida had derived his own name. The ancient Wizard had brought the five tribes the Great Law, and instigated the Grand Council around the Sacred Fire, the flames of which had been tended and warded ever since then by the Onan tribe.

Even more intriguing, one of the major figures in that story was an Onan by the name of Ayenwatha, who had endured a terrible ordeal. In a time of great war and strife among the contentious tribes, the other Ayenwatha had lost his wife and three daughters. The tragedies had been attributed by many to an Onan shaman named Atotarho, a practitioner of magic who was given to dark leanings. Rumored to be under the sway of the Dark Brother, the malevolent shaman lived in the depths of the forest, and was reputed to have living snakes coiled within his hair.

It was in that time of terrible darkness that Ayenwatha had cried out in the midst of his tremendous grief, hesitating in pursuing the revenge that was expected in such loathsome situations. The Wizard Deganawida had heeded his call and come to Ayenwatha, bringing him consolation and revealing a new, more enlightened path for the tribes to take.

Out of that healing time, Ayenwatha had joined with Deganawida, and the two had worked together to found the Great Law, the Grand Council, and the Sacred Fire.

Ayenwatha had even shown compassion to Atotarho during that legendary time, bringing his former adversary to a kind of redemption that was represented with the combing of the shaman's serpent-infested hair. The humbled shaman had renounced his previous ways, embraced the Great Law, and then had taken the second seat upon the Grand Council.

When peace and harmony among the five tribes had been achieved, and everything was set in place, the Wizard Deganawida had abruptly departed. It was said that one day, when the peace of the land had failed, and when the people faced certain destruction, that the powerful Wizard would return to them once again.

Logan found the story to be profound and compelling, rich as it was with the foundational elements of the Five Realms themselves. The tale was also intriguing, in that it contained the namesakes of two of their prominent hosts.

It also had another more immediate effect. By the time that Deganawida had finished, the mood of Logan and the others had been lifted up once again, and the look of serenity on Deganawida's face was unmistakable. The renewed spirits were much more appropriate for a welcoming feast.

GUNTHER

The trespassers had unusually strange clothing, and their speech was like nothing that Gunther had ever heard before, not in even one of the many lands that he had traversed during his lifetime.

While they did not yet appear to be minions of the Unifier, Gunther stalked them with due caution. Life had long ago taught him very hard lessons about taking anything for granted. One erroneous judgement could be lethal.

Times were more shadowy and dismal than ever before. The most recent tidings were a constant burden to Gunther's mind, and he wondered as to whether the strangers had anything to do with the darkness sweeping across the Saxan lands.

Males from the outermost villages of Saxany were being called up by a full-scale, general levy, known in the Saxan lands as the General Fyrd. The distressing news had reached Gunther's ears when he had recently visited Ebba, an older blacksmith who lived within the village of Oak Crossing.

The village was the nearest human habitation to Gunther's solitary woodland abode. It was named after an ancient, majestic oak tree that sat astride the crossroads of a couple of the more remote forest trails.

Not liking the droll field work that so many Saxan villagers were engaged in, Ebba had stepped forward when the village's previous smith had taken sick and died. Having aided the smith often before, Ebba had gained just enough skill, and had scraped up enough equipment, to serve as an adequate blacksmith for the small village community.

As practically everyone needed his services, including all the other artisans, he had soon enjoyed a more prominent position in the village, even though his work was fairly mediocre.

His time was largely spent on simple, practical fare, such as the making of nails, working with small knives, and other common implements. He was also one of the very few people that the reclusive woodsman interacted with more than once a year.

The sight of the thin-faced older man was always amusing in itself to Gunther. Regularly coated with charcoal dust, and with his sparser strands of graying hair disheveled all about his narrow head, Ebba's appearance alone had often evoked a smile from Gunther.

Gunther's latest visit to Ebba had been for some strap-end clasps, a quantity of iron nails, a pair of small cutting shears, and the acquisition of a new hand axe head for use around his homestead. As Ebba retrieved and gathered the items together that Gunther had requested on his previous visit, the blacksmith had related the dire tidings that had cast such a pall over Saxan hearts.

A massive storm front of war had been hurled forth by the Unifier. It was heading directly eastward, rolling steadily towards Saxany, being conveyed through neighboring Ehrengard. Many allies of Avanor were involved in supporting the war effort, from what Ebba had learned from some messengers and Saxan warriors that had passed through the village on their way to designated mustering points.

There had been no choice left to King Alcuin in the face of the impending war but to issue a full levy summons. Even little, remote Oak Crossing had not found itself immune from the demands of the General Fyrd.

Ebba was one of the few remaining adult males left in Oak Crossing, just old enough that he was deemed incapable of holding up to longer marches. Ebba had still been working long hours to help ready the men of Oak Crossing that had since departed for their assigned mustering point.

Ebba had shaken his head sadly, describing what he had thought as he handed over reforged knives to anxious village men, and done whatever he could to shore up the iron heads of picks and scythes normally used for farm work. The only true weapons in the village had been the hunting bows possessed by a few of the men.

In Ebba's opinion, a rabble was being sent out to meet a well-prepared invader in battle, and nothing about it boded well to him.

Gunther tried to comfort Ebba by reminding him that the villagers were just part of a much larger force that would include thanes, household warriors, and many other better trained and equipped men.

Nonetheless, the news had been very disheartening, especially as this was no summons for a localized defense. Ebba would have been expected to take part in repelling such a threat, as he was strong enough to hold a weapon. Rather, the Saxans were moving huge forces far from their home regions, bolstering up a line of defense that was being positioned in the far west of their realm.

The grim news had put Gunther on immediate alert, and he had mulled it all over carefully by the time that he had returned to his dwelling from Oak Crossing. He had kept the news in the forefront of his mind all throughout the far-ranging hunting foray that had now brought him to the very edge of Wessachia's boundaries.

He did not often venture into the nearby County of Annenheim, but a part of him wanted to have a look around the outskirts of the area to see if he might come across any signs of the impending invasion.

A general levy of all able-bodied men, to be sent on a campaign, was no small matter. It heralded a very dangerous emergency, with existential implications for the Saxan Realm.

Gunther had not yet come across the enemy, but he had picked up the trail of the four peculiar strangers. It was clear that the members of the quartet were neither advanced in woodland skills, nor particularly adept at masking their travel.

Any advance scouts sent by a mighty power like the Unifier would be among the best culled from powerful realms. Such individuals would likely prove a challenge even to one as practiced and experienced as Gunther.

The woodsman had now been shadowing the quartet's moves for a couple of leagues. Five of his Jaghuns had accompanied him on the hunting expedition, including the one that had first picked up the strangers' trail. The huge creatures moved dexterously and nimbly alongside Gunther, with nary a sound.

It was fortunate for the strangers that Gunther held such a degree of control over the massive, highly intelligent creatures.

The group of strangers had been walking along the forest's edge for most of the morning, but had just recently turned inward, striding deeper into the woodlands. While still a considerable distance away, Gunther knew that if the strangers kept to their current path that they would eventually come upon his secluded homestead.

Gunther could not assume that they would change directions. He knew that he would soon have to determine whether or not they were truly of the Unifier. The last thing that he wanted was the Unifier's minion's becoming aware of his homestead, especially in the context of an imminent invasion.

If the strangers were innocent of such an association, as a significant part of him suspected, then they would be free to go on their way with Gunther's blessing. If not, then they would not be leaving the woods alive.

Gunther still clung to a faint hope that the affairs of the world at large would bypass his small nook within the woodlands. He was realistic enough to know that such a hope probably would not be justified.

Yet as long as he could do something to affect matters, he certainly would try to guide his fortunes.

Clad in earthy colors, with a knee-length woolen tunic, breeches with narrow lengths of gartering wound snugly about the lower legs from his leather shoes up to his knees, his appearance blended quite well with the shadowy forest environment. Gunther was quite proficient at melting into his surroundings, as well as being adept in not providing his intended quarry with any sign that he was approaching.

Gunther realized that a part of him did not entirely care if the newcomers were investigated or interceded for. He could allow them to amble right into the two Jaghuns currently back guarding his homestead. He knew that his Jaghuns and their bone-crushing jaw strength would make very short work of the four humans.

The stark honesty of the realization was a notion that immediately shamed him, because at one time Gunther knew that he would have sought to protect any creature of the All-Father from avoidable harm.

He had indeed become very hardened over the recent years.

After much travel, pain, and sorrows, he had finally gotten his wish to live the way that he wanted to. He was just over forty, in full health, and still in possession of a very capable body. He was a little slower in reflex and speed than in his youth, but was stronger, more experienced, and far more skilled.

He had fast become defensive towards any unwanted intrusions, discovering a higher degree of sensitivity within himself at each ensuing instance. Most of the occurrences had involved woodland stragglers, whose presence and motives in the sparsely inhabited wildlands were never above suspicion.

Discernment of strangers was becoming an ever greater challenge, as Gunther grew to be fiercely protective of his solitude.

The occasional outlaw or brigand, sometimes appearing in small groups, wandered into his territory. Darker intentions did not always match with courage, as they were easily driven far off from the area. Only a very few had been foolish enough to make a fight of it, and those ill-advised men had met with a very quick fate.

There were a few rare positive exchanges, including some occasional interactions with the men who served Aethelstan, a great thane in service to the Ealdorman Morcar of Wessachia. Aethelstan lived within the nearest burh, a fairly large one called Bergton that lay to the east of Gunther's abode.

The men of Aethelstan, and the great thane himself, respected Gunther's desire to live in peace. They also did not mind Gunther's unceasing tendency to drive off any brigands or outlaws wishing to take up residence within the wilderness area.

As such, they had never tried to pressure him in any way to conform to the usual standards expected of most men. Gunther knew that he did not actually own the land that he lived upon, but it was wild forest, and he did inadvertently provide Aethelstan with a very effective watch close to some Wessachian villages.

Gunther had long ago surmised that Aethelstan had deemed the stalwart's woodsman's shunning of brigands and outlaws as a worthy contribution, in lieu of any other service or material obligation to the Kingdom of Saxany. The King's reeve at Bergton, an honest enough of a fellow named Behrtwald, had never even paid Gunther one visit.

Gunther could also tell that Aethelstan's men were entirely fascinated with the exotic Jaghuns that he raised. They were creatures native to the legendary Shadowlands, which lay far to the east, across oceans and other harrowing lands.

Like Ebba in Oak Crossing, the great thane's men brought Gunther periodic news of the broader world. While remaining isolated, to the point of being fairly reclusive, Gunther was not completely disinterested in word about the happenings in the Kingdom of Saxany and realms beyond.

The larger world had been at the center of his life, up until his self-imposed exile to the woodlands in the Saxan province. Regardless of everything, he was wholeheartedly prepared to live out his life in those woods, with the company of nothing more than his small brood of loyal Jaghuns.

Despite his chosen way, Gunther knew deep within himself that he could not let fellow creatures of the All-Father become needlessly endangered. He still believed firmly that the day would come when he would have to account for his entire life with the Creator of all things.

On that momentous day, no excuses would suffice. Only what he had done, and the choices that he had made, would be weighed in the balance to see whether or not he had truly accepted Emmanu.

Gunther admonished himself harshly for his insular, selfish, and undeniably cruel inclinations, at least until he fully determined the allegiances of the four outsiders.

Even with a modicum of understanding, Gunther was confident that he could determine whose side they were truly on; that of the Unifier, or those that wished to be free in will.

Confrontation on some level was inevitable, but there were no concerns if it turned for the worse. He had five fully trained, matured Jaghuns with him. Furthermore, any of the Ealdormen or Counts in the Saxan Kingdom, even King Alcuin himself, would have given anything to have the martial skill of one such as Gunther in their service.

Gunther quietly kept stride with the group of strangers as he pondered the challenges of his situation.

It was then that a voice, like a soft breeze, came abruptly to his ears.

"Gunther, hold for a few moments. I would speak with you."

Gunther spun around at the sudden words, raising his arm with sword in hand to defend himself. Only at the last instant did he hold back the blow that he was about to deliver.

Standing calmly before him, in long blue robes, was a tall, elderly man, with a bountiful white beard and a similarly snowy mass of hair.

His face was set into a warm smile. He looked out from under the broad brim of his low-crowned hat with one blue eye, which seemed to sparkle with an inner light. The old man showed absolutely no concern over the upheld sword that had barely been held back by Gunther, his right hand resting without any sign of tension upon a tall wooden staff.

"Stranger, you truly show yourself at the most unexpected times," Gunther remarked curtly, not entirely amused at the sudden surprise.

He lowered his sword point, and slowly slid it back into the sheath affixed to his baldric.

Gunther could not stifle a chuckle, as two of his huge Jaghuns bounded right up to the old man. Standing idly, their broad heads came up above the man's waist. They angled their wide, short muzzles upward to gaze expectantly into the old man's face.

The corded muscle massed all around their jaws, thick necks, and shoulders gave evidence to the sheer, awesome power held within their devastating bite. Those massive jaws were now less than an arm's length from the old man.

Yet there was no tension on the part of the Jaghuns, or unease on the part of the old man. It was as if they were simply old friends, and the old man smiled warmly as he reached down and gently patted both of the great beasts upon their heads, scratching them behind their dark ears as they wagged their medium-length tails briskly.

"They really do have a great affection for you, Wanderer. And I do trust their judgements," Gunther said, shaking his head in wonder once again. "You are very unusual among those I have come across in this world, and you give little warning to your visits. We have spoken together a few times, and I find myself with more questions and fewer answers with every new encounter of you. I am certain that you will perplex me again before you depart."

"I must confess that I am sometimes in a world unto myself, and perhaps should be more forthcoming," the old man replied with a grin, seeming to almost laugh. "But then again, you are not the most sociable of men that I have encountered in my journeys, my reclusive woodland friend.

"Your point is conceded," Gunther retorted, a smirk now upon his face.

"And I suppose that you were following the four newcomers too?" the old man then inquired of him. "They are unlike any within our world's realms."

"Yes, I was," Gunther confirmed. "And it seems that you know of them as well, so perhaps you could tell me something more of these strangers. It would be much appreciated."

The Wanderer smiled again. "Yes, I do. And I do know that they are not of the Adversary. You have nothing to concern yourself with about these four. As they are not of the Adversary, they are not of the Unifier either. Those Two are always of common purpose."

"Your words are welcome to my ears, Wanderer," Gunther replied. "I could not tell, as I cannot understand their very strange tongue. I have never heard a tongue such as they have … not in any of my travels."

"They are from very far away, from lands that are far beyond those of your own experience and knowledge," the Wanderer informed him. "But I can be of help to you this day. You will be able to understand their words with this."

He reached into a pouch hanging from the leather belt secured about his robe, withdrawing his hand and extending a shaped pendant of blue stone set into metal, hanging from a long hide thong. The woodsman recognized the form of the pendant as that of a rune, the mystical lettering used by Midragardans.

Gunther accepted the necklace somewhat hesitantly, eyeing it closely, as he held it gingerly in his hand. For an instant, it was as if his mind had become hazy. The blue gemstone in the pendent was rich in hue, holding depths within that far exceeded its diminutive physical size.

"Do not worry yourself, this is not a device of the Unifier's black arts," the Wanderer calmly explained to him. "It is from me, and it will help you to understand their language, Gunther. With such as this, they will be able to understand you as well."

Gunther slowly put on the necklace at the other's bidding.

"If you only knew what I feel about amulets and powers. I have seen my fill of magic within this world," Gunther responded somberly. He then eyed the Wanderer closely. "For me, the mystery is made clearer, with this gift. I have often wondered about your nature. You are no mere sorcerer. No sorcerer would travel these wildlands with such ease, or thwart the senses of my Jaghuns so capably.

"It leaves only one choice in my mind. You are a Wizard. Are you not?"

Gunther's eyes narrowed with his final, declarative words, the last question taking on the tone of a direct challenge that demanded an answer.

The Wanderer grinned broadly, with a flare of evident amusement. "It is you who have said so."

"I fear that I am not wrong in this guess," Gunther replied, "It does not unsettle me, Wanderer. I know that if you bore me any ill intent, as a Wizard, I would have found out long ago."

The Wanderer stepped forward, walking past Gunther. "No ill intent, to be certain. If anything, the opposite, woodsman. But this amulet will come of great use to you for the moment. I expect for you to give it to another very shortly. Let us not tarry further, indulging in speculations. Now come with me, and you will see that you understand the words of these strangers to our lands."

Gunther, certainly no newcomer to the woodlands, had to hurry just to keep pace with the blue-robed man. He marveled at the incredible proficiency of the stranger, as even his Jaghuns lagged behind at first, and had to pick up their own gait to stay close to the long strides of the Wanderer.

In a very short amount of time, Gunther and the old man were close on the trail of the four humans. It was not much longer before they caught up to the woodland interlopers, who had by now come to a full stop.

The four humans were seated upon the surfaces of a couple of thick tree roots, radiating from an old oak tree. The roots that they were seated upon formed boundaries for a little patch of debris-strewn ground, and allowed two of the strangers to face the other two as they talked together.

Gunther and the Wanderer enjoyed the benefit of a steady rise in the ground from the area around the oak tree to a low ridgeline that allowed them to capably shield their own forms. They eased to the top of the ridgeline and looked down upon the four strangers. Talking amongst themselves, the strangers were still utterly inept at concealing their presence in the woods.

Gunther's eyes widened, and he glanced down at the blue stone now resting against his chest.

Unlike the last time that he had heard the voices of the strangers, Gunther could now understand their words as if they were speaking the Saxan tongue with complete fluency. Astonished, he turned to comment to the Wanderer.

His breath caught abruptly in his throat.

There was absolutely no trace of the mysterious figure. It was as if the Wanderer had been just a figment of his imagination, were it not for the presence of three other amulets hanging just a couple of feet away from him, on the end of a nearby tree branch. They were siblings to the one looped about his own neck.

There was no question as to why there were four of the amulets in all, as Gunther reached out and quietly removed the other three suspended from the thin branch. The Wizard, for that was surely what the Wanderer was, intended for them to be given over to the four strangers.

The thought deeply disturbed Gunther. He was not one to trust the whims of Wizards, no matter how benevolent they appeared to be. The tales of them that he had heard in his life had been many. To his knowledge, he had not encountered any himself, with the exception of the elderly, blue-robed man. Furthermore, Wizards were commonly said to have withdrawn in recent ages from open involvement in the affairs of humankind.

There were sorcerers, many legendary, and others such as warlocks and witches, among the mortal race of mankind, but the Wizards were said to be something entirely different, and far more daunting. They were a race of immortals, ageless and powerful, and had been granted gifts unimaginable at the dawn of the world.

As one whose own life occupied a speck of history, Gunther could not begin to fathom the designs of a being such as a Wizard. He wished that the Wanderer would have stayed for a few moments longer, and had not departed before giving Gunther the four amulets.

Gunther wanted to ask the Wanderer exactly why he had entrusted the amulets to Gunther, and why the Wizard had such an interest in the four strangers now gathered just a handful of paces away from the woodsman. Gunther doubted that he would have received any satisfactory answers if he had gotten a chance to ask the questions. If the Wizard had even chosen to respond, his words would have been layered in ambiguities.

Yet at the same time, all of Gunther's encounters leading up to, and including, his current one might be an answer in themselves. The encounters could very well indicate that the Wizards were returning to involve themselves in the affairs of the world once again. If that were true, the implications were ominous, as it was highly likely that only a great reason would draw the Wizards forth.

Gunther shook his head with a rueful grin, remembering his past experiences with the old man. At the very least, he would have to remember to thank the Wanderer for his own amulet, the next time that Gunther encountered him. He already understood and appreciated its tremendous value.

Quietly, he settled himself into a more comfortable position, watching the four strangers with a renewed interest, their words no longer an obstacle. His Jaghuns were pressed in close around him, crouched down and silently awaiting their master's next command.

His full attention honed in upon the four strangers as he listened to their next words. It did not take very long for him to discover that they were almost certainly not servants of the Unifier, and that they were in the midst of a very dire plight.

He listened carefully to their conversation. From what he was able to ascertain, they were traveling without a specific destination in mind, and were hoping to cross paths with anyone that might be able to help them. Fear, frustration, and anxiety were all present just underneath their words, heavily betrayed by their nervous tones.

The shorter, older man appeared to be the leader of the quartet, or at least the most respected.

He had the narrow, tilted eyes and yellowish skin tones like the exotic humans that lived in the lands far to the east, in realms even farther away than the Shadowlands, across many vast lands and great bodies of water.

He had seen a precious few such men within the palace grounds of Theonium, as a result of the risky, lengthy caravan journeys that traversed the Rising Sun Road, bearing loads of spices and silks. The sight of such a man within the woods of Saxany both fascinated and highly intrigued Gunther.

The younger lad, a bit gawky in his maturing body, seemed to be close in alliance to the leader. Gunther could tell from the youth's direct, hardened glances that the younger male held little regard, and likely contempt, for one of the others. The person holding his ire was a young woman with dark hair that had reddish streaks within it, as if dyed.

That particular female was now sitting a little distance off from the rest, having shifted to another root a bit farther back. A sullen expression crouched upon her face, and she rarely met eyes with any of the others in the group.

The final member of the party, a woman of similar age to the other female, seemed to be very attentive to what the two men were saying. Her body language and expressions towards the other woman needed little translation. Gunther could see plainly that she was disgusted with the behavior of the brooding female.

Making a subtle call, indistinguishable from a bird of the forest, he summoned one of his Jaghuns over. The great beast crept up silently on its huge paws to Gunther, its massive head looming just over its human patron and friend.

"Creator's Children," Gunther said in a whisper, gesturing with emphasis towards the four strangers. "Surround."

Nostrils flaring, the Jaghun took in a long draught of scents out of the air, as it regarded the four strangers with an intense, keen gaze.

Suddenly, the Jaghun turned its great head, and roughly licked Gunther on the side of his face, before slowly backing up some distance away. Gunther almost smiled at the spontaneous gesture, but his focus stayed rigidly fixed. Well behind the ridge, the Jaghun rose and loped off into the woods upon its long, muscular legs.

Gunther called another Jaghun over, using a different call. He then gave it the same commands as the first, and sent it onward to join the other.

Gunther kept to his advantageous position. He used three more distinctive calls to bring the remaining Jaghuns in, and uttered the "Creator's Children" command to each as they drew near.

The commands that Gunther had given the large beasts would be welcome news to the strangers, if they knew and understood the potential danger that the woodsman had just abrogated.

Gunther did not plan to lose sight of the strangers until some mysteries were solved, but the precaution settled his mind. He did not want to see his Jaghuns beset the four strangers unless he was convinced that there was a definite reason. Neither did he want to extend them any chance of escape if they turned out to be something darker in nature.

There was no need to rush anything, especially now that he could understand the strangers' speech. Gunther chose to continue observing and tracking the humans for the time being, to see what he could learn. In addition to scrutinizing the four humans, Gunther could also keep a benevolent watch set over them.

There was no mistake that they were vulnerable. The longer that he watched them, the more that he was becoming utterly convinced that they were wholly unprepared for a woodland environment.

AETHELSTAN

A hardened countenance appeared to be engraved into the face of the tall warrior calmly gazing out over the thatch-roofed, timber structures filling up the great burh.

The sky overhead was radiant, a sea of blue-green dotted with rolling masses of pure white clouds, all underneath the beneficence of a beaming sun. The day's weather was pleasantly mild, with a touch of coolness carried along the steady breezes flowing throughout the burh.

Under any other circumstances, the great thane's heart would have rejoiced at the splendor of nature's beauty.

His eyes lingered for several moments upon the square-sided bell tower a short distance from him. It was situated just outside the church, which along with the tower were among the few stone elements within Bergton, a large market town and site of a royal coining mint.

Aethelstan hoped in the core of his heart that the All-Father would be going forth with him, and all of the men gathered that day, once they had set out beyond the walls.

The great thane's spirit was heavy. His stoic expression covered the sorrows that Aethelstan felt churning deep within himself. They came from a number of sources, but the greatest was derived from thoughts of leaving his beloved family behind.

A melancholy had long settled within him over the state of affairs that had been forced upon him in the calling up of a General Fyrd. He did not dispute the absolute necessity of the broad summons, but the harsh reality of its implications was undeniable in regards to a majority of the men who would be marching forth that very day.

The full focus of his authority was on sustaining and furthering the well-being of the newly levied men gathered for the march. This occasion would be nothing like a Select Fyrd, composed of seasoned veterans and household warriors used to the rigors of a military campaign. This time, he would be taking a multitude of farmers, artisans, and craftsmen from the only lives that they had ever known, and ordering them into the depths of unknown dangers. There was no doubt that a great number of the men might well not be coming back.

Even the last moments following the final review of his mustered warriors were turning out to be supremely difficult. A few last echoes of warm, relaxing nights spent in his great hall, surrounded by his wife Gisela, his children, and the men and women of his household retinue, tugged mercilessly at his tormented mind.

He could not deny that he would much rather be taking deep draughts of ale or mead, while listening to wondrous tales of adventure and heroism spun expertly in verses from the lips of a gleeman. An approaching evening would be an anticipation to savor if it were to be occupied listening to the notes of a well-played harp, or putting his mind to games of riddles, as the central hearth fire blazed vibrantly.

While all of that was true, it simply did not do any good to dwell upon such thoughts. Neither could he pity himself, as the burdens were not his alone. Those that went and those that remained behind were both being laden with a very ponderous burden.

Yet despite the unfortunate nature of all of it, there was nothing that the great thane of Wessachia felt the need to question, justify, or regret in regards to what he had to do.

He was grimly resolved. The sudden turn of events in his life was not completely a surprise to him. Aethelstan had long felt the subtle dread common to many Saxans, that even the warmth of life itself was simply a short passage from one vast darkness to another. The good moments in life always had to be cherished and remembered, as no man could stop whatever had been destined for him to face.

A few spear-bearing guards were walking slowly along the inner walkways, running along the top of the timber walls that crowned the earthen rampart ringing the entire market-town, or burh. The walls had been fashioned with wooden crenellations, its outer facing of horizontal wooden planking set between a framing of tall, timber posts. The embankment that the wall surmounted sloped far down into a successive series of three deep, outer ditches.

His eyes swept around the square, stone towers erected at several points along the oval-shaped perimeter. Four held large, iron-banded oak gates set within arches. The other four were placed at even distances in between the gate-towers, providing additional lookout positions and strong-points for defense.

As a whole, the defenses were capable enough, but only if there were enough fighters to man them. Once the column had departed and gathered up other musters, there would be scant few left to defend the burhs of Wessachia, such as Bergton, and even fewer for the outlying villages and hamlets.

Most every man who could bear weapons from the immediate region was now assembled in the masses arrayed all about him.

A number were on horseback, well-prepared for the journey and its considerable demands. These included the men of his immediate household retinue, and warriors from the garrison of the burh itself.

Others similarly equipped and with horse were lesser thanes from smaller, fortified estates who were mustering at Bergton, having come along with their own bands of household followers.

Still others had been equipped collectively, some on horse, and some to travel on foot, to fulfill military obligations to Ealdorman or thane. While not thanes, these men, the ceorls, were qualified for the more commonly utilized Select Fyrd.

All these principal groups would have been expected for a campaign or normal army summons. They were not the elements of the muster that had bestowed Aethelstan with the deep misgivings that he was feeling.

Rather, it was the much larger element of the gathering whose presence at Bergton troubled the great thane, and it was one that was far from common within a Saxan muster.

This larger group was entirely on foot, and included weathered farmers, lifelong craftsmen, simple laborers, and all manner of commoners. They came from within the lands surrounding Bergton, as the territory's populations of able-bodied men had been summoned almost in their entirety to the unprecedented call to arms.

A greater proportion of these men had never gone far beyond their village areas, some having never before even seen the market town that they were now standing within. Rarely did they stray to other villages and hamlets in their vicinity, with the exceptions of special occasions and necessity. There was a great nervousness within this portion of the force already. Aethelstan could see it reflected in their eyes, and feel it coalescing in the air.

A great number of women, children, and older men had gathered to see the massive throng off. They had come in from all the surrounding farm villages, isolated farmsteads, hamlets, and the burh of Bergton itself.

A great trepidation hung over them all.

Aethelstan could not fault them for their anxiety and distress, as he knew in his heart that they had great reason to fear. A General Fyrd was not something that was idly called, and everyone knew it.

A burly man stood near to the front of the massed force. His face was pensive, as he stared out over the gathering. The reeve of the town, assigned to represent the King's authority, Berhtwald would be one of the few able-bodied fighting men remaining behind. With Aethelstan's confidence and insistence, Berhtwald would see to maintaining some semblance of order within the burh, despite the depletion of the overwhelming majority of the able-bodied menfolk.

A fair number of carts and wagons had been readied, piled high with extra weapons, mail shirts, helms, sacks, chests, and barrels of provisions. Helms rested upon the tops of vertical posts in the frames of the wagons, and mail byrnies were carried suspended, with horizontal poles running through their sleeves of circular, iron links. Bundles of spears were tied together and leaning against the sides of the wagons.

Stout oxen with bulging muscles were already yoked and tethered.

The creatures waited patiently for the signal to begin pulling their substantial loads forward. The occasional bellow came from the stalwart beasts, as if they periodically sensed the anxiety looming in the air around them.

A good number of horses were standing idly, near to the carts, their backs loaded with leather packs filled with further supplies. A number of men who would be leading and tending to them were busy making last minute checks on metal buckles and ties on hempen rucksacks.

Aethelstan pulled his gaze from the massed supplies, and looked towards a trio of men from his retinue who were mounted on their steeds nearby.

One bore aloft a large banner that displayed a field of red trees set against a white background.

The second carried a spear-mounted pennon, whose right end had been cut into three triangular extensions. The tapering extensions were red, with the rest of the pennon's body white, reflecting the color pattern of the larger banner.

Both the banner and the pennon were flapping within the clutches of the steady breeze.

The third man carried no banner or pennon, but instead had a large ox-horn. The horn was resting at his right side, hanging from a strap placed over his neck, running across the front of his chest down to his waist.

All three were meticulous men when it came to matters of campaigns and war. Where the three of them could have had their chain mail shirts and helms carried on the wagons, they had the former rolled up behind their saddles, and the latter hanging from the wide pommels of their saddles.

Disciplined, and always keeping in a state of readiness, they were very valued warriors. Their influence would be welcome among a host whose greater number would soon be longing greatly for their homes and hearths.

The great thane slowly nodded to them, as the moment that all of them dreaded could be put off no longer.

The banner and pennon-bearing warriors then turned their horses about at Aethelstan's signal, and started their steeds forward. They cantered down the hard-packed dirt path that led from the open square within Bergton. The path continued out through one of the square tower gates, through an expanse of cleared land, and on into the depths of the surrounding forests.

The third warrior then raised his horn to his lips and blared loudly again upon it, the resonant call carrying far and swiftly throughout the still, tense air.

Last minute hugs were then exchanged, with an open and desperate passion, amongst the commoners of the force with the members of their distressed families and friends that had gathered to watch them go forth.

Aethelstan had a considerable amount of sympathy for the inexperienced commoners about to set out on foot for the long journey. No small number of tears was shed, as feelings and emotions flowed powerfully in those last, precious moments.

Aethelstan turned his gaze from such disheartening sights and inwardly batted down the sharp pangs of empathy that rose up within him. At all costs, he knew that he had to present a visage of determination to all that looked upon him. Serving as a pillar of strength and leadership was an excruciatingly difficult challenge in a moment such as this.

His own personal moment of severance had arrived. Thoughts of the world around him faded into the background as Aethelstan looked to the attractive, dark-haired woman standing just behind his two sons and daughter. Her bright blue eyes were moist with tears that she was trying desperately to keep back.

She rested one weary hand upon the right shoulder of one of the boys, a normally vibrant lad of twelve who now looked quite dispirited. Her other hand lay upon the left shoulder of their young, usually effervescent daughter of seven years.

The two children were gently corralled between her hands before her, looking despondently towards their father.

Their other son, who had just turned eleven, stood a few paces in front of his siblings and mother. He looked up inquisitively and anxiously, peering out from underneath a mop of stringy blond hair.

The little girl remained tucked close to Gisela's side, clutching her mother's leg tightly, as if fearing that she might be leaving too.

Named Wynflaed, Aethelstan's daughter had a cherubic face with a little nose. Her hair was as fair and golden as the light through a bountiful field on the edge of an abundant Saxan harvest. Her eyes were wide and shy, prompting Aethelstan to smile gently at her, even as he could sense the deep sorrow within the child's gaze.

"You be a good girl, and be of help to your mother in all things,"

Aethelstan told Wynflaed, still feeling a little more awkward when he spoke to his daughter than when he was addressing the two boys. "I am counting on you in a big way. Be good and I will take you for some horse rides when I return. Maybe even give you your own horse to ride. Does that sound good?"

The little girl nodded timidly from her mother's side, her sorrow at seeing her father leaving not placated even by the promise of getting her own horse. The subdued response pained Aethelstan all the more.

"Father? Can I not go with you?" the younger of the boys, named Wyglaf, asked.

Aethelstan smiled as reassuringly as he could. He knew that the boy would go with him if he knew his father was walking to face a dragon with just a sword in hand.

"No, Wyglaf, as I need for you and your brother to help guard the burh," Aethelstan said, looking his son straight in the eye, with a serious tone of voice. "It is a very important task. You see all these warriors leaving with me. Who will protect the people of the town? You must help our good reeve Behrtwald, and you must appreciate this task, if you are to lead men some day."

Wyglaf stood up a little straighter and nodded his head, struggling to look dutiful.

"When will you return?" asked the other boy, Wystan.

His thicker dark hair framed the well-defined lines of his face, which seemed to be continually manifesting towards a likeness of Aethelstan himself. His body was showing the first signs of growing into the tall, strong build, replete with broad shoulder and slim waist that his father was graced with.

Aethelstan looked to the older boy, and then slowly brought his eyes up to meet those of his beloved wife. His words were intended for both of them.

"I do not know when I will return …" he said, his words low, somber, and purposeful. "But know that I will do everything in my power to return. Be strong and work hard in my stead. Obey your mother. And in all things place your hearts in the hands of the All-Father, as well as your trust."

He lingered for yet a moment longer, his look intimately holding his wife's gaze, while holding back a wellspring of emotions that started to surge up within him.

Aethelstan said gently to her, "Know that your love goes with me, Gisela, my beloved wife, and mine remains with you. It cannot be broken asunder by anything of this world."

She nodded slowly to him, the longing already present within her face and saying far more than any words could have.

With a great effort, he ripped his gaze away from the anguished look in his beloved wife's eyes, knowing the distress that lingering any further would cause.

Aethelstan kept a resolute mien as he gripped Wind Runner's reins and turned the iron-grey stallion about. He nudged his equine companion firmly in the sides with his heels, spurring the proud stallion forward.

He was not about to show his men anything less than that he was able to move forward at their lead, after leaving his own family behind, as they all set forth under his authority. Their sacrifice was no less than his, a shared ordeal that they would all bear together.

Aethelstan kept his gaze fixed forward as he and Wind Runner trotted off towards the open gateway, moving past the gathered throngs as he headed in the direction of the vanguard elements of the march.

The neighs of horses, shuffling of steps, creaks of wagons, cries of encouragement, and last verbal exchanges between those going and staying filled the air, as the large force began to fall into place and lurch into full motion.

Several bystanders called out warmly to Aethelstan, wishing the All-Father's blessings and a safe return upon him. He acknowledged them with nods and waves to each side, as Wind Runner reached the open gateway and continued on the path passing through the three outer ditches surrounding the burh.

He had always felt strong affection from the people, but also knew that their hopes lay with him to lead their loved ones back alive. Such was an onerous burden for any man, and in the current instance it was tempered only by the absolute necessity of the General Fyrd.

The summons had been urgent enough, conveyed by a spirited royal courier bearing an unmistakable, clear order by sealed parchment. The distinctive seal had been from the court of King Alcuin himself, and was accompanied by another letter bearing the seal of Ealdorman Morcar.

War was thundering towards Saxany, and for the first time in Aethelstan's thirty-seven years of life, a full, comprehensive levy was being called.

CROWN OF VENGEANCE

In his past, it was largely the household retinues, thanes, and ceorls that were called to duty. It was all that was necessary to meet most challenges, whether skirmishes or raids. This time, though, most every male who could bear arms had been summoned.

The full levy had not been called just to defend their immediate territory, and this profound, singular fact was not lost on anyone.

Anyone, even some of the more craven amongst the populace, could be counted on to help defend against an imminent threat to one's own families and homes. The approaching conflict was something much larger, requiring a broad and far-reaching summons intended to bring up massive forces to deploy in strength within the western boundaries of the Saxan Kingdom.

Simple villagers were being called upon to go forth on a long campaign, the duration of which was most uncertain. Even the destination was not entirely assured, as many changes occurred in wars.

From what Aethelstan had been able to glean from the hurried reports and summons, a great army was to be gathered and deployed upon the strategic Plains of Athelney. The Plains lay just beyond the thin neck of land that served as the easternmost border territories of neighboring Ehrengard.

The Plains of Athelney were the gateway to all of Saxany. Once past the Plains, an invading army could strike out in any number of directions.

Through a network of diligent spies, much had been learned about the enemy's intentions and preparations. It was obvious that the enemy was brazenly sending a tremendous force straight towards the Plains of Athelney. It was a titanic spear aimed at the heart of the realm.

Aethelstan had heard many rumors about the nature of the invading force, but all agreed that it was unprecedented in size.

Becoming ever more apparent was that a second force with different designs marched along with the principle invasion. This second force was almost certainly Avanoran in nature, and the leaders of Saxany were now convinced that it had a very specific purpose.

After much deliberation and study of reports, it was clear that the only logical area for a second force to try and strike through would be in the area of Wessachia. The lower areas of Wessachia offered some ideal passages for a considerable mass of warriors to get through the hilly and mountainous terrain, just beyond a stretch of open land that was part of

the adjacent County of Annenheim to the west.

The passage was made ideal, of course, if it went uncontested.

As such, Aethelstan's burh of Bergton, and the other burhs that were under the authority of the great Ealdorman Morcar, were coordinating the formation of a second battle group to go contest this likely thrust of the enemy. All indications showed that the enemy's overwhelmingly best route lay in piercing the hills running south, just beyond the headwaters of the Grenzen River.

Anything north of that area, deeper into Annenheim, would quickly become very problematic for a substantial invading force. The swift and cold waters of the broad river flowing into the seas to the north served as both a barrier and an ancient boundary. It now marked the lands of Count Einhard's lands of Annenheim to the west, and Ealdorman Morcar's Wessachia to the east.

Funneled between the river to the west and the slopes of Wessachian territory to the east, an enemy force moving northward would be placed at a great disadvantage.

Even more challenging to a prospective invader, the large hills of lower Wessachia rose into mountains towards the north. A few easily defensible passes were the only routes through the northern mountains, which could be held for a long time against any force trying to push eastward.

It all left little doubt that an enemy would seek to attack in the south of the Wessachian region, pushing through the lower hills without the dilemma of having a river to its back.

Even though the Saxans were well aware of the general route that an enemy would take, this was still no mere border dispute. Nor was it anything like the common conflicts across the world of Ave through the ages, arising between rival kingdoms or landholders.

A grave and unique moment had arrived, when the very existence of Saxany was under threat from a multitude of kingdoms now in thrall to the singular will of the Unifier.

Wind Runner cantered forth alongside the dense column, and Aethelstan slowed his steed as it neared the front where the large banner of Wessachia was being carried. Aethelstan's ears were filled with the steady tramping of hundreds upon hundreds of feet, and the continual rustles and clinks accompanying the rhythmic tread.

He glanced back along the winding throng of commoners, following along behind the leading contingents of austere-faced, mounted warriors. A great number of smaller pennons were held high among them, carried forward at the end of long spears.

The bonds between men of the same village, and with their immediate neighbors, would be of paramount importance in the face of the adversities that the villagers would soon be facing. More similar contingents would be joining the main column near the outermost villages of Wessachia, having mustered well in advance to meet the main force along its route.

The muster, though hurried, was already going very well by all the latest accounts. Very few of those expected for the muster at Bergton had failed to respond to the summons. It filled Aethelstan with a fierce pride, as he knew that the levy's nearly total presence made a tremendous statement regarding the strength residing within the people's hearts. There was no question that they had overcome much to be standing there that day.

Aethelstan regarded the fearful expressions and anxiety-ridden looks that filled the faces of the commoners as they filed out behind the mounted warriors. Even those who had more calm expressions were betrayed by the tight, white-knuckled grips that they held upon the bows, spears, or farm implements in their hands. Their impending sojourn claimed no end in sight, and promised to draw them very far from the town wall-walks and familiar village surroundings.

There were so many strong feelings that raced through Aethelstan's mind and heart at the sight of the commoners, as they started out on the long journey together.

He had lived and trained with most of the skilled warriors of his household for years. They possessed the best of arms, such as the prized swords on the senior warriors, and the notorious, long-hafted war axes wielded by many of the others.

Aethelstan had already fought alongside them, such as during a few minor border conflicts with Ehrengardian nobles, and he had no doubts as to their hardiness and abilities. His axe-men, he felt, could match the skills of the vaunted King's Guard of their mutual lord, King Alcuin.

The higher level ceorls that were part of the more widespread select levies were capably prepared as well. They were often modest landowners themselves, and some simply had not yet established the fortified enclosure and bell tower that would allow them to officially ascend to the rank of a thane.

CROWN OF VENGEANCE

Whether the land of a couple or several families, a designated amount of land, measured as eight hides in total, was made responsible for providing an equipped warrior to a levy. While not necessarily matching the full skills of a garrison or household warrior, these ceorls were most certainly robust, effectively equipped, and possessed quality training.

It was these more elite portions of the army that Aethelstan was well familiar with; the thanes, garrison warriors, household retinues, and ceorls.

Aethelstan knew the measure of what he could expect from them on a longer campaign. The rest of the general levy was an altogether different situation, holding so many unknown factors within its broad ranks. It gave him much to think about regarding the military aspects of the campaign and looming battles.

It was true that a small number of them had solid lances and sturdy knives, the latter including seaxs of lengths substantial enough to be like a shorter sword. A few of them even had shields and helms.

More often than not, the few better grade weapons amongst the commoners were heirlooms that had been passed down through families for generations. Quite frequently, such items were prizes culled in the aftermath of blood-drenched battles that had occurred long ago.

The matter of bows and archery was much different within the ranks of villagers, farmers, and artisans.

There were a substantial number of very good quality bows carried among the commoners. With strings of linen, and staves of ash or yew, the bows were used by individuals that had honed their skills while hunting within the hilly forests of Ealdorman Morcar's lands.

Most with bows were competent archers, and a fair number were quite excellent in their ability. Aethelstan knew that they would hold a very important place within the Saxan ranks, and he did not even want to begin to contemplate the detriments faced by a Saxan army without an ample number of the peasant bowmen.

Even so, the host of commoners was not of the same sort of martial ilk that his household warriors were.

While most of them were undeniably good, hard-working people, they were not used to the trials and demands involved in an extensive war campaign. How they would respond to the rigors of battle and hardship remained to be seen, and Aethelstan would not know the answer until it was far too late to do much of anything about it. Both he and Saxany were at the mercy of those untested men, in many ways.

In past times, the farmers and artisans had always seen their role as being to support and provision thanes such Aethelstan and their retinues for the more prevalent type of Select Levies.

In truth, they had already performed such a role for this very march. They had worked assiduously, applying their skills tirelessly for day after day, whether it was in the making of barrels and chests, building new wagons, leather repair, the fashioning of iron implements, or any one of the seemingly innumerable elements required for outfitting a large contingent for war.

Yet while they had performed their tasks wonderfully, a growing weight had surely dragged upon their minds. They all were mentally ready to respond to any immediate threat in the vicinity of their villages, or a nearby burh, but it had never before entered their minds that they could be called upon to leave their homes indefinitely, to fight in a far distant war.

This call to arms would take them to fight in just such a battle and war, whose magnitude threatened to take an unprecedented number of lives.

Aethelstan found himself worrying ever more about protecting these people in any way that he could. Never before had he come to the full realization of just how deeply he had come to care for the rugged, plain speaking, soil-tilling people of the hamlets and villages.

The General Fyrd was a terrible burden that he now had to bear, but there was no other choice left to the thanes, ealdormen, counts, and others of the realm. The messengers had been clear about the fearsome war storm that had gathered far to the west, and was now approaching Saxany.

Each and every man would be needed if the Saxan Kingdom were to even have a hope of surviving. The only other path was to submit to the Unifier's growing authority, and to Aethelstan that was no choice at all. To him, and to everyone that he had spoken to, that would be an abandonment of their very souls.

Whether tacit or by overt means, the Unifier was concentrating ever more authority to Himself. Aethelstan could not fail to see that it was pure recklessness to bring so many lands underneath one singular rule. While it might appear to some that kingdoms and empires still existed, Aethelstan knew it was all just illusion.

King Alcuin had been absolutely right in having defied Avanor and the Unifier. Something truly dark and terrible was afoot, as only a kingdom established and ruled directly by the All-Father could be trusted to avoid the kinds of corruption and tyranny inherent in a fallible, imperfect world. Placing such a concentration of power into the hands of mortal men was perilous and foolhardy.

Aethelstan snapped out of his momentary rumination, as there would be plenty of time for thinking once they were fully underway. He did not yet move forth to draw alongside the high banner with the red trees and white background, choosing instead to keep holding Wind Runner back, just off to the side of the proceeding column.

He gazed back upon the long, thick column wending its way down from the tower-gate of the burh. The end of the column had still not emerged, though well over fifteen hundred men were now moving within Aethelstan's sight.

In spite of all the burdens weighing upon his spirit, a flaring surge of pride came over him as he listened to the rumbling marching of the men and watched their ranks file by him.

Saxany was rousing itself to meet a dangerous threat once again, issuing forth in a dark hour to meet its enemy openly and with courage.

Aethelstan and all the men of the column were joining themselves with many honorable generations of Saxan warriors that day, transcending all time as they merged their number to others who had stood forward in times of threat and dire need.

Whatever the result of the coming battle was, the exercise of will, and affirmation of loyalties and values, that was reflected in the great column could never be taken away.

Aethelstan burned with a great pride to be going forward with such men, from the least of the villagers to the most renowned of the veteran warriors. By stepping out of the gates, and setting their foot on the pathway towards the west, each and every one of them was making a firm declaration about themselves.

In the final account of one's life, the measure of oneself, and what one took a stand for, was all that truly mattered anyway.

The recognition of the assertion being made by all the men before him strengthened Aethelstan's spirit greatly, bolstering him at a moment when so many things were battering incessantly upon his mind.

Without thinking about it, his left hand dropped slowly to the leather grip of Aurora, the storied sword sheathed at his left side. His fingers felt the familiar leather wrapping, as they settled between the silver-gilt, tri-lobed pommel and straight cross guard, also gilded with silver.

The blade was named many years in the past, on the very day that it was first wielded in battle. One of Aethelstan's ancestors had raised it high in the morning's light, at the forefront of a Saxan force mustered to face a powerful and determined enemy.

Witnesses later said that the blade radiated the light of the new dawn, just before the Saxans had gone forward to rout one of the last incursions of Midragardan raiders to come into Saxany.

That revered sword had been drawn by others of Aethelstan's line, and it had been a part of many brave exploits done on behalf of the Saxan people.

Aethelstan wondered if the light of the sun would strike the sword once again, when the time came for him to draw it and lead the men of his homeland into the thunder of the coming fight.

His hand squeezed the grip a little tighter, as he uttered a silent prayer that he would measure up to the thanes that had gone before him in a storied and revered line.

Nudging Wind Runner forward into a canter again, his left hand still resting upon the hilt of Aurora, Aethelstan brought the stallion up alongside the warrior carrying the banner of Wessachia just as the front of the column neared the edge of the woods.

The pathway would shortly intersect with a main route for martial forces, or herepath, as they continued westward, where more musters would be linking their numbers to the column as they progressed.

So much lay ahead, and so much remained unknown, but all journeys began with the initial step.

Aethelstan had taken that first step, as had over two thousand other men that day, despite all their fears. That alone made it an equivalent honor for Aethelstan to lead each and every one of them, simple villager and wealthy thane alike.

DEGANAWIDA

Solemnity filled the faces of the modest gathering seated around the hearth fire. The men were assembled in a chamber within the longhouse that displayed the image of a bear, rendered upon the facing of the bark panels suspended over the sheltered porch-entrances at each end.

Situated near to the highly prestigious, central longhouse that housed the revered Sacred Fire of the Five Realms, the Bear Clan longhouse that Deganawida dwelled within was one of the most prominent structures of the village.

The Bear Clan longhouse currently served as the main site for the meetings of the village council. It was the traditionally appropriate location, as Deganawida was the chosen headman of the Onan village called The Place of Far Seeing.

All of the main members of the village council were now present and fully attentive, as Deganawida had expected in light of the unusual, recent developments.

The eight other clan sachems looked expectantly towards Deganawida, their faces illuminated by the flames of the hearth fire. The blazing tendrils crackled steadily within the ponderous silence of the chamber.

Along with Deganawida himself, the sachems represented the nine clans that were present within the Onan Tribe; The Bear, The Wolf, The Firaken, The Beaver, the Shadow Flyers, The Tortoise, The Hawk, The Moose, and The Deer.

The venerated clan matrons of the substantial village had appointed each of the other eight sachems, just as they had appointed Deganawida. The clan matrons could similarly remove any of them, if they were ever deemed to be failing in their charge of guiding the village judiciously.

As of yet, all of the sachems present had served steadily and capably ever since their appointments. It had been quite some time since a sachem had been deposed for perceived failure in their given duty.

In addition to the sachems, the Wise Ones, the elderly men of the village, were also in attendance to give their own counsel and insights.

At first, all of the men had engaged in a sequence of chanted prayers, offering the rhythmic devotions to the One Spirit. As always, the prayers to the Sky Lord had largely centered upon simple thanksgiving, rather than the asking of any favor.

The men had then shared sacred tobacco together. They had smoked it reverently in the special, ornately carved wooden pipes, affixed with eagle feathers, that they passed carefully amongst each other.

A spirit of openness and harmony predominated within the

longhouse when it finally became time to discuss the important village and tribal matters at hand. At this particular council meeting, there was one predominant issue that stood forth from all others.

Deganawida's task, as always, was markedly different than that of the other ruling entities in the neighboring kingdom of Gallea. It was true that Deganawida carried more authority within the village in a more direct manner than he did on his seat at the Grand Council of the Five Realms. Yet his challenge was still to build consensus and wield influence, rather than issue indisputable and binding commands, as did the rulers in the western lands.

The thunderclouds of looming war were most certainly casting broad shadows upon the minds of the clan sachems and Wise Ones. The unexpected appearance of the strange foreigners had not helped matters in the least.

The presence of the foreigners had evoked thoughts of old prophecies and tales, all of which were set within a foreboding, worrisome context. If the foreigners were truly from another world, then there was likely much more to worry about than just the massing forces on the western borders of the tribal lands.

Aside from the daunting, broader implications, there also remained another underlying reality if the foreigners' story was indeed true. Assuming that their tale was sincere, they were still seven fellow humans, vulnerable and lost within an entirely unfamiliar world.

That, more than anything else, weighed heavily upon Deganawida's conscience as he looked out to his fellow council members.

Underneath the wampum banners, signifying the tribe itself, and referencing momentous events of their heritage, Deganawida convened the village council with a few opening words. When finished, he sat back down and waited with an attentive ear and apprehensive heart.

One by one, in the time-honored fashion, all of those wishing to speak rose up to address the council, taking a seat again when they had concluded.

The implications of this particular village council meeting were far reaching. Likely, its conclusions would reverberate all the way to the Grand Council itself. Deganawida was not the only man of the village who was also involved with the Grand Council of the Five Realms. There were three other men present who served as Pine Tree sachems for that august body. Their duties to the Grand Council included the running of messages, and acting as emissaries from time to time on behalf of the Five Realms.

Deganawida could not help but watch the faces of those three men in particular, knowing that they were listening to the discussion with some thoughts already given towards Grand Council matters. Their reactions might well give him a hint of what to expect in the times to come.

The series of speeches that ensued were quite uninhibited, as each speaker spoke frankly regarding their own perceptions and counsel. None would take offense for bluntly given comments during such an assembly. Candor was the way of the Onan, as it was for the other four tribes.

In general, the sentiments that were expressed by the litany of speakers were not particularly harsh. They tended to be ones of caution, balanced with the typical desire to show generosity towards accepted guests of the tribe.

Nearly all of the speakers expressed a concerted desire to keep the guests under close watch, as well as keeping them guarded should they venture beyond the boundaries of the village. It was clear that no man of the council felt comfortable enough to allow the seven free reign, both for their own protection as well as to address concerns of the unknown.

Their impressions of the guests themselves, for the large part, were very positive.

As a whole, the seven were being regarded in good favor, if not yet unconditionally embraced. To a man, the council members that spoke sensed that the seven's claims of being from thoroughly foreign origins were genuine.

Furthermore, there were no troubling suspicions raised by any of the council members in their lengthy orations.

Deganawida's hopes rose incrementally throughout the parade of speeches. He knew that Ayenwatha already felt very strongly about the seven, and Deganawida himself saw something very monumental in the abrupt appearance of the seven strangers.

Deganawida, like Ayenwatha, would abide by the consensus of the village council. Yet also like Ayenwatha, Deganawida greatly desired to have the seven harbored amongst the Onan, as their greater purpose was fathomed.

On a deeper level, he also did not want to see them sent unprepared out of the village, and left to the mercy of the wilderness. Such a thing would be far beneath what the Onan stood for, and would be a failure on many levels.

In addition, there was the very real dilemma facing the tribe of having the seven turned away, only to discover later that they were truly the ones heralded by ancient prophecy.

White Flower, the great Clan Matron of the Bear Clan who had been highly influential in Deganawida's position in the village and Grand Council, also shared his many concerns. Before the council had taken place, Deganawida had spoken with the wizened matron, receiving encouragement and advice that had reinforced him greatly going into the meeting.

Her heavily creased face did not diminish the lively sparkle in her eyes, as she counseled Deganawida to listen to his deepest inclinations on the matter. Her passion for the well-being of her village and tribe richly emanated through her words and demeanor. She had reminded him that he had always based his own positions on what was just, and that he could never really fail in using such a measure.

White Flower never told Deganawida what he should or should not do, or what to think. Yet when he had left her presence just a short time before the council, Deganawida was certain that his heartfelt inclinations had White Flower's full blessing.

Deganawida now brought those deep inclinations into his words when he spoke to the members of the counsel. He freely spoke about his perceptions of the seven, the timing of their appearance, the prophecies, their great vulnerabilities, and his hope that they could find haven among the Onan.

He cautioned the village council to bear in mind that whatever their origin or place in events, the guests were each living human spirits brought into being by He Who Holds the Sky. He implored them to do what was right for the seven on a human level, irrespective of their importance in larger matters.

His advocacy in their favor was strong, but when he sat back down again there still remained a few very influential speakers who had not yet had their turn.

The council meeting grew to be very long in duration, as they tended to be when everyone could speak without being limited in their address. A little anxiety danced at the edge of Deganawida's hopes, as a few more individuals spoke in clear favor of the seven.

Deganawida knew that he was very close to achieving consensus.

Finally, at long last, one of the most respected of the clan sachems rose up to take his turn to speak. Deganawida leaned a little forward, very curious as to the thoughts and leanings of the venerable sachem.

The air was at its thickest, filled with the scents of the smoke, tobacco, and the sweaty musk of the men filling the space.

The clan sachem named Garakontie would be the last one to speak, but his words were the most momentous of the entire council. The sachem could sway consensus with just a few short sentences, something that troubled Deganawida when he knew that he was so very close to securing full agreement from the council.

Long of nose and face, Garakontie, when seen at certain angles, took on an uncanny likeness to the spirited tree dwellers for which his Shadow Flyer clan was named. Like those hardy little forest creatures, he was tenacious, and acutely sensitive in his approaches to strangers.

The Shadow Flyers rendered their judgements very quickly in the wilderness. If something was not deemed to be a threat, the little animals did not hesitate to be seen and heard, whereas a true threat caused them to vanish in a flash of an instant.

While not inclined to make much noise or vanish, Garakontie was never long in his own evaluations of strangers. As far as Deganawida could remember, the Shadow Flyer sachem had always been amazingly accurate about which strangers should be embraced, and which should be shunned. Charm, appearance, and silken words did not deceive Garakontie in the least. He was uncannily adept at getting to the underlying realities, and was never hesitant about expressing any misgivings that came to him. His counsel had been proven correct in hindsight, time and time again.

In such a light, Deganawida listened closely and attentively to Garakontie's words.

"Deganawida, Clan Sachems, and Wise Ones, I cannot say that these are ordinary times, and I am not certain that ordinary answers can be the correct ones," Garakontie stated solemnly. "Much is amiss in our world, at a time when we should be concerned only about the migrations of the eel and salmon, the deer hunts, the clearing of fields, the planting of crops, and matters of trade.

"The appearance of the seven strangers, I believe, is no coincidence with the events that have been unfolding. I also believe that it is no coincidence that they came into the hands of Ayenwatha's war party, so soon after encountering the Wanderer.

"Only He Who Holds the Sky knows the pure truth, but we still must do our best to gain a clear sight of the matters facing our village, our tribe, the Five Realms, and indeed, the entire world. I cannot speak for the entire world, the Five Realms, or even our tribe, but I can say what I see within our village.

"And now, I will tell you truly what I feel.

"I observed the seven carefully at the feast. I can see no hint of the Adversary's touch upon any of them. Not even a shadow or a hint of the Adversary's corruption.

"You all already know that they have passed the crystal test, put to them when Ayenwatha's war party came upon them.

"There is much to them that we do not know, but I say that they are here for a purpose of the One Spirit. I firmly believe that we must shelter and protect them from the Adversary, and from the Unifier. I believe that He Who Holds the Sky will guide us rightly in this path."

It was one of the shorter addresses, but Deganawida could not have asked for any better support. The words of Garakontie were comforting and reinforcing to Deganawida's own inclinations. He knew that the clan sachem wielded a great influence with the others, all of whom valued Garakontie's great ability to fathom the underlying spirit of individuals.

Deganawida slowly arose as Garakontie concluded and took his seat once again. The village Headman was buoyed further by the looks that he now saw upon the faces of the clan sachems and Wise Ones.

It then came as no surprise when the village council fully supported providing a place of refuge and protection for the seven unusual guests.

There were a few parameters put in place, all of which Deganawida found to be very reasonable. The guests would be diligently watched and observed from a distance, and they would continue to be evaluated and measured for any ill signs. They would also be put under guard whenever going outside of the village boundary.

Most importantly, though, they would be given a true place of welcome within the Onan village. They would not be turned away expeditiously, and cast into the woods to fend for themselves.

When the meeting had been brought to a close, and the sachems and Wise Men had departed the longhouse, Deganawida was left with a tranquil and invigorating feeling of relief.

In a way, the village council had just passed a test, further justifying the confidence placed in them by the clan matrons.

They had not had their judgement blinded by the terrible pressure of the looming war. Nor had they rushed to an expedient decision in the hopes of avoiding perceived risks. They had acted reasonably, and with foresight and resolve, and for that Deganawida's own heart was greatly uplifted.

A time of great pressure and imminent threat could easily move men from wisdom to utter recklessness, and see otherwise compassionate men become cruel and pitiless. Courage often gave way to mere self-preservation in the grip of such trying times, bringing about acts that bordered on the heartless and the barbarous.

Yet the true measure of a man, Deganawida well knew, was whether he became a monster during such a time, or still remained a man.

The storm facing all of them had not dissipated, and would only gather in strength as the hours passed, but the early signs regarding the steadfastness of the village leadership were indeed encouraging.

He could only hope that it was a harbinger for the way that the other villages, and even the Grand Council, would be in the difficult days to come.

Deganawida mused to himself in the wake of the council that a small victory had truly been achieved. He would gladly savor it as he sat within the quiet chamber, as all good moments needed to be celebrated.

Without a doubt, one truth had been established. The members of the village council for The Place of Far Seeing were still indeed men.

section v

DRAGOL

Dragol and the other Trogen riders guided their steeds downward, to skim along at a slower pace just a short distance above the uppermost reach of the trees. Fanning out in a wide formation, they were able to survey a fairly extensive swathe of land, doubling and tripling their passes to make sure that no swatch of ground went uncovered.

Though more vulnerable to arrows, as they were within the average range of a Saxan bow, the lower altitude formation still gave them some advantages. It helped to lessen the chances of an advance warning being given by a lookout watching the high skies. An unaware enemy presence along the ground was also more likely to be detected before they could melt among the shadows and foliage beneath the Trogens.

Dragol knew that any Saxans within the woodlands were likely to be very capable in such skills. His own kind was adept at concealment in their own lands, and not just due to the ever-present threats from the Elven menace. Navigating the dangers of the wilderness demanded the ability to become motionless in a flash of time, to be able to quickly shroud oneself in forest growths, and to snap into total silence.

The Trogen's sharp eyes watched carefully for any hints of movement beneath the canopy, but nothing stirred. No signals arose from any of his riders either during the broad search.

Light would be fading soon, and Dragol could not deny the fact that no creature on foot could outdistance the considerable area that they had covered through the sky. Frustration now boiled within him, his patience wearing steadily thinner with the approach of the sun's descent.

One of his riders abruptly cried out.

The tensions vanished instantly, adrenaline sparking within him as the cry reached his triangular-shaped ears. Without hesitation, Dragol deftly maneuvered his Harrak to the left and dug in his heels, spurring the quickly responsive creature to accelerate to full speed.

As a unit, the other riders were doing likewise as they honed in upon the area signaled by their comrade.

LEE

An arduous day's march had ended mercifully, one in which the group had decided to turn inward and continue deeper into the forest. The primary motive was to take themselves farther away from the edge of the woodlands, before they searched out their next camp site.

Lee's argument had won out over the option of continuing along the boundary of the woods. He had reasoned that the horse riders were limited to the open land, as his group had not come across any significant trails leading into the woods. Furthermore, if the bestial warriors were at war with the horse riders then they would also be concentrating on the territory where the horse riders were most likely to be found.

The others found the rationale to be sound, and around mid-day they had headed due east, pushing into the depths of the forest. By the cusp of evening, the energy regained during the previous night's rest was utterly spent.

The hike had gone largely without incident, the greatest surprise coming when Lynn had suddenly given Lee a pinch on the arm. Looking over at her with a startled expression, Lee had followed her gesture to where a black and white plumaged bird with a long tail appeared to be regarding them from a tree branch.

"I heard about these birds once before," Lynn said. "One magpie's supposed to be bad luck, unless you do one of a couple remedies. Can't remember the rest, but pinching a companion was one I remembered."

Lee shook his head and grinned, "Just my luck, that you didn't remember something a little less stinging."

"Don't want bad luck now, do you?" Lynn retorted with a chuckle. Though she was visibly tired, Lee was gladdened to see the sparkle in her.

Lee had raised his eyebrow, and looked over at Ryan and Erin. "Don't forget to pinch each other. We don't need any more bad luck than we've had already."

"I'm not superstitious," Erin had replied in a disinterested tone.

"I'm not too worried either," Ryan had added.

"I think you can salute them too, or at least I think I remember that from the same source I got the other information," Lynn had then said.

"Salute the bird, you say?" Ryan responded with an impish timbre. "Well, why didn't you say so first?"

He had then proceeded to stare at the bird with a mischievous glint in his eyes. A grin had spread upon his face, as he then raised his right hand and prominently directed a vulgar gesture towards the magpie.

The magpie might well have been insulted, as it had emitted a few rather brusque cries in the wake of Ryan's disrespectful acknowledgement. The timing was uncanny.

"There, a single-finger salute for the damn bird, delivered in classic New York style, just in case the pinch didn't work," Ryan had added, chortling. "Thanks for the advice on that, Lynn! That'll make sure we don't' saddle you all with more bad luck."

"You should take issues of bad luck more seriously," Lynn had chided him lightheartedly. She then laughed aloud, "But there's no denying you saluted the bird … or flipped that bird the bird, you could say."

"I figured I could be creative. We're already immersed in bad luck," Ryan had retorted in dismissive fashion, as his waves of self-amused laughter simmered down.

"See? None of the precautions were really necessary, either of yours. I prefer Ryan's version. It was a little less painful," Lee had said to Lynn and Ryan, rubbing his arm where she had pinched him and evoking a little more laughter from the both of them.

He was grateful for the momentary levity. Yet in truth, Lee had felt unsettled all through the day, from the break of dawn until the woodland shadows had begun to grow and deepen.

Lee still felt the unease deep inside him as they finally drew to a halt, taking seats on the great roots of an immense, old oak tree. He took note of some primrose that was spreading within the vicinity of the ancient, mighty oak.

Nearby, high in the branches of another tree, was a large nest belonging to a sharp-beaked bird, whose graceful flight was a joy to watch above the forest's ceiling. The sizeable bird's thin call carried far, its long tail twisting as it changed course in the upper heights.

The four conversed amongst themselves for some time, fatigue doing nothing to dull Erin's sharp attitude, or Ryan's temper. Lynn and Lee had to nurse the overall harmony of the group along as they discussed their frustrations and condition, and took account of their current situation.

Before very long, Lee was fighting back the overwhelming urge to doze, summoning every ounce of his will to remain focused. He knew that the group would have no choice but to muster enough energy to set up a new shelter for the coming night. Day was starting to fade, and there would not be much more strong light left to work by.

Lee was about to get up to his feet, when he was startled abruptly by a forceful outcry that shattered the relative tranquility.

The invasive shouts hurtled down upon them from the sky, from just above the tops of the trees, as a large shadow flitted across the ground. Lee was unable to tell who or what it was, though his heart caught in his throat. The cry evoked the raw memories of the brutal scene that they had witnessed at the edge of the woodlands, but Lee could not be for certain. The form of the flying entity passing overhead was thoroughly distorted by the overlying mesh of tree branches.

Lee cast a glance towards the others.

Lynn jumped up quickly from her place of repose, her eyes wide with fear. Ryan reached quickly for the bow at his side, fumbling with it clumsily in his urgency and frayed anxiety.

Erin was no longer keeping her moody distance from the other three. She stumbled in her maddened haste, crawling on hands and knees to get near the others.

They all looked frantically along the top of the treeline. Even without seeing its form, Lee knew that there was little chance of mistaking the outcry that had come from such a close proximity. Each small patch of unbroken sky was watched assiduously, as they all became statues of flesh and bone.

It only took a few more moments to confirm the nature of what flew above them.

Just visible through a small opening in the treeline, one of the flying steeds passed into view with a rider on its back. There was no urgency in the movements of the creature, as it glided upon the air currents in a circuitous route around their position.

Lee's heart sank as he watched the non-human rider gazing down upon them from its lofty perch. There was little mistaking its intention. It was marking their position for others.

Lee and Lynn frantically grabbed weapons, Lee taking up one of the remaining bows and Lynn grabbing the hilt of the sword that she had claimed. Though very afraid, Lee kept his hands steady and his countenance cool, as he drew long breaths and notched an arrow to the bowstring.

Lynn floundered a little with her sword, in her frenetic confusion about where to position herself, nearly dropping the weapon in the process. She was far from comfortable with the blade, and Lee knew that if it came to fighting on the ground, Lynn would be in great trouble.

Erin was frozen in place, her face a mask of panic. She stammered out, "What are we going to do? Oh my God. What are we going to do?"

"Get a hold of yourself, right now!" Lynn snapped at her friend, her usual patience entirely absent. "Defend yourself. You don't have a choice!"

Lee could not have said it better.

They had all witnessed what the bestial riders were capable of, their deadly skill on vivid display as they destroyed the ill-fated horsemen with efficiency and ferocity. Perhaps the only good fortune that Lee and the others had in that moment was that there was no time to contemplate their odds of survival.

The brevity, urgency, and naked truth of the perilous moment, and their surge of adrenaline, excepting Erin, served capably to steel their resolve towards defense.

"Over here! All of you! Get to cover now!" Lee yelled out to the others, darting for an inviting spot by the trunk of a very large, old tree. Its mass of thick lower branches provided at least some degree of protection and cover over his head, while allowing him to try and monitor what was happening above.

Lynn and Ryan responded immediately, racing towards Lee, but Erin remained behind, still frozen in place. She had not even grabbed a weapon in the interim, and looked for all purposes as if she had been stricken dumb.

Lee cursed angrily under his breath, as he ran out from beneath his protective position by the tree. He raced over to her, his mind of singular focus.

Reaching out, he grabbed her upper arm, forcibly jerking her forward as he half-dragged her to the closest tree. A sibilant hissing of air preceded the dull thud that struck behind him, as an arrow embedded itself into the earth, right in the spot that Erin had just been in.

As they reached the tree, Lee spun her around to face the direction that they had just run from. The long arrow fletched with black feathers protruded from the ground as a visible, sobering lesson for Erin.

"Do you see that? Get a hold of yourself, or you will get killed, or get someone else killed!" Lee shouted quickly at her, incredulous at her stupefied behavior. He had never felt a more searing ire, though he knew that he could not have left her standing there.

He reoriented himself with his bow and set an arrow once again into place, his head tilting up as his eyes locked onto the treeline above.

Ryan was setting another arrow into his bow, having loosed one errant and desperate shot at the hovering rider that had fired upon Erin. The rush of the moment, and his inexperience with the bow, had resulted in missing his mark by a wide margin.

Lee aimed carefully, taking a couple of deep breaths and letting his hands steady themselves. He had once taken archery lessons as a youth, though the compound bow that he had used then was markedly different than the simpler wood construct that he now held.

He reminded himself that the concepts were still the same, even if the feeling was awkward. It took a considerable amount of pull to ready his shot, and in his rigid concentration the creaks of the bow sounded loud to his ears

Through the branches, he could see that the rider on the flying beast was readying another arrow, and searching out a target as it continued to hover in place.

Several other cries indicated that the one firing the arrows down on them was not going to be their only nemesis for very long. The archer was joined just moments later by another, the rider that had originally marked their location. It had broken off from circling and had come into view next to the first archer, readying its own great longbow.

Lee was about to let his own arrow fly, just as a blood-curdling cry rang out from behind and above him. Whirling about, he looked up just in time to see a large shape crashing down haphazardly, bouncing off tree branches and breaking others as it plunged towards the ground.

The wings of the creature folded as it finally tumbled into a free fall through open space towards the hard earth. Its rider had already been cast out from the saddle, shrieking in dismay, and then grunting loudly as it slammed into the forest floor.

Two sickening thumps resonated as the bodies of both steed and rider were crumpled against the hard earth, their forms distorted and broken. There was no life evident in either of them. Lee's eye's widened as he saw the shaft of an arrow sticking out from the neck of the winged creature. It was fletched with a lighter, different kind of feather than the deep black ones of the attackers.

Sparing a glance, he looked across to Ryan and Lynn to see who had fired the accurate arrow that had slain the steed. Both of them looked back at him with expressions of sheer astonishment. Ryan was standing with another arrow in his right hand, his attention drawn to the commotion near Lee. It was obvious that he had not suddenly gained great skill with the bow.

Lee turned quickly to look back behind him, his arrow notched as he strained to pull the string back again.

GUNTHER

Gunther, in his close and careful attention to the four strangers, only became aware at the last instant of the appearance of a large Trogen warrior, mounted upon a Harrak steed in the air overhead.

He recognized their distinctive forms instantly, and he realized their deadly intentions.

Steed and rider crossed through the air slowly overhead, its rider looking down upon the four strangers. It yelled out a cry of warning, before settling into a circling pattern.

Gunther knew what would occur. There would be several others in the vicinity, as the Trogens had been flying over the Saxan forest in substantial patrols during recent days.

That was unnerving enough, as their mere presence was a harbinger of ill-fortune for the Saxan lands. Their hostile posture towards the four strangers, woefully unprepared to deal with the wilderness, much less a Trogen sky patrol, sent a sense of dread racing through Gunther. The quartet was in mortal danger, and now Gunther wished more than ever that the Wanderer had remained with him for a little longer.

The woodsman's biggest advantage was that the Trogen warriors knew nothing of him, their attentions clearly fixed upon the party that he had been shadowing.

Quickly, he made some frantic calls of his own, sounding again much like a bird, though any of the natural fauna within the area had abruptly gone silent at the invasive disturbance from the sky rider's shout.

The coded warning resonated to his accompanying Jaghuns, as the creatures halted where they had been edging themselves into positions creating a perimeter around the four strangers. Three methodically worked their way back to Gunther, crouching down in silence near to his side.

Dexterously, Gunther pulled his large hunting bow out from where it was slung over his back. Made of a select length of yew, the sturdy longbow suddenly became an extension of himself as he readied an arrow.

The Trogens were flying unusually low, and were probably gauging their height based upon the range of the common Saxan self-bow. They were not factoring in the larger type of bow that Gunther carried, based upon the kind carried by the hardy fighters that dwelled in the western edges of faraway Norengal.

Gunther's broad travels had given him a significant advantage this time, even if they had brought him so much darkness. His eyes scanned above in scrutiny as he kept the arrow pulled back, carefully searching out his first target.

As the Harrak circled above the trees, he stepped closer for a better shot. He knew that his Jaghuns would provide plenty enough of a warning if anything threatening to himself were to unexpectedly emerge.

With their eyes and ears applied to warding him, Gunther could afford to concentrate his attentions on the airborne warriors and the four imperiled strangers.

One of the female strangers was currently in a hysterical state, remaining out in the open while the others had taken to a nearby tree for cover. He could not believe her sheer stupidity, aghast at her incompetence.

Showing great bravery and fortitude, the one that Gunther had assumed to be their leader suddenly rushed out and grabbed her, pulling her unceremoniously towards relative safety by a nearby tree. Gunther could see the outrage on the foreign man's face, and the woodsman certainly could not blame him for his furor, as the girl had put both herself and her rescuer at great, and very unnecessary, risk.

Gunther then flinched inadvertently, as an arrow struck the ground where the female had been standing. Looking at the arrow in the ground, he quickly guessed at the trajectory and looked up to find that a second Trogen warrior had taken up a hovering position under the one marking the area. The Trogen archer was already poising to fire another arrow.

Knowing the Trogens as well as he did, remembering their ways and tendencies, he turned and looked back, behind where the group's leader had dragged the fear-paralyzed woman. As he had expected, a third Trogen had taken advantage of the tumult, and had quietly gotten itself maneuvered into position behind the humans.

It was silently hovering even closer to the treeline, its bow drawn back with deadly intent. The two humans on the ground had no awareness of its presence, occupied as they were with the other Trogens. Their backs were readily exposed to its line of sight, providing easy targets to a skilled Trogen warrior.

There was no time to wait, as the war cries of other Trogens were filling the skies. Honing his focus upon the third Trogen, Gunther hit that zone within his mind where the Trogen and its steed were the only things that existed in all of the world.

In the flash of a moment, with immaculately steady aim, Gunther let his arrow fly for the thick neck of the Harrak. There was no doubt about the elite skill that Gunther had developed through the years, and that adeptness was demonstrated once again. The arrow penetrated deep, punching through the winged creature's long fur into the underlying flesh of its neck, as if Gunther had thrust it there from close range with his bare hands.

The Harrak was killed instantly, suddenly becoming dead weight as its lifeless body plunged towards the ground below. It carried its rider towards a doomed fate, though the warrior had remarkable presence of mind as it jerked free from the straps securing it to the saddle, in the desperate hope of avoiding being tied to the beast's movements.

The hapless rider screamed defiantly as it pitched from the saddle. Gunther watched as the bodies of both steed and rider violently struck the upper tree branches, the sounds of snapping and breaking wood accompanying the fatal descent.

Without further hesitation, Gunther readied another arrow and turned back towards the archer that he had originally seen. The Trogen warrior that had previously been circling had joined the fight, hovering near the first.

Raising his bow, he calculated his next shot.

DRAGOL

Dragol cursed with rage as he saw the arrow streak out of the trees and drop the Harrak out of the sky. Even his steed Rodor gave a rumbling growl at the brief yelp that came from the stricken steed, as its wings ceased flapping and it began to fall. The shot had been exceptional, killing the steed nearly instantly and casting one of his warriors to certain death.

In an act of desperate futility, the doomed warrior somehow managed to free himself from the saddle straps, only to be bludgeoned repeatedly by the thick tree branches that rushed up to greet his falling form. The sounds of the cracking branches lasted just a couple of moments, as Dragol gazed down hotly upon the trees that were hiding their unknown adversary.

Calling out orders quickly, he commanded a group of warriors near to him, indicating for them to begin descending towards the ground.

If their enemies were armed, skilled fighters, then having the Trogens all out in the open air would do little good. A few of their number would have to reach the ground, so that they could engage the enemy from both below and above.

There was no time to linger above the treeline, searching for the most favorable spot possible to descend, as they were clearly in a very dangerous position, within range of at least one enemy bow. Dragol could not believe what had just occurred, as it far exceeded his estimation of the bows that they had already seen carried by the Saxans.

It was a new, deadly revelation, one that he would have to keep in mind for future adjustments.

The Trogens obeyed his directive without hesitation, gliding down to just inches above the treeline. They looked hurriedly about for an opening to take their steeds to the forest floor. They were now in a very precarious position, well within the range of the normal Saxan bows, as well as the stronger kind that had just brought the Harrak down.

Dragol guided his own steed downward as he pulled out his great longblade from his sheath. He clenched the leather-wrapped hilt tightly in his powerful hand, his ire rising with each moment as he steeled himself for the impending combat. The invigorating rush that he always felt at the cusp of battle did not overwhelm his discipline, channeling into a fiery resolve and heightening his senses. He swore to give a hundred times more in retribution for the slaying of one of his warriors.

Sparing a quick glance upward, he saw two warriors steadily hovering as they looked for targets for their next arrows. Dragol watched intently, hoping that the enemy bowman who had just felled one of his warriors was more focused upon the two archers, such that his other warriors were unimpeded and allowed the time to find a propitious area to alight.

Three of his warriors flew just ahead of him, and he watched their progress even as he slowed Rodor's pace considerably to look for a potential point of descent. The warriors brought their steeds to a momentary hover, and then started to slowly disappear beneath the treetops. He saw that they had found a wide enough opening in the tree canopy, where the strong wings of the Harraks would not be inhibited as they carefully worked lower, descending towards the forest floor.

Dragol reached the spot a few moments later, and wasted no time in following the trio, guiding Rodor down towards the breach in the forest's canopy.

With flashing speed, three large forms suddenly exploded from the trees and beset the three Harraks setting down just beneath him. The Harraks cried out in agony, as a flurry of movement ensued that was almost impossible to make any sense of at first. Huge claws swept through the air, and powerful jaws snapped before the Harraks had any chance to respond to their assailants.

Reflexively, Dragol jerked upon the reins, and Rodor's wings snapped powerfully downward, abruptly ceasing their descent. Dangerously close to the explosion of fighting, Dragol got a good look at the melee before Rodor lifted upwards. He had never seen creatures such as the ones now assaulting his warriors. They were very large of body, somewhat dog-like, with short, broad muzzles. Their forms rippled with powerful muscles, with long legs that ended in huge paws. They were creatures of both speed and power, and Dragol only had to glance at the structure of their jaws to recognize their bone crunching potential.

Rodor was spurred by the commotion, flapping back vigorously towards the sky as it took Dragol away from the danger. The Trogen chieftain continued to watch the scene in dismay as he was carried back up, mere seconds seeming to take ages to pass before his eyes.

The ambushed riders below had no time to react before their steeds were mortally wounded, crashing into the ground as the four-legged attackers barreled into them. The warriors could not pick themselves up from the disorienting fall, still secured to the saddles of their steeds.

Trapped, unable to maneuver, and having incurred several injuries in the violence of the impact, the beleaguered Trogens were quickly smothered by the horrific, ferocious beasts. The cries of the warriors were cut short, as the beasts' jaws ripped and tore at them in a frenzy, finishing them off swiftly.

Looking back just in time for another dismaying sight, Dragol saw one of the two warriors that had been hovering with their bows falling from the sky. Its steed had been slain by yet another remarkable arrow shot that had come from beneath the trees.

To the right, a couple more of his riders were disappearing below the treeline, through another opening a little farther off. Without pausing even a moment, Dragol cried out at the top of his lungs. He ordered them to come back immediately into the skies.

It was not soon enough, as his own orders were mixed a moment later with the terrible sounds of raging growls and throaty barks, accompanied by the pained cries of Harraks. The noise was followed by the courageous war cries of the two riders, as they faced their adversaries out of Dragol's sight.

There was suddenly a high-pitched yelp of pain, and Dragol's heart surged as he guided his Harrak speedily towards the point where the two warriors had descended. The momentary hope was dashed, as his ears captured agonized Trogen cries, mixed with louder, snapping barks and growls.

He bit back impulsive anger as he crossed over the location, and saw the wreckage that had been made of his warriors and their steeds.

There was nothing that he could do for them, though he took a little solace as he noticed that one of the dreadful beasts that had attacked them was badly wounded. It was trying to crawl away, struggling to pull itself away from the opening in the trees.

With his heels, Dragol signaled to his steed to hover in place. His blood was scorching hot as it raced through his veins, but his mind remained cool and resolute.

With a growl in his throat, and forgetting about the skilled enemy archer that he knew was somewhere out there, he sheathed his great longblade and whipped out his own longbow.

Notching an arrow, he poured his rage and malice towards the slayers of his warriors into one single shot, which raced towards the injured beast. The vengeance-driven shot ripped into the creature's head, abruptly finishing off any chance that it might have had at survival.

Dragol knew that his patrol was unprepared for whatever was below the treeline. Calling out forcefully, and gesturing urgently, he ordered the rest of his surviving warriors to abandon the attack.

He then let loose with a great howl of sheer rage, as his steed climbed back towards the sanctuary of the high skies.

Thwarted and filled with a boiling hostility, Dragol found very little to be comforted about as the remnants of his patrol sped away. The grandiosity of the total destruction of the Saxan patrol had been smashed asunder by the sudden misfortune brought about by the unknown four-legged assailants, and the deadly, unseen bowman.

There was small comfort to be had in such a short period of time where fortunes had changed so drastically, swinging so quickly between extremes. It was true that the Unifier's armies would soon be swarming through the lands that Dragol now left behind him, but that was no solace at all to his embittered heart.

He could only think of the undignified deaths that several of his warriors had met at the jaws of forest beasts, formidable though they were. The feral images of the unusual creatures were stamped indelibly into his mind. He promised himself to see to it that they would be hunted down mercilessly, and slain wherever they were found, once Saxany was held by the Unifier.

His mind then settled upon the black-feathered arrow shaft embedded in the dead body of the beast he had slain, reminding him that he had already exacted the first fruits of vengeance. While only slight, the remembrance nonetheless brought him a little relief, to help endure the return journey back to their camp.

LEE

Lee saw nothing behind him, or anywhere around him, his eyes searching frantically among the trees for even one sign of any other being. Without a doubt, there was another archer very near to his group, one who had just intervened on their behalf. The irrefutable evidence lay not far away, in the form of the dead winged beast with the arrow shaft protruding from its neck.

Despite the unexpected assistance, the notion of an unknown warrior lurking somewhere close by was still unsettling. The friend of the moment could well turn into the foe of the next.

Lee turned his head to and fro, urgently looking for any indication of their unknown benefactor, while keeping his eyes open for the rise of other threats.

Shadows crossing over him brought his head up in a flash. More of the winged creatures were flying at a low altitude just over the tops of the trees. Lee wanted to maneuver over to join Ryan and Lynn, if only so that they could all make a stand together.

He knew that he was effectively trapped where he was. If he emerged from the trunk of the tree, he would come into the clear sight of the two hovering riders, one of whom had already come dangerously close to claiming one of his companions' lives.

Lee peered carefully around the tree that he was behind, looking up towards the two riders imminently besetting them. He then cast a glance across the short distance to where Ryan and Lynn were crouched. If it was only a matter of himself, he might have sprinted out from his position and attempted to join them. With Erin to think about, he gauged that it was too much of a risk to try to reach the others.

Turning his focus back up to the riders, he concentrated on executing a solid attempt with the bow. He steadied his aim as he tilted the weapon upwards, sighting one of the riders as he began to pull the string back.

He wondered if he would have enough range for the shot, as their attackers held the considerable advantage of firing downwards. To his eyes, the distance to the pair of attackers looked daunting to any hope of loosing an arrow that would have even a slim chance of striking one of them.

It was in that moment of rising doubt that a furious commotion broke out somewhere to his left. Flinching, he almost let go of the partially-drawn arrow. His body tingled, and a chill raced over him as he listened to the raucous clamor breaking out just beyond his sight. The growling frenzy was guttural and vicious.

Mixed within the tumult were cries like those of the warriors above, which rang out through the forest. In moments they transformed into unmistakable shrieks of agony, the sounds sending shards of ice into Lee's heart. Very quickly, the forest fell quiet again.

Lee's chest constricted with the fear swelling inside of him, as if someone were pressing down upon it. More crashing sounds brought his attention snapping back to the area on the other side of the tree. He saw one of the two winged beasts that had been hovering plummet to the ground, breaking some branches and careening off of others as the creature dragged its rider down with it. A heavy thud and the sickening noise of cracking bones reached Lee's ears.

Though the body of the winged beast was a little farther off, Lee's eyes spotted the vertical shaft of an arrow coming from the creature's neck. To his guess, it was lodged at almost the exact place of the shaft that had dropped the first winged steed.

Lee turned his head and saw that Ryan still had his arrow notched. He was shaking his head from side to side as Lee's eyes met his, confirming Lee's suspicions.

Another commotion started to Lee's right, and he broke his eyes away from Ryan to rivet upon the sight of two more of the winged steeds trying to land through the trees a short distance away. They were coming down through a small opening in the trees, barely wide enough for the expansive wingspan of the flying creatures.

A huge blur of movement froze Lee's heart a second later. Some manner of creature leaped off of the ground, lunging towards the landing entities. Its momentum hurled its bulk into one of the winged creatures.

Another flashing shape raced in from the other side, as yet another beast came into view, bounding across the forest floor at an incredible speed. Leaping at the last instant, it extended its body as it hurtled towards the second winged steed and slammed into it.

The mass of winged steeds, riders, and their four-legged assailants tumbled in a whirlwind of desperate struggle to the ground. The first beast made quick work of one winged steed, clamping its wide jaws down upon the other's throat, tearing it out with a powerful wrench of its muscular neck. Righting itself, jaws soaked in blood, the creature sprang at the slain steed's rider, who had been badly injured in the fall.

Lee winced. The rider did not have a chance to defend itself, before submerging under a torrent of slashing claws and long fangs driven by powerful jaws.

Just a few feet to the right of the first melee, the rider of the second winged steed hurriedly freed itself from the saddle of its stricken mount. It raised a sword-like weapon up, and shouted out a spirited war cry. Shaking in rage, the non-human warrior charged the second of the attacking beasts, which had found the throat of the rider's steed. The beast jerked its head free, spraying flesh and blood from the mortal wound that it had just delivered.

The heavy blade whipped down with great force, lodging deep into the back of the creature, and eliciting a terrible howl of pain. With a powerful yank, the brawny fighter quickly freed the great blade.

It was about to attempt a second blow, lifting the weapon upward when yet another of the attacking beasts enveloped the warrior from behind. The rider disappeared behind the body of its fallen steed, as the assailant's momentum and size propelled the warrior to the ground.

Lee saw the beast open its broad jaws wide to display a horrific array of large, sharp teeth, snarling balefully right before its head plunged down out of sight. The outcries of the warrior underneath the creature were abruptly silenced.

Hearing a high-pitched whine, Lee turned his head and saw that the beast that had been wounded by the large blade was not dead. Pulling itself forward across the ground on its paws, it strove painstakingly towards a nearby tree, to get away from the unobstructed opening to the sky.

As Lee watched, an arrow streaked down through the hole in the canopy, punching through the beast's skull and instantaneously rendering it still. Just a moment later, an anguished, rage-filled cry filled the air, coming from above the area where the arrow had just sped through.

Looking back, Lee then noticed that the other bow-equipped rider had vacated its position in the wake of its comrade's slaying. Not hesitating a moment longer, he reached back for Erin, clutching her arm and yelling, "Come on! Now! Move it fast!"

Erin appeared to be shocked out of her stupor, putting an effort into rising up as she responded to Lee's directive. Springing forward, the two broke out from the base of the tree. They swiftly covered the short distance over to their other two companions. Ryan and Lynn rose up from their crouches as they reached them.

"Get ready, I don't know what's down here with us now," Lee said quickly. "Some kind of beast, and there's more than one, and they are very close!"

His heart could not have beaten faster, a thundering piston in his chest as a sweat started to break out. The fearsome creatures that had slain the riders and steeds were among the nearby trees. The concern over the unknown archer that had come to their help was swiftly forgotten in the aftermath of his dizzying fear of the beasts.

They were huge, fast predators, and they were anything but solitary. Lee could not assume anything less than that they were a kind of pack hunter, able to work in concert with each other. The situation facing Lee and the others had become even more perilous, with threats both above and below.

"Did you see them?" Lee asked, casting a glance at Ryan.

Ryan nodded rapidly, almost shaking.

"Keep your eyes out, and keep your bow up!" Lee said, his eyes sweeping the forest floor, expecting at any moment to see the long-legged, tall forms of the creatures. The visions in his mind centered upon their crushingly powerful, deadly jaws.

Bows in hand, Lee and Ryan faced in opposite directions, Lynn peering out warily out from between them. Erin, wide-eyed and beyond fright, trembled as she stared out from where she was pressed against the massive tree trunk.

"Yell if you see anything, any movements at all," Lee called out, taking a brief moment to look above him.

Fortunately, it appeared that the riders and their winged steeds were long gone. Yet their absence gave him little comfort, as the causes for it were still lurking somewhere within the shadows beneath the surrounding trees.

Lee, Ryan, Erin, and Lynn kept their places for several tense moments, not so much as moving a muscle. Sweaty hands clasped weapons, as they all anxiously awaited what Lee believed to be an inevitable, terrible fate. The sweat made his skin feel clammy, and an oppressive weight formed in the air. It felt as if the forest was encroaching in upon Lee, confining his group as the sense of threat coiled about them.

The seconds passed as if they were hours, the cries of the sky riders long since faded into the distance. The day was ebbing, and it would not be all that much longer before night fell. It was overwhelming enough even being able to see far into the woods. Lee did not want to consider what it would be like with the woods shrouded in the black of night.

Slowly, he began to take into account other elements, as his mind forced its way through the paralysis of his terror. Calling to mind the unknown being whose arrows had brought down two winged steeds, Lee kept an eye out for the archer, hoping that the individual was some kind of ally. The unknown benefactor was their only real chance at resolving their dilemma, likely being one who knew the immediate woods, and might know more about the nature of the beasts within them.

Lee knew that he and his companions were all at the mercy of sheer chance. He needed no argument to realize that they stood little to no chance against creatures that had made such short work of large winged steeds and well-armed warriors alike.

Lee spared a moment to look over to Erin. Now that she was removed from the necessity of moving positions, the fears were clearly gathering her into their consuming embrace once again. The young woman was shaking, frightened to a nearly hysterical level in the wake of the spectacle that had violently played out before all of their eyes.

"Come on," Lee said gently, mustering steadiness into his voice. He felt compassion for her raw terror, as he was far from immune to its touch himself. "You are going to need to stay focused, and hold a weapon. Where is your dagger?"

Erin did not respond, her eyes staring off into the forest. Her eyes rotated to the left, looked down a little, and abruptly widened.

Lee felt that his heart would stop, fearing that she had just sighted one of the menacing beasts. He followed her revealing glance with trepidation, steeling himself for the sight that would be unveiled to his eyes.

His nerves relaxed slightly, and he let a breath loose as there was no beast to be found. Erin had indicated the dagger, which was lying on the ground several paces away.

Lee was not about to chance another foray out into the open. He already felt a little foolish and reckless for having taken the risk of running with Erin over to join the others. He had taken full notice of the blinding speed that the forest creatures possessed, and knew that predators were often quite attuned to sudden movements.

"Keep your bow ready, and shoot any damn thing that moves," Lee muttered to Ryan.

Ryan shot Lee a nervous grin. His voice was strained. "Like we have another plan?"

Lee forced a smile, his nerves on the extreme edge as well. "No, I guess we don't."

They both almost shot their arrows haphazardly, when a loud voice shattered the heavy stillness permeating the trees.

"Strangers to this forest, hold your arrows!" called a deep voice, from just a short distance away.

To Lee, the voice came from a hidden place that was uncomfortably close. None of the four could see the speaker of the words, though their eyes raced as they hurriedly cast looks all around the encompassing shadows and trees.

At the very least, Lee knew that the voice came from no beast.

Rather, it sounded like the voice of a man.

"I am the one who felled the Harraks with arrows," the speaker continued calmly. "I am not your enemy."

The mystery of the unseen archer revealed slightly, Lee suddenly feared for the man, especially if he was a stranger as well.

"There are beasts out there! Beasts that killed some of the winged animals, and their riders," Lee shouted into the forest, "It is dangerous! They are very close!"

"Beasts?" The voice seemed to carry amusement, much to the abject surprise of Lee. There was not a trace of worry at Lee's pronouncement within the tone of the other. "Oh, those beasts. Nothing to fear from them. They are not your enemies either. They were your defenders. You already know they fought to help you."

A stunned expression crossed the faces of Lee, Lynn, and Ryan, and even Erin's eyes widened at the words of the concealed speaker.

"Come out in the open, then, if you are a friend" Lee addressed the possessor of the voice, not willing to believe how casual the individual was about the ferocious creatures that were prowling somewhere nearby.

Slowly, out from behind the trunk of another large tree, a broad form emerged. Lee knew in his heart that the man walking into view was native to the strange world, or at least someone who had lived within it for a notably long time.

A thick, shaggy beard, and long, unkempt dark locks covered most of the man's head and face, and the brown tunic and trousers that he wore blended in smoothly with the hues of the trees. The man's shoulders were of substantial width, and his thick legs and stout torso indicated great physical strength.

His piercing blue eyes regarded them intently, alert and studious at once. A long bow was gripped in his left hand, and the hilt of a sword, sheathed and suspended from a baldric, poked up from his left side.

"I am Gunther," the man said in the way of introduction. "I am here with my Jaghuns … those creatures that you call … the beasts. You saw them destroy the Trogen warriors and their Harraks, who were out to slay you. Perhaps you will come to understand that my Jaghuns are your friends as well."

The man suddenly cupped his hands to his mouth and made a bird-like call, the sounds uncannily familiar to Lee as a realization dawned on him. He remembered hearing the distinctive calls more than once during

their trek through the forest, discounting the sounds at the time as coming from simple denizens of the forest.

He now understood that the man before him had been following them for quite some time. The notion was sobering, as Lee grasped that their own existence had depended on the woodsman's judgement of them.

Lee had witnessed the skill that the man had with the longbow. The woodsman could have picked off Lee and his companions one by one, with absolutely no difficulty, from the shadows of the forest.

Four large forms suddenly came into view, as if manifesting out of shadow and brush. They trotted forward, continuing up to the man's side. Lee and his companions were mesmerized at the sight of the beasts padding out of the foliage and into the open. The ease of Gunther's posture with the beasts only slightly took the edge off of Lee's renewed stress at watching the creatures emerge, their broad muzzles glistening with dark, crimson stains.

Gunther seemed to sense their fascination with the Jaghuns, as well as their great apprehension. "The Jaghuns are my companions and friends. I have raised each of them from when they were cubs. They will do no harm to you, as long as I will it."

The implied warning was not lost on Lee.

As he looked upon the huge woodsman, a look of concern then started to creep across Gunther's face. His eyebrows narrowing together, the woodsman's eyes cast about the woods, looking past Lee and his companions.

"Mianta!" Gunther called out in a loud voice. His voice held a very noticeable anxiety, as he repeated the name once again. "Mianta!"

A worrisome look encompassed the woodsman's face, as he waited for some kind of response. Lee then remembered the fallen Jaghun that he had witnessed, the one that had suffered the back wound, and had subsequently been impaled with the arrow.

The Jaghuns around the woodsman seemed to become distraught themselves at the woodsman's escalating agitation, whining and slumping their heads, as their tails were tucked in. It was then that Lee fully discerned the nature of the situation, and he held his tongue.

He did not want to be the one to bear the dire news, but his expression must have betrayed his misgivings. Gunther's eyes bored into Lee, and he was unable to meet the woodsman's troubled look, as his own gaze fell to the ground.

"Where is Mianta? My other Jaghun?" Gunther asked, almost pleadingly, taking a couple of slow steps forward. He then queried Lee more pointedly, "Tell me now … what do you know?"

Heavy of heart, Lee was unwilling to deceive the man that had come to their aid. He turned and gave a small gesture off to the left, where the battle had transpired with the last two riders. The body of the Jaghun, arrow lodged in its head, lay still near to one of the slain winged steeds.

Gunther stepped forward, until he saw what Lee had indicated. His eyes widened and he broke into a full run, followed closely by the other Jaghuns. He slumped to his knees, reaching down and lifting the slain Jaghun about its forequarters. He cradled the lifeless body, as he held the creature's head close to his chest.

The other Jaghuns were subdued, their tails sagged down and their ears flattened as they lay upon their stomachs, close to their fallen comrade. They emitted a distinct whimpering sound, which to Lee seemed strangely like a human sob.

Weeping bitterly, Gunther uttered loud, mournful cries that filled the forest. Lee and the others drew close together, watching the man suffer through what looked to be tremendous agony. They made no move to go any nearer to the grieving man.

The sobs gradually lessened, until they finally became silent, but there was no change in the postures of the woodsman and his creatures. Gunther and the other Jaghuns remained in place for a very long time, during which dusk gripped the land.

Stoically, Gunther finally arose in the dimming light and started clearing out the debris around the body of the dead Jaghun. At one point, when the soil had been bared around the corpse, he glanced toward Lee and the others.

Listlessly, he simply said, "Help me."

Without exchanging another word, Lee and the others moved forward to help Gunther, as they worked together to drag the bodies of the winged steeds and fallen warriors to the sides. As large as the winged steeds were, they were not nearly as heavy as Lee had expected. Nonetheless, it took multiple individuals working together to move them.

Seeing their arsenal of sharp teeth and large claws from a close perspective, he knew that they would have been a formidable match for the Jaghuns had it not been for the element of surprise. The musky scent of coarse fur that filled Lee's nose was mingled with the sharper tang from their gory wounds.

Neither Lee nor his comrades could refrain from periodically glancing in the direction of the prone Jaghuns. He did not feel any more at ease around them, not even with the woodsman in their direct midst. The blood of their victims was still caked around their jaws, amplifying Lee's apprehension.

With several grunts and heaves, he labored to pull one of the felled enemy warriors away. Looking down into the canine visage, his mind assailed him with imaginary images of the eyes suddenly snapping open, and the lips curling into a feral snarl. Lee had to keep his eyes focused above him as he lugged the body the last few feet.

At last, a broad clearing was formed around the body of the fallen Jaghun. Lee and his companions backed away slowly, giving Gunther a wide berth now that their task was finished.

"No worm shall gorge upon the body of my friend," Gunther managed to stammer angrily, as he started laying dry branches and brush around the dead Jaghun. It was as if Gunther had forgotten about their very existence. "You have a good servant before you. Loyal and of honor, a triumph of Your creation. It is a loss and tragedy that such should ever fall in this world."

Gunther proceeded to ignite a fire, using some metal and flint that he retrieved from a leather pouch at his waist. Before long, the flames engulfed the body of the Jaghun as night settled in.

The air was filled with the pungency of burning flesh as the Jaghun's physical remains were consumed. The woodsman's dark outline stood motionless before the fire, as he silently gazed into its blazing depths.

After a little more time had passed, he turned and strode back towards Lee and the others, who had continued to remain respectfully quiet from where they observed the woodsman.

"It is my way," Gunther said, as if feeling the need to explain himself. "I will let no friend be put into the ground to be the food of worms. Those of the elder days of Midragard knew best."

His voice was choked with emotion, barely steady in its thickly bitter tone. He continued somberly, almost as if giving them orders, "We must go now, back to my dwelling. The leader of the Trogens will return in time with many more. You may trust me, or you may await the return of the Trogen leader. It is your choice ... but for my part, I am going."

Lee looked to the others, their faces largely obscured in the deep gloom. Inside all of their heads, derivatives of the same rationale were likely proceeding.

Gunther had come to their aid, as had his creatures. All four of them had seen that the beasts were clearly under his control, trained and disciplined. Lee knew that they did not have any ties or allies within the new world, but they had already experienced their share of dangerous enemies.

While still a risk, their agreement was unanimous.

One by one, the others nodded to Lee. He turned back to Gunther. "Let us gather our things, we will follow you."

"Be quick, then," Gunther replied tersely.

Gunther waited a few moments as the four gathered up their packs and new weapons, and returned to stand around him. The light of two bright, rising moons was already cutting through the branches of the trees, casting enough illumination to see the forms of the things around them.

"We are ready," Lee informed the woodsman softly, knowing that the man was bearing incredible pain inside. The others stood silently, clearly not wanting to utter a word and content to let Lee do their speaking for them.

The woodsman remained quiet for a few moments, a pensive look crossing his face as if belatedly remembering something of importance through the morass of powerful emotions that he was feeling. His large hands then untied the bindings on another small leather pouch tied to his belt.

He brought out three amulets suspended from leather necklaces. Wordlessly, he handed one each to Lee, Ryan, and Lynn.

They stared in silence down at the small, blue stones in their hands, set into a metal encasement that framed the shape of the gems. Lee studied his own amulet, fingering it gently. The shape was that of a vertical line, with two lines coming off of it to the right, like an "F" in form, were it not for the diagonal slant of the extensions.

Gunther then transferred an amulet hanging from his own neck over to Erin, which held a blue stone identical to the ones that the others had been given. She took it hesitantly from the woodsman.

Looking back to the others, he said a few words aloud, in a language that was completely unintelligible to Lee. As confused looks came over the others' faces, Gunther then took up the amulet that Lee was holding, and guided it up around his neck.

"I believe you can understand me now," Gunther said. As Lee slowly began to nod, looking in wonderment from the amulet to the woodsman, Gunther then added, "But your friends cannot. Ask them if they know what I have just said."

Lee turned to the others, and from the looks on their faces his question to them was little more than a formality. "Did you understand what he just said?"

The other three shook their heads, all looking at Lee with bewildered expressions.

"No, not a word," Lynn replied in a low voice.

"And I do not know what she just said," Gunther replied. "Have them put the amulets on now, and they will come to know the gift that they bring to their wearer."

"Put the amulets around your necks," Lee conveyed.

As the others slipped their amulets over their heads, Gunther asked, "Now do you understand my words, once again?"

The other three appeared startled, a couple of them flinching, abruptly hearing Gunther's words in their own language once more. They looked to each other in astonishment.

Gunther then read the question still unspoken, perched on the tip of Lee's tongue.

"When you speak, I can understand you, just as when I speak, you understand me," Gunther stated.

The others nodded slowly in response.

"Now you all know what these are used for," Gunther stated. "A very important gift, one that I suggest you take very good care of."

Lee could barely comprehend what was happening, though he could not deny the stark evidence of his ears. The amulet at the end of his neck, while indeed a beautiful stone, looked to be nothing more than that.

"You have quite a benefactor, who desired that I watch over you, and convey the amulets to you," Gunther said, though his words drove the mystery even deeper. "I will tell you more later, but it is best that we get moving."

Gunther turned without another word, and went over to where the makeshift funeral pyre had blazed so recently. He kicked dirt over the ashes and embers, stomping about the area. Once finished, he strode past the four exiles, the remaining Jaghuns loping off into the forest just ahead of him.

Lee and the others stood dumbfounded for a moment, and then started off after the woodsman. His large form was easy enough to make out in the moonlight.

"Keep pace with me, and do not fear. The Jaghuns will scout for us," he muttered back to them, after he had taken a few more strides.

His long stride and brisk pace had the others quickly scrambling to keep up. In the sparse bits of moonlight that reached the ground through the tree cover, they all had to carefully watch their steps.

Lee found that it was no easy task trying to keep their footing, while maintaining the pace silently demanded by the stoic woodsman. More than once, they stumbled on uneven ground, branches, and other small obstacles such as thick tree roots.

Lynn tripped over one such surface root extending off of a very old tree. She fell heavily to the ground before Lee could react, and needed a moment's help to gather her items and get back to her feet.

Despite the difficulty hiking in the night, Lee felt much safer to be in the big woodsman's presence. He was highly relieved that he no longer had to worry about the four-legged ferocities accompanying Gunther. For the first time, he felt relief that the creatures were nearby, evidently warding them as they trekked through the dark woodlands.

DRAGOL

Dragol and the surviving Trogen warriors, with burdened, simmering hearts, returned back to the sprawling encampment where the reconnaissance and sky steed contingents delegated to assist the second Avanoran force were based. There was little permanence to the design of the camp of scouts, as it had to maintain fluidity with the continuing movements of the invasion force that was now marching deeper into Saxany.

A small contingent of light cavalry from Andamoor served as guards for the largely Trogen camp, as well as providing additional scouting upon the ground.

The presence of the Andamoorans was not frivolous. They were extremely mobile, proficient horsemen who could range far from the camp to keep up a constant, flowing perimeter at the ground level. Any approaching enemy forces could be harassed and delayed by ground and air alike, while the evacuation of the camp took place.

As much as humans annoyed him, Dragol had to grudgingly admit that the Andamoorans' endurance, and the swiftness of their steeds, complimented the nature of the camp very well. Most importantly, they enabled the Trogens to remain fully focused upon the tasks that they had been charged with by Avanor. Under the demands shouldered by Dragol and the other chieftains, none of their kind could have been spared to the duties performed by the Andamoorans without it being a detriment to their own efforts.

There were nearly seventy-five Harraks being quartered within the camp, serving almost one hundred veteran Trogen riders. It was a strong sky force in its own right, capable of engagements with modest contingents of Saxans on the ground or in the air. Yet instead of actively searching out the enemy to engage them, the Trogen force was now largely relegated to gathering and providing vital information regarding the lands that the invasion force was moving through.

There was a constant stream of activity within the encampment, as squads and patrols landed and took off, attending to their range of assigned scouting tasks.

As there had not been enough Trogens available to spare even a few for the more basic needs of the camp itself, the Andamoorans had been reluctantly delegated to tending to the Trogen steeds, as well as their own.

As was now routine, a few Andamooran attendants hustled over when Dragol and the others landed. They nervously waited for the Trogens to dismount, so that they could guide their large sky steeds off for food, water, and rest.

Snarling with anger, Dragol forcibly shoved back one of the Andamoorans who lingered too close to him as he got off of his Harrak. The man's dark eyes glittered in fear and resentment, while he trembled in the presence of the outwardly maddened Trogen.

"Away from me, weakling!" thundered Dragol in a growling voice.

The man most likely did not understand a single word that Dragol had said. Only a few Andamoorans understood a smattering of Trogen words, and even fewer Trogens possessed a handful of words from the tongue used by the Andamoorans, spoken by those who followed the ways of the Prophet in the Sun Lands. Nevertheless, Dragol communicated his intention clearly enough, as the Andamooran scrambled to get away from him.

Dragol spat at the ground in disgust with the behavior, for no Trogen thus treated would have failed to defend their personal honor. He could not fathom the weakness that the humans continued to show, wondering what business the Unifier had in putting the Andamoorans to serve alongside the Trogens.

The only reason that he had ever been able to glean was that the Andamoorans and the Trogens did not adhere to the faith of the Western Church. Dragol had already noticed that this fact alone incited almost instant tension whenever Andamoorans were brought together with the other human factions involved in the invasion, such as those from Ehrengard and Avanor.

Perhaps the Unifier wished to isolate the Andamoorans a little, reasoning that the temptation towards conflict would be much reduced if they were placed alongside a non-human race. The Andamoorans could perhaps find it slightly more palatable that the Trogens were non-believers in their faith, given the Trogens' fundamentally different nature. There had been no religious wars between Trogens and Andamoorans, but there certainly had been many among the humans of different faiths.

Whatever the true reasons were, Dragol still despised the arrangement.

Compounding his detestation, he had heard it said that that the Andamoorans had great warriors among them. Word had also spread among the Trogens that the particular Andamoorans within the scouting camp avoided armor as an outwardly visible sign of their courage.

Dragol was highly inclined to challenge any that would make such an assertion, as his experience so far had shown him little to substantiate either of the claims. The unarmored Andamoorans always sniveled and cowered in the face of a Trogen provocation or insult, even though Dragol could easily sense their strong dislike of the Trogens. Confronted, the supposedly courageous men of Andamoor wilted fast.

If the oppressive, westerly Elves dwelling near his homeland had such constitutions, the plight of Dragol's kind would have been lifted a long time ago. The thought of those sufferances, in his present, blackened mood, brought a deep rumble to his throat.

Other Andamoorans, and even a few Trogens, gave Dragol a wide berth as he stormed off into the camp, striding quickly towards his tent. There was no mistaking the aura of absolute wrath that pulsed around the huge Trogen, and nobody within the vicinity wished to voluntarily incur it.

Dragol slowly removed his iron helm, the lining inside the segmented construction thoroughly soaked. His long locks of hair were matted with sweat, and he welcomed the soothing, cool air that enveloped him, caressing his heated crown with the removal of the helm.

The pleasant physical feeling did little to calm his frayed emotions, but at the least it would not add to his agitated state. He could have grimly accepted the day's losses if his warriors had been overcome in hand to hand fighting, pitted in open battle against skilled warriors.

The thought of his warriors being slaughtered by primal animals, and a hidden archer that they had not been able to fight back against, was tormenting his every moment. His face a mask of barely suppressed rage, he stalked morosely past several tents, before drawing the attention of one particular Trogen.

"Dragol! You have returned at last!" called a voice to his right.

Dragol was about to lash out at the interruption of the other, when the more sensible part of him recognized the voice. He held back the heated expletive that he was about to loose, as he turned his head towards Goras and came to an abrupt stop. The Trogen warrior, like him, had just returned from a sky patrol.

Dragol eyed his comrade as he approached, letting his ire recede.

Goras was highly imposing in mass, even when considered among their commonly sizeable race. A little shorter than Dragol, the other Trogen was visibly broader of shoulder, and much thicker of chest. The Trogen's abundant hair sprouting from atop his high forehead, and along the forward half of his head, was pulled back and tied into a ponytail that kept his face completely cleared. The rest of his hair fell freely down the Trogen's shoulders and back.

His unobstructed face gave even more prominence to a large, straight scar, which ran almost vertically down the right side of the warrior's face, from just below the Trogen's eye to the base of his muzzle. It was a mark of profound honor, incurred in single combat with an Elven warrior that Goras had finally hewn down with his longblade.

Goras was clad in a newer style of cuirass being used by some of the higher-ranking Trogen warriors. The leather armor was fashioned in a style of interlaced, rectangular pieces. The pieces were arrayed in patterned rows, arranged opposite of the way that the elements in a cuirass of scale armor lay. It was a more eastern style, echoing the methods used in lands such as Theonia.

Dragol found the new style intriguing. Goras had taken a quick liking to it, saying that it was much more well-suited to movement than were the thick hide jerkins that were natively constructed and worn in the Trogen homelands. Dragol contemplated trying out such a cuirass in the near future.

Goras finally drew to a halt about two paces from Dragol.

"Goras," Dragol finally stated, in a low and restrained voice. The anger continued to seethe within him, and it took an effort not to rage further at the fates that had allowed such a dismal day to pass. "It is by the fortune of Elysium I even returned ... My heart burns for vengeance ... Trogen blood was spilled in a terrible way."

The other's face grew taut, and his eyes narrowed, as a perplexed look rose upon his face. Even with their elongated faces, forming something closely akin to a canine's muzzle, the Trogens were able to display expressions that held some similarities with those of humans.

"What has happened?" Goras inquired. His initial enthusiasm was swiftly replaced by pensiveness.

Dragol continued to temper the fires threatening to erupt inside of him, as he related the events of the recent past with his longtime comrade and fellow member of the Thunder Wolf Clan. He started the telling with the successful destruction of the Saxan border patrol, continuing on up to the forest ambush from the unusual, dog-like beasts. He spoke at length regarding the presence of the exceptionally skilled archer, who had carried a bow whose range far exceeded those normally seen among the Saxans. Most importantly, Dragol iterated his firm desire to return to the area in force, to seek revenge.

Goras' own anger was stoked as Dragol described everything, the visible signs revealing it to have swelled steadily during the tale. His eyes narrowed further as Dragol continued, and his snout began to wrinkle. Before long, he was baring his sharp teeth, as his lips turned back into a snarl. His long canines glinted in the light of the night moons.

Goras nodded slowly as Dragol spoke of his desire for vengeance. When Dragol fell silent, he uttered through clenched teeth, "We will take to the ground, and avenge this treachery. We will find this archer who cowers among the trees. We will hunt these other beasts down, until their skulls decorate our tents!"

Dragol held up a massive hand. "I would like that ... more than anyone. I lost Haza, who has flown with me for many years. His blade was mighty, and his heart very loyal. His spirit finds Elysium now. He did not deserve the kind of death he received ... torn apart by beasts, and given no chance to fight them!"

He had to pause for a moment, a low growl emitting from the back of his throat as his fury almost tore through again. Had Haza been on a great hunt, and found himself locked in mortal combat with a formidable quarry, the manner of his death would have been more acceptable. Standing on his two feet, blade in hand, and willfully engaging a mighty predator was one matter. To die from an ambush was another, as it had robbed Haza of a moment to consciously muster courage, to willingly face an end worthy of a Trogen warrior. The beast had been upon Haza before he could even begin to react.

Slowly and with effort, Dragol regained his composure.

"But we cannot go in where we do not know the enemy's strength, or we shall repeat the folly of today," Dragol conceded, as reason came to the fore. "We will need to speak to those from Ehrengard, and find someone who lives near their eastern border with Saxany.

"We must know about those strange beasts, and see if any know of this archer. He was no common man. I am sure of that. Then, we may go and see that our blades are bathed in the blood of these beasts ... and that this archer can no longer hide from us."

"Then let us send some patrols to seek these answers," Goras suggested. "Since we have arrived in these lands, I have seen no creatures such as you describe."

"A question that demands an answer," Dragol agreed.

"I know you are greatly tired, Dragol, and in need of food and rest. We can send patrols out, after you have eaten," Goras stated.

"Still the accursed dried fish, and hard bread?" Dragol rumbled, loathing the answer that he knew would be forthcoming.

"Yes, and not even in good amounts. It could not feed the scrawniest of humans well, even these puny Andamoorans. ... It barely gives them the strength to clasp the ground each day in their futile prayers. But I will make sure you receive more rations, and some cheese as well," Goras said with a reluctant tone to his voice.

"And the cheese will be like eating rocks too … as this foul, rotten bread is. I think we should soon send hunting parties out, as well as patrols and scouts. Maybe even make these weak Andamoorans earn the right to be in a camp with Trogen warriors," Dragol muttered, flustered at the notion of the meager palette. His eyes flashed in a feral manner as he looked back up to Goras, his sharp teeth unveiled within his sneer. "Perhaps we should really make use of these Andamoorans."

"What I would not give for some juicy meat, and a thick draught of ale" Goras said, a half-smile forming in response to the dark implication of the other's statement. He glared as a couple of the robed, turbaned Andamoorans walked by a short distance away from them. "I fear both those Andamoorans would not have enough meat on their bones to satisfy one of us."

Their banter was the substance of a dark jest. Both Goras and Dragol knew fully well that they would never have eaten the meat of human or humanoid, unless in an act of absolute survival. They also knew that the Andamoorans were not so sure of that.

"You are right," Dragol replied, chuckling darkly. The two Andamoorans took notice that the two huge Trogens were staring intently at them. They picked up their pace and hurried onward, their heads lowered.

"You should eat now. Then we will send patrols forth," Goras insisted.

"And what would Tragan think of that?" Dragol said, posing the most pertinent question.

Goras and Dragol had considerable authority as patrol leaders, but Tragan of the Blood Boars was the commander of the entire Trogen force within the scouting camp.

Even among the most abrasive of the Trogens, his strident attitude was legendary. Yet it was not without purpose. Tragan was not one to frivolously make unnecessary sacrifices, or risk losing resources. He ran an efficient camp, marked by an extreme of discipline, challenging even to the toughest of the Trogens in the force.

In truth, it had been Tragan's absolute directives, derived from Avanor's wishes, that had prevented many Andamoorans from receiving severe beatings from highly vexed Trogen warriors.

Goras grimaced, knowing at once the danger that Dragol was

indicating. "Then curse him, if he would be such a lackey of the Unifier. Sometimes I believe he would run this camp like a prison, to please his new human masters. But if he would not avenge Trogen deaths? He protects the human weaklings infesting this camp. What does that say to you, Dragol?"

Dragol abruptly shot up an arm, palm spread open, to cut Goras off before he said anything further. "Do not speak such words aloud in this camp. Tragan will allow no challenge. You know that. And you know that we are here, fighting and eating our rock-bread, so that we can free our entire race from the vile Elves. Many times I have to remind myself of that, it is true … but we must hold to that."

A hot look flared up in Goras' eyes, as Dragol mentioned the core concerns of the Trogens fighting for the Unifier. They did not fight out of any great feeling of loyalty to the Unifier, or even because they really believed in the strange vision of the Unifier's emerging world.

The allegiance had happened because the Unifier had resolved to help the Trogens end their long-time oppression at the hands of the Elves, in return for their ardent service as warriors. The Unifier had promised to eventually bring about an end to the long plight of the Trogens, which would liberate the great numbers of Trogens living in abominable slavery within Elven territory.

Dragol, Goras, and all Trogens knew readily that no other race or powerful individual in the world had ever openly offered to aid the Trogens against their ages-old nemesis. The decision by the Trogens' Clan councils to send substantial forces forth, and ally with the Unifier in the ongoing wars, had been swift and acceptable by all.

In their own view, the Trogens were fighting as much for themselves in these ongoing wars as they were fighting for the Unifier. The best chance of realizing their own aims lay with the success of the Unifier, and the Trogens were willing to do everything that they could to bring an end to the unrelenting nightmare suffered by so many of their kind.

Goras' great jaws tightened, and Dragol knew that his comrade had realized his momentary foolishness. His eyes darted about, and he looked relieved to find that no one was close enough to have heard his reckless venting. "I cannot argue with you, Dragol."

"We must still seek to take action, but we must be careful," Dragol said more gently. "Remember, a great army will be sweeping through those woods soon enough. If there is a woodsman, we will find his homestead.

We will also have time to hunt in these woods for the beasts. My blade and arrows will have a great thirst when we find them ... I will make sure that thirst is slaked."

"As I will with mine," Goras concurred grimly.

Dragol looked off in the direction of some tents to the right, where there was a collection of packs and barrels stacked.

He gestured off towards the tents. "Goras, join me now, if you do not have to soon leave on patrol. For now, I think you are right. It is best to fill my belly, and get a few moments' rest."

"And to fill mine as well, for I have not eaten yet. Know that we will eat better tonight, or I will spill some blood. I shall get us some cheese, and see about some true meat," Goras said with conviction.

The two large Trogens headed off for the tents. It was no use courting disappointment, and Dragol resolved himself to the simple fare that they would be getting.

The ensuing meal passed with little conversation, the food devoured quickly, though its substance hardly caused the Trogens to salivate. While there was no good meat to be had, Goras did succeed in obtaining a small quantity of cheese, and some bitter ale to help wash the food down, both of which Dragol was eminently grateful for.

They had barely finished eating when a Trogen messenger came up to them, and delivered some new orders directly from Tragan. The messenger, a young Trogen warrior of the Sea Wolf clan, gave a slight bow and took his leave.

Dragol and Goras would have to put aside their individual interests for a time. Tragan was ordering a heavier presence to accompany the initial surge of the ground force as it drove eastward. The two patrol leaders were to be summoned to Tragan's tent soon, to learn the rest of the details.

As the two pondered the messenger's tidings, a commotion rang out suddenly within the camp. Trogen and Andamooran alike were hustling about, and word was quickly spread around that the expected force of warriors for the northeastern thrust had arrived near the camp.

It was a force from Avanor itself, very well-equipped, and highly disciplined.

Dragol was highly curious about the renowned human fighters, especially with his great disappointments in the other humans that he had interacted with. He had learned many things about the Avanorans in recent weeks. He hoped that the tales were true and that he would find them to be worthy allies. Of all the human factions, the Avanorans appealed to him the most.

Their ilk, as part of sovereign realms, as mercenaries, and as ambitious adventurers, had gained a legendary reputation in both the development and overthrow of many realms within Ave. It was almost fitting that the origin of all Avanorans was the same place where the Unifier had risen to power, given the great renown of the warriors of Avanor.

In terms of landmass, Avanor was not an exceptionally large territory, yet it had sent forth a torrent of power that had shaken Ave. Their storied history could not be denied. As a whole, Avanorans possessed an undeniable genius for war.

The Trogens knew that if the force from Avanor succeeded in its aims to curl around to the back of the main army of Saxany, which was deploying out on the eastern plains, the war could quickly be brought to an end. The invasion was also the means by which the location of the archer, and the savage beasts, could be explored. There would be plenty of opportunities during the chaos and upheaval within an invasion campaign.

Goras and Dragol looked to each other, and though Goras' expression remained austere, Dragol knew that they were both gladdened that the war was finally going to escalate sharply.

Their goals, from those of their clans to personal ones, were being brought steadily closer to achievement.

JANUS

Night portended to be a much more peaceful event when experienced within the considerably safer confines of an occupied tribal longhouse. Even so, the environs still demanded a number of adjustments by Janus in order for him to attain a semblance of comfort. It was not an entirely easy task, lying atop cornhusk mats and animal skins spread upon the hard, rough surface of the wooden sleeping platform underneath him.

The air itself was thick to breathe, hindered as it was by very low circulation and ventilation within the domestic chamber. The smoke hole, set directly above the hearth used by both sides of the chamber, was far from effective in filtering out the dense airs of the compartment.

Janus could only imagine how much more ponderous breathing was in the depths of a cold winter, when larger fires had to be lit within the chamber for warmth. He had no doubts that the chamber confines that he was now quartered within could become very congested, if not stifling, rather quickly.

At the moment, no fires were lit within the longhouse compartment. A full stack of firewood lay idle in the storage space set to one side of the sleeping platform. Another such pile rose from the ground in the corresponding space across the chamber, by the other sleeping platform. It was much too warm inside the compartment to even consider putting the wood to use.

Adding to the general discomfort, Janus was beginning to feel the effects from the sheer accumulation of bug bites, though he had not yet given in to applying the grease to his skin that the tribal people used so generously upon their own bodies. At the moment, he was still willing to tough out the irritations brought about by the numerous insects that shared the interior of the longhouse.

Weariness having overridden discomfort, Janus had already slept for several hours, and he did not currently feel like going back to sleep. He lay still within the shadowy darkness, staring upwards at the narrow elm-bark boards comprising the underside of the upper platform. Spanning the full length of the compartment, the higher level was used as a type of garret for storing a number of various items; including the additional pelts which Janus now considered procuring to pad his sleeping space even further.

After a few more moments of consideration and calculation, he thought better of the idea, surmising that the additional effort would not result in very much of an alteration to his current state. Fumbling about in the darkness, he would also risk injury, as well as likely aggravating his slumbering and deeply exhausted companions.

He let out a quiet sigh, while taking in the strong scents of smoke and other odors prominent within the longhouse interior. His thoughts slowly drifted towards the two tribal families that were living in one of the chambers immediately adjacent to the compartment that he and his companions were in.

He had learned that one of the families was a newly wed couple, the woman from the Place of Far Seeing and the man from another Onan village. They had just recently arrived to live in the longhouse of the bride's mother.

Though the new groom was amiable enough, Janus could sense from his brief interactions with him that the man was feeling more than a little awkward. It was very understandable, as the young man was living away from his own family and village for the first time in his entire life.

The other family sharing the compartment was also a fairly young couple. They had one small female child, and appeared to be much more settled, having already lived in the longhouse for a considerable amount of time.

The two families, as were all the families living within the longhouse, were of Ayenwatha's own clan. His was the clan symbolized by the strange, predatory forest cat, whose fascinating likeness was proudly displayed over the longhouse's entrances.

Janus had been as intrigued as he was daunted by the image that he had seen rendered upon the elm-bark panel. He had since learned that the six-legged, cat-like beast was called a Firaken. It was one of the most feared and respected creatures dwelling within the sprawling forests that blanketed the lands of the Five Realms.

As intrigued as he was by the utterly strange beast, the issue was similar to that of the Licanthers witnessed by his companions, the sabre-toothed beasts seen with the army beyond the forest's edge. Janus was not altogether sure that he ever wanted to see a living and breathing Firaken, and certainly not as of just yet.

As far as he was concerned, he had been more than satisfied to experience an entirely mundane evening, wholly uneventful and spent in shelter and relative protection. The calm, uninterrupted night had finally bequeathed to him some solitary time for reflection.

Unfortunately, the tranquility had also proved quickly to be a double-edged sword. In a brief span of time, Janus had found himself nearly overwhelmed with resurgent feelings of loneliness. They had been there all the time. It was just that ever since his arrival within the new world, Janus had been kept far too busy and wary to dwell upon his own inner thoughts for very long. In light of the wrenching sorrows that had continually been tearing at him from within, the pressures and stresses of the unexpected foray into the new world had actually turned out to be a bit of a blessing.

Wounds were opened anew in the silence as Janus slowly succumbed to the onerous weight of his deeply abiding sorrows and fears. His mind drifted to darker places as he thought of the cold and murky road that he had taken ever since his father had so suddenly passed away, into the depths of the unknown. Janus had walked along that icy road shrouded with a stark sense of futility and helplessness, both of which had swiftly taken root and ripened within him.

The shock and anguish had brought the full weight of many other previous sorrows around to bear, forming them all into a bludgeoning amalgam of uncertainty and heartache. Having coalesced so many other older sorrows and fears into one thunderous blow, the nightmare had changed everything about Janus' world. It had tipped him over the edge, shaken his ability to cope, and had shaped and tinted every last perspective of his ever since.

Not even a change of entire worlds could alter it. No matter what emergency might distract him, the wellsprings of sorrow would simply lay in wait to surface again at the nearest opportunity.

He knew all of that for certain, as he felt the weight of it all pressing upon him again, encompassing him with its gray and dampening malaise.

The uglier truth was that this new world had merely served to increase the strains and worries piling up further upon his sorely burdened spirit.

A part of Janus was frightened by the increasing dilemmas that he and his companions were being forced to face. Though he fully recognized the inherently good nature of the people of the Five Realms, he knew that he was still within an unfamiliar world fraught with unknown and terrible dangers.

His mind also wandered back to the deeply troubling thoughts of how, or even if, he would ever get back to the world from which he had come. His mother and sister were now beyond the reach of time and space, effectively as separated from Janus as he was from his deceased father. That thought was enough to shake him to the very core, and he knew that he had to do everything that he could to stop his mind from venturing down that hazardous path.

There was no longer any question of the reality of his new existence. As much as he wished that it were otherwise, it was not a matter of simply needing to wake up from the depths of a very bad, lucid dream.

He would have to come to terms with everything, but a certain irony was also haunting him now.

Janus had always been deeply bothered with the fundamental nature of the world that he had come from. In truth, he often loathed it passionately, with all of its attendant sorrows and tragedies that seemed to rain down so indiscriminately upon its hapless occupants. He had often wished with all his heart that he could somehow find his way to a fresh chance in a brand new world. Now, when he actually had such a chance right before him, the idea was not nearly as attractive as it had been before.

Then again, the fundamental nature of the world that he now found himself in was not really any different from that of his previous one. It was one of the main areas in which this world was much the same as his former one.

Death still reigned with ultimate dominion over all forms of life, the gaping, abyssal maw where all roads of life converged. Sorrow, fear, and grave danger still plagued human life with a relentless, and pitiless, onslaught. The walk to the village with Ayenwatha had made that abundantly clear, as the current plight of the tribal people had been revealed during the conversations that had taken place along the route.

Janus breathed deeply, suddenly catching himself with every last vestige of willpower as he felt his spirit sinking even lower. His spirit already dense and heavy, he knew that he could not weigh himself down much further. The sheer force of negative thoughts was threatening once again to get the best of him, taking him to the threshold of hopelessness.

Quietly, Janus willed himself to action, rousing himself and crawling carefully over the sleeping form of Antonio. He delicately made his way over to the edge of the platform, swung down over the side, and set his feet down onto the hard dirt floor.

Janus paused a few moments in the darkness to stretch his limbs, hearing a couple of faint cracks as his joints and vertebrae responded to the pressure. He listened to the rhythmic breathing of his companions, both those just behind him as well as those on the sleeping platform directly across the cold hearth, on the other side of the chamber.

Taking ginger steps so as not to disturb anyone, he moved slowly across the dirt floor. One by one, he passed through the openings in the walls separating the chambers in the extended sequence of living compartments.

He felt other eyes fall upon him in the darkness, coming from either side, and he heard the sounds of bodies shifting on the bark-panel sleeping platforms. Yet nobody spoke to him, or otherwise moved to halt his progress, as he kept his attention fixed squarely ahead. He concentrated on keeping his step light, though his short, careful strides resulted in many shuffles on the earthen surface underfoot.

Though the litany of similarly arrayed chambers seemed to be endless, he finally crossed through the storage vestibule that marked the culmination of the longhouse structure. Janus pushed aside the hide covering draped over the entryway, and emerged into the open night air.

The air that washed over Janus was refreshingly cool and crisp. It was an instant salve to his body, bringing a welcome relief from the cramped conditions, low circulation, and pungent environment of the chambers; not to mention the collective body heat of the longhouse's numerous occupants.

The night seemed to be lingering idly at the boundary to dawn, passively awaiting the first rays of the new sun to finally drive it away. There was a very faint lightening to the blue-black canopy on the far edge of the horizon, visible from the favorable vantage afforded by the hill-top village.

Janus walked a short distance away from the end of the longhouse, and sat down cross-legged upon the flat ground. He looked out over the elongated, dark forms of the other longhouses occupying the village interior.

He settled himself in and stared away towards the horizons, looking at nothing in particular, content to await the rise of the sun. At the very least, the ascending sun carried with it an uplifting sense of renewal as it ushered in a new day.

"You do not look very happy," a young voice announced softly to Janus.

The calmly voiced words might as well have been shouted out. Janus head jolted upright in complete surprise at the unexpected intrusion of his solitude, his heart immediately leaping up to his throat.

Rapidly turning his head towards the abrupt sound, he beheld a young boy of perhaps twelve years old, crouched down about five feet away. Arms wrapped about his knees, with his smooth hands clasped lightly in between, the youth looked upon Janus with a keen interest.

The child was clad in the typical fashions of the tribe's more matured youth, not far removed from the attire of an adult, wearing leggings, a hide-kilt, and moccasins. The bare skin of his arms and lean upper body was as of yet unblemished by the tattoos so abundant on the adult males of the tribe.

The youth's long black hair flowed freely over his shoulders, and the surface of his large, dark eyes appeared to gleam within the dim ambience of the pre-dawn.

He patiently awaited a response to his inquiry from Janus.

"No, I guess that I am not very happy," Janus replied at last to the youth with a rueful grin, relaxing slightly from his initial shock. His tone lightened as his nerves gradually settled back down. "What brings you out here so early?"

The youth just smiled and shrugged, offering no verbal answer.

"Ah, a mystery," Janus remarked with a slight smile.

"What is wrong?" the youth innocently inquired. He then repeated his initial observation, "You do not look very happy."

Janus gazed upon the child for a long pause.

"I suppose it is because I recently lost a very, very close friend … my father," Janus commented in a weary voice, his eyes lowering as he stared towards the shadow-draped ground.

He did not know how to begin to explain his current situation to the young boy. It seemed to be an insurmountable proposition when he could not really grasp it himself.

"And I also suppose there is more to it now," Janus continued. "I do not know your lands, and I do not know how to get back to my own lands. I am just very sad, and I have much to worry about. I guess that is why I don't look happy."

The child's beaming face dimmed. "I understand sadness. And it is not good to feel lost. It is not good to lose friends … or fathers. But I have something that might help you."

Before Janus could get another word in, the child sprung up, and abruptly bounded off into the depths of the darkness. Though the child was quickly out of sight, Janus could hear the boy giggling in mirth, and wondered what the spirited youth could possibly be up to. His curiosity piqued, Janus looked around after the boy, but it was several minutes before the youth finally returned into sight.

"Here he is," the young boy announced to Janus, striding up and gesturing to his right side.

Though Janus looked closely, he perceived nothing at the child's side. Only empty space occupied the area that the boy was so fervently indicating. Janus said nothing, not quite sure how to respond and having no inclination of what the boy expected of him.

"Can you not see him?" the young boy asked with enthusiasm, smiling luminously.

He looked down to his side again, and shook his head, as if in sheer disbelief towards Janus' lack of reaction and perception.

The boy said matter-of-factly, as he pointed again, "He is right there."

"See what?" Janus inquired at last of the insistent youth, becoming more than a little confused by the strange proceedings.

"A dog for you. Not like the village dogs. One with really long ears. One who will watch over you, and make sure that you have a companion to help you … even here, in these lands that are new to you," the youth exclaimed brightly.

The words froze Janus for a moment. They nearly brought tears to his eyes, dredging up a deeper sorrow, one of those older floodwaters that had been fully released by his father's passing.

On pure impulse, Janus felt that he wanted to scream out that his pain was nothing to make light of, or to play games with. Raw emotion had been poured over raw emotion often enough. Yet even in the strained moment, his heart and mind somehow won out over his immediate, passionate instincts.

He knew that the child had meant well enough, and did not know anything about all of his painful losses. Janus surmised that the imaginative child, in his own way, was just trying to make Janus feel better.

He then decided somewhat grudgingly to play along with the game, at least for the imaginative youth's sake.

"Is it your dog?" Janus asked a little more firmly, acting as if he saw the dog at the boy's side.

The child nodded, and then shook his head vigorously. To Janus, it was an odd response, but the child quickly explained, "Yes … but he is also yours. He is our dog. But I think that you need this friend with you now."

Janus' resistance could not hold everything back indefinitely, as the thoughts poured vividly into his head of older, lost friends. His eyes welled up at the thoughts of his precious hounds, and a few tears escaped and trickled slowly down his cheeks.

The child noticed the change in Janus, and his expression swiftly became saddened. "Do not cry. You did not lose your friends forever."

Something strange seized upon Janus for a brief moment at the child's words, giving him immediate pause. Janus wondered whether he had heard the child correctly, even if he knew in the fullness of his heart that his ears had not lied.

"This dog is one friend to you. There are others, one like him, another that is not," the child then added.

The unexpected words pierced Janus through.

He looked down again at the ground, as the deep-seeded pains within him roared up again furiously, nearly choking him in their vice-like grasp. How badly he wanted to believe the young child, or at least what his mind could imagine that the child was referring to. Yet he did not think that there was any way of proving any relation to his own world within the youth's mysterious, penetrating words.

It was just another trying episode, painfully reminding Janus of times that had left yet more scars on him that would never truly heal.

"Do not be sad," he then heard the young boy say. The clear presence of conviction within the boy's voice was not lost on Janus. "Sometimes, you just have to look with different eyes … eyes that see beyond the things of this world."

Janus fought back his tears, as he recognized a sudden and peculiar change in the boy's tone. Lying underneath the boy's words was the presence of a deeper, resonant wisdom that did not seem quite normal for a boy of twelve.

Raising his head slowly, he brought his eyes up to meet those of the strange youth.

There was no one there.

Swiftly looking about in all directions, all that Janus beheld were the silent pools of shadows, the slumbering longhouses, and the upright stakes of the outer palisade. There were no sounds within the stillness, other than those from the light, whispering breezes gracing the hilltop village.

Janus had heard no footsteps, and he could not believe how quickly the youth had disappeared from sight. He chided himself for being so slow and unaware, and began to wonder if the whole episode was just a mere creation of his imagination, a figment given life by his own powerful sorrows. If it was such, it was likely the first indication that he was truly starting to lose his own grip on sanity.

As before, he found himself entirely alone.

With a brief, exasperated sigh, and a couple of deep breaths, he slowly got back up to his feet. Even though the horizon had grown noticeably lighter, Janus meandered back towards the sheltered porch at the entryway into the longhouse of Ayenwatha's Firaken clan.

Janus no longer had any interest in watching the sun rise.

AETHELSTAN

A small number of higher, bell-shaped tents stood in the midst of a much greater number of elongated ridge-tents arrayed far outward from them. The various tents were now the quarters of a modest host of Saxan warriors, culled from Wessachia and some of the province's immediate border areas.

The dark of the advanced night shrouded the brighter color of the painted, canvas panels upon the larger tents. Most of the bigger tents were currently empty, as the senior thanes who occupied them were now gathered together within Aethelstan's tent, located near to the direct center of the woodland encampment.

The march to the glen had gone about as smoothly as could be reasonably hoped. The outer muster points had joined their numbers to Aethelstan's column towards the end of the trek, continuing a favorable trend as a nearly complete response to the given levy summons had been achieved.

Following the addition of the very last muster point, nearly three thousand men in total had journeyed together for the last stretch. It had taken the better part of another day's hard marching through the wolds to reach the area that the Saxan scouts had identified as a propitious encampment site.

Following the end of the long march, a fair number of scouts continued to work diligently and tirelessly to acquire every last bit of information that they could.

A few of the scouts had set out to try to contact those living in the villages and hamlets just inside Count Einhard's lands to the immediate west. Most fighting men had long since departed with the greater levies, but the observations of those left behind were just as valuable. A village woman or an elderly craftsman could, just as easily as a man in his prime, take note of any unusual happenings in the vicinity of their abodes.

Other scouts boldly scoured the lands right up to the very banks of the Grenzen River, searching for any sign of an approaching enemy.

A few more had carefully surveyed the lands near the edges of Wessachia, to select the best terrain possible for defense, and the most likely routes for enemy incursions.

Upon the column's arrival, the encampment had been efficiently deployed among the trees of the glen. It was a very scenic locale, ringed by hills that fractured the slanting rays of the setting sun. A creek, of moderate size with a gentle current, wended through the midst of the low ground, providing an ample water source for the camp's occupants.

A few trout had already been seen swimming within the clear waters. The discovery quickly prompted a couple of men to occupy themselves with setting baited hooks to lines of nettle-hemp, even in the last light of the day. Another few men attended to the placement of a wicker-trap, the nearly five foot long object well-suited to capturing an array of a Saxan river's common denizens.

As the enemy's presence was not yet imminent, the thanes wasted little time in getting some weapons training organized and underway with the farmers, artisans, and others who had responded to the summons of the General Fyrd. They were hardy, tough men as a whole, woven of an excellent fiber, but they were not given to regular practice in forming up in a shield wall or wielding a combat spear.

Many of the common men were very capable archers, having regularly hunted in the woods near their own villages and hamlets. Such archers would become very valuable in the coming fight.

Yet besides the bow and arrow, it was no mystery that most of the villagers still required much more formal practice in martial skills, where the axe was no longer a tool for menial daily tasks, but rather a weapon for war.

When night fell at last, most everyone was dismissed from their labors and training to seek some rest and sustenance, although the tasks of the higher-ranking thanes were not yet done.

A number of disturbing signs had been recently emerging, heavily burdening the minds of those currently gathered with Aethelstan. At the present moment, the thanes had been assembled in the tent for well over an hour, anxiously hoping for further reports to arrive while discussing the grave matters at hand.

"Your concerns are not without cause. It is certain that far too many scouts have not come back. But take another look. I believe that it is no mere coincidence that most of the scouts that have not returned were sent into this very region," Aethelstan commented.

Already in a terse mood, he looked down somberly towards the crude parchment map spread out before him. It was illuminated by the steady light of a beeswax candle that was set in a holder just next to it.

Rendered on a single sheet of average quality parchment, the small map outlined Wessachia and its border territories. Aethelstan ran his finger slowly over a specific area on the map, indicating the forested hills arrayed just in advance of the headwaters of the Grenzen River.

Though the parchment map was rather simple in its display, it was quickly proving to be a very valuable and welcome gift. It had come from an elderly monk, who resided in the esteemed monastery of Jafarne, located in the neighboring province of Wesvald. It had already become of great use to Aethelstan, both in his planning and in conferences with the other thanes.

He silently pondered the general area where the bulk of the missing scouts had recently disappeared, working to grasp some further insights beyond what his instincts had already told him.

One scout had managed to return from the disconcerting region. Aethelstan had met with the scout privately upon his return, just before the larger conference had taken place. The lone scout had traveled far enough to reach the outlying edges of the marches that bordered Wessachia to the southwest. The area was situated just a little farther away from the core area of Aethelstan's concern, where most of the scouts were vanishing.

The scout had taken a more circuitous route upon his return, avoiding the less traveled woods right along the Wessachian border. In Aethelstan's eyes, it was likely a decision that had inadvertently spared the fortunate scout's life.

The great thane was enormously thankful for the scout's successful return, for the scout's own sake as well as the precious information that had been gleaned. The scout had brought back some very disturbing tidings with him, mostly gathered from a visit to one of the easternmost march forts.

Word had come to the scout of entire horse-mounted patrols, of the kind sent out from the fort garrisons for routine forays, not returning. The number of horse-mounted couriers arriving at the march fort had also dropped sharply in the recent few weeks.

As patrols disappeared and arrivals declined, occupants of the fort had quickly noted that the riders continuing to arrive safely were those coming in from the direct north, south, or southeast.

A few unusually large clusters of sky warriors had been reported within the same period, witnessed in the skies high over the western marches. They had curiously kept their distance from the march forts. They had not visited, or even come anywhere near to the garrisons, as Saxan sky warriors traditionally would have whenever they were within the marches.

A couple men of the garrison had commented to the Wessachian scout that these distantly observed clusters had appeared to be flying in an unusual formation. Instead of flying abreast of each other, or in a discernibly spear-headed type of formation, the observed groups had been crossing the skies in a loose throng.

A few other garrison men had then remarked that the steeds especially appeared to have a different profile in comparison to the winged Saxan mounts that the garrison men had observed on many occasions before.

The men had attributed the anomalous perception to deceptive tricks of the sunlight, the great distance, or fanciful imaginations fueled by anxiety on their part. Apart from the brief mentions of the observation, little else had been said on the matter during the scout's visit.

Aethelstan was immensely glad that the scout had deemed the fleeting observations valuable enough to remember and pass on formally to the great thane. Aethelstan was not quite so sure that the garrison men were deceived by mere tricks of sunlight, or by active imaginations.

It took little to recognize that something was most certainly amiss in that region. Aethelstan could not overlook the possibility that the perceived anomalies could well indeed be dire warnings, of something much worse to follow.

After some further discussion between the scout and Aethelstan, the great thane had come to a firm determination. The areas where the garrison patrols and the scouts had seemingly vanished were both within in the general region around the headwaters of the Grenzen River.

It did not take much further consideration to recognize that the disappearances of the mounted patrols and the scouts were not likely a mere coincidence. It was all but certain that they had a common cause. The faces of the other thanes in the dim firelight within the tent's confines reflected the same worrisome concerns that Aethelstan now held tightly inside of him.

It had now been many hours since the farthest ranging scouts had been expected to return, not to mention a small number of scouts sent out to closer areas along the immediate western boundary of Wessachia. The latter were far past overdue for returning. Aethelstan held out few hopes that the Wessachian scouts would be making an appearance in the camp anytime soon.

The anxiety among even the greatest of the thanes was building towards a very uncomfortable level. Like Aethelstan, most had begun to fear the worst.

"The mounted patrols sent out by the garrison forts that did not return were traveling in the very same area that our missing scouts were probing," Aethelstan stated, sweeping his steady gaze across the faces of those gathered around. "It is obvious that a very serious threat has emerged, one that we need to identify as soon as we can. It may involve the very purpose that we have mustered for."

"And what of the Woodsman? Our missing scouts were not all that far from his hunting grounds and dwelling. Certainly not if they went to the territory immediately to the west. It is said that the Woodsman knows of every beast that crosses through his hunting range … and that no outlaw dares to seek refuge there. If anything threatened and harmed our men, then the Woodsman would know," Ceolric, one of the other thanes, suggested.

"Yes … yes indeed. The Woodsman … Gunther," Aethelstan responded slowly, looking up to Ceolric. "He would surely know of any disturbances. It is excellent advice that you give, Ceolric, and we should dispatch a heavily armed group of warriors to try and make some manner of contact with him. Gunther dwells to the south and west of where we now stand in this encampment. With all our scouts sent to the west not reporting back, I would not desire to send any man out alone now."

"But we have no idea what it is that we face in that area! Should we not be very careful in learning more? Send a larger force immediately to the west? Is that wise?" sharply questioned another one of the thanes, named Ethelred, a thin fellow of about thirty years of age with a haughty expression upon his face.

"You have heard our scout's report, as I have. Yes, the mounted patrols have been said to disappear here, but it would be foolhardy, even disastrous, to be willfully blind to what is happening there," Aethelstan said gravely, pointing again at the map in the area where the scouts and patrols had seemingly vanished.

"What do you think it is?" asked Ethelred, his tone less strident than before.

"I fear that the enemy means to come at us in strength right through this area, but we cannot pass firm judgement on what we do not know. There is something very important to learn here, but we must not be reckless either. … What is the mood of your men?"

As Aethelstan posed the query, his eyes swept again across the faces of the men gathered around him, the question being directed to all of them.

"There is much worry. Many have been drawn away from the fields. … For some there is nobody to shear their herds of sheep, for that season is nearly upon us. Even the newborn lambs are at greater risk, with fewer hale bodies to watch over them. It was fortunate that the plowing of fields was largely finished. The full muster has sorely depleted the villages and towns," Ceolric commented somberly, being the first to voice a reply to Aethelstan's query. "Many have never traveled so far from their village. It is like nothing that even we have known."

The sentiments expressed by Ceolric were soon echoed by the other thanes, all of them pointing out the unique nature of the immense mustering of the Kingdom of Saxany.

"All of you speak truly. What you observe and hear is no different in my own eyes and ears. This is like no time that my father, or father's father, ever knew," Aethelstan replied ruefully. It was the irrefutable truth, and it served no purpose to try and deny it. "We all know that the king would call a full muster for no small reason, and would not ask Wessachia to watch the passes towards the north and east without a grasp of the enemy's intentions."

Aethestan's gaze passed once again across the faces of the stalwart thanes. "Are all the levies in?"

"It seems so," Ethelred replied. "The last group from the villages around the burh at Devonton have arrived in full, five thanes, many ceorls, and a good number of very capable villagers in their force, many of whom possess good arms. These villagers are from thickly wooded areas, and there are also many among them who possess good skill with a bow."

"If the muster from Devonton is in, then we have our full strength here in this camp, as much as we will have available to us. We will need every last man," Aethelstan replied firmly. "And we will also need to learn whatever we can of the enemy's forces, and most importantly, their intended path."

Aethestan's gaze then grew iron-hard, and his tone reflected his conviction. "This means that we must try and make an incursion into the troubled region."

"Then we must decide who it is that will go," Ceolric stated matter-of-factly.

A number of thanes immediately volunteered for the hazardous and uncertain mission, creating some initial disorder within the large tent. The momentary disarray prompted Aethelstan to raise his arms up to quiet them down, to try to bring some coherence back to the discussion.

"We will need to go in some strength, greater than that of an average patrol, as that is our best chance at success. As it is my decision to try and enter this area, I shall personally lead the group," Aethelstan announced, bringing all lingering murmurs and conversations to a full halt. He paused for a moment before continuing. "I will bring several of my own men with me. I would ask no man to take a risk that I would not be willing to take myself."

He straightened up and looked around to the others with a grim countenance that girded the seriousness of his words.

"We must take close assessments of the land," he continued. "The word that has been gathered from spies and scouts tell us that our lands will be facing a great and terrible strength from the west. Our enemies will also know soon enough that we are here, through the eyes of their minions in the air. It is my belief that the men of the march garrisons espied the first of the expected enemy sky riders. I also fear that it is those sky riders that have much to do with the disappearances of so many Saxans in the region of concern. While I am gone, those here must find and prepare the best positions for our coming defense."

In the wake of the great thane's words, a murmur rose up again among the others, as all wanted to accompany Aethelstan on the imminent foray.

Aethelstan knew that the strong-headed thanes would not come to any compromise on the matter, even if they knew that all could not go. To break the impasse, there was little other choice remaining than for Aethelstan to delegate.

Brooking no arguments in the matter, Aethelstan called for total silence. He then proceeded to select about half of the leading thanes from among those surrounding him.

Aethelstan then instructed the others that he had not chosen for the mission to see to the location of the most defensible positions. He then entrusted the map back into the care of an older priest named Father Wilfrid. Clad in a full-length, flowing, dark tunic, the priest had been standing quietly just in back of the Saxan thane.

The old priest nodded serenely to the great thane, as his weathered hands grasped the parchment. He gave Aethelstan a few subtle words of encouragement, barely above a whisper. Aethelstan returned the priest's slight bow, and gave a warm smile in return, very glad for the man's presence. The sight of the old priest always bolstered his spirits, as it did even at that very troubling moment.

The old man had held up very well over the tiring journey from Bergton, having taken extended leave of the church there to accompany the great many men from his parish who had been levied for the looming war. The elderly priest had not complained even once during the arduous travel, spending most of his time among the villagers and common men.

His presence alone had boosted their morale considerably. While it was held among the Saxans that the afterworld was secret and hidden, as no mortal man or woman had ever returned from it, it was nonetheless a great boon to the men of Father Wilfrid's parish to have a beloved representative of that unseen kingdom with them. A priest of the All-Father, especially one that had taken care of their families throughout their life in times of sorrow and joy alike, reminded them of their strongest foundations.

The old priest had given all the young men of the parish the anointing rites of the Three Immersions. He had bonded a good number of them with their wives in the sacred rites of marriage. Furthermore, the priest had given many of their loved ones Transition Rites during their last moments, and had buried them when finally deceased. The kind of bonds that were forged between the men of the parish and the priest during such momentous times in their lives was far stronger than the finest iron.

Aethelstan had been unable to talk the old priest out of going with the Saxan force. He had tried to discourage the priest out of concern for the old man's health, but he was not entirely disappointed that his efforts had failed. The morale of the men, and of Aethelstan himself, was far better with the kindly old priest's imminent presence.

"It shall remain with me until your return. Do not be reckless, my dear friend. Passions triumphing over calm minds can bring you defeat when victory is present," Father Wilfrid then said gently, in the warm, soothing tone that Aethelstan was so accustomed to.

The words were not an admonishment, but simply cautionary and advisory in nature. The sincerity of the priest's concern was indisputable.

"And I shall keep a calm mind Father, here and in the battle to come," Aethelstan responded in a low voice.

Aethelstan placed a hand on the old man's shoulder, and patted him affectionately, in a gesture of reassurance.

Turning back to the men gathered around him, Aethelstan took his leave of them, so that they could all attend to their preparations. Stepping out from behind the low trestle table, he walked briskly through the gathered thanes and exited out the entrance flap of the large tent.

A few of his household troops were gathered just outside. Having been waiting around a nearby fire, they rose to full attention as he appeared before them.

Their looks were expectant in the glow of the firelight, as Aethelstan took a slow, calculated breath of the immaculate night air. The cleansing intake of breath felt good to his lungs as he glanced up at the twinkling night sky above. Yet as clear and beautiful as the night was, there was no time to savor the vast sight spread out to the horizons overhead.

Aethelstan brought his gaze back down with a little regret. He ordered his household warriors to summon ten more of his most senior retainers, even as the major thanes selected from amongst those who had assembled in Aethelstan's tent hurried to gather up their own elite warriors.

If the Unifier had some advance contingents and scouting groups probing the outer borders of Wessachia, ones strong enough to overwhelm small mounted patrols, Aethelstan intended to give them a greeting woven with strength and fury if they were to meet.

It was not very much longer before a solid force numbering just over a hundred well-armed and equipped Saxan warriors were gathered, mounted, and ready for the impending sojourn. Even Aethelstan's own stallion, having rested and eaten, seemed restless and eager to go forth into the night. Wind Runner gave a deep, vigorous snort as the thane climbed into the saddle of his mount and took up the reins.

At Aethelstan's signal they all set out under the silvery light of the two moons; to explore the hilly forest region to the west, locate the woodsman Gunther, and learn whatever they could of the great menace gathering to strike their lands.

LEE

Traveling by night, Lee and his companions were afforded only a scant few, very brief rests. Even those fleeting respites were allowed only in order to prevent the group's total collapse from exhaustion. Lee and the others covered a considerable distance of ground during the forced march, under the steady pressure and guidance of the woodsman Gunther.

The unobstructed two moons far above cast a moderate amount of light down among the surrounding trees. At the least, the illumination was enough to walk by without undue fear of stumbling into some unseen obstacle.

Though his legs felt as if they were fashioned of solid bricks, and his knees and lower back cried out continuously, Lee trudged onward with grim resolve. He glanced often towards Gunther, though he had to concentrate more and more in his increasing fatigue to avoid tripping on the uneven surface of the woodland floor.

The dour woodsman had been fairly silent and withdrawn all throughout the journey. A cloud of tension and dark thoughts had seemed to envelop the woodsman shortly after they had gotten underway.

There were no efforts on the part of Lee or any of the others to try and interject into the man's brooding aura. Lee was more than content to wait patiently until Gunther opted to let them into his private and mysterious world. The woodsman was not the sort of individual to be coerced, and Lee knew that any attempt to do so would be feeble and likely provoking.

For the most part, the four otherworlders had capably handled the exacting pace that they had all been subjected to. Even Erin had been without outward complaint. Gratefully, she seemed reticent about doing anything to offend Gunther. Though Lee felt strongly that she eventually needed some harsh admonishment, he did not want to witness what an irritated response by the stern, grieving woodsman might be like. The man looked to be capable of loosing a hurricane of wrath.

Mercifully, Gunther finally decided to call an extended halt for the rest of the night as they reached the base of a large hill.

The Jaghuns appeared out of the darkness again, soon after Gunther sounded a short series of deep, barking calls. The Jaghuns stayed only briefly, before Gunther dispersed them, sending the creatures trotting off into the shadows of the night.

Lee watched the beasts pad away with nary a sound, their forms swiftly enveloped in the ebon depths of the trees. He knew that they would remain in the vicinity, and was eminently thankful for the presence of such formidable guardians.

Gunther then turned his attentions to the four other humans, and curtly instructed them all to take advantage of the hiatus by taking a nap. The weather was holding clear, and there was no immediate necessity for finding or fashioning any form of shelter.

In moments, Lee and the others had each found a place upon the hard earth. All were soon slumbering under the watchful eyes of the woodsman, as well as those of his inhuman companions.

Dawn gradually spread its burgeoning glow and settled down over the forest, though not before Gunther had already roused his tired wards. In the cool dampness of the pre-dawn, the somber woodsman consumed some pieces of hard bread and dried meat with Lee, Lynn, and Ryan. A perplexed look crossed Gunther's face when the morning's rations were divvied up, as Erin rejected the meat and took only the bread.

Gunther tensed, as if about to make some sort of remark, but then just shook his head and ate his own meager fare in silence.

Lee quickly saw that Gunther's severe mood from the previous evening had changed very little. The woodsman only spoke to them when he needed to give information or issue a directive.

The group was soon on its way again, just as the first piercing rays of sunlight heralded the newborn day, driving the shadows back about the thick tree growth and lower brush. Gunther had informed them just prior to their outset that they were only about half a day's march out from his homestead.

They had not traveled all that far when the group came to a sudden halt, as the faint sounds of a horn reached their ears. Gunther froze in mid-step. When the horn blast was repeated again, Gunther made a whistling sound.

Seemingly out of nowhere, one of the Jaghuns reappeared amongst the party. It trotted immediately up to Gunther, its tail wagging vigorously.

Gunther calmly looked down at the creature, staring into its eyes.

"Bring Saxan," he said firmly.

The creature lurched into motion, and raced off through the woods. Its speeding form was gone from sight in seconds.

Gunther turned back to the others.

Lee did not know what to make of the strange interaction. In the interim, he had gripped the hilt of the sword that he was carrying very tightly. It was the right reflex for one holding to a natural caution, though he sensed no alarm in Gunther.

"The tone of that horn is nothing to fear. It is the warriors of Saxany that sound those horns. They are fighting the ones that assailed you yesterday," Gunther explained. "I know them well enough that my trust is well-placed in them. That unique horn note is their signal for me. Perhaps they have come to warn us of danger. My Jaghun will bring their messenger to us. We do not have to wait for them here. We can find a more suitable place to rest, and to await them."

Without further delay, Gunther started off across the forest floor once again. Lee and the others exchanged several glances, a number of questions coming to Lee's own mind. The curiosities remained unspoken as the four hurried to catch back up with Gunther, and resume the trek.

AYENWATHA

After consuming a light morning meal, consisting of a wooden bowl containing corn meal mush sweetened with a little maple tree sap, a handful of spring berries, and some ample swigs of cool water, Ayenwatha walked about the outer vicinity of his clan's longhouse.

It was well past the time to round up his new guests for a river excursion. The bright morning felt fresh and invigorating, despite the gathering storms of war on the horizon. Ayenwatha savored the moments at hand, looking forward to learning more about the foreigners and gliding down the sun-graced waterways of the Five Realms.

Three of the foreigners were lounging about inside the structure, talking together within their designated compartment. When Ayenwatha had entered the chamber to summon them, the young man named Antonio was laughing boisterously at some jest of the one called Kent. The latter,

Ayenwatha could already sense, was very given to humor, and the war sachem found himself taking an early liking to the spirited man.

The last member of the trio was Mershad, who was politely listening to them nearby. He was definitely a quiet one, and a little harder to read.

The blue-eyed male with the medium length brown hair, named Janus, was found strolling idly about the grounds of the village. Ayenwatha grinned as he saw Janus being trailed at a distance by a few curious children.

The dark-haired, solemn one named Logan was discovered sitting by himself on the shaded side of the longhouse, with his back resting against the elm bark paneling.

The dark-skinned man called Derek and the tall female named Erika were found together in another part of the village. They had been speaking with a couple of the village warriors, standing close to the modest garden plot for ceremonial tobacco lying adjacent to the great longhouse where the Sacred Fire of the Five Realms was kept and tended.

The warriors were showing the guests their curved war clubs, and as Erika watched over his shoulder, Derek fingered one of the weapons with an unmistakable look of admiration. The sight was no surprise to Ayenwatha, as Derek carried the distinctive air of a warrior.

Once Ayenwatha had all seven of the foreigners gathered together, he walked at their head towards the village entrance. Several of the village warriors were already assembled and waiting there.

They joined the stalwart war sachem and the foreigners, as he led them all forth from the village. The party passed through the village's narrow front entrance and headed down the slope of the great hill. A light spread of fog was slowly wafting through the trees below, and a vibrant chill yet lingered in the morning air.

Though the additional warriors took pains not to discomfort the foreigners, there was no denying the warriors' escort function. They were all there at Ayenwatha's behest. The seasoned war sachem was not about to discard reasonable precautions, even if he still sensed no threats present in the otherworlders.

Ayenwatha glanced towards the seven foreigners, and saw that most of them looked quite alert, well-rested for the day's coming foray.

Two of the three that had remained inside the longhouse were still showing signs of being a little drowsy. Antonio and Kent yawned periodically, and stretched out stiffened shoulder and arm muscles as they headed down the hillside. Yet they already walked with a limber step, and it was clear that they were simply shedding the last vestiges of a long sleep's grogginess.

Once they had reached the base of the village's hill, Ayenwatha led the party forward through the trees. They soon passed through the primary areas used for the village's cultivation, in which a number of women had just gotten underway in tending to their day's work tasks.

Ayenwatha watched them idly as his group continued on past the crops. Two of the women had been dear friends to his own beloved wife. They had helped to bring his daughter into the world, one of the most precious, wonderful days in all his life.

The beautiful memories swiftly brought sharp pangs of pain and regret that he quickly pushed back down, before they could evolve into cavernous sorrows. Those shining days were past, and could never be regained. He lived with an abiding hope in the beneficence of the One Spirit, but the only thing that now mattered was what lay right ahead of him.

Laboring with their hoes made of wood and bone, the diligent women paid the group little attention as they passed by. They were far more concerned with the needs of the Three Sisters, the maize, beans, and squash that were so utterly vital to the village and tribe's well-being.

The party left the fields behind and continued onward until they finally arrived at the Winding Stream. Too broad to jump, and moderate in depth, the substantial waterway displayed a robustly flowing current between its banks.

A few of the warriors with Ayenwatha broke away and headed off into the undergrowth. They shortly pulled a number of canoes out from where their elongated forms had been obscured by the dense foliage growing adjacent to the stream's near bank. The light, narrow vessels of stitched bark were subsequently dragged down the bank, and maneuvered to the edge of the water.

The group was then divided up and assigned to the four canoes, separating the seven foreigners in the process. The next moments were spent getting situated in the vessels and pushing them off into the water.

The current quickly gripped the canoes and began to carry them downstream. Without delay, the Onan warriors picked up wooden oars that were lying within the interior of the boats.

With fluid motions, the warriors dipped the oars into the water and pulled vigorously as they began to propel the vessels down the Winding Steam. They traveled in a staggered line, with Ayenwatha's canoe traveling in the lead.

Almost immediately after bringing the boats under control, the quartet was gliding into a curving bend towards the left. It was just one of the many twists and turns that gave the sinewy watercourse its name.

The rising sun's rays glinted off the stream as they slanted through the flanking trees, dappling the water surface with a dynamic blend of sparkles and shadows. A lively chorus of insects along the banks and high among the trees joined their serenade with the bright songs of birds, providing a peaceful accompaniment to the passage of the four boats cruising smoothly along the water's surface.

Before the sun had risen much higher, the Winding Stream merged in a confluence with a much larger river. Looking behind him, Ayenwatha watched the eyes of his guests widen in wonder as they passed into the channel of the considerably larger flow.

The greater river was called the Little Brother. The Little Brother was a substantial river in its own right, but undeniably a lesser sibling to the great Shimmering River that passed through the very heart of the Five Realms.

The Little Brother had cut deep into the tribal lands over the long ages, as it meandered around a number of large, forested hills. Rich green slopes towered high to either side of the river, rising away from the steep banks. The morning fog had dissipated by then, and Ayenwatha relished the brightness of the clear, unsullied day that now dominated the skies above them.

Ayenwatha heard the otherworlders within his vessel begin to speak quietly to each other, where they sat just a few places behind him. Discreetly, Ayenwatha listened intently to their conversation.

"I wonder where we are going today. It seems to be quite the surprise," the one named Logan commented, with a somber tinge to his voice.

Antonio replied in a similarly low voice. "Do you think I know? You tried asking him?"

Ayenwatha knew that they were referring to him. His finely chiseled limbs continued to move with a steady, rhythmic grace, flowing smoothly through each dip, pull, and raising of his oar. The war sachem kept his eyes focused upon the broad river ahead, even if his mind was wholly occupied with his guests.

There was no need to interject with an answer. They would know where they were going, and who would be waiting there, soon enough.

LOGAN

From where he was sitting further back on the canoe, Logan knew that it would be rather difficult to speak directly with Ayenwatha. He had grown highly impatient with the query that lingered upon his tongue. With each moment he found it increasingly harder to wait any longer, and he finally opted to seek some level of answer. Instead of raising his voice and trying to address Ayenwatha, he turned towards the tribal warrior that was paddling immediately behind him.

The warrior's face was implacably stern, presenting a pair of stoic, dark eyes that rested behind a hawk's beak of a nose. His mouth was set in a taut line over his sharp chin. A little taller and broader of back than Ayenwatha, the warrior held a strong posture, and conveyed a supremely confident aura about his person.

The warrior certainly looked as if he was not the sort of man very inclined to harboring a good sense of humor. Nor did he appear to be the kind of individual given to easy conversation.

"So, where are we going today? Nobody has told us yet," Logan asked the warrior in a low voice, careful not to sound too demanding.

"Ayenwatha will explain to you soon. You are in no danger," the warrior replied calmly.

The warrior did not take his eyes away from his task, continuing to work his oar in a consistent rhythm.

Logan waited a few moments longer, hoping that the warrior would elaborate further. With nothing forthcoming, Logan turned back towards Antonio, and shrugged in a gesture of resigned futility.

"Maybe it is a big surprise," Antonio said.

At the moment, Logan was not feeling very enthusiastic about surprises. The new world that had been revealed out of the dense fog had been far enough of a surprise for his liking. Indeed, it was a surprise that was adequate for a lifetime.

A part of him wondered whether it would simply be better to jump out of the canoe and swim for the shore. He glanced back at the warrior, the man's unbending expression showing no acknowledgement of Logan, as if he were invisible.

As Logan casually eyed the warrior, he could not help but take note of the man's strong build, and the sense of strength that his sculpted, heavily tattooed form radiated. The sight brought to mind the stoutly fashioned, ball-headed war clubs, the short-hafted axes, and the bows that the warriors such as him possessed and utilized.

Even the small knife, in the bead and quill decorated sheath hanging from the long cord around the warrior's neck, took on a much more formidable aspect than it would have solely by itself. Its wearer conferred a significantly greater status upon the short blade, reinforced by the thoughts of his skill in wielding it.

Logan shifted his attentions back towards the front. "Right now, I just don't want any more surprises," Logan stated curtly, as Antonio nodded his agreement.

Logan sat in a moody silence for about two hours longer, resigned to simply take in the sights of the hilly landscape passing by around them. The thick mass of trees, running up the slopes of the rises flanking the river, presented a nearly impenetrable upper surface. The intertwined concourse of branches and leaves could easily mask any manner of creature lurking beneath them.

Logan found himself wondering what manner of strange sights that the great span of forest might be sheltering within its midst.

The continuity of branches and leaves down by the river was broken up from time to time by stretches of bare ground. Broad patches of open space were spread out along some areas of the shoreline, especially within a few of the bends in the river.

On one of these patches, a rounded protrusion of land jutting deep into a curve in the river, was a herd of deer with reddish-brown coats. The cluster of deer came into sight as the canoes glided around the bend to the left. Having moved out from the shade of the treeline farther back, the deer were lapping at the clear waters of the river.

Reacting as if one singular body, the startled herd recovered in an instant from their initial surprise at the sudden appearance of the canoes. For a moment, a flurry of snorts broke the passive spring atmosphere. Flashing the white undersides of their tails, they sprang off in nimble, bursting bounds, racing swiftly into the shadows of the forest. In just seconds, it was as if they were never there.

About a mile downstream, along a straighter expanse of the river, Logan happened to be looking towards the bank when he caught sight of a towering, brown-furred form with a set of broad, palmated antlers. The great bull moose was almost hidden from view, standing still under the boughs of soaring trees. As the canoes neared the moose's position, the huge creature turned and lumbered off into the forest.

Shortly thereafter, another capacious swathe of embankment caught Logan's undivided attention, as the canoes rounded another prominent bend in the river.

Logan gazed in sheer wonder as the bank slowly came into full view, steadily revealing a mythic vision that struck him profoundly. A distant age of his own world was brought to life within the scene unveiling before his eyes.

"Unbelievable," Logan whispered slowly, under his breath.

A long, narrow-bodied ship of timber, whose contours flowed elegantly throughout its design, had been pulled up to rest on the ground of the shore.

The grand vessel was meticulously constructed by overlapping rows of horizontal strakes. The eminent level of craftsmanship required for such a ship was evident in its exquisite appearance, each fitted strake and ornamental carving openly testifying to the proficient skills of its makers.

The ship was designed to hold a single mast, rising from a support set near to the center of the vessel. The stout vertical post of pine was currently lowered, and the woolen sail was furled.

A full array of long oars was resting upon a pair of tall racks. The racks were in the form of vertical posts with shaped crosspieces, placed along the centerline of the vessel.

The curving bow of the ship exhibited a carving of a snarling wolf's head at its apex, with the stern displaying the corresponding image of a wolf's tail.

Around thirty very strong-looking men were milling about the immediate vicinity of the vessel, a few of them spread out along the expanse of clear shore. They looked casually towards the incoming canoes, showing no sign of alarm or surprise at its appearance. It was as if they had been waiting expectantly for the arrival of the tribal watercraft.

Logan's eyes absorbed as much as he could regarding their appearances, looking upon them with a sense of awe and wonder.

A few of the men wore protective garb on their upper bodies, a select few with coats of iron-link mail, and others with hide jerkins. The woolen tunics on all of them, whether under armor or not, exhibited a variety of colors. Hues of reds, blues, and greens had been dyed into the wool, and brocaded designs and patterns encircled the cuffs of their wrists, as well as the circumference of their necks and lower hems.

The clothing on their lower bodies was less colorful, largely earthen-colored trousers with either untapered or close-fitting legs. A few wore trousers gathered in below the knee, by cloth bands that were cross-gartered down to their footwear, whether leather shoes or cowhide boots, the latter with furred sides on the exterior.

A few of the men wore cloaks, most of which were pinned at their right shoulders with metal brooches or straight pins. Aside from a few with colorful headbands or round caps of wool, a majority of the men wore conical iron half-helms upon their heads, hammered out of one piece of iron, or fashioned from four iron plates. Several of the helms had straight nasal guards, and a very few had silver-gilt, spectacle-like eye-guards set in front, descending low enough to protect the nose as well.

The men were clearly prepared for combat, many bearing sizeable, round wooden shields, with projecting iron bosses fitted into their centers. A few other shields were set in an outer timber batten that ran down the length of the ship. Vibrant colors were presented on the shield surfaces, paired in most instances to create swirling or sectioned patterns.

All of the men had weapons close at hand, ranging from long-hafted, broad-bladed war axes, to straight swords nestled within their scabbards, and to spears of varying shaft lengths and blade types. A smattering of bows could also be seen in evidence amongst the warriors, the bearers of which possessed quivers full of feather-fletched arrows.

At the approach of the canoes, the men standing closer around the body of the longship trundled down to join the others at the river's edge. Assembled together, they all patiently waited for the arrival of the oncoming vessels.

Logan was impressed with the physical traits of the fair-skinned men, the common characteristics among them becoming clearer as the canoes drew closer.

They were rather tall, very powerfully-built men. Broad of shoulder and thick of limb, most wore full beards upon their faces, some worked into a braided or forked style.

Longer hairstyles predominated amongst them, most having locks cut to about shoulder length. Good grooming was in full evidence, with well-combed tresses culminating in even trims.

Despite the presence of ample color, artistry, and grooming habits among them, there was absolutely nothing soft about the throng of warriors. Their faces and bright eyes formed decidedly hardened countenances, and Logan recognized at once that these were not the kind of men to be taken lightly, or underestimated in any way.

"Eirik! Welcome to you and your men in the land of the Five Realms," Ayenwatha called out loudly, breaking Logan's concentration as the war sachem shouted abruptly to one of the foremost of the waiting figures.

The man identified as Eirik grinned broadly in response, moving at once to intercept Ayenwatha's canoe just as it reached the shoreline. Ayenwatha set his oar down as the bark-lined vessel grated against the ground underneath, rising up and lithely swinging himself over the side of the canoe.

Eirik moved forward and took Ayenwatha into a strong embrace that nearly lifted the tribal warrior off of the ground. Several of his long, blond locks billowed outward as they were picked up and buoyed by the breezy air. The ends of his red, square cloak, clasped by a shining silver brooch at the right shoulder, flapped as it was caught up in the stout gusts.

About six feet tall, he was exceptional of build, even among his own men, being particularly robust in the upper chest and shoulders. He had a multi-lobed, silver-gilt pommel crowning the bottom end of a long sword. The pommel and leather-wrapped hilt protruded upward from where the short, straight crossguard rested flush against the bronze-lined mouth of the scabbard at his left side. The scabbard itself was girded via a leather belt secured snugly around his waist.

Towards the bottom of his brown trousers, his feet were covered in dark, sealskin boots.

Several fingers of his sizeable hands exhibited gleaming silver rings. He wore a couple of silver arm-bands above his right elbow, circling his biceps, the gleaming bands visible right below the short sleeve of his chain mail shirt.

A type of beaded necklace, with two silver pendants hanging down at the bottom of the decorative array, was partially obstructed by the thick, forked beard that the man's face displayed, the farthest ends of which rested upon his broad upper chest.

The fierce-looking man looked markedly relaxed in his posture, adjacent to Ayenwatha's own very casual manner. The pair made for an odd sight; the brawny, fair-skinned man with flowing blonde locks, and draped in his richly colored attire, next to the leaner, reddish-skinned man in his hide kilt and leggings, with a crowning tuft of black hair and his upper body covered by naught but tattoos.

Despite the great variance in appearances, to Logan's eyes both men equally exuded a proud strength and sense of authority. It was also abundantly clear that they held both respect and a palpable liking for each other.

"Ayenwatha! I received your word. Your messenger came in such haste, and told us of your summons. I did not delay," Eirik announced in his deep voice. "I did not know what to expect, so you find my men so armed and equipped, and the wolf's head displayed openly on River Wolf. But I can see from your manner that there appears to be no pressing danger. Am I mistaken in this?"

Eirik's bright eyes gazed intently through the spectacle-like eye guards of his half-helm at Ayenwatha, as he fell silent. Logan could sense a slight flare of tension within the burly warrior as he awaited Ayenwatha's answer.

"No, Eirik. Grave threats to us are building, but none yet calls us to imminent battle. But I have called you here for a matter of great importance. One that cannot be delayed," Ayenwatha responded.

"That there is no immediate danger to our woodland friends is indeed a welcome tiding. I must say that it is very good just to see you once again … in these times we must celebrate all such meetings between friends," he warmly replied, appearing to relax once again at Ayenwatha's words.

His voice had a certain roughness to it, which fairly complimented his tough appearance. His piercing gaze then swept towards the seven foreigners with Ayenwatha.

"So these are your visitors?" he asked pointedly, nodding towards Logan and the others.

Ayenwatha likewise inclined his head towards the seven, who were now standing with the rest of the tribal warriors just a couple of paces behind the war sachem.

"Yes. And before you departed to other lands for the trading season, I wanted for you to meet them," Ayenwatha replied. "I desire to hear your words about them. I have not provided them with new clothes, so that you may see with your own eyes what manner of clothing that they wear. They have said that this clothing is from their own lands. I cannot place the clothing in any land that I know of."

Eirik nodded slowly, his countenance stern as his eyes continued to rest upon the seven. "I am glad that you reached me before I took to the seas for trade. Gunnar will be very interested in this discovery as well."

"I believe that your brother will indeed," Ayenwatha responded.

Ayenwatha then proceeded to explain the incredible amulets that had been given to the otherworlders by the Wanderer, and how the amulets enabled the understanding of languages. Logan took note that Eirik looked very surprised at the mention of the Wanderer, but the warrior held whatever thoughts he might have had to himself.

Eirik then walked past Ayenwatha to come to stand close to where Logan was situated at the forefront of the seven exiles. Having a closer look at Eirik's two pendants, Logan noticed that one was in the shape of a spear, its point oriented upward, and the second was in the distinct shape of a hammer. Logan wondered what the two silver symbols represented as he regarded the bearded warrior before him.

Eirik smiled again, in a genuine expression of greeting, his encompassing gaze taking in Logan and the others.

"I hear tidings that you are not in allegiance to the Unifier, and that you are possibly from another world," he said to them. "It is hard to believe that one can come from another world. But in these very strange and uncertain times, I have come to be surprised by very little. Hopefully, the All-Father has reasons for your presence here. If not, perhaps our patron gods do. I am called Eirik, son of Atli, and I am of the people of Midragard."

As Logan was the one standing right before the Midragardan warrior, he was the first to respond to Eirik's introduction.

"My name is Logan, and yes, this is definitely a new world for all of us," Logan stated, looking straight into the steady, cerulean gaze of the Midragardan.

There was no threat lurking in the man's eyes, but there was an unwavering scrutiny seated in his gaze. Despite the lack of hostility in that look, Logan deemed it wise to be careful not to say anything to offend the

Midragardan.

"It is very good to meet you Logan," Eirik responded, his large hand firmly clasping Logan's arm in a friendly manner, just below his left shoulder.

Before Logan had time to worry about the appropriate return gesture, Eirik released his grip upon his arm. The Midragardan gently brushed past Logan and moved in amongst his companions.

Now in their direct midst, the Midragardan's face could not hide his obvious fascination. More than once, Eirik lingered for several moments as he stared closely at some particular aspect of their unfamiliar clothing.

Logan quietly watched Eirik proceed with his inspection, equally fascinated with the Midragardan.

AYENWATHA

Ayenwatha knew from the Midragardan's reactions that Eirik had never seen or heard of anything like the type of clothes that the otherworlders wore.

He watched with keen interest as the helmed warrior passed onward from Logan, and drew to a halt before Erika. The striking, dark-haired woman briefly introduced herself, as Logan had, though unlike her companion she elicited a slight inclination of his head.

"Your clothes may be strange … and you may not be from our lands, but your mere look threatens to slay me where I stand," Eirik gently commented to her in reply. "Beautiful and strong … one of the Twelve Sisters you could well be."

Erika's face reddened a little in embarrassment at the sincere compliment, though Ayenwatha was all but certain that she had no idea as to who the Twelve Sisters were.

If she had known, Ayenwatha was confident that the shade of red now flushing her skin would have been even deeper. It was a very high compliment to be compared by a Midragardan leader to the deeply revered female Wizards, patrons of Eirik's homelands for ages.

Erika had no verbal reply for the stout warrior, but Ayenwatha could sense that she was flattered and understood the genuine nature, if not the particulars, of the warrior's words.

Eirik smiled softly, and moved past her to stand near to Mershad. He then regarded Mershad closely for several moments after the latter had formally introduced himself. Mershad looked very uncomfortable under the close individual inspection, his eyes glancing downward and staunchly averting the appraising gaze of the Midragardan.

"Like those from Saljuka ... you are indeed like a Sunlander," Eirik commented, after a few more moments had passed.

Ayenwatha understood the reference.

The Midragardan was comparing Mershad to a certain kind of people that Eirik had encountered during his many foreign travels, ones that he had shared several tales about with Ayenwatha. Judging by those engaging and highly descriptive stories, Ayenwatha believed that he could see where Eirik found a resemblance in Mershad to the Sunlanders that lived in the far north.

"Mostly a good people, at least as I have found them to be," Eirik continued. "They have long enjoyed much trade with Midragard, and with those of our kin who settled long ago in Kiruva. I have not met many Saljukans in my life, but the ones that I have met have been fair enough in their dealings with me."

As if perceiving the signs of increasing discomfort in Mershad that Ayenwatha was seeing, the Midragardan quickly added, "Know that they are well spoken of among my people, and take my words favorably."

Mershad merely nodded at Eirik's assurances and mustered a nervous grin, though his eyes continued to remain downward.

"I have heard it said that silver flows in rivers deep in their lands," Eirik then continued. "Their reputation as bold and capable warriors is also oft spoken of. I know that they are very zealous when it comes to matters of their Great Prophet. And they must have courage in their blood, for their people have spread to a great many lands upon the face of this world. Maybe you hold some of their qualities, Sunlander. It would not be a bad thing."

Ayenwatha noticed that Mershad's eyes widened at the open mention of the Great Prophet. Ayenwatha took the distinct response carefully to mind. There was something to be learned about Mershad and his homeland, or world, within that spontaneous reaction.

Mershad looked as if he greatly desired to ask some further questions of the Midragardan. Ayenwatha wished that Mershad had, as he wanted to see if something more could be learned about Mershad in an exchange with Eirik, but such an interaction would have to take place at some other time. By the time that Mershad appeared to have finally mustered himself up enough to venture a query forward, Eirik had turned his attention away towards another of the group.

Eirik strolled a couple of steps to the right, coming to face Derek. Ayenwatha could see something similar in the presence of the two men, from their stout postures to the iron looks held in their eyes.

The Midragardan and the otherworlder both had the confident aura and subtle wariness of experienced warriors. The scrutiny was mutual. Ayenwatha had a strong sense that each man was left with a respectful impression of the other.

Eirik's eyes continued to meet those of the one that Ayenwatha considered as the most stalwart of the newcomers.

The Midragardan warrior remarked, "Many in the Sunlands have a likeness such as yours, ones with the darker skin and a different appearance from that of your friend here. I have heard tales of places even farther away to the northern reaches of the Sunlands, far to the west. It is said that great tribes of brave warriors, with the darker skin and a similar look to you, live in lands of ferocious beasts and a blazing sun.

"The look in your eye is that of a warrior, even if I have not yet witnessed your skill at arms. If you are from another world, I am certain that men would be the same there as in ours, and that one who is not a warrior could not easily deceive one who is."

Ayenwatha could see the briefest flickers of curiosity and agreement in Derek's eyes.

Eirik then turned towards Janus, Kent, and Antonio, regarding each of the last three without much comment, other than to share a brief greeting and introduction with them.

He did linger a little longer before Janus, and the hint of a frown briefly crossed his face. Ayenwatha found the Midragardan's reaction strange, as it was one of perplexity, rather than one born of any discomfort or annoyance.

Finished, Eirik walked back towards Ayenwatha and slowly shook his head. The two of them strode several paces away from the others, so that they could speak together in confidence.

"I cannot say anything for certain," Eirik stated in a low voice, when they had walked far enough to assume that they could not be overheard.

"Then you can tell me nothing?" Ayenwatha asked, speaking in the

Midragardan tongue, a look of disappointment rising to his face. He had hoped dearly that the well-traveled Eirik would have some sort of insight or a few answers regarding the party of seven strangers. Eirik's inconclusive reaction only deepened the mystery.

"I know of nothing like this, from any of my travels," Eirik replied in a low voice. "In the color of their skin, and in appearance, a few of them are akin to the people of distant lands to the north. But I do not think that these people came from those kingdoms. It may indeed be that they are, as they have claimed, from another world."

"Then what do you counsel, my friend?" Ayenwatha asked Eirik pensively, looking past him towards the outsiders. He wondered what Eirik's brother Gunnar would be thinking, as Gunnar was more inclined towards the prophetic tales that so intrigued Ayenwatha. "Could they be the ones that are spoken of?"

"Who can say that they are not? Protect them, and keep them with you, if you think that there is a chance that they are these people," Eirik stated. His eyes then narrowed, "And these amulets from the Wanderer? What of these gifts? Do these guests of yours truly not speak our tongues?"

"There is no doubt about these gifts of the Wanderer. Without the amulets they understand nothing, and without them I cannot understand a word that they say," Ayenwatha said.

"The Wanderer … in the Five Realms, giving gifts to otherworlders," Eirik stated with a contemplative look.

Ayenwatha then fixed Eirik with an unwavering gaze, and his voice carried certitude in its even tone. "These seven know nothing of the things of our world. I have watched them very closely in all manner of things. They are truly strangers to all the things of this world. I can see it in their eyes, in their words, and in their great discomfort with the most simple of matters. I am certain of this. Everything is a wonder to them."

"So I noticed when I first set my eyes upon them. The look that they gave my men and ship was one of sheer amazement, like it was something they could hardly believe they were seeing. Can seven people falsely imitate such a sincere reaction?" Eirik replied with a shrug. "If they are from another world, then there is some true purpose with them being here. And for what it may be worth, I also share your view that they are not of the Unifier."

"Then what should we do while we shelter them?"" Ayenwatha

asked.

"I would teach them the ways of this world, as much as you can, if I were you. Time is a luxury that none of us have, so I would not delay," Eirik advised him firmly.

There was no sense of doubt in the Midragardan's voice. His words were filled with conviction, and Ayenwatha knew that did not come carelessly with Eirik, the son of Atli.

"As for the ways of this world, I will help you get them started now," Eirik said, casting a quick glance off in the direction of his ship, River Wolf. "I think that the things of Midragard might be a little more comfortable for them than the things of your tribes."

Ayenwatha wondered as to what Eirik was getting at, as the Midragardan then turned, took a few strides away, and called out to a few of his men. The men hustled up to Eirik, receiving some rapid instructions from him before continuing on to the longship. They strode up to the interior of the vessel via a long gangplank, which ran from the shore to the top strake about mid-ship.

A few moments later, a couple of the men were carefully moving back down the gangplank, carrying a large, rectangular wooden chest with them. Two others followed behind with a second, similar chest. The small group carried the chests on over to where Eirik and Ayenwatha stood.

At a nod from Eirik, the warriors placed the iron-banded chests upon the ground, unlocked them, and opened them up. Inside of the chests were some of the colorful, brocaded tunics that the Midragardans typically wore.

"Do not attract attention, when you do not have to, Ayenwatha. Clothes similar to these are worn in many lands," Eirik stated to his friend, who immediately understood the gesture. "The differences are much less with these, than with clothes fashioned of buckskin with quill decoration. Certainly much less than what they have on their bodies."

The sight of men and women in woolen tunics was a lot more common across the surface of Ave, especially regarding a group whose members represented many different ethnic heritages. A group of non-tribal people wearing the manner of clothing highly particular to the Five Realms would definitely be peculiar, and would ultimately invite unwanted attention.

"A good suggestion," Ayenwatha remarked.

"Do I not always have good suggestions?" Eirik responded with a light chuckle.

"Then I have one for you," Ayenwatha said, pausing for a moment as his lips turned in a grin, before adding, "Can you and your men join us for a feast in the village?"

Eirik gave a long, wistful sigh.

"Ah, you would beckon to me with this. It is such misfortune that I must return immediately to attend to our trading goods," Eirik exclaimed, shaking his head resignedly. "I do not have to ask my men to know that we all would love a feast in your village. For my own part, I would very much like to visit with your new guests some more. I cannot accept what you offer, but not because I do not wish to. Perhaps on my return, we can feast and share further tales together."

Ayenwatha looked at his friend and nodded, understanding that Eirik had already spared valuable time to heed Ayenwatha's summons.

"I was told that you were already trading in these lands when our messengers found you. Did trading go well on this visit?" Ayenwatha asked him, raising an eyebrow.

Smiling, Erik gestured back towards his ship. "We have some trading vessels, which are waiting for our return at the mouth of this river before we continue onward. They are full, and we are forced to use space on my ship for the overflow. Yes, it has gone well for both parties, Midragardans and the tribes alike. Many useful goods of iron have passed into the possession of your people, and more furs coveted in lands to the east and north will be going along with us."

"That is very good to hear, and I thank you for delaying your return journey, in order to give me your wisdom," Ayenwatha remarked, appreciatively.

He knew that the Midragardans, with vessels loaded with trade goods, would be quite eager to be on their way to their intended destinations.

Eirik lingered for a moment longer, a friendly grin spreading on his face as he turned to face the seven outsiders. He took several steps in their direction. There was no need to summon their attention, as their eyes were all turned towards the large Midragardan.

His voice rose, and carried strongly as he addressed them, "Do not be concerned, seven of another world. In Ayenwatha, you are in the care of a most honorable and brave warrior. It was my pleasure to meet all of you, and it is my hope that we meet again, in future and better days."

He then turned his attention back to Ayenwatha, and the two spoke together in hushed voices. Their expressions were serious as they imparted a few final important messages for each other; Eirik promising to convey tidings of the otherworlders to Gunnar, and Ayenwatha pledging to see to the practical education of the seven.

Before parting, they embraced each other once more, the smiles of friendship coming back to their faces.

Eirik gestured and called out to his full ship crew, and they fell in together as they walked briskly back towards the narrow longship. Once most were aboard, a few men loaded the gangplank onto the ship. The men took a few moments to set weapons down and place shields in the outer railing on the sides of the longship. When finished, they attended to the task of pushing the vessel off of the shore and into the water.

A chorus of grunts and moans accompanied the exertion of well-seasoned muscles straining against the substantial bulk of the timber ship. With a unified team of warriors working diligently, they slid the elongated boat into the water, proceeding to climb aboard with the help of their compatriots.

Oars were removed from the upright racks and set into place through a line of holes in the side strakes, as the men took their places atop chests set at intervals along the length of the ship. The oar holes were aligned efficiently with the exterior rack that held their round shields in place, allowing for the oars to be used with the shields lining the batten.

Lowered into the water, and rowed in unison to the beat of a chant, the ship was turned to align with the river and propelled forward, moving smoothly along the water's surface. The keel cut through the water with a natural grace.

Ayenwatha and the rest of his party remained on the edge of the shoreline, until the ship had glided far down the river. The ship passed around a wide bend and was out of sight in just minutes, right after Eirik gave a final wave from the vessel.

Shifting his attention back to the seven, Ayenwatha commented, "Eirik is a true friend, and he has traded with our people for many years. The Midragardans are a strong people, and are loyal servants of the Creator. They are masters of the seas and rivers.

"They have become good brothers to our people, though it was not always so. Maybe we shall someday go to see their own lands, but for now we will have to be content with tales. Eirik is right. You must learn about our world, about our people and about others … so that you better understand us, and so that you better understand our world."

"We would like that, very much," Erika replied with undisguised eagerness in her voice.

"As much as possible," Logan added quickly, also looking very hungry for more knowledge of their new world.

"And we would like to sample all of your foods as well, maybe many times to make sure that we understand them well. I want to study the turkey and deer meat more carefully … and maybe we can study some ales from all the cultures that you know of," quipped Kent, smirking playfully. "For my part, I want to be an expert in the food and drink of this world."

A light-hearted laughter broke out first among the outsiders, and then among Ayenwatha and the tribal warriors, as Kent's humor quickly dawned upon them. Ayenwatha smiled broadly, glad for the sudden levity.

"We will take your learning of ales much slower than you might like. You should have gone with Eirik if you wished to know more of ales," Ayenwatha replied teasingly to Kent, with easy-going laughter. "But for now, it is probably best to return to our village."

"And you tell me this, right after Eirik's boat goes out of sight? How fair is that, Ayenwatha? How can I hope to learn about the ales of your world?" Kent retorted, with an exaggerated shaking of his head, as guest and tribesman alike laughed again, this time in unison.

JANUS

In the wake of the Midragardans' departure, Ayenwatha's group returned back to the four canoes where they rested up on the shore. All involved in the party helped to get the vessels shoved back into the water, though not before first loading aboard the two chests given to the group by Eirik.

The return voyage on the Little Brother required a little more exertion and time, as they had to row against the light current. The seven guests interspersed with the tribal warriors aided in the rowing, lending the Onan men a much needed, periodic respite.

For Janus, the additional activity was very welcome, though he was not conditioned for sustained rowing. It was not long before he was feeling the effects of the strain. Nevertheless, Janus hardened his resolve, and did not complain, enduring until one of the resting tribal warriors insisted on resuming.

Eventually, the quartet of vessels turned aside from the Little Brother, and continued forth up the Winding Stream.

As the late afternoon shadows grew longer, they finally reached the embankment where they had first begun their sojourn. Though all within the canoes were tired, they joined together to get the vessels lifted out of the water and hidden back amongst the thick underbrush running along the bank.

Ayenwatha then led them back from the Winding Stream, taking them onward to the Place of Far Seeing.

On their way, they came across a couple groups of women that were out foraying with cornhusk baskets, gathering nuts, roots, forest greens, and berries. The fields situated closer to the great hill still harbored a number of women tending to them, as it had on the outset of their journey.

A party of men bearing spears and nets, the latter weighed down with small stones, crossed their paths. The fishing party was also returning back to the village, in very good spirits as they had procured a fair quantity of trout and eels on their own foray.

As they all came to the base of the hill's slope, they saw a second group of men about halfway up the incline. Janus quickly realized that it was a hunting party. They had successfully felled a couple of white-tailed deer, whose carcasses they were now bearing up to the village. Janus' group and the fishing party proceeded up the slope in the wake of the hunters.

Entering the village, Janus saw that it was alive and teeming with activity. Children and dogs were running about and playing, while the adults in view were engaged in a variety of tasks.

The children yelled and giggled as the parties passed through the front entryway, swarming them in an instant. Janus' eyes quickly scanned the young ones for the imaginative boy that had interacted with him in the pre-dawn hour.

His hurried search came up empty, though he was not wholly surprised. He knew that there were several youth still outside of the palisades, as well as many others that were spread amongst the numerous longhouses within the sprawling village interior.

The children ogled the trout and eel that were being carried along by the fishing party, with faces that were both curious and filled with delight.

Janus smiled at all of the youth, as Ayenwatha led his group through them towards the longhouse of the Firaken Clan. Most of the children remained around the fishers and hunters, the interests of their bellies taking precedence over the seven strangers. Janus and his companions continued into the Firaken longhouse with Ayenwatha, and they were soon gathered together within Ayenwatha's own dwelling chamber.

Shortly thereafter, they were sitting together and enjoying a light meal of fresh trout and hominy that had been prepared for them by some of the village women. Janus was utterly famished, and had to restrain himself from simply wolfing down the portions given to him.

As they ate the light fare together, Ayenwatha began to interview the seven calmly about their various interests and desires. He probed them about the things that they enjoyed doing in their own worlds, as well as the things about their new world that were grabbing their attentions.

He listened intently to their responses. Janus was struck by the notion that the war sachem was a man with more than a passing interest in their answers.

The rectangular chests given by Eirik Atlisson were soon brought in by a few tribal warriors and opened up. Janus and the other six gathered around, angling for a good view of the contents, even as Ayenwatha began to pull some of the items forth. Eirik had shown good foresight, as there was ample clothing for seven individuals contained therein.

A series of trousers, woolen tunics, leather shoes, belts, and some linen undergarments were lifted out and distributed amongst the males in the group.

For Erika, there was a long linen chemise, a pair of knee-length cloth leggings, woolen socks, and leather shoes.

Janus was quite happy to receive the new garments, and the reactions of all seven were ones of relief and gratitude. All of their clothes had gotten extremely dirty and sweat-stained since they had arrived in the new world, and a change of attire was long overdue.

The seven spent a few moments changing into their new garments. Erika went into the adjacent, currently unoccupied dwelling chamber to gain some privacy for herself, while the males donned their new clothes right in front of Ayenwatha.

Though feeling somewhat awkward and rough against his skin, the new clothing was welcome. Janus knew that they would have to change clothing at some point, and it was far wiser to start blending in with the cultures that they would be living amongst and interacting with. If they could draw less overt attention to themselves, it was all the better.

After they had all changed into their new attire, shedding their old clothing in a heap to the side of one of the sleeping platforms, Ayenwatha took the seven back outside of the longhouse. He summoned over a few of the tribal warriors who were loitering close by.

Janus watched the others of his group tugging at and adjusting their tunics, trousers, and belts. More than one of the others was scratching at the plethora of new itches brought on by the woolen items now draped over them.

He had almost broken into laughter as he watched his companions walking gingerly in their new footwear, as if each step was fragile and fraught with peril. Admittedly, the feeling of the leather shoes was far different from what he was used to, and he wondered how could ever run at full speed over rock, woods, and soil out in the forest.

A part of him started to consider whether it might be a good idea to retain his old pair of shoes, though another part of him warned him that even that little indulgence would be enough to attract unwanted attention. For the time being, Janus determined that it would be better to strive to acclimate fully.

Kent was wearing a tablet-woven headband that had been found at the bottom of one of the chests. It looked a little out of place on Kent's head, giving him a comical appearance.

When he was in good spirits, Kent's face seemed always ready to break into laughter. Even the new stubble filling in abundantly around his goatee did little to stifle his youthful demeanor. His appearance in the Midragardan attire was so very different from the fierce, scarred, and bearded visages of the other men that Janus had recently seen wearing those same types of headbands. The contrast was hilarious, and it was all that Janus could do not to laugh. He bit back the grin that popped on his face before it could expand any further.

There were still a few hours left in the day, and Janus turned his thoughts to wondering as to what Ayenwatha was about. The war sachem split the seven into three groups. The reason why Ayenwatha had seemed engrossed in their responses, as they had made their personal interests known during the meal in the chamber, was then made very clear.

Ayenwatha told them that it was time for them to learn more about the world that they were now in. They were each to be allowed the chance to develop skills and knowledge according to their own path of interest, which he said would help in speeding up the overall learning acquired by their entire group.

As he made clear, they could always impart the knowledge and skills that they gained amongst each other. With the time available to all of them being so uncertain, and possibly very short, Ayenwatha had deemed it best to concentrate on raising up their collective knowledge. Hence, three groups were being formed to each absorb a different range of knowledge.

Janus immediately saw the wisdom in Ayenwatha's decision, which only increased his already considerable respect for the stalwart war sachem.

A few of the warriors standing with Ayenwatha, particularly strong-looking men with steely expressions, then approached the largest of the three groups. Erika, Derek, Antonio, and Logan were given an assortment of weapons, including bows, short-hafted axes, and the curving, timber-carved war clubs that were common among the tribal fighters.

According to Ayenwatha's ensuing explanation, they were to be sent into the woodlands. The foursome was to practice the art of moving with stealth through the forest, and to learn of its many inhabitants. They would also be learning of its plants, including the many that could provide food and medicine, as well as the others that poisoned and brought sickness.

The quartet would also be learning the use of the weapons that they now held in their hands.

Janus noted that there was no challenge forthcoming to Erika's presence with them, despite the observation that none of the village's warriors were female. Ayenwatha had accommodated her according to her expressed desires, evidently without reservation.

Kent and Mershad comprised the second division of the exiles. They were to be sent onward with a trio of elders, two women and one man, that were subsequently summoned, all three of whom Ayenwatha deferred to with great reverence.

Janus sensed a distinctly greater level of veneration given by Ayenwatha towards the two older women.

The two clan matrons and the older man would be helping Kent and Mershad to learn some of the village's history, including much more about the foundations of the Five Realms. They would be hearing about the establishment of the Sacred Fire, the Great Law, and the Grand Council.

The two exiles would also be learning something of the tribal customs, and a little about the history of the world, at least as it was known to the tribal people. Ayenwatha indicated that they were also to learn the applications of some of the more domestic tools and skills.

The last one left was Janus, who was a little confused at being set apart by himself from the others.

During the meal with Ayenwatha, he had expressed an interest both in acquiring knowledge of the new world, as well as in the skills of survival and combat. In his eyes, he could have fit in very well with either of the two other groups.

He looked inquisitively at Ayenwatha, and was left wondering until Ayenwatha had dismissed the others to begin their orientations in the remaining hours of the day. As the others headed off with their respective mentors, Ayenwatha finally looked to Janus. The sachem took a step closer, the two of them now standing by themselves.

"You may wonder why I have kept you here, alone," Ayenwatha stated, "And why I have not sent you with one of the other groups."

Janus nodded slowly in agreement, wanting to read the mind of the war sachem as he had no answers himself. He did not feel any daunting worries towards the mystery, as he was confident in the good intentions of Ayenwatha, but he was nonetheless filled with curiosity.

"I sense that there is much pain in you, Janus. That I can tell without you speaking openly of it. I see a strong and good heart within you," Ayenwatha stated with an empathic smile, the words catching Janus fully off of his guard. "You can be torn by a pain and be unable to see deeper to the power that it hides from you ... a power that you can take to yourself. While you must fight through that pain alone, to find the greater source that it shields you from, others can help you to see with new eyes."

Janus was left speechless at Ayenwatha's words. The depth of the war sachem's perception was without question.

Ayenwatha did not wait for Janus to answer, merely gesturing for Janus to follow him. Ayenwatha walked off at a brisk pace across the village grounds, with Janus hurrying to catch up and keep in stride.

They moved in among the greater longhouses, eventually threading their way through them towards a far corner of the village, which was on the side opposite the main entranceway. Taking up that far corner was what looked at first to be a longhouse that was about half of the length of the average family dwellings.

Instead of a covered porch area, it had a large, wide entryway. Janus caught a whiff of a distinctive, musky animal scent coming from within the gaping opening.

A couple of tribal warriors were sitting cross-legged nearby. They were occupied playing some type of game that involved a bowl and a small number of sizeable nuts. Each nut was colored half-orange and half-white, such that when they tumbled into the bowl as a group they would produce a varying distribution based upon the revealed topside colors.

The warriors, upon taking notice of Ayenwatha and Janus, immediately ceased the game and got up to their feet.

"That is a game that I have not played in awhile," Ayenwatha remarked, looking over to Janus. "I will have to teach it to you soon, as it is one often played in the village and among the tribes."

"Do you need steeds, Ayenwatha?" one of the warriors interjected in a low voice, a lean, young male who could not have been more than twenty years old.

"I will need two. Bring me Arax, of course," Ayenwatha requested. He then paused for a moment, as if in careful consideration, before adding. "And the second should be Reazl."

Janus listened to the request with increased interest. He had seen the horses within the village perimeter, though he had not yet seen anyone actually riding them. He had little experience in horse riding, but a late afternoon jaunt on horseback sounded very intriguing.

The warriors nodded to Ayenwatha, turning and striding through the opening into the structure. Their forms were quickly swallowed by the shadows of the murky interior.

"You may find what is coming through that opening to be of interest ... it is something about our people that you have not yet had time to learn about," Ayenwatha commented enigmatically, as they awaited the return of the warriors.

Janus watched the opening in growing anticipation. The moments crawled by, as Janus caught the traces of soft spoken voices and shuffling from within the structure.

The young warrior that had spoken to Ayenwatha finally emerged back into the light, leading an incredible sight at the end of a long tether. Brought into the exposing light of day, the revelation stunned Janus.

He stood awestruck and mesmerized as his eyes roved all over the incredible form now standing, living and breathing, just a few paces in front of him.

The creature that was led forth was taller than a large horse and noticeably longer of body. It had very muscular front quarters, which tapered quickly to a much narrower back and hindquarters.

The animal was covered in a blonde-brown fur, the outer hairs of which were tipped in silvery hues. Its head was large and rounded, a broad snout projecting out of a generally inward-curving face. Two rounded ears sat high on the sides of its great head, both oriented towards Janus.

Large, lustrous eyes looked out towards Janus from that massive face, as the creature stepped forward on its lean, muscular legs. Its extended limbs ended in huge, broad paws, each equipped with a stout set of blunted claws.

The characteristic that was most striking about the creature, and the one that took Janus' breath away, were the huge wings that were now folded into its body.

The dark, leathery wings connected to its body just behind the shoulder, meeting a bulging, pronounced mass of muscles that gave ample evidence to an exceedingly powerful strength contained therein. At close proximity, Janus could see that the wings were lined with an extensive network of veins, and covered with a layer of very fine hairs.

Janus was absolutely astonished, and could not fathom what the origin of the winged, bear-like beast could possibly be.

The other warrior then led out a second creature like the first. The second beast was a little smaller in size, and had a darker brown shade of fur, with outer hairs having a more whitish tip to them.

Both of the extraordinary creatures were fitted with a very simple design of harness and saddle, the seat set just behind the base of their broad necks. The saddles were, in truth, more of a low pad-saddle, covered in bead and quill decorated hide, and set atop saddle blankets. A pair of simple, hide-covered stirrups hung down from the sides of each saddle.

His senses slowly returning back to him, Janus reflexively took a couple of steps backward, intimidated by the large, very unusual creatures. Ayenwatha put a firm hand to Janus' back, to stop him from retreating any further.

Janus forced his eyes away from the two creatures, and saw that Ayenwatha was looking at him with a perplexed expression.

"This is a surprising sight to you?" Ayenwatha asked him. "Do you not have mounts to carry you in the lands you are from?"

Janus nodded. "Very much so. I have never seen anything like these creatures. We have horses in our world, like those I have seen in the village, but nothing that can be ridden with wings such as these."

Ayenwatha looked almost as surprised by that disclosure as Janus did towards the emergence of the winged steeds.

"The Skiantha are not in your world? Nothing like these Brega?" Ayenwatha questioned him.

Janus shook his head. "Nothing. Only creatures of our imaginations, such as winged horses, but definitely nothing like this."

"Winged horses? Those are not creatures of imagination in this world, but they are not in these lands," Ayenwatha answered him. "Eirik and Gunnar have told me tales of the Twelve Sisters riding upon such steeds. I would like to see them myself someday."

Ayenwatha became silent for a few moments, dwelling upon some inner thoughts as Janus took in the war sachem's divulgence with even more wonderment.

"And the Brega? The Skiantha?" Janus asked Ayenwatha.

"The Skiantha … races of winged creatures large enough to carry men or women through the skies," Ayenwatha replied. "They can be tamed and harnessed, like the Brega which are found in our lands.

"There are several Skiantha in this world. The Midragardans ride upon a kind called Fenraren, and there are said to be other kinds in other lands, like those ridden by the Elves to the north, and those ridden by the dog-faced ones in lands to the farther east."

"Incredible …" Janus murmured, looking back to the pair of winged steeds before them. His face then took on a look of worry. "Am I ready to ride such a creature then?"

"Have you ridden horses in your world," Ayenwatha asked him.

Janus nodded. "A few times, though I am not an expert."

Ayenwatha regarded Janus for a moment with a serious mien, as if making a final consideration. At last, his features softened as he responded, "The Brega are very intelligent, of good demeanor, and are our friends. They have been companions and steeds for our tribes for many long years. If you have ridden in a saddle, on the back of a horse, you will be able to do this. There is nothing to fear, Janus. Just watch me, and follow what I do."

He looked completely at ease as he strolled right up to the larger of the bearish creatures. He patted it several times on its neck, before stroking the beast affectionately along its broad muzzle. The creature amiably licked Ayenwatha along the face with a wide tongue, eliciting a light laughter from the war sachem.

The creature then lowered its head and crouched down, as Ayenwatha reached for its reins. Ayenwatha slowly mounted it, a task that appeared to Janus to be much more complicated than that involving a horse, due to the huge wings and different anatomy of the winged steed.

"Hello Arax, my loyal friend," Ayenwatha addressed the steed exuberantly, his affinity for the beast plainly obvious in his timbre. "It has been a couple days, long both for me and you. We go to the skies today, with our new friend, Janus."

The creature gave a low rumble as Ayenwatha leaned forward and rubbed its fur vigorously behind its right ear. With a grin, he straightened up and looked towards Janus.

"Now go to Reazl and take the reins as I did," Ayenwatha instructed Janus, as he adjusted his position on Arax's saddle. "Do not fear him. They do not bite without cause, and are very gentle with us."

Janus glanced at Ayenwatha, sucked in a deep breath, let it out slowly, and took a few hesitant steps forward. His natural inclinations were still highly nervous, and a little fearful. He approached Reazl, as the warrior that had led the beast out of the byre structure handed the reins over to him.

Before Janus had time to think further on the matter, Reazl also lowered its body, and angled its head down towards the ground. The gesture gave Janus much more confidence, as he gripped the reins more firmly in his hand.

With a somewhat clumsy effort, he then pulled himself up onto the winged beast. Bracing a foot in one of the hide stirrups, he swung his other leg over to bring himself into an upright, seated position. His heart began to beat faster as the creature stood back up to its full height.

Janus looked down and back, gazing upon the wings of the creature that so fascinated and daunted him. The reality of what he and Ayenwatha were about to do began to fully dawn on him. Trepidation crept steadily into his sense of wonderment, propelling his unease.

"Now, strap yourself into the saddle, like me," Ayenwatha instructed, drawing Janus' attention back from its wandering.

Ayenwatha paused for a moment before proceeding, allowing Janus to watch his demonstration. The sachem tied a couple pairs of long leather straps from the back of the saddle about his waist, effectively anchoring himself into the pad-saddle with a little redundancy.

"With these pulled tight, and with your feet in the stirrups, you will be very safe," Ayenwatha assured him. "It may feel strange at first, but you will soon get used to it. I have chosen Reazl because he is a gentle steed to a new rider. He will be a good steed for one who is on their first sky ride. He will also prove to be very restrained until you are ready to do more."

"I sure hope so," remarked Janus tensely. He tightened the straps in imitation of Ayenwatha, and fit his feet snugly into the leather-covered stirrup loops.

His amazement at the creature underneath him continued to give way to the stark realization that they were going to be actually flying, in mere moments. The thought was bringing a near panic up from within him. Janus had to concentrate hard to fight the disconcerting feeling back down in his mind.

He felt like he was tied down securely, but they had not left the ground just yet. His nerves were undeniably rattled, and it was not getting any better.

It must have shown clearly upon his face, for Ayenwatha was very quick to try to reassure him. "Janus, you will be safe. Do not worry, for Reazl will follow my lead upon Arax. There are just two basic ways to command them," Ayenwatha said. "And never forget, as I have said, they are very intelligent. They will not do anything reckless that would put you in danger.

"Pulling back on the reins slows them, and digging the heels of your feet in will make Reazl go faster. Pressure to the left and right, using the reins, turns them to the side that you choose. Leaning backwards and applying firm upward pressure with your feet makes them rise, leaning far forward in your saddle and putting pressure downward with your feet makes them descend.

"We have also trained them to follow verbal commands, which are to be spoken sharp and firmly. Right, left, down, up, faster, and slower are commands that they will respond to. Know that they will not resist you, and that they will do your will. Use the physical movements if the wind is too great, or if you are going too fast to be understood.

"There are other commands to learn, but those are for another time. The other commands are for use in battle, but you must first learn to ride your steed, and be comfortable with flight, before worrying about combat."

Janus nodded, again extremely grateful for the gift of the blue-stone pendant from the old man in the forest. Without the clear translation empowered by the amulet, he knew that he would probably have had a very difficult time pronouncing even that small number of words with any accuracy. Mispronouncing a command to a steed in the midst of flight was not something that Janus wanted to be worrying about.

"Let us go to a clearing, and let us go up into the skies, Janus!" Ayenwatha stated, palpable excitement rising up again within his voice. "Arax, slow!"

Ayenwatha turned again to Janus, just as Arax started forward. "They also follow the same commands on the ground, as you see … with the exception of a couple of obvious ones."

"This should be quite an adventure," Janus commented, trying to smile about the developing situation. His heart was fluttering as he mouthed his first command to a Brega, "Reazl, slow!"

Reazl started forward at a slow gait, keeping a few paces behind Arax as they moved away from the byre. Underneath him, Janus sensed the ease of balance with which the creature walked across the ground upon its large paws. The two riders and their steeds wended their way back through the longhouses, and headed out into the open clearing closer to the main village entrance.

A number of eyes were drawn towards the two riders as they made their way, some smiling as they saw the slight look of terror upon the newcomer's face. Janus did not find their reactions so amusing, though he reminded himself that the tribal people's mirth at his great nervousness was precisely because of the lack of danger that they perceived.

Once they were clear of the longhouses, and far out in the open ground, Ayenwatha exclaimed loudly, "Up!"

Upon his command, Arax spread its wings outward. The wingspan of the creature was very broad in proportion to the rest of its body. The Brega's thick claws dug into the ground as it powerfully thrust its mass forward. Loping ahead and flapping its wings, the Brega quickly picked up speed. It finally coiled and sprung up vigorously, in an explosive movement.

The great wings of the Brega snapped downward with tremendous force, sustaining the creature as its body hovered in mid-air for just a second.

The wings then bent and rose up in a swift movement, which was a blur to the eye, before widening again and driving downward powerfully.

Gripping the air, the creature ascended on a steep incline away from the ground. A lump forming in his throat, Janus incredulously watched the Brega as it steadily gained altitude.

A light-headed feeling came over Janus, as he knew that his moment had arrived. He swallowed hard, and took a few deep breaths. His knuckles had whitened where they clenched the reins of the creature.

He was barely able to voice the words audibly, but they somehow came out from his lips.

"Reazl, Up!"

He considered the mere utterance of those two words to be one of the braver things that he had ever done in his life.

Reazl dutifully followed the command.

Lurching forward into motion, Reazl bounded a few paces and then lunged, as its own wings spread and powered its body upward. A dizzying, disorienting rush flooded over Janus, as his steed separated itself fully from the sure footing and solidity of the ground.

A discomfiting feeling took root in the pit of his stomach, as the ground fell farther and farther away beneath him. The longhouses rapidly dwindled in size, and the villagers became minute, nondescript figures. Even the hill finally shrank away, melding gradually into the broader landscape.

Reazl kept to a steep incline, rising higher into the sky a short distance behind Arax and Ayenwatha. Janus felt an encompassing wave of light-headedness sweep over him, and he forced his eyes away from looking downward. The wind beating against his face, he concentrated solely upon the form of Arax and Ayenwatha just ahead of him.

"Slow!" called Ayenwatha. He glanced back towards Janus and nodded.

"Slow!" Janus shouted out a moment later, his heart thumping rapidly.

Arax leveled out in its path of flight, followed in turn by Reazl as the two steeds settled upon an even plane. At Ayenwatha's guidance, they set off across the tribal lands at a modest rate of speed, several hundred feet above the ground.

As on the ground, the creatures bore their riders with a smooth and gentle grace. Their wings flapped strongly to maintain height whenever necessary, but they were mostly able to stretch out their broad appendages and glide upon the mild air currents.

Within moments, the pair of steeds had eased into a comfortable pace, bobbing and rocking lightly in the clutches of the upper air.

Janus was immediately taken in by the exhilarating sensation of flight, an elating feeling that juxtaposed sharply with his considerable fears. The fluid breezes washed against his face, as Reazl maintained the steady course.

Looking out to the far horizons, Janus felt that he was witnessing a vision of heaven itself. The beautiful blue-green sky stretched like a silken sheet in every direction. A number of cottony white clouds scudded sluggishly across the heights, gentle and pure of appearance. They brooked no threats of storms, and harmoniously complimented the bright and docile atmosphere that reigned all around them.

Now high in the sky, Janus could truly appreciate the vast expanse of forestland that sprawled out below him. He peered out towards the west, where the green continuity of the forest canopy ended abruptly. Yet to north, south, and east, the rolling hills and hosts of trees reached well beyond the limits of his vision. The hazy outlines of a few distant hills to the north loomed noticeably larger, perhaps indicating a range of small mountains in that region.

The wind continuously caressed Janus, and, as his breathing gradually calmed, he drank in the cool, fresh air, relishing the invigorating feeling as it filled his lungs to capacity.

"Janus, what do you think of flight?" Ayenwatha asked him, his head turned to look back over his shoulder as he smiled brightly towards Janus.

The question snapped Janus out of his hypnotic state, in the face of the incredible, sensational perspective now granted to him. Janus watched as Ayenwatha slowed Arax down and allowed Reazl to draw up alongside.

"This is beyond words," Janus finally said, wholly astounded by the experience.

He felt entirely light of heart, and even a little magical. Janus was touched profoundly by hints of the kind of raw wonder known by children yet unsullied by the ravages of life's harsher experiences. The whispers of such an immaculate sensation were instantly renewing to his sunken spirits, beckoning with glimmers of a deeper and transcending hope.

"I feel that flying allows us to see creation in a truer manner. It also lets us see how large the world really is. We see that we are a part of something tremendous and wonderful," Ayenwatha stated reflectively, looking out serenely over the extensive, green woodlands that his people inhabited. "See how you can only see the horizon itself, but no true ending to it? Your eyes cannot see to the end of any direction that you look. I like to think this vision is like our own lives. We only see what we see in our limits, though there is so much more beyond."

Janus wanted greatly to embrace the sachem's heartening sentiments. Ayenwatha had a vision of forever, of unending horizons opening on to ever-new vistas. If only such a view could be rooted in truth.

Forever was the only chance that Janus would have to heal the gaping losses that his life had accumulated. It was the only chance that the losses would not be rendered permanent, and would someday be made to rights.

Carefully and willfully, Janus embraced the captivating moment, as it settled into the more cherished areas of his memory. He desired to hold the purity of that vivid moment for all of his life, at least as a sign of hope for another existence yet to come.

"I sense that you have a very good spirit, Janus," Ayenwatha said in a low voice, repeating the sentiments that he had expressed on the ground. "I see a joy coming into you at the sight of the One Spirit's workings, and only a good spirit is capable of such a true feeling."

Ayenwatha's voice then took on an undercurrent of sympathy.

"I know that you have many burdens within you, and in time you may decide to share some of them with me."

The sachem fell silent, quietly regarding Janus.

"I may do that," Janus said at last, looking over to Ayenwatha.

For the first time, Janus saw the sachem as someone who could be a genuine friend, given enough time. His tuft of dark hair whipping about in the wind, his eyes sparkling with a youthful energy, and his face wreathed in an affable smile, Ayenwatha was a vision of a liberated, free spirit.

Ayenwatha mischievously chuckled, as if a sudden inspiration had come over him. He nodded towards Janus with a gleam in his eye. "Before we return for the night, are you ready to really see what the Brega can do?"

Before Janus could answer him, Ayenwatha vigorously cried out "Arax ... Reazl ... fast!"

Janus had no time to prepare. He could only react as Reazl surged forward and rapidly accelerated, furiously beating the air with its sweeping wings.

Reazl strained to keep up with Arax, and their rate of speed increased until the ground was rushing by in a blur below. The winds whipped up and beat robustly against Janus' face as his heart leapt to his throat.

Ayenwatha peeked back over his shoulder at Janus, and laughed boisterously, in an entirely carefree manner. Janus knew that he likely had a dumbfounded look etched into his face, but the momentary shock was steadily replaced by the sheer thrill of the racing flight.

The entire experience had allowed Janus to feel an enthralling sense of childlike wonder for the first time in many long, arduous years. For that alone, he was eminently grateful to the sachem, as he previously would have believed that he had become far too numb to feel such an unsullied sense of delight ever again.

A swell of genuine excitement coursed throughout him. Janus found himself smiling again, laughing merrily at the ongoing excitement of the swift flight through the skies over the tribal lands.

The sorrows were still present within him, and the current elation was undeniably temporal. Nevertheless, Janus could not dismiss the reality that he had indeed felt an inkling of true hope. Out of the grayness, it was a flicker of the most vibrant, rich color that he had perceived in quite some time.

GUNTHER

The Jaghun bounded sprightly into sight, just a few minutes before the horses belonging to the Saxan party arrived.

It was enough time for the others with Gunther to patiently compose themselves. Gunther could sense that they were simply grateful for the chance to continue resting their tired limbs.

There were seven horsemen in the approaching Saxan group, all well-equipped, in coats of mail and armed. One bore a pennon upon his long spear, exhibiting several red tree shapes that were set against a white background. The standard of Wessachia at the end of the lance came as no surprise to Gunther, as he had not expected to see anything else.

All of the men but one looked quite startled as they saw Gunther and the others, pulling their horses up abruptly. Gunther directed his attention to the one that had exhibited no significant surprise, though he could read the curiosity plainly enough on his Saxan friend's face.

For his own part, Gunther was curious, and more than a little surprised, at the Saxan's presence.

"Thane Aethelstan? You have come in person?" Gunther inquired, with a readily noticeable hint of concern woven within his voice.

The tall, broad-shouldered horseman at the forefront of the Saxan riders nodded his head towards the woodsman. Aethelstan sat astride his iron-gray stallion with a strong, upright posture, casting a commanding and confident air about himself. His dark eyes peered out from beneath his thick eyebrows, expressive and alert. His strong, angular lower jaw was set firm, covered by his dense, close-cropped beard.

He had his longsword sheathed at his side, the scabbard hanging from a baldric. The shining, silver-gilt pommel, leather grip, and straight crossguard rested upon the scabbard's bronze-banded mouth.

The other six were also armed with swords, with the noticeable addition of long, two-handed axes that were affixed to their saddle harnessing by leather loops. All had long shields slung over their backs, wide and curving at the top, tapering down to a narrow, rounded bottom. Leader and loyal warrior alike, all were in a state of readiness, primed for combat at a moment's notice.

"It has indeed been a long time, Gunther. I wish that it were better times that I found you in," Aethelstan said.

"You know me well enough, Aethelstan. I am not shy of hearing a difficult truth," Gunther responded.

"Then be ready to hear what I have so say. The tidings that I bring are grave indeed, and I have come to seek word from you as well," Aethelstan responded. "Most of my companions remain behind, where your … friend … found us, soon after we had signaled you with the horn."

Aethelstan paused, and took studious account of the strangers, his eyes drifting slowly across their foreign clothing and appearances.

"And I also might ask, who are your companions?" Aethelstan queried.

"Refugees, who are fleeing the Unifier's forces," Gunther replied.

It was a carefully chosen response. Gunther had decided not to delve into the mysteries of their origins, while still telling the truth to Aethelstan. The great Saxan thane happened to be one of the very few people in the world that Gunther deeply respected, and trusted greatly. He could not in good conscience deceive the thane, but neither did he want to broach the confounding aspects of the four strangers; at least not just yet.

Gunther continued, with a steady voice. "I am taking them back to my homestead. We recently fought against several Trogens, who came suddenly from the air, upon Harraks."

He saw the look of worry manifesting rapidly within Aethelstan's face.

"You are certain of this?" Aethelstan asked in a cautious tone. "Trogens?"

"Larger than men, inhuman and feral of visage, and incomparably fierce," Gunther confirmed. "There was no mistake. Their steeds were longer and more massive of body than the Himmerosen of your lands. The steeds were indeed Harraks. It burdens me to testify that they are now within your lands, Aethelstan, but know this without a doubt, and take heed that they are in your skies."

Aethelstan nodded at the somber words with a pensive expression. Gunther truly hated being the bearer of such awful tidings, which portended terrible days approaching, but Aethelstan was the sort of man who wanted nothing less than the full truth.

"It is fortunate that all of these people are still alive, though I lost one of my Jaghuns in the fighting," Gunther continued, the last words feeling like bile in his mouth as he uttered them.

"Your words are heavy to hear, Gunther, and I am sorry for your loss, yet they explain much. We have been suffering many losses of our own," Aethelstan replied dourly. "Patrols in the outer marches have been vanishing, and scouts sent forth by us have not returned. We have feared the worst, and now I think that we finally have our answer."

"So the Unifier has taken to raiding your lands? Gunther asked. "What profit is there in that?"

Aethelstan looked off for a moment, a distant look in his eye. His expression darkened as he looked back to Gunther.

"It is much worse than mere raids. You know of the full levy? The General Fyrd?" the thane asked.

Gunther nodded.

"Then I am afraid that it is only very dark tidings that I now bring you. It is a horrible payment for what you have done for us in these woodlands," Aethelstan said. "I am sure that you know of the large enemy force that has been mustering in the west for some time, as word of it has spread all throughout the land with the calling of the General Fyrd. It marches upon Saxany now, by the order of the Unifier. One great army, striding towards the Plains of Athelney. But it is not the only force. Nor are the Plains of Athelney the only path being taken by our adversaries."

Gunther's brow furrowed as he listened with increased worry to Aethelstan's words.

"Another enemy force is being sent this way," Aethelstan declared. "It is smaller than that which is heading towards the Plains, but it is no less of a threat. Knowledge of it has given us a chance to ready ourselves, to meet this second force in battle before it passes too deeply into our lands."

Aethelstan then fixed Gunther with a stare that conveyed the unprecedented gravity of the specter facing them all. "Be warned, Gunther. It is for no small reason that all have been called to arms across Saxany, farmer, herder, craftsman, bond-servant, and warrior alike."

No person looking could mistake the sharp concern rising upon Gunther's face, as he listened to Aethelstan's solemn words. The calling of a Select Fyrd was one matter, involving the summons of thanes, ceorls, and more veteran warriors. The calling of a General Fyrd, of all able bodied men to arms, was quite another entirely, and Gunther now understood the extent of its cause much clearer.

"Then what could I hope to offer you? I cannot stop an army," Gunther replied in a low, terse tone.

"The word that you give to us is more valuable than a precious gemstone. What forces we have been able to muster within Wessachia are gathered near, and I must know whatever I can about the enemy's approach and strength," Aethelstan inquired. "Every tiding is one less risk we have to fear. It is said that you know of everything that travels through these woods."

Underneath the strong tone of the thane's voice, Gunther could hear the undercurrents of a pleading urgency.

Gunther nodded his head slowly, knowing well the genuine concern that the Saxan leader held for the warriors under his leadership. It was the same concern that Aethelstan had for his people; one that was heartfelt and unrelenting.

"I only know a little. Though what little I know may fully answer your questions on the fate of patrols and scouts ... though these words are difficult to utter," Gunther said disconsolately. "The refugees that you see here were witness to the destruction of a large group of mounted Saxan warriors. I believe this group of horsemen may have been one of those from the fort garrisons in the marches. It was attacked by a much larger number of enemy warriors. ... By their description, these warriors were most certainly Trogens, upon Harrak sky steeds. You would not have heard about this attack, unless you came upon the carnage."

Gunther looked at Aethelstan with a heavier heart, pausing a moment before speaking his last words.

"They were slain to the last man."

Aethelstan looked down for a moment, has face appearing to be covered with shadow. Gunther watched the thane's mail-covered chest rise and fall with the deep breaths that he took.

When Aethelstan looked up to Gunther, his expression remained firm and well-composed, but his eyes reflected the growing weight within him.

"Is there any sign of an army among or near these woods yet?" he asked the woodsman.

"None that I have knowledge of, and I have been ranging about for many leagues over the past few days on a hunting foray," Gunther replied, shaking his head. "But the strength of the war bands in the sky would seem to be a sign of much stronger storms, already at the horizon. From what you have told me, and from what I have learned, I would counsel you to expect the enemy to arrive in this area, very soon."

Aethelstan took another deep breath, and his voice was deliberate and slow as he spoke his next words.

"When we were called to muster, we were warned that the enemy might come with a great number of sky warriors in their ranks. I can only think now of Edmund ... a man who is like a brother to me. ...

"He is a sky warrior, and upon the troubling word of a great enemy sky force he departed swiftly, seeking to gain as many Himmerosen and experienced sky riders as he could, to aid in our defense of the skies.

"He has not yet returned. With these tidings from you, of your own fight, and the one witnessed by these refugees, my fear for him grows even greater," Aethelstan concluded, before falling silent for a few strained seconds. "You speak truly in that the presence of large enemy air patrols on our borders bodes ill. ... Know that we will defend these lands with our lives, but the Unifier indeed sends forth great and terrible might.

Aethelstan paused, and for a moment he was a living image of trepidation. The moment passed quickly, as resolve flowed back into his countenance.

"We will continue to seek signs of the enemy forces, aware of the powerful threats from the air. We will seek the path where this enemy force will likely march," Aethelstan stated, speaking with a stronger presence of conviction. "Gunther, I will do what I can to warn you, if we are able to find the area where the enemy seeks to pass into these lands … and though I know your feelings, I want you to know that you would be most welcome within our ranks."

Gunther swallowed to clear his throat, as he considered his response.

"I am truly honored by your concern, Aethelstan, which you have shown by simply coming here," Gunther replied. "Know that I will do what I can to send word to you, should I learn of anything more."

Gunther halted as the hints of a frown came to his face. He disliked having to say his next words, as he knew how greatly Aethelstan wished for him to join with the Saxans in the face of the looming threat.

The woodsman stated evenly, "As you have known, I choose to live alone from the world of men as long as I have a free choice … and it is for good reason."

Even as he voiced the words, Gunther thought of the widespread muster that had just taken place. He considered all the hundreds and thousands of simple villagers who had been devoid of the free choice that he had.

He could not ignore the stark reality that his warding of that forest area from brigands and outlaws had given him the special privilege of having a choice. That truth was a great tragedy in Gunther's eyes. But despite his sympathies, he felt no regrets about exercising his own free will, other than the disappointment that he knew it would bring to the honorable thane before him.

"Yes, I do know, and I will respect your choice. Know that I will not seek to coerce you, nor will any under my authority," Aethelstan replied quietly.

Gunther then fixed Aethelstan with a rigid stare, his look carrying the unwavering sincerity within his next words. "Aethelstan, I do want you to know that if I chose to live fully within your world, and served in any army, under any man, then it would be a true honor to serve under you."

Aethelstan looked somewhat taken by surprise with the woodsman's sudden, laudatory statement. It was also evident that the Saxan leader was genuinely moved by the declaration.

"I do not know you well enough, woodsman, and perhaps one day you will share more tales of your journeys with me. But my instincts tell me that it is an honor to have been judged in such a way, in your eyes," Aethelstan said, inclining his head towards Gunther. "The refugees are under good care with you ... but also know that I give you my word that I will see to their needs, if you should ever feel a need to place them among my people. I wish you all good in life, and that the coming storms will pass without bringing you harm."

"And you as well, Thane Aethelstan," Gunther replied, giving the Saxan a slight bow.

Aethelstan raised an arm in farewell to Gunther, casting a last glance at the four refugees with the woodsman as he turned his proud stallion around. The men around him also brought their own steeds about, as Aethelstan led them back in the direction from which they had come. The metallic rustlings of their mail and the clops of hoof-steps faded steadily, lasting just a little longer than the sight of their forms amongst the trees.

"Who was that?" Lee inquired in a low voice, when Gunther and the other four were all alone once again.

"That is the thane Aethelstan, who serves the Ealdorman Morcar of Wessachia," Gunther explained. "His market town, which are known as burhs in these lands, is not altogether far from here, called Bergton. He has always seen to the protection and needs of the only villages that I care to visit, at Dragon's Back Ridge and Oak Crossing.

"Aethelstan is well above most men, in heart and honor. There are so few like him in this world. That is a misfortune to our kind. I shall tell you more of these lands, when we reach my home. But we must tarry here no longer. Come, we must get going, if you are to hope to adequately rest, and eat your fill. I do not wish to linger any longer outside of my own domain. Not when such storms are gathering."

Following the dangers that they had already been through, it came as no surprise to the woodsman that there was no dispute from any of the refugees as they started forward, resuming their march. The other four were quiet, lost in their own thoughts as they traveled in Gunther's wake.

They were not the only ones dwelling upon some inner concern, as the brief interaction with Aethelstan had given Gunther plenty to ponder himself. He was grateful for the uninterrupted time to think, as when they reached his homestead, he was certain that he would be faced with a barrage of questions.

A storm was approaching, and it was only a matter of time before it would break. Gunther had some notions of what could be done if the enemy swept through the woodlands, including taking some paths in the woodlands that even the Saxans were not aware of themselves. It was still too soon to make a decision, but it was good to keep all options in mind.

The immediate future boded more favorably. Visions of a good meal and an approaching stretch of repose beckoned invitingly to Gunther. As soon as he reached the sanctuary of his woodland haven, he would be able to partake of both.

The thought put a little extra spring into his step, as Gunther walked briskly forward at the head of the small group.

WULFSTAN

It was about midday when Wulfstan's eyes finally came to rest upon the sprawling, enormous collection of tents that formed the main field encampment for the swelling forces of Saxany. Having never before seen more than a few hundred warriors together at once in his own lifetime, at most perhaps a thousand, the vision before him was entirely breathtaking in scope.

The last stretch of the two-week-long journey had been a particularly difficult, half-day march. All elements of the Great Fyrd had been implicitly instructed to get to the Plains of Athelney as fast as was humanly possible. Every last moment of preparation was critical, according to the word that filtered down to the marching masses.

Wulfstan remembered the earliest stages of the summons well enough. Beacons lit on the summits of great hills soon resulted in a chain of smoking signals whose meaning was as unmistakable as it was urgent. Couriers and messengers dispatched to all parts of the kingdom had spread the alarm with tremendous rapidity. The word had raced throughout Wulfstan's home region in Sussachia, eliciting a great panic amongst the occupants of nearby villages, hamlets, and larger estates.

Wulfstan had quickly gathered up his arms and whatever provisions he could carry. Having said his goodbyes, he had hurried with some men from the nearby villages to the designated muster point for his territory, a place located just east of the fortified market-town of Langstenford.

From the muster point, it had been a most tiring march. More had been added daily as the main column passed by the other muster points set along the way. Like rivulets feeding into an ever-growing river, the many smaller musters combined their numbers with the growing column.

The larger market-towns that they had passed contributed supplies and provisions to the column. An abundance of swiftly collected materials and foodstuffs were given over to the force as it passed by, to be conveyed out to the great plains.

After a few days, more than a few men within the general Saxan ranks greatly envied the thanes and their houseguard, all of whom traveled mounted. The overwhelming number of the men in the column came from the sweeping, expansive levy of the common folk, known as the General Fyrd. There were very few from the Select Fyrd of thanes, ceorls, and the like who did not have a steed to assist their travel.

As a ceorl, Wulfstan was of a rank to qualify him for the Select Fyrd. Yet as fortune had not favored him, he was a ceorl that had not been afforded the luxury of a mount. As such, he had marched among the majority on foot. At the least, Wulfstan was not ill-prepared for the arduous endeavor, having gained some experience with enduring long marches on the two previous campaigns that he had been called to serve in.

Back at his uncle's homestead, near to the village of River's Edge, he was also used to a number of day-long forays into the woods to hunt. He wished that his current exertions were for such a purpose.

Wulfstan sensed a growing anxiety among the common men with each passing day. He could not belittle the nerve-wracked men in his heart.

They were all leaving places where they knew virtually every tree, animal, large rock, meadow, furrowed strip, and, most certainly, every person around them. It was no surprise that their anxiety had risen precipitously as they passed into a far land, where nothing was familiar, and everything hinted at a looming danger.

A couple of mild rains along the way had brought some periods of discomfort, but overall the skies had remained generously clear and bright throughout the long march. The first part of their march was conducted through the forests of Byrtnoth's lands, taking wide, beaten trails through woods that were known to contain outlaws and brigands. Once they had reached the Iron Heart Mountains, they had proceeded through a broad valley, and on into the tree-covered range of low hills that bordered upon the far eastern edge of the Plains of Aethelney.

At long last, the ground had started to level out, and the trees had begun to thin, until one day, on the edge of dusk, they had emerged out onto the great plains. From that point onward, it was little more than a night spent out in the open air, and the half-day brisk jaunt that they had just endured.

Out on the sprawling plains there were hundreds of field wagons and carts, with many more oxen and horses. The animals had been herded and gathered in large throngs far to the rear of the front line tents. The beasts were grazing idly where they dotted a wide expanse of grasses, and Wulfstan had no doubts that the creatures were grateful to be relieved of their burdens. The baggage train and attendant animals traveling with Wulfstan's own column would shortly be added to that mass.

Seeing the staggering sight of the encampment, Wulfstan's left hand inadvertently drifted towards the sword sheathed at his left side, his fingers clenching around the leather-wrapped hilt. His hand rested against the straight cross-guard, where the latter pressed against the metal rim that formed the lip of the scabbard. The flesh of his hand was barely covered by that short, horizontal bar, serving as the base of the untapered, double-edged blade.

His unstrung hunting bow of ash wood was carried in a loose grip in his right hand. A low-hanging, cylindrical quiver full of beech-shafted arrows rested just behind his right hip, affixed to a diagonal leather strap that looped across his body and up over his left shoulder. His current weaponry was rounded out with a long, single-edged seax, carried in a horizontally aligned sheath at his waist.

Wulfstan did not bear all of his means of war upon his own person.

His older chain mail shirt and segmented iron half-helm were currently stored on one of the ox-pulled wagons within the baggage train. So were a long, broad-bladed spear, and a large, newly crafted wooden shield, which had been given to him at the moment of his departure. Having some of the items placed on the wagon had taken a little of the burden off of the extended march, but there was no way that Wulfstan was about to part for even a moment with his sword; a sword that his very own father had directly passed down to him.

He closed his eyes for a moment, remembering a wisp and taste of that very day, when he was just sixteen summers in age.

Wulfstan gently fingered the loose hilt-ring, akin to one that would be worn on the finger, which was attached to a loop solidly attached to the tri-lobed pommel of the sword. He often wondered about the origin of that ring, as the full history of the sword had been lost to time.

His father, Ealdred, only knew that the sword was at least one hundred years old. Regarding the hilt-ring, he had indicated that it might have had something to do with being a symbol of an oath taken by one of their ancestors to their lord.

As his father had insisted that the blade had been passed straight down through their own family, Wulfstan had often wondered whether his forefathers had once fought at the right hands of greater lords. As a youth, it had been an inspiring fantasy to think that Wulfstan's own bloodline had once included renowned warriors.

The heirloom sword was about the only part of Wulfstan's equipment that had not been provided to him by his community.

The collective support of seven other families, totaling eight hides of land between them, had been required to equip him with his half-helm, mail shirt, and some provisions as a warrior of the Select Fyrd. Ever since his father had passed on following a long illness, not more than a year after he had bequeathed Wulfstan the sword, Wulfstan had lived with his uncle, Ealdhelm.

As a young, strong, single male, who had no overriding objections or obligations, Wulfstan had been a prime choice to be the one sent to the main musters to fulfill the families' commitment to the land's defense.

Wulfstan had been feeling fit and strong for the current sojourn, as he had just been engaged in the taxing labor of assisting in the annual plowing of his uncle Ealdhelm's fields.

Of a modest build, his five foot nine inch body was clad in a light brown, knee-length tunic of wool, with loose-fitting trousers wrapped about below his knees with long strips of cloth. Simple leather shoes caked in dried mud covered his feet.

A silver brooch at his right shoulder clasped a dark brown cloak that flowed out behind him. At the moment, his head was covered with a round cap of felt, also of an earthen color.

His face was starting to gain a dense, lengthening stubble, well-advanced and spread all over his cheeks and chin. The nascent growth went along with the pronounced, dirty blonde moustache that graced his upper lip.

Mentally, he had already admonished himself to shave the considerably established stubble, determined to maintain his regular habits, despite the presence of a nearing war. On his two previous campaigns, he had learned that such seemingly inconsequential things helped to keep his inner moorings in place.

Wulfstan's sharp eyes peered diligently outward from beneath his prominent eyebrows, a gaze that always seemed to take in his full surroundings. Sometimes, those keen gray eyes reflected the hardness of stone, and at other times they echoed the gentleness of a misty morning. The great vision of the enormous encampment and the horizon beyond it was enhanced by the clarity of the beautiful day, with nary a cloud in the sky. A bright sun stood out radiantly in the sky above, permeating the plains with a soothing warmth.

The massaging touches of a cool, soft breeze flowed intermittently across the plain. It was hardly conceivable to Wulfstan, in the presence of such a magnificent view, that a great and bloody battle was so very imminent.

That grave thought dampened the elating sensation summoned forth by the sheer breadth of the vision, as much as it reminded him of his troubling, recurring dreams; powerful images of storms, destruction, and the peculiar skyward ascension that the dreams always ended with. The stark visions had begun to revisit him with every passing night.

It was hard for Wulfstan to believe that he was standing on the fabled Plains of Athelney. He had heard the stories told over the years about the old Southern Kingdom, remembering the epic accounts of battles fought within the western Marches, many involving the vitally strategic plains that he was now seeing with his own eyes.

He looked out instinctively for any sign of the enemy on the western horizon, as his contingent continued on their march down towards the broad masses of tents. There was nothing as far as the eye could see to indicate the approach or presence of the enemy army. Beyond the line of tents, and the early efforts to dig camp trenches on the perimeter, the horizon was utterly silent and still.

Wulfstan's loose column was shortly brought to a halt, as materials for tents and other supplies were removed from the baggage train and carried onward by foot.

The slight delay at the cusp of reaching the end of the march was perhaps the most burdensome part of the entire journey. Now that they had arrived, the tired, anxious men were wholly focused on getting settled and acclimated.

Rest and sustenance beckoned tantalizingly close. There was more than a little grumbling by the time that the group of thanes finally roused the column to proceed.

Led by one of Ealdorman Byrtnoth's most senior thanes, Wulfstan's contingent strode through the midst of the vast multitude of tents, until they reached a cleared area towards the northern end of the huge encampment.

A number of Saxans from other parts of the realm hailed them warmly, as the arriving column passed by. Wulfstan and many of the others in his contingent returned the hearty greetings with boisterous salutations of their own.

Already, Wulfstan could feel the bonding undercurrents present with the men from the other regions of Saxany. While undoubtedly existing before the summons, those bonds had already been made much stronger by the shared threat that they were all now facing together. Rivalries existed between various regions of the kingdom, but such things were largely put aside when an existential danger towered over all the Saxan provinces.

Wulfstan's column immediately set about placing and erecting their tents, extending the size of the massive encampment even further. The tents were simple enough to set up, as those used by the common elements of the Saxan force had a nearly uniform size and design.

Wulfstan helped to set vertical poles in the ground at a measured distance, while his comrades laid out a rectangular canvas. A tubular sleeve ran down the middle of the canvases, through which a timber rod was slid to provide the backbone for the tent's ridge. He then helped to secure pegs in the ground along the lower edge of each long side of the canvas, through the holes that already pierced the material.

"We are here at last, at journey's end, and there is no need for any more marching, thank the All-Father," one of the men commented as he drove the last peg into the ground.

The speaker, a burly, middle-aged fellow named Siward, was from a village near to Wulfstan's own home. "I say we find us some good ale," Siward suggested. "And maybe a gleeman that can tell us some poems. Maybe even to a steady tune."

"Or maybe a round of riddles, what do you say?" piped in one of the others, a young, wild-eyed youth of about eighteen years old, whose name Wulfstan did not know.

"My knees can take no more marchin', but my throat is good for ale, and my ears good for poems or for riddles," added an older man, gray of beard, by the name of Bertulf.

"Yer ears for riddles maybe, but not yer brain," guffawed another older man.

A round of spirited laughter gripped the group around them at the jest.

"Put your pence on a riddle tonight, then, if ya feel so," retorted Bertulf, his tone laced with belligerency.

"I cannot, in good conscience, battle one who has no means of doing battle," replied the other, eliciting an uproarious round of laughter, while his belittled comrade groaned and cursed under his breath in frustration.

"Then I will match wits with you, and see your measure, my good man. I could use some pence of my own. But we have not finished yet," Wulfstan remarked with a grin to Bertulf's oppressor.

While he enjoyed riddles, Wulfstan had more of an affinity for the thick, bitter ale that was such a staple of Saxan life. Truly, that heavenly drink was what Wulfstan had his heart set on at that moment.

Yet ale, riddles, and even poems would have to wait.

"And do not forget, my friends, we still have some weapons to get back into our possession," Wulfstan reminded the others, after the levity had settled down a little.

Siward, still looking humored from the verbal exchanges, shook his head ruefully. "Maybe you are right. But it does not mean we cannot keep our minds on returning here for ale and song later! Don't know how long it will be before we fly into the outer dark again!"

Wulfstan smiled at the man's spirited declaration, though he could not help but feel a little bittersweet about Siward's last few words. A heavy weight was carried within Siward's reference to an old saying held among their people.

That Saxan saying likened a person's life to the flight of a bird through the hall of a thane. It described a bird's passage from a cold, outer darkness, into a hall full of warmth and companionship, and on out the other end of the hall, into the icy darkness once again.

Life was not unlike that image, as a man was born from the darkness to live for a brief time, before going back to the darkness from which he had first come. At least for now, Wulfstan knew that there could still be warmth and companionship. He had not yet reached the other end of the hall with its shadowy, mysterious veil, and he intended to stay within the light of life's hearth fire as long as he possibly could.

Wulfstan turned about, sweeping his gaze around as he called out loudly, "Then once we have our weapons in hand again, ale and song sounds good to me too! What say the rest of you?"

A number of the men responded with a vibrant cheer, attracting some attention from other nearby warriors at the sudden burst of enthusiasm. Wulfstan laughed to himself, for even though the specter of war was undeniably hanging over all of them, his people would never omit a good opportunity for ale and song.

"Then let us finish what needs to be done, so we can see to our wants," Wulfstan said to the men around him.

Wulfstan, and the others that had finished erecting their tents, set out to retrieve their weapons and equipment still remaining with the oxcarts, wagons, and packhorses of the column's baggage train.

The walk to where the baggage train was being quartered was a considerable distance. The carts, wagons, and draft animals were purposely set farther back from the frontal areas of the Saxan army's lines. An enemy would not find the baggage trains of the Saxan ranks easy prospects to reach.

Wulfstan found that his great round shield, its iron boss crafted with a pointed apex, was on the same cart as his mail shirt. He donned the mail shirt so that he did not have to carry it back, and then grabbed his shield.

Before going onward, he paused for a moment to run his fingers over the iron rim that went around the outer edge of the shield's face. Underneath its painted, hide-covered facing, the shield was made of stout wood planks, yet undamaged by combat. Soberly, he reflected that the handful of wood planks and thin layer of hide would be all that stood between him and the blades and arrows of the enemy in coming days.

Another nearby cart held his iron half-helm, resting atop one of the cart's posts, along with an elongated lance that was bundled with others in the body of the cart. The lance's broad blade and extensive shaft were to Wulfstan's preference. It was a weapon rather effective for parrying styles of combat that involved slashing and thrusting.

His half-helm was of the time-honored, battle-tested spangenhelm design, a quartet of iron plates riveted to an iron frame, and provided with an iron nasal guard descending from the brow band. Slinging the shield across his back by its leather strap, Wulfstan put on the helm, to wear it for the trek back to his tent.

From his vantage among the numerous ox-carts and wagons, he espied the distant tents of the merchant groups. Despite his deep misgivings about them, he paused and thought for a moment about seeing to some maintenance issues for his gear.

He only had a few silver pennies with him, several of which were only half-coins. After some consideration, he thought better of the idea, deciding to return to the main camp, and opting to hold onto his meager aggregate of coins.

In a short time, there would be even more merchants drawn to the army's presence, like leeches gravitating to the promise of blood under bared skin. The growing numbers of merchants would undoubtedly create much more room for haggling, which was not to the disadvantage of the buyer. In an environment of increased negotiation and options, Wulfstan would find that his few full coins and several half-coins would suddenly grow in their purchasing capacity.

At the very least, the greed of the merchants was firmly limited by the King's own law. They could not exact greater prices from their buyers than those found outside of a time of war. Yet even with the clear writ of the King himself, it still took constant diligence on the part of the King's servants and household guard to watch for violations, and enforce the edict.

If Wulfstan were king, and the entire land were in true danger, he would have demanded whatever was needed without concern for profit. Perhaps that was why his blood was not royal, Wulfstan mused to himself, with a grin spreading upon his face.

As he meandered back towards the teeming expanse of tents, he slowed down in the open ground to watch as a large, oncoming column of mounted warriors approached from the southeast.

In a few moments, their vanguard was passing directly in front of Wulfstan. Triangular pennons hanging from the lances of many of the warriors bore a field of golden stars set upon a purple background. It was the distinctive symbol of the Count Leidrad of Poitaine, whose lands were steeped in lore, a considerable power even in the days of the old Southern Kingdom.

Count Leidrad himself was riding in the lead of the lengthy column, as the heavy cavalry formation was largely comprised of his household retinues and other main garrisons. He sat high in his saddle, the cloth underneath it matching the purple of the pennons. The steady breeze cascading across the plain gently tousled his thick, silvery hair about.

He wore an elegant tunic of deep blue, with elaborate, golden embroidery worked along its collar, hem, and the ends of the sleeves. His great blue cloak matched the hue of the tunic closely. Earthen colored trousers, the bottoms of which disappeared into boots graced with bronze prick spurs, completed the Count's splendid attire.

A squared jaw, a large nose with a pronounced arch to it, shaped as such due to more than one prior breakage, and a pair of deep-set eyes were the most noticeable features of his bearded face. He was a strong-looking man, though he carried a slight paunch in the belly and a little roundness of cheek in his later years.

Wulfstan marveled at the eminent presence of the great Count, while regretting that it was only in a time of war that he was afforded the chance to see the great lords of the Saxan realm in person.

The mounted column behind the Count was a special sight in itself.

Most mounted warriors in Saxany did not fight on horseback, especially in the lands that once comprised the old North Kingdom. The great thanes of both past and present from the latter territories were well content to ride to the battlefield and dismount to fight. Such was the time-honored fashion, for men who viewed their place as within their great shield walls, standing shoulder to shoulder with their fellow men.

The column that passed Wulfstan was part of the other kingdom of old, which had embraced methods of war using both horse and rider. Of course, these were also the lands that were more favorable to such styles, containing broader plains and less mountainous regions.

Contingents such as those under Count Leidrad were now the true cavalry of the Saxan Kingdom. The steeds that they rode came from areas of Saxany that possessed legendary stud farms, which bred formidable war horses.

The superb horses seemed to know their own heritage, as they cantered proudly across the open field. Many hundreds trotted by Wulfstan as he watched, the ground reverberating steadily with their iron-shod steps.

CROWN OF VENGEANCE

A modest host of leather-covered ox-carts, pack horses, and a large contingent of infantry followed the mounted force. Wulfstan knew that there were multitudes of lances, scale armor, mail armor, and shields for the main heavy cavalry piled within the creaking carts being pulled forward by plodding oxen.

Wulfstan waited idly as the multitude of supply carts passed. A number of warriors gathered near to him, several hailing the newcomers as they awaited their passing.

The cries of "Be hale, and be whole!" rang out, from both those marching as well as those watching, as the forces from Poitaine were enthusiastically greeted during their arrival.

As the last of the carts passed by their position, a few of the bystanders continued onward. Wulfstan took a couple of steps along with them, but then hesitated, his curiosity piqued by the sight of a second horse-borne formation approaching. It was just then coming into view, from a more southwestern direction than the force with Count Leidrad had come from.

Wulfstan's interest compelled him to patience, and he took a seat down upon the ground to take in the sight of the second column's approach. As a man that had never gone very far from his home village, he hungered to see the things that he had only heard spoken of before.

The second group of riders finally drew near, and Wulfstan was glad that he had waited. The riders of this group all bore deep red cloaks, as well as large pennons exhibiting a green background, with the figure of a large white horse in the middle.

Another crowd of onlookers quickly assembled, and from their comments Wulfstan confirmed to himself that he was indeed seeing the fabled riders of Bretica. He felt a tingle of excitement as he heard them openly named.

These were the storied riders whose great war horses thundered into battle clad in magnificent scaled armor. He had heard incredible tales of their feats ever since he was a boy, told by traveling storytellers, men of the village, and even his own father.

Fiercely independent and proud, the Breticans were not a people easily subdued or ruled under duress. The host of tales speaking of their ferocious resistance to Midragardan raiders proclaimed such notions boldly. Those accounts were also warnings to any foolhardy enough to try and compel the Breticans to their will.

The Breticans enjoyed great autonomy in the lands under their dominion, and for good reason. Their ire, when roused, was truly something to be feared according to all accounts.

The threat coming from the west had resonated in a rapid and powerful muster of the Breticans, who had unflinchingly, and hastily, moved northwards to stand with the rest of the Saxan realm.

At their head was the famed Count Gerard II, whose own praises had already been sung by famed gleemen, and told by the most renowned of storytellers, all across the kingdom.

A powerfully built man just entering his later years, his thick, wavy locks that had once been midnight black were now laced with ample streaks of gray. His sharp blue eyes scanned the camp and bystanding throng, nodding curtly to various individuals as they hailed him.

His expression remained stern and proud, like the reputation of the stalwart ensemble that he was leading into the huge encampment. His beard and moustache graced an angular, long face with a prominent nose that was decidedly acquiline in its profile.

At the moment, the magnificent horses present in the stately entourage were spared the burdens of the scale armor, having traveled for countless leagues from the farthest southeastern reaches of Saxany.

Wulfstan could only imagine what the Bretican ranks would look like when readied in full battle array. The majority of the Bretican riders matched the character of their stout horses, in that they were proud of demeanor and powerful of build. They were courteous enough to the enthusiastic hails coming from the crowd all around Wulfstan, but they maintained a high posture within their saddles.

The men on foot behind them looked exceedingly tired, and visibly relieved to have reached the camp. Wulfstan's sympathies lay with the infantry. Like the commoners with Wulfstan, they had undergone a very strenuous march without the benefit of having horses to carry them.

"Did ya save any of your storied ale? I want to see if it as good as yer tales say!" yelled out one spirited fellow in their ranks, who was using his tall spear almost as a walking stick.

"Come by our tents, and we will spare ya some. Ya walked far enough, lad. But the question is, can ya southern lads handle our drink? It is not often that we northerners can put you lads to the test!" replied one of those near Wulfstan, a somewhat portly, balding fellow with a broad grin.

His comments drew a lively round of laughter from the onlooking crowd.

"You will know the skills of Hincmar soon enough, when I take you up on your offer," boasted the other, a hearty smile shining through his weary face.

"We shall see, Hincmar of Bretica! Come by my tent, and we will give ya the chance!" the paunchy northerner retorted amiably, waving to Hincmar as the Bretican infantry trudged onward.

When the rest of the Bretican column had passed, Wulfstan felt that his return back to his tent was now long overdue. He did not want to miss the promised ale and song among his own companions. Wulfstan strode quickly towards the sector of the encampment that held the Sussachian tents.

Nevertheless, his witnessing of new arrivals had not quite ended. This time, he did not draw to a halt by choice, instead feeling compelled to come to a stop due to the imminence of yet another column approaching, this one coming from the northwest.

Impatience was now getting the best of him, overriding any curiosities that he had. Spurring himself forward, he hustled across the column's line of approach.

Yet despite his strong urge to continue forward, once he was safely on the other side of the column's path he decided to spare a few moments to indulge his abiding curiosities. The continuing wealth of new and fascinating sights was just too difficult to resist, especially for a man who had seen only Sussachia and a little of the Mittevald in his life.

Wulfstan saw that this third arriving group was wholly comprised of light cavalry. Listening to some nearby conversation, he soon learned that the riders were from northern reaches of Count Einhard's lands. The Count's territory of Annenheim lay just to the north of the most western marches of the Saxan Kingdom.

There were a good number of warriors and horses in Count Einhard's force. Yet as the contingent did not entail infantry or a baggage train, the overall formation was considerably smaller than the previous two columns from Poitaine and Bretica.

The bloodline of these Annenheim warriors was very close in kinship to that of Wulfstan's own ancestors. In truth they had once been of the same tribe of barbarian warriors. He knew this tale very well, and thought about it as he eyed his ancient kin for the first time.

Long ago, a very momentous choice had come to the barbarian

people regarding their religious commitments. Followers of the church of the West had arrived within the lands occupied by the great tribe. Traveling through the lands, they had brought their message of faith, performed signs and healings, and had called upon the populace to embrace the All-Father, and Emmanu the Redeemer.

The response had been fractious for the formerly unified tribe. The people of Wulfstan's lands had chosen to embrace the religion of the All-Father. Their tribal brethren in the western part of the land had rejected the overtures of the new faith's adherents, remaining steadfast in the worship of their people's ancient gods.

The association between the related people had subsequently grown ever more distant over the ensuing ages, due solely to the two factions' chosen forms of religion. The large rift had only begun to heal following the subjugation of the polytheistic occupants of what was now Annenheim, during the period of the Two Kingdoms.

The conquest took place in the age when the lands now under those such as Count Einhard, Count Leidrad, and Count Gerard had been squarely within the rule of the Southern Kingdom. It had happened in the near mythical time of King Theodulf the Great, when the Southern Kingdom stretched even into the easternmost part of what was now the realm of Ehrengard.

Following several grueling wars, and the ensuing final conquest by King Theodulf, the rest of the formerly unified barbarian tribe had been converted to the Western Faith. Though not accomplished by peaceable means, that singular act brought closer associations advancing once again between Wulfstan's people and the ones that they had then acknowledged as their prodigal kin.

The warriors in the horse-riding war band before Wulfstan were equipped with little more than round shields and spears. Only a few had iron half-helms to cap their heads protectively. The tales that Wulfstan was aware of indicated that these lightly armed riders were very capable of conducting fast and damaging raids in the lands of enemies.

They had long been renowned for their style of fighting, ambushing and raiding, spanning times both before and after King Theodulf. How they would be employed in a titanic clash of armies, such as the coming battle with the invaders certainly would be, Wulfstan could not tell.

There was no rider among them to match the preeminent presence of Count Leidrad or Count Gerard. Wulfstan looked over the column in disbelief, as he could not believe that the prominent Count Einhard would arrive in a subdued, unrecognizable manner.

His doubts were answered a short time later. From what Wulfstan was able to gather from snippets of nearby conversations surrounding him, Count Einhard's main forces had already arrived and settled in the camp.

The main contingent from Annenheim was evidently positioned towards the center of the Saxan camp. It stood to obvious reason that the riders before Wulfstan had arrived separately, and later than the main force. The lighter cavalry would likely have been used to shadow the Count's march, warding the main force's flanks and rear from a distance.

Having already witnessed the processions of the warriors of Bretica and Poitaine, Wulfstan was not quite as enthusiastic to watch the Annenheim column pass by in its entirety. The accelerating pangs of his empty stomach finally galvanized him, as he turned away and trudged onward, heading towards the tents of his comrades.

The evening's gloaming was now settling in all around the encampment, the western horizon dimming towards the edge of night by the time that he ultimately reached his own tent.

His fellow Sussachian men, as he had expected, had already procured a moderate quantity of ale. His closest comrades had congregated around one particular campfire, where they were preparing a hearty joint of beef to accompany a quantity of bread that they had begun distributing.

The men were unabashedly distributing prodigious quantities of drink as well. Wulfstan watched the meat slowly roasting upon the spit, as it was diligently turned by one of his comrades. The scents wafting from the campfire caused his mouth to water immediately, and his mind to fixate upon the empty state of his belly.

He realized just how famished and thirsty he had grown. Pulling himself away from the tempting atmosphere, he walked a short distance away and placed his weapons and shield down within the opening of his own tent. When he had finished, he strode back over to the side of the blazing fire.

Fortunately for Wulfstan, the roasting was finished just a short time later. After letting a couple of the others have access to the meat, he withdrew his single-edged knife and sliced himself off a sizeable helping. He added it to his share of the bread and cheeses that were being apportioned.

He was then handed a wooden cup by Siward, which was filled to the rim with thick ale. From the expression and swaying manner of

Siward, it was clear that the fellow from Miller's Creek village had already partaken generously of Saxany's cherished elixir.

Wulfstan slapped Siward on the back thankfully, and took a deep swill of the stout ale. A soft evening breeze caressed his face, as he felt the welcome rush of the thick liquid down his parched throat.

"Now, that is Saxan ale," Wulfstan remarked with satisfaction, taking a deep breath. He shared a grin with Bertulf, who was sitting to Siward's other side with a glazed look to his eyes, and a quite content expression.

"Time for ale, time for song, and a time for riddles," Siward replied. "Been at the ale. You were away for some time, Wulfstan."

"Just got caught up watching some of the new arrivals. Some procession it was! Not often that we've had a chance to see the harvest of Poitaine, Bretica, and Annenheim," Wulfstan answered, before asking with a grin, "So have you been giving troubles to Bertulf while I've been gone?"

"That thick skull?" Siward said, raising his eyebrows and jabbing his thumb in Bertulf's direction.

Next to Siward, Bertulf just continued drinking out of his cup, quite oblivious to the other's words. His stupefied grin accented Siward's words in a very humorous way. Wulfstan rumbled with laughter at the sight.

"No. Figure since Father Dunstan is here among us, I would do as a proper religious man," Siward continued in a voice thick with sarcasm, as he feigned a concerned expression. "Be kind to those who are afflicted, ya know. All-Father did not see fit to give the poor man a brain. He has his burden in this life, and I just don't wanna add to it. It's the right thing to do. "

Siward's mock serious countenance crumbled, as he then broke out into a big belly-laugh. He was clearly amused with himself, and impressed with his own wit. Wulfstan could only shake his head and laugh to himself at the ridiculousness of it all.

Bertulf's brow slowly furrowed, as if he was just becoming aware of the possibility that he was the subject of the outburst of merriment. "What you ... say?" Bertulf responded in a drawling slur, his grin shortening as his eyes narrowed irritably. "Ya think ya know everything about me ... I will have ya know, ya just think ya do, Siward. Ya know nothing ... nothing at all."

"Oh … go back to yer cup, old man," interrupted Siward, still chuckling as he winked at Wulfstan. Siward's eyes then swerved back forward, and he paused as a look of recognition came into them. "Well, well. Father Dunstan looks about ready to sing."

Wulfstan followed Siward's eyes to gaze across to the opposite side of the circle around the fire. Just a moment later, a deep, melodious voice rang out among the gathered men, accompanied by the notes of a small, harp-like instrument. The raucous laughter and conversation died down quickly among those gathered around.

Even the gatherings around nearby campfires quieted down as others heard the sonorous voice of the priest carried on the currents of the night air. Wulfstan grinned widely as the vibrant light from the fire flickered across the thin features of Father Dunstan, whose physical appearance did not substantiate such a powerful and rich voice.

It would be a mistake to assume that the priest's slight frame meant any degree of weakness. Wulfstan had always marveled about how utterly tireless Father Dunstan was. The All-Father seemed to have given him a generously resilient health. In his early forties, Father Dunstan was as robust and energetic as he had always been in Wulfstan's memory.

The kindly, dedicated priest had always attended diligently to everyone that needed help in Wulfstan's home area, no matter the time of day or night. He was there in the darkest of times, and he was there in the brightest of times. The commoners could say in truth that he had been a part of nearly every major incident in the lives of all the peasants who lived within the boundaries of his parish.

It was the major reason that Father Dunstan had come with the men summoned to the great levy. Where he could have chosen to remain back in the small village church, well-removed from all danger, Father Dunstan had made it clear that he was not about to let the men go into a time of great risk and danger, without facing the ordeal right alongside them. His choice engendered a deep loyalty that resounded through the men from River's Edge and the surrounding villages and hamlets.

Wulfstan's sense of gratitude at the sight of the diminutive man came from more than just that willingness to share in the commoners' burdens. Father Dunstan had also found time to help some of the youth of the village learn to capably read and write letters. He had given them a luxurious opportunity, one that village peasants would have otherwise rarely had access to.

Wulfstan was one of those fortunate youth, and had become one of the only ones in his family that could read for himself from the Sacred Writings. It was a deeply precious gift, and had become another of the many reasons why Father Dunstan was so very loved and revered.

The holy man began to sing a tale of valor, the lay of Saint Offa the Martyr. The esteemed story of a brave Saxan King, who had died at the hands of Midragardan raiders in a very brutal manner, was very well-known. It came from a litany of stories of warriors, kings, and saints that graced the Saxans' rich heritage.

Father Dunstan's thin fingers danced deftly along the strings of his instrument, and his eyes sparkled as he looked out among the men. Seeing Wulfstan, Father Dunstan gave him a quick, acknowledging wink, as he headed into another verse. Wulfstan nodded and smiled warmly in return.

The words seemed to flow with the steadiness of a mountain stream, his cadence and rhythm demonstrating that the priest had quite a mastery over the art of oral storytelling. Far from the flamboyance of a tale-spinner in King Alcuin's court, clad simply in a loose-fitting, long dark tunic, with a squared, lighter-colored mantle atop, Father Dunstan gave the common men a rendition worthy of a royal audience.

Father Dunstan had once related to Wulfstan that his father had taught him such arts as a child, before he had gone off to a monastery to learn his letters and start on the road that had led him to becoming a parish priest. Wulfstan had no doubts that the man could have soared to fame if he had chosen another path in life.

Not all men of faith would approve of his singing of tales to the common men. Indeed, Wulfstan knew that some would take great offense at the priest's activity, but Father Dunstan's concern was not for what others thought of him. He was solely focused upon the welfare of those that he administered to.

As the stories Father Dunstan tended to tell were largely oriented on the lives of saints, the subject matter really did not stray far from his convictions and task. A little song to raise the spirit, to Wulfstan, was not such a bad thing.

It was yet another one of the reasons why Wulfstan and the other men so loved their parish priest.

Wulfstan took leave of Siward and Bertulf, and edged his way inward, coming to a free spot in the circle that was situated a little closer to Father Dunstan. He took a seat upon the ground, now close enough to gain more warmth from the fire in the rapidly cooling evening.

An earthenware jug held by another one of his companions was close at hand, to replenish Wulfstan when his cup was empty. His cares steadily relaxed, as many of the men accompanied Father Dunstan on a chorus that sang of a heroic battlefield stand by Saint Offa against a heathen horde.

Wulfstan gave a quick prayer of gratitude in his heart for the special moment. For a time, he would be sharing good bread, ale, and some meat with the men who had come so far together from their shared homeland. As night deepened, they would enjoy even more song and a generous allotment of ale.

Wulfstan chose to savor the moment, and he kept the worries about the future at bay. What would come, would come. Life would bring what it would, and there was nothing that he could do to alter that. For the present, he was still flying through the warmth and companionship of the long hall, wings yet beating strong in between the windows to the outer darkness.

As far as he was concerned, Wulfstan resolved to sustain his presence in that hall of life and friendship.

section vi

LOGAN

As the day finally reached its merciful conclusion, the four exiles trudged wearily back towards the stockaded village atop the large hill's summit.

They possessed an abundance of sore muscles, and four cavernous appetites that begged attention. Rest and sustenance were of the highest priority.

A collective body of knowledge needed to be instilled among the otherworlders within a short amount of time, and the group had once again been split three ways in the early morning. Each unit was to return at the end of the day with more knowledge gained in their designated areas, bringing a greater wisdom and set of skills to the group as a whole.

If there was enough time for it, Logan had learned that they would eventually rotate, but collective knowledge was the initial priority.

For Erika, Antonio, Derek, and Logan, the day had been extremely physical in nature, sorely testing their current levels of conditioning. The hard physical efforts undertaken had undoubtedly obstructed their minds from idly wandering, or thinking too much about their troubling circumstances.

In this way the distractions were a relief in themselves, as they all continued along their path of adjusting to the elements of a new and uncertain world. In a true sense, the arduous day was both an exhausting challenge for the body, as well as a very welcome respite for the mind and spirit. Logan ultimately was quite thankful for it, even as sweat darkened the front of his tunic and spread about his neck, chest, and back.

The four otherworlders had all expressed their heartfelt gratitude for an extended swim in the cool, soothing waters of a wide creek near the end of the day. By that time, their bodies had become caked and sticky with sweat from the day's exertions.

The immersion in the crisp, clear waters had been particularly invigorating to Logan.

Much had been accomplished within a relatively short time, and they were all well underway in their instruction in the nuances of the woods around them. They had also begun to learn the use of some weapons, including archery, axes, and the formidable tribal war clubs.

Their instructors had kept a close eye trained upon them, and had been firm but encouraging in their tutoring and guidance.

When they were left alone at one point for a few moments early in the day, Logan had wondered aloud to Derek as to why the warriors would bring them to an area where they could potentially escape if they meant the village any harm. Derek remarked that he had been perplexed by the same observation.

The answer to the seeming mystery had not taken very long to manifest. After seeing the highly advanced skills demonstrated by the warriors with the various weapons, and seeing the ease with which the tribesmen silently glided among the trees and melted into shadows, Derek and Logan had understood.

The tribal people, without question, truly held the upper hand as it regarded the circumstances of the otherworlders. This was their native realm, and Logan knew that only the most foolhardy of strangers would have thought seriously of setting off through the tribal woodlands under hostile circumstances.

The day itself had proceeded smoothly enough, but the experiences of the guests were quite varied. Out of all of them, Erika enjoyed an advantage on the other guests, even Derek in some respects. She had evidently been steeped with an affinity for the outdoors all throughout her life, something that she spoke openly about during one of their brief respites. Logan did not dispute her claim, seeing the genuine enthusiasm radiating off of her as the group delved into their various exercises.

She also possessed a modest amount of prior experience with the use of bows, though the ones that she had used before were far different in construction from the type proffered to her by their warrior-teachers. The long wooden bows used by the tribal warriors were much simpler in design, and undeniably tougher to use. Yet it was not long before she had adjusted to them.

The group knew that she harbored some pride in this, as it had become more clear that the warriors were not entirely comfortable with the idea of Erika undergoing a warrior's training. The women of the tribes were not warriors or hunters, and though not at ease, the warriors proved reticent to openly judge the ways of their new charges.

After the day was well underway, Logan and Derek had spoken a little more candidly to one of the warriors who seemed more approachable. They had pulled him aside for a moment, as Erika worked with her bow. The two had expressed that Erika was just as vulnerable as they were in the new world, and would need the same survival skills. They had also impressed upon the tribal warrior the idea that Erika came from a world where some women were warriors and hunters.

Erika's aptitude with the bow managed to soften some of the lingering tension in the tribal warriors. They were impressed with her acclimation to the bow, which seemed to help them better accept the idea of her training with weapons.

Logan gained a genuine appreciation for her ability, as he labored with his own bow of ash wood.

Antonio, having led a highly sedentary existence prior to coming into the world of Ave, struggled the most, by a wide margin. He evoked several moments of light-hearted laughter during the day, from both teacher and student alike. He took everything in good humor, often poking fun at himself. The instructors still pushed him hard as the day transpired, but subtly eased their expectations at his ongoing struggles.

Logan and Derek did not suffer quite as much of an ordeal as Antonio. Logan was very studious in his approach to their tribal teachers, asking the most questions. Derek was the most physical out of all of them, and quite zealous to try various actions out, especially with the tribal weapons.

While Logan demonstrated a rapid ability to learn and the physicality to execute new movements, Derek quickly showed his great aptitude with the weapons. He also demonstrated a raw strength and agility that matched the best of their instructors.

He wielded the heavy, curving war club vigorously, muscles flowing with power as he brought the dense, solid orb of wood at the end of the weapon rushing through the air with lethal force. Derek leaped and twisted with vitality as he sliced the air with the blade of an axe. It did not take him long at all before his own shots on his oaken bow were nearly as steady and well-targeted as Erika's. He adapted to movements and techniques very quickly, drawing many outward compliments from their teachers.

The other three exiles had watched Derek's martial display with unfettered admiration. Logan was extremely impressed with their comrade's dexterous and strong execution, and remarked as much to Derek on several occasions. It was clear that Derek's skills with the specific weapons would match his natural ability in due time. Logan mused that their instructors would have readily agreed with the Midragardan Eirik in his esteemed assessment of Derek, in a purely physical sense.

The tribal warriors seemed very pleased with what they had seen with the exiles, other than Antonio, by the end of the day. Logan was glad that they had earned some respect, though he was also quite ready to rest and eat.

His legs protested as he began to surmount the incline of the hill. In his fatigue, the slope seemed to have become much steeper since he had descended it in the morning.

"Would you check that out," Derek remarked, as he walked at Logan's side.

Derek was pointing up into the skies. Logan followed his gesture, just in time to see a pair of winged creatures approaching the hilltop village. Upon the backs of the beasts were two riders, whose identities became clearer as they descended towards the interior of the village.

"If Janus could have one, couldn't they have spared us a few?" Logan posited, recognizing their companion in one saddle and Ayenwatha in the other, feeling a little envy at their comrade's opportunity.

"That is something I will have to speak with Ayenwatha about," Derek replied with a chuckle. "We sure could use a ride up the hill at the end of a day like this."

"At the least, I bet he had a very interesting day," Logan said.

"No doubt that he did, but if we're going to hear about it I want to be filling my belly as I listen," Derek commented.

"I am with you all the way on that," Logan replied with a grin. He looked back up and watched as Janus, Ayenwatha, and their incredible winged mounts disappeared from view, dipping beneath the outer stockade.

MERSHAD

At a location near the sprawling clearings containing the village's growing crops, Kent and Mershad had endured a day much more cerebral in nature. The mental aspect of their particular training was something that apparently burdened Kent much more than it did him, as Mershad had to listen to many whispered laments from his comrade throughout the course of the day. He could tell that Kent hungered for a little physical activity, and did not share Mershad's more academic outlook. Even so, both of them were ultimately weighed down by the day's lessons.

At least they got to bask in the sun, and enjoy the favorable weather. Their teachers were patient enough, tolerating their many curiosities and questions throughout the day-long session.

The instruction was balanced evenly between a village elder and two clan matrons, one from the Tortoise Clan, and another from the Deer Clan. They were all gifted oral storytellers; their expressions and the lilt in their voices making even the drier topics sound fascinating.

When they had begun the day, Mershad harbored one lingering concern that proved to be unfounded. When he gently sought to take a break, so that he could observe his prayers, explaining his desire and regular practice of doing so, the clan matrons and elder were very accommodating, if not openly encouraging. If anything, they appeared to be a little taken aback that Kent did not join Mershad in the observance.

Mershad moved a short distance away to be more discreet in his ritual, but when he rose up after finishing he saw the older man and two women watching him with interest. He appreciated their acceptance very much, though he was becoming ever more aware of the deep spirituality of the tribal people, something that was interwoven with everything about their life.

At the day's conclusion, the two had absorbed much more about the history of their new world, and the customs observed within it. Though Mershad's retention was more extensive than Kent's, he knew that they were both simply glad to unveil some of the mysteries of the world that was now their own.

By the day's end, Mershad knew that they had reached a point where they could take in no further lessons. Kent's attention was beginning to drift as he became more mentally fatigued. For Mershad's part, he hungered for some time to wind down, and digest the wealth of new information more fully.

Kent had quipped that he was on the brink of overload, rubbing his head and sighing as they walked through the trees to rejoin their other companions. Mershad had expressed his agreement with Kent, even as he felt an eagerness to learn what had transpired with the others.

Erika had gone off into the woods with Logan, Derek, and Antonio, while Janus had gone off with Ayenwatha by himself. Mershad could not help but wonder why Janus was singled out, to conduct his training alone. It was a mystery that deepened a short time later, when he saw Janus returning through the skies with Ayenwatha, mounted upon a pair of incredible, winged steeds.

Seeing Janus gliding in on the creature, Mershad found that he had room for at least one more lesson that day, if Janus or Ayenwatha were willing to accommodate him. The matrons and elder had not discussed anything about the winged creatures as of yet, but the possibilities invoked by the idea of flying steeds stoked the fires of curiosity in Mershad.

Mershad shook his head and laughed to himself, thinking about how recently he had been huddling away in a dormitory room. Now, he was wondering if he might have an opportunity to fly, saddled upon a winged beast that looked like a living myth.

THE UNIFIER

"My Lord," came a low, deferential voice, from just a few feet behind Him.

The Unifier had heard the figure emerge out onto the surface of the tower, just moments before.

If the owner of the voice had been able to see the Unifier's face at the moment, he would have beheld solid, bright red eyes that gazed out well beyond the outskirts of the city. The burning stare penetrated far beyond even the outer boundaries of Avanor, piercing the horizons themselves, and worlds beyond.

The Unifier slowly turned His gaze away from the vantage that offered Him such a stunning view of the city, His now-blue eyes attentive upon the lone man standing behind Him.

Dressed in a long white habit, quite similar to that worn by the Clarvasian monks, was one of the most powerful of the Unifier's Sorcerers, and one of His few regular personal attendants.

Baalmon's eyebrows stretched in nearly invisible, white arches over eyes that were usually icy cold, and rigidly impassive. At the present, they reflected a glint of fear, which resonated in the nervous twitch that pulled at the upper lip of the Sorcerer's broad mouth.

Baalmon's nostrils flared briefly as he took in a quick breath of air, almost having neglected to breathe while in the Unifier's immediate presence. His hands remained folded tightly before him, his arms framing the single pendant that hung down his chest. The pendant was crafted into the image of a silver star, with its many straight, extending protrusions, representing rays of light.

"Baalmon, I have been expecting you," the Unifier addressed the other calmly, watching the steadfast breeze tug at the flowing fabric of His servant's linen habit. The Unifier spoke in a voice that was at once pleasing to the ear, an immaculately smooth, low tone palatable to any listener. Underneath the surface, the voice carried a subtle undercurrent of authority, an authority that those such as Baalmon never forgot, not even for an instant.

The Unifier almost smiled in amusement, as He often did at the predicament of His Sorcerers. They were well aware that any errant thoughts or deceits could not be hidden within their minds, which would not hesitate to betray them to the Unifier, despite their best efforts or concentration.

The Unifier drew pleasure whenever He first revealed that aspect of Himself to a person who had no inkling of His deeper natures. He had watched many who had thought that they could obscure their thoughts grovel in sheer terror, at the moment when they had learned of their inner nakedness to the Unifier's pervading gaze.

Adding to the disconcertment of a Sorcerer's private meeting with the Unifier, Baalmon had to endure the conversation without the benefit of the illusory façade that the Unifier displayed with most others. The Unifier did not bother to exhibit the gratuitous smile and eloquent manner that He carried in public situations with His Sorcerers in private. His countenance was implacably stern, void of all masks of compassion, empathy, or selfless concern. His piercing eyes were unforgiving and exacting in their scrutiny, the iciness in them stripped of any mirage of warmth or kindliness. The face that Baalmon looked upon was the most honest expression of the Unifier's incarnate form.

"What word do you bring me?" The Unifier asked. "The war now moves to the south, and will take place there for some time. I can wait no longer concerning those matters."

"Your group of trained Darroks is ready to go forth, my Lord," Baalmmon replied, his eyes lowered towards the tower's surface in front of his feet.

He could not bring his eyes to look into those of the Unifier, and the Unifier knew that it was all that the Sorcerer could do to keep his voice steady. Such was the regular condition of those that knew the Unifier most intimately.

In public, where the Unifier put on many charming guises, the Sorcerers had to muster discipline, careful to hide their fear of Him.

"Ready to be prepared, or truly ready to leave for the east?" the Unifier asked.

"They are harnessed, and their Trogen crews are assembled," Baalmon answered resolutely, to the Unifier's satisfaction.

"That is good," the Unifier said after a tense pause. The Unifier could feel the relief seeping into Baalmon at those three words. The currents seemed to churn faster in the Unifier's swirling eyes as He continued, "The primitive savages of the Five Realms will have a very strong message delivered unto them. Make sure that there is no question about the strength of the message that we send to them. The crews are to hold nothing back.... They are to spare nothing in their path.

"Perhaps it will bring those primitives some last shreds of wisdom, even as their villages are destroyed. It is also My wish to receive clear word of the Darroks, and how they fare. They are My newest weapon, among several that I intend to introduce in the coming months within Ave. I intend for them to be a weapon that I will use against any last realm foolish enough to try and resist My power. They will be as thunderclouds that will bring My storms to bear. Go now, and see to My bidding, by personally seeing these Darroks into the skies and heading eastward."

"Yes, my Lord, at once," Baalmon nodded, before hastily departing.

In moments, the Sorcerer was nimbly descending the steps within the thick walls of the high tower. The contrast between how he behaved in executing his tasks away from the Unifier, and how he acted in the presence of the Lord of Avanor, were incredibly amusing.

The Unifier knew well enough that Baalmon was very stately, intimidating, and even arrogant in his regular dealings with mortals. In truth, among the humans in the citadel Baalmon enjoyed a quite fearsome reputation. He was exceedingly powerful in his own right, steeped in the blackest of arts, and capable of wielding them with titanic fury.

He owed that entirely to the Unifier, who had opened doors into previously unknown depths of the abyss for the Sorcerers. Dark mysteries had been revealed to them, and dark wonders shown. Baalmon had been shown to be one of the strongest and greatest of aptitude, graced in abundance by the Lord of the Abyss, Jebaalos.

Yet all that was reduced in a moment, when the acolyte was before his Master. Baalmon could boast of nothing before the Unifier, who had brought him all his knowledge and powers, and held the strings of both his life and spirit in His hands.

Seeing the Sorcerer like a whimpering, shuffling servant was much more to the Unifier's liking. In time, He would see kings and emperors in modes of even lower obeisance than that shown now by His Sorcerers in private audiences. That glorious day was drawing ever nearer.

For the present, the Unifier would have to allow some mortal rulers to persist in some light delusions. Little did they know of the truth of the nature of the relationship between the Unifier and those most intimate with Him.

Most persons in Avanor, Norengal, and from across the other lands of Ave believed that being closer to the Unifier's side would bring great privileges of position and access. Many of the more ambitious and ruthless were not above recklessly accepting the destruction of their very own souls to gain a step closer to the Unifier's confidence, at least in terms of how they perceived the relationship.

In some ways, they would find out that their initial assessment was correct. Power and privilege of position and access did exist within an individual's closeness to the Unifier, but few anticipated the risks and costs that came with it.

The prices of failure for one with preeminent rank such as Baalmon, as the Sorcerer well knew, were not survivable. He also understood very clearly that the threat of punishment not only regarded his mortal life in Ave, but would be inescapable in the afterworld to come.

No other being than the Unifier could issue such a threat with genuine confidence. The Sorcerer, like all others in the inner circle around the Unifier, was desperate not to suffer even the slightest semblance of failure.

The palpable fear of those tethered closest to Him was simply exquisite, yet the Unifier knew that there was little room for beguiling diversions. The Unifier had to keep His mind riveted on the principle tasks ahead, just as Baalmon would be doing. Still, it was always enjoyable to savor the sweet taste of the world that was to come, if even for just a moment.

As the fearful servant hurried down the steps deep in the tower, the Unifier calmly turned back towards the horizon, gazing towards the south and east. He gently rested His hands on the cool stone between two stout merlons, His long fingers wrapping around the rough edge of the crenel.

His blue eyes shimmered once again, as they transformed into an abyss of deep, blood red.

His lips parted into a wide, feral smile, giving a rare exhibit of His unnaturally sharp, opalescent teeth. The Unifier was indeed pleased with the general course of things, as He turned His thoughts towards several other matters.

JANUS

Out of all the seven exiles, Janus had enjoyed the most adventurous and carefree day.

Their flight upon the Bregas into the lofty skies of Ave had taken them over a far-reaching swath of rolling lands bathed in radiant sunlight. The latter revealed many silvery rivers, shining lakes, and glittering streams, which shone forth brilliantly from the dense green foliage surrounding them. The docile skies were traversed by gentle breezes and dotted with a few small clusters of puffy white clouds.

There were several more unique sights that Janus espied below him within the Onan lands. One such vision involved an impressive group of falls, almost like a sequence of broad, low steps, with sparkling water cascading down them. Janus imagined that the incredible falls were exceedingly wondrous to gaze upon from the ground level.

Over the course of the day, Janus and Ayenwatha had proceeded to visit a few more tribal villages. Some were similar, and others smaller, in size to The Place of Far Seeing. Ayenwatha spoke to Janus about each. A couple of them belonged to tribes different than the Onan, though all of the tribes visited were a part of the Five Realms.

One of the villages belonged to the Onyota tribe, in whose lands Janus beheld a particularly spectacular lake, of tremendous size, nestled among the sprawling forests.

The other tribe that he encountered that day was the Kanienke, whose villages were arrayed along a very prominent river. While within their lands, he saw another incredible waterfall, whose waters tumbled down the face of a towering, rocky escarpment.

CROWN OF VENGEANCE

At each of the brief village stops, Janus found himself to be quite the object of attention. Highly curious villagers gathered excitedly to view the exotic newcomer traveling with the Onan war sachem.

There was much talk of prophecy from the bits and pieces that Janus was able to gather, just at the edge of earshot. The references struck him very oddly, and he wanted greatly to find out more about the intriguing remarks.

He withheld the questions that strained to be voiced on the tip of his tongue. Janus wanted to make sure that he did not inadvertently stumble into some unintended offense of the tribal people due to his lack of knowledge concerning their ways.

Ayenwatha and Janus did not stay long enough in any one place to cause too much of a disturbance. Yet it was very clear to Janus that Ayenwatha enjoyed a high rank and reputation among the surrounding village areas, in Onan villages as well as in the Onyota and Kanienke communities.

The sensations of flight through the skies continued to be exhilarating, even more so after Janus had acclimated further to the newer mode of travel. Janus found himself awash in regret when Ayenwatha finally indicated that they were returning back to The Place of Far Seeing. There was one consolation to the return, in that Janus was the one member of the group that was spared the long climb up the hill slope.

Janus and Ayenwatha landed within the midst of the village without incident, just as the light of the day finally began to fade. For the second time, Janus was astounded at just how smooth of a landing it was, marveling at the grace of the large winged beasts that they rode upon.

Janus accompanied Ayenwatha as they led Arax and Reazl to the far stable building situated near to the outer palisade. The two tribal warriors that had been attending to the steeds when the day began were still there. As Janus and Ayenwatha reached the front of the enclosure, leading their steeds by their long tethers, he saw that the pair of warriors were once again playing the game involving the bowl and colored seed pits.

Janus had smiled contentedly as he lightly stroke Reazl's muzzle, eliciting a soft whine from the amiable creature. He showed no nervousness as he spoke in a low whisper to Reazl, thanking the noble creature for carrying him safely through the skies that day.

Janus glanced away and saw that Ayenwatha was regarding him with a smile. The sachem had evidently been watching the interaction between the learning rider and veteran steed. Ayenwatha had then given

Arax a firm pat on the side of the neck, speaking some words of his own to the bearish winged creature.

The two warriors, having gotten to their feet at the others' arrival, were waiting patiently to tend to the steeds. After Janus and Ayenwatha had expressed their gratitude to the creatures, the warriors had then taken the steeds away into the byre. One of them had paused for a moment, promising Ayenwatha that the hardy Bregas would be fed and cared for immediately.

Janus knew that the comments were not a formality, or even a passionless duty. He could see the genuine reverence that the tribal warriors had for the Brega, echoed in the very way that they handled the large creatures.

Janus felt a calming sense of satisfaction with the day's events, as he traipsed back with Ayenwatha, wending their way through the bark-covered longhouses. They soon found the rest of Janus' group, talking together outside the end of the Firaken-Clan longhouse that they were all lodged within.

Erika smiled buoyantly as she looked up, her gaze meeting Janus' eyes directly. The others, in turn, showed that they were also pleased to see him, even the rather somber Logan.

"The last to return," Erika had exclaimed brightly, though she had a weary look about her. "We'll have to hear your story as well."

"And spared the hike up the hill too! I saw you flying in," jested Derek, with the mirthful grin that Janus knew better than most. "You've got it pretty good, don't you?"

Janus chuckled and shrugged.

"And you couldn't have come down and turned your steeds over to us at the bottom of the hill?" Logan added with a smirk, though Janus could hear in Logan's voice that he would not have objected to such a gesture.

"I'm sure he just didn't know where we were," Erika said with a light laugh of her own, winking at Janus.

"Next time, though, that's a good idea," Antonio remarked, glancing upward from where he was hunched over, diligently rubbing his right knee, as if striving to knead the soreness right out of it. "Don't forget it, Janus!"

Janus could see that all of the others had the same air of weary satisfaction about them. They were in a relaxed mood, and Janus was soon enjoined with their discussion of the day's events.

He was as curious of their exploits as they were of his day-long adventure through the skies. Janus soon got a good feel for the things that they had experienced, and what they had gleaned out of their sessions.

For all of the others, the day had definitely brought a distinct sense of new achievements. The feelings of accomplishment represented a noticeable change, eliciting a more confident tone in the group that had not been seen since the mists had cleared to reveal the strange new world around them.

Janus was finding some things about Ave to his liking, even if many things were radically different from the world that he had known and called his own. There was none of the frenetic nature of the world that he had lived in for over thirty-six years, surrounded by ubiquitous technical devices, and the frenzy of importance attributed to even the most minor, insignificant of things.

Janus and his comrades possessed none of the inventions that his world had proclaimed indispensable, and that sense of dire necessity regarding such implements was eroding with every passing hour that he spent in Ave.

Janus' group was subsisting well enough despite the absence of gleaming devices and modernistic conveniences. There was no sense of being tethered to those implements either, lending a feeling of freedom from the chains of humankind's own inventions. He also found that he quite liked the fact that every moment of communication between people within Ave took place face to face, right in person.

Janus knew that Derek was consciously noting the fundamental changes as well. Earlier that morning, Derek had remarked to Janus that if it were not for the families, relationships, and friends that he had left behind, he would have missed very little from the hectic and relentless pressures inundating their own world. Derek was taking to the relaxed pace favorably, commenting that time itself seemed to move much slower in Ave.

Yet it was also clear to Janus that the people that they had all been separated from, family, friend, and even acquaintance, weighed down heavily upon their hearts. It was just that a distinction had been made, as they had discovered that the new world, its environments, and the things within it, did not seem quite so daunting as before.

The meal that the women prepared for the seven famished exiles that evening was more than ample, not much less of a fare than had been the previous evening's substantial repast.

The cooking pots produced a rather good hominy, accompanied by roasted portions of deer and turkey, bread baked with dried blackberries, and some walnuts and fresh berries gathered from the bounty of the forest.

Janus had experienced venison before in his own world, but the meat provided by the Onan was delicious, as was the turkey. Ayenwatha and some other men of the village took their meal beside the otherworld guests, exhibiting considerable appetites of their own.

After they had all fully attended to their voracious appetites, they had proceeded to relate their various stories to each other. Ayenwatha and the other men sat cross-legged around them, listening quietly as the others described their experiences, and fielded questions from their comrades.

The peace of night settled in softly outside the longhouse, draping a blanket of cool air over the village. The star-speckled darkness brought a serene atmosphere along with it. The deep pools of shadows that formed held no threats, surrounded as they were by the palisades and numerous dwellings.

A more light-hearted conversation gradually ensued amongst the exiles, perhaps the first such one that had taken place since they had all come into the new world. The activity that day had loosened up many lingering tensions, and had obviously given the otherworlders some greatly needed easement of mind.

Janus noted that the others' spirits appeared to lift further as they spoke of their respective endeavors, drawing strength from the presence of a little structure and sense of purpose. The unstable chaos of the unknown no longer held full dominance, as the first rays of understanding and knowledge about Ave began to crest upon their individual horizons.

Ayenwatha and the few men that remained were content to keep listening to the group in relative silence. Janus could see by their shifting expressions that they were very amused by the thoughts and reactions of their guests to the various elements of Ave and the tribal culture.

Janus' companions listened in wonderment to his own description of flight upon the Brega. The more that he gave voice to his incredible experience, the more Janus realized just how very special the adventure had been.

Upon his conclusion, Erika and a few of the others immediately petitioned Ayenwatha for the opportunity to fly upon one of the winged steeds. The warrior sachem resolutely assured the others that they would all be given a chance for an airborne excursion in the coming days.

Mershad, with occasional input from Kent, had then related several fantastic and intriguing facts of their new world's rich history.

His comments had soon inspired many questions from the others. Ayenwatha, or one of the other men present, had to interject a few times with clarifications, or to answer something beyond Mershad and Kent's nascent learning.

It was incredible to contemplate the reality of a people that shared their heritage through an oral tradition. Conveyed dutifully and diligently from one generation to the next, the tradition had bound an entire people together, in a unity that had held strong throughout millennia.

There were also some moments of levity during the discussions. Antonio joked about how he had managed to shoot an arrow almost straight into the ground, just about two feet in front of him. It was an act that Antonio said was undeniable evidence of special skills that only he possessed, and that he had proven to be a very formidable archer against anything within two feet of range.

The truth of the incident was gradually revealed. Antonio had concentrated so hard on pulling the string of the hickory bow back that he had let the weapon slowly tip towards the ground. The men instructing Antonio, in their immense amusement over what was about to happen, had allowed the event to carry forward to its ignominious conclusion.

His next attempt had gone farther, though completely missing an oak tree's broad trunk at close range. It was a target that one of the men had instructed Antonio to aim for due to the relative ease of striking it, even for a beginner.

To everyone's relief, a few shots later, Antonio had managed to bury one arrow into the tree.

Gradually, as the tales of the day's events were exhausted, the direction of the conversation begged some more participation from Ayenwatha and the other tribesmen. They seemed more than happy enough to oblige the exiles.

It could not have been a more perfect environment for the telling of tales. Janus' belly was full, night had fallen outside, and a small fire hissed and crackled in the chamber's central hearth, as all huddled about to listen.

One of the warriors then told the guests some incredible tales concerning the Stone Hides, a large and gentle race of beings that had once lived on the northern borders of the Five Realms, in Osini lands. The legends themselves were not altogether very old, the final events in them transpiring just a few generations prior.

Janus listened in rapt interest as the warrior spoke at length of the strange race of creatures. He knew enough about the unusual nature of Ave to realize that the tales were just as likely to be truthful as fanciful.

The gray-green skin of the Stone Hides was said to have been as tough as any thick leather. It had a stony texture to it as well, which along with the hue of it had given the formidable creatures their name by the tribal people.

The huge Stone Hides had once lived in great harmony with humans within the tribal lands, their presence tolerated fully by generations of the tribes' ancestors. There had been some rogue elements among both the Stone Hides and humans that had resulted in a few unpleasant incidents, but overall relations had been quite good.

It was a time when another race called the Little Ones had also been common within the same woodlands. To Janus, they sounded like a kind of fairy folk, shy and sometimes mischievous, who occasionally aided tribal hunters and interacted with the people. From what the warrior said, the Little Ones still dwelled in the forests, though their appearances to the people were now much more infrequent.

Janus could see that the tribal warrior telling the story looked upon such an age wistfully, and with wonder of his own. The warrior spoke with an unmistakable undertone of regret, as he described what had subsequently happened to the Stone Hides.

The Stone Hides had dwelled primarily underground, but one day the ground itself had suddenly shaken and rumbled violently, all across the woodlands. The upheaval reached the point that the ground broke and crumbled in many places, and had permanently closed off the passages reaching down into their netherworld abodes. In just one terrible day, the Stone Hides' presence had been completely removed from the midst of the tribal people.

The tragic event had been interpreted as a stringent punishment to the tribal people. Evidently, the same age during which the tribes had enjoyed the welcome presence of the Stone Hides and Little Ones was also a period when there was a considerable number of dire and loathsome evils existing within the woodlands.

CROWN OF VENGEANCE

By their relative inaction, the tribal people had been allowing subtle and cunning entities to spread their influences and manifestations. A being called the Dark Brother and those allied to him were beginning to assert themselves more fully and openly, their reach extending even into the village and war councils of the tribes.

The Stone Hides had warned the tribal people of this growing malignancy, even as the tribes had succumbed to more violent passions during wars that had led to grave abominations such as the eating of the flesh of captives.

The consumption of a foe's vital organs was not the only wickedness to sprout in regard to captives, as new practices of cruel torture developed among the people of the Five Realms. The tortures took on a ritualistic, almost ceremonial tone, involving making captives run gauntlets of warriors who mercilessly beat them before they were tied to stakes for burning. Other horrific methods included the tearing out of fingernails and the setting aflame of bark belts filled with pitch and resin, which had been tied about the prisoners' waists.

The abominations had not only been visited upon war captives, but also to some unfortunate Gallean monks that had come among the tribes to propagate the faith of the Western Church. In truth, some of the most brutal practices had been applied to the monks, including the pouring of boiling water over them three times to mimic the Sacrament of Three Immersions that the Western Church used to anoint new converts.

The tribes now looked upon such practices with a shudder of horror, and even an element of disbelief. The warrior telling the tale had been adamant to state as such after relating the blood-curdling details of the past. Janus could sense the sincere shame that the warrior felt towards the atrocities by his lineage, though it was clear that he was determined to render an honest and unfiltered account.

The telling of the dark practices was important to the warrior, in the context of what it eventually led to in the growth, wisdom, and redemption of the tribal people.

The powers of the dark had not spared the Stone Hides in those malignant times either, taking possession of some unstable individuals of their number to commit atrocities upon humans. As with the corruption within the tribes, these hideous violations also involved flesh-eating.

The only difference between the experience of the humans and the Stone Hides was that the latter had been quick in recognizing exactly what was happening. They had moved rapidly to drive out the shadowy influences from their midst, as well as those that had come under the sway of dark powers.

The warrior commented that their ancestors should have seen the trouble coming, long before the warnings of the Stone Hides. It had not been very long before that time that the Wizards Deganawida and the Light Brother had disappeared from sight.

From the perspective of hindsight, it was held by the wise among the tribes that the departure of the two mighty Wizards was a harbinger of the eroding corruption in the spirit of the people. In truth, it had not been much longer following the disappearance of the Wizards that the tribes had started resorting to bloodier and crueler impulses, openly committing horrific acts.

The loss of the Stone Hides, coupled with the people's understanding of the vanishing of the two great Wizards, had served as a terrible shock that had spurred the tribes with a great urgency. As if awakening out of the paralyzing depths of a nightmare, they had begun to see things as they were, in all their naked and monstrous truth. The tribes had then been extremely diligent in rooting out vile witches and malevolent shamans from their haunts within the shadowy, more remote depths of the woodlands.

As they did so, they had come to fully recognize the abominations that they had been committing upon others. They were thoroughly chastened, realizing that the sickness was in truth one of the soul. The Five Realms had abruptly ceased all of the sickening, bloody behaviors, ushering in a period of widespread reform, reaffirming the tenets that underlay the Grand Council's founding by the Wizard Deganawida.

Janus recalled the great caution that had been evidenced, and the quartz crystals that had been brought out, when he and the others had been discovered by the band of warriors. He understood then that the diligence reflected the story he was now hearing, an assiduousness that had not ceased since that period of reformation.

From the way that the warrior talked, it was now unmistakable that witchcraft was truly regarded as one of the most evil of pursuits that a human could ever choose to take, a transgression of the spirit even worse than murder. To the people, it was a direct mockery of the One Spirit, having no presence in the pure light of the world's Creator.

The renewed mandate to oppose the dark arts relentlessly was unquestioned, becoming a major root within the story of the Stone Hides.

It was the very lesson and wisdom that had been derived from what was a great, collective loss to the five tribes. The two Wizards were still gone, as were the Stone Hides, but the tribes had been able to reverse the slide into spiritual devastation.

The warrior finally ended his thorough tale of the Stone Hides and its profound lessons. Upon completion, the other warriors, including Ayenwatha, excused themselves for the rest of the evening.

In the wake of their departure, Janus and the others got up and made their way deeper into the longhouse towards their own quarters. They exchanged polite smiles and nods with the various families settling down for the night within the other chambers.

Janus felt a little awkward walking right through the midst of the families, but could see that there was absolutely no discomfort on their part. Their returning nods and warm smiles were welcoming and kind, and there was no sense of irritation or interruption.

Reaching their own chamber, the seven split up and found sleeping places up on the surfaces of the raised platforms on either side. Setting the cornhusk mats and furs into place, they bedded down for the night.

By then Janus and the others were all at the point of absolute exhaustion. He had already taken notice that more than one of his comrades had had to make a concerted effort during the last parts of the story of the Stone Hides. Heavily drooping eyelids had threatened to transit into sleep, and Janus' companions had done what they could to resist it.

Once six out of seven of the exiles were comfortably arrayed upon their corn husk mats and hides, they had fallen asleep very quickly. The seventh, Janus, did not slumber.

He found that he was still a little restless, not yet ready to give himself fully over to the embrace of sleep. His mind was still churning with the excitement of the day's events, the lingering images of flight yet flowing through his head.

He could not deny that it was good just to feel alive again, even if his inner torments would not completely remove themselves from his mind and heart.

Finding a little solitude was not entirely an easy task within such a communal environment, but Janus decided to seek some anyway. He quietly maneuvered past a lightly snoring Kent, and got down from the sleeping platform. With cautious steps he made his way back down the length of the longhouse, passing through the other compartments.

As with his previous nighttime venture out of the longhouse, he took great care not to let his passage wake up any of the villagers that had gone to sleep. He had to watch his step, and a few more friendly smiles and nods greeted him from the shadowed recesses of the dark compartments as he continued through.

A couple of small children in one of the compartments giggled and ducked their heads under their fur coverlets, drawing a grin from Janus. It encouraged him how he and his otherworld companions had been accepted so quickly by the Onan villagers, and their friendship and generosity continued to amaze him. He wondered if he would ever be able to return even a little of their kindness at some future time. Not being of their world, he strongly doubted it.

At the moment, he figured that simply being cooperative and respectful, and making an effort to learn their history and ways, would at least convey his sincere appreciation of their bountiful hospitality.

The hazy thickness of the air within the various compartments of the longhouse was supplanted by the crisp, clean night as he emerged out from the sheltered porch at the end of the longhouse.

Outside again in the fresh air, Janus took a deep, cleansing breath. A spectrum of stars sparkled in the wide sky above, as the larger moon, and its more distant, smaller companion, had begun their nightly ascension on the far edge of the horizon.

He walked casually towards the front entryway of the village. There were a few warriors standing around the opening, which was now blocked by a removable section of palisade. They regarded him casually as he approached, though their eyes narrowed in curiosity and attentiveness as he drew right up to them.

"Good evening. ... Is it okay to go down to the water?" Janus asked one of the warriors, as he caught the man's eye directly. Then, remembering the parameters set forth by the village council, he added quickly, "Can a couple of warriors take me there?"

The stout warrior to Janus' immediate right considered the request for only a moment. He then replied in an even tone, "It is not always safe at night, and very dangerous if you are not with a war party. There are many dangerous beasts that hunt these lands at night, and we must always look out for enemies. Even witches can be about, and they can take many forms.

"It is not good to go out of the village alone during the night ...

and not even if you have a couple of warriors with you. Your desire is not wise. You must learn these lands well first. You will then know that I am speaking to you truly now, and that your wish is not wise."

Janus was not affronted in any way at the very direct manner of the warrior. He was fast becoming aware of the fact that the tribal people tended to speak their minds openly. He realized that this was their customary way, and not a method of conducting a personal attack.

"Then perhaps I will make a wiser choice than the one that my desires wish to lead me to. I'll stay within the village. Good evening to all of you, and thank you for advising me well," Janus said in return, smiling amiably. He nodded respectfully to the warrior, receiving an affable smile in return, as he turned and left the vicinity of the entryway.

Slowly, he walked back among the silent longhouses, finally nearing the one housing Ayenwatha and his own companions. Out in the open night air, and now living amid a culture so close to the things of nature, Janus found that he was little concerned over getting dirt on himself. He grinned at the sudden recognition, remembering how cautious he had been in his own world to avoid any substantial untidiness.

Lowering himself, he first got down to his knees, and then slowly maneuvered and shifted about to lay upon his back, with his legs stretched out along the bare surfacing of rough soil beneath.

In just moments, he felt his body settling down, as he concentrated his thoughts on letting the tensions in his muscles flow out bit by bit. At first he winced a little as his joints, lower back, and neck adjusted to the flat and even plane.

He looked up dreamily at the ocean of sky and stars above him. Only the faintest hint of scudding cloud vapors tampered with the clear, vivid scene spreading to all horizons above him. Janus had immersed himself into similar visions back in his own world, especially when he was able to go deeper into the countryside, away from the obscuring glare of the city's ubiquitous lights.

The cool, invigorating air, the peaceful serenity of the gentle night breezes, and the unmarred, magical panorama filling his eyes slowly soothed his aching mind and heart, just as similar environments in his former world had done. It afforded him a concerted place and moment to empty out his worries and cares, and to let his mind drift, all the while cradled within the peaceful and encompassing refuge. It was a timeless sensation, one that seemed to suspend the very turning of the world.

His eyes slowly began to close, and Janus started to find himself flickering back and forth on the boundary edge between sleep and full wakefulness.

"There you are!"

Though spoken so very softly, Janus jumped in surprise at the sudden, high-pitched voice, even as the familiarity of it tugged at him.

The speaker, to Janus' complete surprise, was the village youth that had visited with him so very recently. The cherubic youth's face hovered right over him, blocking out the sight of the clear night sky. Despite the darkness, and the silhouetted nature of the boy's form, Janus could see that the youth was smiling broadly and apparently very full of energy.

"And how are you doing, little guy? Well, it seems that we meet once again. Don't get much sleep, do you?" Janus replied, smiling warmly at the youth, as he carefully eased himself up slowly into a sitting position, stifling a slight groan at the labored protest of his body.

"I'm doing very good," the youth replied buoyantly, smile broadening.

"So where did you go off to last night?" Janus asked him. "I tried to look for you, but you disappeared on me. Couldn't see where you went off to."

The child grinned, and shrugged. "I have much to do."

Janus smirked, raising an eyebrow. "At your age? You are too young to be so busy. Enjoy life while you can!"

"I do," the child assured him, before asking, "And did you enjoy your friend?"

"Who?" Janus asked, momentarily confused by the seemingly ambiguous question.

"Your friend. I brought you him last night," the youth said a little impatiently, as if the first reference should have been quite clear enough. Then, he added in a similar, matter-of-fact way, "And he's brought a couple of others today."

Janus had to grin, even as pangs of sorrow tugged anew at him. He remembered the full events of the previous night and the boy's imaginative comments. Janus once had such a vivid imagination, when he was that young.

Janus' voice took on a slightly more somber tone, as the echoes of those unblemished days touched the edges of his now-scarred memory, "Yes, I do remember that. You told me about him … last night."

"He flew with you up there today," the youth said with a flare of excitement, pointing up towards the sky. His eyes seemed to sparkle in the light of stars and moon. "You cannot fly by yourself, like he can, at least not yet."

"Oh … so you saw me on those … what are they called? The winged creatures?" Janus replied, leaning back to rest on his elbows.

"The Bregas? They are really good animals. They have strong spirits. Very strong. They have been good steeds for the people of the villages. They have always been with this land," the youth replied enthusiastically.

"They were amazing to fly on. We have nothing like them where I am from. At first I was pretty scared to get on them, but at the end I did not want to leave," Janus replied, his thoughts going back to the thrilling sensations that he had experienced earlier in the day. His heartbeat picked up a few beats in the mere remembrance of the rush of vivid emotion that he had felt while soaring over the forested hills.

"Trouble is coming, Janus," the youth then said, in an abruptly serious tone.

Janus looked over, and saw that the boy's expression had grown very dour all of a sudden. The blunt change in the youth's demeanor gripped Janus' attention and concern at once.

"What do you mean?" Janus asked, wondering further at the rather brusque shift in the young boy.

As with the end of their conversation the previous night, the boy's tone carried a hint of maturity that belied his seeming age. Janus wondered if the youth was about to suddenly vanish as well.

"Trouble. Great trouble. And I just know it," the youth replied sadly, but firmly, as if to head off an expected question coming from Janus.

The boy had indeed guessed correctly, as Janus had just been about to ask the boy how he had come to know of imminent trouble. Janus paused for a moment, considering his words carefully.

"What kind of trouble is coming?" Janus finally asked.

"Where you were today," the youth said gloomily, looking skyward. The sparkle that had been in his eye now looked like the glistening of sadness. "It will come from up there. Be watchful. Your friends will need you. You must be ready to move. The people of the village cannot protect you from all danger."

Janus followed the youth's sorrowful gaze on up into the star-speckled sky. At the moment, the majestic vision looked as if it was incapable of harboring anything that would put the village even remotely at harm. Such was the strength of the peaceful presence that it was emanating.

Looking away from the sky, Janus turned back towards the youth. His breath caught in his chest. Once again, the young boy had suddenly disappeared. Janus grew silent and turned his head swiftly in each direction. There was no trace of him anywhere that his searching eyes roved.

"Again!" Janus remarked in sharp frustration, shaking his head in disbelief at the child's evasiveness. "Or I'm finally losing my mind."

After waiting a little while longer to see whether or not the child would return, Janus finally roused himself and got back to his feet. With a last glance around, he walked back to the entrance to the longhouse, pushed aside the hide flap covering it, and entered.

As he made his way back through the chambers, he doubted that he would be getting a lot of sleep. Only time would tell whether or not the young boy's warning had any truth to it, but in this strange new world Janus was not about to discount the youth's words entirely.

AELFRIC

The great Ealdorman Aelfric's ebon war steed Midnight galloped thunderously down the long line of tents. The stallion was heading directly towards the center of the encampment, carrying its prominent rider, followed by several others in the Ealdorman's retinue. Bystanders were careful to give the hurrying contingent a wide berth, backing out of their pathway well before the horses reached them.

Aelfric was riding farther away from the westward-most line of defensive encampment preparations, which were being prepared at pressing haste by engineers and many thousands of soldiers and non-combatants.

Aelfric's authority was not one to be questioned anywhere within the huge encampment. King Alcuin's greatest general, designated as the sovereign's majordomo, he had directly received the supreme command of the gathering Saxan forces from the king himself.

The day's inspection had been thorough, and deemed satisfactory, as Aelfric and his entourage completed their survey of the western length of the encampment. The outer defenses were being put into place at a relentless pace, to ensure its full completion well before the arrival of the enemy forces. Virtually every tool or weapon that could find a good use was being employed in the massive amalgamation of digging and ground removal.

Time was no luxury. If anything, it was a baleful adversary.

Scouts ranging beyond the outlying sentry posts had indicated that the vanguard of a staggeringly vast enemy force was finally approaching the plains. The marching juggernaut was estimated to be only a few scant days away.

The invasion army had paused for some time within the borders of Ehrengard, the delay presumably for acclimating and resting the steeds that had traveled far distances to join the diverse force. Now that the enormous invasion force was on the move again, it was certain that the time of battle was drawing very close.

Aelfric was determined to see that the enemy would find a Saxan wall resolutely facing them when they arrived. It was all the culmination of a few months of great anxiety, thorough preparation, and a very rapid response.

The very first whispers of an impending war had come from Saxan agents traveling deep within Ehrengard's cities and ports. They had lingered long after trade had been formally cut off between Saxany and Ehrengard, declared by the Sacred Emperor after the final rejection of the Unifier's overtures to King Alcuin.

Supplies and foodstuffs had begun pouring into Ehrengard just a few months after. The arrival of numerous ships from Avanor, loaded with horses, siege equipment, knights, and other martial elements heralded the existence of dark intentions by the Unifier towards Ehrengard's eastern neighbor.

The mustering of large forces within Ehrengard had also been initiated during that time. Summons to military service had been dispatched from the Sacred Emperor himself, to nobles everywhere across the lands. Ehrengard's forces had soon begun to assemble in great numbers close to Esenshild, a large city located not far from Saxany's westernmost borders.

The levies of their great princes and war-like bishops had streamed in right before the eyes of Saxany's diligent spies. The Saxans had quickly perceived that they were not gathering to be placed upon ships, but were massing near to one singular road that was ideal for the movement of a great army; a road that led directly east towards Saxany.

The signs were obvious, and the interpretations undeniable, but at least the warnings had been long in coming.

Trade had been declining between Ehrengard and Saxany ever since the rise of the Unifier. It had come as no surprise to the wiser Ealdormen such as Aelfric, and the Counts of Saxany, when it had dried up completely at the firm dictate of the Sacred Emperor. The Saxan leaders had adroitly anticipated what was to come, and in their foresight had sent more spies west before the borders between the two lands were all but sealed.

Those spies had taken careful account of everything that they saw. Some periodically returned with extensive updates, traversing dangerous and well-patrolled border regions to bring their highly valuable messages back.

Countless amounts of grain, salted meat, wine and ale barrels, and masses of livestock had been gathered in the eastern territories of Ehrengard, as well as innumerable wagons, carts, and pack animals.

Some stories brought back by the spies told of incredible piles of grain that were so large that they resembled small hills. The surfaces of these 'hills' were even said to sprout a covering of new growths, only to have their surfaces skimmed to reveal freshly kept grains harbored just underneath.

The hills of grain, and every other thing being gathered in immense quantity, were all acute, unmistakable signs of preparations for an invasion.

It had soon become clear to the Saxan leaders that the enormous buildup had not been intended to be a secret either, as emissaries of both Ehrengard and the Unifier had arrived in Saxany for a last audience with the King. Aelfric and a couple of the great Counts happened to be in Aixen when that momentous event had occurred. It happened at a time when many councils were being held in Aixen, in regard to the growing mass of storm clouds within Ehrengard.

As Aelfric thought back to that decisive day, he could still remember the look of utter, incredulous shock splayed upon the emissaries' faces, when King Alcuin had firmly refused the mandate to pledge Saxany's loyalty, or more accurately its submission, to the Unifier.

That moment was forever emblazoned in Aelfric's mind, as that very instant might very well have sounded the end of their proud and free kingdom.

The staunch rejection had taken place right within the King's great reception hall at Aixen. The incensed emissaries dispatched by the Unifier, from Avanor and Ehrengard, had then told King Alcuin that war was unavoidable. They had boasted that Saxany would be conquered and occupied by the Unifier in due time, and that King Alcuin would not stand in the way of the prosperity and order that was being guided out of Avanor.

The emissaries had been unceremoniously escorted out of the hall, whisked away brusquely by the King's royal houseguard. Aelfric had taken a little pleasure in the emissaries' rough treatment, as they had entered so haughtily, and with such ultimate ill-intent towards everything that Saxany was.

For once in his life, Aelfric was not bothered by such a stark violation of decorum. It had been about all that Aelfric could do to refrain from drawing his own blade and striking at the arrogant emissaries.

Word had then been sent quickly of the incident and the King's response, by both airborne and ground steeds, to all parts of the Saxan Kingdom. Parchments bearing the seals of Ealdormen and Counts came back to Aixen with great alacrity, bearing their various responses.

The great Ealdormen and Counts of the land had been unanimous in their support of the King, as had the Gitawan, the great council serving Alcuin.

All seven of the kingdom's Ealdormen and its four great Counts had swiftly pledged their unequivocal support. They had then turned to the immediate tasks facing them, to begin the enormous and extensive summons that would be required to prepare for the expected response from the Unifier.

Hill-top beacons were lit, while innumerable couriers traversed paths and roads all throughout the kingdom. It was to be a momentous time for the most ancient of obligations, a calling out of all the lands' able-bodied males to share in a collective defense of the kingdom itself.

The mustering of invasion forces to the west had also accelerated. The surge of the massing had come so fast that it was clear that the Unifier was prepared for, and probably had anticipated, King Alcuin's response.

Ehrengard had then sealed off the border region, even to the most daring and adventurous of Saxany's hardy spies. Sky patrols, mounted patrols, and teeming numbers of warriors on foot had clamped down on all traffic between Saxany and Ehrengard, and many courageous spies had lost their lives in attempts to get final word out of Ehrengard.

Before all word had been shut off completely, a dire and portentous tiding had arrived in Saxany. Though ominous, the word had been fortuitous, as it allowed the Saxans to perceive the full scope of what was facing them. One of the last spies to make it out of Ehrengard had reported the arrival of an enormous fleet that hailed from neither Avanor nor Ehrengard. The foreign fleet had included many huge, three-masted ships, of a size virtually incomprehensible to a Saxan.

The vessels carried along with them a multitudinous array of unusual foreigners, horses, and even a horde of strange, hump-backed beasts. They were rumored to have come from far to the north, and their presence in addition to the building forces from Avanor and Ehrengard took the threat facing Saxany to an unprecedented level.

The final word concerning the third mass of enemy forces ensured that the Unifier was not hesitating to summon everything that could be brought to bear upon the western border areas of the Saxan Kingdom. Every ounce of strength had to be applied in defense if the Saxan Kingdom was to have any hope of stopping the titanic invasion.

Everything was converging towards a final resolution, as the powerful, massive forces of the enemy trod towards the Saxan encampments out on the Plains of Aethelney.

Flanked by several elite warriors of his household guard, Aelfric turned Midnight aside and cut between a group of bell-shaped tents. The stallion cantered towards a large, pavilion-sized structure that had been erected near the center of the cluster.

Bringing the war horse to an abrupt halt, Aelfric swiveled and jumped down to the ground with a smoothness and agility that belied his age. Though his years said that he should have been beyond his physical prime, he still held onto his vitality with a tenacious grasp.

Aelfric strode towards the great tent without waiting for his immediate companions to dismount and catch up to him. His mind was fixated upon the priorities immediately facing him, no easy task at the apex of such a vast war campaign.

Inside the tent were several familiar figures, many of whom were reassuring presences, quite welcome sights to his eyes. One individual to the left, though, immediately provoked a sense of annoyance, though the conceited man would undeniably serve an important part in the overall Saxan strategy. All the figures nodded respectfully at Aelfric's entrance, and he acknowledged them with a nod.

"Godric, I see that you have arrived as well," Aelfric stated rather brusquely, to the man standing to his left. "I was not sure whether you got our message, for our courier reported that he was unable to gain a direct audience at your fortress."

Though the words were polite, the tone was unmistakably accusing. Aelfric stifled his anger as best as he could. There was no time for pretensions, even though Aelfric expected Godric to suspend his usual arrogance in the face of the deadly wave sweeping towards all of them.

The man being addressed inclined his head. About an inch taller than Aelfric, but more slender of girth, Godric put forth a regal posture about himself, even though he held no throne. His cold, calculating eyes never appeared to look at a person directly, and his small mouth seemed forever set in tension.

Aelfric neither liked Godric nor wanted to have to depend upon him in any way. Godric was beholden to nobody, and the detached weighing of interests would seem to favor the greater strength and wealth of the western lands. Despite the inner misgivings that Aelfric felt, it was undeniable that Godric occupied a most important position in relation to Saxany's current situation.

A substantial fortress belonging to Godric guarded the territory to the immediate south of where the narrow passage of land from Ehrengard to Saxany opened out onto the Plains of Aethelney.

Godric had always enjoyed engaging in solid trade with both Saxany and its neighbor, Ehrengard, a benefit that still continued as his lands were alloidal. A few small farming villages and a smattering of homesteads existed within his free-held land, which was not under the direct authority of either kingdom.

The trade with Saxany was still dangerous for Godric to undertake, as the Saxan lands were currently being barred from transacting commerce with anyone who did not wish to be deemed an enemy of the Unifier.

That Godric still traded with Saxany was the very source of Aelfric's lingering hopes. Perhaps Godric would honor the kingdom that had made his land holding possible.

There was also a certain irony to all of it, one that Aelfric had not missed in the least. As Godric had increased his trade with Ehrengard, he had kept the trade with Saxany more discreet. The irony was simply that Ehrengard had once been an outright enemy to the specific King who had first bestowed the lands that Godric now occupied.

Godric's lands, as Aelfric knew, hailed back to a heroic and honorable lord of the Fourth Era of Ave's history, Conrad the Ironheart. Conrad the Ironheart had rebelled in those days against the unstable, continuously agitating nobility of Ehrengard. It had all transpired during an age when the lands of Saxany were two separate kingdoms. Fleeing eastward, Conrad had sought refuge, beseeching the ruler of the former southern and eastern kingdom, Clovis II.

Not only refuge had been granted, but lands with nominal suzerainty had been given over to him. They were part of the greater buffer zones on the western edge of the southern kingdom, located just to the south of the primary Western Marches. The dominion over that land had evolved into a freehold by the time that the two realms had been united into the Kingdom of Saxany.

Godric, however, was not of the line of Conrad the Ironheart. He had been the most senior among the household warriors of the last direct descendent of Conrad's line, a man named Pepin. He had claimed to have been given the inheritance by Pepin, though no written charter had ever been produced to confirm the claim. Strengthening Godric's position, most of the prominent warriors surrounding Pepin had supported his assertion.

King Alcuin, out of a strong-held belief in honor, had taken Godric at his word. Even so, the circumstances of Pepin's death had been shrouded in dark rumors, a point that had never faded out of Aelfric's mind or suspicions.

It was a point driven further home within Aelfric when Godric had subsequently purged a small number of Pepin's household warriors. Aelfric had regarded all of the purged warriors to be good and decent men, and the purge had left a bitter, black taste in Aelfric's mouth; and a potent, lasting suspicion.

Yet it was not Aelfric's place to question his king, no matter what the thoughts were that went through his own mind. Those thoughts had never seemed to ebb, though, and were brought back to the forefront whenever Aelfric looked upon the darting, shifting gaze of Godric.

"Yes, Ealdorman Aelfric. I received your request. I could see that my presence here was of some importance to you. I came with haste, as we all know that there is little time to spare," Godric replied politely, though his offered smile held little warmth in it.

Aelfric held back his first verbal inclinations, his jaw tightening for a moment as he maintained his composure. The snide attitude wafting off of Godric was more than irritating to the Saxan Ealdorman.

"Good, then we can all speak together, immediately, as you are right, Godric, there is very little time to spare," Aelfric said tersely. He looked gravely towards the others gathered around him, regarding their stern faces for a moment. "The Unifier comes straight at us. He could not be more direct, or confident in His approach. He intends to be as a great hawk diving onto its prey. From everything that we have heard and come to know, the enemy means to break us through the use of brute, overwhelming strength.

"Ealdorman Morcar has placed a force under one of his most trusted senior thanes, Aethelstan, to ward the mountainous forests to the northwest of the corridor of land between Saxany and Ehrengard. Only a fool leaves any possible path undefended, and that route is very inviting to a clever enemy leader. Indeed, there are some new reports that a second force has detached from the invader's main body and is headed precisely that way. Ealdorman Morcar's decision seems to be very wise, and full of foresight.

"To the southwest, we seek the additional help of Godric for supplies, for possible refuge, and to keep something out there that the enemy will have to think about."

Aelfric then turned to look squarely at Godric, endeavoring to hold his eyes, though such was an impossibility with Godric's constantly shifting gaze. The unsettling man blinked more than anyone that Aelfric had ever known.

"Godric, I ask for none of your men, for it is Saxany alone that is being threatened by this invasion. King Alcuin does not wish to try to compel you to come openly into the war, especially as you are one of the first lying in the invader's direct path. We ask only that you honor your lands' long friendship with our Kingdom, and at the least remain neutral in this coming fight."

Aelfric then paused for a moment, to see whether or not Godric would try to make some sort of gesture. His eyes carefully scanned the other's face for some type of indication as to his disposition, coming up quite empty amidst Godric's stony expression.

"As it is, Godric, your fortress and your land are still under threat from the Unifier … that is, if you wish to remain free and the lord of your lands. We can ill afford any shifts in loyalty … such that you might come out openly on the side of the Unifier," Aelfric then said firmly, bringing his greatest concern out into the open.

He waited for the words to sink in to Godric and all of those assembled within the tent.

A fire welled up swiftly in Godric. A scowl crossed his face, and his dark eyes blackened further in anger. When he spoke, his voice was one of barely suppressed indignation. "You mean to question my loyalty? Our land has always been a loyal friend to yours, ever since Conrad the Ironheart, and your nobles have always profited from our friendship. Why should I be different in a time of struggle? Do you have reason to think that it would change now, just because there is a different bloodline ruling over the land bequeathed by Clovis II? Remember that my family has always served the line that received this grant of land from your King Clovis ages ago. Make no mistake, Aelfric, we have been there ever since that day."

"As a man of honor, a certain degree of loyalty cannot change, at least as far as remaining neutral and not becoming hostile to us," Aelfric replied rigidly, his hardened gaze straining to hold the other's eyes as he aimed to make his point patently clear. "I tell you again, I do not ask you to fight, Godric, but we must never mistake your intentions. You must give us assurances that you will keep your fighting men inside of your fortress. Do not let them emerge in formation for any reason during the coming battle. If they do, the honor of your land is forfeit, and if we emerge from the doom that the Unifier intends, then, by the All-Father, I will hold you to account myself."

"Your intent is clear. You disregard my word," Godric gritted angrily, his teeth clenched tightly in his rising ire. "King Alcuin would not question our honor."

"And I will not, if your men remain behind the walls," Aelfric iterated doggedly, inviting no further argument. "Once this fight is over, I shall hope to apologize for any offense that I have given you, and to share the King's full faith in you. As it is, I am the senior commander of this great army gathering for the defense of our homelands, and I can ill afford to take any chances with the coming war. Our position must be made clear."

"Then I look forward to your apology, for you judge me wrongly," Godric said spitefully.

"I shall look forward to delivering it," Aelfric returned without a moment's hesitation. Inside, he was more than willing to render an apology, with absolutely no misgivings, if Godric was something other than what

Aelfric's instincts loudly proclaimed him to be. "I now bid you well, and wish you a safe return back to your land. I shall make sure that you are informed of our movements, to the best of my ability. See that you take stock of foodstuffs and goods, for we may have much need of trade with you. I assure you that you shall be well compensated for any supplies needed. Even should you ask an excess, there shall be no hard feelings during this time of risk and emergency."

Godric did not reply, his wavering eyes drawing as near as possible to locking in a hardened stare with Aelfric. The tension was palpable, thickening considerably in the air within the tent, as Godric was unable to match the steady, calm look of Aelfric's own eyes.

With a curt bow, the other turned and stormed out of the tent. His leather boots drove heavily into the ground with each step, as if to accent his great displeasure with Aelfric.

Aelfric waited a few moments, and then slowly turned his attention back to the throng gathered around him in the tent. Now clad in cloaks and tunics, they would all soon be donning iron helms and coats of mail for the coming fight. Scarred veteran and fiery youth alike, they would all have one common, numerous, and mighty enemy.

Some among the Saxans gathered knew the use of siege engines, and others were experts in cavalry tactics. Others were well-versed in their knowledge of infantry, and there were a couple of men present especially skilled in the use of sky-steeds.

Aelfric was under no illusions. It would require all of them at their best, in order to have any chance of protecting the Plains of Athelney; the western gateway into the Saxan lands.

A Saxan army had never before, in the entire history of the kingdom, or the two that had preceded it, mustered in such power and numbers. The duress of the circumstances had never been greater.

Some good fortune was with the Saxans, in that most of the primary force had arrived safely, and was already in place. At the least, and it was no small matter, the Saxans were no longer facing the danger of having themselves caught unprepared before a full gathering and deployment could take place.

The lines of age were now creasing Aelfric's face with greater prominence and frequency. It surprised him little, especially in the midst of strenuous times such as he was now facing.

He slowly ran his right hand through his gray streaked, long hair, pulling it back from his face. The locks were beginning to thin, and his hairline was sitting a little higher up on his forehead. As much as he set his mind against the ravages of age, there was only so much that he could do.

His aching back and knees betrayed what had once been an exceptionally strong, and nearly indefatigable, body. Still able to wield his blade with considerable force and ample skill, he was certainly far from being an invalid, but he knew that he could not sustain his energies as capably as he had in the past.

The thoughts, at one time, would have been enough to depress his spirits, were it not for one lingering realization.

One aspect about him had gotten stronger and sharper with the years. It was an attribute that was far more valuable to those around him than the presence of another thousand soldiers would have been.

That attribute was the quality of his mind.

A growing reservoir of experience and wisdom to draw from, his mind was an asset that he never would have fully appreciated in his younger days. It was the one part of him that became more valuable, as long as he allowed it, with each passing year. It was a weapon that he would now have to draw upon mightily in the face of the unholy storm coming down upon all of them.

Monks had taught him to read as a youth, on the resolute request of his father, the former Ealdorman of the Wesvald, Cynegils. It was a skill that brought ever more rewards throughout the years.

Since he had learned the immensely valuable skill, Aelfric had pored over many of the parchments that were assiduously stored and cared for within the monasteries of his home province. The rich histories and insights of past warriors, learned clerics, and even kings of long ago had been opened up to him. It had never ceased to amaze Aelfric how many situations and dire challenges in those ancient ages closely reflected those of his own time.

The monastery at Jafarne possessed one of the most prized libraries in any of the kingdoms. The preeminence in its holdings was not a lightly held status.

Among monasteries, there was a constant flow of requests for loans of books and codices, mostly so that the borrowed works could be copied before they were returned.

Works of great prestige brought grand renown to the possessing library, and conflicts sometimes erupted as monks went to incredible lengths to get their hands on such works. Finding a rare, desirable work was not unlike finding a new vein of silver to mine.

Abbots and bishops alike scoured the lands both home and abroad thoroughly for particularly special works, and neighboring monasteries often quarreled over the status of works still not returned between them. Many a book carried its own inscription conveying a staunch admonishment for the reader to return it promptly when finished. Quite often such admonishments took on the tone of a curse.

A great library resulted in a population of monks of high erudition, including the large numbers of visiting monks that such a site attracted. Spending time at Jafarne had resulted in a wealth of opportunity for Aelfric to engage in many lengthy discussions with some of the most learned monks in the land. Those times had enhanced and added to the experiences and lessons learned in the other aspects of his life.

There had even been an opportunity to engage in dialogue with Abelard the Venerable, regarded as one of Ave's greatest minds. The esteemed scholar had been visiting the fabled monastery at Jafarne just seven winters prior. It had been an influential encounter, for in that one day Aelfric had learned to appreciate the ability to forcefully consider, and effectively argue, both sides of any given topic.

It was an art that converted very well to war planning, and the conception of a campaign. The method now helped him immeasurably, to wisely consider all the possibilities inherent with the preparations, to choose the courses that would best confront the coming invasion. That one day, and singular lesson, had been a remarkable treasure that added greatly to Aelfric's accumulation of knowledge gained throughout the years.

Although there was no way of foretelling what was to come, he found himself relieved that he had endured the oft-times arduous task of learning. Most warriors discounted the importance of letters and erudition, but Aelfric had known from an early age that he had been patiently sharpening a new type of blade, on a distinct type of whetstone. Every experience, whether a day spent at one of the monasteries or within his hall, or traveling through Saxan lands, became a new part of that growth and effort.

It was now a time to apply everything contained within him, in a way that was much greater than anything that he ever had need of doing before.

The levy summons had gone very well, far more smoothly than

Aelfric had anticipated. The army would also be very well supplied for several weeks to come.

The Saxans were now in a prime position to offer battle, at a strength that Aelfric knew would be unexpected by the enemy.

"My brothers in arms, what can we expect?" Aelfric queried the gathered thanes, counts, and other leaders rhetorically. "This is no regular force that comes at us. Ehrengard, Avanor, and lands yet unknown are marching against us. The borders have become so dangerous that very little word reaches us, but if my guesses are right, we will fight against many methods and strategies of war."

"Methods?" one of the thanes near to Aelfric asked, echoing the quizzical looks appearing on the surrounding faces. "What can we know other than what kinds of armies gather against us?"

"We have heard word of unusual ships... very large ships from a faraway land. Men shrouded. Men with darker skins. Men of a different faith. Great numbers of strange beasts, with large humps on their backs. I can only believe that they come from the far north ... from the Sun Lands, or lands held by a similar people. I only know what I have learned of some accounts that have been taken of such people and written down. ... These records cannot tell us everything, but they can still warn us of some things that may come ... that is, if we are wise to what is available to us," Aelfric stated, letting the words sink in to the ears of the attentive men. He then added, "And what is available to us can give us some insight into all the elements arrayed against our lands."

He then proceeded to comment at length regarding his carefully read accounts of distant wars in former times, taken from the histories fastidiously guarded in the libraries, and reproduced painstakingly in the monastery scriptoriums.

Aelfric had read the main chronicle of the conquest of Norengal, as well as a few accounts concerning other battles within that large Avanoran campaign.

A copy of a treatise on military theory and strategy, written by a great emperor of Theonia, had also been found in the monks' library at Jafarne. It had referred to many battles in the northern Sun Lands, regions that had seen the constant ebb and flow of great wars all throughout the long ages.

There had also been more than one biography of powerful nobles who had resided in Ehrengard, the vanity of their princely families resulting in the preservation of many great feats of battles, and the details of extensive military campaigns.

The lives of the religious saints were also not without some choice pieces of information, which could be gleaned by the perceptive reader. Often intended to convey a religious meaning, a military lesson could be gathered by correlating the many clues left in the nominally spiritual writings.

Collectively, the various writings represented a witness to the natures of the various forces that were now converging upon the Saxan lands. They were a look through the eyes of those who had lived and experienced the wars and cultures of the coming invaders. The value of those insights, as Aelfric knew very well, was priceless.

"Lands of the far north, such as the Sun Lands, are said to contain warriors that can shoot arrows from the back of a horse... when the horse is in a gallop. ... Their horses are said to be very swift, and they swirl about their enemy and seek to wear down a warrior's resolve.

"There are also accounts from northern lands that great drums of war are used in battle... and that their warriors are very fanatical. If we face such an army, all of us will be facing such warriors for the first time. This is exactly why the Unifier would hurl such an army against us," Aelfric continued, his words uttered deliberately slower so that they could impress more fully upon the minds of the men around him.

"Then the shield wall must hold, and remain firm," another thane commented to Aelfric's left.

The man was one of Aelfric's own thanes, a young and likeable man named Leofwine. It was his first major campaign, having come of age just a year prior, and into his inheritance only a couple of months after that.

Leofwine's eyes sparkled with a brash youthfulness, as he iterated confidently, "If they mean to frighten men with that which is unknown, then we must be steadfast."

"The shield wall must not lose heart. Those on the shield wall must not break ranks, no matter how strange or different the sights," Aelfric stated firmly. "If the enemy is close enough to loose arrows, or hurl javelins, then they will be close enough for us to reach with arrow or javelin."

"And Avanor?" still another thane queried, one with many more years on him than Leofwine. His name Wermund, the thane came from the lands of the Ealdorman Oslac in Mittevald. "Will they seek to fight in such a way? Horsemen shooting arrows from a gallop?"

"No. They will come riding upon the strongest of steeds on the battlefield, and clad in the heaviest armor that we have known. They will use great numbers of archers… and they will use the crossbow. Their fight will not be one to tire us. They will seek to bludgeon us. They will look to open holes in our shield wall for their horsemen to penetrate," Aelfric related somberly. "They have great discipline, and will be fierce opponents.

"The Avanorans are cunning too, and may try to loosen our shield wall by getting our own men to make an opening for them … to make it appear that they are falling back, to lure our men to break ranks in the hopes of a rout. This tactic has been written of, and has been used to great effect before. No man should fall prey to this, no matter how enticing the moment appears. We must make this very clear to all men on the front line of the wall. The entire battle's outcome may rest upon how disciplined we can remain."

"Then it is the shield wall that must be held, at all cost," the older thane Wermund said resolutely, echoing Leofwine. "And of Ehrengard? What unknown means might they bring?"

"Ehrengard we know most of all. Our brethren in the Western Marches have much experience fighting them. They will not all be of a common purpose. The leaders of Ehrengard have the least unity of any that come against us. As many of you know, they constantly war within themselves, among their princes, nobles, and bishops… and this may be to our advantage."

"And the Halmlander? Will they be among them?" Wermund asked. There was a discernable hesitancy and an edge to his voice, accompanying the collective tension that swelled in the room at the open mention of the murderous, fearsome Halmlander from Ehrengard. The vile mercenary company's fame was widespread, and for a very bloody reason.

Aelfric's own countenance grew grim at the mention of them. He slowly nodded his head, taking a deep breath.

His voice remained steady, though he shared the great trepidation that the men around him had. "Ehrengard has wealth, and there is little doubt that they will use it to bring the Halmlander with them. I have received some word of this as well. I expect that there will be a great company of Halmlander on the battlefield. We cannot deny that, and we must ready ourselves for it."

"They must never get through! We have no choice but to slay those mad dogs. Every last one of them," snarled a man named Agobard.

He was a noble with considerable lands in the great County of Rouenum, situated just to the south of the Western Marches. He turned towards a taller man to his immediate left. "Do I not speak true?"

"There can be no compromise on such an evil," commented the tall, deep-voiced man, Count Arnulf of Rouenum.

Aelfric took close account of the highly regarded Count.

One of the most respected nobles in the realm, Count Arnulf had witnessed the brutality of war many times, and had walked more than once upon blood-soaked ground. Aelfric knew that there was little that could startle or surprise Rouenum's great count, as Arnulf's demeanor had been shown to be icily calm amid the worst moments of battle.

Aelfric was well aware that the Count had come across the wake of the Halmlander once before, after the mercenaries had passed through a village situated near the Saxan borders. All reports that had come back to Aelfric had said that the sight of the ravages of the Halmlander had immediately unsettled the Count's battle-hardened eyes, driving him to openly weeping bitter tears.

There was little doubt that the horrific sights had left a deep scar upon the Count's heart ever since. Virtually no man could leave a place that the Halmlander had desecrated with his memory unscathed. Such was the baleful infamy of the vile mercenary company from Ehrengard.

"Ealdorman Aelfric, if these demons are indeed among the ranks of the enemy, we have no choice but to slay them to the very last man. Give us your word that we will hunt them from the moment the battle begins," Count Arnulf said quickly, though his voice held a faint tremor to it.

The sickening fear of having the Halmlander break through the Saxan lines, to gain unfettered access to the vulnerable villages and towns, was rife within the Count's nearly-shaking voice. A panicked murmur broke out within the tent, and Aelfric knew the cause immediately.

The men who knew the Count had never before heard his voice tinged with such dire apprehension.

The feared mercenary band, from deep within Ehrengard, needed no legend to magnify their brutality. Ferocious warriors, they were an advantage to those princes who chose to hire them. Yet once turned loose, they were like a fire unleashed in a dry forest.

They could not be reasoned with, nor could mercy be found anywhere in their darkened hearts. Even the coldest of souls among those that hired them could not help but cringe at the tales of the atrocities that the Halmlander committed in pillaged towns and villages, to sate their seemingly inexhaustible bloodlust.

In battle, the black-hearted mercenaries were indeed well disciplined, fearless, and steadfast. Few commanders could hope to find better infantry. They had turned the course of battles around by themselves, and refused to break ranks, no matter what transpired around them.

Following a battle, especially in a sacked city, town, or village, they transformed into the most rabid and demonic of men. Their depravity knew no bounds.

Despite this, their battlefield value was too great for any prince bent on conquest to ignore. Using them also kept the Halmlander from becoming too restless within the lands of Ehrengard itself.

If left unpaid and unused for too long, the amalgam of former criminals, deserters, heretics, and other manner of rogues would heed no authority. They were not above visiting their devilry upon Ehrengard's own lands, as some royal magnates and nobles had learned in the past, to their great dismay.

"The Halmlander may be the greatest reason why the shield wall must hold and not waver. My heart is as yours. They must not get through, no matter the cost," Aelfric replied carefully, sharing their fears on the matter.

He looked to Count Arnulf, and held the man's eyes. The look in the Count's eyes was nothing like that in Godric's. It was a firm gaze, filled with an honest confidence and sense of conviction. It was also a look that reflected a strong trust in Aelfric.

"The Halmlander will not be hard to find when the battle begins. You may be certain of that, Count Arnulf," Aelfric continued, his steadfast gaze conveying his intent. "When we find them, we will look to strike them hardest of all … and we will look for them from the moment that the enemy first steps onto the battlefield. You have my word on that, Count Arnulf."

A look of relief washed across Count Arnulf's tense face. There was no argument forthcoming from any of the others. Many proceeded to voice their vigorous assent to Aelfric's reassurance that the Halmlander would be actively sought out on the battlefield, without delay. The heavy air within the confined space lightened considerably.

The brisk chatter that was stimulated among them finally died down, as Aelfric patiently awaited the return of their attention.

"And is there anything else? Nay, I should ask, could there be anything else?" Agobard asked with incredulity. Aelfric could read in the man's face that he had come to realize the full breadth of the dark onslaught marshalling to face them. "Are there even more to be sent against us?"

Again, Aelfric nodded, and the assemblage grew very quiet as a look of dismay spread openly on Agobard's face. Every ear in the room was fully attentive to the Ealdorman once more.

"I would hide nothing from any of you," Aelfric began. "As I have said, we have gathered what word we can. You can expect there to be more of the unexpected among the enemy ranks. It has been said to me that the Unifier will bring others who are not of a human nature. Like the army from the Sun Lands, these will be used to frighten and confuse us, taking advantage of our unfamiliarity with their appearances and methods.

"A strong race of beings called Trogens serve as the bulk of the Unifier's sky forces. They are known to be a very fierce race, larger, broader, and stronger than humans. Their bestial appearance may be unsettling, as I have heard that the human warriors of the Unifier call them dog-men, though this is said in derision and mockery of them.

"It is said that they fight with a great and terrible fury. I have heard it said, from our spies and emissaries, that the Trogens speak of a promise given to them from the Unifier. The Unifier has promised to help them in the face of an ages-old oppression upon their kind by the Northern Elves … if they serve Him in this current war.

"Such a promise will only make them fight harder, for I have read that they have suffered a tremendous oppression for many ages, and that many of their kind are held in bondage within Elven lands. They will not enter the battle for lands or wealth, but rather to gain liberation for their kind. Such creatures will not be easy to overcome.

"Some word has also come to us that there are others … of an even larger and more ferocious race than the Trogens, though what these unknown creatures might be, I do not yet know.

"I have no word of any other forces that the Unifier might be sending, but that does not mean that there will not be other strange contingents present in their ranks. We must expect to confront much that we do not now foresee."

His eyes carefully roamed the room in the weighty silence that followed. The word of the Halmlander and the presence of non-human creatures had obviously rattled a number of the men, but he could see the resolve re-emerging quickly upon their faces and within their eyes, as he quietly took his measure of them.

Their reaction was a very hopeful sign.

"No matter what they may throw at us, do not lose heart, good warriors of Saxany. You will see that great strength has been mustered to meet this threat to us all," Aelfric stated.

He then looked towards three figures standing just to his left. Their stoic demeanor had not changed at all during his earlier words with the others. Determined eyes looked back to Aelfric, glinting in the reflection of firelight from a couple of nearby braziers, and what little daylight entered through the entry flaps of the large tent.

In the center of the trio was the tall, regal figure of Count Gerard II of Bretica. He was the senior personage among the three, and the most stout of build. Half a head taller, and standing to Count Gerard's right, was Count Leidrad of Poitaine, a man of very tough appearance.

Both Counts had arrived with strong, experienced forces. The two men alone represented a substantial proportion of the Saxan cavalry that would be taking part in the coming battle. They knew each other very well, and had campaigned several times before within the Western Marches of Saxany.

To Count Gerard's left was Count Einhard of Annenheim. Of medium build, Count Einhard was a little shorter of height than Count Gerard. The youngest of the three by several years, his thick, dark beard, and coarse, shoulder-length locks framed a well-proportioned, attractive face with very defined lines. His smooth skin held no marks or blemishes, and many daughters of nobles regularly bemoaned the fact that he had taken a wife only three years before.

To judge him by his youthful look and slighter build, some would have wondered why he stood so confidently in the company of the two other exalted men. Aelfric knew that to make such a conclusion would be to make an extensive underestimation.

Count Gerard had certainly made no such underestimation, for it was his very own daughter's hand that he had happily given in marriage to the young Count of the northern Saxan province.

Light blue eyes were filled with a sharp alertness and keen intelligence, traits that had earned Count Einhard great respect from both Count Gerard and Count Leidrad. He had long since proven his bravery beyond reproach in the midst of border skirmishes. Like the other two counts, he had also not hesitated to come to the support of the margraves within the Western Marches.

Count Einhard had grown in reputation to become very favored and celebrated throughout the western lands of Saxany, full of spirit and unbridled tenacity. As the count of lands that had also provided a significant number of horsemen to the Saxan army, he shared areas of common interest with the other two nobles standing by him.

Aelfric looked past them towards a fourth man, standing at the left shoulder of Count Einhard. Broad shouldered, with a bullish neck, he was a very powerfully built figure, as if he was made of the rock of the mountains that he had been born among in Annenheim.

He had a high forehead and squared jaw, outlined by dark, wavy hair that descended to just below his shoulders. His face was scarred from an old wound on the right side. His countenance, even at rest, held a look of fierceness. Deeply set, dark, piercing eyes seemed to constantly be evaluating or measuring all those before him.

There was no mistaking his purpose or resolve. He had endured many harrowing adventures during his rise to becoming the leader of a full scara of sky warriors, before Aelfric had designated him to a place of authority over all the sky warriors of Saxany.

The warrior's name was Aldric the Stormblade, and he had earned the bold title by being regarded as perhaps the most lethal sky warrior in the entire realm. It was said that an enemy would rather risk a bolt of lightning than face the stalwart fighter one against one, whose relentless attack was like that of a violent storm's fury.

Aelfric's next words focused upon those four individuals, as he explained their coming roles with depth and detail.

The three major counts, and Aldric, would command the main striking elements, and the most mobile ones, within the Saxan force.

Heavy and light cavalry, positioned at the wings of a vast, long shield wall, would ward the flanks of the great Saxan host. They would be favorably positioned to strike out at the enemy flanks, or to quickly respond to any enemy effort to turn their own flanks.

It was made abundantly clear that even if the mounted contingents from Bretica, Annenheim, and Poitaine contained warriors that were skilled fighters on foot, the necessity for cavalry in the coming fight was going to be most vital. Each and every warrior from the three key provinces fighting from horseback would be sorely needed.

Prince Aidan, who was not among those gathered within the tent, would be positioned behind the shield wall with a large, centrally positioned reserve. The reserve was to include a great number of the fierce, elite axe men that served in the royal household guard of King Alcuin himself.

Key margraves, counts, thanes, and other experienced warriors would be placed all along the front of the shield wall. Layers of lesser thanes, ceorls, and infantry would form ranks behind the initial shield wall, reinforced themselves by a dense mass of levied peasantry.

The warriors trained upon Himmerosen, the race of winged steeds found only in the northern reaches of Saxany, would have the difficult task of defending the skies above them. The numbers of Himmerosen at the camp, according to Aldric, was just over seven hundred strong. Aelfric knew that seven hundred was very few to send against what was coming.

It would nonetheless be the largest force of sky warriors ever gathered together in one place, in the young history of Saxany's sky warriors. The winged creatures themselves, as with all manner of Skiantha, were far from being numerous in their native environments to begin with. The training necessary to master the riding of Himmerosen, and to fight from their backs, was anything but easy. It took time and painstaking effort to build a force of sky riders, and to generate seven hundred required an enormous effort.

While the number encompassed nearly all of the available trained steeds in the kingdom, there was one other concerted deployment of Himmerosen. Aldric had informed Aelfric that a small number of sky warriors had been placed under the command of a thane named Edmund in Wessachia, the mountainous lands that bordered Annenheim to the east.

The two groups, the large one under Aldric the Stormblade, and the much smaller one under Edmund of Wessachia, represented almost the entirety of the kingdom's winged, mounted force. Very few trained steeds could now be found anywhere else within Saxany, and what scant few were left were mostly quartered at the palace in Aixen, serving King Alcuin as messengers.

The true purpose of Aldric's force would be dire and singular in the coming fight: to defend against the fearsome Trogens.

Aldric assured Aelfric confidently that his warriors would not waver in their given charge. He had even boldly asserted that they would drive the Trogens right from the skies.

His deep voice nearly shook with the sheer fervor projected within it. The stout confidence of the sky leader appeared to lift the spirits of everyone in the gathering, as they stood a little straighter, with their heads held higher.

Aldric's words set a good tone for the burdensome discussions that ensued, lasting deep into the day as various elements of the coming defense were proposed, considered, and examined. It was a quite arduous process, but by the time the assemblage finally departed the tent, their tasks and purposes were clear and understood.

For King Alcuin's majordomo, nothing less would have been acceptable.

DARROKS

Outlined in the first rays of the rising sun, a number of massive, dark shapes climbed up slowly into the sky, in the close vicinity of Avalos. The titanic, airborne juggernauts cast vast shadows over the sprawling city, bringing the bustling of many outdoor markets to a complete halt as the winged monstrosities lumbered by overhead.

Thousands upon thousands of pairs of eyes looked up in awe and fear at the skyward behemoths. They found relief only in the fact that they implicitly knew that the creatures were of the realm of Avanor.

The gargantuan creatures had been seen in the skies before. They were commonly known to be in the service of the Unifier, though not a few startled individuals shrieked with fright, trembled in place, or ducked back inside homes and storefronts.

None that looked upon the winged giants would dispute an assertion that there was not a power in the known world that could even hope to wage war with the Unifier. In their minds, nothing could contend with a ruler that could put forth such incredibly formidable powers into the skies above.

The bold sights evidencing such an unprecedented amount of power helped the majority of Avanor's populace put up with the annoyance of the increasingly heavier taxation that they had all been enduring. It also dampened resistance and objection to the many changes that had more recently come into their lives on the insistence of the Unifier.

Most felt that it was now quite futile to consider any form of opposition, even in outwardly expressing their displeasure at the ever-growing burdens. The vivid demonstration of sheer might flying above them did little to discourage that view.

As the hulking shapes gradually passed towards the far, eastern horizon, the people of the city began to turn their thoughts back to more immediate and mundane matters. The areas of the city that had come to a virtual standstill began to ebb and flow once again.

Before the winged forms had entirely passed from view, the people had fully resumed their focus on trade, pleasure, and progress within the streets of Avanor's powerful and wealthy capital. Few bothered to consider the plight of those dwelling in the lands that were the destinations of the winged giants.

LEE

At long last, and with no small amount of grumbling, the hastily marching quartet accompanying Gunther finally reached the edge of his woodland demesnes. The sign of their proximity was embodied by the appearance of a couple of very large Jaghuns, which suddenly leaped forth from the brush to greet their returning master.

Lee and the others involuntarily flinched at the rapid emergence of the large, broad-muzzled beasts from the quiescent surroundings. Their tails wagged furiously, and their exuberant energy boiled over as they sprung about the ground excitedly on their wide paws.

The large, dog-like beasts quickly regarded the quartet of newcomers with great interest, just as the four Jaghuns that had been escorting the group through the forest also emerged from the surrounding trees.

The curiosity of the two new Jaghuns was certainly piqued, as they sniffed and eyed the newcomers carefully between their spirited bouts of bounding and leaping about Gunther.

Even though his mind urged him otherwise, Lee was gripped by a primal fear. He grew very still, and was quite unnerved by the scrutiny of the fearsome creatures as they set their attentions directly upon him.

Gunther warmly embraced his four-legged companions, vigorously rubbing their massive heads between his large hands. He picked them up by their front paws, such that they stood eye to eye with him, and engaged in many more forms of greetings and gestures of familiarity. Lee could perceive that the woodsman's spirits were instantly improved by the Jaghuns' presence.

Erin, Lynn, and Ryan appeared to be very relieved to see the stern man's suddenly buoyed spirits. For his own part, Lee recognized another dimension to the ardor of the woodsman's greeting.

The man's fervent embrace of his creatures was such that he seemed to be reaching for the Jaghun that he had lost, even while seeking a little comfort from those who still remained. When he turned back to them, the sheen on the woodman's eyes was unmistakable. The woodsman was rife with raw emotion, even though he was making an effort to stifle the expression of it in the face of Lee and the others.

Lee said nothing, not knowing what he could even possibly say at such a time. After a few more minutes, Gunther rose back up to a standing position, as his demeanor quickly grew more serious again.

"We should move onward; we are not there yet," he announced curtly.

"So we are not done marching?" Erin queried with a petulant tone, continuing to nervously eye a Jaghun that had cautiously approached and begun to sniff at her.

"He is not going to hurt you, and no, we are not done marching. You may be happy to know that the distance from here is short," Gunther responded firmly, with no trace of humor.

Without another word, the big woodsman started forward with one of the Jaghuns loping along at his side. The others bounded ahead and moved farther off to the sides of the group.

From the first steps into the outskirts of Gunther's territory, the mood of Ryan, Lee, and Lynn continued to lift up. Though tired, the strain of the march seemed lessened with a destination in range. It was a comfort just to know that there was a physical destination to begin with, after having so recently faced the prospect of wandering aimlessly in the wilds.

At the very least, Lee knew that the end of their day's travel was imminently approaching. Only Erin remained dour, her face exhibiting a sulky expression as she seemed to be trying to stare holes right through Gunther's wide back. Her jaw was set firm, and her mouth held tight.

Lee paid her little heed as he focused on his footing through the uneven ground, already irritated enough with her acrimonious attitude. The ground had become noticeably more pronounced in its rises and falls, as they found themselves amid some hills of moderate size. It was to one of the larger hills that Gunther guided the wide-eyed newcomers.

Though the land before Lee had not been entirely cleared of trees, the growth of trees and brush had certainly been purposely thinned to accommodate the woodland homestead that subsequently came into sight. A two-story structure of timber had been built right up against the steep slope of the large hill. The structure was formed around a timber frame supported by thick posts of wood. Horizontal planking covered the spaces within the supportive framing. The steeply pitched roof was densely thatched with straw, and a large wooden door of rough-hewn planks served as the principle entrance to the structure.

There were a couple of small rectangular buildings set off to the right side of the main building. Both were freestanding, shorter in length, and of one level. They were gable-ended, and constructed of timber in a similar fashion to the larger, two-level building. There was also a spacious, fenced holding pen set to the front and left of the building. The space within it was currently empty, and the gate into the pen was closed.

A couple of small Jagoulfs, clearly adolescents of their breed, barked, whined, and yipped excitedly at the sight of the returning group. The little creatures brought a rapid smile to Lee's face, as they expressed their own enthusiasm, albeit in a high pitched, non-intimidating tone that was a far cry from that of their older brethren. One of them tripped over its own legs in its haste to run up to them, going down awkwardly in a ball of uncoordinated muscle and fur.

"Ah, little Skyheart. You have not yet mastered your own body," Gunther remarked, deftly bending over and scooping up the little creature, cradling it tenderly.

The little beast panted rapidly, and started earnestly licking Gunther's face. The woodsman put his mouth to the neck of the juvenile creature, and blew while making a humming sound, eliciting an excited squeal from the little Jaghun as it flailed with its paws.

Laughing, Gunther set the young beast back down. "There you go, now try and make sure you can at least stand up!"

The beast padded around Gunther, looking a little wobbly on its chubby legs.

"And you, Darkmane, could perhaps help your sister in this matter,"

Gunther quipped, as he greeted the second young Jaghun.

Its movements were a little more sturdy than those of its sibling, Lee noticed, as he watched the creature lick Gunther's hand. A little thicker and taller of build than Skyheart, it displayed a line of black fur that ran down from the middle of the back of its head, continuing along the center of its back down to its tail. It was little mystery as to how Gunther had come up with its name.

Gunther looked back to his four new guests. "I do not often have visitors, but there should be plenty of room inside my home for all of you. It may have little in the way of luxuries … but it is a different manner of place than you will find in the villages around this area. I used some ideas that I gained during my former travels. Made some use of a hillside, two-story house design I saw within a Saxan burh, and came up with some things of my own. Took some time to build. Had some failures. But I got it done. It is solid, it is distinct, and this has been my home for some time now."

Gunther sounded both proud and unapologetic as he spoke of his dwelling. Though Lee knew that there were more than a few stories yet to be told by the woodsman, he saved any questions that he might have asked then for a more opportune moment. Gunther was not forthcoming with anything else, commenting no further on his homestead as he strode up to the wooden door leading into the main, two-level structure.

It was not locked, as Gunther unlatched the door and pushed it open. The woodsman then stood to the side, to allow the others to enter first. Lee led the others as they walked inside the woodsman's dwelling, slowly filing into the front room.

The air was a little denser inside, something that Lee noted on his first inhalation. Shadow surrounded them in the dim interior, as the bulk of the light coming into the room entered through the door opening behind them.

There were no windows within the walls of the lower level. Despite the low ambience, it could still be seen that the spacious, open room had some wooden shelving fitted along the right wall, and there were a few rectangular chests lying upon the ground. The floor itself was earthen, hard-packed and smooth, though strewn about with some old rushes that lent a musty scent to the air.

The outside wall planks of rough-hewn timber were covered to a large extent on the inside with great, capacious fabrics. Some of the hangings appeared to have designs woven upon them, but in the dimness Lee could not make out much detail.

A shallow pit or small hearth had been dug out near to the center of the room. Lined with stones, it was filled with cold ash and embers left over from the last fire that had burned within it. A large iron pot was currently suspended over the hearth by a chain, which hung down from the center of an iron tripod.

Looking up, Lee saw that there was an opening set high in the ceiling, visible through the second level. A little further light made its way through the opening in the roof overhead, giving highlight to the central, open shaft. Some wooden steps running up from the back of the room, just off to the left, led on up to the second story loft.

The light through the front door also revealed a last, intriguing feature in the room, which quickly drew the interest of the four guests. Lee became aware that all of his companions had settled their gazes upon it, even as Gunther followed the direction of their stares.

There was another large wooden door centered in the rear of the room, set right in the hillside's outer surfacing.

"Yes, I suppose that doorway looks like a mystery. And yes, it is of importance. I once had a habitation not too far from here … and I relocated myself to this place, after I had learned a little more about these woods. It was a little easier to fashion two levels using the hill, but I chose this particular location for a very good reason, which you will learn about soon enough. But not just yet," Gunther said, disappointing Lee's curiosity once again.

The woodsman unbuckled his leather belt as he walked closer to the wall with the shelves, setting the belt with its attached leather pouches down upon the ground. Straightening up, he removed his great hunting bow and leaned it against the wall, proceeding to place his quiver down next to it. Finally, he removed his baldric, propping his sword in its leather scabbard up against the wall as well. Gunther then directed his four guests to set their own weapons and other belongings down, near to his weapons.

"Please feel welcome in my home. It is about as safe as a place can be in this age," Gunther said invitingly, turning to face the four. "Let me show you where you will sleep. Soon you will eat your fill, though I have only a humble fare, and then you will rest."

Lee was more than ready to take the woodsman up on both offers. Even Erin seemed not to be overly bothered about the rather stark nature of their surroundings, or at least she kept any misgivings to herself. Under other circumstances, Lee had no doubts that a pompous veneer would have shined forth from the young woman.

"This way," Gunther remarked.

He gestured towards the staircase, as he moved forward and led them up to the second level loft. It was difficult to make out all of the features in the upper room, but enough light leaked in to reveal that it was fairly barren.

At present, there was just one rather plain, straw-filled mattress, with a rough-spun woolen blanket heaped atop it, and a couple of hides set to one side. Gunther walked over to the end of the room opposite the top of the stairway, and pulled forth several more coverings out of a deep pool of shadow, mostly turning out to be hides.

"It may not be the most in comfort that you may find within this world, but for now you will have to make use of it," he said, indicating the skins. "I cannot say I was prepared for several visitors, but I have accumulated some extra hides which you may use for warmth, and to cover the floor surface. You may use the mattress as well … though it is for you to decide who amongst you will do so. For the time being, I will sleep below."

He then bid them well, and informed them that he would see to the preparation of the evening meal. Exiting down the stairs, Gunther left them to their own devices, as he turned his attentions to stoking a fire in the cold hearth.

The others remained silent as they quietly listened to Gunther bustling about the hearth below.

"Not the best I've had, I'd say," joked Lynn in a low voice, looking around the room. Walking to the edge of the room's central area, she looked up at the square opening above them, before glancing down upon the cooking hearth on the first level. Lee casually strode over and joined her.

He looked up to the ceiling as well. There was a raised square of timber positioned just above the roof opening, designed to deflect the bulk of any rains out, while allowing smoke from the hearth below to exit.

"I would have to agree," Ryan stated, as he drew up next to Lee, resting his hands on his hips while he looked around. "I come from a poor family, but our little house was a mansion compared to this."

"Well, I don't know about you all, but right now I could use some rest, at least until there is some food to be had," Lee said, as he turned and walked away from the opening.

He pulled one of the large animal skins that Gunther had brought out over to an open space. Lee spread it out along the rough wooden boards that formed the flooring, and lay down upon its surface. He immediately made a little grimace, shifting about as his sore, tired body adjusted to the unforgiving floor surface. He moaned, "Ooohh … I think this is going to take some getting used to."

He rolled his head to the side, looking to see what the others were doing.

With little hesitation, Erin all but dived down upon the straw mattress. A triumphant look was splayed across her face as she stretched out. "I will take this one. Called it first."

Lee saw the irritated looks crop up on the faces of Lynn and Ryan, and also observed that Erin was alert enough to take account of them as well. "For the time being," she quickly added, suddenly seeming a little abashed at her own rash impetus.

"Good diplomacy, Erin," Lynn said, with a noticeable edge to her voice, as she followed Lee's example in pulling out another large skin and claiming a spot on the open flooring.

"Wonder where that door downstairs, in the back, goes to," Erin stated from where she lay, looking back towards the staircase.

"Who knows? Maybe we'll find out after we get a little of our strength back," Lynn said.

"I'll go with that," Ryan said, unleashing a wide yawn as he dragged a skin over, laying claim to some space that was close to the central opening.

"Be careful," Lynn said, watching Ryan lie down. "There's no railing there."

Ryan smirked, and retorted sarcastically, "I think I'll be fine … but thank you for your concern, Mother. …"

Lee chuckled. If Ryan tumbled over the edge, he would not fall terribly far, and would likely be rewarded with a nice singe. All the same, Lee was not too worried over the likelihood.

Letting their bodies relax, and looking forward to dinner, the full effect of fatigue began to descend upon the four.

Before very long, the first tendrils of smoke wafted up through the opening in the center of the floor, accompanied by a glow of light. Shortly thereafter, the scents of something cooking over the hearth reached up to Lee from beneath. It was enough to make his mouth water, but not enough to rouse him.

Despite the discomforts, all four had drifted into sleep by the time that Gunther unmercifully awoke them with a rather forceful greeting. Lee jerked awake, feeling immediately as if his aching body had begun to turn into stone. He felt the series of cricks in his stiff neck as he turned his head to look towards Gunther.

"Come on, get up now! Evening meal is ready!" the woodsman told them, with little expression to his face. He stood at the top of the stairs, and did not depart until he was sure that they were all waking up.

Many winces and groans were elicited from the four newcomers, as they slowly sat up, stretched, and tried to dispel the greatly increased degree of soreness in their bodies. Lee's muscles throbbed with the rigidity caused by napping upon the hard floor surface.

Lee grimaced further as he arched his back, filling the air with some audible pops and cracks. Seeing Ryan's mirthful grin as the youth eyed him, he responded in jest, "You find it funny, don't you? Time is merciless, and will be my avenger, which I guarantee you will discover someday."

"I'll enjoy the here and now, you don't get out of it that easy," Ryan retorted. "Come on, Lee, it's time to eat."

With a little effort, they all got to their feet and went back down the stairs to the first level.

Gunther had set up the room for the meal. There were a couple of narrow wooden trestles, resting upon plain stools. A few other three-legged wooden stools had been pulled up for the guests to sit on.

A few bowls made of undecorated pottery were sitting upon the wooden planks, filled with a steaming pottage. A large hunk of dark bread rested by each bowl. A small wooden bowl held a full portion of some kind of nuts. A clay jug finished out the general arrangement, next to which was a trio of wooden cups.

"I do not have many drinking vessels, so you will have to share what I do have. It is not the offering of a lord or king, but it will fill you up and bring strength back to you," Gunther said without apology.

The others took their seats at the various stools. Erin stared down at the bowl in front of her.

"Does this have meat in it?" Erin said, wrinkling her nose slightly.

Lee listened with amusement, knowing what was about to come.

"Oh yes, and you are very fortunate, as it is some of the best western boar that you can find in these woods. It is the same quality of boar that a great thane would be proud to have served to honored guests in a longhall. And it is all I have until I get to attempt another hunt, which you and your friends interrupted. I admit that what I had left is a bit salty, as I had to store what remained from my last hunt, before I left on the sojourn that ended up with finding all of you.

"It seems that you do not know much of this world, but be assured, you will feel strong again in no time. I may have said that I did not have the full meal of a king to offer you, but even a king would be hard pressed to exceed such fine meat," Gunther replied with a hint of pride. He paused for a moment, before adding in a voice laden with seriousness, "Truthfully, many good men have gotten killed hunting the type of large boar whose meat you will enjoy tonight. It is a very dangerous quarry, for even the best of hunters."

Gunther's brow furrowed, and Lee followed the woodsman's look to see the open grimace spread upon Erin's face. It was exaggerated by the flickering shadows cast by the fire blazing nearby in the hearth.

"She does not like to eat meat," Lee interjected quickly, not knowing how else to explain her sour reaction to the woodsman. He knew that the man would likely find it to be a very odd disposition for someone to have. "It is a belief of hers."

Gunther looked at her for a moment. "It is not one of the fasting days of the Church, if that is what you are worried about. Second day of the week. You should not worry needlessly."

Lee was puzzled for a moment, before comprehending that Gunther had attributed Erin's reluctance to some sort of religious practice familiar to his own world.

"No, it has nothing to do with religious belief," Lee informed the woodsman. "She just ... cannot bring herself to eat meat, at anytime. Please do not feel offended."

"What a terrible affliction," Gunther replied, his eyes widened somewhat with surprise. The man's response was not sarcastic, or in jest, as he had a genuine look of sympathy. "I could not bear to be stricken with such a burden. Your misfortune is truly bad."

Erin said nothing, staring glumly down at the bowl in front of her.

"Well, I do not have such a burden, thank the All-Father," Gunther said with a shrug, leaning over and taking the bowl back from her.

He tore off a piece of bread from his chunk and dipped it into the pottage, waiting for a moment to let it soak, before scooping up a nice portion of it with the bread.

Putting it into his mouth, he chewed on it slowly. After swallowing, he remarked to Erin, "They say that you cannot live on bread alone, but beyond this stew, you will have to do with bread only if you are hungry. Except perhaps for some nuts, I have nothing much else to offer you, until I can scout tomorrow."

Erin's eyes narrowed and her expression darkened. Lee knew what was passing through her mind. She was realizing that Gunther truly deemed her situation to be her own problem to handle, and not his to worry about.

Out of the corner of Lee's eye, he saw Lynn shoot Erin a sharp, warning look. He agreed with Lynn's sentiments, hoping that Erin did not do or say anything to annoy their host.

Erin's face relaxed a little, catching the warning glance.

Lee felt the hard bread, flat and far from leavened, and rather coarse in texture. To his best estimation, it was wheat bread, but he understood quickly why Gunther had dipped his in the pottage.

The others had made similar discoveries, and imitated Gunther as they tore off pieces of the bread and dipped it into their own bowls. Lee could see why Gunther waited for it to soak for a second, as the bread was harder and tougher than any bread that he had ever been given before.

The pottage was predominantly a mix of legumes, grain, and the salted boar's meat. As hungry as he was, Lee was not about to complain. The food was palatable enough. Chewing the bread thoroughly, Lee glanced towards their host.

Gunther was facing towards Ryan, who had an alarmed expression on his face. Ryan had evidently tried to take a bite without waiting long enough for the bread to fully soften, as Gunther commented to the young man, "The bread is good wheat bread. It is not too old. But you must be a little patient and allow it to soften."

Gunther picked up the clay jug and proceeded to pour a dark, rather thick liquid into each of the alderwood cups. Erin sat sullenly, but did not object as the last vessel was filled to the brim and handed over to her.

"I hope your burdens do not include well-crafted mead, for you will not find a better drink in this area. I had been saving this in a small barrel for a special time. I suppose that this is such an occasion," he remarked. "It took my best hunting skills to gain enough to trade for it."

He passed around the other two cups, letting the others drink first before he took a deep draught himself. Gunther gave a light grin as he smacked his lips, a light foam settling upon his beard and upper lip. He uttered a contented sigh, as he refilled the cup in his hands.

Lee had taken a substantial sip, but realized that the mead would be an acquired taste, very different from anything that he had ever imbibed. Though made from the honey of bees, and containing a certain level of sweetness, the drink felt very thick as it traveled down Lee's throat.

One among their number, however, was more than ready to embrace the beverage. Ryan soon was exhibiting the potency of the beverage, after draining a couple of cups. Lee's own blood had already begun to tingle after taking just a few more draughts, and he was not in the least bit surprised that the effects were showing quickly on his young friend, who was downing the mead at a much faster rate.

"I think I will come to like this very much," Ryan announced, the foam giving him an artificial moustache of his own. He looked to be a little lightheaded as he spoke to Gunther, "Can I have more?"

"A man with some good taste," complimented Gunther, who appeared more than happy to oblige the young man. His serious expression was brightened by the trace of a mischievous smirk. "It looks like the mead has chosen to give you the moustache of a Saxan thane."

Ryan, his mouth full with a large bite of bread sopped generously in the porridge-stew, replied slowly, in a muffled voice. "I think I could get very used to this."

Gunther shook his head, and let another amused smirk escape. "We will not always be able to drink so well, though you are fortunate that I am a good hunter, and can hunt these woods freely."

There was no arrogance in his voice, the tone simply being that of a statement of fact. The woodsman then shot a quick glance towards Erin. "Meat is much more scarce in the villages, and I get good trade value for it. Mead, on the other hand, is a real luxury. Elfrida, wife of Leodulf, from the village near Dragon's Back Ridge in Beordenshire, is most skilled in the making of mead. Ale is much more common in these lands. I live with no woman, so I have learned to make my own ale. I will give you some of it soon, so that you can judge my skill for yourself."

Ryan finished off another cup of the treasured mead.

"Slow down, young lad," Gunther cautioned Ryan. "You may not yet realize the full power of that mead. Elfrida puts great strength into it. Nonetheless, I do wish to provide you all a good welcome feast, as best I can."

Taking another mouthful of food, Gunther stood up and took the empty pitcher over to a corner of the room, where he refilled it from the contents of a small wooden barrel. Returning back to his stool, he leaned over and refilled Ryan's cup again, up to the brim, with a little sloshing over the edge.

"If it would okay to ask you, where does that door go to?" Lee asked Gunther, as the woodsman settled back down, pointing over towards the closed door in the back of the room.

Gunther nodded slowly to Lee, his mouth occupied for a moment as he took another prodigious draught of the mead. He set the cup down upon the trestle board, glancing briefly towards the door as all of his guests waited expectantly for his answer.

"To the abode of the Unguhur. It is the reason why I chose this place to build my home … once I made myself known to them, and knew of their presence here," Gunther began, as his eyes took on a more faraway gaze.

"I discovered it all only by the whims of fortune. I had heard of them in tales before. The Stone Hides, they were once called, dwelling in a forested land populated by an alliance of tribes, which lies to the east of the Gallean kingdom.

"Better yet, not long after I discovered them, I was able to befriend them. Not an easy thing, when they diligently keep to themselves in their underground world, and do not concern themselves with the surface kingdoms of humankind.

"Rest assured, they know of the door. It would not be there if they objected to it, believe me," Gunther commented, with a low chuckle. "In a way, I guard an entrance into their world. They do not have to worry about the smaller minds among us, who might try to go down to attack or hunt them, though it would be great folly to even try to do so."

"What are Unguhur?" asked Lynn curiously, posing the question that was on Lee's own tongue.

"They are a strong race that dwells under the surface of the world. A very strong race … of fierce appearance, but quite gentle in nature. You will see for yourselves soon enough. Much taller than a man, and so much stronger. Thick skin … almost like a leather jerkin for a man. There is a good reason why those tribes called them Stone Hides, believe my words. There is a world under this world, and the Unguhur are no small part of it," Gunther informed them.

"Do you go there often?" asked Ryan, nearly finished with his next cup of mead.

Ryan's head was evidently feeling much lighter, as he was swaying a little, and a silly smile was now beginning to emerge upon his face. The young man would have to be cut off from quaffing more mead before much longer.

"I go there when I may. Sometimes they have even let me hunt and fish within their realm," Gunther replied. "That is no small wonder, for one who naturally inhabits the surface world."

"So, what brought you here? To this … place…" Ryan asked, his inhibitions lessening. "You don't live in a village. Just out here by yourself, with all of your creatures … out in the woods. What made you want to live here? Why not around people?"

For a brief moment, Lee could have sworn that Gunther's eyes misted over. If they had, the woodsman made a quick recovery, but he also made it abundantly clear that the question concerned a topic that he did not yet want to address.

His voice was low and steady as he responded to Ryan. "We will speak of it perhaps another time. Good fortune seldom drives a man to live by himself. That is all I can say, and want to say at this time. Do not press me further on this."

Ryan nodded, his mirth curtailed somewhat by the somber tone of their host. Ryan was not so far gone into his drink that he was unable to retract the grin on his face. Lee felt quite relieved for that lingering sensibility, as he could tell that the subject was very sensitive to the woodsman.

"And your creatures? Do you raise them?" Lynn asked, clearly sensing the need to change the subject of conversation between them.

"The Jaghuns? I have raised every one that you have seen here, from their birth," Gunther remarked with a flare of pride in his voice and expression. "The only ones you will see anywhere, except for where their kind naturally lives within the Shadowlands."

"The Shadowlands?" queried Ryan.

"A very dark and brooding land … very, very far from here, to the east. My travels carried me there, many years ago … such a dark and dangerous land. … I was fortunate to get away from there," he told them, staring off with a grim look on his face, as if remembering old fears that had rested dormant in him.

He paused for a few moments, swallowing a mouthful of food, and taking another drink out of his mead cup, before resuming. "I found two Jaghun cubs stranded in the wilderness. Their mother had clearly been killed, as I would have likely been dead to come upon two cubs otherwise. In that terrible land, they stood no chance. … I decided to take mercy upon them, and I took them with me. To my later fortune, one was a male, and one was a female.

"It was a long journey back, fraught with many perils, but they made it to Saxany alive and healthy with me. Those special two have since departed from this world, after living a full measure of life, but their blood still lives on within Ave. Their blood has grown and multiplied with me here in the Saxan woodlands, and they will never be forgotten."

Lee greatly desired to question Gunther further about the Shadowlands, but held his impulse back in order to respect the woodsman's earlier admonishment to avoid asking questions regarding his past. He would have to be content with the information that Gunther was willing to offer, though he hoped that it would not be long before the woodsman was more favorably disposed towards indulging his curiosity.

Lynn then ventured a safer question, which still addressed some of his curiosities.

"So, what are the lands surrounding your home?" she asked him, dipping another piece of bread. "We really have no idea where we are right now."

"The Kingdom of Ehrengard lies to the west of Saxany, connected by a narrow stretch of land. To the north, across the ocean waters, is a land of dense forests and hills, populated by tribal people. A few of these tribes formed a kind of alliance, known as the Five Realms. They have a fierce love of their ways and land, and I am certain that they are not very favored by the Unifier," Gunther said, as an inkling of a grin played about his face. "I truly admire their heart, and my hope is that they are left to their own will.

"Gallea rests along the western borders of those tribal lands. It is a large kingdom, and powerful. Avanor was once a province of that land, giving fealty to Gallea's king, though the Unifier recognizes no sovereign. The Unifier holds His court in Avalos, the great capital city of Avanor, which lies on the western edge of Gallea.

"To the south and east, across ocean waters broken only by scattered islands, is Midragard. The people of Midragard are masters of the sea, and few can match their prowess in arms and war. They were fearsome raiders, whose terror spread far and wide. Even these lands felt the wrath of their plunderers at one time.

"It is good for all lands that strong kings began to rise among the Midragardans, and that a very good and powerful king's influence is felt there now. He is a man of wisdom, who desires different ways for his people other than raid and plunder ...

"Kiruva lies across the ocean to the east. A massive land. Many rivers ... which cross through many great, grassy plains. An abundance of forested flatlands, too. It is a land whose rule I do not understand well, with many princes, and one that is recognized as a Grand Prince.

"Beyond the east of Kiruvar, across another sea, are the Shadowlands that I have spoken already to you of. There are many other lands and peoples in this wide world. Saljuka, Fahtma, the Coastal Kingdoms established in the First Holy War, the Empire of Theonia ... all are in the Sun Lands to the far north. Lambar, Paleria ... to the farthest west. ... It is even said that there are lands of great splendor and exotic ways located to the farthest east ... homelands to an ancient and honorable race of men. And who knows what other lands might not yet be known of?"

For a moment, Gunther appeared to become lost in his thoughts. The mention of the far eastern lands had summoned up a mixture of emotions, the nature of which were shrouded within the mind of the woodsman. His mouth tightened, and he stared down into the cup in his hand, though Lee knew that the woodsman was not looking at the mead that remained within the drinking vessel.

When Gunther finally continued, it seemed almost as if he was talking aloud to himself. He slowly shook his head.

"At one time, I wanted to be one of the few to see those lands to the far east. ... I wanted to travel the Rising Sun Road. But I was held back, right on the cusp of doing so ... Maybe I should have gone ahead and taken that road anyway, right from the beginning. Might have been a better path for me to take."

The woodsman's chest heaved with a long, slow intake of breath.

"You see, to get to those far eastern lands, you would have to journey through Theonia. An empire forged of the natures of both east and west. I called Theonia home for some time, though that time is many years past. Theonia. A land I most want to return to ... and a land I least want to find myself in. Creates quite a problem for me, if ever I wanted to try and go to the far east, does it not?"

A deep sadness clung to the slight, bittersweet grin that came to his face, and his voice had suddenly seemed laden with a heaviness of heart. He drew into himself further, for a few moments becoming much more distant.

Whatever the woodsman's past contained, it was clear that Gunther still carried an open emotional wound in regards to Theonia, something that Lee quietly took to heart as he looked upon the man's weighty, pained expression.

Gunther then looked over towards Lee, as he slowly came out of the momentary trance. His voice lightened a little. "What is done is done, but I still am fascinated with thoughts of the far east. It is hard not to be. I have heard it spoken that the lands in the far east are rich and bountiful lands... filled with a proud and wise people, with spectacular, huge cities teeming with all kinds of splendor. All manner of different and amazing creatures are said to live within those lands as well."

Gunther paused as he continued to gaze upon Lee, as if making some sort of appraisal.

"From what few of those people that I have seen, it would seem that they are indeed akin to yourself ... the hue of your skin, the angle of your eyes. I know little else of their mysterious realms, only what is said, and that is often several times removed from the few adventurers and merchants that have made the great journey on the Rising Sun Road."

"All of it sounds fascinating," Lee said, highly intrigued to hear of the open comparison to himself in regard to the eastern lands.

"And I have only told you of some of the lands that exist within Ave. ... There is the great island of the Northern Elves, the strange lands of Yanith, with its towering forests, the green bounty that is Gael, the lands to the north of Kiruva, where some titanic creatures dwell, and many, many other amazing places," Gunther responded, with an air of reminiscence. "Ave is filled with strange and incredible sights, and a great many lands, whose call pulled me as a youth from my own homeland. Lots of absolutely enthralling places, many that I have seen, and many that I have not."

"Lotsss offf placesss … verrry niccce … verrrry niccceee…" Ryan murmured with a dazed expression, a significant slurring to his speech.

The mead was now exhibiting a potent, highly visible effect. Ryan wavered back and forth, his eyes fluttering, before his head nodded down heavily with a noticeable thud on the trestle table. He just missed plopping his face into his largely emptied bowl of porridge, by just a few mere inches.

"I think he has had enough mead for now," Lee quipped, unable to stop a grin from forming. The image of Ryan's stupefied expression was emblazoned on his mind, pushing out some open laughter even though he was a little nervous as to how Gunther would react to the display.

"I believe that we are all in agreement … even him, as I do not think he will argue," Gunther commented, looking at the youth with a glint of amusement in his eyes. "One must learn to hold their drink well!"

As if to emphasize the difference between the veteran and the youth, Gunther imbibed an extended swill of the mead, emptying his nearly full cup. Some traces of foam held onto his beard as he set the cup down. He casually reached over, grabbed the clay pitcher, and filled it up again.

"Anyone else?" Gunther queried, indicating the pitcher towards the other three remaining conscious guests.

For the first time that Lee had seen, a ray of pure, joyous mirth emerged through the smile that spread on Gunther's face. The big woodsman rumbled with laughter and shook his head, regarding the facedown form of Ryan.

Erin and Lynn laughed heartily, though both indicated that they had taken enough mead for one night, as did Lee. The laughter finally subsided, though it had felt so pleasant, and had relieved a great amount of anxiety in seconds.

Lee smiled as he looked back to Gunther, his inquisitiveness again coming to the fore. "And you've traveled all over many of these lands? That is just amazing."

"A vastness of oceans and lands," Gunther remarked, before adding with a tint of sadness that Lee almost felt guilty for inadvertently evoking, "though I have seen quite enough of it all, and do not have any desire to explore it any further."

The group finished their meal, sharing only a few idle bits of conversation before they finally begged leave of Gunther. The woodsman offered to help with Ryan, though Lee politely declined, as he felt that they had imposed quite enough on the man's hospitality.

Lynn aided Lee as he worked to get their intoxicated friend to his feet, to help Ryan up the stairs so that he could lie down. Ryan groaned as he was jostled, but roused himself enough so that he was not an entirely dead weight.

As Lee reached the base of the stairs, he glanced back to where Gunther was still sitting.

The trance-like look had returned to the man's face, crossed with flickering light and shadow from the hearth fire. The woodsman had retreated inside of himself again, descending to some safe and distant refuge that he had fashioned within his mind.

Lee had a thousand questions that he wanted to ask, but one look at the man dissipated any urgency that he felt. He wondered what paths their host had taken in his life, and what far travels he had undergone. Gunther carried the weariness of tragedy and dreams abandoned, still resounding with the echoes of trauma, as well as the sobered countenance of experience.

He knew that there was much more to the solitary woodsman before his eyes, but his interests would have to wait until a time of Gunther's own choosing.

section vii

DRAGOL

The smaller, second invasion force, comprised mainly of Avanoran warriors, had finally reached the outskirts of the borders of the province of Wessachia, in the northwest of Saxany.

The long column had come to a halt near the headwaters of the substantial Grenzen River, which emerged into its fullness near to the base of the forested hills leading up to the northern Hymaht Mountains.

The Avanorans had distanced themselves many leagues from the massive army marching towards the Plains of Athelney, but their purpose was no less important. The region and the specific site that they approached had been skillfully chosen, and carefully deliberated. It was the northernmost area along the western borderlands of Saxany that they could seek to pierce without unduly exposing themselves to great vulnerability.

A corridor of sorts existed towards the east, ferreted out by diligent Avanoran scouts, through which they could launch a penetrating strike deeper into Saxan lands.

Tents were assembled in a broad encampment that was located close to that of the Trogen sky force and the Andamoorans. Commander, mess, and chapel tents were placed near to the center of the encampment, with the tents of the higher-ranking knights surrounding those, and the dwellings of the common soldiery and camp attendants radiating further outwards.

Banners signifying the various nobles and officers in charge of the army flew from high poles positioned near to the entrance flaps of their tents.

While the Avanorans were situating the encampment, a constant cover of sky patrols had been provided under the orders of the Trogen chieftain, Tragan. Regular waves of Trogens upon Harraks returned and departed from the smaller encampment, keeping a constant set of eyes high in the air to watch over the laboring Avanoran army.

With the exception of the religious volunteers, the Andamooran contingent in the smaller camp had been almost completely emptied out. The entire force of Andamooran light horsemen had been dispatched, to range towards the east and scout far beyond the two camps.

Their absence from the camp areas was probably for the better, Dragol felt. The fanatical, face-veiled horsemen held little affinity for the Avanorans that they regarded as infidels. The Avanoran warriors continuously eyed the Trogens with looks that did little to hide their distaste for the non-human race, considering the Trogens to be little more than barbarous dog-men.

More than one Avanoran knight of considerable rank and lineage, gripping a great lance with a billowing pennon, tensed at the sight of the few Trogen chieftains moving among them, on their way to coordinate their efforts with the newly arrived Avanoran lords.

The Trogen leaders, though restraining themselves from provoking a larger incident, glowered back defiantly at the knights and other human soldiers. Many of the knights would not have been disappointed had the Trogens given in to their urges. More than one knight's hand clenched the hilt of his sword, with a steely look in his eyes.

It was fortunate that the overwhelming majority of the Trogens was in the sky, or set apart in their own camp. Only the strictest orders by the Avanoran leaders, and the severe admonishments of Tragan, could hope to keep the peace among the two races.

The small numbers of Andamooran religious volunteers laboring among the Trogens and their steeds were perhaps the most unfortunate of all. They tried in vain to keep their distance from both groups during the ensuing hours, though not always successfully. Ill-trained and poorly equipped, they tended to the more menial tasks within the Trogen sky steed camp, and were not about to willfully aggravate either the fierce, heavily armored warriors of Avanor, or the massive, aggressive Trogens. The Andamoorans hated and resented all the others, Trogen and Avanoran alike, but were judicious concerning their fate should they provoke either one of the groups.

There was little doubt that tensions would rise between the incoming Avanorans and the Andamoorans, tensions that could well escalate beyond the state of unease with the Trogens. The Avanorans made no secret that they regarded the Andamoorans as heathens and apostates, the followers of a false prophet. As with the Trogens, only the harsh, disciplined command of the Avanoran lords and officers kept a general order.

Nonetheless, when the Andamoorans gathered to say their ritualized prayers at sunset that evening, they grouped together on the farthest side of the combined Trogen and Andamooran camp. Their anxiety having considerably risen, they strove to stay far away from any potential Avanoran derision or incitement.

At the very least, the Trogens left the Andamoorans alone to practice their own beliefs without undue harassment. Dragol had to concede that he respected the ardent zeal of the Andamooran volunteers. He did not believe in their strange deity that supposedly had spoken through some northern prophet, yet he had little doubt that if such a deity existed, that divinity would be quite pleased with such dedicated and loyal followers.

During the onset of the lavender-hued firmament's settling, the gloaming period bridging dusk to night, Dragol and Goras found themselves among the few Trogens that were currently being allowed a short respite from the extensive duties of sky patrols. The two leaders had already incurred a very strenuous day, and even their robust, well-trained muscles ached for some needed relief.

They sat together under the shelter of Dragol's tent, secured safely away from the last, direct rays of the dying sun. Their skin was finally cooling off, their upper bodies now finally freed from the hot, encompassing leather cuirasses that had been worn for so many hours on end.

The two commanders had undergone a vigorous litany of activities since the Avanoran army had arrived at the borders of the Saxan province of Wessachia. Their sky steeds were in little better shape, even though they had each made a change to fresh mounts towards the end of the day.

"It will not be long before battle is enjoined," Goras remarked, watching Dragol slowly massage his tired left shoulder with his broad right hand.

"Not long? At this time, another day is too long," Dragol grumbled, his short muzzle pulled back into an annoyed sneer. "I am tired of floating around in the sky. Skirmishing with overmatched quarry that we stumble across, or being bled by hidden adversaries that we are not allowed to pursue. We must fight a true battle soon. I hunger to get revenge on those creatures that slew my warriors, and to measure myself on a true day of battle."

"You are not wrong to feel such a way, Dragol. There is nothing for us here, but to watch over haughty Avanorans," Goras replied through clenched teeth, reflecting his overall disappointment with their circumstances. The arrogance of the Avanorans only drove the resentments in the likes of Dragol and the others higher. "And there is little sign of the sky warriors of these Saxans. I would feel less angered were it otherwise. At least there would be a hope to look to."

Dragol felt the sympathy that any Trogen would have for another who had long been denied honorable combat. The chance to measure themselves in courage, in strength, and in resolve was held back with each day that passed where there was no true battle.

The Trogens had heard much of the Saxan sky warriors, who flew upon a breed of Skiantha called Himmerosen. Yet they had not seen any significant sign of them in the region, with the exception of some distant elements that could just as well have been larger wildlife, or mirages created by wishful anticipation.

Dragol then replied in a voice that was nearly a growl of frustration. He clenched his great left hand into a balled fist, his arm muscles bulging. "It is not the way of a Trogen, the way that we are used here. The way that we are held back. But we will not wait much longer. I promise you! And when we …"

"Dragol! Look!" Goras said, sharply interrupting Dragol, as his eyes immediately riveted skyward. A couple of gigantic forms crossed over their tent, far above the two Trogens, blanketing the camp in immense, sprawling shadows.

Looking up into the dimming sky, Dragol was awestruck as he watched the two tremendous shapes that were passing through the sky above them. The bulky, winged behemoths were far from an ordinary sight, even compared to some of the incredible denizens of Dragol's own homeland.

If the Trogens had not been told otherwise, the abrupt sight high above would have been great cause for alarm. As it was, Tragan had already informed Dragol and the other Trogen chieftains that the Unifier had prepared new weapons, which had never been used in battle within the world before.

They had been told to look for, and soon expect, the arrival of sky creatures of unimaginable size. Even with the foreknowledge, the imminent, startling sight of the creatures was breathtaking to behold.

"The Darroks! Before our eyes!" Dragol exclaimed with excitement. He rose up swiftly from where he had been sitting and moved out from the tent, turning around and looking to the south and west.

Goras came to stand at Dragol's right side, in rapt attention as they watched the juggernauts flying onward.

Despite their enormous presence, the huge beasts were very capable fliers. They had a narrow body in relation to their seemingly measureless wingspan. The Darroks glided quite gracefully through the air, buoyed periodically by relaxed beats of their expansive wings.

The darkening, velvety sky of the twilight directly over them masked much of the detail of their features, but there was enough visibility to see that the creatures might once have been close kin to dragons.

Dragol studied their lengthy profile, from their great heads, elongated necks, down to their whip-like, tapering tails. Their sinewy, slender legs ended in horrific claws, all tucked up snugly against their undersides during flight.

The silhouettes of some type of carriage could be seen affixed from the middle of their backs to the base of their necks.

The sun was falling below the skyline, and the distant horizon was cast with a rosy hue. It created a majestic ambience that served as a lustrous backdrop for Dragol's first sights of the mysterious, unusual creatures.

"Those two are heading towards the main invasion force," Goras commented in a low voice.

Indeed, the two giant Darroks were heading away from the borders of Saxany, flying resolutely towards the southwest. The Plains of Athelney were directly in their skyward path.

A number of other Trogens and Andamoorans had emerged in the interim, many standing around Dragol and Goras with open looks of sheer wonder and astonishment, as they marveled at the passage of the two mammoth, flying beasts.

Over in the Avanoran camp, a similar, awed standstill had come over its inhabitants, from the greatest knight to the lowest of the paid foot soldiers. An extraordinary, hushed silence had fallen over both camps. All tensions and rivalries had evaporated for the moment, as the collective attention and thoughts of both encampments were consumed with the shared, awe-inspiring experience.

Though flying at an altitude rarely reached by a Harrak, the forms of the Darroks remained large to the eye. The ultimate size of the creatures was almost impossible for Dragol to even comprehend. He could not believe that something so vast could take flight.

"But only two?" questioned Goras, his eyes remaining upon the Darrok forms gradually diminishing on the horizon.

Dragol shook his head slowly. "I do not think that those two are all the Darroks that were sent by the Unifier."

They continued watching silently, until the Darroks were just distant specks on the farthest edge of their vision, at the juncture where earth met sky. The bloated, reddish orb of the descending sun's top crest was still visible, outlining the dark, winged shapes.

As Dragol turned, he caught Goras' eyes, and saw the wonderment and fear mixed in the other's look. "Even two, Goras. Think of two of those, serving the Trogen army against the Northern Elves," he mused aloud.

"A great hope, but for another time," Goras said with a more firm voice, turning to go back to their tent.

Dragol stared off a few more moments in the wake of the Darroks, finally turning away as the sun disappeared completely. Somewhat reluctantly, he oriented his thoughts towards the tasks at hand.

There was still much to be done. Night patrols and sentry posts had to be set, equipment prepared and evaluated for the next day, and orders to be reviewed. He was determined to occupy his mind with immediate labors. He knew that he could not think of the struggle against the Northern Elves, at least until the battles in Saxany were won.

His only relief came from the knowledge that the fight for Saxany had almost arrived, and that the long-awaited, great fight for his own kind lay just beyond that horizon.

AETHELSTAN

Aethelstan and the companions with him had traveled on for several leagues underneath the obscuring coverage of the thick woodlands around them. The going had been much slower than they would have liked, but at least they had been somewhat protected from open exposure to the Harrak patrols that occasionally passed through the skies overhead.

They had made considerable use of the few trails that crossed through the western hills bordering Count Einhard's land, Annenheim. As they were so rarely used, it took some skill to follow the pathways where the forest growth had begun to reclaim them.

There was an overriding tension gripping the contingent, with the constant danger of enemy patrols both in the air and upon the ground. On more than one occasion, Aethelstan had feared that they had been discovered.

The farther and deeper that they pushed onward, the more all of them felt an increasingly sinking feeling within their guts. The stillness in the trees, air, and on the ground gave off a foreboding sense that all was not well within the western woodlands lying between the Saxan provinces of Wessachia and Annenheim. There was nary a sound from animal, bird, or insect, as if the denizens of the forest had chosen to vacate the woodlands or go into deep hiding.

The nervousness within the Saxans welled up to the point that several of them flinched at the slightest rustling of wind-blown leaves, or snap of a twig. Even the sound of their own horses clopping on the trail unnerved them. The sense of edginess among the Saxans was such that even Aethelstan began to feel its hindering weight.

The horses themselves seemed to feel the brooding atmosphere around them. They kept silent as they traveled in the thin column being led by Aethelstan.

Aethelstan turned towards Cenferth, one of his most loyal and dedicated household warriors, who was riding close behind the great thane. Aethelstan addressed the warrior in a whisper. "What do you make of this oppressive silence, Cenferth? It is too heavy for my liking."

The other shook his head, a wary look in his eye. "I do not know, Aethelstan. It could be the quieting of the wilderness lands … as they feel the manifesting of the Unifier's power … or it may be the presence of the army that you suspect."

"I think that it is the army of our enemies, Cenferth. The patrols have not crossed overhead so many times without reason," Aethelstan stated.

The layout of the landscape, and the signs of any large Saxan force, would have been well-scouted by then. The sky patrols, Aethelstan feared, were keeping an eye over their own forces more than foraging about for Saxan patrols.

"Though I wish that it were otherwise, I believe that you are correct," Cenferth replied.

"I only wish we were able to field our own scouts in the sky," Aethelstan stated regretfully.

"We will have to be the scouts, even here on the ground," Cenferth replied gravely. "There are no others, as you have said."

"And find what we may. If we can find definite signs of the enemy army," Aethelstan said.

The deep unease continued for about another hour, during the span of which not one word was uttered amongst the Saxans. As if on a collective conscience, they maneuvered their steeds ever deeper into the vulnerable region, riding towards the edge of the forest itself.

If the Unifier's army were truly near, there would be the signs of scouts or encampments soon enough.

It was not much longer beyond that point when Aethelstan's instincts screamed out to him, and implored him urgently to stop. Snapping up his right hand, the abrupt gesture was repeated quickly among the group as Aethelstan brought his force to a halt among the shadows of the looming trees.

He believed his inner sense. Dismounting carefully, he guided his steed over to a maple tree and tethered it. The others likewise dismounted with care, each stroking their steeds' muzzles and speaking soothingly to the edgy horses. They silently awaited Aethelstan's next instructions.

The stallions shuffled about nervously, ears twitching and nostrils flaring. Aethelstan noticed the breeze coming upon them from the west. His riders were downwind of whatever was agitating the steeds.

The horses continued to whinny and snort, and Aethelstan knew that they could not risk going any farther. Horses were not foolish, and their horses were clearly apprehensive about something troubling that they sensed in the vicinity. A large party could not risk proceeding far beyond their position either. From that point onward, stealth and a limiting of risks was of the greatest priority.

As even the best of the others in the column could only equal Aethelstan and Cenferth in their woodland skills, he deemed it both sensible and honorable that he and his most dedicated warrior should be the ones to explore for nearby signs of the enemy.

Aethelstan stepped without a sound to where the other Saxans were gathered, all of them looking to him expectantly.

"We cannot go farther. Cenferth and I will go forth from here, and be as light of presence and silent as we can," Aethelstan informed them in a low voice. "Remain here with the steeds, and keep them as quiet as you can. If you are attacked, do not be foolish and forget why we have come here. Seek to get to our forces to warn them. They will need to know what we face. The fate of our army on the Plains of Athelney, and our home villages and burhs, depend on it."

Aethelstan let his stare weigh heavy on the others, to reinforce the solemnity of his words. He knew that he was asking a very difficult thing of the warriors, who would not hesitate to fight to the last around their beloved leader. Even so, notions of a warrior's personal honor had to be subordinate to the greater task for which they had all come.

Aethelstan lifted his leather shield strap over his head, grabbing the long, triangular shield and leaning it up against the same tree that his horse was tethered to. Removing his mail shirt to a cascade of light, metallic clinks, he rolled it up slowly, and placed it near the back of his horse's saddle. He also removed his iron helm, affixing it temporarily by the chinstrap off of the pommel.

The countless hours, days, and years that he had spent traveling and hunting amid the woodlands would now govern the best protection that he could have.

With the others standing guard around the horses, Aethelstan and Cenferth stepped lightly off into the forest. Having hunted often together in the forests of Wessachia, Ealdorman Morcar's lands, they were very adept at moving without giving off sound. They knew each other's tendencies well, and could easily convey plans or wishes with a simple glance or gesture.

With nimble footing and close attention to their surroundings, they made excellent progress, until the sporadic sounds of some foliage rustling and the crunching of dry leaves and twigs on the ground reached their ears.

Upon the very first hint of the intrusive sounds that broke the stillness of the forest, Aethelstan was already moving to the side of a particularly large elm tree, and lowering himself down into a crouch. Looking to the side, he saw that Cenferth had done likewise, and they held themselves as still as the high trees around them. Aethelstan gestured just ahead of their position, a little to the left, as Cenferth nodded his agreement with the thane's assessment.

The noises indicated that something was just about to break into view, just a short distance away from them. The two men watched carefully, their eyes fixed upon the trees and ground before them. Aethelstan drew upon his hunting skills, attenuating himself to a fixed, forward stare that took in the full range of his peripheral vision.

The first signs of movement riveted his focus fully upon the disturbance.

A few great black shapes padded across the ground, less than a hundred feet ahead of where he and Cenferth were hiding. The feline creatures moved effortlessly, bounding lithely over any fallen trees with nary a sound. With each burst of motion, they landed in perfect balance upon their wide paws.

The sounds of rustling leaves and scraping brush came from the movements of their handlers, who walked a short distance behind the massive cat-like beasts. They held onto long tethers, gripping them tightly in the elongated, slender fingers of their left hands. In their right hands, they grasped the hilts of long, tapering daggers, with no crossguards.

Aethelstan and Cenferth looked in wonder at the non-human handlers and the powerful creatures that they tended.

The heads of the bestial handlers were like that of some huge rat, with beady, dark eyes and long, tapering snouts. They had long tails, with arms and legs that were skinny in proportion to their bodies. Wherever their dark, waist-length tunics did not cover them, thick, coarse black fur could be seen.

The large cat-like beasts at the end of the tethers moved without any hindrance from their great body mass. With broad chests, stout legs, and massive heads carried high, the latter prominently displaying wicked-looking canines protruding several inches downward, the creatures exhibited a slight slope from their head to their hindquarters. Their stout bodies seemed to be made of solid muscle, as evidenced by the rippling, pulsing bulges just underneath their lustrous coats of dark fur.

There was a pattern to their movements. After a number of steps, the handlers would come to a sudden halt. Both the rat-men and the beasts would sniff at the air, and look all around them. Aethelstan uttered a silent prayer of thanks that they were downwind of the creatures, for he had little doubt that they would have easily picked up the scent of the two humans had it been otherwise.

Aethelstan and Cenferth dared not let even the sound of a breath escape them, as the terrifying creatures passed disconcertingly close by. Each moment seemed to take an eternity as they were condemned to endure a nerve-fraying state of mind.

The first of the cat-beasts showed no hesitation as they walked right in front of the tree that Aethelstan was hiding behind. As the creature passed, Aethelstan hoped desperately that there were no changes in the wind.

The extended canines descending from their upper jaws were veritable sabers, and the glint off of their powerful, horrifically sharp claws gave more than a hint as to what the monstrous cats were capable of.

Just one of the formidable creatures would be more than a match for both Aethelstan and Cenferth, even with coats of mail on their bodies and shields in hand. No less than four of the beasts passed by slowly, within only a few scant feet of the Saxans. Remaining rigid and frozen, they anxiously suffered their unwanted vigil as the creatures moved beyond them.

The light that reached the forest floor through the small breaks in the tree canopy overhead flickered rapidly, as patches of darkness flitted briskly across the forest floor. Aethelstan looked up slowly, bringing his gaze about just in time to see the signs of a large Harrak-mounted patrol as it passed overhead.

The sky patrol's presence did not worry him. Underneath the trees, pressed close to the trunks, there was little chance of Aethelstan and Cenferth being seen from above.

It still did not lessen the heightened tension that both of them were feeling, with impending threats of discovery both in the air and upon the ground. Aethelstan chanced a glance toward Cenferth, and could see the fear shining in the other's eyes. Discovery at the moment meant assured death.

There was little that the two Saxans could do, other than to endure. Aethelstan took long, slow breaths to offset the constriction he felt, as he watched the rat-men guide the cat-like beasts onward, until they finally disappeared among the trees towards the south. Cenferth and Aethelstan sustained their composure and posture, despite the visual absence of their enemies. The thane was simply glad that the rapid beating of their hearts could not disrupt the deathly silence all around them.

At the same time, Aethelstan knew that they had made their own confirmation. The foreign creatures moving about the woods in a patrol-like formation, shadowed by the sky patrol above, left no doubts in Aethelstan's mind regarding Saxany's enemy.

After several more nerve-wracking minutes, Aethelstan finally gave Cenferth the signal to begin their retreat. He knew that they would need to move very cautiously away from their hiding spots, while keeping their attention focused on the areas where the enemy creatures had been sighted.

They had to be ready to fall to the ground at the slightest hint of motion or rustling of the underbrush. The scouts and cat-beasts could double back, without giving any significant warning, and could well catch the two Saxans stranded out in the open.

Aethelstan nodded towards Cenferth, and both men slowly began to rise up from their low crouches. Suddenly, Aethelstan froze, as he heard a light disturbance off to their right.

Something else was heading their way.

His hopes plunged.

Cenferth's eyes were looking off to the left, where the prior group of enemy scouts had just gone. It was fortunate, as he was looking right in the direction of Aethelstan when the thane abruptly held up his hand, and signaled forcefully towards Cenferth to get back down and take cover immediately.

The two men hastily sank back into low crouches, their forms once again masked by the large tree trunks.

Aethelstan's ears had not tricked him. Barely a moment later, two more of the rat-men accompanied by cat-beasts emerged into view from the right. If he had not heard the faint sounds of their movements, he and Cenferth would have been caught in the open, as the oncoming pairs walked with even softer steps than had the preceding group of scouts.

The thane's keen instincts had proven true once again. Cenferth had lowered himself just in time, and had adjusted his position wisely, as the path being taken by the scouts brought them a little closer to the tree where he was hiding. Had he not been in his full crouch, the approaching creatures would have easily noticed him.

No commotion or outcry arose, much to their relief, and they waited silently until the two enemy scouts were past them. The scouts did not pause, continuing steadily forward in the same general path that their brethren had taken. The two men lingered for several long and agonizing moments, with nothing but the lonely stillness of the forest surrounding them.

Aethelstan finally decided to risk movement once again. Signaling to Cenferth, he slowly backed away from the tree, while keeping his eyes looking both left and right. His ears strained to hear the slightest crack of a twig, or singular crunch of a leaf, his muscles poised to react swiftly.

With methodical, cautious steps, they painstakingly moved away from their hiding spots. After covering a short distance, they turned fully, and continued more rapidly on their way back to the rest of their group. They kept their silence assiduously, and were extremely deliberate in their footing until they were far away from where they had encountered the rat-men and the cat-beasts.

Though desiring to break out into a loping run, Aethelstan maintained the orderly pace. It required tremendous discipline, as eager as he was to gain distance and bring the valuable word of the enemy back. Reason prevailed, as there was no way of telling how many scouts there were in the vicinity, or even if the few that they had sighted might be part of a larger war-band.

After what seemed like an eon had passed, they reached the location where their horses were tethered. Their arrival surprised their own men, who whirled about with swords in hand.

"It is us, we have returned," Aethelstan quickly said, as they came into sight. The anxiety-ridden faces of the men around them relaxed, relief flooding their countenances, as Aethelstan turned back to Cenferth.

"It is as we feared," he continued, finally able to speak aloud to his companion. He raised his voice enough so that he could relate the essence of their discovery to the others who were gathering around, pressing in close. "There can be little doubt that the enemy army will come right through this area. They are scouting and patrolling our borders. That is the act of a significant force. Some may say that it was foolhardy to take the risk that we did, yet I am glad that we did so. But I do not know what kind of creatures those were, back there. Our enemy is full of surprises indeed."

Looks of puzzlement arose upon the others' faces.

"Rat-men, handling great predatory cats, of a like that I have never before seen," Aethelstan added gravely, as several eyes widened. "It is not just a human army that we will face. We must make sure that all are alerted, and prepared for this reality."

Cenferth replied heavily, "Then we must return with haste."

"Yes, we must," Aethelstan agreed, though one last favor remained left for him to accomplish. It was a point of honor that he intended to fulfill by himself, now that their aims had been achieved. "But I must warn the Woodsman. This army will march right through these lands, and will find him … and I consider him a true friend. I cannot leave a friend so exposed."

"My lord, forgive me, but should we not return to our forces?" Cenferth asked, plaintively. "We need you there."

"Go and take most of the others with you, but I must now keep my word to a good man," Aethelstan instructed Cenferth, while moving over to his horse. He began to unroll the mail shirt, donning it before retrieving his helm and shield. Putting on his helm, and slinging the shield across his back again, he remounted his steed. "Just remember this. If I did not keep my word, I would not be any kind of man that you would find need of."

Cenferth's morose expression showed that he did not fully agree with Aethelstan, but the warrior knew better than to question or argue with the man that he had pledged himself to.

Aethelstan gripped the reins of Wind Runner. It felt reassuring to feel the saddle under him once again, even though he knew that the massive cats could easily run down a horse in the narrow confines of the thick woodlands.

All of his men volunteered to accompany him, but he was not about to take a large escort. He designated a very select few of his household guard to accompany him, bidding the others to go with Cenferth back to the Saxan camp.

The men assigned to go with Cenferth, having heard Aethelstan's tidings, accepted their charge well enough and did not voice objection. The sooner that they returned, the sooner that their fellow Saxans could brace themselves, and prepare for what was to come.

Aethelstan gently patted the neck of the gray stallion, and said consolingly, "Wind Runner, it is not yet time for us to go back. We must keep a promise."

As if understanding him, the horse started to trot back along the trail at the first nudge from Aethelstan. Its own unease spurred it forward more quickly than Aethelstan wanted, causing him to rein the steed in a little.

Aethelstan's selected warriors fell in behind him on their mounts, as they settled into a steady pace. The light of day had already reached its apex, and the sun was now beginning its long and slow descent through the later afternoon towards night. Soon the growing shadows would begin to permeate the woods, lowering the already dim ambience under the trees even further.

Seeing what he had seen, Aethelstan wanted to be back in the camp when night settled in full. He doubted that any of his men thought any differently, even if they had not beheld the sharp, long daggers coming down from the upper jaws of the massive cats. The raw, frightening image was emblazoned upon his mind, and he did not think that it would fade anytime soon.

Aethelstan and his men rode in disciplined silence among the trees, proceeding towards the demesne of the reclusive woodsman Gunther. Left to his thoughts, the thane simply hoped that Cenferth and the others made it safely back to the main encampment. Both of their groups had important warnings that needed to be conveyed.

JANUS

Janus sat idly, long after the mysterious youth had disappeared. The peaceful scene around him had continued unabated, with no sight or sound of anyone else.

Were it not for the great shadow that snapped his consciousness to a full, wary alertness, he might well have opted to fall asleep underneath the sparkling night sky. The vast form that crossed overhead was like a complete blotting out of the bright moonlight, thrusting Janus into the icy chill of a deep darkness that settled over his heart. He shivered as he stared up into the sky, the sense of serenity that he had been enjoying now shattered.

It looked as if a solid black cloud was spread wide above him, but then some light crept around the edges of the great shape. Outlined in moonlight, the form looked to be a winged body, with an elongated tail. It moved too swiftly in the light breeze of the night, and Janus knew without a doubt that what he gazed upon was no cloud.

He scrambled to his feet as his heart jumped and began to thunder within his chest. Every inch of his being screamed out a dire alarm. A second massive form followed the first, bearing the same ovular outline of a head, a lengthy body with unimaginably broad wings, and an extended tail trailing behind. His body constricting rapidly with fear, Janus recognized the presence above of two mammoth creatures, even as several frantic cries arose from the village warriors serving on the night's watch.

He knew instinctively, to his great chagrin, that the giant forms boded tremendous horrors for the Onan village.

Janus started to run back towards the longhouse where his friends slept, crying out urgently himself. His voice added to the few desperate shouts of warning that were loosed just before the ground reverberated with a number of prominent thumps. The sickening sounds of wood smashing and splintering rose up all around him. Jerking his head skyward, he caught the dismaying sight of a host of large objects raining down from the sky.

Commanding his legs to move as fast as he possibly could, he raced desperately for the hide entry-flap of the longhouse where his companions were resting. He ran faster than he had ever run before in his life, bursting through the flap and nearly falling to the ground as he entered the longhouse.

Somehow keeping his feet under him, he burst through the storage vestibule and the next opening, streaking down the center of the chambers while shouting out hysterically. Many villagers leaped up from where they were sleeping, their eyes wide with fear, as they all felt the thunderous impact of the torrential assault underway outside.

"We are being attacked! Something is attacking the village, from the air!" Janus exclaimed, rousing his friends and the other occupants of the longhouse. "We need to get out of here, now! Everyone! Get away from the village! There's no time! Get out, get away!"

"What is it?" Erika shouted to him as he entered their own quarters, her face reflecting the alarm and confusion gripping her.

The crashing sounds of destruction outside the longhouse were now mingled with cries of terror and pain, as the furious assault mounted with greater intensity.

"Huge creatures, in the sky. Get out, get out!" Janus yelled quickly, roughly grabbing at Antonio and Derek, who were closest to him, and shoving them along. "Get out now!"

As if to emphasize his frantic urgings, a large rock tore through the roof of their own chamber. Its impact cast a mess of shards and splinters all about where it smashed the sleeping platform where Logan had just been lying mere seconds before.

Another great stone crashed through the chamber next to them, and Janus looked in horror as it struck a village woman, killing her instantly in front of her husband and children. Yet another ripped through the roof and landed just beyond the entrance to the next chamber, throwing up a mass of dirt and debris.

"We can't stay here!" Erika cried, pulling forcefully at Logan, who had frozen in indecision. "Come on! Out everyone!"

Following Erika and Janus, the group hurriedly made their way through the chambers to exit the longhouse. They had to hurdle over some debris, and Antonio tripped on a fallen boulder.

Janus doubled back as he heard Antonio cry out, gripping his hand and yanking him back to his feet in an adrenalized surge of effort, born from desperation. He nearly dragged Antonio through the last chambers as they made their way towards the exit of the stricken longhouse.

The other longhouse occupants had been alerted by Janus' passage and the surging commotion. Foreigners and villagers alike shoved and jostled frantically to get to the outside.

A chaotic scene met their eyes as they ran out into the open ground. It was as if the most malevolent and enormous of hailstorms had been unleashed upon the village. Large boulders continued to rain down upon longhouses, crushing the edifices, as well as striking and killing many of the terrified, wide-eyed villagers running about. Some small fires had broken out where falling stones had strewn burning wood and sparks among the longhouse structures. Only the absence of stronger winds prevented the fires from quickly escalating into larger infernos.

Janus and the others did not hesitate for a moment, as they bolted for the main entryway to the village.

"Darroks!" Ayenwatha shouted out from nearby. He yelled to any that would hear him. "Go to the river! Go to the river!"

Heeding Ayenwatha's call, Janus shouted out to his own group and any villagers nearby, "To the river! To the river!"

He saw Ayenwatha racing down amid rows of longhouses, accompanied by several Onan warriors. They were out of sight in just a few seconds.

Janus and the others did not stop to consider why Ayenwatha would race in towards the very center of the bombardment. Janus and his companions hurried across the open ground towards the front gateway in the outer palisade.

Rocks fell to their right, left, in front and in back of them. More cries filled the air, but fortune remained with the outsiders as none were stricken, though Antonio and Janus both came within just a couple paces of being pulverized by one large boulder. They finally won their way unscathed past the open gate of the village and started down the long hill slope.

In his panic, Kent lost his footing, tumbling down the slope. Derek caught up to him, and helped his friend up quickly. The others barely kept to their feet in their own frenzied haste, but all made it safely to the base of the large hill.

Janus, now trailing the others, took long, leaping strides as he covered the last part of the slope. The seven continued forward through the darkness, heading amongst the trees. Enough light filtered down from the clear night sky over them that they did not stumble about blindly, and were able to keep moving forward in a relatively orderly manner.

Though fading, the dismaying sounds of fear and wailing, mixed with the crackling and splintering of wood, followed them as they strove for the river's edge. Above and behind them, a hellish glow now lit the summit of the hill from the fires burning within the doomed village.

From the base of the hill and on through the surrounding trees towards the edge of the river, there were no rocks or other debris falling from the sky. The stillness among the trees was a jarringly stark contrast to the unbridled assault being levied upon the village.

Out of immediate danger, calmer thought processes gradually returned to Janus. The group had slowed their pace to assess their situation, as they finally reached the water's edge.

A number of terrified villagers were now gathering near to them, increasingly becoming a larger assemblage as other survivors streamed in from the beleaguered village.

Janus' heart sank precipitously. The sight around him was anguishing. Mothers and fathers carried small, crying children. Those that had reached the water were frantically looking about for any sign of their family members and friends. Those finding the ones that they sought rushed to embrace their loved ones.

Some children looked around in grief and sheer bewilderment, with no sign of the parents that had urged them to run to safety. Older villagers collapsed to the ground, the surge of energy brought by desperation now betraying the frailty of their elderly bodies.

Janus and many of the others looked skyward nervously, searching for signs of the horrific beasts that had terrorized the village. The creatures were not hard to see, as they circled slowly around in the sky far above the hill, honing in again on the village at its summit.

The immense shapes filled the darkened sky, obscuring large expanses of stars behind them. They were monstrosities evoked from the abyss of nightmares, though what they were Janus could not say. Their wingspan was extraordinary, and it was hard to believe that such titans could remain airborne.

As he observed them, Janus' eyes were gradually drawn towards a most surprising sight, one that was silhouetted against the relatively clear skies.

His eyes straining to make out further details, he could see a flurry of movement occurring along the top of the beasts' long backs, as well as what looked to be some type of artificial structures astride the creatures. He surmised quickly that those concerted movements were the source of the torrent of destruction descending from the flying monsters.

With a sickening sense of absolute helplessness, he could see the shadowy shapes of numerous rocks plummeting down from the creatures towards the hapless village on the hill. As his eyes took in the deadly storm, his ears were filled with the sobs and cries of the adults and children huddled in small groups all around him.

He was only a guest, with little more in his possession than the clothes on his back. The villagers, on the other hand, were watching their homes, families, and friends being destroyed right before their eyes.

As the initial shock of it began to wear off, the terrible scene transpiring was overwhelming. Against the backdrop of the aggrieved litany, his eyes watered up with tears fueled by sorrow and pure, righteous anger.

He sank down to his knees, as his gaze scanned the debilitating sights of the shattered families gathered near to him. He witnessed expressions of tremendous sadness that he knew would stay ingrained forever in his memory.

He stared off as if to gaze beyond the tragic visions, seeking the numbness of emptiness. Yet he could not escape the sights, for there were far too many.

Janus felt a hollow sensation opening deep within him, as a strongly-built tribal warrior stumbled towards them out of the trees. He was straining with an elderly woman carried across his back and an unconscious child in his arms.

The elderly woman was alert, and had her thin arms and legs wrapped around the warrior as he bore her weight.

Janus then noticed the awkward angle of the child's lower right leg, bent at a place where no natural joint existed. That the child was not awake was a great mercy. The warrior's face held both exhaustion and a grim resolve, yet another vivid memory that would remain etched in Janus' mind.

The renewed shock of the moment gradually wore off, though a

feeling of grief subsequently magnified within him. The sight of the elderly woman reminded Janus of the old people in the village who could not have run out as he and his friends had.

He buried his face in his hands, his chest heaving with sobs, as he felt a wave of shame and guilt at having abandoned the village so hastily. He had acted without thinking, rushing out when he should have stayed and tried to help as the warrior had.

"But what could I have done?" he stammered in a low voice, aloud to himself, as an abyss of sadness tore at him. "I should have stayed and helped. I should have stayed …"

He then felt a firm but gentle hand on his shoulder. "You saved me."

Looking up through the haze of his tear-fogged eyes, he saw Logan standing next to him, with a somber expression on his face. The sight of Logan made him think back to the sleeping platform, and where he had seen Logan get off of it at Janus' frantic urging. He remembered the jagged mass of rock that had smashed the platform to shards moments later, exploding down through the bark-paneled roof. His return back into the longhouse had roused Logan just in time. If Janus had arrived even seconds later, Logan would have been killed.

"You came back in, when you could have run out, and you saved me, you saved the others, and you raised an alarm," Logan said firmly. "There are many out here that may well have died if you had not run back."

"But still, I should have stayed," Janus replied, feeling horribly about the elderly villagers who had likely been trapped by nothing more than the weaknesses of their physical bodies.

"Who could possibly think up there?" Logan asked him, looking off towards the fire-encompassed hilltop. "The whole place was coming down. Smashed to bits, set on fire, people running everywhere. There was nothing that we really could do, but react."

Logan sighed and shook his head. "I wish I was not so helpless, and could do something more. I wish I could, but we do not have magic abilities, Janus. We're just human … and until I find a way to something more, I can't expect to have more power than what we have in these limited bodies. …"

Logan deliberately turned his eyes skyward, but not before Janus caught a darker mood spreading across the other's countenance. Janus quietly stared at Logan, wondering what kinds of thoughts were running through his mind.

Even from the side, Janus could see Logan's eyes visibly narrowing, in sudden reflex to something he saw. Janus was drawn to follow Logan's line of sight on up into the sky. Near to the huge flying beasts in the sky, a number of smaller forms could be seen darting amid the behemoth airborne masses.

It was in that moment that Janus suddenly came to realize where Ayenwatha had been headed to, when he had run off into the center of the maelstrom with the other warriors.

AYENWATHA

There was nothing else that the flying hulks could be other than Darroks. Gallean traders had spoken of tremendous monstrosities of the air, flying in the skies around Avalos to the west, which were being trained to serve some purpose of the Unifier's. They had spoken with awe of the sheer vastness of the creatures. Some found them to be a simulacrum of dragons.

The incredible size being unquestionable, most were not altogether certain about the latter claim, as dragons had not been seen in the western lands for so many years. Yet Ayenwatha could not disagree that the beasts before him certainly evoked references to the winged legends.

Ayenwatha guided Arax upward resolutely, in the lead of the nearly thirty defenders that were streaking up from the village towards the bulky forms of the Darroks.

The warriors raced directly at the front of the Darroks, the beasts' forms growing ever larger, with each passing second. Their hearts raced as they sped unhesitatingly towards a desperate battle.

There was no real hope of bringing the creatures down outright, which the warriors with Ayenwatha quickly discovered on their first approach. The thick, leathery hides of the Darroks could easily turn simple arrows aside, and their vulnerable spots, such as the eyes, were provided with armored protection.

The creatures were also not alone, nor were they following their own mind. A great carriage of timber planks and poles, forming a platform surface and railed sides, was lashed to each of the creatures, extending from the base of their necks down to the middle of their backs.

Crews of about twenty figures moved about on the surface of the carriages. Most were tending to the ongoing assault, while a couple of them were occupied in guiding the winged juggernauts via a special harnessing utilizing exceptionally long reins.

The enemy figures labored relentlessly upon the beasts' backs, jettisoning a cascade of larger rocks off of the sides of the beasts, sending them hurling down towards the village far below. As the defenders neared the gigantic forms, Ayenwatha was caught by a sudden surprise.

He recognized that the many enemy fighters serving as the attendant crews were not human. Only a few of the village warriors would have recognized them as Trogens, and even then only from tales and stories. Ayenwatha was one of the few that had heard of the dog-men from the east, huge brutes that were implacable, ferocious warriors.

Muscled and dexterous, the Trogens cried out boldly to each other. Many shouted defiantly at the approaching defenders, as an alarm was raised amongst them. A kind of respite was gained for the village, as the Trogens turned their attentions towards preparing to meet the onrushing defenders.

Ayenwatha discovered that the great Darroks were able to breathe short jets of fire. The ability was unveiled to all of the defending tribal warriors, when one of them strayed too close towards the immediate front of one of the beasts, and barely avoided getting engulfed in the tight column of flame that blasted from the creature's huge mouth.

The creature then swung its head about, trying to find the evasive warrior. The Trogens controlling the beast worked its reins aggressively, working to keep the suddenly-distracted creature moving steadily onward.

Ayenwatha recognized the great danger presented by the fire breath of the winged giants, and swiftly warned his warriors to keep clear of the beasts' heads.

It was not a very hard challenge, as the slow moving beasts could not readily adapt to the sudden changes in direction that the substantially smaller Bregas were able to undertake. A loud outcry then rang out among the Trogens on the backs of the Darroks, a fierce roar erupting to meet the impact of the daring assault.

To Ayenwatha's immense relief, there were no sky steeds, such as Harraks, escorting the Darroks. Yet their enemies were not devoid of a considerable means of defense.

Several Trogens hastily retrieved great bows, each more than the height of a man. They notched arrows fletched with long, black feathers, laboring diligently to train their sights upon the Onan warriors. At the moment, there were few archers fully ready to engage in the fray, as many of the Trogens among the Darroks were still hustling to snatch up weapons. Ayenwatha's warriors would be allowed a small measure of time to try and disrupt or cripple the assaults on their village.

Ayenwatha espied one enemy archer, who had an arrow at the ready and was marking its mental target upon one of the tribal warriors. The Trogen was assiduously focusing its eyes upon the unaware warrior, who was about to fly alongside the Darrok just above the carriage level.

Quickly balancing himself, Ayenwatha set an arrow to his own bow and instantly let the arrow fly towards the Trogen archer.

The shot was loosed just in the right moment. Had he waited even a fraction of a moment later, it would have been too late.

As it was, the bestial archer suddenly jerked about as Ayenwatha's deadly missile found its target. It twisted in the act of its own shot, the arrow going wildly astray of its intended target. Its bow fell from its hands, as it crumpled down to the surface of the carriage.

More shouts of alarm emerged from the felled Trogen's nearby companions. All of the Trogens were readying their weapons, as they endeavored to repel the warriors with Ayenwatha.

The other Onan warriors then let their first volley of arrows streak towards the companions of the slain Trogen.

Several of the tribal warriors' arrows burrowed into the flesh of their intended marks. In just one pass over the Trogens, a great majority of the enemy warriors on the first Darrok were casualties. They were either wounded too badly to continue fighting, or had been slain outright by deadly accurate shafts.

Only a few survived unharmed. The Onan warriors had effectively taken one beast out of the fight. Ayenwatha could see the one remaining Trogen with the reins working feverishly to steer the creature away. The winged behemoth now represented little threat to any village within the landscape below.

The Onan warriors' rapid flight carried them far over and beyond the Darrok. Ayenwatha abruptly gripped the reins of his steed, and brought it sharply upwards. The loose formation of Bregas followed him, emulating his movements as he curled about in a wide arc for an attack upon the next Darrok.

The Darrok that they left behind seemed to recognize the damage done to the crew on its back, and loosed a spiteful, blistering breath of fire after them. The creature was far too slow, and its outburst well too short to be of any danger to Ayenwatha's warriors.

Steadying their steeds in Ayenwatha's wake, the tribal formation leveled itself out as it began to gain speed. At Ayenwatha's lead, the warriors swiftly notched more arrows for a pass at one of the remaining Darroks. The one that Ayenwatha had selected lumbered through the air just a few hundred feet away, a full crew upon its back.

The Trogen warriors on the Darrok were much more prepared for the defenders' approach. There was deadly exchange of arrow fire as the two groups closed within killing range of each other. Ayenwatha and the tribal warriors let loose their barrage, almost at the exact time that the Trogens let fly with their own.

The arrows of the tribal warriors raked the exposed surface of the timber carriage. Once again, the arrows of the warriors of the Five Realms found several targets, but the enemy missiles claimed their own number of victims among the sky riders and their steeds.

With wretched cries and shrieks, a few stricken Bregas plummeted down towards the ground, hundreds of feet below, carrying their ill-fated riders towards certain, gruesome deaths.

A couple of other warriors toppled over, slouching lifeless in the saddles or falling off. Riderless Bregas, left to their own discretion, flew away from the conflict, without any direction or authority to guide them.

Ayenwatha's warriors had still reduced the number of fighters on the second Darrok by about a third, but had suffered their first blows, losing several of their own warriors. They had also suffered another casualty in that the advantage of surprise no longer belonged to them.

The main formation of Bregas with Ayenwatha continued on past the Darrok, and started to turn again in a wide arc so that they could circle back and make another pass. Ayenwatha knew that the Trogens would be braced again for them, but they had to carry the battle relentlessly to the enemy while the villagers on the ground struggled to escape the vicinity of the imperiled village.

As with the first Darrok that they had attacked, Ayenwatha noticed that no stones were falling. The Trogen crew was strictly readying for defense against the tribal warriors.

While he was relieved that they had severely impeded the assault, he also knew what it meant for his small band of warriors. There was little mistaking the situation facing them. With less than thirty warriors remaining, they would not be able to sustain many more passes. A battle of attrition would not be in their favor.

He kept his mind calm, as he thought rapidly of other courses of action. His mind raced through various possibilities as the formation completed its curve and came about to begin another sweep towards the Darrok.

He eyed the harnessing required to secure the high-sided, wooden platform for the occupants on the back of the Darroks. The Trogens were not tethered by any manner of ties or restraint to the platform itself.

If those manning the Darroks were cast overboard from their airborne vessel, there would be no possible rescue for them. Hundreds of feet of empty air and solid ground would seal their fates well enough.

"Stay clear. Shoot arrows at the beast ahead," Ayenwatha cried out to the nearest of his warriors, gesturing forcefully as he spoke. "Keep your steeds to this side. Sky Arrow ... follow me! Keep close!"

The warrior to his right nodded in understanding, and gripped the reins of his steed tightly as he watched for Ayenwatha to take the lead. Ayenwatha then guided Arax off sharply, heading downward to the left. With great skill, he guided the steed tightly as they looped back up towards the Darrok, coming about to fly directly underneath the immense creature.

His years of experience and relationship with Arax enabled the difficult maneuver with a smooth grace of form. Sky Arrow followed skillfully enough, keeping his steed close to the war sachem, as he also made it safely to the underbelly of the Darrok.

The Trogens scrambled frantically to fire more arrows at them as they executed the difficult maneuver. Ayenwatha heard the whizzing sound of an arrow as it passed within just a foot of his right ear. He kept his mind steeled, even as his heart skipped a beat in his chest.

Once underneath the creature, Ayenwatha and Sky Arrow were effectively sheltered from attack by the Trogen archers. Silently uttering a brief prayer of thanks to the One Spirit for the incredibly good fortune, Ayenwatha guided Arax down to the middle of the creature's body. He brought Arax to match the speed of the large beast over them, as Ayenwatha looked upward to study the harnessing. His eyes followed the course of the great leather straps and cords that cross-crossed the creature's body, soon identifying the more crucial concentrations and bindings.

"Sky Arrow, use your axe. Hack the ropes! The ones coming together at the center!" Ayenwatha yelled, making a chopping motion as he pointed out the network of strapping above.

He guided his Brega up closer, while withdrawing his short-hafted war axe from where it was tucked in his belt. Keeping his steed level was difficult enough, as the Darrok bobbed in the movements of its own flight, but he knew that there was a chance to get within close enough range to make his attempt.

It was not difficult for Arax to match the speed of the Darrok. The Brega was able to coast in a smooth glide for several moments, before beginning to lose speed and needing to spur itself forward again. As the stretches of gliding provided the most steadiness, Ayenwatha patiently awaited the beginning of one such span in order to attempt his idea. The Brega went through a couple more cycles, passing close to the desired target as Ayenwatha carefully gauged his range and aim.

After one such cycle, Arax flapped its wings strongly, and then evened out its flight into a glide that carried it right along the central underbelly of the Darrok. Ayenwatha saw his opportunity, as he came within striking range and was conveyed right along what he believed to be a critical juncture in the harness system of the Darrok.

Leaning back, he hacked powerfully at the thick cords and intertwined ropes that passed through one large, iron ring. Several more vigorous, steady blows began the arduous and dangerous task.

Sky Arrow, understanding Ayenwatha's intent, set to work on another concentration of cording set a short distance behind.

The axes quickly cleaved through the taut cords and ropes. The work was disrupted somewhat as the bulk of the Darrok rocked up and down in flight, a few times coming precariously close to smacking into the Bregas and their riders.

Despite several pauses to regain position, and to duck some near impacts with the Darroks themselves, the two warriors were able to keep close and levy a number of solid, successful strikes upon the harness system.

The two warriors took great caution not to strike the Darrok directly, for the beast could easily send Arax and Sky Arrow's steed spinning out of control with an intentional drop in altitude. Ayenwatha was not certain that the beast was incapable of maneuvering its massive, clawed legs to scrape at its underbelly. He could only hope that the creatures were not trained for sudden drops.

Progress continued, but at an uncomfortably slow pace. Ayenwatha nudged Arax whenever they started to fall back a little, and subtly reined the steed in when they were in danger of flying past his target area. Over time, the effort built into a somewhat steady rhythm.

It was a painstaking process for both Sky Arrow and for Ayenwatha, but they continued forward resolutely, maintaining their full focus. At long last, most of the thick, tight straps around the ring that Ayenwatha worked upon had been severed at their underside crossroads. A few robust strikes later, the last few snapped apart with a jolt, as their great tension was suddenly released.

The Darrok must have felt the effect, for the creature suddenly reached one of its deadly, enormous claws back towards Ayenwatha. The huge appendage moved straight towards Ayenwatha and the Brega, as if it was swatting at a mere insect.

In consistency with the creature's lumbering movement, the mammoth claw approached slowly enough for Ayenwatha to react. Arax needed little prodding, having noticed the threatening movement as well, and the two of them banked downward in a near freefall.

The danger of the Darrok's claw swipe was quickly past, but the distance that they had covered in the freefall had brought them within sight of the maddened Trogens on the Darrok's back. The Trogens had also felt the jolt of the harness straps being cut. They knew their tremendous vulnerability, and fear clearly dwelled amongst them. Ayenwatha could hear it within their frantic shouts to each other, watching them clutch at the side rails as they tried to look over the sides.

When Ayenwatha was on the underside of the Darrok, they were impotent. Now that he was in plain view, they moved with alacrity.

A barrage of arrows was loosed towards Ayenwatha and the Brega, most going awry amid the Trogens' hurried, frenzied rush to fire. A searing pain erupted suddenly in the back of his shoulder as one arrow lodged itself into muscle and struck bone.

Arax roared and jerked suddenly. Ayenwatha's heart leaped in that perilous moment, as his life wholly depended on his steed's ability to maintain flight. He had no way of telling where the arrow had struck his steed, and prayed desperately that it was not a fatal hit. He looked around wildly, before finally espying the arrow shaft sticking out of Arax's rear haunch.

Though unsteady, the creature was well-trained and had a natural instinct for self-preservation. It regained control, securing a steady pattern of flight despite the fiery pain that undoubtedly raced through it.

The Trogens above were distracted from their attentions on him, as another outcry rose amongst them. Many fell over as another massive jolt occurred along the platform. Ayenwatha saw that Sky Arrow had succeeded at his end, and was just about to dive away from the Darrok.

Sky Arrow did not have the good fortune of Ayenwatha.

Ayenwatha cried out in helpless frustration as the huge claw of the Darrok swiped and batted Sky Arrow and his steed with full impact, casting them far away from the beast. Their shattered bodies tumbled lifelessly downward.

Ayenwatha cried out in anger, as he watched his friend's body plummet towards the land below. Bitterly, with tears welling in his eyes, he guided Arax towards safety. The Brega was injured and unfit for any more fighting that night, no matter what Ayenwatha might have been willing to do.

He threw a quick glance over his right shoulder, wincing at the biting pain that throbbed within his left. The Darrok was unmistakably altering its course of flight. The Trogens were well aware of their own peril, and likely they were heading away to find some emergency expanse of ground where the Trogens could attend to the repair of the harnessing.

Each moment carried the Trogens within a delicate, precarious position. A little imbalance and the Trogens' fate would be a long plunge through the sky. It was clear that they were not interested in such a foolhardy risk, and had chosen to fight another day.

Ayenwatha closed his eyes, taking a deep breath and uttering two silent prayers. From the wellspring of his gleaming eyes, a couple of tears streaked down his cheeks. He was not ashamed, as the tears were born of loyalty and friendship.

The first prayer was one of thanksgiving for the plan having worked to disrupt the Darrok's attack. The other was for Sky Arrow and his spirit, that he would find his way to the realm of He Who Holds the Sky, the great One Spirit, a place of radiant skies and bounteous hunting.

He had led Sky Arrow forth, bringing the young warrior with

him in the counterattack on the Darroks. In the thick of the battle, he had selected the Onan warrior for the dangerous strike at the Darrok's harnessing. Never was there a greater weight of burden than when his leadership had directly resulted in the death of another. Ayenwatha hoped that Sky Arrow was even now being embraced by their ancestors, and that he was being welcomed into bountiful forests whose illumination required no sun.

"Till the day we hunt again," Ayenwatha whispered, glancing towards the stars above.

Wiping his eyes, he looked around for the other Darroks, to see what had befallen the defenders and the attackers. There were three others moving away in a tight formation, following the Darrok that had suffered the heavy damage to its carriage harness.

Ayenwatha made the best appraisal that he could. The Trogens had taken many losses, had witnessed the vulnerabilities exploited by Ayenwatha and Sky Arrow, and were clearly not in a position to sustain the attack. Ayenwatha felt an instant sense of relief despite his personal sadness, knowing that the assault upon the village was over for the time being.

With a throbbing pain in his shoulder, and now feeling the warm blood trickling down his back, he guided his wounded sky steed back towards the village. It was distressing to take in the sight of all the wreckage as he flew in, but there were no good places to land in the immediate areas surrounding the village's hill. Numbly, he eyed the scattered flames that still licked at the night, guiding Arax towards a patch of open ground. Shortly after Arax had alighted upon the ground, several other surviving warriors set down within the remains of the village, the fighting now over.

On foot, Ayenwatha guided Arax and the others through the village. He ignored the arrow protruding from his body, keeping his eyes fixed straight ahead, not wanting to look towards the broken bodies and shattered remains of the buildings riddling the village grounds. The fires still burning in different sections of the village were not a threat. They were already beginning to die down, having expended their fury as timber was turned to ash.

Once out of the front gate, they carefully started down the slope. Arax exhibited a slight limp, and the hardy sky steed whined with the biting pain that it felt from its wound, aggravated further while walking on the ground and supporting its body weight with its legs. Ayenwatha paused a couple of times and spoke soothingly to the beleaguered creature, the arrow shaft still embedded in its blood-matted haunches.

Nearing the base of the hill, a number of villagers came out from the trees and hastened towards the warriors. Their eyes were laden with sorrow and fear, the burden growing even heavier as they noticed the absence of many warriors who had not returned.

Villagers trained in healing arts, including those of the Healing Societies, were immediately summoned to help injured warriors and steeds alike. They guided those who had suffered significant wounds to open spaces amid the trees. Ayenwatha and Arax were helped over to a space in between the prominent roots of an ancient oak tree.

In moments, the arrows in Ayenwatha and Arax were taken out. Ayenwatha was dizzy with the intense flash of pain that he incurred, but he kept his body under control. His steed thrashed madly about, knocking over a couple of villagers that were laboring to restrain the beast. At a few soothing words from Ayenwatha, spoken through gritted teeth, Arax calmed down enough to be led away to where the rest of the sky steeds were being tended. The wounds were then dressed in a makeshift manner, as there was little access to either material or sacred healing herbs.

Litters were hastily fashioned for a couple of the warriors that were very badly injured. The two warriors would likely require the full rituals of the masked Healers, those of the Healing Societies who wore the sacred masks carved from living trees. Ayenwatha and the others were soon relieved to learn that most of the sacred masks in the village had been salvaged, and that most of the members of the Healing Society had survived.

Ayenwatha lay to one side, his wounded shoulder kept off of the ground. He quietly endured the moans of the injured warriors close by, wishing that he could not hear the sounds that brought him more pain than his physical wound.

It had been all that he could bear to suffer the horrid shriek emitted by Arax, when the beloved steed's arrow had been pulled out. His ears now conveyed without mercy the incessant sounds of crying and lament pouring from his fellow villagers. His heart grew heavy, along with a deadening fatigue that slowly enveloped his body. It took all of his concentration just to confer with the warriors that began to visit him, or to bring him new information.

The word of the extent of the attack and subsequent battle in the sky slowly reached his ears, as he finally rolled over to lie upon his stomach.

Of over thirty courageous riders that had gone into the skies to the defense of the village, only eleven had returned. A couple of riderless Bregas had found their own way back, though the rest of the missing steeds were presumed dead or strayed. The Darroks had indeed been diverted and stymied, but it had been a very costly defense.

The village had taken incredible damage, with nearly every structure absorbing an irreparable amount of destruction. Longhouses had been smashed into so many bits of wood, far past any hope of repair.

The number of killed and wounded villagers, most stemming from the initial onslaught of the unexpected attack, was extensive. Not a single survivor had escaped the devastation without having lost a member of their family, a friend, or a child.

As the various dire tidings continued to stream in, Ayenwatha tried to make some sense of the dreary situation. His understanding of it brought to bear a sobering notion.

With the first shadow of the Darroks falling upon the village, and the first large stone to crash into the village's midst, the people of the Five Realms found themselves in a full state of war with the Unifier. Ayenwatha could not deny that his first thoughts were melancholy, if not devoid of hope. He could not see how the tribes could defend their realm against a power that commanded such hellishly fearsome weapons of war.

The war would likely become one of attrition, a struggle that would be impossible to sustain for the tribes, which had never been great in numbers. The losses suffered in just one melee had been devastating to the village's sky steeds and warriors.

Their losses could not be replaced, while the Unifier could draw upon the warriors of many rulers and lands.

It was inconceivable to think of rebuilding, as the villagers could not begin to think of any reconstruction when winged titans could manifest at any moment to reduce a village to splinters in such an incredibly short span of time. Nonetheless, the fight would have to be fought, come whatever may. It would be an existential battle, waged against annihilation or capitulation.

Ayenwatha clenched his teeth as a spasm of pain wracked him, prompting him to shift his body a little.

The handful of sky warriors had indeed been successful in driving off the attackers. They had also been able to limit the casualties to far below what they would have been had the enemy been allowed free reign in the skies above the village. Once the village had been destroyed, the enemy could well have searched out the villagers as they fled and tried to regroup away from the hill, levying even more carnage and death.

While it was true that a great number of the enemy Trogens had been slain, all of the huge flying beasts that they had arrived on would be returning to their camps alive. The Darroks would soon be outfitted with mended carriages, fresh supplies, and rested warriors to ride them. It was also likely that new precautions would be taken, bearing in mind the approach that Ayenwatha and Sky Arrow had used to render the one Darrok's harnessing unstable.

What was certain was that the next time a force of Darroks came there would be little to nothing that could stop them from raining a torrent of destruction down upon all of the forest villages.

Ayenwatha had also not forgotten that just beyond the western borders of the Five Realms' lands, large columns of enemy warriors had been arriving and assembling. His own war parties had shadowed such formations, and he knew that they were not just a demonstration of force meant to intimidate. The Unifier's emissaries had been unequivocal when the Grand Council had rejected the demand to submit to Avanor's insatiable ruler. The Five Realms were declared hostile enemies of the Unifier, and all those in His burgeoning alliance.

Ayenwatha was under no illusions. The forces massing on the western borders of the tribal lands would soon be invading the territory of the Five Realms, joining their strength to the attacks from the skies.

Ayenwatha knew that he would have to approach the village elders about the only option available to them: the evacuation of all of the villages, and a retreat into the eastern region of their lands.

The villages were very vulnerable to the horrifying new method unveiled by the Unifier. Situated on the cleared summits of hills, they were exposed. The unanticipated attack at night was coldly brilliant, as the enemy knew that the village population would be gathered almost entirely within the palisades. Fires within the village perimeter had probably been used as beacons for the enemy to hone in on the village from the air. There was little question that as long as the enemy had the use of the titanic Darroks, the villages were little more than death traps.

Though there was no denying the realities, it was a tremendously difficult burden to embrace. The land, for a member of one of the tribes, was an intimate part of who they were, interwoven with their very identity. It was what they had always known, an enduring gift of the One Spirit that had always bestowed the means of life to their people for so many generations. The notion of being uprooted in their own lands was unthinkable to any villager, much less a great war sachem.

Circumstances had become mercilessly cruel, and that which would have otherwise been thought unacceptable was now the only viable course of action. There was no other choice, Ayenwatha ruefully acknowledged. If they were to stay in their villages, they would be easy targets for an enemy that would inevitably gain mastery of undefended skies, while simultaneously assaulting the tribes with their many thousands upon the ground.

Ayenwatha had never felt more despondent in his life.

"Ayenwatha," interrupted a low, steady voice.

Ayenwatha slowly looked up, to see the familiar and quite welcome form of Deganawida standing near to him. Ayenwatha gingerly rotated back to brace himself on his strong side, the effort tedious with the weariness that continued to sap his energy.

The village headman and Grand Council sachem looked a little older to Ayenwatha's eyes, his luminous, dark eyes gazing down upon the injured war sachem. Behind the taut expression on the Deganawida's face, Ayenwatha knew that the man was sharing his agony, undoubtedly to an even greater degree.

Despite the physical and mental pains that he was struggling with, a spark of joy nonetheless had leaped up within him at the recognition that Deganawida had survived the terrible raid. A soothing breeze of relief washed all over him, allowing Ayenwatha a brief respite from the withering heat of the inner and outer agonies that he was suffering.

"You fought well ... so very well, against all odds and hope," Deganawida continued after a moment, the unwavering tone of his voice hinting at the substantial inner strength present in the venerable sachem. "You fought so very bravely, for us all. Others have told me how you drove the great sky beasts off, and how you and Sky Arrow disabled one in the face of incredible risk."

No small amount of pride effused the words of the great sachem, though Ayenwatha was not in a condition to take any joy from accolades. "It was what we had to do. But they will return, and we lost two of every three that went up to face them," Ayenwatha replied, in a low, heavy voice, not wishing anyone else to hear the biting pessimism that was rife within him.

"And you must already know that none of the other villages are safe … and that no tribe is safe … and that no man, woman, or child can remain within a village site. You also know of the army that masses to enter our lands, which they certainly will, and very soon indeed," Deganawida replied firmly, the look in his eye conveying that he understood Ayenwatha fully.

Ayenwatha nodded, not entirely surprised to hear such candid words from the old sachem. Deganawida had never been one to waste time trying to sweeten a bitter truth. Ayenwatha knew right then that the old sachem would agree with him about what had to be done.

"It must be done … the villages must be abandoned," Deganawida stated, confirming Ayenwatha's thoughts, as if he had spoken them aloud. Deganawida then spoke in a lowered, compassionate tone, like that of a father giving the wisdom of a hard lesson learned to a suffering son. "Remember … though it is a very cruel time, and though your heart may become all too heavy in the trial to come … it is the people that are the land, and the land that is in the people. That is the wisdom you must hold fast to within your mind, and in your heart. … The people are the land. They are the tribes. They are the Five Realms. Do not forget these truths. As long as you know this, you and yours will never be lost, even if we have to keeping moving as we seek new refuges within our own lands."

The old sachem held Ayenwatha's gaze, seeming to drive the sentiments deep into his being by the sheer force of his will. Deganawida's face had softened into an affectionate smile, his eyes echoing the sadness that Ayenwatha was being tormented by.

The sounds of many hurried footsteps preceded the arrival of a couple of young tribal warriors, both of whom had a look of resolve ingrained on their faces.

They held some thin leather thongs, strung with shells, each thong itself tied to a rough, rectangular piece of wood. Coming to a full stop, they looked expectantly towards Deganawida, who eyed the combinations of shell-strung thongs with attached wood sticks with a look that brooked a hint of relief.

"We were able to enter your quarters from the side, great sachem. The entrances to your longhouse have been completely destroyed … but much of your chamber was left intact," one of the warriors announced. "We found these with little trouble."

"A small bit of good fortune in this darkness. Two notches on each … and make haste," Deganawida then instructed them. "And tell the sachems of each village to move all their people out of their villages and into the forest immediately, without delay. That must be done now. Tell them everything of what has happened here. Spare no detail, no matter how terrible. They must understand what they face, and your account of it may mean all the difference in gaining their cooperation. They must gain the wisdom to empty their villages, before they make their way here two days from now."

Ayenwatha knew that Deganawida's words were no understatement. Unlike rulers in Gallea, Deganawida could not command others outright. He could only urge consensus, and employ persuasion to reach it.

The warriors nodded dutifully, before turning and breaking into a run. Their forms were quickly swallowed up in the darkness, leaving the other two alone again.

"Change has been forced upon us, and we cannot go back," Ayenwatha reflected ruefully.

"Change to the world, perhaps … but not within us, Ayenwatha," Deganawida corrected him, giving a small smile of encouragement to the vigorous warrior. "It is why we will bend no knee to this Unifier. It is why we will fight."

"How can we hope to fight? I lost many of my best warriors this very night," Ayenwatha lamented, concentrating hard not to let his voice choke with the emotion abruptly welling up in him.

His thoughts drifted back to Sky Arrow, and the others that he had seen falling to terrible deaths. As if accenting his feelings, his wounded shoulder continued to throb with a dull pain.

"Our people will find a way. The sons of the World Mother will continue their war, as they have through all time. What may come of their fight is not for us to say, though we know that the Dark Brother has his hand in this time of peril. Remember, the fire dragon helped the World Mother. Perhaps we will find our own fire dragon, in days to come," Deganawida said.

The words brought Ayenwatha back to the many times he had heard the stories told regarding their treasured heritage when he was just a boy. They had impressed many things upon his young heart, not the least of which was that the path of good, honorable men and women often led through periods of great turmoil.

"Then we must not lose heart. There will be no fire dragon if we do," he replied after a few moments, seeing the sliver of light that Deganawida was focused upon.

"That is what I am saying to you, Ayenwatha," Deganawida confirmed gently.

The old man lowered himself down to one knee. For having lived so many years, the old man still exhibited supple movements. Deganawida raised his right hand, which Ayenwatha now noticed was balled into a tight fist. Slowly, he opened his fingers to reveal a dark patch of ash lying within his palm.

"You must keep your strength. Your mind. And your body," Deganawida said softly, as he blew the ashes in his palm.

The small cloud of ash covered Ayenwatha's face, and he reflexively flinched and shut his eyes.

It felt as if a blast of hot, searing wind coursed over his skin, as the ashes settled along his body. As he opened his eyes once again, he felt the tiredness seeping swiftly out of him. The throbbing pain in his shoulder rapidly ebbed, until the last dull aches were completely gone.

For a long moment Ayenwatha was silent, in a state of bewilderment at the sudden shifts in his body. Gingerly, and methodically, he moved his left arm, and felt no sign of discomfort from the shoulder area. It was as if he had never been injured. His whole body felt as if he was fully rested, abounding with energy. Ayenwatha drew himself up into a cross-legged, sitting position, and looked up in wonder at Deganawida.

"Did you think that you knew everything about me?" the old sachem said, smiling, in a brief moment of mirth. "When you are younger, you feel as if you have all answers. When older, you realize how few answers you do have. Maybe I still have a few surprises left, even for the likes of you, my bold young friend."

Ayenwatha smiled warmly back at Deganawida, his spirits buoyed up by the radiant presence of the seemingly tireless old man.

The elder women of the village had selected Deganawida to be the village's headman many years ago, at an age most uncommon for assuming the highest position of influence in the village.

Ayenwatha had known Deganawida as the village's leader ever since he was a young boy. It was said that Deganawida had come to the village not long before Ayenwatha was born, having been discovered by a war party. He had been wandering about the woodlands in a disheveled state, without memory of where he had come from, or what had happened to him. The war party had brought Deganawida back to be adopted by the village.

Whatever his origins were, and whatever trauma he had been through, his wisdom was soon demonstrated to be far beyond his years. His kindness and generosity shined forth in the years that followed, and all within the village were bettered by his presence among them.

It was almost a foregone conclusion when he was appointed as the headman of the village. The wise clan matrons, who alone held the authority to remove a headman, had never once called his guidance of their village into question.

Wise in council, and unsurpassed in compassion, Deganawida's reputation had spread quickly among the villages and tribes. Soon, a great number of village headmen and other sachems found themselves deferring to his sagacity, and he had risen to become the most influential and respected man among the Onan.

When the Onan sachem holding the most prominent seat on the Grand Council had gone from the world to the abode of the One Spirit and the heaven lands, the clan matrons, after having conducted all condolence rites, had appointed Deganawida to the exalted position.

His judicious nature and keen insight stood forth at the unified council that took in all five tribes. Known well among the Onan, he soon became beloved by the other tribal sachems. The ascension brought greater honor to Ayenwatha's tribe. A generous spirit prevailed, as there was no envy or jealousy among the other sachems for the tremendous regard given to Deganawida.

Some even saw a great symbolic meaning in his unexpected discovery and eventual presence among the Onan, leading to his specific placement on the first seat of the Grand Council.

The Onan tribe occupied the central position among the five tribes, and the oral traditions spoke of how the Keepers of the Sacred Fire had been at the heart of the original formation of the Five Realms. To have a remarkably sagacious leader such as Deganawida emerge to assume the place established by the very individual that had brought the Great Law, and formed the first Grand Council, was seen by many as a clear sign of favor by the One Spirit. A strong sense of harmony and common purpose had permeated the five tribes with the guidance of Deganawida and other likeminded sachems.

Ayenwatha's own ascent to become a war sachem of his village occurred within that shining period, something that never left his expressions of gratitude when honoring the One Spirit. Deganawida's guidance and tutelage had contributed so very much to the person that Ayenwatha now was, the man that the village had embraced and trusted to be their most respected war sachem.

With Deganawida's thoughtful guidance, trade had increased with Gallea, Midragard, and others. Even warfare diminished almost to a stop, as hostile tribes were driven back well beyond the northern region of the Five Realms' forestlands. Other tribes that had formerly held enmity towards the Five Realms were embraced in a new spirit of friendship. Witches immersed in dark arts, and similarly evil shamans, had been uprooted.

The elimination of the poisons and threats to their people had allowed the five tribes to focus on cultivating the bounty of their life and culture. The harvests had gone well, hunting was more bountiful than ever, and fur pelts were taken in abundance. Prosperity had never been better among the woodland peoples, and for once they felt as if they had at least a little control over their destinies. A true golden age had emerged for their people, one that had been bought with much sacrifice, resolve, hard work, and wisdom.

Ayenwatha never would have thought that such a wondrous age could be brought to such a horrific end, in just one night. That very evening, everything had seemed to come crashing down, like the large, deadly stones that had ripped through their buildings and indiscriminately slain their people.

What had taken so long, and been so painstaking, to build, could crumble overnight, a sorrowful but undeniable lesson that Ayenwatha was only now learning.

It was then that he fully understood and appreciated what the elders meant when they spoke of life being so fragile and precious. Now, in the midst of the awful turn of events, Ayenwatha marveled at the great strength of demeanor exhibited in the old man before him.

He closed his eyes for a moment, as he absorbed the bit of wisdom to his mind, promising himself to remember it always. He took a deep breath, and looked back up to Deganawida.

"I never said I have claimed to know everything," Ayenwatha replied, allowing himself a small smile. "I am not surprised that there is more to know."

"You have always been wise beyond your years," Deganawida said fondly. "You will need every bit of that wisdom in the coming days. For now, we need to get as much as we can out of the village, and see that we find a good place for our people to establish an encampment."

Ayenwatha rose up to his feet, feeling limber and strong. "Then I will get started now," he replied resolutely.

He took a step by Deganawida, affectionately patting the great sachem upon his upper arm.

AETHELSTAN

The darkness of night had already lain across the land for several hours. The scant moonlight beneath the trees was scattered about by the foliage intertwined above the heads of the small group of companions astride their horses.

They had proceeded as swiftly as they could, their minds fixated on the recent revelations confirming the invaders' imminent presence. Those developments occupied all of their thoughts, as it threatened everything that the Saxans held valuable.

Aethelstan and his few companions, in their haste to warn the woodsman, had nearly stumbled into the Jaghun-warded demesnes before they had announced themselves.

Had they blindly entered the demesnes, they would have risked death. Moving like fleeting shadows, the Jaghuns could be on top of the riders before they even were aware of their presence. In a burst of power, their hurtling forms could easily topple the riders, and bring their tremendous jaws to bear upon flesh and bone.

Aethelstan recognized the features in the terrain that Gunther had been so careful to point out to him just in time. Instinctively, he gripped the horn that hung at his side, but then loosened the grip, as he remembered the admonishment from Gunther earlier.

The admonishment had not been entirely necessary. Aethelstan knew that it would not be wise to use a horn signal. It would attract the attention of any enemy within hearing range, and put them in a state of full alertness. Aethelstan was not about to endanger the woodsman, especially when he had come to warn him.

CROWN OF VENGEANCE

Yet there was another way to signal, one not so obvious to enemy ears. Aethelstan recollected it quickly enough. He reined Wind Runner to a complete halt, and held up his right hand to his mouth. Hoping that he could still deliver the technique accurately, Aethelstan made a distinctive whistle-call, mimicking a bird cry. The melodious call was from a type of bird that lived in a foreign land, a creature that Aethelstan had never seen or heard himself.

Its distinctive cry could not be mistaken for any of the birds that dwelled within the forests of Saxany. Aethelstan sat back in the saddle and waited in the wake of the call, listening carefully. There was no immediate answer, and only the swishing of wind through leaves interrupted the encompassing silence.

After a moment, Aethelstan repeated the sounds again, feeling a little more confident in his delivery. The call raced forth through the sentinel trees, sharply breaking the stillness once again.

The great thane commanded the Saxan warrior to his right to hold his steed steady and calm, and try not to react to the creatures that Aethelstan knew would be arriving soon. In a low voice he turned to his other side, and repeated the message to the two that were on his left.

His heartbeat picked up, and he hoped that his signal had not erred due to lack of practice. He had little doubt that the strange creatures of Gunther would come, but his men's survival depended on that heralding cry.

As the silence became brooding, a part of him worried that it had been foolish to even take the risk. Yet he had given his word to Gunther that he would try to warn him, if he could see a way to do so. He could not deny that he had such an opportunity, and he intended to see it through. Keeping one's honor sometimes meant treading the ground of the foolhardy and reckless.

Aethelstan remained composed as best as he could, knowing full well that the woodsman's lethal guardians would soon be drawing near. He gently repeated his instructions to his men again, if only to distract himself within the nerve-wracking moments.

The formidable creatures emerged shortly thereafter, their great, shadowy shapes seeming to take form right from the ebon shadows pooling amid the encompassing trees. Four of the intimidating beasts formed a perimeter around the horsemen, their intelligent eyes glinting in the moonlight as they regarded the riders closely.

The beasts' presence, though expected, still rattled Aethelstan's nerves. The horses nervously whinnied and stamped about, clearly aware of the dangerous nature of the four-legged creatures silently surrounding them.

"Do not worry, they will not strike," Aethelstan softly stated.

His voice was loud enough for those around him to hear, as he sought to dispel the fears in his steed and the accompanying warriors. He gently stroked Wind Runner's mane, uttering soothing words to calm the horse's great agitation.

His attention was drawn towards the companion at his right side, an ardently loyal household warrior named Cerdic. The sight of the huge, predatory beasts had visibly unnerved the stout young man, who normally had a youthful bravado that bordered on recklessness.

Cerdic was a fierce-hearted warrior who had never shown fear of even the best of fighters in Wessachia, not backing down even when overmatched. Now, the pallor of his skin was ashen and there was a slight tremble to the man's left hand, as he tightly gripped the reins of his steed.

His other hand rested on the hilt of his sword, where it had quietly drifted in the interim. His knuckles were already whitening where they were visible underneath the tri-lobed pommel. The man's eyes were fixated upon the beasts around them. Even as Aethelstan watched, the muscles of Cerdic's hand flexed, tightening further around the hilt of the sword.

"The Woodsman has trained them quite well, I give you my word on that, Cerdic … do nothing to provoke the creatures, and you have nothing to fear," Aethelstan told him.

While each passing, tense moment seemed to last an eternity, in truth the Saxans did not have to wait for long before a human figure finally emerged from the depths of the tree-cast shadows. The sight of the tall, broad-shouldered figure was an instant comfort to Aethelstan's fraying nerves.

"Aethelstan, it is indeed fortunate that I have prepared my friends as well as I have," the Woodsman remarked with a hint of humor to his voice, speaking in a casual manner. Though uttered in a decidedly more lighthearted and confident manner, the sentiments confirmed the Saxan thane's assurances to his household warriors.

Gunther strode forward out of the darkness, his features becoming clearer in a swathe of moonlight pouring through a wider opening in the branches overhead.

CROWN OF VENGEANCE

The Jaghun nearest to the woodsman padded up from behind, and stood alongside of him, its eyes remaining honed upon the mounted warriors. Its tongue lolled about as it panted lightly, the array of shiny, sharp teeth within its broad jaws reflecting the moonlight.

"It is also good that you remember my instructions well, and that you have retained some skill in them," Gunther stated approvingly. "You mimic the Emperor's Songbird of Theonia more than adequately. Someday you should see and hear that magnificent little bird for yourself, and you will know that I speak truly. You are to be congratulated."

Gunther looked about at the gathering of Jaghuns still surrounding the horsemen, and called out emphatically, "Friends!"

Immediately, the inhuman companions of Gunther relaxed their postures, two even going so far as to settle down upon the ground. Despite the loosened appearances, Aethelstan did not overlook the fact that they continued to keep a casual eye upon the Saxans, always remaining on some level of wariness on behalf their master and friend.

Gunther walked forward to stand before Aethelstan and his steed. The great stallion shifted about a little before settling down itself, not quite as assured as its own master with respect to the woodsman's control over his beasts.

"What brings you here, at this later hour of the night?" His eyes darted among Aethelstan's companions, before returning again to the Saxan thane. Even in the dimness, Aethelstan knew that the woodsman could not fail to see the signs of stress and fatigue chiseled into their faces. Gunther's next words reflected that. "You look as if you have undertaken a hard ordeal. I would guess that you did not come here to bring me good tidings."

Aethelstan nodded gravely, his face shrouded with a look of dire concern. "I regret that again I do not have good words to bring to you, but I desired to keep my promise to you. Even now, my warriors prepare for what is coming, but I have come to warn you. It may be the only warning that you will have. I soon may not be able to reach you, even if it was the only thing that I wished to do.

"An army of the Unifier's is approaching through these woods, in great strength. Its passage will almost certainly bring them directly towards your own lands. … I see no other path that they might take … and I fear their intentions do not bode well for any that live within our lands."

Gunther echoed Aethelstan's look of concern, his expression

darkening for several strained moments before a quite unexpected grin broke though. The response took Aethelstan by surprise, and the thane did not know what to make of it at first. Yet knowing the woodsman's personality and disposition, Aethelstan came to recognize the sarcastic irony that was laced throughout Gunther's expression.

"The Unifier's army coming right through here, you say? Seems that I cannot keep to myself, no matter how hard I may try, or how far I run," Gunther remarked, shaking his head ruefully.

"I have traveled through the world to find my own peace … and now they send an entire army to disturb it. … Nonetheless, they can get me only if they find me," he then said with a wink upon his last words. His mouth then straightened, and his next words were spoken in full sincerity, "You have my true gratitude, Thane Aethelstan. I would not have thought ill of you, if you had chosen to remain with your men.

"It is not wise for you to risk yourself to warn me … though you chose to do so. The Saxans need your presence far more than one recluse in the woods. I only hope that I am someday able to justify such a risk, in a time and place that neither you nor I yet know about. You kept your word. It is the measure of a man, and I thank you for it. Such as this is what keeps me from surrender in this world."

Aethelstan nodded, though taken somewhat aback at the outpouring of open sentiments from the usually fiery, and adamantly solitary, woodsman. "Indeed, you are welcome, Gunther. I would have it no other way. I wish with all my heart that I was coming here to simply share conversation, and perhaps a hunt with you. I hope that a day may come when we can do so without worry … if you would suffer a guest for more than a few hours." He could not stifle a chuckle as he thought of the eremitic nature of the woodsman, and the momentous request that an extended visit would be.

"I should also like to try some of the mead from this area, from that village woman that you spoke of. I have no doubt that is one item that you trade for," Aethelstan added, with another amiable chuckle. "For now, I must proceed onward, to begin to prepare the defenses against this imminent threat. I assure you that we will meet the enemy with force, though to what end I do not yet know."

Gunther reached upward and clasped the other's forearm firmly. "I would certainly interrupt my little hermitage for a few hours, nay for a few days, to share your company. May the All-Father keep you strong,

Aethelstan."

"What will be, will be, Woodsman. Though we can always choose to hold the path of honor. … That, at least, is given to our own power. May the All-Father in his mercy and grace give you strength, and protect you in the days to come," Aethelstan replied, sharing the moment of mutual, sincere respect with the tall woodsman.

Though he knew little of the past of the mysterious denizen of the deep woods, Aethelstan knew in his heart that the woodsman was more than worth the risks that he had courted in having kept his word. Aethelstan's warning might well help Gunther to survive for some greater purpose still yet to come. Father Wilfrid had always stated to Aethelstan that the All-Father's ways were a mystery, and that the most unlikely of individuals were often called forth in dire times. Whether or not such a thing applied to Gunther, Aethelstan had no regrets that he had come.

Straightening up in his saddle, Aethelstan gestured to his companions, and nudged his horse to turn about. The horses continued to eye Gunther's Jaghuns nervously, skittish in their mere presence, but the beasts made no move to impede their passage.

The one in their path immediately behind them stood up and loped quietly away, keeping a wide berth as it cleared the passage before the Saxans' horses.

Gunther and the Jaghuns watched until Aethelstan was gone into the night, the soft clopping of the horses' hooves finally fading out as they made their way back towards the Saxan encampment.

Aethelstan did not see the woodsman break out into a run, accompanied by his Jaghuns, as Gunther hurried in the direction of his dwelling.

GUNTHER

"Stay? With an army approaching here?" Ryan exclaimed in exasperation, shaken out of his drowsiness after listening to the first alarming words from Gunther upon the woodsman's return.

No matter how intimidating or formidable Gunther might have appeared to them, Ryan had not hesitated in his blunt response. From what Gunther could tell in looking upon their faces, the youth had adequately expressed the sentiments of the entire group.

The other three had shuffled into the first floor room just behind Ryan, having also been roused abruptly from sleep. They had only recently gotten settled down to rest, probably with the hopes of finally getting a full night of undisturbed repose. Still half-asleep, they had trudged down the wooden stairs to the main room, gathering close around Gunther with inquisitive looks.

Those looks had swiftly become pensive, even a little fearful, as their heads cleared swiftly. It was evident that they perceived that something was very amiss. Gunther had then related to them the troubling news from Aethelstan. His mood was anything but pleasant as he conveyed the tidings.

So much was running through his head as he spoke. He was a formidable warrior in his own right. The recognition of that was not born of any hubris, but simply of honest assessment. His well-trained Jaghuns made him a capable entity within the woodlands, but definitely not for the likes of an entire army.

In the face of the looming threat, there was one option that seemed clear enough. It was the one choice that would allow him to remain close, without becoming embroiled in the futile affairs of humankind again. It was a spark of hope, even if the idea was rather unprecedented, and not altogether certain of success.

As that idea coalesced, he had announced that they were not leaving, drawing the incredulous response from Ryan. It was quickly followed.

"What kind of plan is that?" Lynn stammered, clearly sharing Ryan's feelings. "They'll just flush us out of this deathtrap, and put us all to death. Your creatures out there can't stop an army. I know you can probably fight anyone out there … one on one … but I know you can't fight an army off by yourself … not unless you are some kind of god we don't know about. If you are, it would help if you would tell us."

Gunther nodded, his face showing his increasing irritation at having been so abrasively interrupted by Ryan and challenged by Lynn. He worked to keep his voice controlled, having some sympathy for their exasperation. "I know that I cannot stop an army. I may be many things, but I am not unrealistic," he stated slowly. "If you would let me finish, you would see that I am not planning to stay in this building. I am just planning to stay in these lands. We are far from being trapped. Have you forgotten the door so soon?"

He gestured sternly towards the large, wooden door at the rear of the room. All four pairs of eyes followed, and stared towards the iron-banded slab of wooden planks.

"It is time for you to find out about that door, and what lies beyond it, though I certainly had no idea that it would be under these circumstances," Gunther added gruffly.

Erin asked tentatively. "You mean … the Unguhur?"

"Yes. An underground world, and one that even a small army would not wish to encounter," Gunther retorted curtly, and confidently, the idea seeming better with every second. "The passage beyond that door goes into the depths of the world. You will be quite safe there."

"Won't the enemies just follow us down?" Lee asked.

"It would be a great and terrible mistake for them to do so," Gunther stated firmly, with a dark expression spreading upon his face as he considered the consequences. "But we will go down there only if we truly must … when we truly must. Until then, we stay up here. Maybe there is a chance that this storm will pass us by, or dissipate before breaking upon this area."

He quietly studied the faces of the four strangers.

They were taking the somber news with a dismayed silence. Their all-too-brief respite from the trials and travails of the new world was over, and Gunther could not fault them for feeling great frustration and resentments.

Gunther watched Lee look sadly over to his companions, from Ryan, to Erin, and then finally to Lynn. All of them had beaten, weary expressions, and the glances that they shared amongst each other confirmed his evaluation.

They were exhausted, and not just in a physical sense. There was little that Gunther could do for them except to steel them as much as possible for whatever might come.

"I am sorry … very sorry," Gunther then said to them, in a low and gentle voice.

LOGAN

Walking slowly past the broken segments of palisade at the

entrance, Logan, in a brooding silence, looked around at what remained of the village. He was not alone, as many had begun to return to The Place of Far Seeing to search through its ruins.

Others from villages in the near vicinity had begun to arrive. For the most part, they were fellow members of the Onan tribe, some of the men with blood ties that resided in other villages due to a marriage. Logan's gut clenched as he saw the shocked, horrified looks sprout upon their faces, as the new arrivals set their eyes for the first time upon the interior of the village.

The morning's light had arrived following the devastating events of the previous evening. Instead of bringing a sense of hope, it nakedly revealed the full extent of the monstrous horrors that had been mercifully hidden by the night's shrouding darkness. The sources of countless miseries, shattered dreams, and heavy burdens were brought into the unyielding light of that pitiless dawn. The destruction was spread everywhere that anyone could possibly look.

The crushed, collapsed shambles of former longhouses now littered the village interior. Gaping holes had been ripped in the sides of short segments that were still erect, though much had been consumed by the sporadic fires that had been loosed by the sprawling violence.

Numerous bodies lay amid the wreckage, still awaiting removal. The rubble from the boulders that had been dropped down upon them in the night was strewn everywhere, from large, jagged chunks to smaller fragments, whose sharp edges made Logan careful about where he stepped.

The presence of the rocks caused Logan to reflexively wince nearly every time that he saw one of the badly misshapen corpses upon the ground. He knew full well the brutality with which the contorted, broken villagers had met their ends.

A deeply forlorn and sorrowful assemblage of sights surrounded him. His eyes hardened in anger and regret as he saw some of the village women cradling the crushed bodies of their children or husbands, shaking with sobs and piercing the air with their sporadic wails.

Some children were crying in agony amid the ruins of the village, several newly created orphans just realizing that their parents would never again be there to comfort them. An infant wailed from somewhere off to his left, drawing Logan's attention. He saw that it was just now being pulled out from the lifeless arms of the mother who had used her own body to shield her baby, saving its life.

Young men were openly weeping over the lifeless, still bodies that once held the spirits of their life-mates. Logan tore his eyes away from the delirium of grief within one such young man's face.

Near the shards and splinters of timber that once formed an outer entrance to a small longhouse, a little girl was sobbing with her face buried into the blood-matted fur of a dead dog.

The scenes were overpowering, rapidly draining Logan with each ensuing moment until he was absolutely devoid of feeling. A cold, empty numbness filled him, the depths of which seemed to be without limit, save for the volcanic anger welling up from deep within him. It brought a fierce storm in its wake, as a whirl of emotions surged back to the forefront of his mind.

Before many more minutes had passed, he had to sit down, hanging his head and forcibly averting his eyes from the unrelenting scenes of suffering taking place all about him. His thoughts, fueled by competing emotions of sorrow and rage, whirled about within the tempest of his mind, as if contesting for dominance.

He struggled to grasp anything by which he could begin to feel a shred of purpose or sense. None of the calamity suffered by the doomed village was deserved in any fashion. If anyone had tried to comment that misfortune befalls the just and unjust alike, somehow implying that this carnage was all just a part of some obscene order of life, he knew that he would have reacted violently, smashing his fist right into the face of the speaker with no compunction.

Any order that doled out such terrors to the innocent could be consigned to the fires of hell for all that he cared. The suffering around him was all too vividly real. No matter what sort of eternity lay in wait for those who had died, even if there was one to begin with, there was no justification for the horrid loss and pain.

He thought sardonically about the One Spirit that the villages had so lovingly and loyally spoken of, and wondered how their God could have possibly refused to intervene in something such as this tragedy.

Logan could accept an imperfect world. Mistakes, fallibility, and obstacles were necessary components for the true growth of a person. Even mortality, in its own way, could teach a lesson about the intrinsic value of life. They were things that he could accept, even if sometimes grudgingly or resentfully.

It was the extreme pain and devastating tragedies that he could not reconcile himself with. The more that he reflected on the hideous circumstances of the moment, the more that the totality of it all became a swirling mass of burning confusion in his mind.

For a brief second, Logan wished that he was the One Spirit that these villagers worshiped, just so that he could do some things differently. He knew in the core of his heart that he would have done something different in response, regardless. It was merely an acknowledgement of the true way that he felt.

He shook his head and let a bitter, rueful chuckle escape as he thought of what he would have done. Such was the hapless futility of wishing, without the power to follow it up with. Logan swore to himself that he would never have allowed the same things to happen to powerless, mortal people, knowingly putting them upon great danger's cruel pathway. No child would lose its mother, nor young lady her dearest love, nor husband his cherished wife, if Logan would have been able to have any say in the matter.

In that moment, he came to the conviction that he truly could have done much better by the villagers than their One Spirit had, if he held even a fraction of a god's power. The acrimonious feeling was so strong that if the One Spirit had suddenly manifested physically before him, he would have testified to that certitude with an unwavering intensity.

The same feelings, though they had welled up rather involuntarily in him at first, also made him feel somewhat guilty. His dispassionate intellect could recognize his sheer audacity and presumptiveness in the matter, for a Creator would undeniably hold supreme rights over the creation.

Whatever the case might truly be, Logan knew that all creation did inherently have an element of helplessness in it from the beginning, in that it was eminently subject to its Maker, the prime force that had brought life about. Even if one could not accept a sentient Maker, life was still subject to the primal processes. Yet despite it all, Logan knew that he could not bring himself to lie to himself, or gloss over the genuine feelings that he carried within. In the end, after all of the tumult of his frustrated wishes and rages, he simply felt powerless.

Nothing could be worse to a conscious being made to exist in such a maleficent world. He would have gladly embraced becoming powerful, if but for a short time. At least then he could demonstrate how things should be.

He could not control the things of life, but nor could he hide anything from himself. The feeling was almost like being caught in the undertow of a powerful current, one that he did not possess the strength to break free from.

Logan wished with all of his will that he could somehow, someday, elude the suffocating force of that current before he drowned.

Gradually, the conflicting emotions within him began to resolve. The sorrow within him slowly fused to the anger, as he immersed in the resentment of being powerless. The anguish served to empower the fury to greater potency, even while becoming subordinate to it. Logan's fists clenched in rage as tears of barely restrained anger ran in rivulets down his cheeks, and he shook with deep tremors that reverberated throughout his body and spirit.

Those that saw the lone figure in the midst of the village gave him a wide berth, and none wished to gain his attention.

ERIKA

Erika and Antonio assisted with the carrying of bodies, as well as helping to remove debris from collapsed lodgings for the better part of the morning and early afternoon. The two of them labored unceasingly, until every muscle and sinew in Erika's body cried out for rest.

It was not without some measure of reward, as they were able to free a couple of surviving villagers that had been trapped in the wreckage of the collapsed longhouses. One, an elderly man, had been pinned to the ground by the collective weight of broken planks and frame poles. The other, a boy of about three years of age, was not strong enough to work his way out of a small cubbyhole that had formed around him during another longhouse's collapse. Both were terrified and shaken, though relatively unscathed, when they were finally freed.

Some villagers urged the two foreigners to take a rest, and Erika and Antonio finally agreed to put aside their labors for a few moments. Like everyone, the two of them were sapped to emotional exhaustion by the awful sights spread all around them.

Their minds, hearts, and bodies weary, they trudged slowly back down the hillside, continuing on to the banks of the wide stream that coursed near to the village. They flopped down heavily on the embankment, as if their own bodies were extra baggage.

The two were silent for many long minutes, their faces dispirited as they stared out towards the flowing waters of the stream. Erika found herself wishing that the waters could carry the terrible feelings permeating her away. Finally, Antonio broke the unpleasant stillness.

"Not a wonderland anymore, is it?" he muttered quietly.

Erika looked over to him, before leaning over and putting her right arm around his shoulders. She gave him a brief hug of support and encouragement.

"Was it ever? Not completely unlike where we came from, is it?" Erika replied in a soft voice. "We can change worlds, but can't seem to shake what the worlds have in them. No, it's not a wonderland, even if I hoped it could be so."

Antonio slowly shook his head. "No, it's not ... all my life, I wanted to get away to somewhere else, and here I am. This is what we've gotten into. ... And it's really no better than before."

Erika quietly regarded him for a moment. He was speaking more openly than she had heard him ever since they had met. The fatigue had likely worn away his inhibitions, and his dark eyes glistened with considerable sadness.

"A lot of what happened in our world, we only heard about ... reports, and accounts," Erika stated slowly, after a moment. "Now, we are eyewitnesses too, and we share a burden with a lot of people here, and a lot of people back in our own world. I've never had a feeling like this, and I know we have scars that will remain forever. I know that only comes from having gone through something like this."

"Couldn't have said it better, Erika," Antonio returned ruefully, nodding slowly, before repeating his words. "Couldn't have said it better. ... What good is life anyway?" He abruptly turned his head away from her, and the oppressive silence returned.

"So what are you gonna do about it?" Erika sharply asked him, a spark of fire flaring within her. Something empty and resigned in his voice had touched a bare nerve within her.

She raised her head to look over at Antonio, and her gaze narrowed. Reaching out, she firmly prodded his chin back around so that his head was facing hers. She let her hand linger to force his attention in her direction. Her eyes commanded his to hold to her gaze.

"So what are you gonna do about it?" she challenged him again.

Antonio tried to avert his eyes from hers, but he soon was feeling the firmness of her grip increasing on his chin, and clearly sensed her inviolate will in that moment. He became fidgety at the boldness of the sudden question, and the strength displayed by the young woman.

"Look at me, and you answer me, Antonio," Erika told him a little more forcibly.

With reluctance, he conceded the struggle as he brought his eyes up to meet hers.

"What are you gonna do about it?" she repeated again, for the third time, impatience imbuing her voice with an even sharper edge.

For a few moments, it seemed like the answer to her question would never leave Antonio's lips. It was as if he was stunned, and it was all that he could do just to look into her fiery eyes.

"I cannot sit around and complain ... or feel sorry for myself," he began, in hesitant tones. He took a deep, sighing breath, before forcing more words out. They had an unmistakably resigned quality to them. "I don't like the situation, but wishing it away isn't going to make it go away. I have to deal with it. I know that. You and the others have my support. ... I hope that you know that. I'm just so tired right now. But I'm not going to give up."

Erika nodded, and let a soothing grin cross her face, to replace the stern visage of seconds before. She spoke with a sense of reassurance and gentleness. "We do know that, Antonio. Just keep the fight in you. We cannot surrender within ourselves, or give up in any way. We all are going to need you. Each and every one of us."

"I'll give you my best," Antonio replied, appearing to muster a little more resolve within himself. He gave her a slight smile in return. "We'll get through it."

"We will," Erika replied, confidently. "One way or another ... we will."

"Hey there, you two. ... I've been looking for you," interjected another familiar voice, echoing with sympathy.

Looking around, Erika saw Derek walking towards them. He was wearing only trousers, his upper body bared. His chiseled body glistened with sweat from the arduous work that he had been doing, sweat running down the contours of his well-defined musculature.

He wiped his brow as the corners of his mouth turned up into a gentle grin, though his eyes reflected no joy. A hollow, faraway look rested deeper within his gaze.

"Hey Derek," Antonio said, looking momentarily boosted to see another member from their group of exiles.

Derek strode up to them, placing his hands upon his hips while working to catch his breath in deep gulps. His chest heaved and recessed as he took in substantial breaths of air, obviously fatigued. He wiped his brow again with the back of his hand. More sweat began to muster immediately in the wake of his effort.

"I've been on the other side of the village, and I brought some news with me," he announced to the other two.

"What is it?" Erika inquired.

"Deganawida had some kind of emergency meeting with some elders of this village. It seems that they decided that even the area around the village isn't safe to stay within," Derek related to the two of them. "We are probably going to be evacuating the area pretty soon, to go deeper into the forest. Word has been sent to the other villages of the Onan, and other tribes of the Five Realms, to prepare them for the kind of assaults that hit this village last night. ... It was evidently the first time that kind of attack has ever happened."

"So we are going to be on the move again," Erika remarked, a little regretfully.

Derek nodded grimly, clearly sharing her frustration. "It sure looks that way, but what can we do? With flying creatures like those used in that attack, no village is safe. Well, I'm going back. I just wanted you to know what had happened, so at least you have some idea about what's coming. If you see Janus, let him know about it. I've already located Kent, Logan, and Mershad, though I'm not sure whether Logan even heard what I was saying to him."

Erika nodded. "We'll tell Janus, I promise."

"Hang in there," he said, giving them a brief smile, though Erika could not fail to miss the half-hearted nature of it.

After wiping his forehead clear again, he gave them a thumbs-up gesture as well, though his eyes betrayed the real truth. Erika knew that he was a very tough man, and also knew that his stoic demeanor was not just his own way of handling the tragedy, but was also intended for their own benefit. Casting a presence of strength, even if just a semblance of it, was a lifeline that they could all hold onto within the storm of misery. It was a foundation when everything else seemed so unstable.

"Hang in there, both of you. … It sounds crazy, but I know that it will get better. I know that it will," Derek then added.

"It will, Derek," Erika replied more firmly, giving him a warm smile in return, wanting him to feel a little of the confidence that he wanted to instill in the others.

He returned the grin, though it was laced with sadness. Derek then turned and set off with heavy steps to resume his efforts within the sea of tragedy.

JANUS

It had taken no small effort to force himself to walk into the village on that unforgiving morning. He was not about to let the good people of the village and his friends work through the rubble alone. Heavy hearted, seeing the world shrouded in the coldest gray, Janus had forced his legs to take each step up the hillside and past the outer palisade, taking him into the interior of the destroyed village.

Though he had expected horrific sights to meet his eyes, the lack of surprise in finding them did not diminish the thunderous ache in his heart as his eyes swept across the inner grounds of the Onan village.

All of the calamities in view were more than burdensome to his already fragile psyche. One of them, though, had been nearly enough to shove him over the edge and into an internal abyss.

Though unbeknownst to Janus, it was the very same sight that had compelled Logan to sit down, broken and angry, amid the ruins of the village. It was the scene of the child sobbing into the fur of her dead dog, as she rocked back and forth on the ground, cradling the crushed body.

The image conjured up a thousand upon thousand demons within Janus' delicate mind. The horror and sorrow etched upon the little girl's face, as her tears wetted the fur on the still body in which she had probably once found comfort and a sense of freedom, were far too much for Janus to be able to handle.

Instantly, he connected intimately with the great pain that was embroiling the little girl. The thunder of the agony he felt for her, and felt from the wounds newly ripped open within himself, caused a river of tears to break through and flow outward.

He slowly walked over to the little girl, squatted down, and hugged her tightly, sobbing himself.

Her dog, a large, stout, grey-furred breed, was clenched tightly in her arms. Its head was caked in blood and misshapen, where one of the cruel rocks from the sky had struck it during the dreadful night.

Janus memory invoked a contrasting image, one that made the current scene all the more acrid. He could imagine the little girl, just a day earlier, running through the village, squealing with joy as the dog bounded along playfully at her heels. He could still see the two wrestling and frolicking around, the dog licking her face, barking excitedly, and wagging its tail vigorously, as she threw her arms around it and hugged her furry friend close. The daunting veil of mortality now irrevocably separated the two companions, who had been happily playing together without a care in the world just the previous day.

However the roads arrived at it, this was the ugly culmination at the end of all lives. Through violence, age, or disease, and whether sinner or saint, all paths led to the awful conclusion that extinguished the wonder of a unique, irreplaceable life. That, in its naked reality, was the true face of death.

Death held the countenance of an unbowed conqueror. As always, the only death that Janus desired with all of his soul was the death of death itself.

The little girl continued to cry into the fur of the dog, but after some time curiosity must have moved her to look up to see just who was hugging her. Janus spoke no words, just trying to comfort and console her by his close presence. He understood her pain implicitly, but knew that there was nothing that he could really say.

He wished that he could somehow take the pain away from her, even if it meant that he added it to his own sustained, and continuously worsening, perdition. He hugged her to him even tighter, wishing that he could somehow squeeze the sorrow out of her, and let it seep into his own world-weary body.

Janus silently held the little girl close and snug, for what seemed like an eternity. He did not mind it in the least, knowing that it gave the poor child a slim anchorage to something that transcended the hideousness of the world.

Eventually, he felt a gentle hand lay down upon his shoulder.

Slowly looking up, he beheld a young village woman, whose face was stained with tears. New ones were welling up and moistening her reddened eyes, before beginning their downward trek. She was a very attractive young woman, but a great abyss of sorrow had left her looking haggard and drawn.

"Thank you … for being here, with my daughter … man from afar," she said with great effort, in a voice hollow and exhausted. She tried to force a smile, clearly moved at the compassion that the foreigner had shown to her daughter, a child that he did not know.

Janus nodded quietly to her, knowing what she would ask, as he slowly released his embrace of the girl, and methodically got up to his feet. No words needed to be said that the girl's mother needed to take his place as the comforter. The anchorage that he had instilled in the child, diminutive as it was, would be strengthened tenfold by the presence of her own mother. Many children in the village were now bereft of such a grace, a thought not lost on Janus as he watched the mother's emotion pour forth at the reunion.

The mother instantly dropped to her knees and hugged the little girl tightly, letting the tears flow swiftly again down her angular cheeks. Wordlessly, Janus shuffled away from the scene, feeling numb in his heart, though his chest seemed to throb with the emotional pain that he held within. His legs were weak, barely able to support his weight.

Two times, he tripped on debris and fell to the ground. Each time that he fell, he dragged himself back up and continued onward, heading towards the village's entryway. Janus wanted simply to head away from the village and its immense sorrows. He knew that he needed to get away from everything before he lost control of his tenuous hold on sanity, or could at least deceive himself that he could get away from the pain for a few moments. In truth, one could never escape such an experience, as it left a very unique kind of wound. The bleeding could possibly be stemmed, but the scar would never fade, as Janus knew well enough.

He fell one more time on the downward slope of the hill outside of the village, tumbling down haphazardly several feet before coming to a merciful stop. He ignored the scuffs and burning scrapes that he had incurred in the fall, as he dully got up to his feet and continued downward.

Finally, he reached the bottom, and started forward into the woods. His legs now felt as if they were made of the heaviest stone, though he forcibly picked up his pace and subsequently broke into an unsteady jog.

A few times he wavered, and had to slow down to a stop, to find his balance with the help of a tree.

Eventually, he was deep into the forest, and far away from the village. Ultimately, when his willpower could no longer force his legs to carry him any farther, he collapsed onto the ground. Pulling himself towards the base of a towering oak tree, he curled up into a fetal position and wept bitterly.

At long last, the fatigue of an emotionally drained soul and a physically depleted body overcame his consciousness, and brought him into the merciful arms of a deep sleep.

THE UNIFIER

Everything was so abundantly clear, no depths hidden from the eyes watching the winged form descending from the skies.

The messenger's heart was palpitating rapidly when he landed his Harrak deep within the bailey of the second level of The Unifier's soaring citadel in Avalos. His thoughts were so very exposed, revealed in an instant of transcendent perception by the One watching him.

The Avanoran sky rider had been expecting to be greeted by one of the Unifier's Sorcerers, the ones who attended Him most closely. They often sat within the gable-ended Great Hall that loomed far to his left, diligently conducting the Unifier's affairs.

The Sorcerers of Avalos were quite unnerving in their own regard, though nothing like the Master that they served. Unlike the Unifier, the guardsman could still endure their presence while keeping his wits and composure. He had envisioned that once they had met his arrival, that they would conduct him deeper into the great fortress, or perhaps lead him on up to one of the higher levels of the citadel that the Unifier normally occupied.

The walk would have given him the precious gift of a little time, as he had hoped for a few undisturbed moments to steel his anxieties. The hopes had been brutally dashed when he saw that the Unifier Himself was awaiting him in person within the bailey. To the guardsman's great dismay, he also saw that they were alone, anyone else evidently having been dismissed, as the grounds never went unoccupied by the forms of servants, artisans, or guards.

The eerie silence reigning in the bailey was intimidating enough, unnatural as the winds whistled among the series of buildings all around. A dizzying, icy chill of fear seized upon him with the realization of the Unifier's imminent presence, imbuing his movements with awkwardness. Hurriedly, he got down out of the saddle, his knees nearly buckling as his feet set down on the ground.

The messenger bowed his head immediately, instantly dropping to one knee before the tall, immaculate presence standing before him. He fumbled about as he nervously unlaced and removed his conical iron helm, revealing the short-cropped hair covering his head from his ears forward.

The back half was shaved smooth, as was his face. It was a manner of style that hailed from an earlier age, now embraced by the warriors of the Unifier's Avanoran garrison within the great citadel. Stoic, determined, and well-trained, the warriors that exhibited the strange, half-shaven style were normally to be respected and feared, at least by the populace of Avanor. The Unifier had no respect for the warrior, and was well aware of the man's great fear.

As one of the elite garrison force, the man had been privy to many things that few others knew about the powerful being looming before him. Only the Sorcerers knew the Unifier more intimately.

He had no difficulty keeping confidence concerning certain aspects regarding the true nature of the Unifier, as he had openly witnessed what could happen if he ever failed to do so. Bold, even arrogant, in his dealings others in the realm, he was frightened to the point of paralysis just from being in the immediate company of the Unifier.

The moments spent directly before the Unifier were those that he dreaded the most. Being alone with the Unifier, in the middle of an empty bailey, was staggering to his inner composure. It was all that he could do to function within the oppressive climate.

"What is the report?" the Unifier calmly demanded, ignoring the tremendous fear swarming within the guard, and well aware of everything that the man was thinking and feeling.

The messenger kept his eyes averted from the powerful, penetrating gaze of the Unifier. "The Darroks destroyed a large village, and caused much damage to one of the tribes."

"A village? One village? Did I not make myself clear that five villages were to be destroyed, in the first use of the Darroks?" The Unifier replied in an even tone, intertwined with tendrils of anger. "How was this not clear?"

The guard's heartbeat was now racing precipitously, as he mustered up every ounce of his will to answer. "Your will was clear, my Lord. … They could not continue their attack. … They were challenged by tribal defenders, upon sky steeds. They were able to destroy the village, before losses to the Trogens, and threats to the Darroks, forced them to retreat. The losses to the tribesmen were great. Two of every three warriors that came up on sky steeds were slain."

"And it was said that we would command their skies. That there was no way that the tribes would be able to contend with the Darroks. What can I believe now?" the Unifier stated darkly.

His eyes took on a blazing, reddish hue, with pulsing, swirling movements just beneath the surface of the baleful orbs. Anger rose up within Him at the news that the great Darroks had somehow been forced to suspend their assault, after leveling just one paltry village.

"And of the Darroks?" He inquired in a near hiss.

"They are all healthy," the messenger replied quickly. "All of the losses were to the Trogens upon the carriages. Be assured that there was no harm to any of the Darroks."

The Unifier narrowed His eyes as He focused upon the soldier. He could easily sense the increasing trepidation in the human at having to deliver the less than spectacular tidings.

"There is a threat … yes? Speak now, and openly," the Unifier commanded in a low, threatening voice.

The sky warrior nodded, sweat beading all over his forehead. "Yes, my Lord. … A couple of tribesmen were able to cut a harness free on one Darrok. They flew on its underside, and cut the bindings. The carriage was near to sliding off of its back. The Trogens had to abandon the area, or lose the carriage and themselves."

"How could that be? How could they even reach My Darroks to do such a thing?" the Unifier questioned with clear disgust. The feeble tribesmen had exposed a weakness in Avanor's mighty new weapon, on just the very first use of it. "Why were those savages able to even come near to My Darroks? How did they pass through the Trogen sky warriors?"

A sickening dread gripped the messenger, as he knew that he could not lie, nor could he sweeten his words. There was no use even trying, and a part of him felt that he should simply run for the steps to the circuit wall on the terrace, mount them, and fling himself quickly from the wall.

"They … were not … sent in the carriages. The Trogens were sent without steeds. It was deemed that all room should be used for the stone missiles. The Darroks were loaded with as much stone as they could bear, with enough of a crew to handle it," the messenger responded, the cold sweat surging all over his body. A breeze engulfed him, as it channeled through the rectangular buildings nearby, causing him to shiver.

"It was thought that the tribesmen could do nothing," the guardsman continued. "That their steeds would not be expended on trying to attack the Darroks. That the Trogens would be able to fend any tribesmen off with just bows, if they did emerge to resist. Only a very small number of the tribesmen's sky riders have even been seen in recent weeks … and none in force near this village. Their numbers were underestimated. It is said that they attacked together … concentrating in a group on one Darrok after another, felling as many Trogens as they could."

Had the soldier looked up, he would have noticed no change in expression on the Unifier's face. There was no outward sign of the instantaneous rage that was now churning violently within the tall, dark-haired being. It would not have been unusual, for whether fire or ice surged within Him, His countenance could remain uncannily placid.

The Unifier did not have to ask which magnate or leader had made the errant decision. It would not have been the Trogen leaders, a race of beings that rarely underestimated an opponent. The Trogen warriors had likely had great resentment for the order to go unescorted to begin with. They never would have gone unescorted under their own full command. If anything, the clannish Trogens would probably respect the tribal humans too much. The Trogens that had survived the fight would surely bring word of the debacle back to their own leaders, straining an already tenuous alliance.

The messenger would have been horrified to learn of the torments that the Unifier considered giving to the one responsible for the decision to leave sky steeds off of the Darroks.

The fact that the guard did not know his Master's thoughts also mercifully spared him the brief moment when the Unifier contemplated immolating the guard, simply for having brought word of vulnerabilities that could have been so easily avoided.

The Unifier did not reply to the guard, instead calmly walking past the messenger and on towards the steps leading up to the wall walk.

The Unifier's long, rapid stride carried Him there in moments. The guard remained on his knee behind, not about to follow the Lord of Avanor.

The Unifier simmered, yet what was done, had been done. Another measure would have to be considered in regard to the Five Realms. The ongoing defiance of the tribesmen, like a wind fanning a fire through parched woodlands, had spread growing flames of hatred within Him. The news of their partial success against the Darroks made His spirit boil.

For just a moment, He contemplated the ironies inherent in the moment, as poor tribesmen continued to resist and reject what rich and powerful Kings, Sultans, and Emperors readily embraced.

Once at the wall's crenellated edge, the Unifier swept His gaze across Avalos. He could see the spires of the great Cathedral of Avalos far below, a place nearing completion after many long years of construction. Being constructed with the latest techniques of architecture in the western lands, with towering spires, flying buttresses, and intricate vaults, it would bring a stream of visitors into the city. Though it appeared tiny from His vantage point, the huge edifice served as the most elite church in all of Avanor, the seat of the powerful Archbishop Regnier himself.

The thought of the Cathedral never ceased to amuse the Unifier, especially how it looked so small and insignificant before His towering, mighty citadel. The Cathedral was where many of the wealthiest nobles believed that they offered worship to the Accursed One. While their utterances may have been addressed to the God of the Western Church, an irritant enough, the Unifier was consoled by the reality that their hearts and deeds had long ago fallen to the service of Another.

Other nobles and authorities made their appearances within the Cathedral, but unlike the other nobles, they knew very well to Whom they belonged. The greatest of these was the Archbishop Regnier himself, who was not alone among the bishops and abbots who had been turned to Another's service. Except for the aging Vicar of the Western Church, Celestine IX, and a handful of recalcitrant fools clinging to the old, fading order, the Unifier now held a grip upon a majority of the influential high clergy.

The nobles and ecclesiastical powers of Avalos were just the surface of a broader transformation of loyalties occurring swiftly within many lands and kingdoms.

A large majority of the most formidable and learned that humankind had to offer had readily chosen allegiance to Him, and by extension the

One that the Unifier served. A number of them constituted many of the very individuals that ruled sprawling kingdoms and expansive empires.

The Unifier had not needed to engage in arguments with many of the Kings and Emperors, much less coerce them. For the most part, away from the eyes of the slumbering masses, they had come to submit swiftly, and enthusiastically.

That the men of power and wealth could so willingly bring their rich and strong lands into His service, and that a smaller rabble of wood-dwelling primitives could so vehemently continue to oppose Him, raised His ire and indignation to a white-hot level. That they had exposed a foolish commander in His own ranks, and likely caused severe damage to the Unifier's relations with the valuable Trogen clans, was just one more reason why the Unifier hungered ravenously for immediate vengeance.

It was no time for coercion or even subjugation. It was time for absolute destruction.

Annihilation was the only recourse that would quench the fires burning within the Unifier. The Five Realms had to be cast into a hurricane of retribution, one so powerful that they would not emerge to see any future, even one in willful submission to the Unifier.

Whether they surrendered and bowed to Him or not was no longer of any concern whatsoever. Furthermore, the extinction of the five tribes would be an unforgettable lesson to any who remotely harbored any thoughts of resistance.

The thought brought a brief surge of fiery red into His eyes, as He turned away from the sight of Avalos and slowly strode back down the steps into the bailey. When He reached the messenger, who had not moved at all in the interim, His eyes had returned back to their fathomless blue once again. "See to it that the Darroks are immediately outfitted by our craftsmen with new carriages, ones that cannot be so easily threatened by two tribesman with axes," the Unifier stated bluntly.

"Send word to Viscount Adhemar that the Trogens must be given more authority in matters involving their own kind. I do not think that they will neglect to have Harrak-mounted warriors riding in the carriages. That will answer the presence of any defenders that the failed scouts overlooked," the Unifier commanded in a forceful tone. A slight hint of a grin played about the Unifier's face. "And tell the Viscount that he is then to report directly to Me, in person, and without delay."

The Unifier grew quiet for a moment as He sifted through a few options in His mind. He settled upon a quite intriguing one.

"We will now see if the eastern Galleans can adhere to My desires better than a viscount from Avanor," the Unifier said, articulating the words slow and purposefully. "See that the full authority of command is given over to Count Garnier IV. We will see if commands rendered in the articulations of the Langeoc will be more understandable than those given through the Langeal."

His last words referred to the two versions of the Gallean tongue, the former spoken in the eastern provinces of Gallea, and the latter spoken in the western ones, including Avanor itself. The great Count of Talasae, Garnier IV, was one of those who spoke the eastern version, and he ruled the Gallean lands adjacent to the Five Realms. Talasae was a bountiful province, containing the powerful walled cities of Carcasse and Talasae. It was also home to some heretical religious movements that had deeply aggrieved the Western Church, as well as being a core of the region that had given rise to a newer tradition of epic poets. As if that was not enough, the area had helped give birth to a code of knightly behavior that had been closely embraced by great numbers of the elite warriors of Gallea. Count Garnier would now have a chance to become a subject of one of those epic poems.

"Make sure that it is very clear that Count Garnier unleash destruction upon all of the tribal villages, wherever they are found. Give them no mercy. Accept no surrender. No submission. Have Garnier break the chains on the army massed on the border of the tribal lands. Unleash those forces, and commence with the ground invasion. It is no longer there to influence any thoughts that the primitives might have had at submission. The sun has set upon their land and people. A new sun rises. Begin the invasion. Now go!"

The messenger bowed his head low in deference, and then placed his helm back on his head. His fingers were shaking as he adjusted the leather chinstrap, and it took him another moment to secure it. He rose to his feet, though he kept his gaze fixed to the ground as he turned and hustled back to his Harrak.

Mounting the winged steed swiftly, the guardsman wasted no time in his departure. He spurred the Harrak to lope forward and leap upward, snapping its wings down as it left the ground and began its climb back up into the skies.

The Unifier watched the messenger pass on over the outer walls of the terrace, streaking out towards the horizon as he continued to ascend higher. There was no question that the soldier would gladly hasten to his delegated task, even if predominantly motivated by the desire to flee the presence of the Unifier.

Though the day was bright and the sun unfettered, His face darkened, as if a cloud bank had swept in and cast Avanor's great Lord into a deep shade.

The Five Realms.

Saxany.

Midragard.

One would be destroyed soon. One was facing its final test. One would be dealt with in the near future. Very little remained to stand in His way, and perhaps all three of the last significant obstacles would find their fate to be total destruction before His work was fulfilled.

The new age was coming to the world. An old order would be overthrown, even as a new one ascended, one that would give rise to a new god taking dominion over all creation. The Great War would be finally brought to its end, and Another would come to bathe the world in fire, and recreate it in His image.

The Unifier was that Power's herald and greatest prophet, preparing His Father's coming and unlocking the timeless gates between dimensions. He would be first before all within the new Kingdom, placed even over the greatest of the antediluvian, immensely powerful brethren that had long served that Power. With the fall of the old order would also come the fall of His Father's great Adversary, as well as the Unifier's hated Counterpart.

The scent of the coming victory was exhilarating to every ounce of His being, the culmination of vast ages, meticulous patience, and tremendous sacrifices and suffering. It was all within sight and grasp, a reality both tantalizing and torturous.

His eyes had now become windows upon a raging furnace, glowing hotly with an inner fire of a substance not of Ave. It was an inferno that was borne of His vision of the world to come; a world that would be immersed in oceans of fire before rising anew.

In coming days and months, the Great Prophecies would be crafted to the Unifier's will, brought to fulfillment, and then He would be crowned as the new Son of Man. The thought made Him smile, though there was no benevolence whatsoever in His cold expression.

JANUS

The deep sleep transformed into a rare and special kind of dream, of the sort where Janus was unaware that he was even in the midst of a dream to begin with.

Everything had the essence of stark reality, utterly lucid and full of conscious awareness. All that he sensed was incredibly vivid, his eyes taking in the richest of colors, his ears attuned to every nuance of sound, and his other perceptions similarly enhanced.

Fear gripped him tightly at first, as he wondered whether another transition had taken place like the mist that had taken him unwittingly out of his own world. He took a long, slow look around him, cautiously eyeing his new surroundings.

He found himself entirely alone, somewhere deep among the shadows of an old forest. He recognized immediately that it was a forest far unlike the rolling woodlands around the tribal village. Gigantic trees soared far towards the sky above him, majestic sentinels breathtaking in their lofty reach. The great circumferences of their trunks were a spectacle to behold, a vision of strength and enduring vitality.

Even so, there was a heavy, foreboding stillness to the air. It was an unsettling disquiet that permeated the area, and the only noticeable movements were the rapid beatings of Janus' own heart. His breath tightened within his chest, constricting the coils around his rattled nerves.

Hurried motion off to the right edge of his peripheral vision suddenly grabbed his attention. His eyes widened as he beheld grotesque, shadowy forms that floated through the midst of the air. They moved in and out among the enormous trees, at one moment formless, and at another vaguely humanoid. They were gliding far off the ground, wending their way gradually towards the area where Janus stood.

Looking back to the left, and upward, he saw a couple more of the sable, flowing apparitions converging inward. It seemed as if the shadowy multitude was drifting closer and closer around him, with quite purposeful intent.

At the faint edges of his awareness, Janus began to sense a malevolence effusing from them. His blood chilled as he stared up at the sentient swathes of darkness.

Suddenly, the forms began drifting downwards, drawing closer. An icy chill crept along the tingling surface of his skin. He was riveted in place, as if his very willpower had been chained to a course of unalterable inaction.

To his growing dismay, he saw that the shadow-beings were not alone. With a sinking feeling taking hold in his gut, he realized that the murky entities were actually being hurried and herded along, driven forth by four huge shadows that came into view just a moment later. The larger shadows were gathered lower towards the leaf-strewn ground, but were clearly affecting the movements of the other shifting entities.

The forest area around him then began to darken, as if time was moving so rapidly that he could actually perceive the dimming of dusk into the fullness of night.

The shadowy creatures, both the ones above and those near the ground, pressed in even closer, as the chill saturated deeper into his being. His heartbeat accelerated with the rising fear, driving the panic to a nearly insufferable degree. He could not move a limb, finding himself trapped inside of his own body.

Then, without warning, a new and different creature thrust itself into the midst of the malevolent gathering. Its long, low body shape was supported on four, shadowy legs. It was particularly massive, substantially larger than any dog or wolf. The creature's presence was like a blade of light cutting through dark mists.

It had not come alone either, as a second creature, very similar in form to the first, then manifested into view, just to Janus' left.

A third creature bounded in from just ahead, though this one was notably different in form than the other two. It moved with a feline grace, and had the size of a great tiger. Janus could make out the triangular ears atop its broad head. Its forward-set eyes shined with a pure, radiant white light, as it leaped aggressively into the midst of the shadow-entities.

The abrupt emergence of the three creatures created a frantic scurrying, among both the large and smaller shadow-forms that had been pressing towards Janus.

The two long-snouted newcomers moved with blurring speed, setting immediately upon the shadow creatures with a vengeance. Their mouths opened expansively, lined on the top and bottom with enormous, serrated teeth.

Jaws snapping, they set about consuming the smaller shadow creatures, able to take in an entire entity with only one bite.

Likewise, the monstrous, feline entity assaulted the shadow

creatures. It brought its broad paws to bear as it raked shadow creatures down from the air, and then engulfed them in its gaping maw.

The shadow creatures made no sound, though their distress was obvious as they tried to evade the attackers in sheer futility.

The three creatures were not confined to the ground. They were able to soar into the air in incredible leaps, always landing lightly once they had dispatched their quarry. Though some of the shadow creatures tried to drift up and away, their efforts were in vain, as they could not escape the reach of their three supernatural assailants.

The three ethereal attackers moved with tremendous speed and aggression as they levied their lethal assault. Janus watched the destruction of the shadow creatures with stunned amazement.

In just moments, only the four larger shadow-beings remained. No longer driving the smaller creatures towards Janus, they now seemed to be gripped with fear themselves, flitting about the trees in apparent confusion and disarray.

Able to concentrate entirely upon them, the three four-legged attackers wasted no time in turning their offensive upon the larger entities. The large shadows were maimed and devoured one by one, until nothing of the shadowy, menacing host was left.

Janus watched in awe as the feline-like entity swiped its claws and batted down the last two large shadow creatures in one leap, before consuming each one in turn within its fearsome jaws.

When the creatures had finished, they each turned towards Janus, regarding him intently through their blazing, white eyes.

Strangely, instead of being afraid of the formidable beasts, Janus had a strong sensation resonating all throughout him that there was nothing to fear from the ethereal trio. A calm peace settled over him, as his thoughts became steadily clearer.

If anything, he felt a compelling urge to move towards the creatures, as if by drawing closer to them he would acquire even stronger protection. He also got the distinct impression that the creatures were excited by his presence before them. Though they were not entities of flesh and blood, their forms had much more stability than that of the shadow creatures. He could see without a doubt that the two elongated, canine-like creatures were wagging their tails vigorously.

The feline creature then started to pad slowly towards Janus, moving with fluid ease. He then became aware that he had regained full control of his body once again, feeling his inner authority pass through every extremity of his limbs.

An affectionate warmth flowed abundantly over him within the next few moments, swelling towards a euphoria as the feline drew closer to him. His eyes narrowed, trying to pierce the strange mystery of the creatures that had rescued him.

The canines' tails were still wagging, and he heard purr-like rumblings emitting from the feline that was now just a couple of feet away. The feline stepped in to brush against his side, far too tall to brush against his leg. As it did so, and as his ears heard the echoes of the first jubilant barks coming from the other two creatures, they suddenly vanished from sight.

Janus turned his quickly head from left to right, but he was completely alone. There were no shadow creatures, or sign of the rescuing entities.

Before he could even begin to make any sense of it, a voice abruptly came through the air to him. "Walk straight ahead, around the great tree that is before you."

The voice seemed to come from right next to him, but as Janus turned around in a complete circle, he saw no sign of the speaker.

"Who are you?" Janus called out to the unseen entity.

"More than a friend," the reply came gently, again sounding as if the speaker were standing right at Janus' side. "Now trust me, and walk forward around that tree."

Something inside of Janus had come to understand by then that this all was truly just a dream, and that he had not undergone another experience like the mist. Still fully lucid, he decided to see what might happen if he cooperated with the voice.

He took a slow step forward, and then another.

"It may only take you a week at this pace to reach the tree," the voice came again, resonating with a sparkle of amusement.

"Hey, I'm cooperating," Janus retorted curtly, though he did pick up his stride.

He walked towards the great tree that the voice had indicated, and wended his way around the trunk to the right. Janus blinked his eyes then, as he found himself within a totally new environment. He was now looking upon a cave set into a hillside, under a velvety night sky adorned with diamond-bright stars.

CROWN OF VENGEANCE

A few banks of low clouds were scudding over the terrain, though they blocked little of the sparkling firmament.

Beyond the cave was a hilly, undulating land. In the distance he could see the numerous forms of what he believed to be flocks of sheep moving on some of the slopes. Outlines of what looked to be a few people were at the summits of a couple of the hills, leaning on staves as they looked out over the grazing flocks.

Some tiny, gleaming, reddish lights that undoubtedly came from fires marked the presence of a small village situated just beyond the hills with the flocks. It was too far for Janus to make out any details, other than the existence of many low structures clustered together.

A human cry, unmistakably that of a woman, came to him from the depths of the cave. His attention was immediately riveted upon the dark entrance from whence the sound had emerged.

"Go, and witness," the strange voice instructed him, almost causing Janus to jump in its firm suddenness.

Recovering quickly enough, Janus heeded the words of the unseen speaker. He approached the entrance of the cave and entered it.

A low fire was blazing deeper within the cave, sheltered from the winds outside and the light rain that had just begun to fall. The pattering of the first raindrops faded as Janus walked a few steps further. Shadows flickered along the jagged sides of the cave, and in the midst of thick piles of straw were two human figures.

A woman was lying on her back, knees bent and legs spread far apart, while a man knelt down before her. The man was many years older than the woman, with a thick beard and locks of dark, wavy hair. The woman was young and beautiful, though her brow was beaded in sweat and furrowed in the grips of her considerable strain.

The couple took no notice of Janus as he cautiously took a few more steps into the cave. He then halted and stood stark still, realizing what was occurring before his eyes. The woman was giving birth, right on the verge of bringing a new life into the world.

Just as Janus became curious as to the identity of the couple, he was drawn to the shadows in the area to the left of the woman.

His heart skipped a beat, as he saw something there darker than any blackness or shadow. A great Presence lurked there, though Janus could see no discernable figure within the deep pool of impenetrable shadows.

Janus could feel the sheer intensity pouring forth from that blackness, as it silently observed the woman, the man, and the impending birth. Janus sensed that the Presence absolutely loathed the woman. The Presence was like some enormous serpent, coiled and waiting, whose gaping maw was awaiting the birth to devour both mother and child.

Though the Presence was unmistakably baleful and raging, with a malefic radiance beyond anything that Janus had ever felt before in his life, Janus had no fears for the people in the cave. He knew that the Presence was not there in any kind of manifestation whereby It could do any immediate harm to the woman, the man, or to the newborn.

It was as if Janus was simply gaining a perception of the Presence, as It gazed Itself upon the proceedings from some faraway, unknown region, scrying from a dark place that Janus knew had nothing in common with the two worlds that he knew. He also knew that the looming Presence was far more powerful than he could possibly imagine.

Janus wondered why something as obviously immense as the Presence would have any concern with a couple of simple people and their baby in a cold, lonely cave.

With a sustained cry from the woman, and several gentle words from the kneeling man, a third voice sounded within the small cave.

The cry of a newborn baby accompanied the exuberant and joyous laughter of the man, followed closely by that of the woman, in those next few moments. While the woman sounded exhausted, Janus could hear the tremendous delight and relief in her voice.

The man and the woman spoke excitedly, in the unrecognizable language, as the man carefully attended to the immediate needs of the baby. The man gently wrapped the baby in cloth, handing the newborn over cautiously to the outstretched arms of the mother.

With the warm look of genuine love spread on the man's face, Janus had no doubt that the man had to be the father. Nobody but a father could have given such a tender look to a newborn child. The woman looked so entirely gentle and serene as she accepted the baby from him. The look upon her face embodied the essence of a mother, with boundless joy accompanied by an infinite love as she beheld the face of her new child for the first time.

Like a sharp crack of thunder, Janus' attention was jarred violently as he felt the sudden explosion of pure malignance from the Presence within the shadows. Janus realized with astonishment that it was the mere sight of the baby that had invoked the stark and incredible reaction.

The Presence vanished from the cave instantly, though the echoes of its last expressions shook Janus to the core. An awful understanding was impressed upon Janus' mind. The Presence was murderous, wanting nothing less than the annihilation of the newborn. Janus knew that Its limitless anger at seeing the baby in the world was so great that It could not maintain Its observance, volcanic emotion shattering Its cohesion.

Janus had already comprehended the reality that the Presence was exceptionally powerful, whatever It was, and he found himself fearing greatly for the safety of the mother, the apparent father, and the infant.

However he came to the understanding, he knew that the Presence was the ultimate essence of a predatory hunter, determined to pursue the children of this woman to the ends of the world. Janus felt wholly dismayed, wondering how the woman, the man, and the child could ever hope to evade the black diablerie that was setting its mordant gaze upon them.

As his fear for the small family grew, the veil of the dream faded as he was called back into waking. He found himself lying upon the hard, forest floor, curled up in the fetal position that he had taken when he had first lain down.

At first, he felt a little nauseated, as if he had ingested something wholly unnatural within him. He gagged and heaved as he slowly got up into a sitting position, but the worst of it passed by quickly enough. In a few short moments, the initially strong sensations had settled into a mild discomfort and gentle cough.

The dream-experience had left its images vivid and freshly imprinted upon the eye of his mind. He breathed slowly, as his full orientation returned.

Slowly, he braced himself on his hands and pushed himself back up to his feet. Taking a look all around him, he discovered that there was nothing to be seen close by, yet he did not feel alone.

A sense of wariness brought to the fore, Janus started back for the stream near to the village. On the way back, he recalled the sequence of the dream over and over again within his mind.

Ever since he had arrived in the tribal village, and began to listen more carefully to the tales of his newer hosts, he had heard a lot of talk about dreams and the genuine significance of them. To the people of the village, dreams were not considered to be merely a whimsical or fanciful conjuration of the mind. Nor were they simply a practical process demanded by the subconscious mind, to sift and sort through the things of life's experience. To the villagers, they were something else entirely, experiences to be taken very seriously, if not unquestioningly at some times.

If the dream that he had just experienced was indeed something more, like something that the tribal people spoke so openly of, then there was something important for him to understand within the essence of that vision.

The tribal people would suggest that there was much to discover and learn from the vivid and meticulous dream, whether on the surface or buried deeply.

Whatever the reality was, Janus knew that he would be pondering the incredible dream for quite some time to come.

Preview of Book II

in the

Fires in Eden

series

LEE

"The two of you up there, come down, now!" Gunther yelled up to the loft, before turning back towards the others.

He waited with a worrisome expression on his face, until the two young women had come down the steps to join the others. "No luck is with us. None whatsoever. The Avanorans are coming straight towards this dwelling, in great strength. Far too many to even think about a fight. It is certain that they will find this place, and I am not so naïve to think that they will respect a man's dwelling. We must go!"

"How far away are they?" Erin asked.

Erin, like the others, presented anything but a calm façade. Wide-eyed panic was written all over her face as she looked to Gunther.

Lee's greatest anxieties were spawned by the deep worry etched across Gunther's face. In the short time that he had known the woodsman, there were a few traits in the stalwart man that rose prominently to the surface.

Of his more noticeable characteristics, it was obvious that Gunther was not the sort of man to openly exhibit trepidation, unless there truly was a daunting reason. The entire patrol of the bestial warriors on the winged steeds had not rattled him in the slightest. He had seemed wholly unflappable in the aftermath of that conflict, except for the trauma at the loss of his Jaghun. Lee knew without a doubt that fear did not come lightly to the tall, brawny woodsman.

"They are close enough. Unless you prefer to die gloriously, and take a few of them with you, and hope that some gleeman sings of you one day, I would suggest that we all get moving now. As for myself, I am not seeking glory in a senseless fight, so I am leaving now. You may stay if you like, though," Gunther replied tersely, clearly in no mood for any edgy banter with Erin, sharply preempting any rude responses that she might have entertained.

For her part, Erin made no caustic reply.

Gunther moved swiftly, gathering up a couple leather packs and opening a couple of the wooden chests on the ground. He rummaged through the chests quickly, withdrawing some items of clothing and other incidentals that he packed into the hide pouches.

Lee and the others were sternly exhorted to gather up their weapons, along with any other things that they wished to take with them. There was not much in that regard, as Lee and the others did not have so much as a single change of clothes.

Packs filled, Gunther strode over to the back of the room, heading towards the barred door. He brushed roughly by Ryan in the process, almost knocking the young man off his feet with the brusque impact.

Lee knew that the contact was not intentional, simply a result of Gunther's mind being far away from the woodland abode. Gunther paused to glance back towards Ryan, as if in afterthought, and apparently recognized the confusion upon the younger man's face.

"There is no time, we must go without delay," he said more gently, as he lifted the wooden plank from the great door and swung it open.

What little light there was in the outer room was immediately sucked up inside the door, absorbed into the impenetrable blackness on the other side. Lee reflexively shivered as a robust draft of cold air rushed out of the darkness. Just beyond the door, the sides framing the blackness were revealed to be rough hewn stone

The cooler air emerging from the interior of the cave-like atmosphere had a clean moistness to it, imbued with a damp, musty scent. Only a tiny speck of dim light in the far distance signified anything that he could orient upon with his eyes.

The four awaited Gunther hesitantly, looking between the entrance and the woodsman.

"The door is open for you, to go through, now!" Gunther barked at them. "Walk slowly, and keep your eyes upon the light. The ground underfoot is even enough. You can feel your way along the sides if you wish, but keep your balance."

Lee started through the doorway first, giving some confidence to the others as they followed behind him. The ground a few paces inside the doorway was at a downward slant. Fortunately, it was not terribly steep, and he noticed that it headed straight towards the distant light.

Putting his hands out, he discovered that the passage framed by the entrance remained narrow, as he felt along the rough-hewn rock to the sides. Methodically, he took his first steps forward, careful to maintain his footing. The surfacing beneath his feet, though far from even, did not have any larger projections or dips that threatened make him stumble or fall.

After about twenty paces in the narrow corridor, his hands could no longer touch both sides at once. He could also sense the enlargement of space in the widening passageway, yawning open above and around them. He adjusted over to the side, to move forward along the wall to the right.

Within the surrounding blackness, he could hear the sounds of the Jaghuns padding up from behind, shortly passing by Lee and the others. The presence of the creatures in the passageway was reassuring, though it did not entirely quench his sense of apprehension as they made their way through the darkness, towards the unknown.

Lee heard the shutting of the wooden door behind them, followed by a sliding sound and a loud "pop", as if a wood plank was being shoved into place from the inside.

It came as no surprise to Lee that Gunther had taken both sides of the door into consideration when he had built his dwelling. Heavy, swift footsteps then echoed along the passage, as Gunther hurried down the corridor. Within a few moments, he drew up alongside Lee.

"The enemy will find my home, but there will be no easy path for them to take, to come against us down here. Remember, we are calling upon friends, in a time of need," Gunther said to Lee, loud enough for the others to hear. He then spoke louder, addressing the quartet. "Now keep going towards that distant light."

Gunther's voice trailed off as he started forward, taking the lead. Lee and his three companions fixated their eyes upon the distant glow, still far ahead and below.

Moving slowly through the deep gloom, the rest of the descent seemed to take an eternity to complete. The light before them was a welcoming beacon, reassuring and calling to the party as they carefully navigated the engulfing darkness of the downward pathway.

Gradually, the speck of light grew to become a definable circle, which in turn became an oval-shaped portal, one that was easily big enough for the group to walk through. The light gradually illuminated the ground and sides around them, though it revealed little other than rock.

Off all the strange things that Lee had seen in his life within two worlds, what awaited the group at the end of the passageway was perhaps the strangest yet. He had expected something unusual, but found that he was completely unprepared for the sight that greeted his eyes.

The light was not generated from any sun or artificial means.

The luminescent glow came from many broad, amorphous patches, spread high up the sides of a huge rock cavern that the passageway opened upon and revealing what looked to be a rather bizarre forest that stretched out far and wide in the vast cavern. Even at first glance, in the midst of an entranced awe, Lee saw that there was a definite order to the strange forest. It was as if the growths had been cultivated according to a well-organized arrangement, evincing a specific purpose for the forest. Lee's initial impression was that the forest was similar to an agricultural farm.

The forest was a mixture of soaring vertical growths, some varieties resembling giant mushrooms. The growths continued on down in size to much shorter stalks, the smallest of which were barely taller than Lee.

The footing underneath was very strange, as algae-like growths and a spongy loam covered the ground. Lee could see that it was the substance of the thick layers that served as the foundation for the greater forest. The path that they were walking on was like a channel cutting through the deep organic material. The amount of loam that the towering stalks were rooted in throughout the cavern was incredible to consider.

Lee drew to a complete halt just a few steps into the cavern, gazing all around. The bright, glowing patches on the walls, bathing the great expanse with bluish light, added considerably to the mystical beauty of the extraordinary place. He looked about in a state of wonder, nearly breathless as his eyes adjusted further to the glowing light. The overall effect of the place was simply magical, unlike anything he had ever seen.

"I don't think I believe this," Lynn remarked slowly, her eyes drinking in the astonishing sights surrounding them.

"Unbelievable," Ryan added, craning his neck back to look up at the underbelly of one of the tall mushroom caps. Had the cap been upon the ground, all four of the exiles could have stood comfortably within its circumference.

Lee hardly bothered to notice the Jaghuns grouping swiftly around them. Just ahead, Gunther had come to a stop himself, though it was not out of awe for the sights around them. His eyes darted among the growths, as if searching for some sort of sign, or presence.

Gunther slowly stepped back to where Lee was.

"What is it?" Lee asked in hushed tone.

"The Unguhur might wonder why I bring companions who can speak their language well ... as they know that I possess only a small number of their words. Best not to give rise to suspicions where we are needing friends," Gunther said, keeping his attention riveted upon their surroundings. "I will have to meet everything about the four of you in time, including your amulets from the Wanderer."

"Should we take ours off?" Lynn asked him, voicing the first question that came to Lee's mind.

"They will know you are of another world, no matter what you do. The instant that they see you will tell them enough. I may suggest that you simply keep your own words few at the beginning, if speaking any at all. But keep your amulets on you. At least it will help you understand what they say. We have little other choice," Gunther replied evenly. He then paused, as if thinking further on the matter. "It may also be wise not to reveal that you can speak with them, and understand them. They may speak more openly, if they do not know you can understand their words."

The four exiles nodded. Lee was relieved to know that they could retain the pendants. Once he had come to understand the nature of his amulet, he had regarded it as indispensable. In a world where he knew not one of the languages spoken upon its surface, the amulet was a lifeline.

The group remained silent, as Gunther continued to look out into the wondrous forest around them.

"As a friend I come, Gunther, of the upper world," Gunther called out loudly into the stillness about them. His voice carried far and vibrantly, echoing within the enormous space of the cavern.

His shouted words brought Lee, Lynn, Ryan, and Erin closer in towards him. Lee was now fully out of his enraptured state, thoughts of the forest retreating as he looked to see who, or what, Gunther was speaking to. He found himself gripped by a nervous anticipation.

Movement drew his eyes, as a grayish shape could be seen moving amongst the growths, emerging from a deeper part of the fungus-forest and striding towards them. The figure was not alone, as several other large shapes came out from the forest growths all around the party just a few moments later.

The great size of the approaching beings became increasingly apparent with each long stride that they took. Were it not for the relaxed nature of the Jaghuns, and the placid, entirely unruffled demeanor of Gunther, Lee would likely have sought to take flight, and run as fast as he could back towards the passage.

The hulking creatures approaching them were humanoid, each one standing well over eight feet in height. They had large, triangular ears that were pressed close against the sides of their wide heads.

The shape of their faces had a distinctive concavity, lending them all a naturally melancholic expression. Large, forward-set eyes rested deep within their wide sockets, beneath pronounced brow-ridges, while their prominent lower jaws jutted forward.

Their thick, bullish necks were connected to immensely muscular bodies, warning any who looked upon them of an inherently tremendous physical strength. They were also long-limbed creatures in proportion to their powerful bodies, the considerable lengths of their arms and legs rippling with corded muscle.

There was little mystery as to the identity of the creatures. Lee knew that the beings coming towards them were the Unguhur.

Lee could see why the creatures had once been called Stone Hides. Their grayish skin did indeed have a stony texture, though at close proximity Lee could see that the creatures possessed a very light growth of thin, gray hairs covering their outer skin.

Most of the creatures wore a type of hide-skirt, similar to a kilt, which was wrapped around their waist and hung down to just above their thick knees. A select few wore plain hide tunics along with the kilt, both items appearing to be fashioned of a thicker, different kind of leather hide. The Unguhur wearing tunics also looked to be larger and more muscular than the rest.

The massive hands of the Unguhur exhibited fingers that ended in what looked like of small spear blades. The same was true of their rather long feet. Lee could not help but conjecture that the creatures could readily tunnel through hard-packed ground without the need for any tools.

The ones wearing the tunics were armed with great lances. The lance blades were crafted out of a black stone that had been shaped long and sharp, making the weapon propitious for slashing or for thrust.

Those with the hide-skirts alone carried much shorter weapons, club-sized for the scale of the beasts. The crude, mace-like weapons held a large, obsidian stone lashed tightly to the end of their thick shafts.

The creatures bearing the lances moved to the forefront of the bare-chested ones, the latter clustering into a loose throng behind them. Altogether, sixteen of the creatures came to stand before Gunther's party. The huge beings made no hostile moves, though they kept some distance between the two parties. The ones in the front retained a firm grip upon their huge spears, though the sharpened points were tilted upwards, towards the cavern ceiling.

Gunther turned to Lee and the others, and spoke in a lowered voice. "We must wait for one of the Unguhur leaders, versed in our language. One will come. These were the closest to us, warriors and laborers attending to this cavern."

Lee nodded wordlessly to Gunther. He was not about to divulge the nature of their amulets to these creatures, for there was no telling what interest or alarm the brutish-looking beings might harbor for the magical devices.

After what seemed like an age had passed, five more of the Unguhur walked into view out of the forest. Like those in the forefront of the group before Gunther, four were wearing the tunic-kilt combination, and bore great spears. The four warriors walked in escort around the fifth member of their group, keeping the distinctive being centered in their midst.

The protected Unguhur, alone among the twenty others in sight, was unarmed. Clad in a full-length tunic of softer material, flowing almost like a robe, the creature wore a necklace made up of an array of very long, sharp teeth. Tan-hued hide armbands were wound snugly about each of its upper arms. Each exhibited a single line of raised scutes, gleaned from the hide of whatever creature had been used to fashion the armbands.

"Hail, Eranthus," Gunther greeted the guarded Unguhur, lowering his head towards the approaching contingent.

"Gunther. You come. Been long. No wood? No trade? You bring others?" the robe-wearing one stated, when the last group of Unguhur had finally reached the larger gathering.

Lee listened with the benefit of the amulet, knowing by the stilted, hesitant words that the Unguhur was speaking in the Saxan tongue to Gunther. The creature spoke in a low, gravely tone of voice that fit well within the atmosphere pervading the strange world of deep, underground rock. It was obvious to Lee, from the great deference given to the creature by its surrounding brethren, that the being held great authority amongst their kind.

"No trade. We seek refuge here. A danger comes to us above," Gunther replied.

It was difficult to read the expression upon the creature's broad face, but the look in the large being's eyes seemed to convey familiarity, and even a sense of affinity, towards Gunther. The same eyes shifted to study the four humans with the woodsman very closely. The creature's eyes narrowed, bringing furrows to the prominent, broad ridge of its forehead, applying great scrutiny to the clearly unexpected human guests.

"Enemy come?" Eranthus asked.

Gunther nodded, and as he spoke he used physical gestures to illustrate and emphasize his words. "Bad times come in world above. Work of Unifier. Big army comes. There are many enemy. Had to leave home. Could not stay above. Come to warn Unguhur. Need home with Unguhur."

At the mention of the Unifier, the Unguhur leader Eranthus' facial muscles tensed into something that looked much like a snarl. The lips curled back enough to reveal that the Unguhur had large teeth, along with a set of extremely prominent, and very sharp canines. Lee could tell that there was no love lost between the Unifier and the Unguhur, something that made Lee feel much more reassured about their prospects with the intimidating creatures.

"You safe. In Unguhur lands now. Come now. Who friends?" Eranthus asked, his eyes looking back inquisitively towards the four exiles.

"Will give story. Maybe prophecy. Friends. Protect from Unifier," Gunther replied.

"Gunther friends welcome. Gunther beasts welcome. Come. We go to Oranim," Eranthus stated. "We watch tunnel to above world."

Eranthus turned and spoke in an even lower tone to the warriors that had escorted him. Lee picked out several words, listening as the Unguhur leader instructed the warriors to summon others, ordering them to watch over the long tunnel that lead up to Gunther's dwelling.

When Eranthus was finished speaking to the warriors, two of the spear-carrying Unguhur had cupped their hands to their faces, and bellowed back in the direction of the forest.

In mere moments, a number of other voices were raised from places near and far within the forest. There were evidently several more Unguhur in the cavern, as a trickle of Unguhur appeared shortly into view, covering the ground in swift, loping strides.

Gunther did not have to explain to Lee that each of the giant creatures was worth several human warriors, if combat were to ensue. Lee found himself intensely grateful for the fact that Gunther was regarded as a friend by the creatures, as over thirty of the creatures now surrounded them. If the Unguhur had decided to become hostile, there was nothing that Gunther and all of his Jaghuns combined could have done to protect Lee and his companions.

Most of the warriors gathered together, leaving with the ones that

Eranthus had instructed towards the lower tunnel entrance. Eranthus then motioned for the humans to follow, adding the invocation, "Warriors there. Now, come."

Only a couple of the warriors had remained behind, and these now escorted Eranthus, as the club-wielding Unguhur dispersed and headed back into the bizarre forest.

Eranthus led them a path that meandered through the forest-like environment, the loam on each side sloping up to the base of the lofty growths flanking the pathway. Walking in silence, Lee took in the sights of the forest around them. They moved through many varieties of unusual growths before finally stepping out of the forest and entering a broad clearing. His feet stepped once again onto a hardened surface, the ground no longer covered with the organic material that saturated the area underneath the tall growths.

A short distance ahead of them, at the end of a gentle, downward slope, an underground river flowed. The dark waters of the river coursed with a slow current, patient and confident within the channel that it had carved out of the rock over long ages.

There was an area along the shoreline where there were a number of broad, crude rafts. They were fashioned from even lengths of some kind of thick stalk, though whether the stalks were from something in the fungal forest, or a kind of tree, Lee could not yet tell. The stalks were lashed tightly together with hide rope, and the rafts looked sturdy enough.

Several large stones rested at the edge of the river's shore. The end of a long rope of hide was looped and secured around each stone, the other tied at the end of a raft. There were two such anchoring points for each individual raft, arranged so that the length of a particular raft could be tethered securely, right alongside the landing area.

A cluster of long paddles, and some considerably lengthier poles, lay prone upon the stony shore. There were a few Unguhur standing around the bobbing rafts, all looking upon the party's approach with great interest reflected in their deep-seated gazes.

As they all neared the edge the river, Lee and his companions stayed back a little, keeping some distance between themselves and the flowing waters. The rock surface near the edge looked dangerously slick.

Peering down the river, Lee could see that it traveled along the outer edge of the forest, curving out of sight into the depths of a tunnel whose mouth was not far downstream. Off to the right, he saw that the river emerged from a similar tunnel at the other end of the cavern.

It was in that moment that Lynn suddenly flinched, bumping into Lee and then aggressively nudging him. A startled, fearful look was splayed upon her face, and Lee followed the line of her sight to see what had suddenly unnerved her.

A distinct pair of impassive eyes was poking above the water's surface, set into two rising protrusions. The creature's pale eyes reflected the glowing light within the cavern, giving them the appearance of lustrous gems. A little distance in front of the eyes was what looked to be a very pale, light tan bump that broke through the surface of the water. The creature was hovering just a short distance beyond the rafts, staring intently towards the group of newcomers and the Unguhur alike.

At first, Lee could make out very little of the organism's full form, concealed as it was by the dark waters. Finally, as realization dawned upon him, his eyes stretched wider with an upsurge of astonishment and fear.

Lee did not need to be an expert to judge the great size of the jaws belonging to the floating creature, from its eyes to the tip of its elongated, tapering snout. He instinctively shuddered to think of the enormous size of the body extending beyond those unblinking eyes, easily larger than any crocodile or alligator that he had ever heard about.

"Gunther! What's that? Tell me that's not what I think it is," Erin blurted out excitedly, as she became acutely aware of what Lee and Lynn had been staring at.

The Unguhur, most especially Eranthus, looked upon Erin with a look of stunned surprise, even as Erin cast a look of alarm towards Gunther. Lee tore his gaze away from the creature in the water, and looked towards Erin, seeing immediately that she had just realized her mistake.

"Wizard Gift. Will tell story soon," Gunther quickly said to the Unguhur, while shooting Erin a highly annoyed glance.

Lee could not entirely blame Erin for the inadvisable lapse in discipline this time. The massive creature in the water was absolutely terrifying to even comprehend, and he could not fault her for being shocked into committing the blunder. Nonetheless, he froze as he awaited the response of the Unguhur.

The Unguhur leader nodded to Gunther, although some tension had clearly manifested between them. Eranthus replied to Gunther with a pensive voice, "You tell soon. What this is. All new ones speak?"

The leader glanced towards Gunther's four human companions in the way of emphasis.

Gunther's face tensed, as he replied, "Yes, all new ones speak."

Eranthus regarded Erin and the others with confusion apparent in his expression. "You understand my words?"

Erin nodded silently, looking reluctant to reply.

With a sigh, Gunther held his hand out towards Erin, indicating the amulet with his gaze. She took it off slowly, and handed it over to the woodsman, who placed it around his neck. Eranthus's already large eyes widened further, as Gunther opened his mouth and spoke again.

"A Wizard's gift. It enables us to speak your language, perfectly," Gunther explained in a resigned tone. "I wanted to talk to you about this first, to explain it carefully, so that you would not be alarmed. I do not much like the things of magic myself."

"What Wizard?" Eranthus asked Gunther, with palpable apprehension.

"The Wanderer," Gunther replied. "In the forests above. He sees something of importance in these four."

Lee could see Eranthus visibly relax at the open mention of the Wanderer. He was grateful for the Wizard's apparently widespread reputation.

"That is a good tiding," Eranthus commented, the edge now absent from its voice.

"Nice going, Erin," Ryan muttered under his breath, with more than a little disgust in his voice.

Lee did not reprimand the young man, as there was no use in hiding their capability anymore.

Ryan had also taken notice of the cause for Lynn and Lee's surprise, and he glanced back towards the creature in the river. "So what are they, Gunther?" Ryan asked the woodsman uneasily. "I can't say I'm thrilled to see those things either."

"Those are Gallidils," Gunther calmly informed Ryan and the others. "Do not be afraid of them, but be cautious. They have lived alongside the Unguhur race for much longer than I have."

"They are so enormous," Lynn remarked, in clear awe.

"The ones dwelling in these caverns and tunnels are among the greatest of their kind," Gunther replied. "There is some talk in the world above of an even larger surface kin, living somewhere within the Shadowlands. Thankfully, I did not encounter such monstrosities when I traveled in those lands. These are not of that breed, but you will likely find nothing to rival them anywhere else in Ave."

"Doesn't surprise me," Ryan retorted.

"How can the Unguhur live so close to something like that?" Erin asked fearfully.

"They do not have a taste for the Unguhur," Gunther said. "There is also some interaction between the Unguhur and the Gallidils, which shows a rudimentary level of relationship. But all of you should just use reason. I will give you one simple piece of reason. Stay on the shore or the rafts. Do not swim in the waters and tempt the Gallidils."

Gunther grinned with a humorous sparkle to his eye, albeit brief, as he looked upon the faces of the four otherworlders. The woodsman was undeniably deriving more than a little enjoyment from the sight of their collective agitation.

"Stay out of these waters, and you will be fine enough," Gunther reiterated, shaking his head and chuckling. "Is that clear enough? Difficult to understand?"

"That one stays by rafts often. It is a young bull of their kind. We feed him plenty enough," Eranthus remarked.

The Unguhur leader then gestured towards the cluster of its own kind, the ones that had been standing down by the rafts when the party had emerged from the forest.

One of them turned, took a couple of steps to the side, and bent down to pick up the prone body of a large fish. The fish was one of a row of several rather sizeable fish lying upon the ground, near to one of the anchorage boulders.

Lee got a good look at it as the Unghur lifted it up. The pale-hued fish was highly unusual in appearance. It had an extended dorsal fin, with a similar fin running along its underside, adding to a general form that to Lee brought to mind an eel.

Yet he knew without question that it was certainly no eel. If anything, it was something like a catfish, judging by the long, whisker-like barbs protruding from the rounded end of its rectangular head. In proportion to its body, the fish had very tiny eyes. For a creature that lived in the dark of underground waterways, the existence of a diminutive set of eyes was not a surprise to Lee.

As the Unguhur raised the fish up, the Gallidil immediately started drifting towards the shore, as if it were well familiar with the gesture. Lee watched the giant creature gravitate closer, gaining a better perspective of the reptilian beast's substantial girth and length. It was truly a monster, and the fact that it apparently had some sort of routine encounters with the Unguhur was of little comfort.

As the water parted and coursed around the contours of its tapering snout, Lee received some glimpses of the short spikes visible on the creature's exterior, lining its upper and lower jaws. The fearsome array of interlocking teeth included veritable daggers protruding up from the lower jaws, towards the end of the snout, one on each side.

Lee did not even want to think about what it might look like when the creature opened its extensive jaws wide. Even closed, they were incredibly intimidating to behold.

With a great heave, the Unguhur slung the fish carcass out towards the incoming Gallidil. The creature's great jaws exploded out of the water, flashing amidst a burst of water as they clamped down upon the tossed meal.

Lee quivered slightly at the sheer power and speed exhibited by the leviathan, even as he heard an audible gasp from Lynn and a curt exclamation from Ryan. Erin was left in a state of near paralysis, a faint trembling having come over her body.

"Keep him eating. Keep belly full. No room for Unguhur then," Eranthus commented with a throaty rumble that Lee took to be laughter. Eranthus saw the dumbfounded expressions on the faces of the four with Gunther, and a mild look of irritation came across its face, "Second fish in short time. That one has eaten much. Now no room for Unguhur. Do you understand?"

"They do not have much humor in them right now," Gunther quipped wryly, chuckling again. "I will explain it to them later, Eranthus … if they can remember to stay out of the water."

Gunther's reply caused Eranthus to suddenly break into loud laughter, accompanied by several of the other Unguhur. Thinking that they had just inadvertently caused some offense, Lee was very relieved to see their open mirth.

Gunther winked at his four guests, and turned back to Eranthus. "Many thanks, for keeping the Gallidils full. I am not sure whether or not I would like to find out if they like the taste of humans."

The Unguhur within earshot rumbled merrily for a few more moments. The display of joviality in creatures with such robust and outwardly intimidating appearances was quite a juxtaposition, at least to Lee's perspective. Admittedly, he expected the creatures to be far more given to far less friendly manners of expression.

The lighthearted reaction, and a few snippets of explanations, did much to allay the fears in Lee. He could see the others with him starting to relax as well. Lee looked from Gunther back out towards the river, to see if his calming nerves would still hold up at the direct sight of the Gallidil.

As if no longer interested in seeking another meal, the huge Gallidil had turned away, and was already swimming slowly from the raft area. The sight of the Gallidil distancing itself was admittedly more reassuring than anything that Gunther or the Unguhur could say.

A couple of the Unguhur then stepped out onto the broad rafts. The rafts jostled a little as they took the creatures' full weight, but the great size and mass of the rafts kept them fairly stable upon the water's surface.

At a gesture from one of the Unguhur upon the raft, Gunther guided his four human wards forward, towards the edge of the natural quay. His Jaghuns followed in a loose cluster closely behind him.

The Unguhur appeared fully relaxed, despite the fact that another Gallidil manifested itself in the wake of the one that had just been fed. Lee's breath caught in his throat as he took notice of the new creature, which was significantly larger than the former one.

The tremendous creature was hovering uncomfortably close to the edge of the raft that Lee was being guided onto. It slowly crept inward, as Lee took his first step upon the lashed stalks of the raft.

The ease with which the Unguhur went about preparing the raft only marginally lessened his suddenly renewed anxiety. Erin looked as if her nerves were about to swiftly fray apart as she hung back a few paces. Ryan's face held little conviction as he tried to gently coax her forward. Lynn had managed to board the raft, but her eyes were fixated downward, clearly laboring to shut out any sight of the creature.

"Hah! Now you want extra meal!" one of the Unguhur on the raft shouted to the Gallidil, while slowly shaking its head.

The Unguhur's attitude showed its high annoyance, and also its familiarity, with the evidently freeloading beast. It looked back to one of the others on the shore, continuing to shake its great head in apparent resignation. "Give him one too."

The Unguhur that the one on the raft had just addressed snatched up another one of the large fish lying upon the shoreline. The fish that was selected was a grander specimen of the same type as the first. The Unguhur lugged it over to the shore's edge, and heaved it deeper into the river.

Swiftly, the Gallidil rotated about, darting off with surprising dexterity towards the ample offering as the Unguhur on the raft scowled after it. The carcass was snapped up in an instant, spraying water all about in the violence of the water-born hulk's movements.

The Unguhur turned back to the four humans with Gunther, staring quietly at them. To Lee, it seemed that the creature took notice of the great discomfort exhibited on the faces of the four exiles with the woodsman.

"Gallidil no danger," the Unguhur said. "We know that old bull too. Do not worry."

Eranthus then gently implored them, "Go. Get on the raft. The Gallidil will be no trouble."

Ryan stepped onto the raft, and turned around to help Erin. He held out his hands to her, to offer her some assistance.

Erin paused for a few more moments right at the cusp of the river, shivering in fright, before finally grasping Ryan's hands and taking a ginger step onto the raft. A look of panic remained etched across her face, as she kept looking past Ryan towards the water. Once on the raft, she swiftly moved to join her companions towards the middle of its surface.

A second Unguhur followed Erin onto on the raft, holding two of the longer poles and two paddles. It handed one of each of the elongated implements over to the other Unguhur.

The small group of Jaghuns was then divided amongst the two rafts. Gunther aided each of them in getting onto the watercraft, as they showed little enthusiasm towards the endeavor and had to be cajoled one at a time.

The beasts were clearly agitated and fidgety around the water, especially the youngest amongst them, Skyheart and Darkmane. Gunther's presence aided the younger creatures' willpower, and he kept the younger Jaghuns with him on the raft that he was to ride upon.

"Come now Fang, you are the most fearless! And yet you are little better than the pups!" Gunther commented gruffly to the greatest of his Jaghuns, as the creature eased itself nervously towards the center of the raft.

The Jaghun eyed the water with great intensity. Its rippling chest was taut, and its broad paws were pressed firmly into the raft as it stoutly braced itself.

"Can't blame them," Lee remarked, staring out at the dark, flowing waters. It was a sight that was understandably unnerving for any terrestrial creature, especially with the knowledge of what lurked within the river's depths.

"No, I sure can't," Lynn agreed at his side.

"Fang's been here before, he should know better by now" Gunther replied curtly, with a dismissive air.

The more that Lee stared, the more his mind began to conjure up visions of exaggerated depths, and hidden leviathans. He pulled his attention away from the murky river to watch the rest of the group boarding, knowing that the sight of the river was doing him little good.

In a few moments more, all of the passengers were finally settled aboard. The Unguhur raft pilots untied the pair of rafts from the anchoring rocks upon the shore. With a shove, and a few dips of the paddles to orient the rafts, the party was heading down the river.

The rafts, though rather simple, were sturdy, and provided amply for the larger forms of the Unguhur. For the much smaller humans, they were more than adequate watercrafts. The rafts were easily able to accommodate all of the humans and Jaghuns, with plenty of space to spare. Ably handled by the Unguhur piloting them, the floating platforms remained amazingly steady within the waters as they traveled along the slow currents.

Lee's nerves were given little respite, however, as he was quick to notice that the rafts were accompanied by their own set of waterborne escorts. A couple of very sizeable Gallidils were keeping pace effortlessly, swimming in the wake of the rafts.

"We don't have any fish on this raft to give them," Erin commented to Lee tersely, in a whisper.

"We'll be fine," he whispered back to her, though the sight of the pursuing giants was quite unsettling. If he could have edged any further towards the center of raft, he would have, but he was already as far as he could go.

While Erin pressed in closer to him and kept watching the Gallidils, Lee relaxed his guard enough to start noticing the other aspects of their travel. They passed by the teeming stalks of the underground forest to the left, as they made their way towards the gaping tunnel entrance ahead.

There was not much activity within sight, but on a few occasions Lee espied Unguhur a short distance from the shore. They invariably came to a halt in their tasks and stood quietly, staring at the unusual group of visitors riding upon the rafts.

They left the huge cavern with its mystical forest behind as the rafts entered a wide tunnel that had been burrowed out by the river. The continuous passage of water had rendered the surfaces of the tunnel walls fairly smooth. The rocky ceiling hung a little low, just barely high enough for the Unguhur to stand up straight on the rafts.

Patches of the glowing, algae-like substance that lit the great cavern grew at periodic places within the tunnel, swathes of it clinging to the damp passage's walls. The regularity of positioning, and the general uniformity of the size of the patches themselves, gave a strong indication that they had been willfully placed and cultivated by the Unguhur. The ambience generated by the patches was more than enough to help with their navigation of the long, dark tunnel.

Their large hosts were not extremely talkative, even amongst each other. He looked over to the woodsman, who was cradling Skyheart and Darkmane close to him. While the two Jaghun cubs whimpered and whined, Gunther appeared to be completely at ease, even though he shared their hosts' subdued demeanor in the sustained silence of the travel.

Deep within the rock, at the end of a prolonged, curving stretch of river, the rafts abruptly emerged out into a sprawling, gargantuan, underground lake. Like the strange forest, the sight was instantly breathtaking.

Lee's mouth went agape at the immensity of the lake-cavern, as he looked out across the huge body of water. On the far shore, at the end of the enormous cavern, a subterranean metropolis arose. Even more spectacular, the mass of edifices looked to have been carved out of the very rock of the cavern itself.

Stretching from one side of the cavern all the way to the opposite end, the semi-circular city was recessed back into the rock, rising in distinctive terraces. The glowing, algae-like substance used in the forest and tunnels was applied in great quantity within the vast cavern, casting a considerable ambience over the city and around the lake.

A gossamer shimmering was spread like a thin, dynamic membrane, all across the rock facing of the great cavern. Its glimmering nature flowed from the rippling and undulating lake surface, reflecting the cerulean light of the widespread swathes of luminous growths from water to rock. The effect was at once ephemeral and dazzling, holding Lee spellbound for many moments as he gazed upon the majestic entirety of the spectacle.

Most of the luminance within the city emitted from among the ascending terraced structures. A sprawling cascade of shadows was cast along the jagged cavern walls that bordered the city on three of its sides, as well as the rock ceiling above it.

Moving, merging, and separating, the host of shadows paraded across the rock surfaces, likely emanating from the movements of a substantial number of Unguhur, whose activity was visible all throughout the city of stone. A considerable number of rafts of various sizes, were tethered along the far shoreline, and many others were floating out upon the surface of the great underground lake.

Those out upon the water were each attended by two to three Unguhur, whose purpose was very evident. Standing rigidly in place, as if statues, they stared intently downward at the gleaming surface of the water.

In their huge hands they gripped forked spears, poised and motionless above the water, with their powerful arms drawn back on the verge of a downward thrust. Tensed and ready, they were patiently awaiting a very specific moment.

As Lee looked on, one of them abruptly lashed out with blinding speed and force, thrusting the spear down into the water. When the Unguhur retracted the spear, a splashing form had been skewered upon its far end. The Unguhur strained as it brought the flopping, thrashing body of a large fish aboard the raft.

It was a different type of fish than the kind that had been fed earlier to the Gallidils. The fish had a flatter head shape, provided with a lower jaw that jutted out noticeably farther than the upper. Its back and underside fins were set further back along its body.

Like the other type of fish that Lee had witnessed, this fish was also very light in coloration, its pale hue shaded by the light blue ambience radiating from the growths on the walls.

Though the raft was very large, the throes of the fish, and movements of the Unguhur, as it pulled the catch towards the center, caused the raft to rock significantly.

Some of the Unguhur that were engaged in fishing, either distracted, or having already secured a recent catch, paused to look up at the newcomers on the incoming rafts. They hesitated for a moment, and Lee could see a few of them getting the attention of their companions.

He knew that they had taken note of the human and Jaghun occupants of the rafts, apparently not a very common sight within their subterranean domain. They stared quietly at the rafts, but did not seem to be alarmed as they eyes took in the presence of Eranthus and the two warriors. A few finally turned their attentions back to the task of fishing, while the gazes of others still lingered.

Several more of the great Gallidils could be seen resting out of the water, their ample bulk pulled up on the bank in little clusters along the far shoreline. Still others were traversing the surface of the lake, their extensive mass drifting gracefully through the dark waters.

The ones in the waters did not react to the two rafts, though a couple of the creatures altered their courses so as to avoid any chance of colliding with the watercraft.

Once in the colossal cavern, Eranthus' raft took the lead, pulling a little ahead of the second and keeping its quicker pace. The Unguhur upon it paddled with strong vigor, heading for the midpoint of the vast crescent that formed the far shoreline.

One Unguhur on each raft then shifted to the longer poles as they drew closer, having reached much shallower waters. The Unguhur used the poles to aid in their final approach, as they deftly positioned the rafts, and brought them towards an area on the shoreline where several large anchorage-rocks were set down by the water's edge.

A few Unguhur, of the type wearing only the hide-kilts, hurried down to the edge of the shoreline, to help the arrivals secure the rafts and disembark.

The Jaghuns bounded nimbly onto the shore, appearing more than pleased to find a solid rock surface underneath their paws again. Gunther set Darkmane down, as Skyheart leaped to the solid ground behind him. The woodsman strode away several paces from the rafts, waiting quietly for Lee and the others to join him.

Lee hardly saw the woodsman, as his eyes were bombarded with an abundance of sheer wonder, as were those of his companions. They all stood nearly dumbfounded as they drank in the full sight of the astonishing city from up close.

The great terraces now towered far over them, with evenly demarcated sections of them running down to either side. The sections, to Lee's best guess, were likely groups of individual dwellings.

Each section contained a series of four units, stacked upwards and back in the terraced arrangement. The terrace-sections ran all the way to the very ends where the lakeshore culminated in the cavern's walls.

It was a colossal and breathtaking mass of edifices, which could provide for a large number of the huge Unguhur, maybe a thousand or more. Lee could not begin to fathom how much effort had gone into the incomprehensible undertaking to initially fashion the subterranean city. It was now abundantly clear that the terraces had been carved out of the very rock of the cavern.

Not far ahead from where they were standing was the base of a very broad set of stone-carved steps. The steps led far upwards, towards a massive, unique structure that exhibited a smooth, curving outer facing. Whatever the rounded-faced structure was, it was set within the deliberate center of the entire metropolis, with everything else arrayed in the balance.

A couple of the lance-bearing Unguhur wearing the tunics stood attentively to each side of the stone steps, down at their base. Though they undoubtedly observed the arrival of the human and Jaghun newcomers, the expressionless Unguhur warriors made no move to come forward from their positions.

Another set of rafts was disembarking just a short distance down from where Lee's group had landed. Several of the warrior-Unguhur were busy offloading the bounty of a recent hunt. Erin wrinkled her nose in distaste, as Lynn gawked at the unusual contents of the rafts.

Lee found the quarry of the hunters to be fascinating, giving him some more clues regarding the nature of the underground world that he and his companions now found themselves within. The evidence indicated a world as strange as it was daunting, and not one to be approached with a trivial attitude.

Great woven baskets rested idly on the shore, containing several huge crayfish. The great crayfish were, on average, longer than the distance from Lee's elbow to his fingertips. Lee did not want to imagine the pain that their sizable pincers could inflict.

A warrior lugged the bodies of two substantial eels to the shore, dragging the ends of their over ten foot long bodies to scrape along the stony surface. The bodies of the eels were greater around in circumference than Lee's upper leg, and the sight of them and the crayfish instantly brought a greater understanding to Lee of the underground water's formidable denizens.

Yet it was not only water-bound creatures that had been obtained in the hunt.

Two other warriors picked up a long pole, along which were strung the bodies of several very large bats, a couple of which had wingspans of well over two feet. One bearing up each end, the warriors conveyed the pole high off the ground as they made their way away from the shore. They headed down the shore to the right, lugging their leathery-winged quarry.

Three other warriors labored with the massive coils of a great constrictor. Its immense bulk and length made Lee shudder, as he realized with certainty that the giant serpent was large enough to swallow a human being.

Even more troubling, the serpent was a creature that was not limited to just water or land, but could hunt in both environments. He could only hope that such creatures had been ridded from the immediate vicinity of the metropolis and cavern that he and his companions were now standing within.

The last warrior among the rafts of the hunting party carried another carcass ashore, which had a bulbous, rounded body. Its long, thin legs were all folded, pulled in tightly against its lifeless body.

"A great cave spider. A delicacy among the Unguhur, and one that your friend probably would not appreciate very much," Gunther commented, nodding towards Erin with the hint of a smirk on his face.

Lee chuckled in slightly detached amusement, as Erin proceeded to confirm Gunther's words. Having taken notice of the great spider, Erin had immediately blanched.

Though he found some humor in the reaction, he did not find the idea of a great cave spider altogether appetizing.

"All that is down here? In these caves?" Lee asked Gunther, as the implications of the hunters' quarry continued to dawn upon him.

"It is an enormous cave system, and this hunting party has likely been out for quite some time. It is a dangerous undertaking for them, but the Unguhur do not want to eat fish constantly," Gunther stated, another grin escaping him, as he eyed Erin's continuing discomfort. "And, like all of us, they like to test themselves, though I admit that they do indeed choose difficult tests."

"Nothing I would like to test myself with, anytime soon, or even remotely encounter," Lee said, glancing back to the nearly forty foot length of the serpent, and the massive head at one end.

"I cannot say I disagree," Gunther said, also looking upon the dead snake.

Most ironically, Lee got the impression that he and his companions were every bit as exotic to the Unguhur as the warriors' underworld catch was to the newcomers. Lee caught the successful hunters more than once stealing curious glances towards his own party.

Though they continued in their labors, there was no mistaking that the hunters were greatly intrigued by the sight of the humans. Lee surmised that it was Eranthus' presence as an Unguhur of great authority that prevented them from giving in further to their manifest curiosity.

Lee then noticed that Eranthus had just sent the two warriors, who had escorted them from the cavern-forest, on towards the metropolis. The two creatures headed briskly in the direction of the steep flight of stone steps. The two lance-bearing sentries made no move to hinder them as they drew up to the base of the climb.

The two Unguhur then quickly ascended the steps in fluid strides, their movements looking effortless to Lee's eyes. The warriors finally reached some manner of stone platform or landing at the end of the long staircase, disappearing from view as they proceeded towards the massive, circular structure looming at the summit.

"Welcome to Oranim, the great city of the Unguhur," Gunther informed Lee and the others. "There are other underground forests, such as the one that you have seen, but this is the only city for this population of Unguhur. From what I can tell, several hundred live here, perhaps as many as a thousand, a population that has dwelled beneath Saxany for many, many years."

"This is just amazing. ..." Ryan stated, his voice trailing off. He looked around thunderstruck, his eyes panning along the sights of the stone metropolis.

Lee could add nothing to his young friend's assessment, content to stand in place, and quietly take it all in.

More from Author
STEPHEN ZIMMER

Begin Another Epic Adventure in *The Exodus Gate*, Book One of The Rising Dawn Saga.

For Benedict Darwin, a prominent radio show host whose broadcasts cover the supernatural, paranormal, mythical, and conspiratorial, a new virtual reality device with a mythical setting promises some fascinating diversions. That the device was a gateway across time and space, designed for a very specific purpose, was the last thing that he suspected.

A shadow is falling over the world, as a group of financial and political elite work to bring the world together under one authority, a centuries-old process called The Convergence. They are guided from the depths of the Abyss, where Diabolos, The Shining One, rules from the Risen Throne. Diabolos hungers for not just the world, but also dominion over Heaven itself. Great powers are mustering in the Ten-Fold Kingdom to assault Adonai's realm like never before, to bring a great war that has gone on since before time began to a triumphant end. Only then can all worlds be remade in the image of Diabolos.

Bringing back the Nephilim, the monstrous offspring of Fallen Avatars and humans that existed before a terrible deluge destroyed them ages ago, is part of this gathering of infernal power. The virtual reality device in Benedict's possession is a key component of that plan, and the hunt is soon on to recover the gateway device. For Benedict, Arianna, high-school student Seth Engel, and others, the path becomes harrowing and filled with peril and encounters with the fantastical; but a device can be used for other purposes, than those for which it was originally intended.

An epic adventure that takes place in a world like ours, and incredible worlds and realms beyond, The Exodus Gate opens The Rising Dawn Saga.

Praise for

THE EXODUS GATE

"With The Exodus Gate author Stephen Zimmer sets the stage for an adventurous new science fiction fantasy series that is sure to entertain the reader from beginning to end. Zimmer has weaved a tale of fantastic realms populated with exotic creatures. Keep a sharp eye out for this new series."
—Mark Randell ---Yellow30 Sci-Fi

"The first book of the Rising Dawn Saga, The Exodus Gate is a promising beginning to what will probably be a thrilling trilogy in a style that is a cross between Clark Ashton Smith and C.S. Lewis for its usage of mythic and religious symbols in a fantastic mixture of the ancient and modern worlds."
-H. David Blalock, Pure Reason Review.

"Zimmer's writing style is very to the point and forces you into the story very quickly."
-Jon Snow-Best Fantasy Books

What I loved the most about this book is the way that the author blended several different genres together. You've got Sci/Fi, Fantasy, Techno-Thriller, all rolled up into one and it works. It manages to follow the conventions of all of those genres and still come off fresh. I don't think I've ever read anything quite like it."
M.Y., Nashville, TN. from Amazon.com review

ISBN Number   978-0-615-26747-0

ABOUT THE AUTHOR

Stephen Zimmer, originally born in Denver, Colorado, currently resides in Lexington, Kentucky where he is an author and a filmmaker. Stephen wrote and directed the feature-length, indie fantasy/supernatural thriller <u>Shadows Light</u>, as well as the 30 minute short horror film <u>The Sirens</u>, included on the <u>Indie Movie Masters Festival of Horrors Vol. 1 DVD</u>.

The Exodus Gate, Book One of The Rising Dawn Saga, was Stephen's first novel. The epic modern fantasy novel was released in March of 2009 through publisher Seventh Star Press, with the second installment of the series scheduled for a late spring 2010 release.

Crown of Vengeance is Stephen's second novel, and the first book of the new epic fantasy series Fires in Eden.

Stephen maintains an active online presence at

WWW.STEPHENZIMMER.COM

where information on his literary, movie, and other endeavors can be acquired, as well as links to his social networking and blog presences.

www.ingramcontent.com/pod-product-compliance
Lightning Source LLC
Chambersburg PA
CBHW070537030726
47505CB00001B/66

* 9 7 8 0 9 8 2 5 6 5 6 1 2 *